Robert Merle

THE ISLAND

Translated from the French by
HUMPHREY HARE

ST MARTIN'S PRESS

New York

THE ISLAND

Preface

I dislike reading prefaces and writing them still more. And I would gladly dispense with writing this one, if I did not feel that this book required certain elucidations.

The event which originally inspired this novel is an historical one. At the end of the eighteenth century, some mutineers from *The Bounty* fled from Tahiti, where it would have been too easy for the British Admiralty to find them, and discovered in the middle of the Pacific a little deserted island which, from the configuration of its coast, was almost inaccessible. It was called Pitcairn. The island was fertile, and the mutineers could have lived there happily till the end of their days had they not quarrelled with the Tahitians who accompanied them. The British and the natives engaged in a merciless struggle, of which the details became known only twenty years later from the possibly inaccurate account given by the one survivor to the British captain who discovered the little colony.

The captain was honest, religious and sentimental. He was the less inclined to doubt the story since the old sailor from *The Bounty* had, in his later years, become extremely pious, and governed the population, which consisted of women and children, in the most admirable way. The captain was both moved and edified, and on his return to England recounted, in charming English, the story of the Pitcairn war as he had heard it from the repentant mutineer.*

From this not very detailed report, which is the only and, as we have seen, a somewhat uncertain source, are derived all the accounts that have since claimed to record the fate of the little community which lived and fought an internecine war in the island, while massacres on a greater scale were deluging Europe with blood.

The story, for reasons which will appear later, has attracted me for years. In 1952, I think it was, I told it for the first time

* I wish to thank Miss Nancy Mathers for the research she has done for me into the history of Pitcairn.

7

to Maurice Merleau-Ponty in a restaurant in Rennes. The reason I have not written it earlier is that I conceived it at that time as an historical novel. And this, it was clear, I could not write. What was known of the Pitcairn war was too concise, uncertain, and enigmatic in its very brevity.

In 1958 I made the decision that has resulted in this book. I decided to throw history overboard and tell a story which, by reducing the true events to a mere outline, would leave me free to imagine the characters and situations. From that moment, I ceased to feel the boredom that is the price paid by the historical novel for the imaginative laziness it permits; not to mention the style, the pastiche which it would have been all too easy to sustain from one end to the other; nor the ready-made events to which, somehow or other, I should have had to attach my characters as best I could.

Not, of course, that I despise a most legitimate literary form, one indeed in which I have indulged myself. But it is legitimate only to the extent that its history is important, and not merely local and anecdotic. I cannot believe I shall be taken to task for having placed on a Pacific island characters other than those who actually lived there.

This book is not therefore the story of what happened on Pitcairn. It is an imaginative novel, with no other justification than its own vitality and the revelations I have made in it – deliberately or unconsciously – about my own life, of course, but also about the afflictions that threaten man's existence on our frail planet.

R.M.

1

As Purcell crossed the forecastle he avoided looking at the men. Whenever he went among them, he was ashamed of being so well dressed and so well fed. He went to the prow and leaned over. There was a fine moustache of foam each side of the stem. *The Blossom* was making headway.

He turned. The men were washing down the deck with a clatter of buckets. He sighed, looked away, leaned back with his hands behind him on the rail, and cast an eye over the ship. She was a beauty! As far as the eye could see, the sun was shining on the long Pacific swell. And *The Blossom* was tilting her three masts to port, under a breeze from the south-south-east on her beam. She was steady with all sails set to the wind, she rose without rolling on to the crest of each wave that passed under her hull, and slid smoothly down into the next hollow. She was a beauty, Purcell thought lovingly. From stem to stern she was shipshape and well-found; her hull slipped through the water; and her rigging was new. Eighteen months ago, when coming down the Channel, *The Blossom* had outsailed a St Malo privateer.

Purcell listened. Though there was an island nearby, he could hear no cries of birds. The sea was silent except when a wave broke. But all about him were the sounds that always gave him pleasure in a good wind: the clatter of the great wooden blocks, the vibration of the shrouds, and beneath him, behind his back, the soft continuous sounds of the stem moving through the water, like the tearing of a piece of silk.

Purcell looked at the men again. As ever, he was struck by their thinness. He reproached himself with his pleasure in admiring *The Blossom,* and his hands tightened on the rail as he thought angrily: 'The madman! '

He pulled out his watch, looked at it and shouted harshly: 'Jones! Baker! '

The two sailors carefully belayed their brushes and ran over to him.

'The log!' Purcell said.

'Aye, aye, sir,' said Baker; and though his brown face, with its regular features, showed no expression, his eyes smiled at Purcell. Casting the log was an easy job. Jones was his brother-in-law, and Purcell had not chosen him as his mate by chance.

'Get on with it!' said Purcell in the same harsh voice of command.

He added almost in a whisper: 'Be careful. Particularly you, Jones.'

'Aye, aye, sir,' Baker said.

Purcell watched them go off; and crossing the forecastle again, he went to his cabin.

The poop was empty, and Baker said in a whisper: 'A piece of advice. Keep quiet.'

He pointed to the deck beneath his feet and added: 'The bastard's got antennae.'

'I'm not a child,' young Jones whispered, looking annoyed and expanding the muscles of his chest.

He took up the sand glass, and at the precise moment Baker heaved the log into the sea, turned the glass over and held it carefully vertical on a level with his eye. It gave him pleasure to watch the grains of sand flow in a fine rain into the glass, while the line ran off the reel and passed overboard. The sight had not yet palled on Jones. It gave him an agreeable sense of power, as if it was he who was making the ship move forwards.

When the last grain had fallen, he looked at his brother-in-law with an air of importance and said: 'Finished!' Baker immediately stopped the reel, hauled in the line and counted the knots.

'Nine and a half,' he said in a low voice, looking nervously towards the companion ladder which led to the poop.

'Splendid!' Jones said.

'God damn it!' Baker said in a low, furious voice. 'What the hell does it matter to you whether this blasted ship's making headway or not?'

He finished rolling the line on to the reel, raised his head, and seeing Jones looking out of countenance, smiled at him.

At that moment there was a sound of steps on the port companion ladder to the poop, and before Burt even appeared they were standing to attention.

'Don't look at him!' Baker whispered, and his heart began beating. Burt was always apt to go for the young ones, and Baker was afraid for Jones.

His eyes reduced to slits as if against the setting sun, Baker watched Burt come towards them, gazing with hatred at the elegance of his gigantic figure. From the top of his cocked hat to the points of his buckled shoes, all was neat and perfect: the lace cravat as white as snow, the coat with deep cuffs to the sleeves, the smooth white stockings, the gilt buttons shining like mirrors. 'The bastard,' Baker thought, allowing a little gleam of hostility to appear in his eyes. He preferred that Burt's attention should be fixed on him rather than on Jones.

A couple of paces from them Burt straddled his long legs and asked in a metallic voice: 'How much?'

'Nine and a half, sir,' Baker said.

'Good.'

With his legs set wide apart, and his hands behind his back, Burt slowly inspected the two men. The red and white striped trousers were clean, the chins shaven, the hair short. Baker's head reached about to the level of his stomach, and Burt looked with interest at the bright dark eyes fixed on him from below. The little Welshman was full of guts. Polite, impeccable, discreet, there was hatred underneath. Burt felt an agreeable tremor of excitement. Impeccable? It was a mere matter of waiting. There would be a false step. There always was.

'You may go,' Burt said.

They rejoined the party washing down the forecastle deck. Boswell was leaning against the rail, whip in hand, the thong coiled on the deck at his feet. When the two men passed him, he raised his dog-like face and breathed threateningly through his nose. They were doing no wrong and Boswell bore them no ill-will. The sound was merely a habit. He made it unconsciously each time a sailor passed within range of him.

Jones and Baker freed their brooms from their lashings with an appearance of haste, though they purposely entangled the knots.

Washing down was progressing slowly. When Boswell turned

his little eyes on the men, they immediately pretended to be busy but without putting their backs into their work. And even this pretence ceased as soon as he looked away. The men then merely made a noise with their brooms and got as little done as possible.

This manoeuvre had not escaped Boswell, but he hesitated to interfere. He was afraid of this crew. It was the worst *The Blossom* had ever had. Little Smudge was a snake. MacLeod was sly and dangerous. White, the half-caste, had a temper. Baker was violent. The rest were inoffensive. But those four were enough to corrupt them all. The thought angered him. He shouted raucously and slapped his whip on the deck between the men, taking care to touch none of them.

From the poop, Burt could not see the party washing down the deck, but he heard the shout, and from the slap of the whip that followed it realised that Boswell had hit merely wood. He stood bolt upright, his head high, his eyes watchful. Something unusual was going on. His watchdog was frightened. Burt decided to go and see for himself, and began a slow manoeuvre to reach the forecastle without being seen.

At the same moment, Jimmy, the cabin boy, put his innocent young head up through the hatch. He emerged little by little, carrying a bucket of dirty water. He had been helping the cook in his galley all morning, and it was his first breath of fresh air.

The appearance of the cabin boy was a distraction to the sailors. Boswell felt it, turned his back and looked at the sea. It was a tacitly accepted pause. While still continuing to make a certain amount of noise, the sailors straightened up, their lack-lustre eyes seemed to become more lively, and two or three of them made little signs to Jimmy, though they did not speak to him. Above their striped trousers, their naked torsos were thin, their shoulders drooping, and their backs criss-crossed with long scars.

Jimmy blinked at the sunlight pouring down on the deck, glanced quickly round, waved his left hand at the sailors, and laughed without any particular reason. Two years younger than Jones, and much less athletic, he had the round face of a child, and when he laughed there was a dimple in his right cheek. Carrying the bucket of dirty water, he went to the starboard rail and glanced at the scroll of foam passing down the side. Then he raised his head and stood there, his heart beating. On the horizon, sharply defined in the morning mist, was a flat island, crowned with coconut palms. A scent of leaves and wood smoke reached him on the wind. He knew from the sailors that they were approaching the Tuamotu Islands, and though there was no question of dropping anchor there, the mere sight of land delighted him. He craned his neck and stared at his first South Sea Island lying on the horizon, his mouth open and his porcelain blue eyes moist with happiness.

At this moment, a compact flight of terns came skimming over the sea towards them, suddenly soared up to the topsails with incredible speed and began circling round the foremast with shrill cries. Jimmy watched them, automatically smoothing his short hair that fell over his forehead in two childish locks. He spent several seconds scratching his head and watching the birds before the weight of the bucket in his hand reminded him of his task. He then made the most surprising mistake for a cabin boy: he emptied the bucket of dirty water to windward instead of to lee. Much of it was naturally blown back in his face. Jimmy heard a curse behind him and turned round. Captain Burt was standing there. His coat had received a splash or two.

'I'm sorry, sir,' Jimmy said, looking up and standing to attention. He gazed at Burt's impassive features high above him. The chin, seen from so low, jutted like the prow of a ship and the nostrils curved with a thin, implacable precision. Burt had a curious way of straddling his legs and standing in an attitude that lent him something of the appearance of being his own statue. He was dark and his face was so sunburnt and immobile that he gave the impression of being made of bronze. Only the eyes were alive, and they were as cold and piercing as blades of steel.

Burt stared down at Jimmy. Though the boy was not aware of it, there was a half smile about his lips, and his face still reflected his happiness at the sight of the island.

'Are you smiling?' Burt said in his metallic voice.

'No, sir,' Jimmy said.

Captain Burt stood utterly still, his legs set wide, his arms crossed. Jimmy's round features, his ingenuous eyes, and the two locks of hair on his forehead, were far below him. Burt could make no mistake. There was not a trace of insolence on that childish face. The cabin boy looked at Burt with the expression of confidence that was his when he spoke to adults. A few seconds went by; Jimmy was embarrassed by the prolonged silence and smiled timidly.

'Are you smiling?' Burt repeated, his voice so threatening that it froze Jimmy so that his smile, far from disappearing, became fixed in a grimace.

Burt shivered with anticipatory pleasure. There was a certain formal quality about his cruelty. Before he punished or struck, his victim must at least give the appearance of being in the wrong. Burt was not concerned to impress witnesses. What they thought or said meant nothing to him. This formality was for Burt's own pleasure. In the game he played day after day with his crew, he had made certain rules for himself and he respected them.

'So you were smiling,' he said quite calmly. 'You were laughing at me.'

'No, sir,' Jimmy said tremulously. He could not control the nervous reaction which parted his lips in a sort of grin. He was frightened, was fully aware of the danger he ran at that moment by looking at Burt as Burt accused him of doing, but the more he tried to bring his face back to normal, the wider his lips parted.

Burt exaggerated his immobility and the fixity with which he stared at the boy. He knew that by prolonging the silence, he would force the boy to imitate the very gesture he was reproaching him with.

'You're smiling!' he shouted in a terrifying voice, and Jimmy began irresistibly to smile.

Burt savoured his triumph for several seconds. He had played the game correctly. The cabin boy was at fault. The rules had been respected.

'You've asked for it,' he said, simulating to his own satisfaction a perfect tone of regret.

He took a deep breath and his cold eyes glittered. Then, advancing one foot, and resting the weight of his body on it, he pivoted his powerful torso from left to right, and hit Jimmy as hard as he could with his fist. The boy had time neither to duck nor guard himself. He received the blow in the face. The sailor Johnson, who was a few yards away when the incident occurred, declared afterwards that he had heard the bones crack under the violence of the blow. Jimmy, he added, collapsed 'like a bran doll'.

Burt blew on the fingers of his right hand, opening and closing them two or three times on a level with his face as if they had gone numb. Then he looked expressionlessly at the sailors, stepped over the body, and returned slowly to the poop. As soon as he had gone, the sailors stopped work. They looked at Jimmy. Even Boswell hung his head, dumbfounded. He realised the captain had put everything he had into the blow and could not understand why. After a second or two, he ordered Johnson to throw a bucket of water over the boy's head; this from Boswell could pass almost as an act of kindness. Looking round, he at last became aware of the men's inactivity. He shouted at them, distributed a few blows with his whip, though they seemed to be without conviction, and then went off.

Johnson was old, bent, lame, grey-haired and so thin that the muscles of his forearms stood out like ropes. He unfastened the line holding one of the buckets, drew up some sea water, and poured it over the boy's head. Since it had no effect, he bent down to give Jimmy a few little taps. Johnson's sight was not good, and it was only on bending down that he saw what Burt's fist had done to the boy's face. He started, knelt down beside the inert body, and put his ear to Jimmy's chest. He remained like that a long moment, terrified. Jimmy's heart had ceased to beat.

When old Johnson got to his feet, the sailors understood from his haggard expression that Jimmy was dead. Their hands clenched about the handles of their brooms, and they gave a low inarticulate murmur.

'I'm going to tell Mr Mason,' Baker said in a low voice.

Mason was the first-lieutenant and Jimmy's uncle.

'Don't,' MacLeod said. 'Boswell hasn't given you permission It's too risky.'

'I'm going all the same,' Baker said.

He was trembling with anger and pity. He had need to act to get rid of the temptation to go and plunge his knife into Burt's guts.

He handed his broom to Jones and disappeared down the hatch. The sailors set noisily to work again to cover his absence. To leave your job without permission meant a dozen from the cat at the gangway.

When Richard Mason appeared on deck, smartly buttoned into his uniform, everyone stared at him. Mason saw Jimmy's body lying twenty yards away, looked at the sailors and came to a halt. He was a man of some fifty years of age, solidly built, with a square face and a narrow forehead. Baker had not had the courage to tell him that Jimmy was dead, but from his expression of horror, and from the sudden silence of the crew, Mason felt his heart contract. His legs began to tremble, and it was with difficulty that he crossed the intervening space to the boy.

When he came within a yard of him, he was able to see his face distinctly. The boy's eyes were half shut, his nose crushed, almost pulped by the force of the blow, and the bloody swollen lips revealed the teeth in a grimace that resembled a smile. Mason knelt down, raised Jimmy's head, placed it on his knees, and said quietly, as if talking to himself: 'Jimmy's dead.'

His mind became a total blank, and he felt as if time was flowing on and nothing happening. Then, with sudden awareness, he heard a low voice saying with extraordinarily distinctness: 'The old man's going off his head.' He looked up but could see nothing at first except the deck drenched in sunlight, and hazy faces floating above it. The faces became clearer. The sailors were staring at him. Then Mason remembered that Jimmy was dead. He looked down at the head on his knees, and began softly calling: 'Jimmy, Jimmy, Jimmy . . .' His mind became a blank again. He was seized with panic, and forced himself to look up at the watching sailors. At first there was only a sort of haze of light in which everything was pale and confused. He stared at it in desperation, and little by little their eyes emerged, fixed on him. Mason clung to them. He knew he must cling to them.

He gropingly laid Jimmy's head back on the deck, got up,

and went over to the sailors. When he was two yards from them, he stopped and said tonelessly: 'Who did this?'

He stood there before them, bowed, his arms hanging, his eyes bewildered, and his mouth open as if he could no longer control the muscles of his jaw.

A voice whispered: 'Burt.'

'Why?' Mason said in the same toneless voice.

'Because he had splashed him.'

The men were struck by the sunken appearance of Mason's face, which was ordinarily so firm.

In the same dull, listless voice Mason said: 'Because he had splashed him?'

His eyes went vague and he repeated automatically, expressionlessly: 'It's horrible, horrible, horrible . . .' It was a sort of a sad, continuous, almost inarticulate wail, as if he found difficulty in pronouncing his words.

'Christ,' said Jones, 'I can't stand this!'

'Is there anything we can do, sir?' Baker asked.

It seemed as if he had asked the question merely to interrupt Mason's lament. Mason slowly raised his eyes to him.

'Do?' he echoed.

He suddenly straightened up, and his face became firm and rigid. Squaring his shoulders, he made an almost drill turn, and walked straight past Jimmy's body to the hatch. The sailors watched him till he disappeared.

They heard Burt's powerful voice from the poop.

'Mr Boswell! The work seems to be slackening off!'

Isaac Boswell appeared like a jack-in-the-box. He was square, thick-set and red faced. As he rushed at the men, he barked like a dog, and ran from one to another distributing blows. He went on shouting for a good minute. Then he suddenly saw Jimmy's body lying at his feet and fell silent. Ten minutes had elapsed since he had ordered Johnson to throw water over the boy's head, and now a big black fly was buzzing round the open wound of the nose, and the eyes were already glassy.

Boswell craned his big pug-nosed face forwards in an effort to grasp the situation, but his instinct, more agile than his brain, was already alert. The sailors were washing down the deck without allowing themselves so much as a glance or a groan. But

Boswell was not deceived. Their very silence concealed a threat. They seemed to be waiting.

'Well, Boswell,' Burt's voice suddenly said behind him, 'are you taking a rest?'

Boswell trembled like a dog being beaten by its master. Yet he felt relieved; Captain Burt's six feet seven inches were at his back.

'The boy's dead, sir,' he said.

'So I see,' Burt replied.

He turned to the sailors, embraced them with a glance, and said calmly: 'Have the body thrown overboard.'

'Without a burial service, sir?' Boswell said in stupefaction.

'You heard me,' Burt said curtly.

Boswell, whose head was on a level with the captain's chest, looked up at the icy features and understood: Burt was deliberately provoking mutiny so as to nip it in the bud.

Boswell turned to the crew and shouted in a tone of command: 'Hunt, Baker, throw the body overboard!'

Several seconds went by. Baker went on washing the deck as if he had not heard. As for the enormous Hunt, he took two or three wavering steps towards Boswell with a bear-like gait, but little Smudge came quickly up beind him and whispered: 'Do like Baker. Don't go.' Hunt came to a halt, and gazed stupidly from Boswell to Baker out of his pale little red-rimmed eyes.

Burt's face was like a bronze mask fixed in a perpetual expression of contempt. Arms folded and head held high, he was standing with his long legs set wide apart. Motionless as a tower, he watched the quiverings of these little men of whom he was the master from on high.

'Well, Mr Boswell?' he said calmly.

Boswell hurled himself on Hunt and began beating him. Hunt was usually so docile – for lack of the imagination to disobey – that he had never received the whip before. He stood quite still, and his pale astonished eyes moved from Boswell to the captain and from the captain to the sailors. Boswell beat him furiously. But his blows seemed to have no effect; he felt as if he were whipping a mattress.

'Captain Burt,' Lieutenant Purcell's clear voice said suddenly, 'will you allow me to say the proper prayers over the cabin-boy before he's committed to the sea?'

The words fell on the deck like lightning, and Boswell stopped beating of his own accord. Purcell was standing face to face with Burt, and looked so absurdly small and frail by contrast that he might have been a band-boy at the foot of a citadel demanding its surrender.

A few seconds elapsed before Burt replied. The sailors looked at Purcell's fair, handsome, clean-cut face with stupefaction. His religious convictions were well-known, but no one would have suspected that he had so much courage.

'Mr Purcell,' Burt said, 'I have ordered the body to be thrown overboard.'

'Yes, Captain Burt,' Purcell said politely, 'but it's against the law. . . '

'I am the law in this ship.'

'Certainly, Captain Burt, you are the only master on board . . . after God.'

'I have given an order, Mr Purcell.'

'Yes, Captain Burt, but it is not decent to set Jimmy adrift without a prayer.'

There was a murmur of approval from the men. Burt turned and stared at them fixedly.

'Mr Boswell,' he said finally, pointing negligently to the third officer, 'that man is a mutineer. He is encouraging mutiny among the crew. Arrest him, take him below and put him in irons.'

Boswell stared at the captain in stupefaction.

'I protest, Captain Burt,' Purcell said quietly. 'It is grossly illegal to put an officer in irons.'

'If the man resists, Mr Boswell,' Burt said, 'you may use force.'

Boswell hesitated, and his red face, large as a York ham, betrayed his embarrassment. He went slowly to Purcell and, with an awkward gesture which lacked all violence, took the young man by the arm. He seemed frightened by the sacrilege he was committing. For the first time in his life he was raising his hand to an officer.

'Come, sir,' he said in a low voice.

And with an almost comically shame-faced air, he added: 'Please.'

Burt did not wait till Purcell had left the deck. He took two steps towards Hunt and hit him with his fist. The blow lacked violence and even had a sort of grace. Hunt collapsed. The sailors were struck by the contrast between the moderation of the blow that felled Hunt and the brutality of the punch that had killed Jimmy.

'Smudge, MacLeod, throw the boy's body overboard,' Burt ordered.

Little Smudge hung his head but showed no hesitation. Cringing like a frightened dog, he went quickly across to Jimmy's body. Burt looked at MacLeod. The Scotsman could have borne being flogged with Smudge bravely enough. But he disliked the idea of being flogged alone. He assumed an expression of disgust, shrugged, and went to take the boy by the feet. Smudge took the shoulders. It was all over.

Burt stared at the crew with his cold eyes. He had subdued them once again. And now he would make them dance! He would spare no one, not even little Smudge who had obeyed so promptly.

'Stop!' a voice cried.

Richard Mason's head and shoulders appeared through the hatch. The men were surprised. They had almost forgotten him. Smudge and MacLeod stopped. Mason emerged on deck, thrust Boswell and Purcell, who were about to go below, aside without seeing them, and walked across to Burt with a sort of automatism. His face was rigid and seemed pale in spite of his sun-tan. He came to a halt three paces from Burt, stood to attention, and said with an odd solemnity: 'Captain Burt, I regret to have to inform you that I consider you a murderer.'

'Take care what you're saying, Mr Mason,' Burt said calmly. 'I shall not allow myself to be slandered. It is perfectly obvious that it was an accident.'

'No,' Mason said curtly. 'It was no accident, it was murder. You killed Jimmy deliberately.'

'You must be mad,' Burt said. 'I had no quarrel with the boy.'

'You killed him,' said Mason in a sad, passionless voice, 'because I loved him.'

There was a sudden tension among the men. None of them had yet thought of it in that way, but now that the accusation had been made, it was clear to them that it was true.

'If that is your opinion, Mr Mason, it is up to you to prove it in a court of law. As for me, I shall sue you for slander.'

There was a silence and then Mason went on tonelessly, as if he were talking to himself: 'I have just spent ten minutes in my cabin considering all that.'

And as he fell silent with a sort of absent air, Burt said drily: 'Well?'

'Well,' Mason said absently, 'it is quite clear that if I accuse you, the court will acquit you. I shall then be accused in my turn of slander, ruined by the damages awarded you, and broken.'

'I'm delighted you see the matter so clearly, Mr Mason,' Burt said. 'That, I think, is precisely how things will turn out.'

'Yes, Captain Burt,' Mason said, in his dull, automatic voice, 'and that is why I have taken the decision I have. I shall make no legal accusation.'

'I congratulate you on your good sense, Mr Mason,' Burt said.

He gave a brief smile and went on: 'But your decision does not alter mine. You have slandered me in the presence of the crew and, as soon as we reach London, I shall hail you before the courts.'

'You won't have the chance,' Mason said in a more decided voice.

Putting his right hand in the inside pocket of his coat, he drew out a pistol, aimed it at Burt with a steady hand and fired.

The explosion rang out with stunning force. Burt swayed on his feet for some seconds like a gigantic statue, then fell backwards in one piece with a terrific clatter. His body bounced twice on the deck, then lay still on its back, the legs stiff, the arms spread wide. Where his nose had been there was a gaping hole.

There was suddenly a deep silence on deck. From a distance, the sailors stared at Burt's body. They had never before seen their captain stretched out full length, and he seemed taller than ever. At last they made up their minds to draw near, but they did so slowly, and with a sort of caution, as if Burt's very stillness was a menace to them. Though half his brains were scattered on the deck, they almost expected, so much did they believe in his superhuman strength, to see him get up. For eighteen months they had been subjected to the most appalling tyranny; it had taken from them their dignity and had reduced them to slaves. And now that Burt was dead, they felt no joy at the sight of his corpse, and it surprised them.

'Who fired?' Purcell cried, hurrying up the hatch by which he had only just disappeared.

'It was Mr Mason, sir,' Baker said.

'My God, that's what I was afraid of!' Purcell cried, hurrying forward, Boswell at his heels.

'Just take a look at him, sir!' Smudge cried in a piercing voice. 'He's properly dead, the bastard!'

The sailors looked coldly at Smudge. Burt was dead; there was no point in insulting him, and in any case it was not for Smudge to do so.

'May God have mercy on his soul,' Purcell said.

Mason was holding the pistol hanging at his side. He looked bemusedly at Burt's dead body.

'Stand back there!' a loud voice shouted suddenly.

The Blossom's second-officer, J. B. Simon, was standing a few paces away, a pistol in each hand. He had a yellow complexion, thin lips, and a long thin nose. Though he was not brutal, the men disliked him. Simon felt that he had not succeeded in life, and it made him bitter and inclined to find fault with them.

'Stand back!' Simon shouted, pointing the pistols at them. 'Get back to work. I'm captain of this ship now, and there's a bullet in the head for the first man who doesn't obey me.'

There was a moment's astonishment. The men did not stand back as Simon had ordered. It did not occur to them to be frightened. In the first place, they were shocked by the second-officer's taking the initiative and failing to keep to his proper place.

'It's for Mr Mason to take command, sir,' MacLeod said. 'Mr Mason is the first-lieutenant of this ship.'

Simon had a violent prejudice against the Scotsman. For the last eighteen months, he had never missed an opportunity of finding fault with MacLeod. His interference infuriated him.

'You damned Scotsman!' he yelled, pointing one of the

pistols at him. 'Another word from you and I'll send your brains to feed the fishes.'

MacLeod turned pale, and his eyes glittered. He felt the handle of the knife in his pocket. No one had ever dared insult his country before.

'For God's sake, John!' Purcell cried, going across to Simon. 'For God's sake, put those pistols away. Enough harm's already been done. You know very well it's for Mr Mason to take command.'

'Mr Mason has killed his captain,' Simon said hoarsely. 'He's a mutineer. He's no longer qualified to command a ship. As soon as we get back to London, I shall hand him over to the police and he'll be hanged.'

'John!' Purcell said, his eyes wide with horror. 'You're not speaking seriously!'

'Devil take you and your sentiments, Mr Purcell!' Simon shouted, the pistols trembling in his hands. 'By God, if you take another step towards me, I'll make a sieve of your guts!'

Purcell stopped in his tracks, abashed by the gleam of hatred he saw in Simon's eyes. He had lived with him in comradeship for eighteen months, and Simon had never let him see that he hated him; and now this unreasoning hatred filled Purcell with stupefaction and deprived him of all power of action.

'Mr Boswell!' Simon said furiously.

Boswell looked at Simon, turned his head away and glanced questioningly at Mason. He had the unhappy look of a dog uncertain which of two masters to obey. The hierarchy demanded that he should obey Mason, but Mason gave him no orders. Indeed, the first-lieutenant was still standing perfectly immobile, a haggard look on his face, the pistol hanging from his hand, an his eyes fixed on Burt's gigantic body.

'Mr Boswell!' Simon repeated, his yellow face contorted with anger.

Boswell gave Mason a last glance, then slowly and as if regretfully went over to Simon.

'Aye, aye, sir,' he said in a low, hoarse voice, looking submissively at Simon.

'Mr Boswell,' Simon said, 'make those men obey.'

Boswell grasped his whip more firmly, turned his pug-nose

towards the men and stared at them. They stared back without flinching and he realised what had happened. The men no longer saw the captain's figure behind him. Burt's strength was not the only explanation of his ascendancy. Burt had been a brave man. On more than one occasion the sailors had seen him advance on them with bare hands, while their own were clutching the open knives in their pockets. They had known Burt was not bluffing; he really wanted a fight, alone against them all. His inhuman courage astonished them. But Simon was merely a mean officer who liked bullying them. Even his malice was mean. They were not afraid of him.

Boswell ought to have gone first for Baker, since Baker had refused to obey Burt. But, leaning on the handle of his broom and without moving an inch, the little Welshman defied him with his dark eyes. Boswell did something he would never have done in Burt's time; he flinched, walked past Baker as if he had not seen him and immediately made another mistake. He went for Hunt.

Hunt had already been beaten by Boswell and struck by Burt. He did not understand why he was being beaten again; and he had not understood what Simon's intervention was about. Now his clouded mind became suddenly aware of a sense of injustice. He bared his teeth and uttered a growl of anger. Hurling himself at Boswell with unexpectedly agility for one so massive, he tore the whip from his hand, threw it on the deck and was on him in a second.

What then took place was quite unprecedented. As far as the men were concerned, everything else became subordinate to their interest in the fight. They moved forward the better to see the combatants, who were rolling on the deck, and Simon had to retreat several paces to avoid being surrounded. His situation had suddenly become both comic and desperate. He mouthed threats, but even to himself they seemed absurd. The men's interest was fixed on the fight to the death, and they paid no more attention to him than if he had been brandishing property pistols on a stage.

Sweat was trickling down Simon's forehead and along the deep flaccid lines that wrinkled his yellow skin each side of his mouth. Scarcely five minutes ago, it had all seemed so simple.

With pistols in his hands, he could seize command, return to London, hand Mason over to the law, and be confirmed in command of *The Blossom*. And now Boswell was fighting for his life. Even if he won, Simon was no longer sure he could succeed. He felt very lonely and his hands trembled. With all his might he resisted the temptation to press the trigger and shoot a man at random. Supposing the making of an example did not intimidate the men? Suppose they all turned on him?

That he should be the only man on deck who was armed and yet not be able to impose his will seemed to Simon appallingly unjust. Anyone else with pistols in his hands, he thought bitterly, would have aroused fear. But fate, which had so often caused him to fail in life, was mocking him once again. He was carrying death in each hand and the men merely turned their backs on him.

Simon watched the fight in agony. The two men had become a single roaring monster. And when the monster ceased to be, one man would rise to his feet. Simon's eyes grew wide with horror and fear clutched him by the throat. He knew suddenly that Hunt was going to kill Boswell. His pistols shook in his hands. With Boswell dead, it would be his turn next. He had failed. Once again, he had failed.

Hunt had succeeded in getting his enormous hands round Boswell's neck. He was squeezing, wholly insensible to Boswell's fingers clawing at his face and to his knee jerking at his stomach. Simon became panic-stricken. His hands were shaking and he was blinded by the sweat trickling down his forehead into his eyes. He moved forward like an automaton into the circle within which the two men were fighting. Almost without taking aim, he fired at Hunt. He was immediately seized from behind, disarmed and held still. He felt a sharp flash in his chest, a red veil closed over his eyes, and he knew he was sinking backwards into the void.

When Hunt got to his feet, there was a little blood on his shirt where Simon's bullet had grazed his shoulder. Boswell was lying on the deck; his face was purple and his mouth twisted. Simon had fallen beside him, and their heads were touching. His eyes were wide open, and the two deep yellow lines each side of his thin lips lent his face an expression of bitterness.

Purcell suddenly came alive, forced his way through the crowd of sailors, and came to a halt, his eyes horror-stricken, incapable of uttering a word. MacLeod bent down. He withdrew his knife from Simon's body, wiped the blade carefully on the dead man's shirt, replaced it in its sheath with a click and put it in his pocket. At that moment, he met Purcell's eyes, shrugged, looked away, and said awkwardly like a child found in fault: 'He'd asked for it, sir.'

Purcell made no reply. He was struck by MacLeod's manner and thought sadly: 'They're children. They're cruel as children are.' As he turned to go, he was surprised to see Mason standing on his right, his face pale and his head lowered. Then Mason looked up and swept the group of men with a sad, despairing glance.

'Mutineers!' he said with a sort of sob. 'Mutineers! That's what you are!'

'You too!' Smudge shouted angrily.

Mason's face crumpled as if he had received a blow, his eyes blinked, and his lips trembled.

'I too,' he whispered.

2

The next day, at one o'clock in the afternoon, the seaman White padded up to Lieutenant Purcell, who was checking the helmsman's course, stood to attention, removed his cap and said in his sing-song voice: 'The captain's compliments, sir, and lunch is ready.'

Purcell raised his eyebrows and looked at White.

'The captain?' he said with a half-smile.

'Yes, sir,' White said, his jet black eyes gleaming through the narrow slits of his lids.

White was the son of an English sailor and a Chinese woman. He had been fostered by a rather drunken Anglican missionary who was amused by the baby's yellow skin and thought it a good joke to call him White. The name had made the half-caste the butt of every ship in which he had served till the day he had knifed a wag and thrown his body overboard. The crew had not given the murderer away, and White had been left in peace from then on. But peace had come too late; White spoke little, never laughed and readily took offence. When Purcell turned to him, raised his eyebrows and repeated: 'The captain?' White, who had not understood the sense of the question, thought the lieutenant was mocking him, and from that moment cherished a violent grievance against him.

Mason was already sitting in Burt's chair when Purcell entered the wardroom. Without a word, he signed to the lieutenant to sit opposite him, in the seat he himself had occupied when Burt was alive. 'Here I am promoted first-lieutenant,' Purcell thought ironically. The day before, there had been four of them about this same table at breakfast. And now he was alone with Mason. Purcell raised his eyes and looked at him. All trace of emotion had disappeared from his face. He was ahead of Purcell and was eating solidly, with peasant precision, his square jaws chewing carefully.

It was a sort of unwritten law in British ships of the period that the captain remained silent throughout the meal, and thereby imposed silence on the officers dining at his table. The idea behind this custom was doubtless that, since the captain had no equal on board, there was no one worthy of conversing with him. Purcell had not been there five minutes before he was aware that Mason intended conforming to the rule. He did not even open his mouth to ask for the pepper or the pickles but, like Burt, pointed to them so that Purcell should pass them. Purcell secretly observed Mason's neat, square features, his grey-blue eyes, his rather low forehead and his bushy hair. His whole appearance was one of honesty, narrowness and devotion to duty. And yet this impeccable officer was now commanding an outlaw ship. He was peacefully sitting in the place of the captain he had killed, and was surrounding himself, as the captain had done, with the august silence appropriate to his rank.

At the end of the meal, Mason raised his head and said curtly: 'I wish to speak to the men, Mr Purcell. Will you assemble them?'

He got up. Purcell had not finished eating, but he also got

up, somewhat vexed. That also was an unwritten law: when the
captain had finished, the lieutenants' meal was over, even if
their plates were still full.

Purcell went on deck and ordered White to ring the bell. The
men came aft dragging their feet and gathered on the half deck.
Once again, Purcell was struck by their thinness. He faced them
in silence, embarrassed because Mason, as Burt had done, was
keeping them waiting.

The 'captain' finally appeared. Straddling his legs, he faced
the crew, clasped his hands behind his back, and looked the
men up and down.

'Men,' he said in a loud voice, 'I intend making for Tahiti to
take in water and food, but I have no intention of staying there.
Tahiti is now too well known to His Majesty's ships. The arm
of the law would soon reach us. I therefore propose to leave
Tahiti as soon as possible and seek an island, which is not
marked on the charts and lies far from the usual shipping
routes . . . However, I do not propose to compel anyone
to accompany me. You'll be free either to remain in Tahiti or
sail with me.'

He paused. When he went on, it was clear that he was making
an effort to keep calm.

'You must know that the law considers as mutineers not only
those who have taken part in a mutiny, but also those who have
witnessed it and done nothing to prevent it. For the first – whatever their rank – it's the rope. For the second, it is possible – I
say it is *possible* – that the Court may show indulgence. In any
case, there's a chance of it. I tell you this, men, to help you weigh
the odds before reaching a decision.'

He stopped and seemed to be questioning the crew with his
eyes.

'May I ask a question, sir?' said MacLeod.

'Yes.'

'If we come with you, is there any hope of getting back home
one day?'

'No,' Mason said curtly. 'Never. In no circumstances. You
may be quite certain of that, MacLeod. When I've found the
island, my first care will be to burn *The Blossom*. Not to do so
would be pure folly. *The Blossom* is the tangible proof of

mutiny, and so long as she's afloat there's no safety for any of us.'

He paused, looked gravely at the crew, and continued, emphasising his words: 'Once again, I am compelling no one. Those who wish may remain in Tahiti. They'll see England again even if,' he added sombrely, 'it's from the height of the yard-arm of one of His Majesty's ships. But, I repeat, for those who come with me there'll be no return.'

He turned to the lieutenant.

'Mr Purcell, you will take the names of the volunteers and, when you have done so, you will come to me in the cabin.'

He fixed his grey-blue eyes on Purcell, then looked at the sea billowing to the horizon, glanced up at the sails, and seemed on the point of adding something. But he changed his mind, drew himself up, squared his shoulders and, turning on his heel with a sort of haste, went towards the wardroom.

It took Purcell no more than half an hour to make out his list. He was surprised by the small number of volunteers. The sailors seemed to prefer risking the rope to the prospect of never seeing their country again. 'How odd,' Purcell thought, 'these men are very poor. They have nothing to attach them to the old world. Most of them have neither wife nor children; they have never been able to afford them. And what can England mean to them, except poverty? But they know that poverty. That's what it is. It's the unknown which frightens them . . .'

When he entered the captain's cabin, Purcell thought the heat would suffocate him. But there was not a drop of sweat on Mason's forehead as he sat at the table, cravatted, buttoned tightly into his coat, a glass of rum in his hand, and a big chart spread before him.

'How many?' he asked briskly.

'Nine including yourself, Captain Mason.'

'That's what I feared!' Mason said anxiously. 'I shan't have enough men to work the ship.'

'We may be able to ship some Tahitians . . .'

'I fear we shall be forced to,' Mason said. 'We, Mr Purcell?' he went on, suddenly looking up. 'You've included yourself among the volunteers?'

'Yes, Captain Mason.'

Mason raised his eyebrows, but said nothing. He took the list from Purcell, cast a rapid eye over it, nodded his head, and slowly read it aloud, stopping at each name, except at his own and Purcell's:

Richard Hesley Mason, Captain.

Adam Briton Purcell, Lieutenant.

MacLeod, seaman.

Hunt, *id.*

Smudge, *id.*

White, *id.*

Johnson, *id.*

Baker, *id.*

Jones, *id.*

When he had finished, he raised his head and looked at Purcell: 'What do you think of this crew?'

'Some of the best and some of the worst.'

'Yes,' Mason said, shaking his square head.

And without considering how disobliging the remark must be to his second-in-command, he added: 'Pity I can't work *The Blossom* by myself! Will you take a glass of rum, Mr Purcell? . . . Ah, it's true, I forgot,' he went on, as if vexed that the lieutenant did not drink. 'Do you know,' he continued, 'what has led the volunteers to choose as they have? . . . In MacLeod's case, it's obvious. He killed Simon. And Hunt killed Boswell. Those two had no choice. But what about White, for instance? . . .'

'There's a rumour, Captain Mason, that he once knifed a man. He may fear that the story will come to light if there's an enquiry.'

'Yes,' Mason said, 'and it would not surprise me if Smudge also had a past. But Jones, Baker, Johnson? I'd swear those three were as white as snow.'

'Jones would follow Baker to the end of the world,' Purcell said. 'And Baker must consider himself guilty because he refused to obey Burt.'

After a silence he went on: 'Only Johnson's choice remains to be explained.'

Mason had not invited him to sit down, and since the beginning of the interview he had been standing in front of the table at which Mason was sitting. Purcell's fair, open face betrayed a certain uneasiness. The distance the 'captain' was placing between them seemed to him a useless piece of play-acting, and it embarrassed him.

'Yes,' Mason said, 'there remains only Johnson's case to be explained.'

He added: 'And yours, Mr Purcell.'

Since Purcell said nothing, he went on: 'You have nothing to fear from a court martial.'

'I can assure you,' Purcell said with a half-smile, 'that I have no past.'

'I am convinced of it,' Mason said imperturbably.

And he waited, grave as a judge. He was captain of *The Blossom* and had a right to know why his lieutenant had decided to accompany him.

'Well,' Purcell said, 'perhaps you don't know it, but I asked Burt to read the burial service over Jimmy's body. Burt ordered Boswell to put me in irons. I am therefore a mutineer.'

Mason opened his grey-blue eyes wide.

'I didn't know that!'

He looked at Purcell. For a brief moment his face lost its impassivity and he said with emotion: 'I thank you for your action with regard to Jimmy, Mr Purcell. It was very courageous of you.'

He went on: 'You think a court martial would convict you as a mutineer?'

'I'm sure of it. Besides, I would be blamed for having done nothing after the murder . . . after the death of Burt.'

Mason blinked. The slip had not escaped him.

'You're no doubt right,' he said stiffly, his eyes staring at the floor.

He went on: 'You have no ties in England?'

The indiscreet question surprised Purcell. He hesitated, but it was better to answer. The question was not ill meant, and he was going to have to spend the rest of his life with this man.

He said quickly and with embarrassment: 'My father is dead. My mother . . .' – he looked away – '. . . does not care for me.'

Mason looked down at the chart. Then he went on with a smile that seemed forced.

'Well, we're in the same boat, Mr Purcell.'

The lack of warmth in his tone wounded Purcell and he made no answer. Mason went on: 'You've already made a stay in Tahiti, I believe?'

'Six months, four years ago. I lived with a Tahitian chief. It was he who taught me the language.'

'What?' Mason said. 'You speak Tahitian? That'll be very useful to me. You speak it fluently?'

'Yes, Captain Mason.'

'After six months! You must have a gift for languages, Mr Purcell,' he added with a little propitiatory laugh, as if it were an insult to an officer to suppose he had intellectual gifts.

'Do you think,' he went on, 'that the Tahitians will supply us with food?'

'As much as we require.'

'Without a *quid pro quo*?'

'Without a *quid pro quo*. Though there'll be a certain amount of thieving.'

'Much?'

'Continuously.'

'Scandalous!' Mason said, his face turning red with indignation.

'Oh, no!' Purcell said. 'They'll give you everything they've got and they'll take from you anything they want; it's their idea of friendship.'

Mason tapped the table impatiently.

'This Tahitian chief with whom you lived . . .'

'Otou.'

'Is he important?'

'Very important. He has great prestige. He's got blue eyes, and claims he's descended from Captain Cook,' Purcell added with a smile.

Mason's expression became stiff and cold, and it was a moment before Purcell understood: Captain Cook was a captain, and therefore irreproachable.

Mason got to his feet. He was not much taller than Purcell, but so broad and solid that Purcell felt almost frail beside him.

'Mr Purcell,' Mason said, and once again his face was twisted with emotion and his voice quivered, 'believe me, when I say that I feel the full weight of my responsibility towards these men who, because of me, will never again see England. However,' he added after a second's silence, 'if what I did was to be done again, I would do it.'

He uttered the words with some force, but they sounded false. Purcell looked away and said nothing. He did not approve of Burt's murder, and he knew Mason would never be able to forgive himself for other reasons. For Mason, the moral problem did not arise. He was thinking purely as a sailor. Ashore, the murder would have been justified. At sea, he had led a crew to mutiny and made the ship an outlaw.

'With your permission,' Purcell said, 'I'll go on deck and attend to the foretopsail. It's ill-set.'

'I noticed it just now,' Mason said. 'The topmen in Burt's time . . .'

There was a silence in which the two men avoided each other's eyes. Mason went on: 'Do you think maintaining discipline has become difficult?'

'It has not become difficult,' Purcell said tonelessly. 'It does not exist.'

He added: 'If we ran into bad weather, I don't know if I could get the men to go aloft.'

As Mason stared silently at him, he said: 'I pray God it won't be long before we find your island.'

Otou was standing on the threshold of his hut, looking into the distance and rubbing his chest with his large, elegant hand. His pectoral muscles were still powerful, though slack with age, his belly was not precisely obese, but ample, and Otou had no desire to hurry off with the young men to meet the *Peritani*.* He felt he was growing old, but since the idea was not a pleasant one, he persuaded himself it was dignity which forbade his running to meet the foreigners. The *Peritani*'s big canoe was in the lagoon, its huge sails furled, and the white men were lowering their little canoes to come ashore. A flotilla of canoes had already left the beach and had almost reached them. In the first of them were the children, followed by the scarcely less prompt *vahinés*. '*Aoué, the vahinés!*' Otou said, smiling. Crowned with leaves – the sun was already high – the men waved their hands

* The British.

in a friendly way, but they had stayed on the beach. Otou approved their reserve.

The Tahitians, including Otou himself from the threshold of his hut, began laughing because the foreigners' boats moved so slowly across the calm waters of the lagoon. By *Eatua*, they were heavy, and the movements of the *Peritani* were so slow and jerky! However, it was pleasant to watch the dipping of the long, curious white paddles that looked like mosquitoes' legs on the water.

The boats ran up on to the sand and Otou saw the *Peritani* clamber out. They were hirsute, bearded, and dressed only in their striped trousers. Otou nodded his head *Aoué*, how thin they were! The great rainswept island could not be as rich as people said.

Otou suddenly uttered a great cry. He raised his elegant hands, spread them out in a wide gesture and called loudly: 'Ivoa! Mehani!' Without waiting for an answer, he hurried towards the newcomers, his bare feet trampling the hot sand.

'Adamo!' he cried from afar.

Adam Purcell turned his head, saw Otou running towards him so fast that his stomach was jerking a little above his *pareu*, and he set off as fast as he could to meet him, his fair hair shining in the sun.

'Adamo!' Otou cried, clasping him in his arms.

He pressed him several times to his vast chest, rubbed his cheek against his and repeated with every possible inflection of surprise and affection: 'Adamo! . . . Adamo! . . . Adamo! . . . Adamo! . . .' Purcell blushed a little and his lower lip trembled.

A compact crowd had formed about the two men, and Purcell noticed with amusement that it mimed and commented, like the chorus in a Greek tragedy, the dialogue between the two protagonists.

'Adamo!' Otou cried, his eyes moist, pressing Purcell to his chest again. 'You've come! . . . Adamo, my son! . . . You've come! . . .'

'Adamo has come!' the crowd echoed in joyous clamour.

Suddenly a beautiful girl with naked breasts rushed at Purcell, snatched him from Otou's arms, embraced him and began kissing him lip to lip, in the *Peritani* manner, which made the crowd laugh because it seemed to them so childish. Purcell tried to draw back, but the girl, who was almost as tall as he was, and certainly quite as strong, clasped him vigorously to her breast and continued to rain kisses on him. Purcell was at once amused and touched and let her have her way, merely glancing questioningly at Otou over the girl's shoulder.

'What?' Otou exclaimed. 'It's Ivoa! Don't you recognise Ivoa? Adamo does not recognise Ivoa!' he cried, taking the crowd to witness with a gesture of his big hands.

There were immediately a great ebullition of affection, much loud laughter, and many little friendly taps on Purcell's shoulders.

'Adamo!' the Tahitians cried with affection and surprise as if the fact that he had failed to recognise Ivoa merely redoubled their friendliness towards him.

'Adamo!' Ivoa cried in a clear voice. 'Don't you recognise me?'

She released him, placed her hands on his shoulders, held him at arm's length, and smiled at him, revealing her brilliant teeth. Purcell looked at her. Her long black hair, growing rather low on the forehead and divided in the centre by a parting, fell over her shoulders in big curls and, as she leaned forward a little, half concealed her naked breasts and flowed down to her hips. Ivoa was not black, but the colour of amber and her big blue eyes, shaded with dark lashes, stood out against her warm complexion. Purcell stared once again at her long hair, black as a raven's wing; it was scarcely frizzy at all, but thick and luxuriant, dense as a mane. There was a lump in his throat and he could not utter a word.

'Well, I have changed!' Ivoa said in her clear voice. 'Could you still carry me on your shoulders, Adamo?'

'He wouldn't get far!' Otou cried with a great happy laugh, and his two big hands, which the moment before had been reposing on his stomach, now fluttered round his head like so many birds.

The Tahitians all began laughing. *Aoué*, Otou was right! What a beautiful girl Ivoa had become. Slender, but round where she should be. And she was certainly some weight.

'Look!' Ivoa said. 'I've still got the medal of your God Jesus round my neck. I've never left it off! Not for a single day! I've even kept it on while bathing! And every night I've stroked it and asked your God Jesus to bring Adamo back. And He's done so!' she added triumphantly. 'He must be a very powerful god, for He's managed it! Adamo has come!' she cried in a paroxysm of happiness, raising her arms and extending her palms to the sky. And the crowd round Purcell shouted for joy.

'Yes, you've grown,' Purcell said, smiling and turning his head slightly away.

Each time he looked at Ivoa's hair, his throat constricted.

'Don't stand in the sun, your head will cook like a tern's egg!' Otou said amid the laughter. 'Come to my hut, Adamo! Are you hungry?'

'Very hungry,' Purcell said.

And once again the Tahitians gave vent to exclamations of affection. Ivoa took him by one arm and, kissing his neck, immersed him in her scented hair. Otou seized the other arm, and preceded, accompanied, pushed, indeed almost carried, Purcell covered the hundred yards to Otou's hut amid acclamation.

He had reached the threshold when an athletic Tahitian came running up. He was head and shoulders taller than the crowd. He burst through it, hurried smiling broadly to Adamo, took him under the arms, raised him effortlessly to the level of his eyes, and held him thus amid the laughter, flourishing him above the heads of the crowd as if he were a baby.

'What about me?' he cried happily. 'Do you recognise me, Adamo?'

'Mehani!' Purcell cried, his eyes bright, forgetting the absurdity of his position in his pleasure.

'He recognises him!' Otou cried happily, and with a wide gesture of his hands took his people to witness the prodigy.

'Adamo recognises Mehani!' the crowd cried, as affectionate and surprised as if Purcell had not recognised him.

Mehani, his eyes glowing with happiness, restored Purcell to the ground as if he were afraid of breaking him, and the shouts redoubled.

'Your children have grown, Otou,' Purcell said. 'I can hardly believe it's scarcely four years . . .'

'Adamo's hungry,' Otou cried. 'Come in, Adamo,' he went

on with a wide gesture of his hand. He prolonged the gesture with consummate elegance, extending its curve as it were, dismissing the crowd with a truly royal dignity.

Mehani placed Purcell on a mat, sat down opposite him and devoured him with his eyes. His skin was darker than his sister's, and there was a remarkable contrast between the lower part of his face – which was tender and almost feminine with its wide mouth, shapely lips and round chin – and the upper part, to which an aquiline nose and deep-set eyes, shadowed by very black lashes, lent a thoughtful, almost severe aspect.

'É Adamo é!' he said. 'É Adamo! É Adamo é!' And by the way he modulated his voice, the tone at once melancholy and happy, he expressed all the memories, now four years old, which were besetting him at this moment. At the same time, he beat the mat rhythmically with the flat of his hand, as if the muffled, repeated sound could reflect all the pleasure his friend's presence promised for the future.

'É Adamo é!' he said at last. 'I remember how frightened you were of the sharks in the lagoon . . . !'

He burst out laughing and Otou and Ivoa echoed him. It was true! Adamo had been frightened of the sharks! The harmless lagoon sharks! Mehani rose like an expanding spring, leaned over towards Purcell, took his head between his hands and placed his forehead against his own in sign of affection. Then he let go of him and, putting his fingers on his shoulders, gave him repeated little taps on the tops of his arms, looking at him meanwhile with an expression of delight.

'É Adamo é!' he said, incapable of expressing all his affection for him in words.

'Aoué!' Otou said. 'You must let him eat! You can't eat well and talk at the same time!'

Ivoa handed Purcell a wooden plate filled to the edge, and even before he saw what it contained, he recognised the fruity odour of raw fish marinated in lemon juice. Mehani was sitting opposite him, leaning against a doorpost, and Otou sat with his back to the other, so as to leave a view of the beach and lagoon to their guest. When she had served her father and Mehani, Ivoa took her place on Purcell's right, not sitting, but crouching on her knees, and a little behind him, for Tahitian etiquette forbade her to eat at the same time as the men. She kept the flies off Purcell's face with a palm leaf and, from time to time, gave him a little teasing tap with it on the shoulder. Purcell knew she never took her eyes off him. He could see the mass of her dark hair out of the corner of his eye, and he dared not turn his head towards her.

Purcell was wearing only trousers and shirt; and the sun, flooding into the hut, reached his bare feet. Part of Mehani's shoulder stood out in silhouette against the light on the left side of the doorway, and on the right was Otou's, as large, but less solid and less round, the muscles grown emaciated and flaccid with age. Purcell was hungry. Ivoa lightly stroked his neck with her fingers, but he pretended not to notice. He breathed deeply of the scent of her hair, and gazed out at the slender trunks of the nearby coconut palms and, farther off, brilliant under the sun, the great mauve patches and indigo reflections on the blue surface of the lagoon.

There was a profound silence in the hut. For Tahitians, Purcell remembered, eating was so agreeable an occupation that it sufficed in itself. His body at ease in the shade of the hut, his feet caressed by the sun, he had a delightful sense of quiet and coolness. The world was well ordered: Otou and Mehani opposite him and, on the perimeter of his right eye's vision, Ivoa leaning forward to brush his cheek with her hair. He looked at his friends, and felt profoundly happy. What affection there was in their eyes! What repose in their souls! It was a moment he would remember; and at the very moment of thinking it, he felt a poignant sense of regret, as if the moment were already in the past.

'Adamo!' Mehani said anxiously. 'What's the matter? Your eyes look sad.'

'A thought has just come to me, Mehani.'

'*Peritani! Peritani!*' cried Otou, shaking a long finger in front of his nose, as if he had known for a long time past that a *Peritani* was incorrigible. 'Eat! Eat! One must not think too much with one's head!'

Purcell smiled and looked down at his fish. Otou was right. To be really happy, you should be conscious of your happiness, but not too much so. You needed to find the point of balance, to use guile, to realise you were happy, but not to the point of telling yourself so. A warm, scented breeze from the centre of the island swayed on the coconut palms, and Purcell could see, high above the hut, tall palms waving like manes with a gentle rustling. He breathed the air with delight.

'It's the scent of Tahiti,' he said aloud.

'What is the scent. of Tahiti?' Ivoa asked, leaning on his shoulders with both hands.

'The tiaré flower.'

'É Adamo é!' Ivoa said. 'There are many other scents in Tahiti. There's the scent of hibiscus, of frangipani, of the big ferns, and of thyme. And the scent of jasmine, which is as fresh as a baby's skin. And there's the scent that comes from the plateau when the wind blows from the mountain and it's going to rain. It's a scent that makes you want to work.'

Otou began laughing and, extending his huge hands in front of him, the thumbs spread wide from the other fingers and the palms almost perpendicular with his forearms, he shook his head and said: 'When you're young, you shouldn't work too much, Ivoa. It's when you're old, and have nothing else to do, that work becomes a pleasure.'

Purcell turned his head, looked into Ivoa's big blue eyes and felt his throat go dry. He said: 'And there's the scent of your hair, Ivoa.'

Ivoa smiled a slow smile and Purcell felt his heart beating. 'She's mine, if I want it,' he thought.

A dark figure suddenly filled the doorway. Purcell looked up and saw Mason, tightly buttoned, cravatted, and wearing shoes. Purcell was particularly astonished by the shoes. They were highly polished and the buckles glistened in the sun. Mason must have taken them off before landing, and then put them on again.

'Mr Purcell,' Mason said, very cold and correct, and without giving the Tahitians so much as a glance, 'can I have a word with you?'

Purcell got to his feet, went out of the hut and joined Mason a few paces away.

'Mr Purcell,' Mason said rather distantly, glancing quickly at the lieutenant's hair, bare back and feet, 'you seem to be very popular with these savages. Will you introduce me to their chief?'

'I shall be very happy to introduce you to Otou,' Purcell said drily. 'Otou is a gentleman.'

'Well, then, introduce me to this . . . gentleman,' Mason said, 'and explain the situation to him.'

'Without concealing anything?'

'Without concealing anything, and tell him our plans.'

As soon as Otou and his children saw Adamo and the chief of the *Peritani* returning, they rose to their feet, and Otou came to the threshold, smiling, his stomach well to the fore, his big demonstrative hands indicating his house to the newcomer and inviting him to enter with a certain nobility.

Mason had observed from afar Adam Purcell's arrival on the beach through his telescope; he had thought the embraces with which he had been welcomed wholly disgusting, and he feared he might himself be subjected to them. But nothing of the kind occurred. Mehani and Ivoa bowed their heads without coming near him and Otou, although prodigal of courteous gestures, did not even extend his hand.

Mason sat down on a mat. There was a long pause. The Tahitians were gravely silent. Mason, almost intimidated by the reserve of their greeting, coughed, blushed, blinked, and finally without looking at anyone, explained *The Blossom*'s situation in English and the request he wished to make to Otou, who listened and nodded his head as if had always foreseen this speech. And while Adamo translated, he continued to nod and smile urbanely, as if it were quite normal for the first-lieutenant of a British ship to kill his captain and lead the crew in mutiny.

When Purcell had finished, Otou got to his feet, filling the hut with his great stature. He made a long speech, at once flowery and precise, and accompanied it by eloquent gestures from his big hands. He made no reference whatever to the events on board *The Blossom*. He dealt merely with Mason's requests. Yes, he would supply the chief of the big canoe with food for a long voyage. Yes, he would give him a goat and a he-goat to breed from, and also a couple of dogs; and since he wanted them, a couple of wild pigs, though the *Peritani* chief would find these animals in abundance in all the South Sea islands. Moreover, the chief would find taros, yams, sweet potatoes and breadfruit trees everywhere. But since he wished from precaution to take roots and plants with him, Otou would supply them. Otou would do better. Otou possessed, as his personal property, the single cow and the single bull in Tahiti. They were descendants of the couple the great Captain Cook (Otou pronounced it '*Touto*', the 'K' sound not existing in Tahitian) had in the past given Otou's family. Otou would make a gift of these animals to the chief of the great canoe.

Purcell translated, amused by Otou's guile. With what a magnificent air he made a present of these cattle to Mason! In fact, he was delighted to get rid of them. The Tahitians liked neither the meat nor the milk of these animals. Besides, they were far too large. They ate too much, and devastated the gardens. Had it not been for the memory of the donor, Otou would have had them killed. He had at least taken care to separate the bull from the heifer so as to limit the consequences of the gift which, in the view of the Tahitians and of Otou himself, had greatly honoured his father at the time when his mother was still beautiful.

As Purcell was completing his translation, Otou uttered a cry, leapt quickly to his feet and rushed towards the door, shouting: 'Taboo! * Adamo! Taboo! There, on the beach, Adamo! Tell your chief that it's taboo in Tahiti!'

'What's the matter?' Mason said frowning. 'Why all the shouting? These natives are so emotional. What's taboo, Mr Purcell?'

'Muskets, Captain Mason. MacLeod's on the beach with a musket. He no doubt intends to go hunting.'

'Tell him to take the musket back on board,' Mason said. 'I don't want any trouble with the blacks.'

Purcell ran down to the lagoon and hailed the Scotsman. MacLeod turned, looked him disdainfully up and down and, as Purcell went towards him, decided to go slowly to meet him. He was tall and very thin, all legs, his shoulders narrow and pointed, and his eyes were small, grey and bright in a face like a knifeblade. He disliked everyone on principle and officers most of

* The word is really '*tapou*', since there is no 'b' sound in Tahitian.

all. He made no exception for Purcell. However, he did not detest him altogether, for Purcell was a Scotsman.

He came to a halt ten yards from the lieutenant and stood casually with his weight on his right leg, the left leg spread wide, the musket in the crook of his arm, determined not to stand to attention. Since the mutiny, his behaviour towards Mason and Purcell had bordered on the rebellious, though he had not absolutely refused to obey them.

'MacLeod,' Purcell said, pretending not to notice the insolence of his attitude, 'take that musket back on board. It's the captain's order. Muskets are taboo in Tahiti.'

'I wanted to shoot a wild pig,' MacLeod said, shaking his head, and his hard, morose face suddenly took on the childish look Purcell had noticed before. He felt like a schoolmaster confiscating a naughty schoolboy's marbles.

'A wild pig!' Purcell said with a laugh. 'You need only ask the Tahitians for one! They'll give it to you.'

'I know that,' MacLeod said contemptuously. 'I know them well. I've been to this part of the world before. The idiots'll give you anything they have. They've got no sense, that's what I say! It's lucky they don't wear shirts, they'd give them away!'

'Why should they bother to economise?' Purcell said. 'They've got everything in abundance.'

'It may not last for ever,' MacLeod said mistrustfully, as if he expected the climate of Tahiti to become like that of the Highlands one day, 'and anyway I'd like to have shot a pig rather than be given one by these damned naked idiots! Give! Give! That's the only thing they know about here! Proper savages! And I don't like people giving me things! The MacLeods have never owed anybody anything. Never! I don't give presents!' he went on proudly. 'And I don't want people to give them to me either!'

'I'm sorry, MacLeod,' Purcell said, 'but muskets are taboo in Tahiti.'

'Taboo! Another piece of their damned foolishness!' Mac-Leod said, shaking his head contemptuously. 'If I were the captain, I'd bring these blacks to heel! . . . God damn me,' he went on with a wide threatening gesture that seemed to include the whole island, 'we've got the muskets, haven't we? So it's we who should be laying down the law, that's clear enough! '

He turned away without saluting and went towards one of the ship's boats that was still afloat. Purcell watched him move away, tall, thin, ungainly, his tow-coloured hair thin on the crown of his head, the musket in the crook of his arm, its barrel pointing at the ground.

As soon as Purcell returned to the hut, Mason got to his feet, asked his second-in-command to thank Otou, and went away. His abrupt departure astonished the Tahitians. They stood on the threshold and followed the *Peritani* chief with their eyes. When he reached the edge of the lagoon, Mason sat down, took his shoes off, got up again, hailed the duty boat and returned on board. They could see him sitting in the stern, putting his shoes on again.

'Why doesn't he stay with us?' Ivoa asked in astonishment. 'What's he going to do in the big canoe?'

'Nothing,' Purcell said. 'He's decided to stay on board all the time we're at Tahiti.'

'Why?' Mehani asked. 'Doesn't he like us?'

'He hasn't even asked himself that question,' Purcell said, sitting down again.

He looked at his friends. Once again, he felt free and happy. Mason had not been unpleasant, but his mere presence had been enough to extinguish all his pleasure.

'You're going to live on an island with that man . . .' Otou said, a gesture of his large hands completing his thought.

'He's not at all ill-natured,' Purcell said smiling, 'and I get on well with everyone.'

But he suddenly thought of Simon's hatred of him and his brow clouded.

'É Adamo é! ' Ivoa said. 'Don't be sad! I don't want Adamo to be sad,' she went on petulantly, addressing her father and Mehani as if they were responsible. 'As for me,' she went on, 'I don't like that man with things made of skin on his feet.'

'Ivoa! ' Otou said, surprised that Ivoa should express so decided an opinion.

Ivoa lowered her long lashes over her blue eyes and hid her head against Adamo's shoulder.

'Why don't you like him?' Purcell asked.

She raised her head and said with a pout: 'He didn't look at me.'

Purcell laughed.

'It's quite true!' Mehani cried, hitting the mat, then clapping his hands together. 'I noticed it! The *Peritani* chief was frightened of Ivoa! And he scarcely even looked at my father. He was sitting there like a tortoise, his head and his four legs inside his shell.'

Ivoa burst out laughing.

'Ho! Ho!' Otou said. 'That's no way to speak of a guest!'

But he was laughing too. After a moment, Ivoa gave Purcell a long plaited basket containing oranges, mangoes, avocados and wild bananas.

'I'll peel your orange,' she said, when he had helped himself.

Mehani looked up and glanced quickly at Otou who smiled. 'Perhaps this has a significance I don't understand?' Purcell thought. He looked questioningly at Ivoa. She caught him looking at her, turned her head and gazed at him from her luminous eyes. In an ordinary conversational tone, as if it was a question of going for a walk, she said: 'Adamo, if you want me on your island, I'll come with you.'

Purcell looked at Otou, then at Mehani. They were smiling. They seemed to be neither surprised, nor upset.

'Do you understand what it means, Ivoa?' he said at last in a choking voice, taking her by the wrist. 'If you come with me, it's for always. You'll never see Otou again.'

'I understand,' Ivoa said, lowering her eyes to the orange she was peeling.

There was a silence and Otou extended his large hands in front of him, the palms forward, the thumb separated from the other fingers.

'It's you who do not understand, Adamo,' he said with a smile. 'Ivoa has but one life, and which of us is the more important in her life, I or you, Adamo?'

3

'Well,' Mason said, 'since we're sailing tomorrow it's time we made the acquaintance of the Tahitian volunteers. How many have you got, Mr Purcell?'

He was sitting in his cabin, in precisely the same attitude as a week ago, a chart spread out in front of him, and a glass of rum in his hand. However, there was one difference: he asked Purcell to sit down.

'Six,' Purcell said. 'Here are their names: Mehani, Tetahiti, Mehoro, Kori, Timi and Ohou.'

'Do you know them?'

'I know Mehani and Tetahiti well, the others less well. In any case, they're athletic fellows and we shall be glad of their weight on a halyard.'

'Six Tahitians,' Mason said, inclining his square head with an anxious look. 'Six and our seven men, that makes thirteen. It's none too many to work *The Blossom*.

'I've not read you all my list,' Purcell said, 'there are also twelve women, and Tahitian women are perfectly capable of going aloft . . .'

'Women!' Mason cried. 'Women on board my ship!'

He started to his feet and upset the chart and his glass of rum. Purple in the face, blinking, his lips closed in a tight line, he was for a moment incapable of speech. He squared his shoulders as if he were about to attack Purcell and thrusting his stubborn face forward he exploded: 'Never, Mr Purcell, never!'

There was a silence. Purcell bent down, picked up the chart with two fingers and handed it to him.

'I fear we have no choice,' he said calmly. 'The Tahitians won't sail without their women. Nor will our men. They're afraid the island you're looking for will be uninhabited . . .'

'Women on board, Mr Purcell! Whoever heard of such a thing?' Mason repeated, his grey-blue eyes wide at the enormity of the proposal.

'The fact is,' Purcell said, 'the circumstances are exceptional . . .'

'But women on board!' Mason repeated, forgetting himself

45

so far as to raise his hands in the air as the Tahitians did.

Purcell allowed a few seconds to elapse.

'I fear,' he went on, 'that you're in no position to prohibit them. The Tahitians will refuse to come; and the men are quite capable of seizing the ship, putting us ashore and setting sail without us.'

'They'll cast her away on a rock,' Mason said contemptuously.

'Perhaps, but you and I will be on the beach at Tahiti . . .'

Mason sat down again, placed the chart in front of him, lowered his eyes and said: 'How many of them are there?'

'Twelve,' Purcell said, sitting opposite him. 'Here are their names.'

'Their names don't matter,' Mason said angrily, sweeping them away with a gesture.

There was another silence, and then he went on more calmly: 'They must have quarters apart from the men.'

Purcell screwed up his eyes. The precaution seemed to him absurd.

'Certainly,' he said in a flat voice. 'I'll arrange separate quarters for them.'

Mason emptied his glass at a single gulp, put it down and seemed resigned to the inevitable.

'You'll attend to all the details,' he went on. 'I don't want to hear these women mentioned.'

'Aye, aye, sir.'

Purcell replaced the list in his pocket, but did not get up.

'With your permission,' he said, 'I still have something else to talk to you about.'

He added: 'Something that's worrying me.'

'Go on,' Mason said, his expression becoming suspicious.

'He's already closing his mind,' Purcell thought. He went on: 'If the island you're looking for is uninhabited, a problem will arise. Our colony consists of nine British and six Tahitians. Fifteen men in all. There are only twelve women.'

'Well?' Mason said curtly.

'There'll be three men without women.'

'Well?' Mason said again.

'I fear it may give rise to a very dangerous situation. I therefore propose we either disembark three Tahitians . . .'

'Impossible,' said Mason drily.

'Or embark three more women . . .'

The effect of this suggestion was quite extraordinary. Mason looked at him, his eyes began blinking, his hands trembled and he turned red with anger.

'Never!' he cried, drawing hiself up to his full height. 'Mr Purcell, you should be ashamed of making such a suggestion to me! We already have too many woman! They're of no interest to me whatever!' Raising his right hand as if taking an oath, he went on: 'I do not even wish to speak of them! The reason I chose the career of a sailor was that on board at least . . . Mr Purcell,' he continued, leaving the sentence in the air, 'you know very well that if I consulted my own convenience, I would take none at all! And you sit there, in front of me, cool as a cucumber, and suggest . . . Mr Purcell! I've known only one decent woman in my life; and that was my sister. All the rest are . . . are . . . As for me,' he went on without defining the enemy sex, 'I have no wish to leave progeny behind me . . . Twelve women,' he exploded with a renewal of anger. 'Twelve! In my ship! Twelve half-naked creatures who'll go cackling and screeching about my deck from morning till night,' he said disgustedly, as if the Tahitian women were terns or parakeets. 'Let me tell you, Mr Purcell, and you can tell the men from me, that I'd rather remain in Tahiti, and hang myself if need be with my own hands, than take one more woman aboard *The Blossom*!'

He took a deep breath, and said more calmly, though his tone forbade further argument: 'That'll be all for the moment, Mr Purcell.'

Purcell saluted stiffly and left the cabin in a rage. It was mad! It was an incredible folly! Mason was taking more trouble to couple his goats and pigs than to pair off the citizens of the future colony. 'How absurdly stubborn!' Purcell thought with another gust of anger. What difference could it make whether he took fifteen instead of twelve!

Merely from the point of view of their strong physique, the Tahitian women were undeserving of Mason's contempt. They learnt almost as quickly as the men to go aloft, to reef down or take in sail. *The Blossom* had not left Tahiti a week before they had become excellent topmen. To Purcell it was a curious sight to watch them climb along the ratlines at the word of command to the dizzy end of the spars, laughing, singing and uttering shrill cries.

On the ninth day after sailing, *The Blossom* ran into a fairly violent storm and Mason gave the order to take in sail. Purcell sent the crew aloft. The sailors, aware of the danger, obeyed with a promptness they had not shown for a week. But apart from Mehani and Tetahiti, the Tahitians refused to move. Perhaps the bad weather would have frightened them less had they been in their own canoes. But the dizzy pitching, the shock of the waves against the hull, and the wild lurching of *The Blossom* as she righted herself on her keel, terrified them. They had taken refuge in the crew's quarters, and lay there, seasick, huddled together and grey with terror. Naked as they were, they were frozen with cold. Nothing could persuade them out of their inertia. They thought they were lost.

The storm lasted scarcely a day; and the ship was never really in danger. But the episode spoilt the relations, which till then had been friendly, between the Tahitians and the crew. The sailors could not forgive the 'blacks' for having 'let them down' at a difficult moment.

The fine weather returned, but with it the wind dropped, the heat became stifling, and *The Blossom* lay becalmed in a sea as heavy as oil. All was still. There was not a breath of air, not a ripple at the stem. The sun alone seemed to move. The sails hung pitifully slack, wrinkled, MacLeod said, as an old woman's skin. The horizon seemed to imprison the ship in a circle of fire, and Purcell had the impression that the sea was little by little closing in on *The Blossom* like solidifying jelly.

One morning old Johnson pointed to the rubbish he had thrown overboard the day before still floating alongside. In fifty years at sea he had never seen the like.

Leaning on the rail, the sailors put out fishing lines from morning till night. The Tahitians went out in boats, and stood on the thwarts, harpoon in hand. But the sea, though full of fish, would not yield up a single one. As if disgusted by her immobility, even the sharks had deserted *The Blossom*.

The empty sky, the dead sea, the leaden colours, all gave them an impression of having reached unawares some petrified planet that would not release its prey. A torrid sun bleached the sails, and melted the tar in the seams. Though buckets of water were thrown over them twice a day, the timbers above the waterline were beginning to open. The sailors had to wear wraps round their feet because of the heat of the deck.

Fresh water was beginning to run short and Mason rationed the food. Nevertheless, the bull had to be killed, and a few days later the heifer. Then they ate the goat and its mate, the wild pigs, the two dogs, and there was nothing left alive on board but humans.

Another week went by, and then the wind came from the west, rippling the sea as it approached. The sails filled to splitting, and the rigging vibrated from one end of the ship to the other; the deck trembled beneath their feet, and the heavy three-master, raising her prow to the waves, sprang forward with the lightness of a bird.

An hour later they sailed through a shoal of flying fish. A great number of them landed on deck and through the transparent water they could see the big fish chasing them. Purcell ordered the quartermaster to heave to, lines were thrown, and they caught as many as they wanted. It was a happy carnage and in a few minutes they had the first real meal for a week.

It was scarcely finished when the sky grew cloudy, the air turned deliciously fresh, and rain began to fall. They dragged every sort of receptacle on deck, including casks and awnings. The Tahitians took off their *pareu*, and raising their hands to the sky, threw their heads back and shouted for joy, their mouths full of rain.

Little by little their bodies moved into the rhythm of a dance. The men began to clap their hands, and the women chanted an inarticulate song that grew louder and faster till it reached a breathless crescendo. Their hair dishevelled and their dark bodies gleaming in the rain, they each danced on one particular spot. They scarcely moved either their feet or their shoulders, concentrating all the life and movement of their bodies in their wide hips.

The sailors, with the exception of Smudge, had also taken their clothes off, and for a moment Purcell thought, so contagious was the Tahitians' excitement, that they were going to join in the dance. But they remained on the forecastle, washed by gusts of rain, and watched the Tahitians from afar, slapping each other's backs and apparently rather embarrassed by their nakedness. Purcell thought with amusement that the whole scene was rather Biblical. The Tahitians represented man in a state of innocence; and the *Peritani* man after the fall.

While pretending to watch the rain collecting in the awnings, Purcell missed nothing of what was going forward on deck. He was struck by Smudge's behaviour. The little man had retained his shirt and trousers, and was standing rather apart from both groups. He had taken up his position against the rail between two boats, and there he stayed, as if shrinking into a hole, bowed, hollow-chested, one shoulder higher than the other. His grey hair fell over his forehead, his eyebrows frowned above his pointed nose, and his lower lip jutted contemptuously. Coiled in on himself, as it were, he stared at the Tahitians with his sly, malevolent, rat-like little eyes.

Purcell suddenly heard a woman call: 'Jono! Jono! Jono! '

He turned, but the rain was falling more heavily and half blinded him. He saw a tall massive figure leave the group of Tahitian women and go towards that of the sailors. She stopped half way. It was Omaata.

Everyone suddenly turned to look at her. She had a splendid brown body and was six feet five inches tall. Though each detail of her anatomy seemed larger than human proportions, the whole had a certain harmony. The sailors fell silent while they watched her. Since *The Blossom* had left Tahiti there was no woman on board of whom they talked more often. They had a sort of respectful admiration for the size of her thighs, the amplitude of her back and the hugeness of her breasts. Her strength had already become legendary and had given rise to a fund of stories: she had given MacLeod a friendly tap on the back and had inadvertently sent him sprawling twenty feet across the deck. She had broken a spar merely by leaning on it. She had heedlessly parted a rope thick as your wrist. There was some joking as to what would happen if she fell in love with little Smudge. It formed the basis for many salacious witticisms. The general conclusion was that little Smudge would be overlaid.

Omaata took a further two or three steps forward. A ray of sunlight piercing the dark sky shone on her, and the sailors were able to gaze at the curves of her body at leisure. Purcell screwed up his eyes. The sailors were like so many tom-cats contemplating with an admiration not unmingled with awe the vast contours of a tigress.

'Jono! Jono!' Omaata called in her deep voice.

'Go on!' MacLeod said to John Hunt, giving him a little shove in the back.

Hunt docilely left the group and went heavily towards Omaata. He was as tall and broad as she was, scarcely more massive, and hairy from eyebrows to toes, which gave him a prestige with the Tahitians who were generally beardless. He gazed at Omaata out of his little porcine eyes. His red, hirsute face seemed to have been crushed and flattened by some gigantic blow which had doubled its width and destroyed all profile. However, he seemed more alive than usual and to be almost on the point of smiling. As for Omaata, she was laughing with all her strong white teeth and there was a gleam dancing in her eyes which were as large as pools.

They stood face to face for some little while, as if Omaata realised that Hunt thought slowly and must not be hurried. Then she seized his hand, dragged him into the group of dancers and took up her position in front of him. She began swaying her hips while staring at him and chanting in a deep voice: 'Jono! Jono! Jono!'

The Tahitians gathered round Hunt, clapping their hands. Mehani gave him a little tap on the shoulder and danced beside him as if to encourage him.

Omaata went on chanting: 'Jono! Jono! Jono!'

Hunt suddenly began to move. He half raised his eyes and began to jerk about like a bear, his arms dangling and his little pale eyes fixed on Omaata. Meanwhile, though the warm tropical rain kept falling, there was a little rent in the dark clouds that obscured the whole horizon, and the sun appeared very low in the west. The deck, the masts and the sails of *The Blossom* were lit up, silhouetted in white, unreal relief against the inky sky, and the light, shining across the surface of the sea in long parallel rays, struck the group of dancers almost horizontally, lengthening their shadows unnaturally on the deck, and setting Hunt's red hair aflame.

'Jono! Jono! Jono!'

Omaata's deep voice seemed to coo and roar at once, and Hunt jerked from side to side, nodding his great bearded head to the rhythm. He looked very red and white among the brown bodies of the Tahitians.

'Jono! Jono! Jono!'

Omaata gradually drew nearer and nearer to Hunt, undulating her vast hips, her huge dark eyes fixed on him and the palms of her hands turned towards him. She came within arm's length and they danced face to face for a whole minute. Then Hunt uttered a groan that had nothing human about it, drew himself up to his full height and brought his big red paws down on Omaata's shoulders. She gave a cooing laugh, disengaged herself with extraordinary speed, and began to run with Hunt at her heels. She ran in circles round the deck, turning every second to see if Hunt was following her, and continuously laughing her deep laugh. Finally she disappeared like a whirlwind down the companion-way to the crew's quarters. Hunt dashed down the steps after her. The sailors were laughing themselves sick. Smudge, all alone in his hole, uncrossed his little legs, turned his head away and spat contemptuously into the sea.

'Sir,' White said, 'the captain's asking for you.'

Purcell sighed, went to his cabin to change and reported to Mason.

The captain's mahogany table was screwed to the deck by little wooden wedges round each foot; and Mason himself seemed screwed to his chair behind the table. Neatly dressed and cravatted, he seemed as remote from what was going forward on deck as the inhabitant of another planet.

As soon as Purcell presented himself, he placed his finger on the chart and said: 'There it is.'

Purcell moved round the table and leaned over. About half-way between Rapa Island and Easter Island, Mason had drawn a pencil cross on the chart. Purcell looked up questioningly, and Mason went on: 'There it is. That's the island we're looking for. If the wind doesn't fail, we should make it on the evening of the day after tomorrow.'

Purcell looked at the chart.

'At Tahiti you were talking of an unknown island.'

'It is unknown,' Mason said sharply. 'Jackson mentions it in his *History of a Voyage in the Southern Hemisphere,* but it appears in no Admiralty chart; even in the most recent, such as this one. Officially, the island does not exist. Nevertheless, Jackson gives its longitude and latitude, and that's how I can mark it on the chart and lay a course.'

Purcell looked at him.

'What if another captain who has read Jackson's book should find himself in the neighbourhood? . . .'

'I have thought of that, Mr Purcell,' Mason said. 'It's a risk but it's a very limited risk since the island is almost inaccessible. According to Jackson, it is very mountainous, is surrounded by steep cliffs and has no bay or anchorage of any kind. It seems it's even difficult to land by boat owing to the surf. Jackson himself did not land there. However, he approached near enough to describe it. It's about five miles in circumference, covered with luxuriant vegetation, and is cut by a stream. I must add that Jackson discovered it in the dry season, from which one may suppose that the stream is not intermittent. That is clearly an important point.'

As Purcell remained silent, Mason went on: 'I should like your opinion, Mr Purcell.'

'Well,' said Purcell hesitantly, 'if the island is where Jackson places it, and if it is as he describes, I think it would suit us perfectly, except . . .'

'Except what?'

'You said "five miles in circumference", I believe . . . That is perhaps rather small.'

Mason thrust his square brow forward and said peremptorily: 'It is quite large enough for thirty people.'

Purcell went on: 'Now, yes. But in a few years' time . . .'

Mason set the argument aside with a sweep of his hand. 'When I read Jackson's description in Tahiti, the objection occurred to my mind, Mr Purcell. But I rejected it.' He fell silent without explaining why he had rejected it. Purcell felt irritated. Mason had already known where they were going in Tahiti and had kept him in ignorance for three weeks.

Mason went on: 'I would be obliged to you not to reveal to the crew what I have just told you.'

'Is there any reason for concealing it?'

'None. They are not to know it, that's all.'

There was no point in the secret. It's only value was hierarchical. The commander was exercising the privilege of a commander to leave his subordinates in ignorance of what the commander knew. Thus the secret of *The Blossom's* destination had placed a distance between Purcell and himself and, now that it was shared between the captain and the second-in-command, it was to maintain a similar distance between the officers and the crew. It seemed laughable to Purcell. Mason was continuing to employ all the little mean tricks of command, when his command no longer existed. And he was not even aware that it did not.

'Well, we're agreed, Mr Purcell,' Mason said at last, as if the prolonged silence had served to dissipate Purcell's reservations about the size of the island.

Purcell drew himself up.

'If you please, Captain Mason?'

'Yes, Mr Purcell?'

'I have a request to make.'

Mason looked at him. 'He's already withdrawing into himself,' Purcell thought with annoyance. 'His first reaction is always negative.'

'Go on,' Mason said.

'As captain of this ship,' Purcell said, 'you have, I believe, should occasion arise, the right to marry couples who express their wish to be united.'

'Quite correct.'

'I desire,' Purcell went on with a certain gravity, 'that you make use of the prerogatives of your position to unite me by the ceremony of marriage to a Tahitian woman.'

Mason got to his feet, blushed, put his hands behind his back, and said without looking at Purcell: 'You wish to marry a black, Mr Purcell?'

'Yes, Captain Mason!'

He said it with such energy and restrained violence that Mason was disconcerted. He never would have believed that

Purcell could be so aggressive. Standing with his profile towards Purcell, he had fixed his eyes on a picture showing *The Blossom* in process of building. Though he sniffed haughtily to show his displeasure, he was weighing the situation with a certain wariness. Purcell was rather too fond of the blacks and, like all Scotsmen, was a damned barrack-room lawyer, but apart from that there was nothing to reproach him with. Mason did not want to quarrel with him and realised it might be dangerous to reject his request. On the other hand, to marry his second-in-command to a native was clearly unthinkable.

'You're a Dissenter, I believe,' he said contemptuously.

Purcell looked at him. He did not see where this was leading.

'I have, indeed, sympathies with the Dissenters,' he said after a moment.

'As captain of a British ship,' Mason said, 'I can marry you only in accordance with the rites of the Church of England.'

'So that's it!' Purcell thought, repressing a smile. Mason was attributing to him his own formalism.

'There is nothing shocking to me in the Anglican marriage rite,' he said at once. 'My objections to the Church of England are on other points.'

Mason was surprised to hear Purcell speak so coolly of his 'objections' to the Church of which His Majesty was the head. In expressing himself thus, Purcell was, in Mason's eyes, doubly at fault: he was lacking in loyalty to his sovereign and he had the bad taste to attach importance to religion.

'You do not understand my objection,' he said stiffly. 'I do not admit my right to marry a Dissenter according to the rites of the Church of England.'

Purcell realised irritably that he had been wrong. This was not formalism, it was mere evasion. Mason was trying to refuse by heeling over backwards. 'I did not say I was a Dissenter,' he replied drily. 'I said I had sympathies with the Dissenters. Officially, I am a member of the Church of England. You will find it mentioned in the ship's papers.'

'And now,' Mason thought, 'if I refuse, it's a break.' He sighed, turned suddenly to Purcell and said loudly: 'As far as I'm concerned, Mr Purcell, I cannot understand your decision.

But, after all, your private life is your affair. I do not feel I have the right to reject your request.'

'A change of course in extremis,' Purcell thought. The two men were standing face to face, silent and embarrassed. Both knew they had been within an inch of a break. They were both relieved not to have reached that point, and yet they were annoyed with each other. One because he had had to fight to obtain his rights; and the other because he had had to give way.

'Select two witnesses among the crew,' Mason said in a tone of command, 'and punctually at noon tomorrow . . .'

He left the sentence in suspense as if it was repugnant to him to finish it. Purcell bowed his head and said with some stiffness: 'Thank you, Captain Mason.' And he withdrew without waiting for Mason to dismiss him. He felt irritated, anxious and hurt. Without either of them desiring it their relations were deteriorating every day, simply because they were so different from each other.

The next day, in the presence of the seamen Jones and Baker, and before the crew assembled on the half deck, Captain Mason, commanding *The Blossom,* baptised Ivoa, and then united her, according to the rites of the Church of England, to Lieutenant Adam Briton Purcell.

None of the rest of *The Blossom*'s crew followed the second-in-command's example.

On 10 July, at about seven o'clock in the morning, a large black cloud became visible in the south under a perfectly blue sky; it appeared to be advancing directly towards *The Blossom.* The crew gazed at it in surprise, for its course seemed improbable owing to the fact that the wind was blowing from the north.

The cloud came nearer and spread at an abnormal speed, taking the shape of a triangle, and Jones shouted joyfully, 'Birds!'

There was a clamour of joy. Seamen, Tahitians and women all hurried to the bows.

'White,' Purcell cried, 'inform the captain!'

Purcell turned and found Ivoa standing behind him.

'Adamo,' she said in a low voice, 'I thought we should never arrive.'

Purcell put his hand on her shoulder, pressed Ivoa to his side and stood there silent and motionless, his head raised. They were approaching their goal. The land on which these birds nested was to be that in which they would spend their lives at each other's side to the end.

'Terns!' Mehani said, pointing to the birds.

There were much excitement and chattering among the Tahitians.

'What are they saying, sir?' Baker asked.

'That their eggs are as good as chickens'.'

'I mistrust them,' MacLeod said.

The terns were now flying round *The Blossom*, darkening the sky with their numbers. They looked rather like small seagulls, but their beaks were longer and their tails forked. They began diving on the port side and the crew went to the rail. No doubt seeking protection beneath her shadow, a compact shoal of bright little sardines was swimming parallel to *The Blossom*'s hull. The terns fell on them by thousands, so that the whole surface of the sea turned white with the splash of their diving. Purcell was astonished by the sight; it seemed to be raining birds.

'Look, sir!' Baker said, pointing to the sardines. 'The poor little brutes get eaten by everyone!'

Splendid bonitos with black and blue striped backs were flashing through the transparent water and throwing themselves on the sardines with incredible voracity. But the massacre did not stop there. The bonitos themselves were being chased by sharks that beat the sea with their huge tails and seized them with a great snapping of jaws.

The seamen gradually fell silent. At first they were amused by the terns' fishing, but it was turning into carnage. The sharks, after tearing the bonitos to pieces, devoured each other, and the sea was stained with their blood.

'By God!' old Johnson said. 'I don't like the sight of it. It's no life being a fish.'

'It's the law,' MacLeod said, his thin elbows on the rail. 'The small fry get eaten up by the big. There's nothing to make a fuss about. It's the law. One's simply got to be the strongest, that's all.'

Mason came up on deck, rather red in the face and carrying his telescope.

'Is land in sight, Mr Purcell?' he called, his voice quavering.

'Not yet, Captain Mason.'

There was a silence. Mason seemed disappointed as a child. 'Those birds are disgusting,' he said crossly, looking at the deck covered with their droppings.

'It seems their eggs are edible,' Purcell said.

Without asking Purcell to accompany him, Mason went forward to the bows. Meanwhile, the shoal of sardines moved away from the ship's side and the terns left *The Blossom* in pursuit. Purcell ordered the seamen to swab the decks. He had to repeat the order twice before he was obeyed.

When it was done, he went forward. Mason's eye was glued to his telescope. He was standing absolutely still, his face red and the muscles of his neck taut. After a while, he lowered the telescope, drew himself up, and opened and closed his right eye several times. He began rubbing it with the tips of his fingers.

'I've been looking too long. My eye's going cloudy. Will you take a look, Mr Purcell?'

Purcell put his eye to the telescope and adjusted it to suit his vision. He had imagined the island to be like Tahiti: mountains separated from the sea by a protecting reef, a calm lagoon, and a coastal plain. The reality was quite different. The island rose like a black, crenellated cliff, dominating the sea from over a thousand feet, its base battered by huge white scrolls of surf.

Purcell handed the telescope back to Mason. 'It's a rock and not very hospitable,' he said without looking at him.

'It needs to be inhospitable,' Mason said with a good humour Purcell had never seen in him before.

He pointed the telescope towards the island again and went on with animation : 'Yes, Mr Purcell, it's a strange thing to say, but I should have been very disappointed if this island was not, as Jackson says, almost inaccessible.'

'We've still got to land on it ourselves,' Purcell replied.

Mason straightened up, lowered the telescope, and began to laugh without apparent reason. Purcell noted that it was the first time he had seen him laugh since Jimmy's death.

'We shall land, Mr Purcell!' he said gaily. 'We shall land, even if we have to use ropes to climb the cliff!'

And he added with unusual exuberance: 'And I hope they'll be as steep everywhere! We can't afford the luxury of visitors! They'd be fatal to us! Devil take it! A man has only one neck to carry his head! We could wish for nothing better, Mr Purcell! It's a true natural fortress! No one will come to interfere in our little affairs, I can guarantee that! No, no! No curious visitors! We shall be quite private there! The island's a little marvel! If we can find enough earth to grow our yams in and enough water to prevent our ever suffering from thirst, we can defy the whole world!'

He turned and leaned against the bulwark, his arms spread wide, his hands on the man-rope, and looked at the terns still fishing a cable's length from the ship.

'It's an astonishing sight, isn't it,' Purcell said, 'to see them all dive together?'

'We shan't lack eggs for breakfast,' Mason said with satisfaction.

A little after two o'clock that afternoon, *The Blossom* made a bay which was wide open to the north-east wind. Mason decided to anchor there nevertheless, for he was in a hurry to get ashore. He had a boat lowered to make a tour of his domain, and to Purcell's surprise took command of it himself. He had no intention of leaving it to anyone else to make a detailed reconnaissance of his fortress's defences.

He returned three hours later, and both he and the seamen were delighted with what they had seen. The west and south coasts of the island consisted of steep cliffs, jagged promontories and huge piles of rock. On the east, however, they had found a little creek which led to a beach of fine sand. But the beach was defended by a girdle of reefs, and on the landward side by an overhanging cliff. There was only one possible conclusion: the sole practicable anchorage was *The Blossom's* present one, though it was a very bad one. And the only possible place to land was undoubtedly the beach lying two cable lengths from the ship, provided a boat could reach it without being swamped by the surf.

Shortly after Mason's return, they had to put out another

anchor since *The Blossom* was dragging towards the shore under the north-westerly wind. Purcell joined Mason on the poop and listened for some time in silence to the wild surf defending the approaches to the beach. Its low roar seemed to fill the horizon, only to cease suddenly as the backwash met the oncoming wave. Then the two waves would rise in a huge breaker that beat down on the sand like a thunderclap.

There was certainly a cave somewhere in the high rocks that shut off the beach on the right, for it seemed to fill and empty at intervals, when there was a bigger wave than usual, with a sharp detonation as the air decompressed and a long siphoning sound as the sea flowed out of it. The crash and the gurgle that followed it made an even more sinister impression on Purcell than the roar of the surf.

'I'm wondering,' Mason said after a moment, 'whether the island's inhabited.'

'If it is,' Purcell said, 'there's a fair chance the natives will be hostile.'

'Yes,' Mason said, looking anxious, 'that's what I think. For, if they were friendly, they would have surrounded us with their canoes long ago.'

Purcell looked at the thick foliage crowning the cliff and said: 'There may be dozens of eyes watching us from under those leaves.'

'Yes,' Mason said, 'and it would be tiresome to have to start our occupation with a minor war.'

Purcell looked at him in amazement. Was Mason really contemplating occupying the island against the will of the inhabitants and at the price of a fight?

'It would be inhuman, Captain Mason!' he said with decision. 'We can't kill the poor people to take their island from them!'

Mason stared at him for a full second. Then he turned red from the neck up, his eyes blinked several times, he thrust his head forward, and Purcell thought he was going to explode. But to his great surprise Mason restrained himself and a weighty silence fell between them; when he spoke again it was perfectly calmly, indeed as if Purcell had raised no objections whatever.

'Mr Purcell, you will take command of the whaleboat and endeavour to land.'

'Aye, aye, sir.'

'Take six men with you, with muskets and ropes. If you succeed in getting through the surf, you will haul the boat up on the beach and scale the cliff. Your task is to discover if the island is inhabited. If you are attacked, return to the boat and re-embark. There will be a second boat a cable's length from the beach to cover you with musket fire in case you're pursued. If you are not attacked, take a look at as much of the island as you can between now and nightfall and return on board to report to me.'

'Aye, aye, sir.'

Purcell was silent for a moment and then said: 'If you please, Captain Mason?'

Mason glanced coldly at him.

'Yes, Mr Purcell?'

Purcell looked him straight in the eye. This time, he was determined not to let Mason cover his objections by one of his silences.

'I pray God that the island is uninhabited,' he said firmly. 'But if it is inhabited, you cannot count on me to fire on the natives, even if I am attacked.'

Mason turned purple in the face, his eyes blinked, he lowered his head, and shouted with extraordinary violence: 'God damn your conscience, Mr Purcell!'

'Captain Mason!'

Mason's eyes glittered.

'I said: "God damn your conscience, Mr Purcell".'

Purcell was silent a moment and then said gravely: 'I do not think you should talk like that.'

There was a silence. Mason was making so violent an effort to control himself that his hands trembled. He saw Purcell look at them and put them behind his back.

'I beg your pardon, Mr Purcell,' he said at last, turning his head away.

'It's of no consequence, Captain Mason. Everyone becomes exasperated from time to time.'

The exchange of courtesies relaxed the tension, but it was only superficial.

'In any case, there's no point in quarrelling, since we don't yet know whether the island is inhabited.'

Purcell felt his anger rising. Mason's whole attitude was one of evasion and denial. He took refuge in silence, anger or postponing a decision.

'Forgive me,' Purcell said firmly, 'it's before we land that we must determine our attitude to the natives. As far as I'm concerned, I must repeat that even if I'm attacked I shall not open fire on them.'

There was a silence, and Mason said: 'In that case, you'll be running a very grave risk, Mr Purcell, and I do not feel justified in asking you to run it. I shall command the whaleboat myself. You will remain on board.'

Purcell understood that Mason intended to open fire at the sight of the first spear.

'I think,' he said, his throat constricted, 'that it would be better if you let me command the whaleboat.'

Mason drew himself up.

'Mr Purcell, I recognise your right to say that you will not defend yourself if attacked, but I do not recognise your right to tell me what I should do.'

After that, there was nothing more to say. Purcell turned away. He was so indignant that he felt too unsure of himself to add another word.

He went to his cabin and threw himself down on his cot, his head on fire. He could not control the trembling of his legs. He shut his eyes, breathed deeply and tried to recover his serenity. *The Blossom* rose gently to the swell from the north-west and the golden afternoon sun flooded in through the square scuttle. 'And yet,' Purcell thought, 'men are going to massacre each other.'

After a while, he felt a cool hand on his brow and opened his eyes. Ivoa was sitting on the edge of his cot and looking at him in silence.

'Adamo,' she said in her low musical voice, 'are you ill?'

'No, Ivoa. I'm angry, that's all.'

She smiled, showing her bright white teeth, and her magnificent blue eyes seemed to light up her face. She said mischievously: 'The *Peritani* quarrel. The *Peritani* worry their heads. The *Peritani* are never happy.'

Purcell raised himself on an elbow and smiled at her.

'The *Peritani* think of the future. That's why they're never happy.'

Ivoa shrugged her beautiful shoulders.

'When misfortune happens, it happens. Why think of it in advance?'

'The *Peritani* think one should struggle against it.'

Ivoa raised her brown hand and put her fingers lightly on Purcell's lips.

'The *Peritani* are very proud. And sometimes they're crazy. The chief of the big canoe is quite mad.'

Purcell sat up and looked at her in astonishment. Ivoa could not know of his conversation with Mason. They had spoken in English.

'Why do you say that?'

She blushed, lowered her lids over her eyes, and hid her head against Purcell's shoulder. She had gone further than Tahitian discretion permitted and she was ashamed of her bad manners.

'Why do you say that?' Purcell asked.

But it was useless. She had already said too much, and she would say no more.

'Let's go on deck,' Purcell said, intrigued.

As they emerged from the half light of the companion-way, the bright day dazzled him. He blinked. There was an unusual silence on deck. The Tahitians and the crew were gathered in a group near the foremast and he could see the tall figures of Mehani and Tetahiti. Purcell looked at them, the sun in his eyes, wondering what they were doing and why they were so silent. He went over to them. The women and the seamen made way for him. He stopped and stood rooted to the spot in astonishment. The six Tahitians were drawn up in line. They each had a musket. Mason was explaining to them how it worked.

'Mehani!' Purcell cried. 'Muskets are taboo!'

Mehani looked at him in astonishment.

'They're taboo in Tahiti,' he said with a broad smile, 'but not on the great canoe.'

He seemed surprised that anything so obvious should be misunderstood. The taboo had no general incidence. It was limited to a single place.

'Mr Purcell!' Mason cried, having understood the word 'taboo'.

His voice was curt and his grey-blue eyes bright with anger. But he did not continue his protest. Mehani turned to him and watched him attentively. Purcell's interference had clearly been ineffective. Mason turned his back on him and continued his task.

Purcell had never seen him so patient with 'the blacks'. He went from one to another, showing them how to load, aim and fire. He repeated each movement a dozen times, and the Tahitians copied him. They were so keen to do it properly that they were sweating heavily. Purcell noted that their firing positions were already almost correct.

'Captain Mason,' Purcell said, making an effort to control the quivering of his voice, 'may you never regret what you're doing at this moment!'

Mason made no answer. He was pleased with the progress of his recruits. He ordered a seaman to place a small rum-keg on a chest. It was the size of a human head, and so balanced that it would topple over at the impact of a musket ball. In fact, the range was short and the target fairly large. Mason wanted to encourage his pupils.

The muskets were loaded with ball and the Tahitians began firing. There was some jostling among the group of women and seamen standing behind the Tahitians. They wanted a better view. Purcell nearly fell over Jones who put out an arm to save him. He noticed he had a musket in his hand. He looked about him. All the seamen were armed.

He said in a low voice: 'Where do all these muskets come from, Jones? I thought we had only five or six on board.'

'A whole heap of them were found in Burt's cabin, sir. New muskets. We thought he probably wanted to barter them for pearls.'

Shot succeeded shot, interrupted by fairly long intervals. Mason stood beside the firer and corrected his stance, aim and the position of his left hand on the musket before allowing him to fire.

'Do you know what the captain's planning, Jones?' Purcell asked.

'Yes, sir. Before handing the muskets out he gave us a short talk.'

'I don't like it,' he added. 'Why should we go and annoy those chaps if they don't want us?'

Purcell looked at him. He had porcelain blue eyes which reminded him of Jimmy's.

'What do your comrades think?'

'Apart from Baker and perhaps Johnson, they're for it.'

He blushed, stood on one leg, hesitated and said in a low, embarrassed voice: 'They think it will be easy.'

'You mean they're for it, because they think it will be easy?'

'Yes, sir.'

He added: 'They think that with the muskets they'll kill the lot.'

'And what do you think about it?'

He lowered his eyes and said with a shake of the head: 'Even if it is easy, I don't like it.'

There was a sudden clamour. A Tahitian had knocked the keg over. It was Mehoro. Cheered by his companions, he thrust out his huge chest and brandished his musket with an air of triumph. Purcell was struck by the behaviour of the Tahitians. They seemed to have lost their gentleness and kindness. They talked loudly, gesticulated, challenged each other truculently, jostled each other to fire before their turn, and were by now scarcely listening to Mason's instructions.

The women were silent. Dominating their group by her head and shoulders, Omaata stood quietly watching the firing with large dark eyes. Not a muscle of her face stirred.

The firing was going more rapidly, and whenever the keg fell the excited sweating Tahitians uttered cries of victory and brandished their muskets. There was an acrid odour of powder in the air, and the excitement was so great that Mason could not maintain even a semblance of discipline among the firers. He had been imprudent enough to distribute a dozen balls to each Tahitian, and they were now firing all at once, paying no attention to his shouted orders. Mason seemed ill at ease. He looked once or twice towards Purcell, but could not bring himself to ask his help. The firing had got completely out of hand. The Tahitians shouted and stamped their feet like madmen, and there

C

was such an atmosphere of unhealthy and dangerous hysteria that Purcell saw the seamen's faces beginning to look anxious. In contrast to the Tahitians, they stood silent and quiet, while the dark faces of the women had turned grey with fear.

There was a sudden tension. With a sweep of his arm, Kori pushed Mason, who was trying to prevent him firing before his turn, roughly aside. The keg fell. Mehoro claimed the success by brandishing his musket. But Kori had fired at the same time. Indeed, he claimed to have fired before him. Mehoro frowned angrily and, as Kori advanced threateningly towards him, levelled his musket at him. The women screamed, Mehoro lowered the musket which was not indeed loaded, but Kori seized Timi's musket in a fury and fired point-blank. Mehani knocked up the barrel just in time, and the ball made a hole in the foretopsail.

After that, a deep silence fell over the deck. Omaata left the group of women and, with unexpected speed in so huge a body, advanced on the Tahitian men. She drew herself up to her full height before them and her dark eyes flashed.

'That's enough!' she said in her deep voice. 'You'll fire no more! It is I, Omaata, who says so!'

They stared at her, amazed that a woman should address them on that tone.

'You ought to be ashamed of yourselves!' she went on angrily. 'I, a woman, am ashamed of your bad manners! You have shouted! You have not listened to your host! You have jostled him! Oh, I am ashamed! It makes me blush to see you behave so badly. The muskets have sent you mad!'

One by one, the Tahitians lowered their muskets to the deck. They hung their heads, their faces grey with anger and shame, furious that a woman should teach them a lesson, yet not daring to reply, for what she said was true.

'Yes,' Omaata went on, 'I, a woman, have made you ashamed of yourselves! You have behaved with less good sense than sons of pigs! What was the point of firing at a little empty keg? And yet, because of it, Kori nearly killed Mehoro!'

Kori, who was broad and squat and had arms like a gorilla's, pointed at Mehoro and said childishly: 'He began it!'

'Be silent!' Omaata said.

She went to him, took him by the hand and led him to Mehoro. The latter showed reluctance, but Omaata seized him by the wrist and forcibly placed his hand in Kori's.

The two Tahitians looked at each other for a moment, then Kori placed his right hand behind Mehoro's neck, pulled him towards him and began to rub his cheek against his. He was shaken by the horror of what he had nearly done. His thick lips parted, almost forming a square like those of a tragic mask. Tears trickled down his face, great hoarse sobs came from his throat, and his strong body trembled. He had nearly killed Mehoro! He was inconsolable! With his hand behind his victim's neck, he tried in vain to speak, his dark eyes fixed on Mehoro's face in an expression of despair.

Then the Tahitians surrounded him. They gave him little pats on the back, pinched his upper arm, and their voices softer than a woman's set about consoling him. Poor Kori, he had lost his temper! Oh, yes, he had lost his temper! But nothing serious had resulted. Poor Kori! Everybody knew how nice and kind and gentle he was. Everyone loved him. Everyone loved him.

'Mr Purcell,' Mason said, cutting these effusions short, 'tell the blacks to hand in the balls.'

Purcell translated, and Mehani immediately went from one to another to collect the balls, which he then handed to Mason. He then made an elegant and dignified speech, his gestures, though less rotund, recalling those of Otou.

'Mr Purcell?' Mason said.

'He is making an apology for the bad manners of the Tahitians, and assuring you that in future they will treat you with the respect due to a father.'

'Very well,' Mason said, 'I am very glad we've got them in hand again.'

He turned to go.

'Thank him,' he said over his shoulder.

'Is he angry?' Mehani asked, frowning. 'Why is he going away without making a reply?'

According to Tahitian etiquette, Mason ought to have answered the speech with another of similar length.

'It is I who must reply,' Purcell said.

And he improvised a speech in which the reproaches were so

veiled that they might have passed for compliments. But the Tahitians did not mistake his meaning. The whole time Purcell was speaking, they kept their eyes on the ground.

Purcell had not time to finish his speech. Mason called him. He was standing on the poop, gazing at the surf.

'What were you saying to them?' he asked suspiciously.

'I was thanking them for their apology.'

'Is "thank you" so long in Tahitian?'

'With the flowers and the thorns, yes.'

'Why all this talk?' Mason said, thrusting his square forehead forward.

'It's the custom. Not to make a speech after Mehani's apology would be to break with them.'

'I see,' Mason said, but he did not look convinced.

He went on: 'I have altered my plans, Mr Purcell.'

Purcell looked at him in silence.

'I shall land not one but two boats, and a third will patrol and cover them. The blacks give me six more muskets,' he explained, as pleased as a general who has had an extra division added to his force. 'The whites,' he went on, 'number nine – eight, without counting *you*, Mr Purcell – which gives me in all fourteen muskets. I can therefore arm the three boats. The two boats with the landing-party will each have five muskets and the covering boat four. The blacks will be divided so that there are two blacks in each boat; in that way they will be well surrounded by whites.'

He added tonelessly, looking away from Purcell: 'You will stay on board – with the women.'

Purcell's handsome, clean-cut face gave no flicker of expression, and he continued to look attentively at Mason.

'In any case,' Mason said, 'the anchorage is unsure, and someone capable of taking command should necessity arise must be on board.'

It was almost an apology. He realised it, was displeased at it and went on curtly: 'You will have the boats lowered, Mr Purcell.'

Mason went below to his cabin and drank two glasses of rum straight off. The damned argufier! As if fighting the blacks was a pleasure. If the island was inhabited, one really couldn't set sail again, without food, and for God knew where, with a mutinous crew, and a lot of blacks who would simply lie down at the first squall.

When Purcell saw the three boats laden with men and muskets, he felt a curious sensation of unreality. Perhaps the seamen and the Tahitians felt it too for they ceased talking and silence fell. The sun was already fairly low and Mason issued orders that no food should be taken. The expedition would dine on such fruits as it could find on the island.

The three boats were grouped in a circle on *The Blossom*'s starboard side, one moored to the gangway, awaiting Mason. He went down the ladder heavily and took his place in the stern. With one knee on the helmsman's thwart, he put his telescope to his eye and began studying the beach.

The men watched from the boats and the women leaned silently on the bulwarks. On Purcell's right, head and shoulders taller than he was, Omaata stood, watching gloomily, still as a statue.

'Mr Purcell,' Smudge shouted shrilly from below, 'I daresay you won't be bored among the women!'

The intended insolence was so obvious that the seamen hesitated for a moment. Then Mason turned and smiled, and they burst out laughing. Purcell remained impassive. He was vexed that Mason should have encouraged the men to mock him.

Omaata leaned her massive head towards him and turned her large dark eyes on him.

'What did he say, Adamo?'

'He suggested I would not be bored among the women.'

Knowing the Tahitian taste for this sort of joke, Purcell expected laughter. But the women remained silently staring at the boats, their expressions cold and disapproving.

'Adamo!'

'Omaata!'

'Tell him that if there's a fight he'll be killed.'

Purcell shook his head.

'I can't tell him that.'

Omaata drew herself up to her full height. She threw out her chest and clutched the bulwarks with her enormous hands.

'It is I who am telling him!' she said in her deep voice, beat-

ing her chest with the palm of her right hand. 'I, Omaata! Tell
him it from me!' she added, pointing her finger at Smudge and
inclining her colossal torso over the sea. 'Tell the little rat he'll
be killed! Tell him, Adamo!'

She leaned down from *The Blossom*, her finger still
outstretched, her eyes flashing and her wide nostrils dilated in
anger. The men in the boats looked up at her, fascinated by her
roaring and the finger pointing at Smudge like a sword.

'Tell him, Adamo!'

Purcell looked at Smudge and said quietly: 'Omaata insists
I tell you that if there's a fight you'll be killed.'

There was an embarrassed silence. Apparently it had not
occurred to anyone that the expedition might end in a death on
the British side.

Jones, who was in No. 1 boat with Mason, suddenly shouted
out: 'Smudge killed! Impossible! He's chosen the covering
boat!'

It was true. The seamen looked at Smudge and laughed aloud.
Purcell did not so much as smile.

Mason gave the signal to cast off. His boat was to try to get
through the surf first. If he succeeded, they would haul the boat
up on the beach and boat No. 2 would then follow. The covering boat would patrol a cable's length from the shore and would
endeavour to land only if the enemy tried to seize the boats to
cut off the retreat.

Purcell followed the operation through Burt's telescope. They
got through the surf without difficulty, nor did the seamen have
to use the ropes and grapnels to climb the rock.

Some twenty minutes later, the landing-party had disappeared
among the trees crowning the cliff, and Purcell felt reassured. If
there was to have been an attack, it would have taken place when
the men were climbing the rock. The defenders could easily have
stoned them from above, while remaining hidden in the bushes.

For a long while Purcell waited, his anxiety diminishing with
each minute that went by.

A little before noon, there was the sound of a single shot. Ten
minutes later, there was another, and that was all. The seamen
must be hunting.

The glorious armada returned at nightfall without having had to fight. It was still hot and the men seemed tired. Mason was the first to come aboard.

'You may be reassured, Mr Purcell,' he said loudly, 'the island is uninhabited. There will be no fighting.'

Purcell looked at him. It was impossible to tell from his expression whether he regretted it, or whether he was relieved.

4

The next day, at seven o'clock in the morning, Mason took advantage of the slack water at high tide to try to beach *The Blossom*. The ship would be at hand for the crew to strip her of such useful objects as would be of value on the island. The beaching was not an easy operation for *The Blossom* was much less handy than a boat and might easily turn broadside on to the surf. However, all went well and, since a piece of good fortune never comes singly, it so happened that it was the last day of the spring tides, and it was to be hoped that during the next days *The Blossom* would be high and dry even at high tide with her stern safe from the bludgeoning of the surf.

The manoeuvre was assisted by another lucky chance. There was a rounded rock, some forty feet long and ten feet high, where the ship was beached. Indeed, they nearly hit it as they went in, the starboard side being no more than some three feet from it when the keel hit the sand. Mason saw at once how he could use the rock. He gave orders to make fast to it with grapnels so that when the tide fell the side of the hull would rest against it thereby giving the ship only a very slight list. At low water, the position was secured by placing props here and there, so that the ship had the comfortable air of being in dry dock.

Both luck and ability had played their part in beaching the ship. The crew felt as they did when there was a fair wind, and they busied themselves from eight o'clock in the morning until eight o'clock at night fixing the props with unusual zeal. The Tahitians lent effective help and the seamen, who had been contemptuous of them since the episode of the storm, were beginning to look at them with a more friendly eye by the end of the day.

Next morning, the first to be up and about became aware that the bows of the ship lay under an overhanging rock. This gave MacLeod the idea of setting up a windlass to haul the materials they were to strip from *The Blossom* to the top of the cliff with comparative ease. Without consulting anyone, he organised part of the crew and the necessary tackle to put his plan into execution. When Mason came on deck at eight o'clock, with Purcell at his heels, he was amazed to see what the men were up to. MacLeod was directing operations as well as working harder than anyone else. His pale face was alight with the fire of creation and he was swearing continuously at the incompetence of his party. Mason turned red with anger. The thing had been done without his knowledge. His authority was being brought openly into disrespect.

'Mr Purcell,' he cried in a quivering voice, 'did you give the order?'

'Certainly not, Captain Mason.'

Mason strode to the bows, followed by Purcell who could scarcely keep up with him, looked at MacLeod who was working some thirty feet above him, and said curtly: 'What are you doing?'

'Setting up a windlass,' MacLeod replied, going on with his work.

'Who gave you the order?'

MacLeod, who was bending over his work, nonchalantly straightened up his long bony body, glanced at his companions, shrugged, bent his knife-blade of a face down towards Mason and said in a slow, rasping voice: 'Captain Mason, I need you to sail the ship, but I do not need you to construct a windlass. It's my trade.'

Purcell screwed up his eyes and looked from Mason to MacLeod. MacLeod was insolent, but he was replying indirectly rather than entering upon an overt struggle.

'It is not a question of your trade,' Mason said curtly. 'I gave you no order to set up a windlass'.

'Well,' MacLeod said, glancing at his companions again, and

suddenly assuming a dull-witted expression, 'a windlass is a good idea, isn't it?'

He was being evasive again. Mason blinked several times, and the veins in his neck stood out. But he managed to contain himself.

'Once again,' he said fairly calmly, 'that's not the point. You must understand, MacLeod, that good order and discipline must be maintained and that it is I who command on board.'

'Aye, aye, sir,' MacLeod said. And he added in a low voice but so that Mason could hear: 'I'm not on board here. I'm ashore.'

The seamen smiled. It was a good point and it was what they all felt, even those who liked the Old Man. On board, you obeyed, but ashore, you were no longer a seaman.

'Must I undo what I have done?' MacLeod asked with feigned submission; and he glanced round at his companions as if to take them to witness how stupid authority could be.

Mason was aware of the trap. He hesitated. If he said: 'Take the windlass to pieces,' he would have the whole crew against him for everything would have to be humped from *The Blossom* to the top of the cliff; but if he said: 'It's a good idea, carry on,' he would appear to be abdicating his position.

'Mr Purcell will inspect what you're doing,' he said at last, 'and will give you my orders. ' He, too, had evaded the issue. But it did not lower his prestige with the crew. On the contrary, indeed. The Old Man had tacked brilliantly. He had not taken up a position and had passed the helm to the lieutenant.

'Aye, aye, sir,' MacLeod said, nonchalantly putting a finger to his forehead.

He bent his long sharp nose over the windlass and said: 'Purcell knows about as much carpentry as I know of the Bible.'

Smudge laughed. Mason and Purcell turned away. The seamen glanced happily at each other and watched the two officers moving away along *The Blossom*'s deck. From the cliff they seemed very small and insignificant. 'The Old Man mustn't think he's going to be king of the island,' MacLeod said.

'Nor Purcell either,' Smudge said in a grating voice. 'To hell with his Bible, and with him too.'

There was a silence. Since Tahiti Smudge had taken a particular dislike to Purcell although no one knew why.

'He's not done you any harm,' young Jones said, looking at Smude with his clear eyes. 'Why are you always down on him?'

Smudge looked down his long nose, pursed his big lips and said nothing. Johnson coughed and said in his cracked voice: 'I don't care a damn for the Bible, but I shall always remember how Purcell asked Burt to recite prayers over the boy's body. He looked all pink and white as he stood up to Burt. He looked like a girl. But, by Christ, he wasn't one! He needed a hell of a lot of guts to cross Burt.'

'The old fool's always bum-sucking,' MacLeod said, spitting contemptuously. 'Show him an officer and he'll go down on his knees to him.'

Old Johnson opened his mouth to reply but MacLeod gave him such a venomous look that he preferred to keep quiet. Since MacLeod had coolly stabbed Simon in the chest the crew were afraid of him and MacLeod played on their fear.

Mason was pacing the poop with a grim face and paying no attention to Purcell. The seamen were ashore; his authority was growing less every day; *The Blossom* was beached and would soon be dismantled, broken up and destroyed to build huts. Thirty-five years at sea were ending today.

'Captain Mason,' Purcell said, 'since you're sending me ashore, with your permission I'll take the opportunity to inspect the island.'

'In that case,' Mason said, 'take two or three armed men with you. I can't help fearing the island is inhabited and that the inhabitants are in hiding.'

Purcell looked at him, and Mason went on in a calm, level voice as if he wished to prove to the lieutenant that the incident with MacLeod had left him unmoved: 'In fact, it's unlikely enough. We found no trace of fires, paths or cultivation. But you'll see that the island is surrounded by a collar of bush. And the bush is more or less impenetrable. It would afford ideal hiding places for guerrillas. Imagine a host of little palm trees, thousands of them growing close together. In places you have to part their trunks to get through. In other places there are giant ferns as in Tahiti, with trunks as thick as my . . .'

He was going to say 'as my thigh', but restrained himself. The word 'thigh' seemed to him indecent.

'. . . Huge trunks, Mr Purcell! Huge leaves! Bigger than those in Tahiti! You take three paces and you're lost to view . . .'

'All the same,' Purcell said, 'if you found no trace of fires . . .'

'I didn't visit the mountain at the south end of the island. I merely went round it. It's a chaos of rocks and not very attractive. It's difficult to believe people can live on it. And yet it's possible. The one stream on the island has its source there and there's therefore a water supply . . .'

He stopped, and then went on in a curt, official voice, as if he had suddenly remembered he was talking to a subordinate: 'Be back by noon.'

'So early?' Purcell said in astonishment. 'Is there any particular reason?'

'I shall expect you at noon, Mr Purcell,' Mason said curtly.

'Aye, aye, sir,' Purcell said, looking away.

He felt embarrassed. Poor Mason, it was childish. MacLeod had had a disastrous effect on him. He felt it necessary to assert his authority over a minor detail. 'As if it was I who would upset it,' Purcell thought, turning away.

Mason called him back.

'Take this map,' he said more gently. 'I drew it yesterday. You'll find it useful.'

Purcell returned to the deck and selected Baker, Hunt and Mehani to accompany him. When she saw 'Jono' join the lieutenant, Omaata came majestically forward and asked Purcell to allow her to come too. He agreed. Then Ivoa's blue eyes looked at him in silent pleading. He nodded; upon which two other Tahitian women, Itia and Avapouhi, also came forward; and all the others would have followed if Mason had not shouted from the poop to take no more, since unloading the ship would require a great number of hands.

It took twenty minutes of hard climbing under a burning sun to reach the top of the cliff. Throughout the whole climb the thousands of terns which nested in the rocks circled aggressively round the little group and deafened them with their cries. Purcell had expected that on reaching the top of the cliff they would have to make their way through the little palm trees Mason had described. However, immediately above the beach there was a gap of some twenty yards in the collar of bush. It contained splendid trees and sparse undergrowth.

Nevertheless, Purcell did not make for it at once. He made a detour through the rocks to the point where MacLeod had set up his windlass. The little group followed him. Silence fell at his approach and the seamen grouped themselves round the windlass under construction as if it were the symbol of their freedom. As for MacLeod, he did not raise his angular face from his work for an instant, but Purcell felt from the tenseness of his thin body that he was only awaiting an opportunity to renew his insolence. 'He's an offensive fellow,' Purcell thought, 'but he's not altogether wrong. Why should *The Blossom*'s officers rule the island?'

He walked slowly towards the windlass and, the closer he got, the more he was aware of a sort of tension among the seamen. To them he was at that moment the second-in-command of *The Blossom* sent by the captain to decide whether the windlass was to be completed. Purcell suddenly felt furious with Mason. He had given him an impossible part to play. If he played it properly he would make himself hated by the men. If he did not play it, he would still be suspect as far as they were concerned. He thought the best thing to do would be to stay just a minute and not to say a word. Then he thought: 'To hell with prudence.' He went a pace nearer. To hell with it; he would attack them frontally.

He had no time to do so. MacLeod attacked first. Oddly enough, it was not Purcell he went for, but Baker against whom Avapouhi was leaning at that moment. He gave him a hostile glance and, without even looking at Avapouhi, said in his drawling voice: 'Some people go for a stroll while others work.'

'You haven't asked me to do anything,' Baker said, giving him look for look and placing his hand on Avapouhi's shoulder.

The exchange stopped there, and Purcell said: 'Men, you're expecting me to tell you what I think. Very well, I'll do so. The windlass is a good idea, and I have every confidence in MacLeod. But it was quite unnecessary to be insolent to Captain Mason. If we're all going to live together on this island, we might as well live in peace.'

MacLeod slowly raised his sharp face, spat a long jet of saliva at his feet, and Purcell thought: 'That's done it, he's not going to miss his opportunity.'

'If you think the windlass a good idea,' MacLeod said in his slow, grating voice, 'no one is going to prevent your giving us a hand. After all, I'm working for everyone here. And, in my view, everyone should get down to it.'

It was clever and a sort of shiver of pleasure ran through the men. MacLeod had suggested a wholly pleasant thought: an officer working with his hands under the orders of a mere seaman.

'And the worst of it is,' Purcell thought, 'he's right. He's odious, but he's quite right.' He said curtly: 'As you yourself remarked, I don't know enough about carpentry to be of any use to you.'

But he did not want to leave things on the basis of a snub, and he added more conciliatingly: 'But if you need me to translate your instructions to the Tahitians, I'll be delighted to help.'

It was an overture, but MacLeod scorned it.

'I need no interpreter,' he said so arrogantly and insolently that Purcell blushed.

'That's all right then,' Purcell said, controlling his voice with difficulty.

He went off, furious both with MacLeod and himself. Perhaps it would have been better to say nothing after all.

He made his way into the undergrowth, followed by his companions.

'Are you upset, Adamo?' Omaata said, putting her huge hand lightly on his neck.

Even so, her hand was heavy. Purcell stopped, gently removed Omaata's fingers, but kept them in his own or rather round his own for his immediately disappeared, were swallowed up and became invisible. At the same time, he looked up and saw far above him the giantess's dark face, her huge nostrils and immense, dark, liquid and affectionate eyes. They made him think of pools under the moon. He suddenly felt Ivoa's cool hand in his other one. He turned to look at her. She smiled at him. He glanced at his companions. Standing round him in a circle, Mehani, Avapouhi and Itia were looking at him. His heart glowed with the warmth of their affection. How kind they were, he thought gratefully. How friendly!

'Is it as obvious as all that when I'm upset?' he said at last.

'Oh, yes,' Ivoa said. 'When everything's going well your face is like a Tahitian's, but when something's upset you, your face becomes like a *Peritani*'s.'

Mehani burst out laughing.

'What's a Tahitian face like?' Purcell asked with a smile.

'Smooth and happy.'

'And a *Peritani*'s?'

'Look,' Itia, 'I'll show you.'

She frowned, stiffened her neck, drooped the corners of her mouth, and her pretty childish face suddenly assumed an expression of anxiety and importance. Mehani and the Tahitian women roared with laughter.

Purcell caught Baker's eye and said in English: 'Itia's imitating the anxious expression of the British.'

Baker smiled.

'I don't understand a word of their jargon. I shall have to set about learning it.'

Avapouhi leaned towards Purcell.

'What did he say?'

'That he doesn't understand.'

'I'll teach him,' Avapouhi said.

She put her hand on Baker's arm and said in sing-song English: 'I . . . speak . . . you.'

'To you,' Purcell said.

'To you,' Avapouhi repeated, chanting the syllables.

Purcell looked at her with friendliness. She was pretty, but it was not her beauty that struck him. There was an extraordinary sweetness about her.

Omaata took Hunt's arm. He uttered a little grunt of pleasure and she led him to the head of the group. Purcell could hear the rumbling of her voice but could not make out what she was saying. The shade and freshness were delicious and as soon as they had taken a few steps into the undergrowth they ceased to hear the terns. But after five minutes the silence ceased to be grateful and seemed to Purcell to become almost abnormal. He remembered the forests of Tahiti. Walking in them aroused no sound at all, no rustle in the grass, no noise of falling or flight, not even the scraping of a leaf. In these fertile lands, in the most clement climate in the world, the fauna consisted only of wild pigs and birds.

The birds were so bright and small that Purcell had taken them at first for butterflies; and they were so friendly that they perched on your shoulder. If the island, as they thought, was uninhabited, their confidence in the kindness of the human race was not surprising. Purcell never grew tired of watching them. They flew about making patches of brilliant colour. Some were purple and azure; others scarlet and white; and the most exquisite of all black and gold with blood red beaks. Purcell noticed one peculiar thing about them: they neither sang, nor even chirped. The whole forest was silent. Even the birds were mute.

As they walked on, Mehani and the Tahitian women uttered exclamations of joy. They were constantly able to recognise Tahitian trees and they enumerated them on their fingers: the coconut palm, the breadfruit tree, the mango, the avocado and and the pandanus. The last was most useful, Omaata remarked, for cloth could be made from its bark and the clothes they were wearing would not last for ever. Among the shrubs Mehani discovered yams, though they were rather small, taros, sweet potatoes and a plant he called 'ti', an infusion of whose leaves, he explained, made an excellent remedy 'when you were ill'.

The island made a strange impression on Purcell. There was a paradox about its fertility. It contained everything necessary to man, and yet man was absent. However, from the presence of yams Mehani deduced that the island had once been inhabited, and to prove he was right he discovered in a clearing a heap of stones which had formed a *morai* and three gigantic figures roughly carved in the black stone of the cliff. The Polynesians who had once lived on the island must have had barbaric religious ideas for the effigies had terrifying faces. Mehani and the Tahitian women gazed at them in silence, impressed by the malignant expression of these gods. In Tahiti, the religion was amiable and the god beneficent.

Since entering the forest, they had marched continually towards the south, though they had not made much headway since there was no path through the undergrowth. The terrain from the top of the cliff formed a gentle and regular slope so that this part of the island was a plateau. About half an hour after they had left MacLeod the forest ceased and they were faced by a steep, stony hill. However, it was crowned with trees which led them to think that the forest began again on its summit. They climbed it with some difficulty for it was steep and rugged, and the sun was hot. They were glad to reach the shade again. They then found that there was a second plateau covered with the same vegetation as the first, but the trees were spaced farther apart, the undergrowth was less thick and the slope steeper.

Purcell stopped and took Mason's sketch-map from his pocket. According to it, the island ran north and south and was oval in shape. If Mason's figures were correct it was two miles long, but not more than three-quarters of a mile broad. Mason had divided the island from north to south into three almost equal parts. In the northern part he had written: 'First Plateau'; in the middle part: 'Second Plateau'; and in the southern: 'Mountain', adding in parenthesis: 'very arid'. The whole perimeter of the island was hatched and across the hatches Mason had written in one place: 'Small palm trees', and in another: 'Ferns'. In the 'Mountain' third he had shown nothing but a wavy line ending on the south coast.

Purcell turned to Baker. 'I suppose that's the stream?'

Baker took a look at the map. 'Yes, sir, that must be it. But we didn't follow it to its source.'

'Thanks.'

Baker went and sat at the foot of a pandanus and Avapouhi followed him. Purcell glanced at Ivoa. She smiled and said in a low voice: 'Ouili is nice.' 'Ouili' was the Tahitian version of Willie Baker. Purcell nodded and looked at Mason's map again. It confirmed his impression of the day before from *The Blossom*'s deck. The island was really very small. It did not, indeed, appear to be so, but that was no doubt due to the slope, the difficulty of walking, and the thickness of the undergrowth. If the mountain, as Mason had said, was a 'chaos of rocks', it was obvious that the future village would have to be built to the north, on the first plateau. It had the only possible access to the sea. On this basis, the second plateau, on which they were at the moment, would be cultivated. Thus the really habitable part of the island consisted of these two plateaux, which meant, if one had faith in Mason's map, that it consisted of a rectangle one and a quarter miles long and three-quarters of a mile broad, the rest of the island being occupied by the mountain. Owing to its fertility, this area might suffice to feed thirty people. It was doubtful, however, whether they would be very comfortable in the long run. It might well have been the smallness of the island that had compelled its first inhabitants to leave it and risk the sea in search of more land.

Purcell put the sketch-map back in his pocket, called to his companions who had strayed into the undergrowth, and they set off again. Considering they were so close to it, he was surprised not to see the mountain between the tops of the trees; but it was concealed by a mass of bright green foliage dominating the forest from above. Purcell directed their march towards it and ten minutes later they debouched into a little clearing. On the farther side of it stood a gigantic banyan.

There were shouts of joy and the Tahitian women ran towards the tree. Purcell hurried after them. He could not yet see the trunk, which was hidden by the innumerable shoots that grew downwards to take root in the ground and thereby support the branches from which they sprang. The tree gave an impression of issuing from the earth, returning to it and issuing from it once again. Its vertical branches had proliferated with such exuberance that the banyan covered an area of some sixty feet square and resembled a temple supported by columns. Lianas with huge leaves clung to the columns, hiding the interior of the 'temple', and Purcell wondered whether there were not, in fact, several banyans making up one single mass. Some of the vertical shoots were as thick as an ordinary trunk, and their support was clearly effective, for one of the horizontal branches, which had been split and almost detached from the trunk by lightning, was still held up by the aerial roots which its tremendous weight had bent but failed to break. The Tahitian women disappeared among the columns with shouts of joy. The whole band followed them, and before reaching the main trunk they found a series of leafy rooms, enclosed by curtains of liana and thickly carpeted with moss.

The women wandered in astonished delight through the leafy rooms, laughing with pleasure. Then Itia picked up a handful of moss, threw it in Mehani's face and fled. The other women imitated her, uttering shrill cries, and the men dashed off in pursuit of them through a maze of rooms in which one could easily lose oneself, the pursued being often separated from the pursuers by no more than a screen of leaves.

Purcell played and shouted like the rest, and yet he was not really happy and could not wholly abandon himself to the game. After a while, he left the banyan, went a little way off and lay down in the clearing. 'Why can I no longer enjoy myself as they do, without reservations, like a child?' he wondered. What had he lost that the Tahitians still had? He was depressed to discover that he was a prey to habitual anxiety, to a general disquiet.

Baker and Hunt joined him, and a few minutes later Mehani and the women, breathless and happy. They were surprised that Purcell should have put an end to the game so soon.

'It's already late,' Purcell said, pointing to the sun. 'We'll rest a little, and then return on board.'

Once again, he took out Mason's map and studied it.

'Baker,' he said after a moment, 'will you show me on the map the route Captain Mason followed yesterday?'

Baker came and sat beside Purcell and bent his brown, clean-cut face over the map.

'It was like this, sir. When we reached the first plateau, we set our course east as far as the bush. There we veered and made south. And we went round the mountain, keeping the bush to starboard all the time. It was not a very pleasant walk, I can tell you.'

'In fact, you went round the perimeter, and we've come through the centre. I was merely wondering why Captain Mason had not marked the banyan on the map.'

Purcell went on: 'I see from the map that the captain estimates the collar of bush to be a hundred yards wide. Did he reconnoitre it?'

'Twice. Once on the east. Once on the west. The first time, I did it. It's very unpleasant inside there, sir. It's dark and stifling. You scratch your hands on the trunks of the little palm trees, and since they're whippy, they hit you in the back if you let them go too quick. And then it's so dark that after a while you don't know where you are. Luckily I'd arranged with the captain for him to call out every minute. It was due to that I was able to find my way.'

'What's on the other side?'

'The cliff.'

'Nothing in between?'

'Nothing.'

'And from the forest to the cliff, you counted a hundred paces?'

Baker gave a slight smile.

'To tell you the truth, sir, I lost count several times. It was dark, I was a bit jumpy and the damn musket kept tripping me up.'

Purcell looked at Baker. The Welshman was lean and dark, his eyes were bright with intelligence in his clean-cut face.

'And then,' Baker went on, 'you must realise you can't go in a straight line in the bush. You zigzag. And counting your paces doesn't really add up to much in the end.'

'Yet you told the captain you had counted a hundred paces.'

Baker's thin, brown face broke into a smile and his dark eyes shone mischievously.

'I even said "a hundred and four paces", sir. I was very precise.'

'Why?'

'If I hadn't been, the captain would have made me do it again.'

'I see,' Purcell said without moving a muscle of his face.

He looked at the map and went on: 'How did it happen that the man who reconnoitred the bush on the east also made it a hundred paces?'

Baker paused for a moment. Then, with his eyes sparkling, he said gravely: 'It was Jones, sir. I told him.'

'Thank you, Baker,' Purcell said, his face impassive.

He glanced at Baker, and there was a twinkle in his eye as he said in a calm, official way: 'You made a remarkable contribution to the drawing of this map.'

'Thank you, sir,' Baker said imperturbably.

Purcell got to his feet.

'Where are the women?' he called to Mehani in Tahitian.

Mehani was lying full length on the grass a few paces away. He raised himself on his left elbow and pointed over his shoulder with his right hand.

'They've found a thicket of hibiscus.'

At that moment, Avapouhi, Itia and Ivoa appeared. Omaata followed them, so much taller than they were that she looked like a mother driving her little girls before her. All four of them had put the large red flowers of the hibiscus in their black hair, and they came forward smiling, their arms supple as lianas, and their round thighs making the bark fringes of their short skirts sway at every step.

As soon as he saw Omaata, Hunt raised his little pale, anxious eyes to her. He had not noticed her leave him, and for several minutes had felt lost.

'Jono, Jono,' Omaata said in her deep voice.

In the twinkling of an eye she was beside him, patting the red hair on his chest, and uttering caressing words in an unintelligible lingo. After a moment, Hunt leaned his face against her huge breasts, and remained there in an attitude of tenderness and abandon, giving little grunts of pleasure like a bear cub in its mother's bosom. Lowering her voice, which was as deep and powerful as the roar of a waterfall, Omaata continued talking to him in her incomprehensible jargon. Meanwhile, she put her powerful arms round Hunt's neck, and pressed him to her as if he were a gigantic baby.

'What's she saying, Mehani?' Purcell asked.

Mehani began laughing.

'I don't know, Adamo. I thought it was *Peritani.*'

'There are words that sound like *Peritani,*' Purcell said, 'but I can't even understand those.'

Omaata raised her head.

'It's a private language for Jono and me,' she said in Tahitian. 'Jono understands me very well.'

The enormous Hunt heard his name and grunted tenderly. Since Omaata had taken him in hand, he was as scrubbed and clean as a ship's deck. 'He's her baby,' Purcell thought. He looked at the giantess and smiled: 'How old are you, Omaata?'

'Since I've been a woman, I've seen twice ten summers.'

Thirty-two. Perhaps less. She was young, therefore. Younger than himself, younger than Jono. But her dimensions put her in a world apart.

At that moment, Avapouhi came and knelt in front of Baker, raising her gentle face to him. She looked at him gravely for a few seconds, then slipped an hibiscus flower between his hair and his ear, smiled, fluttered her eyelashes, got quickly to her feet and ran away. She crossed the clearing and disappeared into the undergrowth.

'What does that mean?' Baker asked, turning to Purcell.

'She has chosen you as her *tané*.'*

'Oh!' Baker said, blushing under his tan. 'With them it's the women who choose?'

'In England, too,' Purcell said, his eyes smiling. 'But in England it's not so obvious.'

'And why did she run away?'

'So that you should chase her.'

'Oh, I see!' Baker said.

After a moment, he got to his feet. Avoiding their eyes, he said with an embarrassed smile: 'It's too damned hot to start playing hide-and-seek again.'

He went off towards the undergrowth. He dared hot hurry and was very conscious of the eyes staring at his back.

'What did he say?' Mehani asked.

He had observed Baker's embarrassment with intense amusement. He realised once again that the *Peritani* were quite mad; the simplest things embarrassed them.

'I'm surprised,' Omaata said. 'I thought she had chosen the Skeleton.'

'The Skeleton' was the nickname the Tahitians had given MacLeod.

'On the big canoe,' Itia said, 'she did choose the Skeleton, but she doesn't want any more of him. He beats her.'

It was to be seen, Purcell thought, whether MacLeod would accept the fact of Baker's succeeding him. There was going to be no lack of difficulties on the island.

Mehani raised his powerful torso on both elbows, and put his

* A man, a lover or a husband.

head back to look at Itia.

'I shan't beat you, Itia,' he said meaningly. 'Or only a very little,' he added, laughing.

Itia gave a saucy shake of her head. She and Amoureïa were the youngest and physically the smallest of the Tahitian women. She had a slightly snub nose, and the corners of her mouth turned up towards her cheeks, which gave her face an expression of gaiety. Itia was liked for her vivacity, but from the point of view of Tahitian etiquette her manners were not good; she lacked reserve. She criticised people too much.

'Well,' Mehani went on teasingly, 'aren't you going to give me a flower?'

'No,' Itia said, 'you don't deserve one.'

She threw a pebble which landed on his chest.

'A stone,' she said with a little pout, 'that's all I'll give you.'

Mehani lay back full length and clasped his hands beneath his neck.

'You're wrong,' he said placidly.

Itia threw another pebble at him. Mehani removed his hands from his neck and put them over his eyes to protect them. He smiled, but said nothing.

'To begin with,' Itia said, 'you're not handsome.'

'That's quite true, Itia,' Ivoa said laughing. 'My brother's ugly! There's no uglier man on the island!'

'It's not only his ugliness,' Itia said. 'As a *tané* he's no good.'

'Oh! Oh!' Mehani said.

Lying in all the majesty of his magnificent body, he stretched, threw out his chest and made the muscles of his thighs ripple.

'Stop showing off!' Itia said, throwing all the pebbles she had in her hand at him. 'I wouldn't have a *tané* like you for anything in the world. It would be me today, Avapouhi tomorrow and Omaata the day after.'

'I have Jono,' Omaata said in her deep resonant voice.

Purcell laughed.

'Why are you laughing, Adamo?'

'I'm laughing because I like your voice so much.'

He said in English: 'It's like the roaring of a dove.'

He wanted to translate but could not find the word for 'roaring'. There were no wild beasts in Tahiti.

'In my opinion,' Itia went on, 'the best *tané* on the island is Adamo. He's not tall, but his hair is like the morning sun through the palms. And, oh, his eyes! I love his eyes! They're clearer than the water of the lagoon at midday. And his nose is quite, quite straight! When he smiles, he has a dimple in his right cheek and looks as gay as a girl. But when he doesn't smile, he looks as impressive as a chief. I'm sure that Adamo is a great chief in his own island and owns many coconut palms.'

Purcell laughed.

'There are no coconut palms on my island.'

'Oh,' Itia said in amazement, 'how do you live then?'

'Badly. That's why we go to live on other people's islands.'

'No matter,' Itia said, turning her bright eyes on him, 'even without coconuts, you're a good *tané*. You're the best *tané* on the island.'

Ivoa raised herself on an elbow, and smiled at Itia with a mixture of kindliness and dignity.

'Adamo,' she said, with a wide, expressive gesture of the hand which recalled Otou, 'Adamo is Ivoa's *tané*.'

The reprimand made Mehani roar with laughter, and Omaata smiled with disdain. Itia hung her head and hid her eyes behind her right arm like a child about to cry. She had been called to order and was ashamed of her bad manners.

They all fell silent. It was hot and Purcell, lying full length on the grass, Ivoa's hand in his, began to feel sleepy.

'I wonder,' he said thoughtfully, 'what happened to the people who lived on this island.'

'Perhaps,' Omaata said, 'there was an illness and they're dead.

'Or perhaps,' Mehani said, 'there was a war between two tribes, and they all massacred each other.'

'Even the women?' Purcell asked.

'When the priests of the tribe decree "the disembowelling of the chicken"*, the women are killed too. And the children.'

Purcell raised himself on his elbow.

'But everyone doesn't die. There's always a victor.'

'No,' Mehani said, shaking his head sadly, 'not always. At Mana, they all killed each other, all of them, men and women! There was only one survivor. He didn't want to go on living on

* The total annihilation of the enemy.

the island with all those dead. He jumped into his canoe, and succeeded in reaching Tahiti, where he told the story. Then, two weeks later, he died. It is not known what he died of. Perhaps sorrow. Mana was a little island, no bigger than this, and now it's empty. No one wants to go there.'

'I think,' Itia said, looking up, 'that the people who lived here left in their canoes because they were afraid.'

'Afraid of what?' Purcell asked.

'The *toupapahous*.'*

Purcell smiled.

'You're wrong to smile, Adamo,' Omaata said. 'There are *toupapahous* so wicked that they spend their time tormenting human beings.'

'What do they do?'

'If you light a fire, for instance, and put some water on to heat, the *toupapahous* will make the water overflow and put the fire out as soon as you've turned your back.'

There was a space between Mehani and Purcell. Itia came and occupied it. She lay curled up on her side. Her little face had gone grey. She turned to Purcell and said: 'Give me your hand.'

'Why?' Purcell asked.

'I'm frightened.'

Purcell hesitated and glanced at Ivoa. But Ivoa at once said: 'The child's afraid. Give her your hand.'

Purcell obeyed. Itia clasped his hand in her warm fingers, and put it under her cheek with a sigh.

It was clear that the Tahitian women played at frightening themselves so as to enjoy being reassured.

Purcell looked at the sun, withdrew his hand from Itia's, got to his feet and picked up his musket. Hunt and Mehani followed his example.

'And Avapouhi?' Itia asked.

Purcell gave a little wave of his hand and Mehani said in a teasing voice: 'Come with me. We'll go and look for her.'

'No,' Itia said, 'I want to stay with Adamo.'

After a moment, Purcell joined Mehani at the head of the little band.

'What do you think of the island, Mehani?'

* The ghosts.

'It's not good,' Mehani said without hesitation. 'It's fertile, but not good.'

'Why?'

'First,' Mehani said, extending the fore and middle fingers of his right hand, 'there's no lagoon. When there's bad weather, we won't be able to fish. And then, because of the crops and the shade, we shall have to build our huts on the north, and the stream is the other side of the island. We shall have to go and fetch water every day – an hour there, and an hour back.'

'Yes,' Purcell said, 'you're quite right.'

He looked at Mehani and was struck by his thoughtful expression. What an astonishing face he had! At once virile and feminine, at one moment gay and then suddenly serious. Mason looked on the Tahitians as so many children, but he had not realised, as Mehani had done at the first glance, the drawbacks to the island.

'You'll regret having come with me,' Purcell said after a moment.

Mehani turned his face to him and said gravely and decisively: 'Better this island with my friend than Tahiti without him.'

Purcell felt embarrassed. But he realised at once how foolish it was. In England, it was not done to express your feelings, and still less to express them eloquently. But why should he suspect Mehani's sincerity? He had left his island for him.

He heard Mehani laugh and glanced at him.

'You're embarrassed,' Mehani said. 'You know I'm speaking the truth, and yet you're embarrassed.'

'The *Peritani* don't say things like that,' Purcell said, blushing.

'I know,' Mehani said, putting his left hand on Purcell's shoulder. 'They never say the things that are good to say. And as for the things that are good to do . . .'

He laughed.

'. . . they do them, but with a wry face.'

Purcell laughed and Mehani echoed him. They felt happy, walking shoulder to shoulder through the patches of sunlight and shade in the undergrowth.

Purcell turned and smiled at Ivoa. The vision of her big blue eyes fixed on him accompanied him as he walked on. When they had left in the morning, the women who had stayed behind with Mason had been preparing a wild pig to stew. As they drew nearer, Purcell could smell the good odour of wood smoke. He felt delightfully hungry and mended his pace. His lungs full of pure air, he suddenly felt young and gay, so alive and happy that he had a feeling of bounding over the ground. From time to time, his shoulder touched Mehani's and the contact sent a wave of warmth through his body. The island was beautiful, sweet smelling, and bright with birds. A new world was opening before them. He glanced round with a feeling of joy and possession.

'É Adamo é!' Mehani said. 'You're a pleasure to look at!'

'Yes,' Purcell said.

He wanted to say: 'I'm happy,' but could not bring himself to do so. Instead, he said quickly and confusedly: 'As far as the water is concerned, you're right, Mehani. It's an inconvenience. I hadn't noticed it. I merely thought the island rather small.'

'No,' Mehani said with a smile, 'it's not too small. There are still many places in which to play hide-and-seek.'

Then his face turned serious again, and he said anxiously: 'No, Adamo, it's not too small – if we get on well together.'

'What do you mean? If the *Peritani* and the Tahitians get on together, or if everyone gets on together?'

'If everyone gets on together,' Mehani said after a moment.

But there was a note of uncertainty in his voice.

5

Two days after *The Blossom* reached the island, Mason drew up a plan for the village. It was diamond-shaped and the four angles pointed to the four cardinal points of the compass. The sides of the diamond consisted of 'avenues' (this was the name Mason gave them) and the huts were placed outside the diamond on a perpendicular north-south axis; they were regularly spaced and all faced south. Each hut was therefore in echelon to its neighbours, and none of them blocked either sun or view from the hut behind it.

This advantage, which became apparent only after the huts had been built, was accidental. In making the plan, Mason had no other consideration than to follow the compass-card, and he would have given the village a circular shape, had a circle not seemed more difficult than a diamond to lay out on a terrain cut up by trees. To Mason, the important consideration was that the position of each hut round the diamond should correspond to a point of the compass. Starting from the north, Hunt's and White's huts lay on each side of the northern point of the diamond; then, following East Avenue (for this was the name Mason gave to the two eastern sides of the diamond), you passed, one after the other, Smudge's hut at the north-east, MacLeod's at the east, Mason's at the south-east, and Purcell's at the south. Turning up West Avenue, that is to say the two western sides of the diamond, you passed Johnson's hut at the south-west, Baker's at the west, and Jones's at the north-west.

In the centre of the diamond, Mason had planned a square whose sides were each ten yards, and this he called Blossom Square. Four paths, which Mason termed 'streets' joined the 'avenues' to the little square. It would have been logical for them to run from each angle of the diamond. But when Mason drew his plan he was concerned about his own access to Blossom Square, and traced the first 'street' from his own hut at the south-east point of the compass. For this reason, he called it Trade Wind Street. Wishing for symmetry, he traced the second from the north-west, opposite Jones's hut, and called it Nor'-wester Street. Two other streets completed the design: Sou'wester Street, which started opposite Johnson's hut, and Nor'easter Street connecting Smudge's with the square.

Though the village consisted of only two avenues, four streets and a square, Mason had seven signboards made. They were nailed to wooden posts, and on them he painted the names he had given the arteries of his town with his own hand. Once these streets and avenues had been laid out (and rather sketchily metalled) the British, who had been assembled punctually at noon by the captain, set up the signboards at the angle of each street with a ceremony that intrigued the Tahitians, who however did not adopt the English names, which seemed to them unpronounceable. They contented themselves with calling the 'streets' by the name of the nearest *Peritani*. Thus Trade Wind Street became for them 'the path of the chief' (Mason); Sou'-wester Street, 'the path of the old man' (Johnson); Nor'wester Street, 'the path of Ropati' (Robert Jones); and Nor'easter Street, 'the path of the little rat' (Smudge's nickname). Later, when their relations with the *Peritani* became strained, they no longer gave the 'streets' the names of the British but of the Tahitian women who lived with them. Thus, 'the path of the little rat' became 'the path of Toumata'; and 'the path of the old man', 'the path of Taïata', etc.

Both 'streets' and 'avenues' (which were about the same width, approximately a yard) failed to achieve the fine straightness Mason gave them in his plan. The wish to keep as many trees as possible necessitated a certain amount of winding. Indeed, they cut down only such trees as were strictly necessary for building the huts and clearing the little gardens attached to them. The advantage of keeping most of the trees was that the huts were concealed by them, and the view from each limited to its immediate neighbours. The diamond arrangement, though originally due to a whim of Mason's, was nevertheless excellent from this point of view too, since about an acre and a half of woodland was preserved within its borders.

Mason had placed his own hut at the south-west so that he would be the first to receive the trade wind which in the island, as elsewhere in the South Seas, brought a refreshing breeze in summer and good weather at every season of the year. On the other hand, he had taken care to place the Tahitians' hut outside the village and some twenty-five yards from the most northerly point of the diamond, as much to keep them apart from the whites as to make use of their hut as a wind-break against the northerly winds. This calculation, though cunning, turned out to be a mistake. When he drew his plan, Mason had not realised he was in fact exposing his hut to the sou'wester which brought cold and rain to the island, while the 'blacks'' hut was protected from it by the acre and a half of wood which had been left within the diamond.

Mason had also drawn on his plan a path running from the

northerly point, between Hunt's and White's huts, to the Tahitians' big hut. It then turned eastwards and ran north-east towards the sea. He called this path Cliff Lane. He also laid out another path running from East Avenue between Purcell's hut and his own towards the south. This path which, like the preceding one, had already been traced by the islanders when Mason made his plan, led towards the second plateau, and stopped at the banyan. Mason called it Banyan Lane, but the British preferred to term it Water Lane, for it was by this path that they went to fetch water.

The six Tahitians had said from the first that they intended to build a hut in which they could all live together with the women who might choose them as *tanés*. They had large ideas, and their hut was the only one in the island which could pride itself on an upper floor. This upper floor consisted of one room twenty-four feet by eighteen. Like Ulysses' bed in Ithaca, the beam at each corner supported a bed, which was large enough to receive three or four occupants. A central trap-door and a ladder led down to the ground floor, which contained two beds, built like those on the upper floor, out from the angle beams. Neither floor had any of the furniture which ornamented and often encumbered the huts of the British: cupboards, chests, tables, stools. Each of its inhabitants had been content to fix shelves on which his personal belongings were kept beside his bed. It had not occurred to any of the Tahitians to secure their belongings, precious though they were, from borrowing or stealing. There was moreover no door to their hut; anyone who liked might walk in. The walls were made of wooden screens which ran in grooves and could be opened or shut according to whether they wanted to admit the sun or protect themselves from it.

The British huts, both in conception and detail, showed a far greater tendency to suspicion of their neighbours and a desire to keep their distance from them. There were nine British on the island. There were therefore nine huts, since each wished to have his own. And each hut was not only fenced in but had a door, chests and cupboards, all of which were fastened with locks from *The Blossom,* or with complicated sailor's knots which made opening them difficult even for the owner.

It had been decided, so as to achieve both speed and equality, that the huts should have an identical plan and similar dimensions (eighteen feet by twelve). This simplified the carpenters' task. Since the kitchen, as in the Tahitians' hut, was a lean-to, the huts might well have consisted of a single room to serve both as dining-room and bedroom. But British decency was revolted by the idea of a double-bed forming part of the furniture of the room in which you received your friends. Except for Purcell's, the huts had been divided up. The wooden walls were immovable and had each two or three portholes, either round or square, from *The Blossom*. These were effective as protection against wind and rain, but in fine weather – the most usual weather in the island – admitted much less light and sun than the Tahitians' sliding walls.

The nine huts were solid enough. Their walls were made from the oak bulwarks of *The Blossom* and were so thick and of such close grain that it was difficult to drive a nail into them. But no personal caprice entered into their construction, and they were all built on the same model. In fact, the British did not in the least mind this similarity and Purcell was the only one of them to show any originality. For the south side of his hut he had adopted the sliding walls of the Tahitians, and had extended the roof in the form of a verandah so that he could enjoy the view of the mountain without being inconvenienced by the sun. When this had been done, Purcell saw with pleasure that it lent dignity to his hut by extending the line of the roof.

Each morning, after dressing in the lean-to, Purcell went to admire it. He turned his back on the house, walked down the one path his garden possessed to a thicket of hibiscus which marked its limit, and turned to gaze with satisfaction at his handiwork. At this hour, the sliding doors were already open, awaiting the first oblique rays of the sun, which had as yet scarcely touched the threshold. From where he stood, Purcell could see Ivoa busying herself with breakfast. He waited for the moment when she would have completed her preparations and would come to the threshold of the sliding doors, like the manager of a theatre coming to the front of the stage to make an announcement. She looked at him from afar, smiled and chanted in a long sing-song: 'A-da-mo! Come and eat, A-da-mo!' Since they were only some twenty yards from each other and could see each other perfectly well, there was no need for this summons. But it had become a habit. Purcell listened and smiled, watched Ivoa's figure and made no answer. She repeated the tender, caressing chant: 'A-da-mo! Come and eat, A-da-mo!' The tonic accent on the 'da' of Adamo was strongly marked, and the rest of his name was uttered on a high modulated note of indescribable charm. It moved and delighted him, and he would let her repeat the call yet a third time before signing to her by raising his hand that he had heard.

On the heavy oak table her *tané* had made, Ivoa would have set out an open coconut, a mango, a banana and cakes of breadfruit, cooked the day before in the common oven. Ivoa had adopted with a good grace the strange *Peritani* habit of laying the table. Could it be useful or important to eat twenty-six inches above the floor? But on one point she had remained inflexible: she would not take her meals with Adamo, but only after him. The Tahitian religion held (as does Christianity, moreover) that man had come first in the order of creation, and woman second, as a sort of later corrective to man's solitude. But the Tahitians, more imaginative than the Hebrews, or perhaps merely having a better appetite, had made a culinary application of this masculine priority. A man must eat before his wife, and she must be content with what is left over.

When he had finished his meal, Purcell left the hut by the front door, crossed West Avenue, and went into the undergrowth. After a few paces, he heard laughter and singing. He smiled. The *vahinés* were already at work. He had never seen them work so hard! Some of the huts had not yet been roofed and they were making the screens to cover them.

'You've come without your wife,' Itia said, as soon as she saw Adamo. 'Is it to choose another?'

The *vahinés* laughed and Purcell smiled.

'No, I've come to say good morning to you.'

'Good morning, Adamo,' Itia said.

Purcell went up to the *vahinés*. He admired the speed and precision of their movements. They distributed the tasks among them. One group cut the branches of pandanus. Another wove the leaves round the branches on which they grew And a third bound the branches together with strips of bark from the trees.

'Do you know who's going to take me for his *vahiné*?' Vaa asked.

'No,' Purcell said.

'And me, do you know?' Toumata asked.

'No.'

'And me?' Raha asked.

'No, no,' he said. 'I know nothing.'

As they talked, they hurried on with their work. At the moment they were all living together in a huge tent made from *The Blossom*'s sails, and they wanted to get their huts finished. In Tahiti, and then on board, there had been a certain promiscuity; but in the end everyone had grown weary of it. On reaching the island, the British had said publicly that they had decided to choose their women, once and for all, as soon as the huts were finished.

'I'm off,' Purcell said, making a little sign to them with his hand.

Itia straightened up.

'You'll come back soon?'

'I've got work at home.'

'Can I come to see you?'

'My little sister Itia is always welcome,' Purcell said.

This dialogue had been listened to in silence by the *vahinés*, but as soon as Purcell had gone there was laughter and a rapid flow of talk.

Purcell found old Johnson waiting for him outside his door.

'Sir,' Johnson said in a low voice, glancing furtively round, 'may I borrow your axe? I've got a damned stump in my garden I want to get rid of.'

Purcell picked up the axe which was lying against the wall of the kitchen lean-to and handed it to him. The old man took it and let it hang from his thin arm, while stroking his beard with his other hand. He could not make up his mind to go away.

'Sir,' he said, still furtive, 'I hear you've got a nice verandah.'

'What?' Purcell said with surprise. 'Have you never seen it? I'd have thought after all this time . . .'

Johnson made no move, and his faded, watery blue eyes shifted restlessly from one object to another. His temples were sunken, he had a big nose with a wen on the end of it, and his brick red face had purple patches on the cheeks which ate into the white hair of his beard.

'May I see?' he said at last, his eyes shifty.

'Of course,' Purcell said.

He led him round the hut into the garden; and it soon became obvious that Johnson did not want to be seen talking to him from West Avenue.

'You're very nicely here, sir,' Johnson said, 'very nice and snug. Nothing but the forest and the mountain.'

Purcell looked at him and waited.

'I've got something to ask you, sir,' Johnson said.

'Go on.'

'Sir,' Johnson said hoarsely, 'I don't want to be impertinent, particularly after the way you behaved at Jimmy's death . . .'

He fell silent, looked at the top of the mountain, and said very quickly as if he had prepared the sentence: 'Sir, will you allow me not to call you "sir" any more?'

Purcell laughed. So that was it!

'What do you want to call me?' he said, laughing.

'Oh, it isn't me,' Johnson said, holding the axe to his chest as if to defend himself. 'I'd never have thought of it! We had a meeting,' he went on, apparently embarrassed. 'We voted and decided not to call you and Captain Mason "sir" any more.'

'You voted?' Purcell said in surprise. 'Where did you do this?'

'Under the banyan, sir. Yesterday, after the midday meal. It's as if you and Captain Mason aren't our officers any more. Everyone voted for it.'

'You too, Johnson?' Purcell said calmly.

Johnson hung his head.

'Yes.'

Purcell fell silent. Johnson felt the edge of the axe with his big red hand and said in his hoarse voice: 'You must understand. I daren't go against them. I'm old, I haven't much strength left, and it's the same here as it was in *The Blossom*. I'm just tolerated.'

D

Purcell looked away. He disliked Johnson's humble tone.

'After all,' he said after a moment, 'why should the men continue to treat us as officers? We no longer exercise the functions.'

Johnson opened his eyes wide.

'That's what MacLeod said, sir,' he said in a low voice, surprised at finding the same argument on the lips of one of the interested parties.

He added: 'I didn't think you'd take it like that, sir.'

'Purcell.'

'What?' Johnson said.

'Purcell. Not "sir". Purcell.'

'Yes, sir,' Johnson said.

Purcell laughed and Johnson echoed him with a little cracked laugh that had no gaiety.

'Thank you for the axe,' he said, turning away.

Purcell looked after him, as he went limping off, dragging his left leg behind him, the axe hanging from his emaciated arm. Bent, used up and frightened, he seemed to have no place in this adventure.

'Johnson,' Purcell called quietly.

Johnson stopped and turned. He waited, almost standing to attention.

'If I understand you,' Purcell said, going to him, 'your comrades didn't lead you an easy life on board.'

'The fact is,' Johnson said, looking at the ground, 'I'm old. I've got these spots on my face, and I've no more strength than a chicken. So they naturally take advantage of me.'

'In that case,' Purcell said, raising his eyebrows, 'why the devil did you follow them here instead of staying in Tahiti? You weren't one of the mutineers. You ran no risk by staying there.'

There was a silence. Johnson raised his free hand to his chin and rubbed the sparse white hairs of his beard. His rather watery blue eyes looked down his big nose.

'Well,' he said, suddenly raising his head with an expression which might have been defiance, 'I don't want to go back to England, that's what it is. It can happen to anybody to have done something wrong when they were young, can't it?'

'You committed a crime? '

'When I was young,' Johnson said, looking down his nose again. 'Sir,' he went on, suddenly raising his voice, 'even if I have committed a crime, is it just that I should be punished for it for the rest of my damned life? That's what I want to know! '

'It depends,' Purcell said. 'It depends on whether you did someone a great wrong.'

Johnson thought about it for a few seconds and said: 'It's certainly done me a great wrong.'

There was an absent look in his eyes as if the events of the past had suddenly coalesced in his mind. A moment later, he turned crimson from ear to ear, the veins of his forehead and temples swelled disquietingly, and his head seemed to be on the point of bursting under the pressure of memory.

'I can't say I did anyone else a wrong, sir,' he said indignantly 'No. I can't say that! '

Waving a finger in front of his long nose, he went on: 'And the other has no right to say it either. And if there was a case, though there can't be for a matter like that, God damn me and forgive me, sir, like Job on his dunghill, but I've never done any harm to anyone. But the fact is, if there was a case I know well what all the neighbours would say, God bless the good souls, if they were *bona fide* witnesses, as our squire says, and not damned liars, like some I know. The other profited by me, that's the truth, sir, and if there's a roof over the other's head at this moment, and the wherewithal to whet the other's whistle with a drop of beer on Sundays after service, who does the other owe it to, by Christ, if it's not to me, and may God damn the other to hell if it's not the truth, sir, as true and *bona fide* as my name's Johnson.'

He went on: 'I'll tell you what I did, sir. I got married.'

There was a silence and Purcell said, intrigued: 'You can trust me, you might as well tell me the whole thing. I don't understand. What has your marriage got to do with the "other"? Who is "the other"?'

'Mrs Johnson, sir.'

'Oh, I see,' Purcell said.

Johnson looked at him and said: 'You'll perhaps say it was not a very serious crime to get married. But don't say it, sir,' he said reproachfully, as if Purcell had indeed put forward that opinion. 'It must have been a serious crime, since I've been punished for it all the rest of my damned life.'

He looked at Purcell as if expecting agreement, and as Purcell remained silent, he went on with a sort of pride: 'I wasn't poor, sir. If I was at home at this moment, I shouldn't be a charge on the parish. I had a little cottage, sir, and nice bit of garden with rabbits and chickens. Well, I preferred to leave it all and sail in *The Blossom*. At my age, sir!'

'I imagine,' Purcell said, 'that, like me, you didn't know what Burt was like.'

'I did,' Johnson said. 'I'd already sailed with him.'

Purcell looked at him in amazement.

'And you preferred . . .'

'Yes, I preferred it,' Johnson said soberly.

There was a silence and then Purcell went on: 'And that's also the reason you've come with us?'

'Yes, sir.'

'It seems to me,' Purcell said after a moment, 'that you've chosen a curiously radical solution. After all, you could have left Mrs Johnson and yet stayed in England.'

'No, sir,' Johnson replied.

And he said with complete certainty: 'She would have found me.'

He stopped, made a gesture with his free hand as if to drive away all his memories at once, and went on: 'Oh, I'm all right now, sir. I'm not complaining.' Then he added humbly: 'Perhaps I shall have a bit of peace at last.'

There was a sound of hurrying steps in front of the house and someone shouted excitedly: 'Purcell! Purcell!'

'Here I am,' Purcell cried.

He went round the hut, Johnson at his heels. It was White. He was breathless, his eyes were starting from his head and his lips were trembling. He said in a staccato voice: 'Everyone's on the cliff with their muskets. I was looking for you.'

He regained his breath, swallowed, and added: 'There's a sail.'

Purcell felt as if someone had hit him in the face.

'Distant?' he asked calmly. 'Heading this way?'

White shrugged his shoulders, turned away and ran off without another word.

'Come, Johnson,' Purcell said, resisting a desire to run. 'No,' he said impatiently, 'leave the axe here, you won't need it.'

Instead of going by West Avenue, he cut through the undergrowth, Johnson stumbling along beside him.

'What a business, sir!' the old man muttered.

'Yes,' Purcell said, clenching his teeth, 'you may not have found the right place to get a bit of peace.'

As they crossed Blossom Square, they passed beside a group of women. They stared at them in silence. They already knew; and must have been forbidden to go to the cliff. They were gathered in front of their tent, and had stopped work.

As Purcell came to the passage through the bush which opened on to the north cliff, Mason shouted to him not to show himself. At the moment, it was in fact a useless precaution for the ship was still far away. No more than the outline of the island could be visible to those on board.

The men, both the British and the Tahitians, were sitting with their muskets on their knees at the edge of the bush under cover of a few small palm trees, scarcely taller than a man. Mason was standing, his eye glued to his telescope. No one uttered a word. They were all staring at the sail.

'She's on an easterly course,' Mason said at last. 'She's not making towards us.'

But this meant nothing, and they knew it. The island appeared on no chart. The captain would certainly want to reconnoitre it.

Mason lowered his telescope, changed it to his left hand, and began rubbing his right eye. This gesture of Mason's was so familiar to Purcell that he was almost astonished to see him repeating it at such a moment.

Mason stopped rubbing his eye and handed the telescope to Purcell. This was also part of the routine.

'Mr Purcell,' Mason said calmly, 'can you see her flag?'

Purcell's hands were sweating on the telescope, he could not concentrate enough to distinguish the colours. Then he felt a lump in his throat and said in a scarcely audible voice: 'She's wearing the white ensign She's a frigate.'

'The telescope!' Mason said tonelessly.

He almost snatched it from his hands. Purcell put the palm of his hand over his right eye and, when he removed it, he saw the men's strained and anxious faces. They were looking not at the sail but at Mason.

'You're right,' Mason said.

There was a moment of sudden tension, and the silence became almost intolerable.

'Sir,' said Baker to Purcell, 'do you think they're looking for us?'

Purcell glanced at him. The Welshman's brown, regular features seemed impassive, but Purcell noticed that his lower lip was twitching. There was nothing Purcell could say. He had just realised his own legs were trembling, and he tried to control them by stiffening the muscles.

'I don't care a damn whether she's looking for us or not,' MacLeod said with sudden violence.

His Adam's apple moved upwards in his thin neck, and he added: 'What I do know is that it's us she'll find.'

After that, no one said any more. A frigate! How could they resist a frigate? Purcell looked at the men. Their faces were pale under their sunburn, but none, except Smudge, showed panic. Smudge's eyes were rolling, his lower jaw was hanging open, and he was incessantly rubbing his hands together.

Purcell sat down at the foot of a little palm tree. He was wearing only trousers and shirt; and was not very comfortable. The north-west wind was blowing fairly strongly and the thick woods to the east of the cliff were so dense that they cut off the sun. He put his hands in his pockets, leaned forward, and tautened the muscles in his back. At that moment his eyes fell on his legs. They were trembling.

Purcell swallowed and looked round him. No one was looking at him. They were all staring out to sea. He drew a deep breath, put out a hand to lean on and touched the muskets. There were twice as many muskets as men on the island, and Mason had had the reserve muskets placed on trestles to keep them off the ground.

'Be careful,' Baker said, following Purcell's glance, 'they're loaded.'

Purcell shrugged. It was mad! Muskets against a frigate! As far as he was concerned, nothing on earth would induce him to fire at anyone. He picked up the musket his hand had encountered, put it on his knee, and looked at it with sudden attention. What a pity the musket should have so inhuman a purpose! It was a beautiful thing. The strong butt was of highly polished wood, and the metal of the barrel shone with a dull, reassuring lustre. Purcell stroked the butt and felt the weight of the weapon against his legs with pleasure. 'I can understand being fond of a musket,' he thought. 'It has both elegance and strength.' The men who had invented the infernal machine had known how to give it grace. He caressed the weapon on his knees, its weight against them was heavy, warm and friendly. His legs had ceased to tremble.

Mason lowered his telescope, looked round at the men, and said tonelessly: 'She's running down towards us.'

For a few seconds no one said anything, then MacLeod said in a low voice: 'We're done for.'

Everyone looked at him. With his right hand he made the motion of passing a slip-knot round his neck, pulled the imaginary rope tight and, twisting his head down on his shoulder, put out his tongue and turned up his eyes. Since Mac-Leod normally looked like a corpse, this piece of mimicry was very effective. The men looked away. Mason turned red, blinked, thrust his head forward and said, without looking at any of them, but with so much energy that his words seemed to explode one by one: 'They won't take me alive!'

He raised his head. He could see in the men's eyes that his determination had found an echo in them. I am their leader, he thought with a touch of pride, and they expect me to save them.

'Captain Mason,' Purcell said, 'may I have the telescope?'

Mason handed it to him, saw the musket on Purcell's knees and thought: 'Even Purcell, even that weakling . . .' He felt a wave of pride. He felt as if the island was a ship of the line under his command and that he was bearing down on the frigate to cut her in two. Never had his life seemed so full. 'Destroy the frigate!' he thought furiously. 'What does it matter if I am killed? Destroy it! It's her destruction that counts!'

'Sir,' White said.

The half-caste was so taciturn that they were surprised to hear his voice. He seemed surprised himself, looked round in embarrassment and hesitated. Purcell noticed that he showed emotion, as the Tahitians did, by his skin turning grey.

'Sir,' White went on, 'this is what I think. There's a bit of a sea running, and a great deal of surf. Perhaps the frigate won't risk a boat . . .'

'They might well hesitate if it were not for *The Blossom*,' Mason said.

Indeed, they had not thought of that! They were betrayed by *The Blossom*. Dismasted, dismantled and reduced to a hulk, she was nevertheless visible from a great distance as she lay on the only beach on which it was possible to land.

'Sir,' Baker said.

MacLeod uttered so hostile a snarl that Baker fell silent. Since mimicking the hanging awaiting the mutineers, MacLeod had affected to take no interest in either the danger or the discussions. He was lying on his back, his hands beneath his head, his eyes half-shut and his musket beside him.

'What did you say?' Baker asked, glancing sharply at him with his bright dark eyes.

'I say,' MacLeod said contemptuously, 'that some chaps forget today what they decided on yesterday.'

Baker blushed under his tan. It was true he had called Mason 'sir', but since morning everyone had been doing the same, and now MacLeod was picking on him. He stared at MacLeod. He was furious with him, annoyed with himself and could find nothing to say.

'Well?' Mason said impatiently.

'Is there no way of defending ourselves except by firing on the chaps as they land?'

Mason's face went hard and he said curtly: 'Why?'

'Well,' Baker said, embarrassed, 'to fire on unsuspecting chaps without warning . . .'

'It's either them or you,' Smudge said through his clenched teeth.

White with fear, sunk into himself, he stuck out his lower lip, and from behind the white locks that half covered them his little rat's eyes gleamed, anxious and furtive.

'Smudge has answered you,' Mason said.

'Yes,' MacLeod said, opening his eyes. 'He's answered and yet not answered.'

He got to his feet and picked up his musket. He slowly straightened up, and when he had done so stood there loosely, leaning on his musket with a certain nonchalance and looking round at the seamen. His trousers were so tight they showed the bones of his hips and you could count his ribs under the dirty white vest he alone wore. His eyes half-closed, his legs straddled, looking at once haughty and more than ever like a sneering skeleton, he took his time before speaking. Every eye was on him. Mason deliberately turned his back and put his right eye to the telescope.

'Yes,' MacLeod repeated. 'I say Smudge has not answered, and the proof that he hasn't, my lads, is that he answered evasively. I don't care a damn about knocking off every bastard in the frigate, including the captain, but as I said, that's not the point. The real point is this, my lads: the frigate lowers a boat, and in the boat are a dozen bastards. They get through the surf and they land. What then? We fire, kill one or two, wound as many, and the rest re-embark. And what does the frigate do? Up anchor and set sail? Is that what you think? We've killed two of His Gracious Majesty's sailors, and the frigate clears out? Christ! Do you believe that? Perhaps you haven't noticed that the frigate has guns?'

He looked round contemptuously.

'Well, I'll tell you what'll happen, my lads. The captain of the frigate will say to himself: "Two of my bastards have been killed, so they don't seem to like us around here! They're bandits! Pirates! Perhaps even French! Very well, I'll blow that island to pieces, and when I've blown it to pieces, I'll hoist a flag on it and give it my name, and it'll be one island the more for His Most Gracious Majesty . . ." That's what the captain'll say! So he lowers half his boats with half his crew, but before he sends them in, the bastard'll turn his fifty guns on us for an hour or two. And what'll happen after that, my lads, won't matter to any of us, for there won't be any survivors.'

Mason looked over his shoulder at the men. It was obvious

that the Scotsman had affected them by his animation and convinced them by his reasoning. The description he had given of
what would happen was so expressive and dramatic, as well as
so probable, that none of them doubted it was prophetic.

Mason handed the telescope to Purcell, and suddenly turned
to face MacLeod.

'Well, what do you suggest?' he asked, his voice quivering
with anger. 'That we should surrender? To sow panic is not
enough, MacLeod. We must have a plan.'

'I'm not sowing panic,' MacLeod said, furious at being put on
the defensive after the success he had achieved. 'I'm stating
things as they are. As for a plan, we must discuss it among us.
We've got plenty of time. The frigate won't be here for an hour.'

'Discuss it!' Mason burst out violently. 'Discuss it! This isn't
a parliament! While we discuss, we can make no preparations.'

'Listen, Mason,' MacLeod said.

'How dare you address me like that!' Mason cried, red with
anger. 'I won't put up with your damned insolence any longer.'

'You'll just have to put up with it, Mason,' MacLeod replied
in his drawling voice, 'for I've no intention of addressing you in
any other way. We're not on board here. *The Blossom*'s rotting
on the beach and she's no more use to anyone. Nor, I regret to
have to tell you, Mason, is her captain. You know how to sail
a damn ship, Mason, I'll give you that. But on land you're
no more than the next man. You've a right to express an
opinion, but that's all. As for there being a parliament, I don't
mind telling you, Mason, you've put your finger on it. There is
a little parliament here, and no later than yesterday we voted
unanimously, and do you know what? No longer to give you
and Purcell your ranks. You no longer count here, Mason, and
you'd better get used to it. As I've already said, you've a right
to your opinion, but that's all.'

For a full second Mason gaped, deprived of speech and
almost of movement. Then he recovered himself, straightened
up and looked sternly at the seamen.

'White?' he asked curtly.

'I agree with MacLeod.'

'Baker?'

'I've nothing against you,' Baker said, embarrassed. 'But I

agree. We're no longer aboard *The Blossom* here.'

'Jones?'

'I agree with Baker.'

'Johnson?'

'I agree, too,' Johnson said, hanging his head.

'Hunt?'

Hunt grunted, but made no answer.

'Smudge?'

'Do you think, Mason,' Smudge said, thrusting his long nose forward with a sort of impudence, 'that we're going to lick your and Purcell's boots? We don't want any damned officers here! We've had enough of them . . .'

'Stow it,' Baker said. 'There's no need to be rude.'

Mason turned to Purcell, who was leaning against a tree and watching the scene impassively.

'Did you know about this, Mr Purcell?' he asked suspiciously. 'Did you know about this vote?'

'I'd only just heard about it,' Purcell said.

He straightened up, feeling annoyed. Mason's suspicions had destroyed at a blow all the pity he felt for him.

There was a silence and then Mason said aggressively: 'Well? What do you think of it?'

Purcell was silent for a few seconds. He was seeking some means of making Mason understand that he was not with him, but without actually disavowing him in front of the men.

'Well?' Mason repeated.

'As far as I'm concerned,' Purcell said curtly, 'I shall continue from deference to call you Captain Mason, but if the men wish to call me Purcell, I don't mind.'

'You don't mind?' Mason cried indignantly.

'No, Captain Mason.'

'Well, aren't you . . .' Mason began contemptuously.

He was going to say: 'Aren't you disgusted?' but he stopped, his mouth hanging open. He had nearly forgotten. Officers must never quarrel in front of the men. His mouth closed like an oyster. He turned suddenly on MacLeod, looked him up and down and said furiously: 'Of course, you plotted all this, Mac-Leod! You're the leader! It's you who have turned the men from their duty!'

'I'm no one's leader,' MacLeod said, drawing himself up with dignity, 'and I've done no plotting at all. I've a right to my opinion, and I've stated it. And since you're talking of duty, Mason, I'll tell you this: I didn't advise you to kill your captain and lead his ship's company to mutiny . . .'

Mason turned scarlet, and his hands gripped his musket. Purcell thought he was going to fire at the Scotsman. MacLeod must have thought so too, for he put his own musket under his right arm. He waited, his finger on the trigger and the muzzle pointing at Mason's legs. Two or three seconds went by. Then Mason slung his weapon with an appearance of calm, and the tension relaxed.

'Men,' he said in a fairly firm voice, but without looking at them, 'if you think you can do without your captain, very well!'

He hesitated, realised his left hand was trembling, put it behind his back, and repeated with a rather pitiful effort to put irony into his voice: 'Very well!'

He fell silent. He wanted to abdicate with some firm, well-chosen phrase suitable to a commander. But his mind was a total blank. He was unable to speak.

The seamen waited, motionless. Even MacLeod said nothing. They realised that Mason was seeking some final word but could not find it, and far from seeing anything ridiculous in the situation, they were embarrassed for him.

'Men,' Mason said, scarlet, stiff, blinking his eyes, his left hand clenched behind his back. 'I . . .'

He could get no further. Smudge sniggered and Baker dug him in the stomach with his elbow.

'Very well!' Mason repeated at last with another derisory effort at irony.

Then he squared his shoulders, turned on his heel, and went off.

There was a silence, and then they all turned back to the sea and stared at the frigate. She was growing larger every second, carrying death on every square foot of her deck.

'Well,' Smudge said, thrusting his nose forward aggressively, 'what's your plan?'

'My plan?' MacLeod said, glancing angrily at him.

'Well, we've got to do something!' Smudge went on. Fear of

the frigate had lent him the courage to confront MacLeod. 'If you've thrown the captain overboard, it must be because you know what course to set . . .'

There was a murmur of approval from the men. MacLeod put a hand on his narrow hip and looked at them contemptuously.

'My lads,' he said, in his sardonic drawl, 'you've lost a captain. You needn't count on me to replace him. I've no taste for rank. And I'll tell you one thing. If there are chaps here who need a daddy to tell them what to do, they needn't come to me. Get that into your heads, my lads. I'm nobody's daddy. And I've got no plan either.'

He stopped, looked at them defiantly and went on: 'It's up to all of us to make a plan.'

There was a silence, and then Purcell said politely: 'I have a suggestion to make.'

They all looked at him. He had been sitting at the foot of a palm-tree, his musket on his knees and the telescope to his eye. He had kept so still that they had nearly forgotten him. Now they were almost shocked by his presence. They would have thought it more natural that he should have gone off with Mason. Purcell sensed it in the silence with which they greeted his remark. He said stiffly: 'Of course, if you don't want to hear my suggestion, I'm quite prepared to go away.'

'Purcell,' MacLeod said gravely, looking round at his companions as if to make them witnesses to his liberal attitude, 'as I said to Mason, everyone here has a right to his opinion, and you're no exception.'

'Very well,' Purcell said, 'to begin with I think the nor'wester has freshened considerably, there's a sea running, and I don't now believe the frigate will drop anchor in the bay or lower a boat.'

The men turned to look at the sea and gauge the swell. After a moment, Johnson shook his head and said in his hoarse voice: 'It's no worse than the day we landed.'

He was immediately contradicted, but with a certain lack of assurance. They dared not give way to hope, or even formulate it, for fear fate would retaliate.

'As for the muskets,' Purcell went on, 'Macleod's right. To

use them is to commit suicide. Here's what I suggest. If they land men, the Tahitians alone will show themselves on the cliff, utter war cries and, if necessary, throw stones. The frigate must believe she's dealing with natives.'

There was a silence, and then Smudge said peevishly: 'I don't see any difference between that and Mason's plan.'

'Nor do I,' White said, his eyes gleaming malevolently in the slits between his lids.

MacLeod chewed his underlip and said nothing.

'But there is one,' Purcell said. 'Before leaving London, we received an Admiralty instruction forbidding all landings in the Pacific where the natives adopted a hostile attitude.'

There was a silence. MacLeod scrutinised Purcell's face.

'You have read that instruction, Purcell?' he said slowly.

'Yes,' Purcell said.

He kept his guileless eyes on MacLeod, and thought: 'May God forgive me for the lie.'

'I'm for it,' Baker said.

'So am I,' said Jones.

The others were silent. Purcell looked at them. Hunt was staring into space out of his little pale eyes. He had understood nothing of what was going forward and now looked appealingly at MacLeod as if asking for help. Old Johnson was nodding his head as if in approval, but from the furtive glances he gave Mac- Leod, Purcell realised he dared express no opinion before the Scotsman had given his. White and Smudge were hesitating. They were so hostile to Purcell they could not bring themselves to approve his suggestion. They, too, were waiting for MacLeod to give his view. 'If there's a parliament,' Purcell thought suddenly, 'it's a parliament dominated by MacLeod.'

'Yes,' MacLeod at last said slowly, 'your plan wouldn't be a bad one, Purcell, if it weren't for the damned hulk of *The Blossom* on the beach. Even her name's on the stern, and in twenty minutes from now the captain'll be able to see it through his telescope. And when the bastard does see it, believe me, my lads, he'll begin asking himself questions. He may well come to the conclusion that the natives on the island have killed *The Blossom*'s crew. And, in that case, I wouldn't be surprised if he insisted on paying us a little visit, even if the blacks do throw stones at him.'

'Well?' Smudge said.

'Well,' MacLeod went on, 'here's my opinion. First, we must do as Purcell has said. Then, if the chaps from the frigate press on, we must take to the bush by the mountain with the women, the food and the muskets.'

He stopped, sniffed the wind and glanced at the sea. The nor'-wester seemed to have freshened again, or was it an illusion?

'Why by the mountain?' Smudge asked.

'Because there's water there.'

'And what the hell shall we do in the bush?'

'Outwit them,' MacLeod said, sniffing disdainfully.

Suddenly turning red in the face, he bent his tall body down towards Smudge and said furiously: 'Christ! Don't you understand? What have you got inside your head? Nothing? Empty, is it? An empty shell? Can't you see that if we fight the bastards we're done for!'

'Then why the muskets?' Smudge asked.

MacLeod straightened up and went on in a calm, sardonic voice: 'Our beloved countrymen are tenacious. They may track us down. They may starve us out. They may even set fire to the bush to drive us out.'

'What then?' White asked.

'Then we'll come out and sell our lives dearly.'

There was a silence. White raised his hand and said in his shrill, sing-song voice: 'I'm for it.'

They all followed his example, with the exception of Hunt. The raised hands reached to about the level of his mouth and his little pig's eyes stared at them anxiously.

'Well,' Smudge said, nudging him on the hip, 'aren't you going to vote?'

Hunt raised his hand.

'Purcell,' MacLeod said, 'will you tell the blacks to collect all the food they can in the village and be ready to take it to safety in the bush.'

Purcell translated and the Tahitians, looking perfectly impassive, at once set off to obey. Since Mason had distributed muskets to them, they had remained apart and had not uttered a single word.

'I wonder what those birds are thinking,' MacLeod said, rubbing the side of his nose with his finger. 'They mustn't betray us when we take refuge in the bush.'

'They won't betray us,' Purcell said curtly.

He put the telescope to his eye and took a moment to find the frigate. This time, there could be no mistake. The sea had risen, and occasional waves were so high that at times they hid the ship's bows.

'In my opinion,' Purcell said, controlling the trembling of his voice with difficulty, 'she can't come any closer inshore on this wind.'

He handed the telescope to MacLeod, who began to swear because he had difficulty in adjusting it. He stood perfectly still, tendons and muscles showing on his thin neck, which started to turn red. The seamen were all gazing out to sea, but a curtain of mist had fallen over the island and they could not see the frigate's sails clearly enough to be certain of her course.

'She's running before the wind!' MacLeod shouted. 'Look, Purcell! She's running before the wind!'

Purcell took the telescope and, while he was adjusting it, heard the man's quick breathing. The frigate had in fact turned back on to an easterly course. She had taken in a lot of canvas, the wind was on her port quarter, and she was pitching considerably. As soon as she had doubled the island, it was clear she would turn south-east to ride more easily. The sea was rising every minute.

Purcell lowered the telescope and took a deep breath. He felt as if his lungs had been closed and he was now opening them to the air again.

'To make for land's the last thing she's thinking of,' he said happily. 'She'll be out of sight in an hour.'

They all wanted to look through the telescope to reassure themselves about the frigate's course. The danger was still too near. Merely to talk of it made them fear it would return. They were all astonished by the telescope. When it came to Johnson's turn, he said proudly that he had watched Burt put his eye to the instrument all his life, and he had never thought the day would come when he would put his own to it. It was true. It was Burt's telescope. And now it belonged to them. Burt was dead, Mason no longer counted and they were free.

MacLeod had slung his musket and, propping himself against a little palm-tree with his hand, was watching the horizon. When Johnson returned the telescope to Purcell, he stood up straight and said: 'I've one suggestion to make. Let's set fire to *The Blossom*. And let's do it at once.'

There was a silence, and then Baker said, looking shocked: 'To all that wood?'

The objection carried weight. The men looked at MacLeod and then looked away again. They dared not contradict him, but they did not approve of setting fire to *The Blossom*. In the first place, *The Blossom* was theirs. For jacks of all trades, even her hulk meant enormous wealth. Hundreds of useful little things could be made of all the wood and metal she contained.

MacLeod looked at them contemptuously.

'Christ!' he said in his rasping voice. 'The danger's scarcely over, and you've already forgotten it. There's the seaman for you! No more brains than a fish! Baker may want to carve a pipe for himself out of *The Blossom*'s hull, but I tell you, my lads, I'm not going to risk my precious neck for Baker's pipe. The only purpose *The Blossom* serves is to give us away. Haven't you realised that yet? She's an invitation card to the island: "Here are *The Blossom*'s mutineers. Welcome to His Majesty's frigates!" And she's an invitation card that can be seen over miles of sea! If there's a ship in the vicinity, *The Blossom* will attract her like sugar attracts flies. You should realise that captains go mad at the sight of a wreck. Whenever they see one, they make straight for it, even if they're in a hurry. They get excited and start asking a whole heap of questions. Believe me, my lads, there's not a damned captain in the whole Pacific who wouldn't come ashore to put his nose into that hulk.'

Purcell looked at the men. MacLeod had convinced them once again.

'MacLeod,' Purcell said, 'if there's to be a vote, I think Captain Mason should be here.'

'It's his right,' MacLeod said.

He added with a shrug: 'But I'll bet you a penny he won't

come. White, go and fetch the . . .'

He was going to say 'the captain', but corrected himself: 'Go and fetch Mason.'

White obeyed. There was no captain any more. But he was still acting as steward. He was sent with messages from one end of the village to the other. Everyone thought this quite natural, including White himself.

White returned a few minutes later.

'He won't come,' he said, out of breath.

MacLeod raised his eyebrows and gestured with his open hand as much as to say: 'I told you so.'

'You told him this concerned *The Blossom*?' Purcell asked.

'Yes,' White said, and once again Purcell saw an inexplicable hostility in his eyes.

'Did you tell him it was a question of burning *The Blossom*?'

'No,' White said.

'I put my suggestion to the vote,' MacLeod said with dignity. Every hand was raised, except Purcell's.

'I think,' Purcell said, 'that if Captain Mason had been told it was a question of burning *The Blossom,* he would have come.'

'It would have made no difference,' Smudge said. 'Even without your vote and his, there's a majority.'

'That's not the point,' Purcell said patiently. 'Personally, I agree with burning *The Blossom*. But I think Captain Mason should be given the opportunity to protest. I demand that a second attempt be made to get Captain Mason to come.'

'I put the suggestion to the vote,' MacLeod said.

MacLeod, White, Smudge, Hunt and – after a certain delay – Johnson voted against. Jones, Baker and Purcell for. The vote upset Purcell. It was clear that MacLeod had a personal majority in the 'parliament'. White and Smudge would vote with him from conviction; Hunt from stupidity; Johnson from fear.

'Purcell's suggestion defeated,' MacLeod said.

He paused and then went on: 'Proposal to burn *The Blossom* at once.'

They all voted for it. Purcell gave no sign.

'Purcell?' MacLeod said.

'I abstain,' Purcell said.

'What does "I abstain" mean?' Johnson asked.

MacLeod shrugged.

'It means you don't vote either yes or no.'

'Well, really!' Johnson said, opening his eyes wide. 'You just say: "I abstain" and it means neither yes nor no. Are you allowed to do that?' he went on doubtfully.

'Of course.'

Johnson shook his head in astonishment.

'Really,' he went on. 'I'd never have thought it. "I abstain",' he repeated with a sort of respect, as if surprised so simple a word should have such power.

'Well, now that you know, shut up,' Smudge said.

MacLeod coughed and said solemnly: 'Proposal to burn *The Blossom*: seven votes for. One abstention. One absent. Proposal adopted.'

'Let's get on with it!' Smudge said eagerly.

Once decided, setting fire to *The Blossom* became a party of pleasure. What a splendid bonfire the damned ship would make! Even the stones in the creek might melt! The seamen hurried to the cliff, and Purcell could hear them jumping from rock to rock as they descended the steep path leading to the beach.

Purcell turned his back on the sea, went towards the village and entered East Avenue. He wanted to avoid Blossom Square and being questioned by the women.

An hour later, Purcell was naked to the waist, chopping wood in his garden, when he heard himself hailed. He looked up. It was Baker. He was pale in the face.

'Come quick!' Baker cried. 'Quick! Please! Let's run! You're the only man who may be able to stop it!'

Baker sounded so anxious that Purcell joined him and set off running beside him through the wood towards the cliff.

'What's the matter?' he shouted as they ran.

'There's a terrible scene going on with Mason. The blacks must have told him. The Old Man's been behaving like a madman! He screamed. He almost wept. He wanted to throw himself into the flames. In the end, he turned his musket on MacLeod!'

'Did he kill him?'

'No, they managed to disarm him. They tied his hands and

took him to the top of the cliff. They sent the blacks away. Run, sir! Run!'

'What's happening?' Purcell cried, fear in his heart.

Baker tripped, recovered himself, and turned his head towards Purcell.

'They want to hang him!'

6

Purcell took in the whole scene at a glance: the noose hanging from the main branch of a pandanus; Mason standing at the foot of the tree with his arms and legs bound; the men gathered in a half-circle round him; and, behind them, leaping, roaring flames and a cloud of smoke rising from the beach.

As he ran, Purcell noticed that the rope was not tied to the branch, but simply passed over it. MacLeod was standing on Mason's right and holding the loose end in his hand. Hunt was standing massively on the prisoner's left and, since he was very tall, the noose was swaying on the level of his face.

Purcell stopped running as soon as he saw Mason was alive. He was breathless and put his right hand to his side as he approached the group. He glanced at Mason, his eyes wide with anxiety, but Mason was looking at no one. He was standing almost to attention, his face rigid, his eyes staring straight in front of him. Encouraged by his stillness, multi-coloured little birds from the undergrowth were fluttering round him. At the very moment Purcell came up, one of them perched on the prisoner's shoulder and pirouetted there gaily and encouragingly. Mason neither moved nor turned his head.

MacLeod!' Purcell cried breathlessly.

'Don't worry, Purcell,' MacLeod said. 'I would not have put it to the vote without you or Baker. Everything will be done in accordance with the rules. Everyone will have the chance to say what he likes. And Mason will have all the time he needs in which to defend himself.'

'But you're not seriously thinking . . .' Purcell cried.

'I'm as serious as it's possible to be,' MacLeod replied. 'If Mason hadn't been prevented from firing, the fishes would be making a meal of me at this moment.'

'But he didn't fire!'

'He didn't have time to,' MacLeod said. 'White was quicker than he was!'

'I wouldn't say that,' Jones said suddenly. 'I wouldn't say he didn't have time. At least two seconds went by before White leapt at him.'

'He was taking his time aiming at me,' MacLeod said.

Jones's young and honest face frowned with the effort to remember exactly how things had happened.

'No,' he said, 'I wouldn't say that either. I'd say it was more as if he was wondering whether he'd fire or not.'

Jones looked at Mason as if asking his support. But Mason did not move his head so much as an inch. His mouth was closed, his eyes fixed, and his expression disdainful; it was as if he were not even listening to the discussion on which his life depended. He seemed determined to remain silent and to ignore his judges. 'He's a brave man,' Purcell thought irritably. 'Very brave and very stupid.'

'You see,' Purcell said urgently, 'even if White hadn't leapt at him . . .'

'That,' Smudge said violently, 'is what Jones says. I say the opposite. I say he was going to fire.'

For a moment Purcell said nothing. He realised at once that Smudge wanted Mason's death. He felt an overwhelming disgust and Smudge's presence was so intolerable to him that he could no longer look at him.

'Purcell,' MacLeod said, 'you must understand me.' And Purcell thought: 'This is it, he's going to take control of the discussion.'

'Listen to me,' he cut in, 'we must not begin our life on the island by a murder. For it is murder!'

He wanted to speak with authority, and it was with despair that he heard his voice flowing weak, pale and emasculate from his lips. The very strength of his emotion prevented his communicating it.

'It's murder,' he repeated. 'Mason was wrong to aim his

musket at you, but he was not in control of himself. Whereas you, if you hang him . . .'

He stopped and looked at the men. He had made no effect on them. It was all over. White, Smudge and MacLeod would vote for. Hunt was staring at the noose with his little pale eyes, his big stupid face expressionless, but it was clear he would vote with MacLeod. Johnson, his big nose pointing to the ground, was rubbing the purple patches that ate into his beard with his left hand. He had not looked at Purcell once.

'It's murder!' Purcell cried.

But it was useless. He felt as if he were talking to stones. MacLeod glanced at him. Of all the seamen, he was the only one who had listened to him with attention. He was waiting. He was in no hurry to speak again, as if he wanted to make it quite clear that he was leaving the opposite party every opportunity to have its say. His grey eyes were bright in his eyebrow-less sockets, and between his sharp, curved nose and his nutcracker chin, his thin lips were pressed together. There was not an ounce of fat on his face; the skin covered nothing but bone, and the muscles of his jaw pulsed in the two frightening hollows under his cheekbones.

'Purcell,' he said at last with a sort of dignity, 'you say we mustn't begin our life on the island by a murder. That's just what I say! It's precisely because we're beginning our life on the island that we must be severe with bastards who start using their muskets. What'll happen if we aren't? We'll all be killing each other! And that's certain! When you quarrel with your neighbour, or prefer his field to your own, or want his woman, what'll happen? It'll be the man who fires first who'll be the law-maker! And that's anarchy! It's massacre! I'll tell you this, Purcell, though Mason wanted to shoot me, I bear him no grudge. He was mad about his ship, and he saw red. But we need law and order,' he went on violently, 'and we need to make an example! Particularly at the start, Purcell. That's where you're wrong! Any man who threatens to kill a comrade, or even makes as if to do so without saying a word, I say deserves the rope! At once! On the spot! Otherwise there'll be no law and order on the island. We'll all be killed down to the last man!'

Purcell looked at him in stupefaction. It was obvious he was perfectly sincere. This mutineer was the incarnation of respect for the law. This murderer wanted to protect the life of his fellow-citizens. He thought as a man who was on the side of the law.

Baker said suddenly: 'We didn't hang Kori when he fired at Mehoro.'

'Quite right!' Purcell said at once. 'There's a precedent. It wouldn't be just to have two yardsticks.'

MacLeod was too much the lawyer not to be shaken by the word 'precedent', but it only lasted a few seconds. He recovered himself.

'They were blacks,' he said with contempt. 'The blacks can look after their own affairs. It's no business of ours.'

'After that, there was a silence, and then MacLeod went on: 'Mason, have you anything to say in your defence?'

Mason made no reply. MacLeod repeated the question and waited patiently. Purcell looked away. He could feel the sweat running down his back between his shoulder blades. It was now inevitable. It was as impossible to stop as a rock rolling downhill. MacLeod would say: 'I propose that Mason be hanged for attempted murder.' Jones, Baker and himself would vote against. The others, for. Purcell put out a hand and leaned against the trunk of the pandanus. He felt weak and somehow out of his element. He looked round at the undergrowth and at the men grouped about him as if he had never seen them before. The sun made bright patches here and there, and the brilliant, multi-coloured birds fluttered round the sailors and Mason. One of them perched in the noose. Two others joined it, and the noose began swaying gently above their heads.

'I propose . . .' MacLeod said.

At that moment, Hunt grunted. It was so unexpected that MacLeod ceased speaking and everyone looked at the giant.

'It was in *The Swallow*,' Hunt said suddenly, his little pale eyes fixed on the noose. 'I remember. It was three years ago. Or perhaps four.'

There was a silence and, as he said nothing further, Smudge turned his little rat face towards him.

'What do you remember?'

'A chap called Decker,' Hunt said.

He fell silent again, as if surprised at having spoken, looked at Smudge, puckered his red-bearded face and said: 'What have you put that filthy thing up there for?'

'What filthy thing?'

Hunt put out a hand and touched the noose. The multi-coloured birds flew away.

'It's for Mason,' Smudge said. 'He tried to shoot MacLeod. He's going to be executed.'

'Executed?' Hunt echoed.

His pale eyes became veiled and he said confusedly: 'This chap called Decker had struck an officer. They put this filthy thing round his neck, and they hauled on it.'

Everyone waited, but Hunt had fallen silent again. His little pale eyes were staring into the distance. It was as if he were no longer there.

After a moment, MacLeod said: 'I propose that Mason be hanged for attempted murder.'

Upon which old Johnson raised his head and said in a loud, determined voice: 'I abstain.'

He had had the phrase ready from the start and had found it difficult to wait until MacLeod had finished before uttering it. When he had said it, he glanced round, screwed up his little eyes and stared at the wen on the end of his nose with an expression of extreme satisfaction. So it was not inevitable, Purcell thought, with sudden hope.

'You're mad!' Smudge said threateningly.

Johnson turned on him with the courage of the weak.

'It's my right,' he said. 'MacLeod said so.'

'And talking of rights,' Purcell said, looking coldly at Smudge, 'you have no right to influence votes by intimidation.'

'Stow it, Smudge,' MacLeod said.

MacLeod turned and his glance passed over Mason's head to Hunt. Hunt looked at him irritably and uttered low guttural grunts.

Hunt's face seemed so crushed, so lacking in relief when seen in profile, that it might have served as an anvil to a sledge-hammer. In his youth he had been a prize-fighter, and over many years his poor silly head had been hammered by the fists of his opponents. This may well have been the cause of his stupidity and irritability; and perhaps it accounted for the hunted look in his little, pale eyes.

'What are you looking at me like that for?' MacLeod said.

Hunt merely grunted and MacLeod shrugged.

'Let's get on,' he said. 'Smudge?'

'For,' Smudge said with a sort of enthusiasm.

'White?'

'For.'

'I'm also for,' MacLeod said. 'Jones?'

'Against.'

'Baker?'

'Against.'

'Purcell?'

'Against.'

Hunt groaned, stared sullenly at MacLeod and said slowly and distinctly: 'Take that filthy thing away.'

There was a silence.

'It's for Mason,' Smudge said. 'He nearly shot MacLeod.'

'Take that filthy thing away,' Hunt said, shaking his head from side to side like a bear, 'I don't want to see it any more.'

MacLeod and Smudge looked at each other. Purcell drew himself up and said incisively, his heart beating: 'Before any further attempt is made to influence the voting, I would like to put it on record that Hunt does not appear to be in favour of the hanging.'

No one replied. The seamen were all looking at Hunt, waiting for what he was going to say. But Hunt merely uttered angry and inarticulate little grunts, which could not be interpreted as words. After a moment, he looked at the noose again, drew down the corners of his mouth as if about to cry, ran his eyes slowly up the rope to the branch, and then gradually down again to the end MacLeod was holding.

'Hunt,' MacLeod said, looking him firmly in the eye. 'You must vote. You're either for or against.'

Hunt grunted, and suddenly his arm passed in front of Mason with the speed of lightning, caught hold of MacLeod's hand, and opened it as easily as he would have opened a child's clutching a toy. The free end of the rope fell loose from MacLeod's hand and began swinging. Hunt seized the noose and pulled. The rope came down slowly at first, then with increasing speed till it fell to the ground, where it lay in a coil and was still. Hunt pushed it with his foot and emitted a series of little grunts, as brief and triumphant as those of a dog that has just killed a snake.

No one said a word. Purcell looked at the object at his feet which was so representative of man's ingenuity. It was a strong hempen rope, stained with tar in the centre, bleached by the sun and frayed in places by use. Lying on the ground, the noose hidden in its coils, it seemed inert, inoffensive and without significance.

'I suggest,' Purcell said, controlling the convulsive quivering of his voice, 'that Hunt be considered as voting against.'

Looking pale, his lips compressed into a thin line, MacLeod was massaging his sore hand. With Hunt voting with Purcell and Johnson abstaining, there were four votes against, and three in favour. He was defeated.

MacLeod felt the seamen's eyes on him. He drew himself up and, rather surprisingly, smiled. His lips parted, but his cheeks, instead of filling out, became hollower, and his face looked more than ever like a death's head.

He gazed calmly and sardonically at his comrades.

'My lads,' he said at last in his rhythmical, drawling voice, 'I don't consider that Hunt has voted. No, my lads, I won't agree to his vote being counted since he hasn't voted like a Christian with the tongue the good Lord has given him to speak with . . .'

His pious language surprised them, and their astonishment gave MacLeod a respite. No one thought of protesting or interrupting him.

'However,' MacLeod went on, 'we must be just. If Hunt isn't counted and Johnson abstains, that makes three votes against and three in favour. There's no majority in favour. There's no majority against. So, I put the question to you: what are we to do?'

The question was purely formal, for, before anyone had time to reply, he went on: 'I'll tell you, my lads: I withdraw the motion.'

And he looked round at the seamen to invite them to witness his generosity. He was a born politician, Purcell thought. Though defeated, he was giving himself all the airs of victory.

'Very well,' MacLeod went on, 'it doesn't count. We wipe the slate clean and Mason goes free. And so,' he went on dramatically, 'what happens? One day or another, Mason does it again, and this time he blows my brains out. There are some chaps,' he went on, looking at Hunt, 'who are so thick they can stand upright without brains, simply by their weight. But I need a brain to give orders to my bones, or I'd be floating about in the air like a kite in the slightest nor'wester . . . I ask for another vote, my lads, and at once. I propose that in future any bastard who threatens to kill a comrade, or draws a knife on him, shall be condemned and hanged within twenty-four hours.'

There was a silence, and then Baker said suspiciously: 'It being understood that the present vote does not apply to Mason?'

'It is understood.'

'I'm against it,' Purcell said. 'No one has the right to kill his brother.'

'Amen,' Smudge said.

Smudge's hostility to Purcell was so impudent that it embarrassed them all. Purcell remained impassive.

'I put my motion to the vote,' MacLeod said.

Johnson abstained. Hunt did not answer. Purcell voted against. The others in favour.

'It's carried,' MacLeod said with satisfaction. 'White, you can unbind Mason.'

White obeyed and everyone watched Mason. When he was free of his bonds, he bent and unbent his arms two or three times, straightened his cravat, which had been displaced during the struggle, and without a single word or glance turned his back on them and walked off.

The seamen watched him go.

'The old man's got guts!' Johnson said in a low voice. 'The way he stood under that rope!'

'No,' MacLeod said, sniffing disdainfully, 'it's not guts. It's training. Those bastards of officers are taught to keep a stiff upper lip in their damn schools. Keeping a stiff upper lip's dinned into them! Even if your mother gets drunk, keep a stiff upper lip! So they naturally do keep a stiff upper lip, even under the noose . . .'

'All the same,' Johnson said.

Since he had abstained, he had gained courage. MacLeod made no reply. He had turned away and was watching the flames mounting from the beach.

'I'm going back to look at the fire!' he said with enthusiasm. 'I've not often seen a fire like that! And it's not every day a simple seaman has the chance to burn a ship like *The Blossom* with his own hands.'

They all laughed, and MacLeod echoed their laughter at his own joke. His sharp face suddenly assumed an expression of childish happiness. The sailors shouted, all talked at once, and slapped each other's backs. Purcell watched them disappear down the cliff path, laughing and jostling each other. The whole thing was already forgotten. They looked like schoolboys glad of their freedom after a tiresome lesson. They were not even wicked, Purcell thought.

He moved a few paces away. He had no wish to return to the village. He felt tired. He sat down at the foot of the pandanus which had nearly had to bear Mason's weight, drew up his knees and clasped his hands about them. He was amazed by the pitiless chain of events. Because a frigate had appeared on the horizon at eight o'clock in the morning, a few hours later Mason had been standing, hands and feet bound, under a noose. And because Hunt, three years ago, had seen a comrade hanged and had disliked the sight, Mason had escaped death. He owed his life to this minute chance, to a memory lingering somewhere in Hunt's poor confused brain.

Purcell heard a slight noise behind him. He had no time to turn round before cool hands were placed over his eyes and he felt a woman's breast against his back.

'Ivoa!' he said, seizing her hands. But he did not recognise them. They were smaller than Ivoa's. He pulled them from his eyes. There was a shrill laugh. It was Itia. Kneeling behind him and leaning against his shoulder, she looked gaily and mischievously at him. Purcell smiled at her, but let go of her hands and drew away from her.

'Oh! Oh!' Itia cried, clutching at his shoulders in feigned panic. 'You're going to make me fall, Adamo!'

'Sit down then,' Purcell said.

She pouted, lowered her eyelashes, raised them again, shook her shoulders, undulated her hips, wrinkled her little snub nose and finally obeyed. Purcell watched her with amusement. Amid the tall, majestic women, her short stature and slender round body gave Itia the charm of a child.

He smiled at her.

'Where have you come from Itia?'

He looked at her. She at once assumed an air of importance, and began her miming all over again. Where she had come from was a secret. She was not sure whether she should tell him. There was a gay little spark flickering in her dark eyes. What a round laughing face she had! All her features seemed to turn upward, eyebrows, eyes, nose and the corners of her mouth.

'From the village,' she said at last.

'From the village? Why do you say things that aren't true? I'm sitting opposite the path. I'd have seen you coming.'

'Yes, yes,' Itia said, looking as if she were about to burst into tears. 'How unkind you are, Adamo! You're calling me a liar!'

And she burst out laughing as if pretending to tears were the height of comedy.

'I came by the path,' she went on, 'but I left it when I saw the *Peritani* under the tree. I knew very well that the *Peritani* did not want me to come near. So I slipped between the trees till I reached the bush. And from there,' she said with a circular wave of her arms, pivoting her body on her hips and throwing her chest out, 'I made a detour. I saw everything!' she said with an air of gaiety which could clearly have no connection with the spectacle she had witnessed.

'What did you see?'

'Everything.'

'Well, since you saw everything, you'd better go back to the village. You must have a lot to tell them.'

Itia pouted, tucked her legs under her, and leaned her shoulder against Purcell's; she turned her head towards him and looked at him from under her lashes.

'Aren't we very comfortable here?'

She smiled. It was impossible to look at her round face and bright eyes without wanting to smile too.

Purcell gazed at her with a sort of tenderness. Itia was full of naïvety and cunning, but her cunning was in itself a sort of naïvety.

A few seconds went by, and Itia said politely, in a low, soft, gentle voice: 'Kiss me, please, Adamo.'

The *vahinés* had nearly all adopted the *Peritani* kiss on the lips. But they attached no amorous significance to it. They even practised it for fun among themselves because they thought it amusing.

Purcell leaned towards her, but as he was about to kiss her, he saw her eyes behind her lashes. He got to his feet.

'Go back to the village, Itia.'

She too got up, and hung her head like a child caught out being naughty. As Purcell went to her to console her, she suddenly threw herself on him, seized him in her arms, clasped her hands behind him and pressed him frantically to her breast. He felt her breasts crushed against his skin, and as Itia's head only reached to his chin, he could smell the spicy odour of her hair and mingled with it the scent of hibiscus flowers.

He took her by the shoulders to push her away, but she was stronger than he thought. She pressed herself against him, thigh against thigh, as if she wanted to fuse with him.

'Let me go, Itia.'

'Oh no!' she said, her lips glued to his neck. 'Oh, no! No! I shan't let you go! I've got you!'

He laughed.

'Where are your manners, Itia?'

'That's just it,' she said in a choking voice. 'I haven't any. Everyone says so.'

He laughed again, put his hands behind his back, seized her wrists and tugged. He had to use all his strength to loose her hands. He held them, brought them round in front of him, pushed Itia away to the full length of his arms, and held her there a moment. He knew, if he let her go, that she would try to clasp him in her arms again.

'Itia,' he said, 'aren't you ashamed of yourself?'

'Oh, yes! ' she said.

She pushed her left shoulder forward and hid her face against it. Out of her dark, veiled eyes she looked at Purcell with the effrontery of a squirrel.

'I ought to be more severe with her,' Purcell told himself. 'But she's so funny she always disarms me. Oh, don't lie to yourself,' he thought immediately. 'It's not only that she's so funny.' He looked at the two hibiscus flowers in her hair and frowned.

'Listen to me, Itia,' he said. 'And please don't forget it. I'm Ivoa's *tané*.'

'Well, what does that matter?' Itia said. 'I'm not jealous.'

Purcell laughed.

'Why are you laughing?' she said, screwing up her mischievous eyes in astonishment.

'You see, it's the other way round. It's for Ivoa to be jealous or not.'

'Is that what you think?' Itia said. 'When a woman's in love, she's jealous, and even of a man who's not her *tané*. You see, I'm not jealous of Ivoa, but I hate it when Omaata kisses you and presses your head to her big breasts.'

'That's quite enough,' Purcell said. 'I shall be very angry, if you go on like this. Go back to the village at once.'

He was still holding her wrists. He dared not let go of them until he had her promise to leave him.

'All right,' Itia said. 'I'll go, if you explain.'

'If I explain what?'

'Why you don't want to be my *tané*.'

Purcell said angrily: 'I'm the *tané* of one woman alone.'

'Why not of two?' Itia said, resting her chin on her left shoulder and looking at him ingenuously out of the corners of her eyes.

'Because it's wrong.'

'Because it's wrong,' Itia said in stupefaction. 'Why is it wrong? Wouldn't you like it?'

Purcell looked away. 'I certainly would,' he suddenly thought. 'Of course I would. Unfortunately.'

'In my country,' he said at last, 'it's taboo to have two women.'

'You say things that aren't true,' Itia said. 'All the *Peritani* of the big canoe had two women in Tahiti. Sometimes, three. Sometimes, four.'

'They weren't obeying the taboo,' Purcell said patiently.

'But you obey it?'

He nodded.

'Why? Why you alone?'

He smiled.

'Because I have . . .'

He was about to say 'because I have a conscience,' but he could not translate it. There was no word for 'conscience' in Tahitian.

'Because I respect taboos,' he said after a moment.

There was a silence and Itia said suddenly with a triumphant air: 'It's a taboo in your big island. It's not a taboo here.'

He ought to have thought of that. For a Tahitian, a taboo was local. He said aloud: 'For a *Peritani* things are different.'

He added: 'Wherever he goes, his taboos follow him . . .'

He fell silent, astonished at having so well defined himself and his fellow-countrymen.

After a moment, he went on: 'Well, I've explained it to you now. You promised. Go back to the village.'

'You're not angry?' Itia said.

'No.'

'You're really not angry?'

'No.'

'Then kiss me.'

He had to make an end. He could hardly stay there all day holding her wrists. He leaned down. Itia's lips were soft and warm, and the kiss lasted a fraction of a second longer than he had intended.

'Well,' he said, straightening up, 'you promised. Go away.'

She looked at him. She forgot her miming.

'Yes, Adamo,' she said gently and as if her obedience was a sort of homage to him. 'I'm going. Yes, Adamo. Yes.'

He let go of her, and watched her walking away down the path, looking so small under the ancient trees. He smiled and shrugged his shoulders. She was only a child. But he immediately recollected himself: 'Don't lie to yourself. She's not a child.'

Above all, he was astonished that his conscience was so tender as to have pricked him. He shook himself and began walking towards the village. But after a few yards, he slowed his pace. He was struck by the notion that sin seemed to lose its force in this climate. This thought seemed new to him and he turned it over pleasurably in his mind. He suddenly raised his head. It was a Tahitian idea! What did it mean, but that the British taboos lost their force in this island? That was what Itia had said. 'Which means,' he thought anxiously, 'that I'm admitting that religion is not universal . . . This country's too soft, my theology's becoming corrupted.' He came to a halt, disquieted. 'But if it's corrupted by the effect of the climate, doesn't that mean that Itia's right?'

It occurred to him that this train of thought might have been inspired by Satan, but he at once rejected the idea. To see Satan everywhere was a papistical idea. On that basis, Satan would become more important than God in everyday life. He shook his head. No, that would be too easy. As soon as you ceased to understand, you brought in Satan, frightened yourself a little, and ceased to think. He would have to think it all out. He would meditate upon it. He knew he could not be happy without being at peace with himself.

He heard a sound of steps and voices. He looked up. The Tahitians and the women were coming down the path towards him. They passed him, scarcely stopping.

'Aren't you coming, Adamo?' one of them asked.

They had seen Mason come back. So, in the end, everything had turned out all right. And now they were going to watch *The Blossom* burning. It was a great festival. Their laughing, eager faces were all turned towards the high red flames.

Last in the group was Ivoa. Itia was walking beside her, leaning on her shoulder and being polite. 'Well I'm damned!' Purcell thought angrily.

Ivoa stopped.

'Aren't you coming, Adamo?'

'No,' he said, 'I'm going home.'

There was a silence, and Ivoa said: 'I'll come back with you, if you like.'

Purcell realised what a sacrifice this would be and said: 'No,

E

no. Go and watch the fire.'

She went on: 'Does it make you unhappy to see the big canoe burn?'

'A little, yes. But you go on, Ivoa.'

Itia took Ivoa's arm and leaned her head against her shoulder. They looked like members of the same family waiting for an artist to paint them. 'It's extraordinary,' Purcell thought, half-irritated, half-amused, 'she already considers herself my "second wife".'

'See you soon,' he said.

He left them and turned from Cliff Lane into East Avenue. There was utter silence. 'There's not a soul in the village,' Purcell thought, 'apart from Mason. And apart from me. The captain and second-in-command of a ship being destroyed by fire. When one thinks of the amount of effort and thought that goes into building a ship . . . And now, in a few hours . . . The Old Man must be eating his heart out in his hut.'

Purcell went towards Mason's hut. Their relationship, since the incidents at the time of the landing, had become somewhat cool, and this was the first time Purcell had visited him.

Mason had used the rails of the poop to enclose his garden, and as he put his hand on the gate, Purcell had an agreeable sense of familiarity. He had recognised the oak rail of the quarterdeck. It had been replaced before sailing from London and so hastily that there had been no time either to polish or varnish it. It had merely been anointed with linseed oil, and all the roughnesses of the wood had remained.

As he crossed the few yards to the hut, Purcell was struck by the smallness of the enclosure. Mason had not made use of a tenth of the space allotted to him.

He knocked gently on the door, and after a moment knocked again. There was no reply and Purcell said: 'It is Purcell, Captain Mason.'

A few seconds went by. Then Mason said from behind the door: 'Are you alone?'

'Yes, Captain Mason.'

There was another silence and then Mason said: 'I'll open to you. Take two paces to the rear.'

'What?'

'Take two paces to the rear.'

There seemed to be a menace in Mason's voice and Purcell obeyed. He waited another few seconds and, just as he was beginning to think Mason would not open the door, it turned slowly on its hinges, revealing Mason standing on the threshold with a musket under his right arm, its muzzle pointing straight in front of him.

'Put your hands up, Mr Purcell.'

Purcell blushed, put his hands in his pockets and said curtly: 'If you no longer trust me, our interview is useless.'

Mason stared at him for a moment.

'I beg your pardon, Mr Purcell,' he said more mildly, but without lowering the musket. 'I thought those ruffians had changed their minds, and were using you to make me open my door.'

'I allow no one to make use of me,' Purcell said coldly. 'Besides, you need fear no change of mind. The men have voted, and they'll never go against the vote.'

'Their vote!' Mason said derisively. 'Pray come in, Mr Purcell, and shut the door yourself.'

Purcell obeyed. As he advanced, Mason retired into the hut and, so long as Purcell had not shut the door, kept the musket pointing at the opening.

Purcell found himself in a tiny hall from which led another small door.

'Come in, come in, Mr Purcell,' Mason said, looking disapprovingly at the lieutenant's naked torso.

He himself was, as usual, dressed, shod and neatly cravatted.

He passed behind Purcell. There was a sound of iron against iron. He was bolting his fortress.

Purcell opened the little door, glanced inside, and stood on the threshold in astonishment. Within the room, Mason had reconstructed his cabin in *The Blossom* down to the smallest detail. Everything was there: the bunk with its raised protective oak edge, the big chest, the table and its two dumpy chairs, the square ports, their white curtains, the barometer, the prints showing *The Blossom* being built, and even, opposite Purcell, a whole bulkhead of varnished mahogany, in which there was a low door with a brass handle. In the ship, this door had given on to a passage, but here it must lead to a second room, no doubt as large as this one was small. For Mason had faithfully reproduced on land the narrow dimensions of his cabin.

'Sit down, Mr Purcell,' Mason said.

He himself sat down on the other side of the table and leaned his musket against the bunk. There was a moment of embarrassment. Purcell stared at the feet of the table, and saw with astonishment that the little oak wedges which had surrounded them in *The Blossom* were here too, firmly screwed into the floor, as if Mason feared that the island might start throwing his furniture about by suddenly beginning to pitch and roll.

This detail, which might have amused Purcell on some other occasion, depressed him. He suddenly felt how useless his visit was.

Mason was not looking at Purcell. His grey eyes were fixed on the barometer. After a moment, he became aware of Purcell's eyes on his and said anxiously: 'It's falling, Mr Purcell. It's been falling continuously since morning. There's bad weather on the way.'

'Captain Mason,' Purcell said, 'with your permission, I have a suggestion to make to you.'

'Carry on, Mr Purcell,' Mason said, looking at once haughty and suspicious.

'Already!' Purcell thought. 'He's closing his mind to it. Any idea put forward by someone else is *a priori* suspect.'

'Captain Mason,' Purcell went on, 'there's one thing about which we can do nothing whatever, neither you nor I. There's now a *de facto* power in the island.'

'I don't understand you,' Mason said.

'Well,' Purcell said, embarrassed, 'this is what I mean: since this morning, I'm the only man on the island to allow you your rank.'

Mason blinked, turned red and said curtly: 'I shall not thank you for that. You're merely doing your duty.'

'Yes, Captain Mason,' Purcell said, discouraged.

The Blossom would soon be nothing but a heap of cinders on a Pacific beach but the myth of 'the only master on board after God' went on . . . There was no longer a helm, but Mason was still navigating the ship. There was no storm, but he consulted the barometer. There was no rolling, but he had screwed wedges to his table legs. There were no manoeuvres to order, but the men were still the men; Mason was still their captain, and Purcell still his second-in-command.

'I think, Captain Mason,' Purcell went on, 'that we must take into account the fact that the men have formed a sort of parliament.'

'A parliament!' Mason said haughtily. 'A parliament!' he went on in a violent crescendo of contempt, raising his arms to high Heaven. 'A parliament! Mr Purcell, don't tell me you take this parliament seriously!'

'I have had to,' Purcell said. 'It nearly hanged you.'

Mason turned red; and his face quivered with anger. A whole second went by before he was able to control himself. He looked at Purcell resentfully.

'As to that, Mr Purcell,' he said coldly, 'you might have spared yourself the trouble of coming to my defence against those ruffians. I assure you I'd have been quite content to be hanged at the same time as they were burning *The Blossom*.'

Purcell looked at the table legs. It was incredible. The whole thing was a fantasy. The captain died with his ship. Since he could not go down with her because he was ashore, he would at least have the satisfaction of being hanged while his ship was being burned! 'That's what he was thinking,' Purcell thought, 'when he stood so stiffly under the noose.'

Purcell looked at him. 'I thought I was doing my duty, Captain Mason,' he said conciliatingly.

'No, Mr Purcell,' Mason said with emphasis, 'you were not doing your duty. Your duty was to oppose the mutineers with force – I say advisedly: with force – instead of treating with them.'

He rubbed his hands on his knees and went on more mildly: 'But I do not reproach you. I had a moment of weakness myself. I had their leader at point-blank range and I failed to fire. I should have fired,' he went on, his grey eyes staring into the distance. He banged his knee with his fist. 'With that blackguard dead, the others would have returned to their duty.'

'The men,' Purcell said after a moment, 'may had thought they were merely anticipating your orders. You yourself said in

Tahiti that, as soon as we had installed ourselves on the island, *The Blossom* would have to be burnt.'

'But not like that!' Mason cried indignantly, sitting up straight in his chair. 'Not in that barbarous manner. In certain circumstances, Mr Purcell, a captain may consider it his duty to destroy his ship. But when I thought of the destruction of *The Blossom,* do you really think I ever imagined such a scene of anarchy, such shouting and laughter? No, I saw it after this fashion: the men drawn up on the beach in perfect silence, myself addressing a few simple words to them, the flag being struck, the order being given to set fire to her, and the ship being saluted as she sank, as it were, into the flames.'

He fell silent, and was clearly so moved by the scene he had imagined, that, to Purcell's stupefaction, there were tears in his eyes. 'He's living in a fantasy,' Purcell thought. 'He's quite simply forgotten that he's killed Burt and has stolen the ship.'

'It's fallen another degree since you arrived,' Mason said, gazing at the barometer.

He got to his feet and carefully shut the two portholes, as if fearing the sea might damage his furniture. Purcell already thought the room too hot; it now became stifling. But it appeared not to inconvenience Mason, fully-clothed though he was. 'He's lucky,' Purcell thought. He could feel the sweat running down his back and the intolerable itching of prickly heat along his arms.

Mason sat down again.

'Captain Mason,' Purcell said firmly. 'I've come to make a suggestion to you.'

'I'm listening,' Mason said distantly.

Purcell looked at the square head, the stubborn brow and the determined jaw. The whole face was solid and all of a piece, as impenetrable as rock.

'Captain Mason,' he went on with a poignant sense of impotence and failure, 'broadly speaking this is how things stand in the parliament the men have formed: there are two parties, one consisting of MacLeod, White and Smudge, the other of Baker, Jones and myself. Between the two parties, there are the waverers: Hunt and Johnson. One can never tell for certain how they'll vote, but they'll usually vote with MacLeod. Being assured of a majority, MacLeod is more or less king of the island.'

He paused for a moment and went on: 'This seems to me to be a very dangerous state of affairs; and I've come to you to suggest two possible ways of rectifying it.'

'He's scarcely listening to me,' Purcell thought. 'And yet his life on the island, mine, the seamen's, our relations with the Tahitians, everything, absolutely everything depends on the decision he'll take. He must understand!' he thought with all the intensity of a prayer. He plucked up his courage, looked Mason in the eye and said as forcibly as he could: 'I suggest two things, Captain Mason. The first is that you should attend these assemblies and take part in the voting; and the second is that, by the use of your vote, you should help to bring the Tahitians into them.'

'You must have taken leave of your senses, Mr Purcell,' Mason said faintly.

He stared at Purcell with his eyes starting out of his head. He was so amazed he seemed almost to have lost both the power of speech and the faculty of indignation.

'Let me explain!' Purcell continued heatedly. 'In the first place, it's mere justice that the Tahitians should form part of the assembly, since its decisions will also apply to them. Further-more, they have a great respect for you, and their votes, together with yours, mine, Baker's and Jones's, will give you a majority and enable you to keep MacLeod in check . . .'

A whole second elapsed. Mason sat up straight in his chair. He clutched the arms and looked angrily at Purcell.

'Mr Purcell,' he said at last, 'I can hardly believe my ears. Are you suggesting that I, Richard Hesley Mason, captain of *The Blossom*, should join that rabble of mutineers, argue with them and *vote*! You did actually say: "*vote*"! . . . And as if that were not enough, you also suggest that the blacks – I say it advisedly: the blacks – should be allowed to take part in discussions with the men who, ruffians though they may be, are at least British! Mr Purcell, this is the most outrageous suggestion . . .'

'I can see nothing outrageous about my suggestion,' Purcell interrupted curtly. 'The choice is a simple one: either you shut yourself up in your hut and lose all control over events, or you decide to act. And there is only one way to do so; it is to take your place in the assembly and supplant MacLeod with the support of the Tahitians.'

Mason got to his feet, his face rigid. He was putting an end to the interview. Purcell also rose.

'There is a third way, Mr Purcell,' Mason said, his eyes fixed severely on a point in the ceiling above Purcell's head, 'and it is the only one compatible with my dignity.'

He paused and then went on: 'It consists in waiting.'

'Waiting for what?' Purcell said roughly.

'Waiting,' Mason said with an air of complete certainty, 'till the men grow tired of MacLeod's follies and come to me in my hut to ask for orders.'

It was disarming. He lived by stereotyped phrases. He could see the men knocking at his hut door, shyly removing their head-dresses, scratching their heads, looking down at the floor and saying: 'Sir, we've come to ask you to take the helm again . . .'

'Have you any further suggestions to make?' Mason asked coldly.

Purcell looked at him. Mason was standing in front of him, massive, upright, his chest thrust out, his shoulders back, his square head set on his tanned sailor's neck: thirteen stone of courage, seamanship, obstinacy and prejudice.

'I have no other suggestion,' Purcell said.

'In that case,' Mason said, 'I'll open the door for you.'

He picked up his musket, went to unbolt the door and stood to one side. While Purcell went out, he kept the musket pointing at the opening. No further word was said.

The door banged behind him and Purcell heard the sound of the bolts and the lock.

He crossed the five yards of the tiny enclosure and leant down to put his hand to the latch of the gate. He suddenly understood. Mason had given his enclosure the precise dimensions of *The Blossom*'s poop.

7

The women had to wait another long week before all the huts in the island were roofed. In his capacity as carpenter, MacLeod had decided not to leave it to anyone else to fix the frames of palm-leaves to the rafters, and he performed the task with a slow meticulousness. Nor was the care he took unnecessary, for the nor'wester sometimes blew violently across the village despite the screen of trees protecting it from the sea.

It was on December 3rd, after working all day under a hot sun, that MacLeod announced the huts to be finished. At noon, the British gathered in the centre of the village and, after a brief discussion, decided that the assembly should meet at nine o'clock that night to proceed to the sharing out of the women. Purcell translated the news, and it aroused considerable excitement in the tent in which the Tahitian women lodged. For each of them, that very evening would be the happy or unhappy climax to three months of waiting, planning and intriguing.

The last assembly, which had decided to set fire to *The Blossom* and had tried Mason for attempted murder, had been held impromptu on the cliff. But now there was time to select a place and the banyan was chosen as the scene for the debates. Though the giant tree was some distance from the village, since it stood on the second plateau and to reach it you had to climb the steep slope linking the first plateau to the second, there were sentimental reasons for the choice. It was under the banyan that the seamen had met recently for the first time and resolved by a unanimous vote no longer to allow the officers their rank. Though this particular vote had been concerned with a matter of comparative detail, it was nevertheless at that moment the men had first felt free of the slavery of shipboard.

A shelter had been erected in the middle of the village to protect *The Blossom*'s bell and the big clock from her wardroom from the weather. Everyone had access to the hour and, in case of need, could ring the bell to alert the community. The evening meal was scarcely over when all the women, except Ivoa, gathered round the shelter and watched, minute by minute, the brisk, jerky movement of the clock's big hand. As none of them could yet tell the time, there was little point in their vigil. Purcell, who had seen them assemble under the trees, went to tell them they were much too early.

They laughed. It did not matter, they would wait, they liked waiting. They laughingly surrounded Purcell. Did Adamo know which of the *Peritani* would choose Horoa? Itihota? Toumata? Vaa? Purcell pretended to stop his ears, and they laughed all the more. He was surrounded by big dark eyes and teeth gleaming whitely in brown faces. White too were the tiaré flowers in their splendid frizzy black hair that reached down to their hips. Purcell looked at them with friendliness. Their charmingly curved lips candidly revealed their cannibal teeth, and their laughter rose to a crescendo, clear, pearly and musical. They all talked to him at once. É Adamo, é! É Adamo! Was Adamo going to choose a woman other than Ivoa? 'No, no!' Purcell said decidedly. There were murmured congratulations. Adamo was so nice! So faithful! The best *tané* on the island! 'My baby!' Omaata said, making her way through the crowd of *vahinés*. And she crushed him so forcibly against her bosom that Purcell uttered a cry. There was a ripple of laughter. 'You'll break him, Omaata!' The giantess relaxed her embrace, but without freeing her captive. Her big dark eyes were moist with affection, and she ruffled his fair hair with her big strong hand. 'My baby, my baby, my baby . . .' Purcell made no attempt to struggle. Held by the huge arm weighing on his shoulders, his face crushed to the enormous naked breast, stifled, embarrassed and moved, he could hear the echoes of Omaata's deep voice rumbling like a waterfall in her chest. Above Purcell's head, Omaata's eyes were pools of tenderness. Little by little, her emotion took possession of all the *vahinés*. They ceased laughing, closed in round Purcell and tenderly touched his back with the tips of their fingers. Adamo was so fair, so clean, so nice. Our brother Adamo, our little brother Adamo, our kind brother Adamo. At last Omaata let him go. 'I tell you,' Purcell said breathlessly, his face red and his hair rumpled, 'you've got plenty of time. You've got time to go to the beach for a bathe.' No, no, they would wait. 'Good-bye, Adamo. Good-bye, brother. Good-bye, my baby.' At that moment, the big hand of the clock gave a jerk forward and stopped with a slight backward movement as if it were applying the brake. There were laughter and exclamations. But no, there was plenty of time. Adamo had said there was plenty of time. '*Aoué,* I shall do my hair,' Itia said.

At eight thirty-five, White appeared on Nor'wester Street, crossed the Square and went to the shelter. The women stopped talking when they saw him and moved aside to let him pass. The half-caste's silent progress, his yellowish skin and his jet black eyes, which were scarcely visible in the slits between his lids, all made their impression on them. Yet, they had a certain regard for him. He was always so polite. White nodded to them, and turned to lean with extended arm against the post of the shelter. He screwed up his eyes to watch the big hand moving in the falling dusk. He too was early, and he remained in the same position for a good five minutes. He turned only once, and his expressionless eyes glanced over the faces about him, stopping for a brief moment at Itia's. When the big hand pointed to twenty-to, he seized the clapper of the bell with a sort of solemnity and swung it to and fro for several seconds to a powerful, regular rhythm.

Purcell and Ivoa left their hut rather late. They saw the bright light of two torches moving along Banyan Lane and then, as they drew nearer, the long file of the islanders, whose silhouettes stood out against the illuminated undergrowth. They heard laughter, snatches of song and exclamations in Tahitian. As it was very warm, they were all, except for MacLeod, naked to the waist, and as he drew nearer Purcell could distinguish the British by the paler colour of their skins. The two torches, one at the head of the file, the other at the back, did not give much light, and it was only by his white vest that Purcell recognised MacLeod, who was walking in front of him. When his eyes had become accustomed to the dark, he noticed that the Scotsman was carrying a coil of rope over his shoulder, two pegs in one hand and a mallet, hanging from his long thin arm, in the other. Beside him, Purcell recognised the frail figure of Smudge. He was carrying an officer's cocked hat. The two men were silent. When Purcell joined the file, neither of them paid any attention. Yet, after a moment, Smudge turned and looked at Ivoa.

When they reached the second plateau, the leading torch

moved out of the file, and approached them. Its bearer was brandishing it at arm's length, no doubt to avoid being burnt by the sparks spluttering from it. The torch and its halo of light high above their heads, the long dark arm of its bearer below, and lower still the dark silhouette of a figure coming silently towards them, all created a striking effect.

'Purcell?' said White's singsong voice.

'Here,' Purcell said.

'Purcell,' White said, 'I have a letter for you from Mason. He's not coming to the assembly. He says that if his name is mentioned you should read the letter.'

'Thank you,' Purcell said.

He took the letter, noticed it was sealed with wax, and put it in his pocket.

Under the end of the lowest big branch of the banyan, Mac-Leod hammered in the two pegs at a distance of about five feet apart. When he had done this, he took some fishing line from his pocket and tied the thin end of a torch to each peg. Then, indicating a wide circle with a gesture of his outstretched arms, he signed to the British to take their places round the torches. He himself sat with his back against one of the vertical roots hanging from the banyan branch.

There was a moment of embarrassment and hesitation. Until now, all discussions had been carried on standing. As soon as it was decided to sit down, the choice of places seemed to become almost too important. In fact, it turned out as might have been foreseen: Smudge sat on MacLeod's right, his back to the banyan, White on his left. Opposite MacLeod, and separated from him by the two torches, Purcell took his place, with Jones and Baker on each side of him. At the two ends of the circle were Hunt and Johnson. Everyone, except Hunt, was struck by the fact that this disposition was in precise accordance with the parties in the assembly. 'And I am the leader of His Majesty's opposition,' Purcell thought with bitter irony. 'We've come to that. We've already come to that. And it's that fool Mason's fault.'

The Tahitian women sat behind Purcell laughing nervously and whispering continuously. The six Tahitian men remained standing and a little behind Hunt. They had expected MacLeod to ask them to sit down round the torches, and when they realised they were excluded from the circle their impassive faces betrayed neither disappointment nor anger. Their manner showed a certain reserve, however, and they watched the *Peritani*, trying to make out what was going forward. They were less good at languages than the Tahitian women, and none of them yet knew enough English to follow the discussions.

Their distant attitude and the taciturnity of the British ended by impressing the women. They ceased laughing. A tense, anxious and rather solemn silence fell over the thirty human beings who were to live together on this exiguous rock till they died.

MacLeod, his back to the banyan root, was sitting cross-legged, his torso upright. In his hand was the coil of rope with which Mason had nearly been hanged. Even the noose had not been untied. It did not run, however, because the rope was rather damp, and the patch of tar a little above the noose, which Purcell had noticed on the day of Mason's trial, now looked grey and dirty instead of black. The light of the torches, falling on the Scotsman's thin face from above, showed up his narrow forehead, made of his eye-sockets two deep holes, and threw his hooked nose into relief, giving his face the appearance of a curved knife-blade. In the general silence every eye was turned on him. He, too, was silent, well aware of the important position he had assumed on the island, sure of himself and of the resources of his eloquence. His grey eyes stared straight in front of him, his skeletal torso was stiff and motionless within his dirty white vest, while he prolonged, with all the ability of an actor, his audience's suspense.

'Shall we begin?' Purcell said curtly.

'Just a minute,' MacLeod said, solemnly raising his right hand, 'I have a word to say. Gentlemen,' he went on at once, as if 'lads' or 'chaps' was not suitable to so grave an occasion, the moment has come to share out the Indian women.* For a long time past, we've been saying we'd do it, and now it must be done, gentlemen, since we can't go on living in sin and lewdness as we did on board *The Blossom*. It's not that I've got anything

* British sailors at that time called all the women of the Pacific 'Indians', whatever their race.

against sin. It's all right for a time, when one's young and sailing about the world. But now, God damn it, that we're ashore and each of us has his own hut, there must be order! Every man must have his legitimate wife. Otherwise, no one will ever know who's the father of the children. And to whom would I bequeath my hut if I didn't know who my son was?'

He paused. 'He's been at sea for twenty years,' Purcell thought, 'but he's still the Highland peasant. All he's got in the world is four planks of wood on a remote island, and he's thinking of bequeathing them to his son . . .'

MacLeod went on forcefully: 'We'll therefore share out the Indian women. And this is what I propose. Suppose some bastard doesn't agree and wants the same woman as his neighbour, it'll be decided between them by a vote. And what's voted will be done! That's the law! And if anyone thinks he hasn't had a fair wind, I'll say: my lad, the law's the law. We're white men here, and the assembly makes the law. If Mason prefers to stay in dry dock instead of coming alongside of us, that's his business. But the law's the law, even for Mason, officer though he may be! We don't want any fighting here. If any man pulls a knife against any other damn bastard, let him remember the law that was voted on the cliff after Mason's trial. There's a rope here, that's all I'm saying. And here it is, my lads! Its strands may be a bit worn, but it's a good hempen rope for all that, and there's not a bastard on the island so heavy that it won't take his weight . . .'

He fell silent and, holding the coil of rope in his left hand, he raised the noose in his right and dangled it to right and left and in front of him as if he were a priest offering a relic to the adoration of the faithful. Then he smiled, his cheeks became hollows each side of his sharp nose, the muscles of his jaw showed beneath the skin, and his thin lips formed a sardonic line.

'My lads,' he went on, 'if there's any bastard here who wants to take his last look at the sky through this noose, he need only draw his knife.'

He placed the rope back on his knees, his eyes glittered in their dark hollows, his lips tautened in silent laughter, and he glanced round at the assembly. Purcell felt Baker nudge him with his elbow. He turned his head. Baker leaned towards him and whispered: 'I don't like all these threats. He looks as if he's hatching something. ' Purcell nodded silently. Behind Hunt, the Tahitians were talking in low rapid voices among themselves. Then Tetahiti shouted across to the women: 'What's the Skeleton saying?' Omaata rose to her knees and said: 'He says they're going to share out the women, and anyone who's not content will be hanged.' 'Always this hanging!' Tetahiti said scornfully. The Tahitians began murmuring more loudly, but still too low for Purcell to hear what they were saying.

MacLeod raised his hand to demand silence and waited. Seen thus, his arm raised, his knees bent under him, his body straight and hieratic, he looked by the light of the torches like a sorcerer celebrating a rite. They could just make out the high dark wall of the banyan and its supporting columns behind him.

'My lads,' he went on, 'we'll proceed this way. Smudge, who can write, has written your names on pieces of paper. I'm going to ask Purcell to make sure he's left no one out. When that's done, the papers will be folded, placed in Burt's cocked hat, and the youngest, that's to say Jones, will draw the lots. The chap who's drawn will say: "I want Faïna, or Raha, or Itihota . . ." And if there's no opposition, he has her. But if anyone says: "I oppose it", then we'll vote, and whoever has the majority has the girl . . .'

Purcell got to his feet and said indignantly: 'I refuse to support this procedure. It's scandalous. It doesn't take the woman's consent into account.'

MacLeod sniffed disdainfully.

'God damn me,' he said looking round, 'if I ever thought there'd be an objection of this kind. One might think you knew nothing about blacks, Purcell. As far as they're concerned one man's as good as another. We saw that on board *The Blossom* . . .'

There was some laughter, and Purcell said sharply: 'What you say of the Tahitian women on board *The Blossom*, could be said with equal justice of a certain number of His Majesty's respectable subjects. The Tahitians were not alone in being promiscuous.'

'It's not the same thing,' MacLeod said with an air of superiority.

'I don't see why not,' Purcell said. 'I really don't see why you demand of the women a virtue you don't practise yourself. However, that's not the point. When you say: "there must be order", I agree with you. But where I don't agree with you is when you want to proceed without the women's consent. That's not order, MacLeod, it's violence.'

'You can call it what you like,' MacLeod said contemptuously, 'it doesn't matter to me. I've my own ideas about marriage, you know, and I didn't invent them either. Suppose I'd gone back to the Highlands instead of mouldering here, and I'd found a lassie I liked. I'd have gone to her old man and said: "Mister, I own this and that, will you give me your daughter?" And if the old man shook hands on it, I scarcely think the daughter's consent would be asked! No, sir! And I don't think she'd have shown any reluctance either. After all,' he went on with a sardonic smile, 'I don't differ physically from anyone else, except that my bones rattle a bit when I sit down, but you can be sure I'd have chosen a well-upholstered girl so as not to hurt my ribs when I fell on her . . .'

There was some laughter. When it died down MacLeod went on: 'That's how things would have happened in the Highlands, Purcell, and I can see no reason, merely because I'm condemned to live in this blasted island of savages in the middle of the Pacific, why I should go down on my knees to a damned negress and pander to her every whim.'

'It's not a question of pandering to her every whim,' Purcell said, irritated by MacLeod's speech, 'but to get her consent before taking her for wife.'

Old Johnson raised his hand as if he were asking permission to speak, looked anxiously down his long nose, and said in a hoarse voice: 'With your permission, sir . . .'

He glanced at MacLeod like a dog that knows it's done wrong and immediately went on: 'With your permission, Purcell. Suppose I say: "I want Horoa", and Horoa doesn't want me. I say: "I want Taïata," and Taïata doesn't want me. In short, I name them all, and none of them want me . . .'

He raised his eyes to Purcell and said anxiously: 'As a result,

I don't get a woman at all.'

'Believe me,' Purcell said, 'it's better not to have a woman than to have one without her consent.'

'I don't know about that,' Johnson said, shaking his head doubtfully and rubbing the purple patches in his beard. 'When women are bad they're altogether bad, inside and out. But when they're good, Christ, it's like honey!'

There was laughter. Johnson stopped with a look of astonishment, glanced timidly round, and said: 'It ought to be said.'

'What ought to be said?' Smudge said laughing.

MacLeod nudged him in the chest with his elbow.

'Let him speak. You're always nagging him . . .'

Johnson looked gratefully at the Scotsman and Purcell suddenly realised what Smudge's and MacLeod's game was. The first bullied the old man, and the second 'protected' him. Half afraid and a half grateful, Johnson became the more closely linked to them.

'It ought to be said,' Johnson went on, reassured by MacLeod's intervention.

He got to his feet with a somewhat pitiable attempt at dignity, and said with an air of authority, as if he was accustomed to be listened to with respect: 'I was thinking it over when you were talking, Purcell. There's this matter of consent. Well, as to consent, I'm in agreement. No, no! Consent isn't what you think, Purcell. Take Mrs Johnson. She consented all right, but things were none the better for it.'

There was more laughter, and MacLeod said: 'Does anyone else want to speak?'

There was a silence and MacLeod glanced at each of them in turn.

'If no one has anything more to say, I propose we vote on it. Who agrees to the negresses being asked for their consent?'

'Ask rather who does not agree,' Purcell said.

MacLeod glanced at him, shrugged his shoulders, and said: 'Who does not agree to asking the Indian women for their consent?'

He raised his hand, Hunt immediately followed suit. Then, in order, Smudge, White and Johnson.

'Five votes out of eight,' MacLeod said in a neutral voice.

'Purcell's motion is rejected.'

There was a silence and then Purcell said: 'Hunt has no need to fear that Omaata will refuse him. I wonder why he voted with you.'

'Ask him,' MacLeod said drily.

Purcell stared fixedly at him, but said no more.

'Smudge,' MacLeod said, 'pass the hat to Purcell.'

Smudge got to his feet, crossed the space between the two torches and handed Purcell the cocked hat. After Burt's death, the sailors had shared out his effects and Smudge had received his cocked hat. It was much too big for Smudge ever to be able to dream of wearing it, but he had hung it up as a trophy on the wall of his hut, and swore many oaths at it whenever he remembered Burt's tyranny and his own cowardice.

While Purcell took the papers out of the hat, turned them to the light of the torches to read the names and then folded them over twice, there was a certain relaxation of tension and the conversations began again. The Tahitians, who had been standing behind Hunt, now sat down, and began commenting in low voices on what they had seen. Omaata joined them and Purcell heard them questioning her about the vote. Hunt, his pale little eyes staring into the distance, was humming to himself. Having made a great but unsuccessful effort to follow the debate, he was relieved that no one spoke to him. With his huge fists reposing on his enormous thighs, he stared at Omaata, and waited patiently for her to come and sit beside him. The Tahitian women behind Purcell had begun laughing and whispering again. They had perfectly understood what the vote was about, and were mocking the pretensions of the *Peritani* to choose their *vahinés,* instead of being chosen by them as was the custom.

While checking the papers, Purcell was watching the opposite party out of the corner of his eyes. Smudge was having a long conversation in a low voice with MacLeod, and it was apparent that MacLeod was not agreeing with him. White remained apart from it. At one point, he got to his feet and went to straighten a crooked torch. Only once did Purcell surprise him glancing anxiously at the women. On his right, old Johnson was rubbing the purple patches in his beard with nervous, jerky movements. Though the vote had made it certain that he would not have to return alone to his hut, he was only half reassured.

Purcell heard Baker whisper: 'They've been intimidating Johnson and working on Hunt.' Purcell nodded, and Baker went on in a low quivering voice: 'MacLeod's going to oppose me over Avapouhi, and the vote will go to him.' Purcell turned and looked at the Welshman's thin brown face three inches away from his own. His eyes were anguished. 'He really loves her,' he thought. 'I'm just going to check these papers again,' Purcell said. 'Meanwhile, go and tell Avapouhi to take to the bush if you raise your right hand, and to stay there. As for you, if the vote gives her to MacLeod, choose Horoa.' 'Why Horoa?' Baker asked, doubtfully. 'I'll explain later.' Baker hesitated, then seemed to understand and got to his feet. Purcell did not turn his head. He picked out the papers again with his left hand, unfolded them one by one, folded them again and replaced them in the cocked hat.

He had scarcely finished when Baker came back to resume his seat beside him. MacLeod, opposite, was still talking in a low, vehement voice to Smudge. Baker said: 'Put your right hand on the ground. I've something to give you.' Purcell did so, and felt a hard cold object in his palm. He closed his fingers on it. It was Baker's knife. 'Keep it,' Baker said, 'I'm afraid of losing my head.' Purcell put his closed hand into his pocket.

'Well?' MacLeod said, raising his hands for silence.

'I have read and counted nine papers,' Purcell said. 'All nine are in the names of the nine British. I have seen no paper bearing the name of a Tahitian. I presume you intend to exclude them from the sharing out.'

'You're dead right,' MacLeod said in his drawling voice.

'It's not fair,' Purcell insisted. 'You'll be gravely wronging the Tahitians by doing so. They have as much right as we have to choose a wife.'

MacLeod looked in turn at Smudge, White and Johnson with a triumphant expression that seemed to mean: 'I told you so.' Then he pointed his sharp chin at Purcell, let his pale lashes cover his eyes, and said contemptuously: 'Coming from you, Purcell, that doesn't surprise me, since you're pretty well heart and soul with the blacks. God damn me, I've never seen a white who loved savages as you do! You're always on their side.

Always licking their arses or getting them to lick yours. Taking them in your arms, slapping them on the back, fondling them, embracing them. Man or woman. Why, it's a passion with you!'

Smudge laughed, and Johnson smiled, quickly turning his head away in embarrassment as if he had wanted to smile at MacLeod without letting Purcell see him do so. 'The bastard!' Baker said between his teeth. Young Jones touched Purcell's elbow and whispered: 'Shall I kick his arse?' Jones was small, but very strong. Purcell made no reply. His handsome, fair, severe face seemed chiselled in marble. After a moment, he glanced at a point above MacLeod's head and said calmly:

'I presume you have other arguments.'

Baker looked at him with admiration. Disdain for disdain, Purcell could beat MacLeod any day. It had more class too; you did not feel the intention to wound.

'Yes,' MacLeod said, 'yes, Purcell, since you want to know, I have other arguments, and they're weighty ones. Give me a chance, and I'll tell you what they are. There may be some sons of bitches on this island who've perhaps not noticed we're fifteen men here, British and black, and that there are twelve women . . . Suppose now we put all the names in the hat. What happens? It means the three last to be drawn don't get a woman.'

He looked round sardonically.

'They might be blacks . . . But they might equally well be whites, and I'm damned if they're going to be whites, Purcell. I'd rather your darling blacks went without women than Smudge, White or Jones . . .'

'Don't you worry about me,' said young Jones squaring his shoulders. 'I'll make out all right.'

'MacLeod,' Purcell said leaning forward, 'we don't often agree but now listen to me, this time it's serious. Imagine what will happen when the Tahitians remain alone under the banyan with the three women you'll have left them.'

'Well, what?' MacLeod said. 'Three women among six isn't so bad. It makes half a woman each. That's not too bad, one woman for two. I've not always had as much.'

'Don't you realise that this will shock them more than anything else you could do?'

'Well they'd better unshock themselves,' MacLeod cut in.

'I've nothing against them, you know, Purcell. I won't spend my time licking their boots, but I've nothing against them. But if it's a case of choosing between them and us, I say we come first.'

'You're contradicting yourself.'

'What do you mean?' MacLeod said, sitting up straight, cut to the quick in his Scottish logic.

'You've insisted that on the island the officers should not be privileged in relation to the seamen, and now you're giving the British privileges in relation to the Tahitians.'

'I'm not privileging anybody,' MacLeod said in his drawling voice, 'but I tell you, Purcell, there's an order in my preferences. And the one who comes first, on land or at sea, come fair wind or foul, is number one: James Finchley MacLeod, his mother's own son. Then I think of my comrades. Then of the other chaps from *The Blossom*. Then of the blacks.'

'It's an egotistical point of view,' Purcell said indignantly, 'and, believe me, it'll have terrible consequences.'

'Terrible or not, it's mine,' MacLeod said, his hands on his knees, his death's head, hollowed by the light of the torches, laughing silently. 'And as to egotism, you're quite right, Purcell, I yield to no one on that score. Nor do these gentlemen either,' he added with a gesture of his thin arm which included the company. 'Egotists! They're all little egotists to the last man! And there's going to be a big majority of damned little egotists against your motion, Purcell.'

He paused for a moment and said still smiling: 'Has anyone else anything to say?'

He went on, almost without a pause: 'Let's vote. Who's against it?'

He raised his arm, followed at once by Hunt, then Smudge and finally Johnson. White did not move. They all looked at him in surprise. With his arm still raised, MacLeod turned his head to the left and looked at the half-caste. White, his dark eyes scarcely visible, withstood his glance without flinching, then slowly turned his head away and looked straight in front of him.

'I abstain,' he said in his soft, sing-song voice.

'You abstain?' MacLeod said with restrained fury, his right arm still raised and his little grey eyes flashing.

'I must remind you,' Purcell said sharply, 'that you have no right to influence the members of the assembly, and White no more than Hunt or Johnson.'

'I'm not influencing anybody,' MacLeod said, suddenly raising his voice.

Even though White abstained he still won. He had four votes. Purcell only three. But White's abstention disquieted him. He was no longer sure of his troops.

He lowered his arm, but continued to look at White.

'I don't agree with you,' White said in his sing-song voice.

His face was calm and relaxed, his arms were quietly folded across his chest, and there was something inflexible about the softness of his polite voice.

'In that case you should have voted for me,' Purcell said.

White remained silent. He had said what he thought. He had no more to say.

'That was a surprise . . .' Baker said, leaning towards Purcell.

'No,' Purcell said in a low voice, 'not altogether.'

'Four votes against,' MacLeod said after a moment. 'One abstention. Purcell's motion rejected.'

But it was clear that White's abstention had taken some of the spirit out of him.

'Purcell,' he said angrily, 'pass the hat to Jones. It's time we got on with it if we're not going to be here all night.'

Jones knelt, sat on his heels, and put the hat on his bare thighs. Alone of the British, he wore a *pareu*, and indeed he was the only one of them whose physique could compare, though it was on a smaller scale, with that of the Tahitians. The youngest member of the crew after Jimmy, he was just seventeen. He had a handsome, slender, athletic body and wore his fair hair cut short. His freckled nose was short and slightly snubbed, and his almost beardless chin was short and rounded, as if he had not yet finished growing. His china-blue eyes looked at people frankly and were reminiscent of the cabin-boy's. But he was more virile and more aggressive than Jimmy. Very conscious of his muscles, he was always contracting the muscles of his chest, partly from vanity and partly in the hope of increasing their size.

'Well,' MacLeod said, 'are you going to begin?'

Jones held the hat against his thighs with his left hand and stirred the papers with his right. He was very excited and could not make up his mind to begin drawing the lots. He was afraid the owner of the first name he drew would choose Amoureïa. When, after the mutiny, *The Blossom* had touched at Tahiti, Jones had known love for the first time in her arms. She had been just sixteen. Neither at Tahiti nor on board had he been faithful to her, but as the novelty of his conquests wore off he had gone back to her. And since the landing, they could have been met in all the paths of the island, childishly solemn, holding each other's hands.

'Well,' Purcell said, 'what are you waiting for?'

'I've got a needle,' Jones said, 'a terrible needle. I'm afraid they'll take Amoureïa from me.'

'Go on!' Purcell said smiling. 'I'll bet you my shilling you'll get her.' He took a shilling with a hole in it from his pocket and threw it on the ground between himself and Jones. Jones looked at the shilling and was impressed.

'Go on!' Baker said from Purcell's other side, and putting his hand on the ground he leaned forward the better to watch his brother-in-law.

Jones drew out a paper, unfolded it, turned it to the light of the torch and read it. He opened his mouth, shut it again, swallowed, and finding his voice at last said: 'Jones.'

He looked to ingenuously astonished at having drawn his own name that everyone except Hunt laughed.

Jones contracted his pectoral muscles and squared his shoulders to show that he would not be laughed at. But behind his aggressive manner he felt weak, and so terribly moved he could not speak.

'Well,' MacLeod said, 'don't take all night! Since you're the first, you've got a dozen women to choose from, my lad. But hurry up and make your choice.'

'Amoureïa,' Jones said.

And frowning over his childish nose he looked anxiously round the circle to see if anyone was going to dispute his choice.

'No opposition?' MacLeod said, brandishing the end of the rope like a cudgel. He held it behind him, let a few seconds go by and then brought it sharply down on the ground between his legs.

'Awarded!'

'Amoureïa!' Jones said in a choking voice as he turned towards her.

She at once came forward into the circle of light, smiled, knelt down beside him, and took his hand. She was pretty and slender and had a rather ingenuous expression like her *tané*'s. Jones relaxed his muscles with a long exhalation of breath that was half-way between a whistle and a sigh. His shoulders fell forward, his chest became hollow and, tilting his head to one side, he looked at Amoureïa in wonder. She was there. She belonged to him. He almost floated off the ground with joy. He felt the whole of life lay before them and that it would never come to an end.

'If you'd let go of your Indian's hand,' Smudge shouted harshly, 'you'd perhaps be able to continue drawing the lots.'

Jones took a paper out of the hat.

'Hunt!' he said loudly.

Hunt stopped humming, groaned, raised his head and fixed his little pale eyes in astonishment on Jones, the hat and the paper Jones was holding in his hand. Then he looked anxiously at MacLeod, as if asking his help.

'It's your turn,' MacLeod said. 'You can choose your woman.'

'Which woman?' Hunt said.

'Your woman. Omaata.'

Hunt seemed to reflect and then said: 'And why should I choose her?'

'So that she'll be yours.'

'She is mine,' Hunt said thrusting his face forward and clenching his enormous fists on his knees.

'Of course, she's yours. You simply say: "Omaata," and she sits down beside you.'

Hunt looked at him suspiciously.

'Why did you say: "choose"?'

'There are eleven women. You choose one of those eleven women.'

'To hell with the eleven women!' Hunt muttered, making a gesture with his hand as if to sweep them out of his life. 'I have Omaata.'

'Well then, say: "I want Omaata", and Omaata is yours.'

'Isn't she mine now?' Hunt said looking menacingly at MacLeod.

'Yes, she's yours. But listen. Do as I say. You say "Omaata", she sits down beside you, and it's all over.'

'And why should I say "Omaata"?'

'Christ!' MacLeod said, putting his hands to his head.

Purcell said caustically: 'MacLeod, tell me how you set about getting Hunt to vote for you. It must take a lot of time.'

MacLeod looked at him angrily, but made no reply.

'Let's put an end to this,' Baker said irritably. 'I suggest Purcell tells Omaata to sit beside Hunt and that the matter be considered closed.'

MacLeod nodded and Purcell translated. Omaata's massive figure at once emerged from the shadows behind him. He turned round in surprise. He thought she was still with the Tahitians. Seated as he was, she seemed even taller than ever, and as she passed between Baker and himself to cross the circle, he was surprised by the huge size of her thighs. She stopped a moment in front of the torch, dazzled by the light, seeking Jono. She thus had her back to Purcell whom she covered with her shadow, and the flame, outlining the contours of her colossal silhouette, made the reflections flicker on her black shoulders and, for a second, made them look like polished marble.

She sat down beside Hunt, and in a low cooing voice addressed a flood of words to him in her incomprehensible jargon. Hunt grunted softly in return. 'He's purring,' Jones whispered. Purcell smiled, but Baker's thin brown face remained tense. His eyes seemed sunk in his head, and his lower lip was quivering.

There was a long silence. MacLeod and Smudge were talking to each other in low voices, as if their disagreement of a few minutes before had been suddenly renewed. Jones was waiting for them to finish before drawing a third name from the hat.

Purcell shivered a little. Like all the rest of them except MacLeod, he was naked to the waist, and a fresh breeze was blowing from the sea. The torches suddenly seemed to pale. The tropical moon had risen. It was enormous, and so bright that it was like dawn breaking. The clearing was lit up and the leafy labyrinth of the banyan's alleys appeared behind MacLeod with its shadows and patches of light, stretching away into mysterious depths through a perspective of columns. Purcell turned, smiled at Ivoa and looked at her companions. Bathed in a soft light, their teeth and the whites of their eyes gleaming amid their dark hair, they were waiting patiently. Purcell was struck by the indestructible power emanating from their charming faces, from their bodies without arrogance, whose every curve, rounded as amphoras, spelt the bearing of life. The *Peritani* might wave their muskets, shake their rope, argue and 'choose'. What incredible futility! What would the island have been without the women? A prison. 'And what,' Purcell thought, 'would have remained of us in a few decades? Nothing but the dust of our bones.'

'Adamo,' Ivoa said teasingly and with an eloquent gesture of her hands to her breast, 'are you sure you're really going to choose me?'

'Yes,' Purcell said smiling. 'You, always you, and you alone.'

'Are you asleep, boy?' MacLeod drawled.

Purcell turned and saw Jones take his hand from Amoureïa's with a guilty look and plunge it into the hat.

'Mason!' he called clearly.

Purcell raised his hand.

'I have a letter from him.'

He took it from his pocket and turned it to the light. It was closed with a wax seal bearing Mason's initials and the address, written in a small clear neat hand, ran:

Lieutenant Adam Briton Purcell,
First Lieutenant of *The Blossom,*
Ashore at 130° 24′ Longitude West
and 25° 2′ Latitude South.

Purcell broke the seal, unfolded the letter and read aloud:

'Mr Purcell, you will see to it that I am assigned a woman capable of doing my cooking and taking care of my linen.
Richard Hesley Mason, Captain,
Commanding *The Blossom.*'

Purcell stared at the letter. He could scarcely believe it. Mason wanted a woman after all!

Purcell saw him in *The Blossom*'s cabin on leaving Tahiti.

Red of face, his arms raised to heaven, he had indignantly refused to take another three women on board.

'We already have too many women, Mr Purcell! They hold no interest whatever for me. Had I consulted my own convenience I would have taken none on board.' And now 'he was consulting his own convenience' and demanding one!

'The Old Man doesn't want a wife, he wants a housekeeper,' MacLeod said.

The seamen laughed and began exchanging remarks about Mason's supposed impotence. It was an enjoyable subject and the exchanges went on for a good five minutes.

'I'm a generous chap,' MacLeod said, raising his hand to stop the joking. 'Even if the Old Man did want to shoot me, I won't have it said that I left him to wash his own linen.'

He glanced round at them, his nose jutting sharply above his thin lips. 'Generous when it costs him nothing,' Baker muttered.

'If no one wants her,' MacLeod went on, pretending not to have heard, 'I propose giving him Vaa.'

No one disagreed. MacLeod banged the end of the rope on the ground and asked Purcell to translate.

Vaa got to her feet, looking solid and plain. She came into the circle and stood firmly on her strong peasant legs, her big feet set wide apart, the toes curled down as if to grip the ground more firmly. She put her two strong hands behind her back and said politely that it was an honour to have the chief of the big canoe for *tané*. The women laughed and Itia cried: *É Vaa, é!* Your *tané*'s a frigid one! . . .' Vaa's wide rustic face broke into a smile. She said: 'I'll warm him up,' and she immediately departed for the village to set about it.

Jones unfolded another paper. 'Johnson!' he called loudly.

Johnson started, looked down at the wen at the end of his long nose and rubbed his scanty beard with the back of his right hand. Then he uncrossed his legs and, putting a knee to the ground, rose with more vigour than might have been expected from his age. He stood first on one leg, then on the other, rubbing his beard and looking furtively round. Despite the thinness of his body, his paunch projected. It was round and hard, curving up to his stomach where it seemed to want to join his chest which was hollow and bent by the weariness of his many

years. Johnson was so bowed that he had to thrust his neck
forward in an effort to stand upright and his arms had long since
given up the attempt to remain in the same plane as his
shoulders. They hung forward, so thin that they resembled a
bundle of cords; there were little black patches on their inner
sides and they were streaked with huge, blue, projecting veins.

Johnson glanced timidly and suspiciously round as if he were
wondering whether the silence greeting his name contained some
trap. He had long determined on his choice, but he hesitated to
reveal it, not knowing whether there would be opposition and
fearing, despite the assembly's decision, that the woman in question might want none of him. He looked furtively from Mac-
Leod to Purcell, as if seeking support from the majority and
the minority in turn. Then he looked at the women, and his
wrinkled eyelids fluttered continuously as if to dissimulate the
direction of his gaze. His red-rimmed eyes stared at them with
an extraordinary expression of fear and covetousness. He was
like a boy holding a stolen penny in the hollow of his hand who,
gazing at a pastry-cook's window for the cake of his choice, cannot make up his mind either to go in or go away.

'Well?' MacLeod said sharply.

Johnson glanced at him timidly, ceased rubbing his beard and,
looking away, said in a piping voice: 'Taïata.'

His choice was a modest one. Taïata was the least young and
the least pretty of the Tahitian women.

'Any objections?' MacLeod asked, raising the rope's end
above his head.

Almost without a pause, he brought it down on the ground.
Johnson looked up and called in a voice that quivered with
excitement: 'Taïata!'

There were whisperings among the women, but none got to
her feet, none answered. Johnson's mouth began to tremble. He
raised his arms to the horizontal, and began rubbing his right
thumb with the thumb and forefinger of his left hand in a slow,
automatic movement. 'He's going to cry,' Purcell thought.

'Taïata!' MacLeod called loudly.

There was a silence among the women, then the whispering
began again. Taïata got to her feet. She came slowly into the
circle. She was short and strong, slightly bow-legged and wad-

dled a little as she walked. Her eyes were concealed by puffy lids, and her face looked hard and stubborn in the light of the torches. Johnson uttered a thin little laugh, went to her, took her by the hand and made a sort of little skipping dance-step which was so ridiculous and pathetic that no one thought of laughing at it. He sat down, but as soon as Taïata had taken her place beside him, she roughly disengaged her hand from his and looked coldly at him, her little dark eyes seeming lost within her swollen lids. 'Poor Johnson,' Purcell muttered. But no one answered him. Jones was looking at Amoureïa, and Baker was staring straight in front of him, looking pale and with his teeth clenched.

'Jones!' MacLeod said severely.

He too seemed nervous and tense. Jones released Amoureïa's hands, seized the hat and drew another name.

'White!' he cried as loudly as if White had been at the other end of the clearing.

White made no move and his face remained impassive. At first he said nothing. Sitting cross-legged, his hands flat on his knees, he made no movement except to tap his trousers with the first and second finger of his right hand. His other fingers, short, knobbly and square at the tips, were raised with a sort of airiness, as if he were about to play a harpsichord. Two or three seconds went by.

'Itia,' White said softly.

There was sudden excitement among the group of women, and their murmuring grew louder and more passionate than before. Purcell turned round. Itia was on her knees. Her eyes lowered, her lips firmly closed, she was shaking her head. Itihota was on her right, with her arm round her shoulders. On her other side were Raha and Toumata. Itihota said: 'Take him He's not bad. He won't beat you.'

'No, no!' Itia said.

'Itia!' MacLeod shouted.

Itia got to her feet, advanced into the circle and took up her position between Amoureïa and Johnson, opposite MacLeod. Her eyes were flashing.

'Listen, you *Peritani* Skeleton,' she said looking angrily at the Scotsman, 'you ought to blush for shame behaving as you do.

What sense is there in choosing a woman who has not chosen you?' She spoke exactly as though it was MacLeod and not White who had chosen her. She went on: 'You know what happens when you choose a woman who hasn't chosen you: you're cuckolded.'

The women could not repress their laughter and the Tahitians echoed them more loudly. *Eatua* be praised! Itia's bad manners had some use!

MacLeod stood up.

'What's she saying?'

'She's asking you,' Purcell said in a flat voice, 'if you want to be deceived by your wife.'

He added: 'The question is purely rhetorical. She's not attacking you directly.'

MacLeod's eyes blazed with anger, but he controlled himself.

'Tell her to hold her tongue,' he said calmly, 'and to go and sit by White.'

Purcell translated.

'I don't hate the yellow man,' Itia said with an effort at courtesy. 'His hand is not icy-blooded,* like the Skeleton's. The yellow man behaves politely. He is always as gentle as the shade . . .'

She held her head high, arched her firm little body, and said with determination: 'But I don't want him for *tané*. I want Mehani.'

Mehani got to his feet. He had been chosen. By rising he signified that he accepted. Mehani loved all the women impartially. But he felt friendly towards Itia.

MacLeod glanced from Itia to Mehani. There was no need to translate for him what Itia had said. He clenched his teeth, brandished the end of the rope and said furiously: 'Tell her that if she doesn't go and sit by White, I shall beat her.'

'I shall not translate that threat,' Purcell said. 'It is a very dangerous one. Mehani now looks on her as his wife. If you touch her, he'll attack you.'

'There's a law,' MacLeod said. 'We'll hang him.'

'If you can,' Purcell said, staring him in the eyes.

MacLeod raised his sharp chin and veiled his eyes,. If it came

* He is not an egotist.

to a fight he would have Purcell, Jones, Baker, the six Tahitians and perhaps the women against him. He bitterly regretted not having brought a musket.

He turned his head to the left.

'White, get up and fetch your wife.'

It was a disguised defeat. He was putting the onus on White.

White made no attempt to seize Itia by surprise. He got up with slow dignity and went towards her. She was out of his reach with a couple of bounds, then turned on her heel and with extraordinary lightness scampered away into the clearing, her long hair flying behind her. She was making straight for the west towards the bush.

'Stop, Mehani!' Purcell shouted.

Mehani halted on the point of following her. Poised on one leg, his athletic body in profile, his head held high and his nostrils dilating, he was like a coursing greyhound stopped in its tracks.

'If you go after her,' Purcell said in Tahitian, 'they'll track you down with their muskets. Stay here. Come back to the village with us.'

He added: 'The night is long . . .'

Mehani sat down, his eyes fixed on Purcell. White remained perfectly still, watching Itia fleeing away under the moon. To go after her would have meant losing face. When she had disappeared into the undergrowth, he slowly crossed the circle again and went back to his place. Since saying 'Itia', he had not uttered a single word.

'We'll find her,' MacLeod said. 'She'll have to eat and drink.'

There was a silence. Purcell screwed up his eyes and said in a flat voice: 'I propose that White choose another woman. Itihota, for instance. Itihota would accept White willingly.'

White opened his mouth, but before he had time to speak, MacLeod intervened.

'Yes, sir,' he said sarcastically, 'certainly, sir. With all my heart, sir. Itihota for White and Itia for Mehani. Very cunning, Purcell, but God damn me if that's how it's going to be. You've perhaps forgotten that this is an assembly. And no black is going to lay down the law for us, even if he happens to be your dearest friend. As for Itia, don't you worry, Purcell, we'll find her.'

Purcell said coldly: 'Three miles of bush in a collar round the island. A mountain with a spring. Seventeen active adherents.'

'We'll find her,' MacLeod said, and he signed to Jones to go on.

Jones put his hand into the hat.

'Baker,' he said almost in a whisper and looked guiltily at his brother-in-law.

Since Amoureïa had been sitting beside him, he had not once thought of Baker and his fears.

Baker raised his brown face and said curtly: 'Avapouhi.'

There was a silence. Everyone looked at MacLeod. The Scotsman had been waiting for this moment. But now that it had come, it seemed to surprise him. Two or three seconds went by. The end of the rope lay on the ground between his legs; his eyes were lowered, though he held his death's head straight and rigid on his thin neck; he was sitting absolutely still. 'He's hesitating,' Purcell thought. 'Itia's flight has made him think. If it were not for the presence of the others . . .'

'Opposed,' MacLeod said, and he looked up and stared at Baker.

Baker stared back at him but said nothing. MacLeod put a hand to the ground, got to his feet and leaned against the root of the banyan. He was expecting Baker to go for him, and he preferred to meet the attack standing up.

'My lads,' he said in his drawling voice, glancing round at his companions, 'if I demand Avapouhi, it's not because I want to do Baker down . . .'

'Oh, no!' Baker said, his voice vibrant.

'But there must be order,' MacLeod went on, paying no attention to the interruption. 'We can't tolerate the women passing from one man to another on this island. Who had Avapouhi in Tahiti? Old man MacLeod. Who had her on board *The Blossom*? This mother's son. But you know what they're like! Hardly had we landed on the island, when off goes my Indian with Baker. Just a freak of fancy, my lads! That's all! All these black women have them. And I tell you,' he went on, raising his voice, 'if you allow them to treat you like that, it's the end. No more order. No more family. We should no longer even be the masters. My lads, I'm telling you: we might as well wrap skirts round our bottoms straight away and do the washing-up!'

Smudge and Johnson laughed, but not very heartily. Baker's eyes left no doubt as to his intentions, they feared that the fight might become general and, if it did, they could not even count on Hunt's strength. Enclosed in Omaata's arms, he was taking no interest in the scene, and was purring like a great cat.

'Right,' MacLeod went on, 'let's go on from there. When Avapouhi deserted me, I said nothing. I'm a peaceful chap. I didn't want a fight with Baker . . .'

'You prefer a vote to a fight,' Baker said, his voice so calmly insulting that MacLeod blanched.

Purcell glanced at Baker. He was sitting cross-legged, his hands in his pockets. Apart from the occasional quivering of his lower lip, his face was impassive. But his dark eyes, black-ringed and feverish, were fixed on MacLeod's with an expression of intense scorn.

'I refuse to be provoked,' MacLeod said, recovering his calm. 'If it's a fight you want, you won't have it, Baker. There's a law, and I shall keep to the law.'

'And who made the law?' Baker said, speaking very slowly. 'Didn't you make it yourself? And now you're taking refuge behind the law to avoid a fight. When it comes to talking, you're afraid of no one. But I've never noticed you in the front rank when there are blows about. When Burt told you to throw the boy's body overboard, you obeyed, didn't you? You and your friend Smudge were all submission. You were obeying the law then, too . . .'

He detached each word with such force that he seemed to be throwing them one by one in the Scotsman's face.

'I shall not reply to your provocations,' MacLeod said, standing still as a rock. 'I've said what I had to say about Avapouhi. It's up to you to speak. When you've done, we'll vote.'

Baker went on in the same slow, implacable voice: 'You're in a hurry to get to the vote, aren't you, MacLeod? Voting's easy, isn't it, MacLeod? As easy as putting a knife into the chest of a man who can't defend himself, as you did to Simon.'

F

Then something singular happened: the Tahitians murmured in approval. They had never heard of Simon and they had not understood a word Baker had said. But they realised from his tone and his eyes that he was abusing MacLeod, and this delighted them. The Scotsman did not even turn his head. He was standing with his back to the banyan root, his hands behind his back, his chin raised, his eyes half-closed. He waited till the Tahitians' murmuring had died down, looked at Baker through the slits of his eyes, and said: 'Have you finished?'

'I have not finished,' Baker said, his voice cold and insulting. 'I was talking of easy things, MacLeod. Hanging Mason, for instance, when his hands and feet were bound, that was an easy thing. It requires no guts. Merely a vote.'

'I'm not preventing anyone from having a majority,' MacLeod said.

'The majority is easy too,' Baker went on in his slow, calm voice, which was nevertheless charged with incredible tenseness. 'It's easy enough to get round a chap who's never understood anything about anything. Easy enough to intimidate a poor old man who can't defend himself. Just look . . . ! '

He suddenly turned towards Johnson and pierced him to the marrow with a furious glance. Purcell was astonished by the force, or rather, by the extraordinary brutality of his gaze. Johnson opened his mouth as if he was short of breath and seemed to curl up, like an insect when boiling water is poured on it. He clasped his knees with his arms, lowered his head and remained in that position, sunken, dominated, crushed.

Baker shrugged in pity and turned to look at MacLeod again.

'Another thing that's not difficult,' he went on, the vibration of his voice lending his words a peculiar intensity, 'is to beat a woman. Particularly a woman who doesn't defend herself like Avapouhi. That's why you regret her. It's not the same with Horoa. She hits you back. And you don't like that. Hitting's all right. Pulling someone's hair's all right. Kicking someone's all right. But fighting's not. Not even with Horoa. Oh, no, Horoa's tough! When you touch Horoa, she'll throw things at you. Last night, it was your hammer . . .'

'I didn't know that! ' Jones said, and he laughed like a child. It was a sudden outburst of youthful, heedless gaiety and it caused a silence in the circle. MacLeod had borne the insults without flinching. Jones's innocent laughter broke his nerve. He suddenly felt all the banderillas Baker had placed in his flesh. His eyes lost their lucidity. They became anxious and curiously staring. He let his shoulders sag forward and put his right hand in his pocket.

At the same instant, Baker put his left foot to the ground; with his right knee slightly raised, he looked like a runner at the start of a race. He had forgotten he had given his knife to Purcell, and in the cold rage driving his compact, wiry little body on, he was prepared to fight MacLeod with bare hands. Panting, tensely gathered, all his muscles taut, he stared at the Scotsman, his eyes furious, glowing with the absolute certainty that he would kill him.

MacLeod had opened his knife in his pocket, and the sweat was trickling down his forehead. He was making a desperate effort to resist the impulse to fight Baker. He thought derisively: 'To fight over a black!' It was absurd, he could have her by vote and without risk. 'I'm letting myself be manoeuvred,' he thought with contempt. Meanwhile, he moved forward with the stiff gait of an automaton, his hand clutching his knife.

'MacLeod!' Purcell cried.

MacLeod started like a man being woken from sleep, looked at Purcell for a full second, took a deep breath, and removed his hand from his pocket. Still facing Baker, he drew back till he felt the vertical banyan root behind his back. It was over. Purcell noticed how his thin sides raised the white vest in his effort to master his breathing.

'If no one has anything else to say,' MacLeod said after a minute, 'I suggest we proceed to the vote.'

Baker made a movement and Purcell put his hand on his arm. 'You should have let me do it,' Baker said in a low furious voice. 'I would have killed him.' Purcell increased the pressure on his arm. Baker sat down and closed his eyes. He seemed suddenly exhausted.

MacLeod sat down again, picked up the end of the rope and said dully: 'Proposal to assign Avapouhi to me.'

He raised his arm, imitated by Hunt, Smudge, White and, two seconds later, Johnson.

'Five votes out of eight,' MacLeod said in the same dull, spiritless voice. 'Proposal adopted.'

He had won, and his victory gave him no pleasure. Among the plans that filled his active mind, that of taking Avapouhi from Baker by a vote had seemed particularly enjoyable. And now that he had done so, it was he who felt defeated.

'Avapouhi!' he said at last.

Baker raised his right hand, there was a stir among the women, and Purcell resisted the longing to turn round.

'One moment,' Baker said, as if he had raised his hand to demand the right to speak, 'I presume I have a right to choose another woman?'

'Of course you have, man!' MacLeod said, trying to recover his verve, 'of course you have, of course! I'm not the chap to leave any member of *The Blossom* without a companion. Even Mason had the right to his Indian woman. Make your choice, man!'

But his truculence rang false. Even his voice rang false. He seemed disappointed and tired.

Baker looked him in the eye and said curtly: 'Horoa.'

MacLeod showed reluctance. 'Does he care for her?' Purcell wondered. 'And, if he does, why did he want Avapouhi? To show his power? To humiliate Baker?'

MacLeod repeated automatically: 'Horoa?'

'Perhaps you want her too?' Baker said bitingly.

There was a silence. MacLeod half closed his eyes and raised his chin.

'Is there any opposition?' he said in a flat, toneless voice.

He waved the end of the rope, and without further delay, smacked it on the ground.

'Awarded!'

'Horoa,' Baker said.

Horoa entered the circle with a powerful, supple movement of her crupper, like a mare bounding from a river. She took up her position in front of MacLeod with all the elegance of her five feet ten inches. Her eyes flamed and, pointing an accusing finger at him, she began a vehement speech, gesturing widely. While speaking, she moved to and fro, caracoling as it were, and as if impatient to set off at a gallop. Proud necked, generous breasted, with long, sinuous legs, she raised her quivering nostrils with impatient movements of the head that shook her mane.

To the accompaniment of the Tahitians' laughter, encouragement and even, from time to time, the rhythmic clapping of their hands, Horoa spoke with extraordinary impetuosity for five full minutes without ever seeming to draw breath or search for a word. She neighed and pawed the ground as if preparing to depart for more attractive horizons. She finished as abruptly as she had begun, and her bosom still heaving from the effort she sat down by Baker, took his head in her arms, drew him to her, and crushed her strong lips against his.

'Translation?' MacLeod asked.

Purcell looked amused and raised his eyebrows.

'Literal?'

'In general,' MacLeod said quickly.

'In general she has made a jealous scene because you have preferred Avapouhi to her.'

Purcell watched MacLeod attentively and it seemed to him that a shade of pleasure passed over his cadaverous face. He went on: 'She ended by saying that Baker was nicer than you are and that she was delighted to have him as her *tané*. I imagine,' Purcell added generously, 'that she was speaking from spite.'

'In any case, it makes no difference to me,' MacLeod said, his face a mask. He paused a moment and then called: 'Avapouhi.'

There was no sound or movement among the group of women. MacLeod called again: 'Avapouhi!'

Since no one replied, he got to his feet. The women were all staring at him, and he looked from one to another of them.

'Itihota,' he said severely, 'where is Avapouhi?'

Itihota got to her feet like a docile pupil to reply.

'She's gone,' she said in English in a sing-song voice, and raised her right hand towards the west.

'You may sit down,' MacLeod said calmly. He went back to his place. His face showed nothing. 'He's taking it well,' Jones said in a low admiring voice. Purcell nodded.

'We shall find her,' MacLeod said quietly.

He looked at Jones and said: 'Go on.'

Jones put his hand into the hat, drew out a paper, unfolded it and read: 'MacLeod.'

'I've made my choice,' MacLeod said composedly. 'Go on.'

Jones drew another paper from the hat and called: 'Purcell.'

Purcell smiled a little. It seemed to him rather absurd to have to choose his own wife. He said in a low voice: 'Ivoa.'

She was standing behind him. She came and sat on his right. Her magnificent blue eyes were fixed on his and she leaned her shoulder against him.

'Opposed!' Smudge shouted loudly.

Purcell heard the shout but it did not at first get through to his consciousness. It was the tense silence that followed it which brought its significance home to him. At that moment, his head was turned on his shoulder and he was smiling at Ivoa. His mouth remained fixed in a smile for a whole second after Smudge had spoken. Then the smile slowly faded, and Purcell's usually calm features registered amazement. He opened his eyes wide, turned his head, looked at Smudge as if to make sure that he had correctly heard him, and then glanced round at the assembly. He looked as if he doubted the reality of the scene.

His incredulity was so obvious that Smudge repeated surlily: 'Opposed.'

Purcell stared at Smudge, his eyes wide. He looked at him without anger and as if he had difficulty in admitting his existence.

'Are you trying to say,' he asked with extreme deliberation, 'that you are demanding Ivoa?'

'Of course I am!' Smudge said.

There was a silence. Purcell could not take his eyes from Smudge's face. He looked at him as if he were trying to solve an enigma.

'It's incredible!' he said as if talking to himself, and he stared at Smudge's features as if one among them could reveal to him the secret he sought. Then he said in a low voice: 'But we're married!' with the same air of profound incredulity and as if he were reluctant to state anything so obvious.

'To hell with that!' Smudge said.

He was sprawling on the ground, supporting himself on one elbow. He had not moved on shouting: 'Opposed!' Between

his retreating chin and retreating forehead, his big nose projected with a sort of impudence, and as his cheeks in silhouette
seemed to be drawn forwards, the whole conformation of his
face had the appearance of an animal's muzzle. He was not looking at Purcell. His bright little eyes, dark as boot-buttons and
sunk deep in their sockets, glanced from right to left with a
sort of ferocious anxiety; and he kept pushing his big nose forward with continuous little movements he seemed unable to
control and which gave him the appearance of a hog digging
into its food with its snout.

Purcell remained silent and MacLeod turned to Smudge
with all the gravity of a judge and said: 'If you oppose, you
must explain why.'

'Course I shall!' Smudge said, his Cockney accent lending
his least word an indefinable insolence. 'And it won't take me
long to explain neither. Now I ask you, chaps, did we or didn't
we say we'd share out the women? If we did, then Purcell must
put his back into the common pool with the rest. I know very
well Purcell's going to say his Indian has been living with him
for three months. But I don't see what rights that gives him. On
the contrary! Why should he always have her? Why shouldn't
someone else have her for a change? Why not me? Ivoa mayn't
be the prettiest, but she's got class. She acts like a lady. Proud
and all that. I've had my eye on her from the start. And God
damn me if I haven't as much right to her as any blasted
officer!'

'You're out of your mind,' Purcell said, still more astonished
than indignant at the enormity of this speech. 'You're demanding my wife! It's monstrous!'

'Your wife!' Smudge said, sitting down and poking his big
snout forward with an air of triumph, as if he had found a titbit
at last. 'Your wife! I thought that's what you'd say! But I'm
telling you once again: I don't care a damn about your marriage.
It don't mean nothing to me. It's just a bit of parson's play-
acting! And I don't care a damn about it, I tell you! I'm going
to take Ivoa from you, married or not, parson or no parson!'

Purcell was paying less heed to Smudge's words than to the
fact that he could not manage to meet his eyes. He looked slowly
round the 'majority'. Hunt was humming and looking at him

without seeing him, but MacLeod, White and Johnson were all looking away. 'They knew about this,' Purcell realised suddenly. 'They're prepared to be accomplices to this infamy.'

He felt Baker's elbow against his. He turned to look at him. 'We shall have to fight after all,' Baker said in a low voice. Jones heard him, leaned forward to look at him, let go of Amoureïa's hands, and tightened his *pareu* round his waist. 'Give me back my knife,' Baker said in a low voice, putting his left hand on the ground beside Purcell. Purcell shook his head. He got to his knees, in the position Baker had adopted a few minutes earlier when defying MacLeod. The movement awakened him from his stupor. He turned pale, his heart beat faster, and his hands began trembling. He put them in his pockets. He felt Baker's knife under his fingers. The handle was warm and hard and its contact gave him pleasure. 'I understand how one can reach the point of killing,' he thought, his fingers clasping the knife. But he immediately felt ashamed. He let go of the weapon, and took his hand from his pocket.

A few seconds went by. He wanted to speak, but could not, and he realised that his jaws were so clenched that he could not open his mouth. He swallowed. At the third attempt, making an incredible effort, he succeeded in uttering a sound at last.

'Smudge,' he said in a stifled voice, his face betraying the violence of his effort to retain his self-control by the pallor and trembling of his lips, 'you don't know what marriage is. It's not a piece of play-acting, it's an oath. The rite doesn't matter. What matters is the promise to live together till death.'

'Well, it'll be just one more promise that won't be kept,' Smudge said with a sort of laugh, pushing his snout forward and his hard little eyes flashing with rage. 'And don't try to come it all soft over me with your marriage and the Bible and everything! I've got my own ideas about your marriage. There's one chap at least you haven't deceived with all your play-acting, and that's me! I saw what you were up to, Purcell, and how you planned it all. You're a cunning one, Purcell, I'll say that for you. Always soft as Jesus, but with an eye to the main chance. When you saw that there were twelve women for fifteen men aboard *The Blossom,* you said to yourself: "There'll be trouble sharing out the women on the island!" So off you go, seize the prettiest, manners and all, get round her with your Jehovah nonsense, baptize her and marry her in front of Mason. And so, when you reach the island, you think: "No trouble! Clear of the whole business! A covert keepered by God Himself!" On account of a prayer at the gangway, the woman's yours.'

Smudge thrust his nose forward, drew breath, and as if the speech he had made had aroused all his rancour against Purcell, he went on in a tone that almost resembled moral indignation: 'That's what you thought. That's how you figured it out, Purcell. Like a man who says: "I come first", and the others afterwards, if there's anything left. As an officer who's used to being served first, and of the best. Always the top of the basket and the cream off the milk. And offal for the rest. What am I? A dog? Have I got four feet? Do I lie down when I'm told? What chance have I had in life compared to you? Toiling in the London docks at fifteen with a crust of sour bread and a drop of gin in my stomach? Unloading bales of cotton sixteen hours a day? For whom were the ladies in lace who came to the docks with two horses in front and two flunkeys behind? For me? You bet your life they were! I was mud, like the mud of the docks. No question of soiling their pretty little shoes. They didn't even get out of their carriages. "Boy, go and find Lieutenant Jones . . . Or Lieutenant Smith . . . Or Lieutenant Purcell",' he added in an explosion of rage which brought tears to his eyes. 'And just a penny for me! A penny to watch him kissing their hands, the fluttering of their eyelashes, the tapping of a fan on his fingers. It was hell! All those pretty manners. And I, nothing but a little heap of mud in the docks. But we're not in London here, Purcell,' he went on, grinding his teeth. 'There are no carriages here, no officers, no lace. Nor judges who send a good lad to Tyburn for stealing five shillings. We're among equals here, Purcell. God damn me, I'm as good as you are, that's what I say! And it's up to the chaps to decide which of us two is to have your woman, married or not, and even if it'll break her pretty little heart to leave you!'

Smudge was affected by the evocation of his childhood. He felt justified by his emotion, and for the first time he had the courage to look Purcell in the face. He was surprised to find no resentment in his eyes. This discovery redoubled his rage. And since Purcell said nothing, he pointed his nose aggressively at him and said with furious insolence: 'Well, what have you got to say to that?'

'Nothing,' Purcell said quite calmly. It seemed to him there was no longer a problem now that he had understood what was in Smudge's mind when he had demanded Ivoa. The easiest part remained to do. There was nothing for it but to fight.

'I consider,' he said levelly and with a sort of gentleness, 'that this discussion is at an end.'

'In that case,' Smudge said, his little rat eyes suddenly aflame, 'I demand that it be put to the vote.'

He turned towards MacLeod, but MacLeod did not look at him. His eyes were fixed on Purcell, and he was trying to master his anxiety.

'If someone demands a vote,' he said in a curiously hesitant voice, 'I must naturally put it to the assembly.'

Purcell got to his feet and looked at MacLeod.

'You will not put it to the assembly, MacLeod,' he said firmly. 'This vote is shameful. I refuse to allow it.'

'You refuse to allow it!' MacLeod said exactly in the tone of an outraged magistrate in court. 'You refuse to allow a vote of the assembly? We don't need your permission, I can tell you that!'

Purcell said quietly: 'In that case you can legislate alone.'

There was a silence and MacLeod said in a tense voice: 'What do you mean by that, Purcell?'

'I mean that from the moment you put it to the vote, I shall retire from the assembly and cease to recognise its authority.'

Baker got to his feet and came and stood beside Purcell. Jones looked at them in turn, got up and went to Purcell's left. He stood there with one leg thrust forward, for once forgetting to tense his chest muscles, though his eyes were watchful.

The Tahitians all began talking at once and in great excitement. Unable to understand the language of the protagonists, to them the whole scene had been a mime whose significance they were not always able to grasp. But now there could be no doubt. The three *Peritani* facing the Skeleton were defying his power.

'I would like to avoid this rupture,' Purcell went on calmly. 'And I had determined to make a good many concessions to avoid it. If it takes place, it'll create a very dangerous situation. Don't push me too far, MacLeod. If Jones, Baker and I leave the assembly, the whole atmosphere of the community will soon become intolerable. There'll be two parties on the island; two clans at war with each other or, at best, ignoring each other. It's a small island. In the long run, life will become impossible.'

'If you leave the assembly, you'll be treated like rebels,' Smudge cried vehemently. 'We'll hang you!'

'Shut up,' MacLeod said.

Though his attitude remained apparently firm, he was in fact hesitating. If Purcell went, all the Tahitians would join his camp. Purcell would have numbers, strength and the complicity of the women. And all this because of that maniac Smudge, he thought angrily. There was no way of dissuading him from his folly. He was even obliged to support him to preserve his vote. MacLeod was discovering with bitter surprise that, if he reigned on the island thanks to his partisans, he was also their slave.

'Think it over, MacLeod,' Purcell went on. 'I'm not hostile to the assembly. On the contrary. As long as one votes and discusses one doesn't draw a knife. But if the majority takes advantage of its power to bully the minority, then it's a far worse tyranny than that of Mason, and even violence won't make me accept it.'

MacLeod realised what these words meant. It was an ultimatum. It was veiled in the sense that, far from making threats, Purcell was suggesting it was he who would resort to force. But veiled or not, the ultimatum was there, with all its implications.

Smudge sensed MacLeod's hesitation. Red with anger, fear and excitement, he clenched his fists, drew his little body to its full height and, thrusting his head forward, suddenly began shouting hysterically: 'Don't be done down, MacLeod! Don't listen to him! Put it to the vote! What are you waiting for? You're not going to allow a damned officer to lay down the law!'

His shouting and gesturing filled the Tahitians with astonishment. '*Maamaa*,'* Tetahiti said, tapping his forehead with his forefinger. There was laughter, and Omaata shouted at the top of her voice: 'What's the matter with the little rat, Adamo?'

* Mad.

Purcell turned to her.

'He wants to take Ivoa from me, and the others will vote with him.'

There was a murmur among the Tahitians. It gradually increased to a growl, and was accompanied by angry exclamations from the women. Mehani got to his feet with decision. Ivoa was his sister. He felt almost as offended as Adamo by Smudge's impudence. He extended his two hands in front of him to demand silence, and made an indignant, though elegant, speech in which he reproached Smudge and the Skeleton with their unfriendly proceedings. He regretted having to say it, but these two *Peritani* were behaving towards Adamo like sons of pigs, and equally badly towards the Tahitians. It was clear that the Skeleton had excluded them from the sharing out and the six of them would have to be content with three women. Not that this made any difference. He, Mehani, intended to take his pleasure with all the *Peritani*'s women (laughter). But it was an affront. It was an affront to Tetahiti, the son of a chief. It was an affront to himself. It was an affront to all of them. He, Mehani, was the son of a great chief. And everyone knew, he added modestly, of whom his father, the great chief Otou, was the son . . . That was why Otou had been kind and generous to the *Peritani*. And now the chief of the big canoe was *maamaa*. He shut himself up in his hut all day. The Skeleton had seized power. He treated the Tahitians worse than prisoners of war, and he wanted to despoil his brother Adamo of his wife. That was why he, Mehani, the son of Otou, said this: everyone must fight beside Adamo against the Skeleton. And let anyone who agreed say so.

Mehoro and Kori immediately got to their feet, shortly followed by Ohou and Timi. Tetahiti stood up the last. Not that he was any less decided than the others but, being the son of a chief and having the advantage of Mehani by reason of his age, he wanted to show that he had reflected more deeply before taking his decision. As etiquette demanded, however, he was the first to speak, and he said gravely: '*É a roa*.'* The phrase was echoed by his companions.

MacLeod glanced at the six Tahitians, then turned to look at the group formed by Purcell, Jones and Baker. His lips formed

* I entirely approve.

but a single line, thin and sinuous under the sharp edge of his nose.

'I propose,' he said, 'that the debate be adjourned. We cannot deliberate under pressure from the blacks.'

'That's no way out, MacLeod,' Purcell said curtly. 'The Tahitians are threatening no one. If the assembly adjourns now without a resolution, we shall leave it.'

'Don't listen to him!' Smudge shouted. 'Don't listen to him! Put it to the vote, MacLeod!'

MacLeod had no time to answer. Omaata got to her feet. Hunt uttered a plaintive groan, but she paid no attention to him. She took a pace forward, and the circle was at once filled with her presence. Frowning and dark of eye, she stared round at the Tahitians and the *Peritani*.

'You, men,' she said in her cataract of a voice, 'you talk and you talk . . . I, Omaata, am going to do something.'

In two strides, she passed in front of White and MacLeod, and went to where Smudge was sitting. He tried to draw back, but Omaata was too quick for him. She bent down and, seizing him by the waistband of his trousers, raised the little man to the level of her eyes, holding him effortlessly at her enormous arm's length.

'*Iti ore,*'* she said in her deep voice.

And with her right hand she began slapping him. Indeed, they were taps rather than slaps. Precisely the kind of little taps one gives a cat that has forgotten itself. But Omaata did not know her own strength. Smudge screamed. Held in a vice by the fingers twisting his trousers across his stomach, his head red from the blows, he struggled like a madman, kicking his legs, beating the air with his ridiculous little fists, and uttering continuous and strident cries.

The Tahitians were hugely delighted. All the humiliation of the evening was being avenged. While the *vahinés* shrieked shrilly, the men roared with laughter. Raising their bent legs to the level of their hips, they loudly smacked their thighs.

'Omaata!' MacLeod cried.

'Let him go, Omaata!' Purcell shouted in Tahitian.

'*Iti ore,*' Omaata said, her teeth clenched.

* Little rat.

She would listen to no one. She continued to administer little taps, and the screaming, struggling, scratching Smudge thrust his head forward and looked like an animal caught in a trap. His arms were too short for his fists or nails to reach Omaata's face. He managed, however, to kick the giantess in the stomach with his bare feet, but this apparently did not discommode her in the least. 'What abdominal muscles she must have!' Jones said, lost in admiration.

MacLeod got to his feet and advanced on Omaata. That fool Smudge had asked for it. Nevertheless, as leader of the majority he had no choice. He had to intervene. Smudge was a vote.

Deafened by the victim's screams, MacLeod approached Omaata circumspectly. He was afraid she would turn her powerful arm against him, or that Hunt would attack him to defend her.

'Stop, Omaata,' he said severely.

She did not even turn her head, but at last finding it a little fatiguing to hold Smudge at arm's length, she stepped to one side, pushed the Scotsman out of the way with her right shoulder, apparently without even seeing him, and propped Smudge's panting body against the root of the banyan against which MacLeod had been leaning. She had, however, considerably diminished the severity of her blows. They were scarcely more than flicks now.

'Mr Purcell! Sir!' Smudge cried, his face crimson. 'Tell her to stop!'

Purcell crossed the circle, looking anxious, and placed his hand on Omaata's shoulder. He shouted: 'Please let him go. You'll kill him.'

'*Oa!* Man!' Omaata said, her voice rolling like thunder. 'They are just the taps of a baby.'

'Stop, Omaata,' Purcell shouted into her ear.

'He'll remember it!' Omaata said, shrugging her colossal shoulders. Deaf as justice, she went on slapping Smudge, striking him impartially on each cheek. As he tried to protect himself with his hands and elbows, she obliged him to lower his guard by jabbing him from time to time in the stomach. Each time her monstrous finger poked him at this sensitive point, Smudge's screams became one long sharp piercing cry like that of a rat in a trap.

'No, no!' Purcell cried.

And with both hands he seized, or rather hung on to, Omaata's arm. She gave a little jerk. And Purcell rolled on the ground.

'Baby,' Omaata said, looking down at him with solicitude, 'I haven't hurt you?'

'No,' Purcell said, getting up, 'but please let him go. Let him go, Omaata!'

'Sir!' Smudge shouted. 'You shall keep Ivoa! Tell her to stop!'

MacLeod placed his hand on Hunt's shoulder. It was his last hope.

'Hunt,' he said, 'stop your wife. She's killing Smudge.'

Hunt turned stiffly towards Omaata as if his neck and his body were soldered together. His little pale eyes stared at the scene. It was as if he were taking it in for the first time. An expression of something like surprise appeared on his crushed, scarred features, and he grunted: 'Killing Smudge?'

'Can't you see?' MacLeod shouted in his ear. 'Friend Smudge! Stop her, Hunt! She'll kill him!'

Rubbing the red hair on his chest with his right hand, Hunt considered Smudge's correction. He did not understand why Omaata was doing this to Smudge, but he had no doubt that there were good reasons for it.

'She'll kill him!' MacLeod shouted.

Hunt ceased rubbing, appeared to meditate, and said: 'Why not?'

He shook his head like a dog coming out of water. He was pleased with his reply. For once, things were clear and easy. Everything Omaata did was right. If Omaata wanted to kill Smudge, that was right.

'Friend Smudge!' MacLeod shouted.

Hunt rose to his full height, pushed MacLeod out of the way with the flat of his hand and said: 'I'll help you, Omaata.'

'Stay where you are!' Omaata cried, glancing at him out of the corner of her eye. And since he took another step forward, she cried: 'Sit down!'

Hunt sat down again.

'Omaata, I beseech you!' Purcell cried.

He returned to the charge. He clutched her arm again. For fear of hurting him, she dared not shake him off. But she continued slapping. Purcell's weight affected the strength of her blows, but completely failed to arrest them.

'Omaata!' Purcell cried.

There was a ripping of cloth. Smudge fell flat on the ground. His trousers had given way, leaving a large strip of cloth in the giantess's hand. Smudge immediately got to his feet, and clutched his trousers with both hands to conceal his nakedness as best he could. The Tahitians laughed all the louder.

'*Iti ore!*' Omaata said, retracting her thick lips over her huge teeth.

She started off after him. Purcell at once threw himself against her and seized her in his arms, his head on a level with her breasts. Taken unawares, Omaata tripped over his legs and lost her balance. She had the presence of mind to roll to one side as she collapsed, so as not to fall on Adamo and crush him with her weight.

Smudge had taken to his heels, his little legs weaving across the clearing. Since it sloped down, his little backside, by an effect of perspective, looked as if it was bouncing along the ground. Everyone stood up, and laughed and shouted to see him flee. As they watched him, an ink-black cloud veiled the moon, and Smudge disappeared as if swallowed up into the earth.

In spite of the two torches, the disappearance of the moon seemed to plunge the whole scene into dusk and Purcell had a curious impression of twilight as he regained his place. The wind had risen, and rain began to fall on his bare shoulders. He shivered.

Jones leaned towards him, a wide smile on his boyish face.

'I've never laughed so much in my life.'

'Well, you were wrong,' Purcell said curtly.

Omaata went back to her place, applauded by the Tahitians. MacLeod was leaning against the banyan root, but he had not sat down again. He waited till the noise abated, raised his hand and said dully: 'I propose we adjourn.'

Jones looked into the hat.

There's one name left.'

'Well, draw it,' MacLeod said, passing his hand across his

face with a weary air. Smudge's flight had avoided an open rupture with Purcell, but White and himself were without women, Smudge had been made ridiculous, Purcell was stronger than ever, and the blacks were on the verge of rebellion.

Jones unfolded the paper and read: 'Smudge.'

He laughed youthfully. Why hadn't he thought of it earlier? There had been nine names in the hat. The last could only be Smudge's. No one echoed Jones's laughter. An air of melancholy and weariness had fallen over the assembly. The opposition was no more satisfied with the result of the proceedings than the majority. As for the Tahitians, they had ceased laughing and were talking in low voices. Of the three parties on the island, theirs was the most wronged.

'Since Smudge isn't here,' Baker said acidly, 'we cannot assign him a woman.'

'Nevertheless, that's what we're going to do,' MacLeod said, recovering some of his aggressiveness. 'For if we don't do so before separating, and leave the blacks with four women, there'll be the devil to pay later, when we take one from them.'

No one replied. No one wanted to argue. The rain was beginning to fall in large slow drops that made as much noise on the hard banyan leaves as if on tiles.

'I propose Toumata,' MacLeod said. 'I think she gets on well with Smudge.'

Purcell turned and said: 'Toumata, do you want Smudge for *tané*?'

'Yes,' Toumata said, getting to her feet.

She looked at Omaata reproachfully and said: 'He has always been kind to me.'

This impressed Purcell. He looked at Toumata with more attention. Her features were commonplace, but her eyes were gentle and there was something firm about her face.

'Any opposition?' MacLeod asked.

'There can be no opposition,' Jones said. 'Everyone else is fixed up.'

Jones had spoken in all innocence, without thinking that Mac-Leod was not 'fixed up'. But the Scotsman read sarcasm into his remark, and gave him an ugly look. Baker, who was always ready to fly to his brother-in-law's help, saw the look and returned it with interest. The battle of eyes lasted scarcely a second, but when it was over, a heavy silence fell over the circle. 'Already!' Purcell thought. 'The least word now, the least gesture . . .'

'Let's make an end,' he said aloud.

'Awarded!' MacLeod said, making the gesture of hitting the ground with the rope, but without carrying it through.

He added sullenly: 'The assembly is adjourned.'

As if the storm had been merely awaiting these words to break, the rain began falling with extraordinary violence. The British and the Tahitians had different reactions. The first fled with their women across the clearing towards the village. The second retreated into the leafy chambers of the banyan. Purcell followed them, Ivoa's hand in his.

It was very dark within the maze of the banyan, and it was by the sound of their voices that Purcell found the Tahitians. As soon as he came among them, they stopped talking.

'Who's there?' Purcell said, embarrassed by the silence.

'We're all here, Adamo,' Mehani said. 'All six of us. And also Faïna, Raha and Itihota.'

'The three women the *Peritani* have left us,' Tetahiti said drily.

Purcell was disconcerted by the tone of the remark and made no reply. His eyes had become accustomed to the dark. He could make out the outlines of the faces round him and could see the whites of their eyes.

'I'm going to join Itia,' Mehani said.

He was addressing Purcell and his voice sounded normal. Purcell looked up.

'In this rain?'

'I must. She'll be frightened.'

'Frightened of what?'

'The *toupapahous*.'

There was a silence and Purcell said: 'Will you find her?'

Mehani laughed: 'I've already played hide and seek with her.'

He added: 'Good-bye, Adamo, my brother.'

It was the accustomed formula, and there were the usual warmth in his voice, the usual trustfulness. No, Mehani had not changed.

Purcell tried to follow him with his eyes. The Tahitian moved away with no more noise than a cat. When he came to the edge of the huge banyan, his athletic figure was silhouetted for a brief instant in a gap in the leaves against a patch of the paler sky, then it leaned forward and disappeared.

After Mehani's departure, the whole atmosphere seemed colder to Purcell. The rain beat on the leaves of the banyan above their heads with a sort of anger. The Tahitians were silent.

Purcell said: 'I asked the assembly to put your names with ours.'

Tetahiti said in his grave voice: 'We know that. Omaata told us.'

Purcell waited, but no one made any comment.

'Brothers,' Purcell said after a moment, 'you have been done an injustice, but I have not associated myself with that injustice. On the contrary, I have tried to fight against it.'

There was a silence, then Tetahiti said with cold courtesy: 'We know it. You tried.'

What did that 'you tried' mean? Were they reproaching him with not having succeeded?

Purcell waited a long moment, but no one spoke. Ivoa pressed his hand and whispered: 'Let's go.'

'Good-bye, Tetahiti, my brother,' Purcell said. 'Good-bye, all. Good-bye, my brothers.'

'Good-bye, Adamo,' Tetahiti said.

There followed a polite murmur of voices. Purcell listened till it was over and his heart sank. None of the Tahitians had called him 'brother'.

8

The rain continued all night. Coming out of his hut in the morning, Purcell realised that the wind had changed from north-west to south-west. It was the first time a sou'wester had blown on the island, and the sudden change of weather made the sailors suspect that they were in for a spell of cold and rain. In fact, the sou'wester continued for the next three weeks and it rained every day. The sky was permanently covered by heavy clouds, the long swell of the Pacific turned greeny-grey, and there was even a little snow, though it melted before it touched the ground.

To the Tahitians this bad weather was a disquieting novelty, for they had never in their lives known such cold. By bringing rain, however, the sou'wester did some good. It watered the plantations of yams and taros that had just been completed, and for as long as it lasted it did away with the water fatigue. Indeed, to fetch sufficient water from the mountain required ten people with buckets and calabashes, and a two hours' walk there and back. Since some of the receptacles were rather heavy, it had been decided that all the inhabitants of both sexes should take part in the fatigue. The twenty-seven islanders were formed into three teams, and since the fatigue only took place once every two days, each team performed the duty only one day in six. Mason sent his woman, but refused to take part in it himself. They were almost grateful to him for his refusal, for wherever he appeared his presence created embarrassment.

As soon as the rain began, MacLeod built a big wooden frame and lined it with one of the tarpaulin covers of *The Blossom*'s boats. They had kept three of these tarpaulins, and MacLeod built two more of these cisterns. Placed in the open, their total capacity in time of rain was sufficient to supply the colony with water.

Before the huts had been finished and the women shared out, life in the island had been communal. They had found it convenient to build only one kitchen and take their meals together. This custom largely came to an end with the beginning of domestic life. Nevertheless, if cooking became a family matter, the supplying of food remained, for the moment at least, a communal business. While awaiting their first harvest, they thought it wise, in order to prevent waste, not to leave the picking of fruit and wild yams to the whims of the individual. This was also arranged by teams. Fruit and vegetables were gathered in appropriate quantities, brought to Blossom Square and distributed equally among the households. Next to the shelter protecting *The Blossom*'s bell and the wardroom clock, they laid a few planks on trestles. The British called this the 'market' and to it the fruits and vegetables were brought, though only the central portion was used for them. The stall was divided into three parts by planks nailed across it. The compartment on the right was for fish, and that on the left for meat.

When the fishermen – British or Tahitian – brought back their catch, they placed it in the right hand compartment and rang *The Blossom*'s bell. The women hurried to the 'market', politely admired the fish whatever their size or quantity, pretended, with much laughter and shouting, to quarrel over them, and prolonged the distribution to well over an hour, so much pleasure did they take in it. The British fished with lines, and the Tahitians with harpoons. But this was not the only difference. When fishing was good, the Tahitians never caught more fish than were needed, whereas the *Peritani*, carried away by a sort of intoxication, brought back many more than the colony could either consume or keep. Half the catch had to be thrown back into the sea before it went bad. The women remarked that the *Peritani* always wanted to have everything, and were so greedy that they could never content themselves merely with what was necessary.

To the right of the market was a round hole in the ground, its bottom and sides lined with a mosaic of stones. It was the communal oven. When a wild pig had been killed a big fire was lit in the oven. On the stones becoming white-hot, the fire was removed, and the pig, having been skinned, drawn, washed and sewn up again with a hot stone in its stomach, was placed in it. It was then covered with banana leaves on which were placed yams, taros, avocados and mangoes. Another armful of leaves was placed on top and the whole covered with earth. The meal was thus cooked all at once in successive layers.

When the pig was cooked, it was placed on leaves in the left-hand compartment of the 'market'. Omaata cut it up into equal parts, while the women queued up with banana leaves in their hands. The wild pig was the only mammal on the island and had multiplied considerably. However, it was prudently decided not to kill more than one a week so as not to exhaust the supply. The Tahitians knew its habits and tricks, and were given the job of hunting it. For this purpose, they were lent muskets which they now handled as well as the British.

As soon as they had arrived on the island, the Tahitians had gathered a great quantity of the fruits of the breadfruit tree. These fruits, the size of a human head, contained a pulp which they set to ferment in silos. After two months, when they considered that fermentation had taken place, they began to use small quantities of it. They kneaded it with water, made little loaves of it and set them to cook in the communal oven. At first, they did not bake too often, for fear their stock would run out before the next year's harvest. But after a month, it was estimated from the amount consumed and what remained, that they had been needlessly parsimonious, and from then on they baked each week. When the loaves came out of the oven, they were a fine golden colour, but they had neither the taste nor consistency of bread. As soon as you had bitten into the crust, the interior melted on the tongue like almond paste, and the taste, agreeable if a little sharp, was more like that of a fruit.

There was plenty of food on the island but the greater part of it consisted of vegetables and fruit. The weather was not always suitable for fishing, nor was the fishing always successful, so that the islanders had fish on the average only three or four times a week. The British had greatly relied on terns' eggs, and they were very disappointed to discover that terns laid only in June and July, so that they would have to wait another six months before having, as Mason had said, 'eggs for breakfast'.

During the first week of rain, advantage was taken of a few bright intervals to strip large pieces of bark from the pandanus which the women beat in mortars to make a sort of paste which they then spread out and rolled thin till it took on the appearance of cloth. Once dry, the paste looked rather like rough linen, and had the peculiarity, when new, of making a slight crackling sound as it was folded. Sometimes in one hut, sometimes in another, the women worked at its manufacture throughout the rainy period.

Neither MacLeod nor White made themselves ridiculous by mounting an expedition to recover their women. It was obvious, moreover, that they could not have taken a single step towards the interior of the island without their approach being announced to the fugitives by that signalling system in which the natives excelled. The day after the sharing out of the women MacLeod said that the rain would make the rebels come back more surely even than the fear of solitude. But the rain fell day and night for three weeks without anything of the kind occurring. From certain signs, Purcell became aware that the 'majority' had passed the word round to watch Mehani's movements. He warned him through Ivoa and, when he asked her how her brother had received the news, she replied: 'He laughed. He seemed very amused.'

'Was that all?'

'He said that the *Peritani* would make very bad warriors . . .'

'Why?'

'Because they don't know how to follow a track. Then Timi said that, if there was a war, the Tahitians would defeat the *Peritani,* even if the *Peritani* had muskets and they had not.'

'He said that!'

'Yes, but everybody told him to shut up. You know Timi . . .'

Moreover, Purcell never saw Mehani now. He spent all day sleeping in the Tahitians' hut, wearing over his *pareu* because of the cold a shirt that had belonged to Burt, and whose frilled front and lace cuffs delighted him.

The rainy days seemed interminable. There was no sound in the village but the rhythmic beating of the pestles in the mortars. Assembled in one of the huts, the *vahinés* made a happy noise as they manufactured their cloth. They were usually singing, but sometimes stopped to gossip about the village, or to compare in detail the merits of their *tanés*. There were exclamations and laughter, and then after a few minutes the pestles started their work once more. The low, mysterious beating began again to the rhythm of a song whose tune was as sad as its words were gay.

Johnson's hut was the nearest to Purcell's on the west and, during the first week after the sharing out of the women, Purcell heard the sounds of quarrelling, followed by dull blows and groans to which succeeded a deep silence. This happened after the midday meal, and three days later at the same hour Purcell heard similar noises succeeding each other in the same order, though he was unable to tell whether it was Taïata or Johnson who was beating the other. He questioned Ivoa. Shaking her head, she replied that everyone in the village knew that they were not getting on together. And this was not astonishing considering Taïata's character, for she had had several *tanés* in Tahiti and had never kept one of them for more than a month. When *The Blossom* had dropped anchor in the bay, it had been some five years since she had had a husband, even from among the old men on the island, and this was no doubt why she had decided to sail with the *Peritani*.

On the other hand, nothing was known of the relations between Mason and Vaa, who had become rather haughty with her companions since becoming the *vahiné* of the chief *Peritani*. She went out little, and then only to go to the market. As for Mason, he never appeared in the village, and if he happened to meet anybody at the corner of a path he made no reply to their salutations. Whenever the weather was fine, he set off alone for long walks on the mountain. When it rained, he contented himself with pacing his 'quarter deck' three times a day. His 'quarter deck' consisted of planks laid on stones between two handrails. This may have been so as to avoid getting his feet wet, but perhaps also to give himself the illusion of being on board ship. When Purcell sat at his table behind his porthole and raised his head from his book, he could see him pacing to and fro. The rain beating down on his cocked hat and shoulders apparently did not affect him at all. Every four or five turns, he would stop, grasp the handrail and, standing very upright, his chin held high, would stare fixedly into the distance, as if the view, instead of being cut off by coconut trees a few yards away, extended in billowing waves to the horizon.

Rain fell from morning till night. Purcell read. In front of him was one of the square portholes from the wardroom, and behind him was the sliding door giving on to the mountain. When building his hut, it had seemed to him a good idea to be able to open it wide to the warm sun. But it had also opened it to the rain and terrible sou'wester. The wind now shook the door in its grooves, and the wet filtered in everywhere, making a little lake on the floor and dripping between the boards in spite of their joints.

Even in London, even in his native Scotland, Purcell had

never seen such rain. You woke up to a white mist floating in clouds between the trees and accompanied by a fine icy rain. Little by little the cotton-wool grew clearer, as if the sun was about to pierce it. And indeed the mist rose, but only to give place to rain. During a single day there was every variety of it: fine rain, heavy showers, and windy gusts. The island's soil failed to absorb it and you waded up to your knees in mud. There was nothing but vegetables to distribute, the weather making fishing and hunting impossible. MacLeod's three canvas cisterns overflowed and they had hastily to dig a ditch to drain the overflow to the cliff. The paths gradually became impracticable since the stones had sunk into the earth, as if sucked down by the mud. They had to go and fetch more, selecting the largest and flattest they could find, transport them with great difficulty, and lay them on top of the others. They had left as many coconut trees in the village as possible for shade. But now the trees created a sort of stifling humidity.

Everything dripped with water. The whole place was an aqueous, rotting sponge. A sweet musty smell hung on the air and impregnated everything. The boards at the angles of the houses were covered with mould, and tools rusted in twenty-four hours, in spite of the grease with which they were smeared.

Blossom Bay was to the north, sheltered from the wind and relatively calm. But on the west coast, the sea enfiladed the cliff and battered it with huge waves. The spray sometimes reached prodigious heights and, borne on the sou'wester, fell like salt rain on the village. Towards the end of the second week, a dull rumbling sound shook the island, awakening the islanders in the middle of the night. In the morning, they found that part of the overhang of the north cliff – where MacLeod had constructed his windlass – had collapsed, undermined by the sea. Purcell sometimes felt that the island would part the cables that attached it to the bottom under the buffeting of wind and waves, would be set adrift and, fissured by the rain, would break up and dissolve into the encompassing sea.

Behind the portholes in each hut the *vahinés* lit *doédoés* at nightfall to show the *toupapahous* that their presence was undesired. So as to be able to continue reading, Purcell, for his part, lit three. The extravagance was unimportant since *doédoés* abounded in the island. They were a sort of nut, and the tree which bore them had the same name. The nuts were full of half-solid oil, and the British had learnt from the Tahitians to use them as candles by stringing them on palm fibres which acted as wicks. The light they gave was less bright than that of a candle, and the flame spat at times like a cracker, but the smell of the oil was agreeable and fruity, and produced no ill-effects.

From time to time Purcell would go to his porthole and look at the little points of light shining here and there among the trees. It was terrifying to think that this rock and the thin crust of mud, which bore the trees and their fruits, formed the only habitable land within a radius of five hundred sea miles. The island was surrounded by nothing but waves, wind, rain and darkness . . .'And we,' Purcell thought, 'clinging to this thin crust of mud, can still find strength enough to form factions . . .'

There was a loud knocking at the door, but before Purcell had the time to get up, Ivoa ran to open it.

Vaa appeared. Her hair was soaking, but she was wearing with dignity a blanket from *The Blossom* over her shoulders. She came in, greeted Ivoa with a mere nod of the head, and crossed to the table at which Purcell was reading. Without pre-amble she said: 'My *tané* wants to know if he can come to see you this evening.'

Vaa's manner astonished Purcell. Only a great Tahitian chief would have permitted himself so abrupt an opening.

'This evening?' he said, raising his eyebrows doubtfully.

'This evening,' Vaa said.

She was standing very upright in the middle of the hut, her short legs straddled. She was dripping with rain and there was a little pool at her feet. Her big honest peasant face revealed a certain haughtiness that was derived from her consciousness of the social rank to which she had attained by marrying Mason.

'It's late and it's raining,' Purcell said, somewhat surprised by Vaa's grand air. 'But if your *tané* desires, I can go to see him tomorrow morning.'

'He said you'd say that,' Vaa replied with an indefinable air of addressing an inferior. 'He doesn't want that. He said he'd prefer to see you this evening.'

'Well, let him come then! ' Purcell said.

Once again Vaa gave Ivoa a little distant nod, and off she went.

As soon as the door closed behind her, Ivoa burst out laughing.

'The airs she gives herself!' she cried. 'Vaa, man, Vaa! She's as stiff as a *tavana vahiné*! * And you know she's of very lowly birth!'

'There are no two ways of being born,' Purcell said, looking vexed. 'She was born. That's all. Don't be vain, Ivoa.'

'I?' Ivoa said, and with a charming gesture she put her hands to her breast. Purcell admired her grace, but clung to the truth of his remark.

'You're proud of being the daughter of a chief . . .'

'Of course, I am! Otou is a great chief!'

'Otou is a good and intelligent man. Be proud of being Otou's daughter, but not of being the daughter of a chief.'

'I don't understand,' Ivoa said, sitting on the bed. 'It's because Otou is Otou that he's a chief.'

'No!' Purcell said peremptorily. 'Even if he were not a chief, Otou would be Otou.'

'But he is one!' Ivoa said, spreading wide her hands in a demonstrative gesture.

'Listen,' Purcell said, 'if you're proud of being a chief's daughter, there's no reason why Vaa should not be proud of being a chief's wife. It's no more absurd.'

Ivoa gave a little pout. There was a knock at the door. Ivoa ceased pouting. She had not time to be aloof before becoming reconciled. She gave Purcell a brilliant smile and hurried to open the door.

'Good evening, chief of the big canoe,' she said courteously.

'Humph!' said Mason.

He never knew the names of the native women. They were impossible to remember. They all ended with 'a'. Besides, they all looked alike. They were always half-naked and chattering. Or banging away at their mortars with their damned pestles.

Purcell got to his feet and waved him to a stool.

'I believe this is the first time you've visited my house.'

'Humph!' said Mason.

* A chief's wife.

He sat down and looked about him.

'It's cold here,' he said stiffly.

'Yes,' Purcell said with a smile. 'It's my sliding door. I shall have to perfect it.'

There was a silence. Mason looked at his feet. Purcell had an odd feeling that he was shy and did not know how to begin.

'You burn three *doédoés* at once,' he said at length. There was a certain reproach in his voice as if Purcell was still on board *The Blossom* and wasting oil.

'I was reading.'

'So I see,' Mason said.

He leaned over Purcell's table and read the title of the book aloud: *'Gulliver's Travels'*.

'Have you read it?'

Mason shook his square head.

'Just enough to know that the so-called Captain Gulliver was never a sailor. And as for what he says about the countries he pretends to have visited, I don't believe a word of it . . .'

Purcell smiled. There was another silence.

'Mr Purcell,' Mason went on, 'I want to thank you for having had Vaa assigned to me.'

He added without a touch of humour: 'She gives me complete satisfaction.'

'I'm glad of it, Captain Mason,' Purcell said. 'But it's Mac-Leod you should thank. It was he who thought of Vaa.'

'MacLeod!' Mason said, turning red. 'Well, I'm sorry to owe anything at all to that . . .'

He was going to say 'to that damned Scotsman', but he remembered just in time that Purcell was also one.

'Do you know,' he went on indignantly, 'I met that man yesterday. He was carrying Burt's sextant. Naturally, I demanded it of him. Do you know what the fellow had the impudence to say? "It's my share of Burt's effects. But if you want to buy it off me, I'm prepared to sell it to you." '

'Sell it!' Purcell cried. 'What use does he think he can make of money here?'

'That's what I asked him. He replied that in twenty years time there would be a prescription for the mutiny and then, if a British vessel happened to call here and take him back to

Scotland, he'd prefer not to arrive home without a penny in his pocket . . .'

Purcell laughed, but Mason did not echo him. His eyes were fixed on the ground and he seemed preoccupied. After a moment, he looked up, shook himself and said almost aggressively: 'I have a service to ask of you.'

'At last,' Purcell thought.

'If there's anything I can do,' he said with a nod.

Mason waved his hand impatiently as if to sweep the courteous formula aside.

'Of course,' he said almost offensively, 'you can refuse . . .'

'But I've not said I'll refuse,' Purcell replied smiling.

'This is what it's about,' Mason went on, impatiently cutting Purcell's protestations short. 'During my walks on the mountain, I've discovered a cave on the northern slope which is difficult of access. You reach it by an extremely steep path . . . Well, a path . . . That's a manner of speaking. It's so steep you have to cling to the rocks to get up it . . . What's interesting is that it's the only means of access to the cave. In fact, it's flanked on both sides by high walls of rock, peaks I might say . . . And they're impossible to climb. Moreover, the roof of the cave overhangs the opening, so that it's impossible to reach the entrance from the top of the mountain, even with the help of a rope. I'll add that there's a spring inside the cave . . .'

He paused. He seemed surprised at having spoken at such length.

'I examined the cave carefully,' he said, his grey eyes suddenly bright, 'and I'm convinced it's impregnable to attack . . .'

Suddenly raising his voice, he added: 'Mr Purcell, I assert that one man alone – I say: one man alone – with arms, sufficient ammunition and of course enough food, could hold a whole army at bay from the entrance to the cave . . .'

'The frigate,' Purcell thought. It was becoming an obsession. In spite of its formidable defences, to Mason the island no longer seemed impregnable. He had found something better: a second line of defence. The island was the castle, and the cave its keep . . .

'Of course,' Mason went on drily, 'I'm not asking you to fight with me. I know your views. And naturally I'm not counting on the men either . . .'

He paused and went on in a voice whose assurance rang false: '. . . so long as they have not returned to their duty.'

He paused again and said solemnly: 'Mr Purcell, I am merely asking you this: to help me transport arms and ammunition to the cave.'

He fell silent and fixed his grey eyes on Purcell. After a moment, since Purcell said nothing, he went on: 'I could have asked Vaa. She's very strong,' he went on, casting a glance at Purcell, as if he regretted that he did not look tougher. 'But it seems the natives are frightened of these caves; they believe they're haunted by *toupapahous*. From one point of view, it's an excellent thing. There'll be no fear of theft as far as they're concerned.'

'And the seamen?' Purcell asked.

'Why should they be tempted by the muskets, when they've each got one already? Besides, there's no danger of their ever finding the cave. Except for the water fatigue, they practically never leave the village. Like true sailors, they hate walking. We've been here for several weeks, Mr Purcell, and which of them has ever wished to go to the top of the mountain? Only two of us ever have: you and I.'

He paused and then went on: 'Of course, I'm asking you to keep this secret.'

'I can promise you that,' Purcell said at once.

There was a long silence and Purcell said: 'To my great regret, Captain Mason, I do not feel able to perform the service you ask of me. By helping you transport arms to the cave, I should be making myself an accomplice to the murders you might commit with them in case of a landing.'

'Murders! ' Mason cried.

'What else?' Purcell said calmly.

Mason got to his feet, his face purple, the veins on his forehead blue and swollen, his lids flickering across his eyes.

'I consider, Mr Purcell,' he said, his voice shaking with anger, 'that I should be in a state of legitimate defence . . .'

'That's not my opinion,' Purcell said curtly. 'Let's not mince our words, do you mind? We're all guilty of, or accomplices to, the crime of mutiny. By opposing the armed forces of the Crown with weapons in our hands, we should be committing another crime: that of rebellion. And, if we had the misfortune to kill the sailors sent against us, of aggravated murder . . .'

'Mr Purcell!' Mason cried with such violence that Purcell thought he was going to hit him. 'I have never in my life . . . Mr Purcell,' he went on angrily, 'I cannot tolerate . . . It's the most intolerable . . . How dare you coolly . . .'

His lips trembling and his eyes staring, he began several phrases without being able to finish any of them. His inability to express himself redoubled his fury. He clenched his fists, abandoned his speech, and said coldly: 'I have nothing more to say to you.'

He turned on his heel, crossed to the door, opened it and went out like an automaton. The door banged two or three times in the wind before it occurred to Purcell to shut it.

He went thoughtfully back to the table. There had been something almost abnormal about Mason's violence.

'By *Etua!*' Ivoa cried. 'He shouted! Oh, how he shouted! . . .'

She was sitting on the bed, her legs tucked under her, a blanket round her shoulders.

'He asked me to do him a service; and I refused.'

Her *tané's* reticence did not escape Ivoa. She was devoured by curiosity, but Tahitian good manners forbade her to ask questions, particularly of her husband.

'*Maamaa,*' she said, shaking her head. 'Adamo,' she added teasingly, 'why are the *Peritani* so often *maamaa?*'

'I don't know,' Purcell said smiling. 'Perhaps they've got too many taboos?'

'Oh, no!' Ivoa said. 'That can't be the reason. The Skeleton has no taboos, and he's more *maamaa* than all the rest . . .'

She went on: 'If he was not *maamaa*, he wouldn't have insulted my brothers by excluding them from the sharing out.'

She fell silent and turned her head away as if she had said too much.

'They're angry with him?'

'Yes,' she said, her head turned away. 'They're angry with him. Very.'

Something in the tone of her voice disquieted Purcell and he asked: 'And with me, too?'

'With you, too.'

'That's unjust!' Purcell cried indignantly.

He got up, went over to sit on the bed beside her, and took her hand.

'You saw yourself . . .'

'I saw,' Ivoa said.

She went on: 'They say you treat your friends as if they were enemies.'

'But it's not true!' Purcell cried, profoundly distressed.

'They say the little rat wanted to take your wife from you and yet you prevented Omaata beating him. And that's true,' she added, suddenly giving Purcell a look that upset him.

He thought: 'She's angry with me, too.' He got up in astonishment, and began walking up and down the room. Hated by one lot and suspect to the others . . . He suddenly felt appallingly alone.

'And Mehani?' he asked, coming to a halt.

Ivoa turned her head away and went on as if she had not heard him: 'They say you stopped Ouili killing the Skeleton.'

'Killing!' Purcell cried, putting his hands over his ears. 'Always killing!'

He began walking up and down the room again. He felt powerless to explain his conduct, even to Ivoa.

'And Mehani?' he asked, stopping in front of her.

There was a silence. Ivoa crossed her arms on her breast and said ironically: 'Be happy, man; Mehani still loves you.'

Purcell's face cleared and Ivoa said vexedly: 'I believe you love Mehani better than you do me.'

Purcell smiled and went and sat on the bed beside her.

'Don't be like the *vahinés Peritani* . . .'

'What are they like?'

'Jealous, more often than not.'

'I'm not jealous,' Ivoa said. 'For instance, Itia runs after you to make you play with her. And what do I do? Do I make a fuss?'

This last speech perplexed Purcell and he made no reply to it. After a moment he went on: 'What does Mehani say?'

'He defends you. He says you're different and must not be judged like the others. He says you're *moa*.'*

She looked at Purcell from under her lashes and asked ingenuously: 'Is it true? Is it true, Adamo, that you're *moa*?'

He was on the point of shrugging his shoulders. But he restrained himself and continued walking up and down the hut. To be *moa,* in the Tahitian view, was not the result of heroic effort. It was innate. One was *moa* as one might have a clubfoot: from birth. It was a peculiarity admirable in itself, but implied no merit. 'Well, let them believe it!' Purcell thought. 'Let them believe it, if it helps them to understand my behaviour . . .'

'Yes,' he said seriously, coming to a halt. 'Yes, Ivoa, it's true.'

'By *Eatua*!' Ivoa cried, and she looked so happy that Purcell felt ashamed. 'What an imposter I am!' he thought with embarrassment.

'É Adamo é!' Ivoa went on. 'I'm so happy! I once saw a *moa* in Tahiti, but he was so old! Oh, how old and decrepit he was! And now, I've got a *moa* here in my house every day! And he's handsome! And he's my *tané*!' she concluded in rapture, throwing up her hands.

She threw the blanket off her shoulders, jumped from the bed, ran to Purcell and, taking him in her arms, covered his face with kisses. Moved and disconcerted, Purcell looked at her. As she lightly kissed his cheeks, his chin and his lips, her face moved continually, and Purcell saw the glow of her magnificent blue eyes passing to and fro before him. How beautiful she was! Light, warmth and generosity emanated from her!

'And so you're *moa*!' Ivoa said delightedly.

She clasped him in her arms, and began moving backwards, slowly at first, then faster and faster, as if she were dancing with him. Purcell felt a sort of glow of amusement. She was leading him towards the bed. Suddenly, she fell backwards and he fell on top of her, laughing. Then he ceased laughing, sought her lips, and yet had time to think: 'Tahitian women have a peculiar idea of sanctity.'

The next day, there was a bright period and the sun appeared

* A saint.

G

for the first time in three weeks. At eleven o'clock, Purcell left his hut, turned into West Avenue and knocked at Baker's door.

Horoa opened to him. She looked lively, mettlesome and indomitable.

'Good morning, Adamo, my brother,' she cried.

Clasping him on the very threshold, she embraced him impetuously in the *Peritani* manner. When Purcell was able to draw breath, he saw Baker behind her, smiling calmly in the middle of the room.

'Come,' Purcell said without going in, 'I'm taking you with me. I'm going to pay MacLeod a visit.'

'MacLeod?' Baker said, his delicate brown face immediately changing its expression.

'Come on,' Purcell said. 'It's time to negotiate.'

When Horoa saw Baker on the point of going out, she stood in front of him and, shaking her arms, her eye fiery, made him a vehement speech.

Baker looked questioningly Purcell.

'She's reproaching you with going out before you've cut wood for her.'

Baker slapped Horoa's bottom and said with a smile: 'Later on, Miss.'

This had no effect. Her breast heaving, her nostrils dilated, Horoa pawed the ground and arched her crupper, while continuing to air her grievances.

Baker turned to Purcell: 'How do you say "later" in Tahitian?'

'*Aroué.*'

'Horoa,' Baker said sternly, '*aroué! Aroué!*'

He slapped her bottom again and went out. While the two men walked away, Horoa stood in the open doorway and continued her harangue.

'She's fatiguing,' Baker said.

He went on: 'Not a bad girl, you know. But fatiguing. Always dramatising things.'

He stopped, waved his hand and cried: '*Aroué! Aroué!*'

They went on their way.

'I expect she regrets MacLeod. Life with me must seem too quiet.'

Purcell turned to him.

'That's what she was saying.'

Baker laughed.

'Well, that's splendid. There won't be any difficulties in that direction.'

The sun was already hot. It was wonderful to see the sky shining through the palms again, and the brightly coloured birds about them. They had disappeared during the rain, and they had thought them dead, since they were so small and fragile. And now here they were, more lively and tamer than ever.

'Do you think you'll succeed with MacLeod?' Baker asked in a different tone.

'I think so,' Purcell said.

They passed Johnson's hut and Purcell said in a low voice: 'From what I can hear from my hut, they like dramatics there too.'

'She beats him,' Baker said.

Purcell stopped and looked at Baker.

'It's she? You're sure of that?'

'I saw her chasing him in the garden with a stick.'

'Poor old man,' Purcell said.

To have come so far, to have placed so many countries and oceans between a shrew and himself and, having reached the end of the world, to fall into the hands of another!

Baker screwed up his face: 'You see, sir . . .'

'Purcell.'

'Purcell . . . You see, Purcell, Johnson calculated wrong. He chose an ugly woman. He thought, because she was ugly, that she'd have good qualities. Well, it's not true. If it were true, everyone would be after the ugly ones. They'd be at a premium! The fact is, ugly women are just as tiresome as pretty ones . . .'

Baker paused and then added: 'And they're ugly into the bargain.'

Purcell smiled.

'You're a pessimist. It seems to me that Avapouhi . . .'

'Oh, I've got nothing against Avapouhi,' Baker said, shaking his head. 'I'm speaking in general. You see, Purcell, women, in general, seem to me . . .'

He rubbed his forehead above his right eyebrow:
'. . . fatiguing.'

He added: 'They're never content with their lot. They always
want something other than what they've got. Another husband.
Another dress. Indeed, anything.'

'You're unjust. Tahitian women aren't like that.'

'Horoa's like that.'

Purcell glanced at him. He was a highly strung type; but of
the calm sort. His face was impassive, but there was a dark line
round his eyes and his lower lip twitched like a pulse.

Baker went on: 'Won't you tell me what we're going to
MacLeod about?'

'I've got an idea,' Purcell said. 'It occurred to me when talking to Mason last night. I don't know how much it's worth.
And in case it doesn't come off, I'd prefer not to tell you about
it in advance.'

They were passing Mason's hut, and they saw the captain
walking to and fro on the wooden path of his quarter-deck, shod,
cravatted, buttoned, his cocked hat on his head. 'Good morning,
Captain Mason,' Purcell said without stopping, and Baker also
said 'good morning', but without adding 'sir'.

Mason did not even turn his head. His eyes fixed on the horizon, he was walking straight ahead, placing his feet with care,
his body carefully balanced as if to counteract the rolling of a
ship. From time to time, he waved a hand impatiently about his
head to chase away the birds that were flying too close to him.
This gesture reminded Purcell of a man chasing away mosquitoes, and it seemed to him somehow out of place.

'The birds don't seem to have suffered from the rain,' Purcell
said.

He looked at Baker and said in a low voice: 'What about
Avapouhi?'

'She hasn't either.'

'And Itia?'

'Nor she.'

'When did you see Avapouhi?' Purcell asked.

'Yesterday. Horoa was pounding at Omaata's and I was able
to escape.'

'You may not have to wait much longer,' Purcell said.

He looked at Baker. He was suddenly very aware of his friendship for him. His brown face was so frank; his whole demeanour so straightforward. There was a glint of humour in his brown eyes. His manner was gentle though there were re- serves of strength behind it. 'And of violence,' Purcell thought. 'That's the only thing in him I dislike.'

As soon as Purcell put his hand on the gate to MacLeod's garden, the Scotsman appeared at the hut door, and behind him, half concealed, and looking absurdly short and fat in compari- son, was White, naked to the waist, his hands behind his back.

'What do you want?' MacLeod called in an unfriendly voice.

'To see you,' Purcell said without entering.

There was a silence.

'Both of you?' MacLeod said suspiciously, and it occurred to Purcell that he was afraid they would attack him.

'I want Baker as a witness to what I have to say to you, but White can stay too, if you wish it.'

'Very well,' MacLeod said. 'Come in!'

As they crossed the garden, he stood in the doorway watching them. His long gawky body was balanced on one thin heron's leg, his right hand was nonchalantly placed on his hip, but his eyes, set deep in their sockets, watched their every move- ment.

On entering the hut, Purcell was struck by the number of cup- boards. They reached from floor to ceiling, surrounded the door and the two portholes, and had little doors at varying heights which were all either locked or padlocked.

Apart from the cupboards, there were only a solid oak table in the middle of the room and a number of stools, which made it look as if MacLeod's house was the meeting place of the 'majority'.

MacLeod took up his position behind the table as if he wanted to place an obstacle between himself and his visitors, then sud- denly stretched out his skeleton hand towards them – the arm and hand seeming so long that they appeared to reach across the room – and silently indicated seats. They sat down. White went quietly round the table and took his place beside MacLeod. He put his hands on his knees and began tapping them with his first two fingers, his dark eyes watching Purcell attentively. MacLeod remained standing, his hands in his pockets.

The four men looked at each other for a moment without uttering a word. Purcell had expected MacLeod to attack first and overwhelm them with his invective. But MacLeod seemed disinclined to speak. He preserved a wholly dignified silence. His attitude suggested that Purcell's and Baker's presence in his hut was so unusual as to require an explanation. 'It's extraordinary,' Purcell thought. 'Only three months ago, he was a mere seaman like the rest. And now there he stands, leaning against a cupboard, as cold and distant as a diplomat giving audience.'

'What have you to say?' MacLeod asked.

That was precisely what it was: he was giving them audience . . . William Pitt receiving ambassadors.

'It seems to me,' Purcell said, 'that the present situation cannot continue. It does no one any good. In the long run, it'll destroy all mutual relations. I think the moment has come to reach a compromise.'

'A compromise?' MacLeod said.

Purcell looked at him. He was inscrutable.

'As I see it,' Purcell went on, 'the present situation is satisfactory to no one. Baker and Mehani have not got the women they want. As for White and yourself, you have no women all.'

He gave them time to swallow the bitterness of the pill.

'Well?' MacLeod said.

'I suggest a compromise,' Purcell repeated.

There was a silence and MacLeod said: 'I'm not opposed to an agreement. What do you suggest?'

'I can see only one solution,' Purcell went on. 'An exchange. White yields Itia to Mehani and receives Faïna from him. You give up Avapouhi, and Baker gives you back Horoa.'

MacLeod was silent for a moment, then he raised his head, took a deep breath and dug his hands still deeper into his pockets.

'Is that what you call a compromise, Purcell? Where's the compromise? I see clearly what I'm losing, but I don't see what I'm gaining! And, cool as a cucumber, you call it a compromise! A compromise of what? The only things I can see that are compromised are my own interests! Let's go back over the facts, in case you've forgotten them. Baker takes Avapouhi from me. All right! Then there's a vote, and the vote gives her back to me. Upon which she disappears into the landscape, and you say: "Let's have a compromise: we'll make Avapouhi come back and Baker'll take her again! . . ." You've got a damned cheek, Purcell, I'll say that for you! . . . There you sit, looking like the Angel Gabriel, innocent as Jesus Christ, your bottom scarcely touching the chair, just as if you were on the point of ascending into heaven, and you propose this sort of compromise! . . . It's unbelievable! And what about the law? We've an assembly here, Purcell, though perhaps you've forgotten it! There are laws! There are votes! And what's been voted's been voted, that's what I say . . . ! '

He drew breath.

'As for Avapouhi, she'll be found, don't you worry about that. Perhaps sooner than you think. It's not the sailor who sails closest to the wind who makes most way! And because I'm paying out the main-sheet at this moment it doesn't mean I've no intention of arriving. No, sir, I'll get there! And when I get alongside that little sloop, I'll trim her properly, you can be sure of that, and God, wind or devil won't make her drag once I've got her lying at anchor.'

'Let's admit,' Baker said suddenly, cold anger quivering in his voice, 'let's admit you manage to lay hands on her and bring her home. What then? What do you do? Nail up your portholes? Put an iron bar across the door? Shut her up in a cupboard? Padlock her to your bed? Is that the idea?'

'What I do with my legitimate wife,' MacLeod said with dignity, 'is my business.'

He fell silent. It was clear that he had no intention of getting into an argument with Baker. Purcell waited, but MacLeod said nothing. He had refused, and his refusal was categorical.

Purcell looked at MacLeod and something in his attitude warned him. His refusal was not perhaps so categorical as all that. MacLeod was not dismissing them. He was not breaking off negotiations. He was a cunning beast. Both clever and cunning. Subtle even. He had scented something, and he was waiting. His refusal was a phase in the negotiations. Nothing more.

'If you think you can find Avapouhi,' Purcell said, 'or if you think that, having found her, you can keep her in your hut, well that simply means the moment's not yet ripe. That being so, I propose adjourning these negotiations.'

They looked at each other in silence. MacLeod said neither yes or no. He appeared to have no opinion about putting an end to the interview. He was neutral. He was effacing himself. It was as if he were not there. 'He's a fox,' Purcell thought. 'He's not going to make things easy.'

Purcell shrugged and got to his feet. Then White ceased tapping his knees with his fingers and said: 'I accept.'

'You mean,' Purcell said, 'that if you're given Itihota, you'll leave Itia to Mehani?'

'That's what I mean.'

Purcell looked at Baker and sat down again.

'Good,' he said, without showing his satisfaction. 'I think you're wise. When I leave you, I shall go and see Mehani and the Tahitians. Since they've only got one woman between two of them, it's not only a matter for Mehani. But I don't expect there'll be any difficulties.'

He glanced at MacLeod. The Scotsman was staring into the distance. He seemed neither pleased nor annoyed at White's initiative. It seemed not to concern him. His own position remained unchanged.

'If I go now,' Purcell thought, 'he'll let me go. He's too certain I'll come back. When did I betray myself?' he thought with annoyance. 'Why is he so certain I've got something to offer him?'

'Think it over, MacLeod,' Purcell said. 'Think it over, before I go.'

MacLeod seemed unmoved.

'I've thought it over,' he replied nonchalantly.

There was a note of sarcasm in his voice, as if he knew Purcell would not put his ultimatum into effect.

'Very well,' Purcell said, 'let's return to the problem.'

He took a black leather purse from his pocket, untied the laces, opened it, and spilled the contents out on the table. It contained a number of gold pieces, and he made a careful pile of them in front of him as if about to play dice. In the silence, Purcell could hear the others breathing. He looked at his companions. They seemed bemused, paralysed. Only their eyes were alive. Ali Baba's treasure could have produced no greater effect. Then someone coughed. MacLeod took his hands from his pockets. A board cracked under his feet as he moved the weight of his body to draw nearer. He leaned his sharp nose over the table and Purcell heard a sucking noise, as if the air had difficulty in entering his throat.

'There are ten pounds sterling there,' Purcell said. 'They're yours, MacLeod, if you leave Avapouhi to Baker.'

'Purcell!' Baker cried.

Purcell raised his hand to silence him. MacLeod straightened up.

'God damn me!' he said hoarsely. 'I've sailed before the mast for twenty-five years but, God damn me, if I've ever seen the like of it!'

On the ill-planed oak table, which had been hastily darkened with linseed oil, the gold lay in a neat pile, and the sun shining in through the portholes lent it a peculiar brilliance. It was a modest, even an insignificant pile; merely a little collection of flat, round, rather nicely engraved objects that could be of no possible use to anyone on the island. One of the pieces was slightly out of place, and Purcell corrected its alignment with a quick, careful hand.

'Well?' Purcell asked.

MacLeod drew himself up to his full height and put his hands in his pockets

'It's a disgrace,' he said indignantly at last, 'but with an ironical curl at the corner of his mouth, 'it's a damned disgrace, that's what I say! An officer bartering women for gold! It's scarcely worth being brought up in the schools and trained to stand to attention with all the other damned little officers of His Majesty's service to end up in a trade of that kind! It's a disgrace, I say, Purcell! And am I,' he went on with mock dignity, 'a vagabond of the London docks, to be offered a bribe in exchange for my legitimate wife, awarded me in due and proper form by a vote of parliament? And morality, Purcell? What of morality? Are you throwing it overboard? Casting it over the side with the refuse to feed the sharks? God damn me,' he went on with a wink, as if he was suddenly passing from feigned indignation to a parody of indignation itself, 'is that what your

Bible teaches you? To serve as go-between to a legitimate husband and his wife's former lover?'

Purcell got to his feet and said drily: 'I've no time to listen to your nonsense. If it's no, say so and I'll go.'

Meanwhile, he went to the table and put his hand over the pile of gold as if about to return it to the purse.

MacLeod said: 'Twenty.'

'What?' Purcell said, leaving his hand where it was.

'Twenty. Twenty pounds. I accept, if you give me twenty pounds.'

'I thought so,' Purcell said.

He took his right hand from the table, put it in his pocket, and drew out another purse, saying calmly: 'Since you may regret not having asked for more, I'll tell you now it's absolutely all I've got.'

He untied the laces of the second purse and spread its contents on the table. Then, picking up the pieces in his left hand, he placed them one by one beside the first pile.

'That makes twenty pounds in all,' he went on. 'However, I'm not going to give you the whole twenty pounds. Only nineteen. The twentieth is part of another bargain.'

'What else do you want?' MacLeod said with an arrogant, long-suffering expression as if it was he who was being despoiled.

'Burt's sextant.'

MacLeod opened his mouth. But Purcell did not allow him to speak. He said sharply: 'You can take it or leave it.'

MacLeod sighed, drew a key from his pocket, opened the cupboard behind him, took out the sextant and placed it with a bad grace beside the gold pieces.

'We're agreed, aren't we?' Purcell said. 'You leave Avapouhi to Baker and you take back Horoa.'

'Agreed,' MacLeod said sulkily, lowering his eyes.

Purcell pushed the gold towards him like a gambler who has lost his stake. As he did so the piles collapsed and as the coins spread out they suddenly looked more numerous. MacLeod spread his thin fingers over them and gathered them up, but without arranging them in piles. Purcell noticed that he gave the heap a circular shape.

'MacLeod,' Purcell said.

MacLeod looked up impatiently. He seemed displeased to be interrupted in his task.

'MacLeod,' Purcell continued gravely, 'I'm glad we've reached an agreement. As far as I'm concerned, it seems to me very important there should be a good understanding between us.'

'To me too,' MacLeod said casually, waving his hand as if to put an end to the conversation.

He seemed impatient to be alone. Baker looked from MacLeod to Purcell; he was irritated by his friend's ingenuousness.

'You see,' Purcell went on, his blue eyes fixed gravely on MacLeod's face, 'it seems to me very important to avoid serious disagreements between the inhabitants of the island. Given the rather peculiar conditions in which we're living, the least quarrel can take on tragic proportions.'

'Of course,' MacLeod said vaguely. Both his hands were on the gold and he was impatient. 'I won't contradict you there, Purcell,' he went on, almost compelled to agree by Purcell's clear, persuasive gaze.

'I must admit,' Purcell went on, 'that I'm very much concerned about our relations with the Tahitians. They're not very good. From now on nothing must be done to make them worse.'

'Of course, of course,' MacLeod said absently.

Baker nudged Purcell with his elbow.

'Let's go,' he said in a low voice.

He was embarrassed that Purcell did not realise how little his words counted with MacLeod.

Purcell paused, got up, blushed and said with an effort: 'I've got something more to say to you ... I ... I don't want you to look on me as an enemy. I'm not your enemy.'

And quickly, stiffly, without bending his elbow, he held out his hand to him.

MacLeod drew back a little. For a whole second he looked at Purcell's hand, then at the pile of gold his own were covering. He succeeded at last in detaching his right hand from the gold, took Purcell's and shook it across the table.

'Nor am I yours,' he said without warmth.

When he had let go MacLeod's hand, Purcell turned to Baker

as if to invite him to follow his example.

'Good-bye! ' Baker said.

He went to the door. He was furious at Purcell's blindness. As far as he himself was concerned, he felt far from kindly disposed.

He held the door open for Purcell. White got to his feet and followed Purcell. He too must have noticed MacLeod's impatience for them to go.

As they passed through the little gate in the garden, Purcell turned to White.

'I'm going to see the Tahitians and, as soon as I've arranged matters, I'll come and let you know.'

'Thank you,' White said in his gentle voice.

And he went off with his cat-like tread. His hut was at the northern point of the lozenge, opposite Hunt's.

Baker and Purcell walked some way in silence down East Avenue. They were glad to be in the sun again. MacLeod's hut had seemed cold to them.

Baker had an appointment to meet Avapouhi at nightfall. He would have to wait the whole long day before telling her . . . He could see her slowly opening her beautiful dark eyes, and placing her hands in his: 'Is it true, Ouili, is it true?' How sweet she was . . .

Baker looked at Purcell and said with great feeling: 'Thank you, Purcell.'

Purcell turned his head away and said coldly: 'It's nothing.'

They were embarrassed. Baker thought his thanks too little, but had not the courage to repeat them. Purcell's tone had surprised him.

'I expect MacLeod's biting each coin in turn,' Purcell said.

'The damned Scotsman! ' Baker said through clenched teeth.

'I beg your pardon?' Purcell said, coming to a halt.

Baker stopped too. Purcell drew himself up, frowned and looked coldly at him. Baker stared back in surprise.

'I'm a Scotsman too.'

'I'd forgotten,' Baker mumbled. 'I'm sorry.'

He added: 'Evidently there are exceptions.'

Purcell turned red in the face. 'I've put my foot in it again,' Baker thought.

'No, no,' Purcell said indignantly. 'No, don't say that, Baker! There are no exceptions! There are no exceptions, do you hear? When one has a prejudice against a race, one extends the faults of individuals to the whole race, and limits their qualities to the individual. It's stupid! It's . . . indecent! Believe me! It's more generous to do the opposite.'

'The opposite?' Baker asked gravely.

'To generalise the virtues and consider the faults as exceptions.'

This gave Baker food for thought. After a moment, he began to smile.

'Well,' he said with a mischievous gleam in his brown eyes, 'I'll employ your system, Purcell; and I'll begin by saying that all Scotsmen are shrewd except you.'

'Except me?' Purcell said, looking annoyed as he began to walk on. 'Why do you say that?'

Baker felt he should not have said that either! But the moment of embarrassment had passed. The warmth of friendship lay once again beneath their quarrel. 'By dint of dropping bricks,' Baker thought.

Looking severe, Purcell awaited his answer. He really does look like an angel, Baker thought affectionately. And to think he believes himself to be shrewd!

'Well,' he said quickly, 'when you lectured him at the end, he wasn't even listening. He was simply thinking he wanted to be alone with his gold . . .'

'I noticed it,' Purcell said, suddenly looking sad and tired. 'I had no choice. I wanted him to understand.'

'He added: 'It's completely mad. He doesn't realise. He's created a very dangerous situation.'

'Dangerous?' Baker said. 'Why dangerous?'

They had reached Purcell's hut.

'Are you coming in, Baker?' Purcell said without answering.

Ivoa ran to meet them. Tahitian etiquette prevented her asking questions, but as soon as she saw Baker's face, she went to him: 'É Ouili é!' she said, putting her hands on his shoulders and rubbing her cheek against his. 'É Ouili é! I'm so happy for you!'

Baker smiled, his lower lip quivering. Seeing Ivoa in her hut made his joy at recovering Avapouhi the more present to him.

He said with difficulty, like a schoolboy spelling out a lesson: '*Oua maourou-ourou vaou.*'

'I wonder,' he said, turning to Purcell, 'why "thank you" is so long in Tahitian?'

'They're never in a hurry,' Purcell said.

Baker laughed, looked at Ivoa and repeated gaily: '*Oua maourou-ourou vaou.*'

Ivoa tapped him on the right cheek with the tips of her fingers and spoke to her *tané* in Tahitian.

'She wants to know,' Purcell said, 'when you'll be seeing Avapouhi.'

'Tell her . . . No, wait a minute!' he went on, raising his hand, happiness dancing in his bright brown eyes, 'I'll tell her myself in Tahitian. Ivoa,' he said solemnly, '*aroué!*'

He repeated it with an air of satisfaction: 'Avapouhi, *araoué!*'

'Oh, how happy he is!' Ivoa said, putting her arm round Purcell's shoulder and pressing herself against him. 'Look, man, how happy he is!'

'Sit down,' Purcell said smiling. 'No, not on the stool. In the chair. I've just finished it.'

'Those sliding doors are a good idea,' Baker said, sitting down and looking round him with pleasure. 'It's as if you were on a terrace. The sun's right in your house.'

'When there is any sun,' Purcell said with a grimace. 'Will you stay and share our yams, Baker?'

'Oh, thank you very much,' Baker said. He turned to Ivoa, raised his hand, and repeated, laughing like a drunken man: '*Oua maourou-ourou vaou.*'

Ivoa laughed and spoke to Purcell in Tahitian.

'What does she say about Avapouhi?' Baker said, listening.

'She says she's happy for Avapouhi, for she's as soft as silk.'

'That's it!' Baker said, his eyes bright, 'that's just what she is! She's as soft as silk! Her hands, her eyes, her voice, her movements . . . For instance,' he said, clapping his hands, 'the way she has of raising her eyelids to look at you! Like this!' he said, mimicking her. 'Slowly! Ever so slowly!'

He stopped, surprised at having let himself go. Purcell watched him, smiling.

There was a silence and Baker said abruptly: 'Why did you say that MacLeod had created a very dangerous situation?'

'The Tahitians have a grudge against us.'

'I can see their point,' Baker said. 'One has to admit we've not treated them very well.'

He went on: 'Is it dangerous that they should have a grudge against us? They're such nice chaps.'

'I know a Welshman,' Purcell said, looking him in the eye, 'who's such a nice chap he finds it necessary to give me his knife before starting an argument.'

There was a silence. Baker frowned and said: 'That's what I regret. We'd have no more worries now.'

'Don't talk like that,' Purcell said curtly.

Baker was silent a moment. Then, his brown eyes fixed gravely on Purcell, he said: 'I've been thinking about all this for the last three weeks. I don't agree with you. I understand you, but I'm not of your opinion. For you, a man's life is sacred. But that's where you deceive yourself, sir. You'll see what it'll cost us to have held MacLeod's life sacred.'

As Purcell made no reply, Baker sat up in his chair and went on: 'When we've finished eating, would you mind sending Ivoa to tell Horoa. I don't intend going home till evening, and I'd rather she'd gone. She'd make a scene. She'll be delighted, but she'd make a scene just the same. And another when she arrives at MacLeod's! She's the sort of woman who's only happy when she's having a row!'

He smiled, shrugged and added indulgently: 'The great mare that she is!'

Purcell nodded and Baker leaned back in his chair.

Purcell sat on the floor, his back against the post of the sliding door, his right leg bent under his chin, his left resting on the earth of the garden. His fair hair was shining in the sun.

'There's one thing I don't understand,' Baker said suddenly. 'Why two purses?'

'I knew he'd raise the price.'

'Yes, but why take your whole fortune in those purses? Why not only half?'

'What does it matter?' Purcell said, screwing up his eyes in the sun and looking towards the distant mountain. 'It's as if I were giving him stones.'

'Now, yes, but in twenty years' time?'

Purcell shook his head.

'Whether a frigate arrives here in twenty, twenty-five or thirty years' time, MacLeod won't have the time to enjoy his gold. He'll be hanged.'

'Hanged? Why hanged?'

Purcell looked at the mountain again and said with a detached air: 'There's no prescription for the crime of mutiny.'

Baker sat up in his chair and stared at Purcell in stupefaction. After a moment, he said: 'Oh, so it was you who took him in? Good God!' he went on. 'Scot against Scot! I shall have at least seen that in my life! And it was you who played the more subtle game!'

Purcell smiled, then his smile faded, his eyes turned back to the mountain and his expression grew anxious.

'I know what you're thinking,' Baker said after a moment. 'You're thinking we'd be so happy on this island if it weren't for those bastards. And how many of them are there, in all? Not more than three or four! Smudge, MacLeod, Timi . . . Timi may be a black, but you're not going to tell me he's a nice chap . . . If I were God, do you know what I'd say? I'd say those three were going to spoil things on the island. Well, I'd see only one solution. I'd recall them to Myself . . .'

'But you're not God,' Purcell said.

9

The fugitives returned that evening. It was a great triumph for the women, some little satisfaction to the Tahitians, and a loss of face for the Skeleton. Omaata rang the bell in Blossom Square and, except for the members of the majority, all the village assembled. Itia and Avapouhi were crowned with flowers as if for a sacrifice. Their eyes glowed, their laughter rang out and they seemed bursting with health.

There was much merriment. Everyone rubbed their cheeks, poked them and gave them little taps. Purcell arrived, took them by the shoulders, put his nose to their necks and sniffed them. This made everyone laugh, for it was how Tahitian mothers embraced their babies. Purcell adored these women's skins, which were so soft and perfumed, and seemed to melt under one's fingers.

Omaata made a speech. Things had returned to normal. In the end, it had been the women who had chosen their *tanés,* and not the other way round. When she had finished, the fugitives were cross-questioned: why weren't they wet? Where had they taken refuge during the great rain? How had they fed themselves? But they obstinately refused to reply and, smiling, their black lashes lowered on to their cheeks, their heads close together, they kept their secret.

In the evening, by the light of the *doédoés,* there were dances and singing in the market-place. It surpassed in joy and lasciviousness anything Purcell had hitherto seen. Ouili and Ropati took part and were almost as wild as the Tahitians. There were cries of pleasure when Jono arrived with Omaata, and began dancing like a bear. After a while, they went to fetch the yellow man. No one bore him any grudge. He had been so gentle and so polite. Itia rubbed her cheek against his and, to console him for having had to give up the *vahiné* he desired, two or three women made advances to him which pleased him.

The next day, the sou'wester gave way to the trade wind, and sunny days and bright nights began again. For the Tahitians, who counted by nights and not by days, the Christmas of the *Peritanis* fell on the ninth night of the eleventh moon. This night like every night in the month, had a name. It was called Tamatea, or 'the moon that lights the fish at sunset'.

Its sign was propitious. And, indeed, Mehani was lucky enough to kill a wild pig at his first shot during the afternoon. He took it to Omaata who cleaned it while the women prepared the oven. It occurred to Purcell to send White to Mason and the members of the majority to suggest they should all dine together that night in Blossom Square, by the light of the moon, to celebrate Christmas and memories of home. He also asked

Mehani to invite the Tahitians to join the *Peritanis*.

But within the hour Purcell realised that his hopes were illusions and the extent to which their positions had already hardened. His invitations were refused. MacLeod said he much regretted it but he was entertaining his friends that night. All the members of the majority refused in turn. They were dining with MacLeod. Purcell had the impression that MacLeod had used White to send out his personal invitations at the same time as his own.

Mason was ruder. 'He says there's no answer,' White reported, embarrassed to have to transmit such a snub to Purcell.

'And the sextant?'

'I gave it to him from you.'

'What did he say?'

'He said: "Good".'

Purcell raised his eyebrows.

'Is that all?'

'Yes.'

'Did you tell him how it came into my hands?'

'Yes.'

'What did he say?'

'Nothing.'

'He didn't give you any message for me?'

'No.'

Purcell scrutinised White's face. But the half-caste never lied. He was so scrupulous that he was not even content merely to repeat a message word for word. He reproduced the intonations and even mimed the facial expressions that had accompanied it. For instance, when he said 'good' there could be no mistake but that it was Mason's curt and haughty 'good'.

The Tahitians' reply bore every appearance of courtesy. They thanked Adamo a thousand times. They were very honoured to be invited, they and *their three women,* to share the *Peritani's* meal. But they regretted that circumstances forced them to decline the invitation.

Purcell was weeding his garden when Mehani brought him this reply.

'They said "our three women"?' he asked, looking up.

'Yes.'

'Who said that? Tetahiti?'

'Yes.'

'He was speaking in the name of them all?'

Mehani nodded. After a moment, Purcell went on: 'Why is he the chief here? In Tahiti, your father is as important as his.'

'He's old; he's thirty.'

'And if I invited him to dine in my hut tonight?'

'He would refuse.'

And as Purcell remained silent, Mehani added: 'He says that you are not *moa*.'

'I have lied to no purpose,' Purcell thought sadly. 'And now that I've begun, I shall have to go on lying. To Ivoa, to Mehani . . .'

'But you know,' Mehani said, 'I don't believe it either.'

And as Purcell looked at him in stupefaction, Mehani began laughing.

'And I hope you don't either, Adamo?'

Purcell looked at him, not knowing what to reply. Mehani tapped him on the shoulder, stopped laughing, and said seriously: 'They don't believe it. That's why I have to go on saying you are.'

There was a silence and Purcell said: 'What's all this comedy about?'

'Well,' Mehani said, looking away, 'if I didn't say you were, I couldn't come to dine with you tonight.'

'If you didn't say it and came, what would happen?'

'I would be a traitor.'

Purcell started.

'So we've reached that point, have we?' he said slowly.

He went on, his throat constricted: 'What do they think I am, if I'm not *moa*? An accomplice?'

Mehani made no reply. After a moment he took Purcell's hand, raised it to his face and placed it against his cheek.

'You'll come?' Purcell said.

'I'll come, brother,' Mehani replied.

He looked at Purcell with a glow of affection in his eyes.

'With Itia,' he went on.

'What?' Purcell said. 'They'll let Itia come?'

'You should know, Adamo, that no one can give Itia orders.'

'Not even you?'

'Not even I!' Mehani said laughing.

On Christmas Day, therefore, they all ate of the same pig cooked in the same oven by the same hands, but they ate it in different places: the Tahitians in their hut; the majority at Mac-Leod's; the minority, Itia and Mehani at Purcell's; and Mason in his own hut.

At noon three days later, there was a knock on Purcell's door. It was White. He did not come in.

'MacLeod has sent me to ask if you have had any fish.'

The table was laid three paces away from the half-caste, and the fish was on it, lying white and smooth on a banana leaf. But White saw nothing. His eyes were tactfully lowered. And Purcell had the impression that if he said 'no', White would repeat his 'no' to MacLeod without comment.

'Have a look,' Purcell said.

White raised his eyes, looked at the table, said 'thank you' and turned on his heel.

'White,' Purcell said quickly, 'what's it all about? Haven't you had any?'

White turned and said tonelessly: 'None of us has had any.'

Purcell turned to Ivoa and said in Tahitian: 'Where does this fish come from?'

'Mehani brought it.'

'Were they fishing this morning?'

'Yes,' Ivoa said briefly, looking away.

'But they didn't ring the bell when they got back?'

'No.'

'Apart from me, to whom did they give fish?'

'To no one. It was Mehani. Mehani caught some extra for us, Ouili and Ropati.'

There was a silence and Purcell said: 'They no longer want to fish for the *Peritani*?'

'No.'

Purcell sighed and turned to White: 'This is what she says . . .'

White shook his head.

'I understood what she was saying. Thank you.'

'White!'

White stopped at the door.

'Please tell MacLeod I wasn't aware of what was going on.'

'I'll tell him.'

Two days later Jones visited Purcell in the afternoon. He was dressed only in a *pareu,* as was his habit.

'Am I disturbing you?'

Purcell shut his book and smiled.

'Do you know how many books there were in the ship's library?'

'No.'

'Forty-eight. And I have all my life to read them in. Take the chair.'

'I'll put it in the sun,' Jones said.

Bending down, he seized the heavy oak chair by one leg. Then he stood up, holding it at arm's length, the muscles of his shoulders standing out with the effort. He took three paces forward, crouched down and placed it on the ground, the chair's four feet touching down not only at the same instant but so gently that they made no noise at all.

'Bravo! ' Purcell said smiling.

After this exploit, Jones sat down, his eyes lowered, looking shy and distant.

Ivoa came in.

'É Ropati é! ' she said, raising her right hand and fluttering her outspread fingers.

She went to him smiling, and placed a maternal hand on his short hair. His blue eyes fixed on the distance, Jones offered his cheek to her. He was like an affectionate child impatiently waiting for the effusions to cease so that he could go on with his game.

'Your hair's like mown grass,' Ivoa said.

Purcell translated.

'My hair's not green,' Jones said.

He laughed. Then he frowned again above his short nose, crossed his arms, clasped his biceps and felt them with an expression of severity.

'MacLeod and his lot went fishing this morning,' he said almost as if making a dramatic announcement. 'I saw them coming back. They'd caught masses of fish! '

On the word 'masses' his voice suddenly rose to a falsetto.

Jones blushed. He disliked his voice playing tricks on him.

'Well?' Purcell said.

'They didn't ring the bell,' Jones said indignantly. 'They preferred to throw some of the fish away rather than give us any.'

'That's bad,' Purcell said, and fell silent.

'After all, by not giving the Tahitians any, they were merely paying them back in their own coin. But what have we done to them?'

Purcell shrugged.

'Do you know what we'll do?' Jones said, uncrossing his arms and thrusting his chest out aggressively. 'We'll go fishing tomorrow, you, Ouili and I . . .'

'An excellent idea!' Purcell said, interrupting him. 'I see what you mean. When we get back, we'll ring the bell and distribute fish to everyone . . .'

Jones opened his eyes wide and his mouth formed an O.

'Very well,' Purcell said, giving him no time to protest, 'go and warn Baker and collect worms with him. It's already late in the afternoon.'

He got to his feet, accompanied Jones to the door and watched him going off along West Avenue. Jones walked with a certain deliberation, his head high, and the muscles of his back held taut to square his shoulders.

'Why are you smiling?' Ivoa asked.

Purcell turned.

'He's a nice boy, funny and nice.'

Still watching Jones, Purcell went on after a moment: 'I should like to have a son.'

'May *Eatua* hear you,' Ivoa said.

The 'minority' had good fishing, but Purcell's generosity had no effect. The Tahitians refused his fish. The majority accepted them, but omitted to return the politeness when they went fishing themselves. Vaa accepted her share both on this occasion and on the following ones. As for Mason, he either did not know, or refused to know, the origin of the fish that appeared on his table, for during the whole of the following month he continued to ignore the greetings of those who fed him.

January went by. Ivoa was pregnant and beginning to count the days, or rather the nights, till she would be brought to bed.

She placed the date in the month of the sixth moon, and hoped that it would be in the last quarter (which was auspicious) and, if Eatua granted her desire, on the wonderful night of the Erotooéréoré, or the 'Night when the fish come up from the depths'. She was very proud of the fact that Adamo's child would be the first to be born on the island. She considered it a splendid omen for his future.

Tahitian women, in general, are not considered to be very fecund. Captain Cook considered this a wise dispensation of heaven, considering the freedom of their morals and the smallness of their island. In any case, Ivoa was still at this date the only one to have become pregnant, and they had to wait till April before they knew in which hut the second baby would be born. In fact, towards the end of March, the Tahitian women began to have their suspicions. But it seemed so unlikely that they preferred to attribute the appearance to increasing stoutness due to a sedentary life. By April, however, there could be no further doubt. And when Vaa, the day after the night of Tourou (the night on which fish and crabs visit each other), appeared at the market to fetch her share of wild pig, her stoutness was so obvious that a deep silence fell over the queue of *vahinés*. The news created a sensation on the island which lasted for a fortnight. And Itia even made up a naïvely obscene song about it. But after they had had a good laugh, the women began to hold Vaa in respect. At the time of the sharing out of the women, she had said in public that she would 'warm' the chief of the big canoe. To all appearances she had succeeded.

April also brought a disappointment: the yam harvest was poor. It was carefully shared out among the community. Everyone made a clamp beside his hut in which to store his share, which was to be used with the greatest economy, so that there should be no interregnum before the next year's harvest, and no inroads made on the wild yams. These, indeed, were an important reserve in case next year's harvest turned out to be an even greater failure.

At the beginning of May, MacLeod told Purcell that, when passing the blacks' clamp, he had noticed it was already much reduced. At the speed with which they were using up their yams, they would not last six months, in which case the blacks would

obviously eat the wild yams and so make inroads on their reserve. MacLeod asked Purcell to intervene. They must be told
to consume less.

MacLeod was quite right, as Purcell realised when he went
to have a look at the Tahitians' clamp. He talked to them, but
did not mention MacLeod's name.

At his very first words, he became aware of obvious incom-
prehension. In Tahiti, nature provided everything in such
abundance that the notion of depriving oneself in the present for
the sake of the future seemed to the Tahitians to be one of
those *maamaa* ideas peculiar to the *Peritani*. Indeed, when there
were no cultivated yams left, there would be wild ones. When
there were no wild yams left, there would be fruit. And when
there was no more fruit, there would always be fish. As long as
a man had a good harpoon in his practised hand, he would
never die of hunger. Purcell began his explanations all over
again. He persuaded no one. And, after an hour, he realised that
the Tahitians thought his intervention impertinent. He said
good-bye and left them.

A week after this conversation. White came to tell Purcell
that there would be an assembly after the midday meal at
MacLeod's hut. The meeting place surprised Purcell. Why not
under the banyan as usual? White shook his head. He did not
know. But the meeting was very important. MacLeod had said
so.

At about two o'clock, instead of going directly to the Scotsman's hut, Purcell went along West Avenue to see Baker and
Jones. He found neither of them. They had left for the Skeleton
five minutes ago. He then turned into Nor'wester Street with the
intention of going to MacLeod's through the coconut plantation.
He had scarcely taken ten paces into the trees when he saw Itia
sitting at the foot of a pandanus. She watched him approach
with lowered head, her eyes bright behind her lashes. He
stopped.

'What are you doing here, Itia?'

'I was waiting for you,' she said with effrontery.

'Waiting for me!' he said laughing. 'How did you know I'd
come this way? It's not my usual road.'

'I followed you. You didn't see me. I was in the undergrowth.

Man, it was funny! I followed you from your house. I knew from Horoa that you were going to the Skeleton's.'

'Well,' Purcell said, 'what do you want?'

She got to her feet and came towards him, her round laughing face raised to him. She stopped a yard away, put her dimpled arms behind her back, and said sweetly: 'I want you to kiss me, Adamo, please.'

'That's quite enough,' Purcell said severely. 'I don't kiss the woman who belongs to Mehani.'

'And to Tetahiti,' Itia said. 'And even a little to Kori.'

'Precisely,' Purcell said, 'you have three *tanés*. Isn't that enough?'

'Two,' Itia said. 'Kori's only a little bit.'

Purcell laughed.

'Why are you laughing?' Itia said, hiding the lower part of her face in her shoulder, but leaving her bright eyes showing. 'It's not taboo to have two *tanés*. And why shouldn't you have two women, Adamo? I'm sure it would do you good to have two women.'

Purcell was disarmed and laughed. Itia was a child of nature: instinct, kindness and guile were there in a naïve state, but already concentrated on one object with the indomitable persistence of her sex.

She was no longer laughing. She was watching him.

'You've got a new necklace,' Purcell said.

'They're pandanus kernels. See how good they smell,' Itia said, rising on tiptoe and holding her necklace out to him.

The kernels were a beautiful orange colour and strung on a liana. Purcell smelt them and his temples began beating. Never had he smelt anything more intoxicating. He realised Itia's intention too late. She threw herself against his chest, put her arms round his waist, clasped him with all her might and clung to him. She was using the tactics that had succeeded so well on the day *The Blossom* had been set on fire.

She was exquisitely perfumed. To the scent of the pandanus kernels was added the sweet warm odour of the *tiaré* flowers she wore in her hair.

'Itia,' Purcell said in a low voice, 'will you let me go if I kiss you?'

He saw his mistake at once. He was capitulating too quickly. She was going to exploit her advantage.

'Yes,' she said, her eyes bright, 'but not just a little kiss like last time.'

He felt her little fresh supple body against his. He leaned down and kissed her. Then he detached her two little hands from behind his back, brought them round in front of him and said: 'You'll go away now?'

'Yes,' she said, looking at him with moist eyes.

And she ran off. She seemed to be flying through the undergrowth like a sunbeam. 'It's disgraceful,' Purcell said in a low voice. But there was no point in lying to himself. He did not feel disgraceful. He saw Itia's little face and her expressive little body before him. Her manner, her mimicry, her attitude, her whole feminine dance of seduction . . . All these were clearly intended to produce a certain effect. Indeed, it was all so obvious. But the irony was that, though one saw it and knew it, the desired effect was produced all the same.

When Purcell entered MacLeod's hut, all the British on the island, with the exception of Mason, were there, crowded round the table. MacLeod, cadaverous and important, was lording it over them, his thin hand lying flat on a big sheet of paper covered with an irregular network of lines.

Baker indicated to Purcell an empty stool between himself and Jones, and Jones got up to let him pass. Purcell murmured: 'Good afternoon', without looking at anyone in particular. There was a silence, and then MacLeod said: 'We were waiting for you.' His tone was not aggressive. He was merely stating a fact.

When he had taken his seat, Purcell glanced at the sheet of paper. He recognized it as a rough map of the island, or at least of the non-mountainous part of the island. The shape of Blossom Bay seemed to him rather fanciful, but he identified the map from the lozenge of the village and the rectangular houses flanking it.

'My lads,' MacLeod said, 'we've got to discuss the question of the land.'

He paused and Purcell felt that, for once, it was not part of his usual play-acting. At the word 'land' his expression had become grave.

'We've had a bad harvest,' MacLeod went on in his drawling voice, 'but that's not so much what's worrying me, seeing that harvests are like women; there are good and bad ones and, taking one with another as you might say, they even out. No, what's worrying me, my lads, is that there are some people on this island who're no more provident than a sparrow on a branch and who've already made a hell of an inroad into their clamp. At the speed they're going, I can see very well what's going to happen. In three months' time, they'll be going after the wild yams. And who'll suffer for it? I! You! All of us! The wild yams are our reserve! They're sacred! But do you think the blacks'll care about that when they've got nothing left to eat? So what can we do? Mount guard? It might be possible by day, but by night the blacks have only to strip themselves naked and we wouldn't see them even if they were stealing our vegetables.'

MacLeod put his hands flat on the edge of the table and glanced round at his audience as if to impress on them the seriousness of the situation.

'In short,' he said, 'there's one thing that just won't do, and that's holding everything in common, as we've done. It was bound not to work. And you've already seen it over the fishing. The blacks have decided there'll be no more fish for the rest of us. All right. The result is that there are three teams fishing in this island.'

'It's your fault there are more than two,' Purcell said drily.

'Of course!' Baker cut in resolutely. 'We made you a present and you didn't reciprocate it.'

Jones had not been listening very attentively. He was taken unawares and contented himself with a vigorous nod. MacLeod and his friends made no reply. MacLeod must have warned his followers against being provoked by the minority.

'As for the Tahitians' decision,' Purcell went on, 'I don't approve of it. But there are excuses for them. They've been despoiled. If you'd included them in the sharing out of the women, things would never have come to this.'

MacLeod's thin lips parted in a smile and the dark hollows beneath his eyes became accentuated.

'You may say that, Purcell,' he said in his drawling voice, 'but if Ivoa had been put in the pool to be shared out with the others, you wouldn't have agreed! Oh no! You wouldn't have agreed at all! You want everything to be in common! And you'll put everything in, except the main thing.'

'There's no connection!' Purcell said with irritation. 'You don't share out women as you do yams. They've got a say in the matter.'

And he added cuttingly: 'As, indeed, you saw for yourself.'

After that remark, there was a silence. MacLeod did not flinch. As for Baker, he wisely said nothing. He did not even smile.

'Suppose,' MacLeod said at last with a wave of the hand, as if he were sweeping aside an irrelevant argument . . .

'Wait a minute,' Purcell said, 'I haven't finished. I want to remind you that there are still several things we do in common on this island, and that they're very important to us. For instance, the water fatigue. Imagine a situation in which each of us had to go and fetch water for himself . . .'

'There's another thing we have in common too,' Baker said. 'Wild pigs. Till now there've been no separate teams to go after pig. And why? Because it's more convenient. And it's more convenient, when a pig has been killed, to hand it over to Omaata and the women. It has to be drawn, washed, cooked in the oven with all the things that go with it, and cut up. There's no one team that would care to do all that work. And the moral of it is,' he concluded, looking at MacLeod, 'that when it suits you, you share; and when it doesn't suit you, you don't . . .'

'Well said, my lad!' MacLeod said with a wide smile, glancing triumphantly round as if Baker had summed up his own thought.

He went on: 'And one would be very stupid to share when it doesn't suit one!'

As Baker made to speak, he went on : 'And as for the land, my lads, it suits me that it should be shared out, because I want to be able to say: "I put my back into it, I dig, I weed and I hoe . . . My plot's properly worked. And what it yields, I eat." And now, Purcell, I'm going to tell you this: if there's a bastard next door who contemplates his navel instead of getting down to work, and has to tighten his belt to the bone because he's got no harvest at the end of the year, well, I'm sorry for him, but there it is. It's each for himself, and that's how I see things . . .'

Purcell looked at him. He was a Highland crofter. As the result of toil, his heart was stone. His head, too.

'Well, what have you got to say about that?' MacLeod went on, as Purcell remained silent.

'I'm against the principle,' Purcell said. 'In my view, the best solution was the communal one. But since things have reached the point they have – with three or even four parties on the island – it may be better to do as you suggest so as to avoid quarrels. On condition, of course, that the land is shared out . . .'

He paused and said emphatically: '. . . equitably.'

'You can count on me for that,' MacLeod said with a brilliant smile.

And Purcell suddenly understood the nature of the ascendancy the Scotsman exercised over the majority. MacLeod was not only the most intelligent. With all his hardness, he strangely enough had charm.

'I also think it better to divide the land,' Baker said. 'I don't want people coming to my place to see if I'm eating too many yams.'

MacLeod did not take this up.

'We'll be fair to every bastard on the island,' he said gravely, placing his hand on the map. 'Everything'll be done in a regular way. I've made a survey of the cultivable land with White. We used *The Blossom*'s log, and I bet it's the first time the damned log's measured land instead of being dragged through the sea from a ship's poop. When we'd finished we made a plan, as I said, and we've divided it up into equal parts. So that there'll be no argument, I suggest we draw lots for each plot . . .'

He turned to Purcell and gave him another disarming smile.

'You won't say that's not equitable, Purcell?'

'It seems to be,' Purcell said with some reserve.

So much sweetness and light put him on his guard.

'But I warn you, my lads,' MacLeod went on, looking round at them, 'not to get too excited. The plots aren't big ones. Don't start imagining yourselves to be landed gentry. No! The fact is we mustn't touch the fruit trees and, if we clear the wood, the soil's so thin on the rock that a strong sou'wester will blow it all into the sea. I've worked it out, my lads. There's no more than eighteen acres of cultivable land, and that comes to two acres each . . .'

Purcell started.

'Two acres!' he said in astonishment. 'You've divided it into nine parts!'

'What of it?' MacLeod said, raising his eyebrows. 'Aren't there nine of us?'

'What about the Tahitians!' Purcell cried.

'I haven't forgotten them,' MacLeod replied. 'They'll help the whites work their land, and they'll be paid in kind for their labour.'

'You must be mad, MacLeod!' Purcell cried, pale with anger. 'You ought to be shut up! You're making serfs of them! They'll never accept!'

'I don't care a damn whether they accept or not,' MacLeod said. 'I'm not going to give good land to people who are too lazy to work it. You should see what they do with their land in Tahiti. It's a disgrace! The black's all right for fishing, or for climbing a coconut tree. But he's no good at cultivation. That's what I say.'

'MacLeod,' Purcell said, his voice trembling, 'you don't understand. In Tahiti, even the poorest has his garden and his clump of coconuts. The people who have no land in Tahiti are those who've been deprived of it, the criminals, the dregs of the island. You don't realise what you're doing by depriving our Tahitians of land! It's to insult them in the gravest possible way! If you smacked their faces in turn, you'd be doing no worse!'

MacLeod nodded towards Purcell and looked round at the majority as if to say that this was what he expected.

'Everyone knows you've got a kind heart, Purcell,' he said sardonically, 'and that you dote on the blacks. But I'm here to tell you that I don't care a damn what the blacks think. The blacks don't count with me. They don't interest me at all. The only thing I found them rather useful for was fishing. And that's now finished. So what use are they? None. Useless mouths, that's what they are. As far as I'm concerned, they can put their damned carcasses on a raft and go and drown themselves between here and Tahiti. It'd mean nothing to me.'

'We were very glad to get them to crew *The Blossom*,' young Jones said, squaring his shoulders. 'If it hadn't been for the blacks, we should never have got here.'

'And that's true! ' Johnson said.

Everyone looked at Johnson. He had openly approved a criticism of MacLeod by the minority.

They were even more astonished when he got to his feet. He stood there awkwardly for a moment, his pectoral muscles slack, and his thin little stomach projecting. He hesitantly rubbed the purple patches in his beard.

'You must excuse me,' he said in his hoarse, quavering voice, 'this looks as if it'll be a long discussion. I must go. I've got to cut wood for my wife.'

'Sit down,' MacLeod said. 'Your wife can wait.'

'I've promised to cut some,' Johnson replied, rubbing his beard and gradually disengaging himself from his stool. 'And what's promised is promised. I'm not the man to go back on my word,' he added, drawing himself up with a pathetic attempt at dignity.

He began edging almost imperceptibly towards the door.

'For Christ's sake sit down,' MacLeod said. 'Sit down, I tell you! We're discussing something important and everyone ought to be present! '

'I give you my vote,' Johnson said, continuing his retreat with scarcely visible steps, his feet dragging on the boards. 'What's promised is promised,' he went on, raising his voice rather ridiculously and putting his hand on the latch of the door. 'And when old Johnson's given his word, he's not the man to go back on it.'

'I know what's the matter,' Smudge said laughing. 'You're frightened your trollop will beat you.'

Johnson turned pale, drew himself up and said almost firmly: 'I allow no one to talk of my wife like that.'

'I should care,' Smudge said. 'Meanwhile, come and sit down, or I'll come and get you.'

He got to his feet. But Baker leaned forward and gave Smudge a little tap above the knee with his forefinger.

'Leave him alone,' he said quietly, fixing his glittering eyes on him. 'You've got his vote, that should be enough.'

There was a long silence which became almost unbearable so strange was the situation. The two men on their feet were perfectly still. Johnson with his hand on the latch had been turned into a statue by Smudge's threatening glance. And Smudge himself was pale, furious and petrified by Baker's eyes.

'Sit down, Smudge,' MacLeod said suddenly in a loud easy voice. 'And you, Johnson, go and cut wood for your Indian, no one will blame you for that.'

His intervention saved his lieutenant's face and also deprived Baker of the advantage of his interference. Smudge sat down, and as he did so seemed to shrivel up on his stool, his rat's face looking flat and shrunken with fear.

'Thank you, MacLeod,' Johnson said, his red watery eyes fixed gratefully on the Scotsman.

And he went out, humble, bent, and dragging his feet, without a glance for Baker.

'We were talking of the blacks,' Jones said, frowning over his little nose.

He was proud of his last intervention and wanted it to be remembered.

'MacLeod,' Purcell said, 'the Tahitians came with us out of friendship and because they wanted to share in our adventure. We can't deprive them of their share of the land, it's not possible.'

'They gave up during the storm!' Smudge cried, suddenly recovering all his virulence. 'And that, I'll never forget! We had to go aloft alone! The bastards have got no guts! They've got no more guts between the six of them than a chicken!'

'It's scarcely up to you to talk of guts,' Baker said.

'And talking of guts,' Jones said, 'you won't go swimming among the sharks as they do. Nor will I.'

He felt his biceps and glanced severely round at the others. He had made short work of Smudge.

'Jones is quite right,' Purcell went on. 'We're not afraid of a bit of bad weather, and the Tahitians aren't afraid of sharks. Courage is a question of habit. Besides, it's not a question of judging them, but of giving them land. Having decided to steal their share from them, you're finding every possible fault in them. They're cowardly, they're lazy . . . It's absurd. The truth is you don't want to admit they've got the same rights as you have.'

MacLeod slowly spread wide his long arms, clasped the two corners of the table with his thin hands, and said with exasperation: 'I don't care a damn for their rights. Do you hear, Purcell, I don't care a damn for their rights. A fish also has a right to live before it's caught, but that doesn't prevent my hooking it. If we shared the land with the blacks, it would mean fifteen plots of scarcely more than an acre each. I say it's not possible. I need two acres to live comfortably and enough food for my wife, myself and my children, if I have any. We must think of the future. I'm not going to be generous towards people who don't even give me fish.'

'It's not a question of being generous or not. You're defrauding them.'

'All right,' MacLeod said, raising his hands and letting them fall back on the table with a bang. 'All right, I agree. I'm defrauding them. So what?'

There was a silence and Purcell said hoarsely: 'It means war. Don't you understand?'

'So what?' MacLeod said in the same tone of exasperation. 'They don't frighten me. We've got muskets. They haven't.'

Purcell stared him in the eye.

'That's a horrible thing to say, MacLeod.'

MacLeod uttered a little laugh, and said in a voice vibrant with anger: 'I'm much concerned for your feelings, Purcell, but if you've nothing further to say, we might put it to the vote.'

Purcell drew himself up.

'We'll put it to the vote,' he said bitingly, 'and I'll tell you what'll happen. Smudge will vote with you, because he shares your opinion; Johnson has given you his vote, because he's afraid of Smudge; and Hunt, because he doesn't understand. And White, who probably doesn't agree with you, will abstain out of friendship. You'll therefore have four votes against three. There's no longer an assembly on this island, MacLeod, there's a tyranny. And it's yours. I won't tolerate it any longer.'

'What's all this song and dance?' MacLeod said.

'Let me speak,' Purcell said, getting to his feet. 'You're committing a folly and I won't be associated with it. I lack words to

H

describe what you're about to do. It's . . . it's . . . it's indecent. And all this simply to have one acre the more!' he added, suddenly raising his voice. 'I shall not take part in the vote, MacLeod, neither in this one nor in any others. From this moment, I'm no longer a member of the assembly.'

'That goes for me too,' Baker said. 'I'm disgusted with your tricks. And I shall be delighted not to have to see so much of you, you and your henchman.'

'And for me too,' Jones said.

He sought for something cutting to add, but could think of nothing, so contented himself with frowning.

'I'm not detaining you,' MacLeod said calmly. 'You're as free as air. But talking of feelings, I can't ever remember my heart beating at the sight of Baker, and perhaps in time I'll be able to console myself for not seeing him. But let me tell you, Purcell,' he went on with sudden warmth, 'that you don't know what you're talking about and that an acre's an acre. Perhaps not for you who've never lacked for anything. But I can tell you this, if my mother had had an acre more, I'd have had enough to eat as a boy, and she wouldn't have had to work herself to death. All right. Though I tell you this, it's of no interest to anybody. You want to go, and you go. Perhaps I'll weep a little on Smudge's shoulder when you've gone, but I shall reconcile myself to it. All right,' he went on, 'you're going. We'll draw the plots of land by lot, and we'll send White to tell you which are yours. You can trust MacLeod. It'll all be done according to rule. Blacks are blacks, and whites are whites. And I shan't do a chap of my own colour out of one square inch, tyranny or not.'

Purcell went to the door, looking pale and tense. There was nothing he could do. He had not a card in his hand. To leave the assembly was the only possible solution. The act of resigning did him good, but it was wholly ineffective.

'Good-bye, Purcell,' MacLeod said, as Purcell reached the door with Jones and Baker at his heels.

Purcell looked at him, surprised by the tone of his voice. It was odd, but at that moment there was regret in MacLeod's eyes. 'He's going to be bored,' Purcell thought. 'He loved organizing the assembly against me. No opposition, no assembly, that's obvious. I've broken his toy.'

'Good-bye,' Purcell said after a second's silence. 'If you want to reconstitute an assembly, you know my terms.'

'I know them and I don't like them,' MacLeod said with dignity.

Purcell was scarcely aware of the warm sun on his chest. He was at once furious and very anxious. Baker was on his right, and young Jones on Baker's right.

'Well, that's done it!' Jones said after a moment.

Purcell made no reply. Baker nodded and young Jones said in a happy, excited voice: 'Well, what do we do now? Do we form a second assembly?'

Baker nudged his arm.

'That's it. Purcell will be the leader. You the opposition. And I shall abstain.'

'I was being serious,' Jones said frowning.

'And aren't I serious?' Baker said.

They had reached Mason's hut, and Jones said sulkily: 'I'll go by Trade Wind Street. I'm going home. I'll leave you.'

'Stay with us, Ropati,' Baker said smiling. 'You can go round by East Avenue. Stay with us,' he went on, taking him by the arm. (And Jones immediately flexed his biceps.) 'Stay with us. You don't know how much I learn by listening to you.'

'Shut up.'

'Why "shut up"?'

'Shut up, you beast.'

'What language,' Baker said primly. 'This island's full of vulgar chaps. I shall leave it.'

'Do you see this huge fist?' Jones said, brandishing it under his nose.

'I have eyes and I see,' Baker said with a pious air.

'I shall hit you in the ribs with it.'

'I put the proposal to the vote,' Baker said, assuming a Scottish accent. 'A vote is a vote, my lad, and it'll all be done according to rule. Ropati's proposal. Who's for it?'

'I'm for it,' Jones said.

'I'm against. So is the angel Gabriel.'

'Hush!'

'He can't hear. He has ears and he can't hear.'

'Amen,' Jones said. 'How does the vote stand?'

'Two votes against. One for. Ropati's proposal rejected. The law is the law.'

'Whoever violates the law shall be hanged.'

'Well said, my lad,' Baker said.

He resumed his normal tone.

'I'm glad not to have to meet those two any more. If there was another island near this one I'd go and live on it.'

'What are you talking about?' Purcell said suddenly, raising his head.

'About another island near this one.'

'MacLeod would want to conquer it,' Jones said.

'Listen,' Purcell said, 'I've got a proposal to make.'

'What did I say?' Jones cried, his porcelain blue eyes laughing. 'We're forming another assembly!'

'This is what I propose,' Purcell went on.

He stopped and looked at each of them in turn.

'We'll go and see the Tahitians and share our land with them.'

'You mean our three plots?' Baker said, coming to a halt. 'We won't have much each.'

'Two-thirds of an acre.'

There was a silence. Baker looked at the ground, his brown face suddenly serious and tense.

'What a shame!' he said after a moment. 'MacLeod and his lot will have two acres each, and we and the Tahitians two-thirds of an acre!'

He went on: 'Rich and poor. Already.'

'You can say no,' Purcell said.

'I've not said I'll say no,' Baker said frowning.

He walked on and said after a moment: 'But I dislike the idea of my children being a poor man's children.'

He came to a halt and, raising his face to the sky, suddenly cried aloud, his brown eyes bright with anger: 'And all because of those bastards!'

The phrase rose in a crescendo to the word 'bastards', which he yelled out with incredible violence.

There was a silence and Baker said: 'I'm sorry.'

'I expect you feel better now,' Purcell said.

'Much better. Let's go now.'

'Where?' Jones asked.

'To the blacks to tell them we'll share.'

'But I haven't given my opinion,' Jones said.

'Give it.'

'I'm for it,' Jones said. 'Three votes to four. Purcell's proposal adopted.'

And he began laughing. Baker looked at Purcell and they exchanged a smile.

The Tahitians' daily siesta was scarcely over when the three British reached their hut. The Tahitians went to bed late at night and rose early in the morning, but they slept for three or four hours in the middle of the day. It was this habit which had given the British the idea that they were 'lazy'.

The big hut's sliding wall was wide open to the south. As he drew near, Purcell could see them stretching and relaxing after their siesta. The Tahitians must have seen them too, but with the exception of Mehani, who was already coming towards them down Cliff Lane with a smile on his lips, none of them greeted them or even seemed to see them.

As they approached, Tetahiti came out on to the wide open space in front of the hut, took up an axe and began splitting tree-stumps. Purcell admired the long, athletic line of his body as he raised the axe above his head. His body curved backwards like a bow. For a second, axe and body seemed suspended in the air, and then came down in a semi-circle with the speed of a whip. The movement was so quick that the axe appeared to leave a blue wake against the silver-grey sky.

Purcell stopped within two yards of him, but Tetahiti did not deign to interrupt his work. Tahitian courtesy was compensated by a whole range of minor insolences. This one was marked. Purcell was irritated and said drily: 'Tetahiti, I want to talk to you. It's important.'

This *Peritani* abruptness was unusual in Adamo and Tetahiti realised he was hurt. He felt rather ashamed of having offended him without provocation, arrested the movement of his axe as he was raising it and laid it on the ground. Then he made a gesture towards the hut to attract his comrades' attention, sat down on one of the stumps, and signed to the three *Peritani* to do likewise. It was a half-courtesy. He accepted the meeting,

but did not ask them to come into the hut and sat down before
they did.

It was a moment before Purcell spoke. He had never been
very intimate with Tetahiti. His cold exterior disconcerted him.
Tetahiti was as tall and strong as Mehani but, though he was
only thirty, all trace of youth had left his face. There were two
deep lines each side of his mouth, a vertical wrinkle on his forehead between the eyebrows, and his eyes, behind heavy lids, had
not the gentleness of Mehani's.

Purcell began with polite formalities about the weather, what
the prospects were, about fishing and the harvest. Baker and
Jones sat behind him, resigned to a long and incomprehensible
conversation. And while Purcell was talking, Mehani came and
sat in front of him on Tetahiti's right. His elbows on his knees,
he kept clasping and unclasping his fingers, his head lowered
and his eyes on the ground. Ohou and Timi took up their positions on Tetahiti's left, but slightly behind him. As for Mehoro
and Kori, who had become great friends since Kori had nearly
killed Mehoro on board *The Blossom,* they remained sitting on
the edge of the hut with their legs hanging down.

'Tetahiti,' Purcell said at last, 'something very serious has
happened, Ouili, Ropati and I have left the *Peritani* assembly.'

Tetahiti gave a slight nod. It meant: 'I'm honoured by the
confidence.' It was a courtesy, but a courtesy that kept a
distance between them. From under his heavy lids, his attentive
eyes were continuously on Adamo, though they expressed no
impatience to hear more.

'The assembly has decided to share out the land,' Purcell went
on, 'the division is unjust, and that's why we have left the
assembly.'

Tetahiti remained silent. His face showed neither interest nor
astonishment.

'The assembly,' Purcell said straight out, 'has decided to
divide the land into nine instead of fifteen lots.'

Purcell's eyes were fixed on Tetahiti and he sensed rather than
saw the reaction of the Tahitians. There was nothing very precise, neither exclamation nor gesture. But there was a sudden
tension. Tetahiti himself never moved, but his eyes became
harder.

'The Skeleton,' Purcell went on, 'proposes that the Tahitians should work on the *Peritani*'s land and be paid in kind.'

Tetahiti gave a short derisive laugh and that was all.

'That is an offensive proposal,' Ohou said, bounding to his feet. 'We are not the *Peritani*'s servants.'

Ohou was tall and strong and had an ingenuous expression. He scarcely ever spoke and normally left Timi to express his opinion. His intervention surprised everyone, since he was considered incapable of speaking in public. They waited for him to go on with a certain curiosity. But he said nothing more. Ohou's two sentences had exhausted his eloquence. And, as he sat down again, he felt ashamed of having spoken first and of having done it so badly. He knew he lacked the poetic gift which, in Tahiti, was the first of a politician's virtues.

'What you say is true, Ohou,' Purcell said. 'The proposal is offensive. I mentioned it, because the Skeleton proposed it. As far as I'm concerned, I've another proposal to make.'

He spread his arms wide to include Jones and Baker.

'I propose to share our three parts with you.'

There was a silence and at last Tetahiti spoke: 'That's not just,' he said in his deep bass voice. 'Ouili, Ropati and Adamo, that makes three. We Tahitians are six. We would share three parts among nine of us. They would have six parts among six.'

He said not a word of thanks to Purcell. And now he fell silent, as if he were awaiting another suggestion. Purcell remained silent too, and there was a moment of embarrassment.

Mehoro left Kori's side, got to his feet and came over to crouch beside Tetahiti. He looked up at him as if asking permission to speak. Mehoro had a wide, round face, full of candour and gaiety.

Tetahiti lowered his heavy lids in assent.

'You, Adamo,' Mehoro said standing up, 'and you, Ouili and you too, Ropati, are not selfish. It is generous of you to say: "Our three parts are yours." Your offer moves me. But what Tetahiti says is true: it's not just. Why should the Skeleton have more land than Adamo, or Ropati, or Mehoro?' he went on, placing his large hand on his square pectoral muscles. 'No, indeed, it's not just.'

He had spoken with great emphasis and drew breath as if blown.

'In Tahiti,' he went on, 'when a chief has committed an injustice, we all go together to see him and say: "You have done what should not be done. And now you must undo it." And we wait a moon. And if at the end of that time, the chief has not repaired his error, two men come at night and put a javelin in the door of his hut. And, after that, we wait another moon. And if at the end of that moon, the chief has still done nothing, we surround his hut by night, set fire to it and, when he comes out, we kill him.'

'And suppose the chief has friends?' Purcell said after a moment.

'If they've not deserted the chief, we kill them too. '

'And suppose the chief has many friends and defends himself?'

'Then, it's war.'

'And how does one end the war?'

'When the chief and all his friends are dead.'

'That means spilling a lot of blood,' Purcell said.

He looked at Tetahiti and said calmly: 'In my view, one should not spill blood.'

Tetahiti slowly raised his heavy lids, looked at Adamo and said solemnly as if giving a verdict: 'In that case, you are the friend of the bad chief.'

'I am not his friend,' Purcell said emphatically. 'I have left the *Peritani* assembly to show that I disapprove of it. And I have come to share my land with you.'

Tetahiti nodded.

'Adamo,' he said, 'you are a good man. But to be good is not enough. You say: "I will share the injustice with you." But that does not remedy the injustice.'

There was a murmur of assent. When it had died down, Mehani unclasped his hands, placed them on his knees and said: 'What my brother Tetahiti says is true. However, it is not true that Adamo is the friend of the bad chief. He has fought him with courage, words and cunning. He has fought against him from the start. We must not turn from my brother Adamo because Adamo does not wish to shed blood. Adamo has *moa* ideas about blood. I, Mehani, son of a chief, uncover my shoulder in Adamo's presence,' he said, getting to his feet.

He drew himself up to his full height, took a deep breath, then rested the weight of his body on his right leg, and stood completely still, his two round, muscular arms hanging at his side, his head inclined towards his shoulder. He looked as relaxed and majestic as a statue.

He went on: 'Friends, you must not judge Adamo as you would judge another *Peritani*. Many *Peritani* came to the big island of Tahiti, but no one had clearer eyes, more golden hair or pinker cheeks than Adamo. Look, brothers, at Adamo's pink cheeks!' Mehani cried with an elegant gesture of hand and body, as if Purcell's complexion was in itself a guarantee of his integrity.

The argument seemed to Purcell absurdly irrelevant, but it had an effect on the Tahitians. They looked at Purcell's cheeks with a sort of respect, and their respect seemed to increase when Purcell blushed.

'And now,' Mehani went on, 'this man whose cheeks are like the dawn has come to us and has said: "I will share my land with you." To me, Mehani, the son of a chief, the offer is welcome. It is not justice. But it is welcome.'

He made a wide, elegant gesture of the hand that was reminiscent of Otou and said, chanting his words as if they were a poem: 'Adamo has not brought justice. But he has brought friendship.'

His hand fell beside his body as he bent his knee, and he sat down with a graceful prolongation of the movement. 'Well spoken!' Mehoro said warmly and Kori echoed him: 'Well spoken!' Then Kori got to his feet, and swinging his long gorilla-like arms, went to sit beside Mehoro, his shoulder against his.

Timi got to his feet, and Purcell at once felt a certain threat in the air. Outwardly, there was nothing menacing about Timi. He was the smallest, the slenderest and certainly the most handsome of the Tahitians. His beardless face was lit by long, slit gazelle's eyes turning up towards his temples and shaded by long lashes thick as leaves. The iris was so large that it occupied nearly the whole of the slit, leaving little room, except at the corners, for the blue-white of the eye. This conformation gave his glance a melancholy sweetness, but one had little opportunity of admiring it, since Timi more often than not kept his lids lowered like a virgin.

'Mehani,' he began in a deep musical voice, 'has said and yet not said that Adamo is *moa*. And it may be true that Adamo is *moa*. Perhaps Ouili is *moa* too. And perhaps Ropati also. Perhaps there are many *moas* among the *Peritani* . . .'

The insolence of this beginning was obvious, and Timi's affectation of not looking at Adamo more obvious still. 'That one's an enemy,' Purcell thought.

'These three *Peritani*,' Timi went on, without looking at any of them, 'come and say: "You Tahitians have been done an injustice. We have protested against this injustice. And we are prepared to share our land with you." And we Tahitians say: "This sharing is not justice. We will have nothing to do with it." Then these three *Peritani* will go away, take their land and cultivate it. And we shall have no land.'

Timi raised his right arm, stretched his hand out in front of him and opened his fingers. The effect of this gesture was striking. One had the impression that he had earth in his hands and that it was slipping between his fingers.

'And so,' he went on, his fingers still apart, 'these three *Peritani* enjoy their land and we have none.'

He let his hand fall to his side and added with biting irony: 'However, these three *Peritani* are protesting against injustice.'

He paused and looked at Kori and Mehoro as if he particularly wished to convince them. He went on ironically: 'At the time of the sharing out of the women, these three *Peritani* also protested. It was pleasant to see them protest, because we could tell that they were indeed our friends. However, their protests had no result. And after the protests, the six Tahitians had three women among them. And these three *Peritani* had a woman each.'

Timi sat down and Purcell admired the art with which he had demonstrated that, though the three *Peritani* had protested against the injustice, they had nevertheless profited by it.

Purcell looked up and saw Kori's and Mehoro's eyes fixed on him. They were friendly and encouraging him to reply. Then he looked at Tetahiti. He also was awaiting a reply. As for

Mehani, he was staring upwards and his eyes were dull. He was yawning fit to dislocate his jaw so as to show how little he thought of Timi's speech. 'The speech may have done me more good than harm with the others,' Purcell thought.

'Timi,' Purcell said, drawing himself up, 'what you have said amounts to this: all the *Peritani* are bad, and the three *Peritani* here are as bad as the rest. And, what's more, they're hypocrites into the bargain.'

Purcell paused as if to give Timi time to protest against the meaning he was attributing to him. But Timi did not flinch. He was sitting cross-legged on the ground on Tetahiti's right and staring at his knees.

'Timi,' Purcell went on, 'if that's what you think, your thought is unjust. At the sharing out of the women, for instance, it would have been just to allow each to choose her *tané*. But in that case, as you know very well, Ivoa would have chosen me; Avapouhi would have chosen Ouili; and Amoureïa would have chosen Ropati. So, you see, as far as the women are concerned it would have made no difference.'

He paused and then said decisively: 'We have not profited by the injustice.'

Kori and Mehoro nodded their heads and Mehani smiled. As for Tetahiti, he turned his head slightly towards Timi and said firmly and disdainfully, though without raising his voice: 'What Adamo says is true. The women he mentioned would certainly have chosen the *Peritani* who are here. On that point there is no reason to harden our hearts against them.'

He paused and then went on: 'We must be careful to treat Adamo with justice. Perhaps one day, I, Tetahiti, will be obliged to treat Adamo as an enemy for the reason I have given and will repeat in a moment. But we must not forget: Adamo speaks our language. Adamo loves us. Adamo is as polite as the shade. Adamo,' he went on with a sudden flight of poetic fancy, 'is gentler than the dawn he carries on his cheeks. Moreover, he does not want injustice.'

He paused. His face gradually became stern and he went on: 'However, Adamo will not act to prevent injustice. It is in this, as I have said, that he is the friend of the bad chief. And the friend of the bad chief is not our friend.'

Purcell swallowed and said tonelessly: 'I am prepared to act if there is any way of acting other than the one Mehoro described.'

Tetahiti looked away and replied: 'Judge of it for yourself; there is no other way.'

'Is that the opinion of you all?' Purcell went on after a moment.

'Let anyone who does not agree say so,' Tetahiti said.

Purcell looked slowly round the Tahitians. None of them spoke. Mehani was perfectly still, his right fist clasped in his left hand, his eyes on the ground, his face resolute. He, too, agreed with Tetahiti.

'I pray *Eatua* that there will be no war,' Purcell said.

There was a silence and Tetahiti said gravely: 'If there is war, you will have to choose your camp.'

Purcell got to his feet.

'I shall not bear arms,' he said in a low voice. 'Neither against the bad chief, nor against you.'

Tetahiti's heavy lids fell over his eyes. He picked up the axe he had placed at his feet, got up, and, turning his back on Purcell, began splitting the tree-stump again.

10

When Mason had made the first tour of the island in a boat, he had noticed a little cove on the east. It was shut off on the land side by the steep semi-circle of the cliff, and defended on the sea side by a belt of rocks. At the end of this little bay was a beach of black sand which was inaccessible by boat, and accessible from the interior of the island only by means of a rope that was tied to the base of a banyan and hung down the basalt wall. The British called this cove Rope Beach from the rope by which it was reached.

It was this creek the minority chose as their fishing place when each clan set about fishing on its own account. By a tacit agreement, the majority and the Tahitians left it to them. Climbing down to it and particularly up again was laborious, but the cove was full of fish, faced east so that it got the early sun and was sheltered from the nor'wester by the cliff. Baker and Jones fished in the calm water at the sides of the cove, but Purcell preferred to fish from one of the points, at a place where there was considerable surf. The first day he was nearly swept away by a wave and owed his life to the fact that, as it withdrew, it hurled him violently against a rock which happened to be between him and the sea. He now took the precaution of attaching a line to his waist and tying the other end to a point of rock a few yards behind him.

Purcell had been fishing for two hours, happy enough not to have to talk to anyone for once. The island was a small island, and the village a small village. They all lived on top of each other. And since the recent events, his hut had been full of *vahinés* who came to get news, or brought news themselves, which was sometimes true and sometimes false.

Purcell pulled in his line and then let it out again. Life was stifling in the village now. He felt as if the state of tension now reigning on the island had made it even smaller. When he went down to Blossom Bay, he was surprised to find himself looking longingly at *The Blossom*'s boats which were drawn up in a cave and sheltered from the sun. Ivoa must have had the same idea, for she had asked him the day before how far away the nearest land was. But it was impossible to sail five hundred sea miles in an open boat with a woman near her time. Alone, he might have tried it. 'The island is a prison,' he thought with a sudden sense of discouragement. 'We've escaped hanging but not imprisonment for life.'

Once again, he had allowed his bait to be taken. He was dreaming too much. He had to bait his line again. He moved back a few yards and sat down behind a rock, which afforded some shelter from the wind. A few minutes before he had thrown down a fish's head, and now the sea slaters were gathering. They had hard avid little feet and ovoid bodies of a doubtful brown. It was an obscene mêlée. They were swarming with a continuous sort of buzzing noise, climbing on top of each other, wounding and killing each other as they fought over the feast. To all appearance, their cruelty was useless. The fish's head was big enough for there to be enough for all. It would take them several hours to polish off their prey. Purcell looked at them for a moment in disgust, not even daring to push them away with his foot. How loathsome these insects were! They were all mouth and carapace. There was nothing vulnerable about them, nothing human. A limitless hardness. An avidity which did not even know the limits of its own interest.

Purcell felt a hand on his shoulder. He turned round. It was MacLeod.

'I called to you,' the Scotsman shouted as if in excuse as he removed his hand. 'But with this wind . . .'

Purcell was so surprised to see MacLeod in his fishing area that he could find nothing to say.

'I've got to speak to you,' MacLeod said.

'All right,' Purcell said. 'But let's not stay here. You might be washed away.'

And, jumping from rock to rock, he made his way to a little cave which lay beside the rock to which he had attached his safety line. MacLeod followed him and, when Purcell sat down at the entrance to the cave, he took up his position a yard from him and stared out to sea.

'It's not because you've left the assembly you're angry?' he said at last, looking questioningly at Purcell.

'I'm not angry with anyone,' Purcell said.

'I went to your hut,' MacLeod went on. 'It was your wife who told me you were at Rope Beach. It's not a bad spot,' he said doubtfully, looking round the bay. 'At least for chaps who're prepared to act like topmen on the end of a line. But it wouldn't suit me. I've been doing that job for thirty years, and it's a miracle I'm still alive.'

Relaxed, perfectly at his ease, presenting Purcell with his displumed eagle's profile, he was leaning back against a rounded rock, his long spidery legs stuck out casually in front of him. His red and white striped trousers had been patched at the knees with large squares of sailcloth and were as dirty as the white vest which clung to his ribs.

'I saw your new sliding door,' MacLeod went on. 'As I was in your hut, I took the liberty of having a look at it.'

He added after a moment's thought: 'You're handy at it,

Purcell, for an amateur. I noticed it when you were building your hut. You're the only one beside myself who thought of building with lap joints. As a result yours and mine are the only two that are watertight. All the same, it wasn't very clever,' he went on with animation, 'to lay the boards edge to edge, as they all did, since there was no covering for the joints. The result is that you can caulk as much as you like but there'll always be draughts. No, as I was saying, the lap joint was the only solution. And I'm not complimenting you when I say you're handy with wood, Purcell.'

Since Purcell said nothing, he gave him a quick sideways glance and went on: 'As for your sliding door, I'll tell you. It's the work of a man who has principles. Perhaps too much so. As I always say, the good amateur can do as good work as the professional. The difference is that he doesn't go so fast and pays too much attention to the rules. I'll tell you, Purcell,' he went on confidentially, leaning towards him as if he were about to sum up the secret of his trade in a word, 'the ultimate success is to break one of the damned rules and do the job as well as if one hadn't.'

'Thank you for the hint,' Purcell said.

'Delighted. And if you ever need a tool, let me know. There are *The Blossom*'s tools and my own, which I don't lend to anyone. But I'll make an exception for you, since you're so to speak one of the trade.'

That MacLeod should offer to lend him his tools was incredible! The mere suggestion struck Purcell dumb. He turned to look at his companion. MacLeod was staring at the horizon, his eyebrows raised, his mouth half open. He seemed surprised at his offer himself.

'The blacks came to see me last night,' he went on suddenly. 'All six of them. With Omaata.'

'With Omaata?'

'She acted as interpreter.'

'Oh!' Purcell said.

And he fell silent. There was nothing but the 'Oh!' and the silence.

MacLeod went on: 'You can guess what they had to say to me.'

Purcell did not reply and MacLeod went on: 'Of course, I said: "No". Then they gave me this little packet and went away.'

MacLeod took the packet from his pocket and handed it to Purcell. It was a bundle of little twigs bound together with a liana.

'Do you know what it means?'

'I've a vague idea,' Purcell said, and he set about counting the twigs.

'Don't bother. There are twenty-eight.'

Purcell tied the twigs together again and handed them back to MacLeod.

'In my opinion, it means they're giving you a moon to change your mind.'

'A moon?'

'Twenty-eight nights.'

'I see,' MacLeod said.

After a moment, he went on: 'And if I don't change my mind?'

'They'll come by night and put a javelin in your door.'

'And then?'

'It'll mean they're giving you another moon.'

'And at the end of that moon?'

'They'll kill you.'

MacLeod whistled and put his hands in his pockets. His face remained impassive, but when he spoke again his voice was slightly off key.

'How will they set about it?'

There was a silence. Then Purcell shrugged and said: 'Don't imagine they'll come and defy you to single combat. That's not their style. War, for the Tahitian, is an ambush.'

'Two can play at that game,' MacLeod said.

Purcell got to his feet.

He went a yard or two into the shelter of the cave, the wind ceased, and he at once felt the heat of the sun on his chest. It had been there all the time, but the freshness of the breeze had prevented his feeling it.

'Play!' he said after a moment. 'If you were playing only with your own life.'

'It's only me they're threatening, isn't it?' MacLeod said arrogantly.

And since Purcell said nothing, he went on: 'Or are they thinking of a massacre, in your opinion, Purcell?'

'They're not thinking,' Purcell said. 'They're not whites. They don't think about what they're going to do and they don't discuss it among themselves. They give way to their emotions. And then one day they act. And without ever having discussed the matter, they'll be in agreement.'

'Emotions!' MacLeod said contemptuously. 'What emotions?'

'Rancour, hatred . . .'

'Against me?'

'Against me, against Smudge, against all the *Peritani*.'

'You too?'

'Me too.'

'Why you?'

'They don't understand my attitude about you.'

'I don't blame them,' MacLeod said.

And he gave a harsh laugh which sounded false. Purcell went on: 'They think I ought to join them in killing you.'

There was a silence and MacLeod said: 'And that's just what I'd do in your place. And that's what Baker would do, if he weren't your friend. You'll say, as far as I, Purcell, am concerned, it's my religion. I've been sailing about the world for twenty years and I've never noticed that religion has changed a man. If he's bad, he stays bad, with or without Jesus Christ . . . And the explanation? I'll tell you. As far as talking's concerned,' he went on, clasping his hands like an effigy on a tomb, 'I agree. But as regards actions, nothing doing. As a result, there's not one bastard in ten thousand who takes his religion seriously. And that one bastard's you, Purcell. It's just my luck to have fallen on you! I appreciate it, I can tell you,' he added in a tone of voice that might have been either ironical or respectful. 'If it were anyone else but you, there'd be three muskets in the blacks' camp at this very moment.'

MacLeod blinked as if dazzled by the sun, but he gave Purcell a sideways glance from behind his lashes. Purcell surprised it and it gave him a shock. MacLeod was not as certain of his neutrality as he made out. He had come to reconnoitre the ground. 'But in that case,' Purcell thought, 'are the charm, the friendly tone, the praise of my carpentry and the compliment to my religion nothing but play-acting? He seemed sincere. I could have sworn he was sincere.' Purcell swallowed. He always gave people too much credit. Once again, he had been taken in.

He said with a certain irritation: 'I shall not take up arms against you, if that's what's worrying you. As to what Jones and Baker will do, I haven't asked them.'

'It doesn't worry me,' MacLeod drawled, 'but I tell you straight out, Purcell, that it would have sickened me to see whites in league with blacks against chaps of their own colour.'

Purcell turned red with anger and put his hands in his pockets.

'You make me sick, MacLeod,' he cried, his voice quivering. 'You dare to take a moral tone after what you've done! . . . It's abominable! As for my being on your side, let me tell you that I'm not! I think you're wrong from start to finish! You've bullied, frustrated and offended the Tahitians in the most . . .'

He could not find the right word and went on in another explosion of indignation: 'It's really disgusting! Disgusting to bring fire and bloodshed to the island to satisfy your avarice. You're a criminal lunatic, MacLeod,' he went on. 'That's what you are! I shan't raise my little finger against you, but if the Tahitians kill you I shan't shed a tear, you can be sure of that!'

'Splendid!' MacLeod said calmly.

He smiled and slowly got up on his long legs. His tall figure, in silhouette against the sun, seemed to Purcell almost incredibly thin.

'There's nothing like being frank, is there?' he said in an almost friendly tone. 'And thank you for your good wishes . . . But don't you worry about me. I may have all the makings of a decent skeleton, but you won't be able to open your Bible and say your prayers over my corpse just yet. No, sir! I'll see to that. You can trust old MacLeod to keep his eye on the wave and give her helm at the right moment. As for war with the blacks, you say: "It's your fault." All right, suppose it is my fault. It would have come sooner or later anyway. Have you ever seen a country that hasn't had a war? And I'll tell you something else, Purcell, that you may not have noticed: the island's too small. It's already too small for us. What will it be for our children? Well, let's have a war then, it'll make more room. And after it we'll be able to breathe more freely.'

'Provided you haven't been one of the people to make the room,' Purcell said coldly.

This reply had more effect on MacLeod than the previous upbraiding had done. He blinked, looked away, and did not reply for a moment.

'Don't try to frighten me,' he muttered at last.

Purcell looked at him. If that hurt it might be worth putting more pressure on.

'MacLeod,' he said, 'I'm going to tell you what's wrong with you. You lack imagination. You can't imagine your own death. Only that of the Tahitians.'

'We've got the muskets,' MacLeod said, staring at the ground.

Purcell got to his feet.

'Your muskets won't be any use to you,' he said with emphasis. 'You think you're invincible with your muskets. But you're wrong, MacLeod. You don't know how wrong you are. Believe me, I've seen a tribal war in Tahiti. Their warriors have incredible stratagems. You'll be struck down, and you won't have the time to see what's hit you.'

MacLeod shrugged.

'We've got the muskets,' he said, his face rigid.

He had become unreceptive. He had shut himself into his carapace, sheltered from fear, and even from thought.

He turned his back as if to go away, then changed his mind, faced Purcell again and said in a low voice: 'Johnson tells me you cured him of fever a month ago.'

'Yes,' Purcell said, raising his eyebrows, 'but why? I'm not a doctor.'

'What do you make of that?'

MacLeod held out his right hand. The whole back of it was swollen and the centre red.

'What is it?' he asked anxiously. 'Is it a *feefee*?'*

Purcell looked at the hand without taking it, then raised his eyes and stared at MacLeod. He was struck by his pallor. MacLeod was ready to risk his life for an acre of land but was afraid of a spot.

* Elephantiasis.

'It's a boil,' Purcell said. 'A *feefee* is rarely localised in the hand. There's nothing the matter with your testicles?'

'No.'

'That's where it usually starts. Sometimes also in the legs.'

'So it's just a boil?' MacLeod said, passing his tongue over his lips.

'Yes, I think so. Bathe your hand in hot water.'

'Thank you,' MacLeod said gratefully. 'When I saw my hand swelling, it worried me. I remembered the chap in Tahiti, who had to hold his balls up with both hands to be able to walk. Christ,' he said indignantly, 'it's no Christian disease!'

Purcell said nothing.

'Thank you, doc,' MacLeod said with a charming smile and, putting two fingers to his forehead in a half-serious, half-joking way, he turned on his heel and went off, jumping from rock to rock on his long thin legs. 'A locust,' Purcell thought, as he watched him go. 'A big, hard, greedy locust.'

Purcell fished for another twenty minutes, then he picked up his catch and his lines and joined Jones and Baker at the end of the cove. The sun was already high. It was time to climb the cliff.

'You've had a visit,' Baker said.

'I'll tell you about it.'

When they had reached the plateau, Jones offered to take part of the catch to the 'market'. Purcell smiled agreement. He knew Jones liked ringing *The Blossom*'s bell as loudly as he could, waiting for the *vahinés* to arrive, and receiving their compliments on his fishing.

Baker turned into East Avenue with Purcell. They remained silent the whole way. They were beginning to be suspicious of the trees and the undergrowth and to be afraid of talking in the open air.

Purcell's hut was empty. Like that of the Tahitians, it was open to the winds and Purcell saw with annoyance that someone had 'borrowed' his chair. The Tahitian habit of borrowing from your neighbour anything you wanted was annoying. His chair might be returned to him in a week or in a month. He would have to wait. It would have been bad manners to enquire where it was and, of course, the height of meanness to ask for it back.

Purcell made Baker sit on the stool, and himself sat down against the sliding door his legs hanging out into the garden. After a moment, he said: 'MacLeod wanted to know what we were going to do. He was afraid our "three muskets" would join the Tahitian camp. He probably doesn't know that I haven't got a musket.'

'What did you say?' Baker asked.

'You know my position. But I made no promises about you and Jones.'

Baker was sitting with his elbows on his knees and looking straight in front of him. The dark circles round his eyes in his brown, regular face, and the twitching of his lower lip gave him the appearance of being overworked. In fact, he worked no harder than anyone else. But Purcell had always seen him like this: nervous, tense and impatient.

'I don't agree with you,' he said after a moment. 'When you've got a poisoned leg, what do you do? You have it cut off, before the poison invades your whole body. MacLeod is poison, you'll agree, and he's in process of poisoning the island, and what are you doing to stop him?'

There was a silence, and Purcell said: 'I'm not preventing you from joining the Tahitian camp.'

Baker shrugged.

'I shan't do so without you, you know that.'

Purcell was touched. He lowered his eyes and said quietly: 'You can do so. We shan't fall out over that.'

Baker shook his head.

'Of course not. I don't see how I could fall out with you. But, in the first place, I don't understand the blacks' language, I wouldn't be at my ease . . . But it's not only that,' he went on hesitantly.

He looked away and said with some embarrassment: 'It's really because we wouldn't be together any more . . . We've always been together, ever since *The Blossom.*'

He suddenly raised his head, blushed and said with restrained anger: 'Christ, sir! You ought to have let me do it on the night of the sharing out of the women.'

Purcell remained silent. It was always the same argument, the same grievance . . .

'And Jones?' he asked after a moment.

'Jones will do as I do,' Baker said.

There was a sudden draught, and the door behind them banged. Purcell turned. It was Itia. She was standing in front of the closed door, a crown of hibiscus flowers in her hair, the kernels of her pandanus necklace hanging between her bare breasts. She was staring at Baker's back in disappointment. She knew Ivoa was with Avapouhi and she had not expected to find anyone with Purcell.

'What do you want?' Purcell said curtly.

He at once regretted his tone and smiled at her. Itia smiled back. The corners of her mouth turned upwards, her shining eyes slanted towards her temples, and her little round face brightened.

'Adamo,' she said in her gay clear voice, 'Mehani will await you at Omaata's.'

'When?'

'A little after the belly of the sun.'*

'Why at Omaata's? Why not here?'

'He didn't say.'

'I'll be there,' Purcell said.

He turned his back on her. But she did not go away. She stayed there by the door, her hip against the jamb, the fingers of her right hand playing with the kernels of her necklace.

'Won't Ouili go away soon?' she asked at last.

Purcell laughed.

'No, he's not going away.'

'Why? Isn't he going to eat?'

'When he goes, I shall go with him. Go away, Itia.'

She lowered her head like a child about to cry and he added gently in English: 'Go away.' It was a particular kindness. Itia was always flattered when Adamo talked to her in *Peritani*.

'I go,' she said importantly.

She went on: 'You see, Adamo, I put on my pandanus necklace. When I come to see you now, I always put it on.'

'Why?'

'What!' she said, suddenly laughing aloud and putting her fingers to her mouth to hide her laughter. 'Don't you know?

* Noon.

Man! Don't you know?'

She went off laughing, and the door banged behind her.

'She's after you,' Baker said.

Purcell made no comment and Baker went on: 'Avapouhi must be waiting for me.'

'I'll come with you.'

They walked in silence along West Avenue, and then Purcell said: 'We'll have to think about laying more stones. Otherwise it will become impassable with the next rains.'

'In my view,' Baker said, 'each of us should be responsible for the section leading to his neighbour. For instance, you make up the road as far as Johnson. Johnson as far as me. I as far as Jones. And Jones as far as Hunt.'

'No,' Purcell said. 'With that system there'd be good and bad sections. Believe me, it'd be better if we all worked on it for an hour a day, including the women. Everyone could bring a stone back from the beach. It'd be finished in a fortnight.'

They had been talking of making up the road every time they had walked along West Avenue during the last month. But nothing had so far been decided. The listlessness of the tropics was affecting them.

There was a tremendous row coming from Johnson's hut, and Purcell recognised above the old man's querulous voice the shrill shouting of Taïata.

'Listen to that,' Baker said. He added: 'I'd love to know what she's saying to him.'

Purcell listened.

'Son of a pig... Capon... Rat's sperm...'

'Well!' Baker said.

Avapouhi and Ivoa were sitting on the threshold of Baker's hut.

As soon as they saw their *tanés*, they got up and went to meet them.

'I'm going to Omaata,' Purcell said.

'Be careful, man!' Ivoa said, laughing. And she added: 'I'm going home.'

'I'll come with you,' Avapouhi said at once.

Since Ivoa had become pregnant, she could not take a step in the village without a *vahiné* hurrying to give her an arm. She was the object of more consideration than a queen bee in her hive.

As soon as he had left Ivoa, Purcell hurried on. He was expecting Itia to appear at any moment. Jones's door was wide open, and Jones was sitting there completely naked, eating, with Amoureïa standing behind him. When he saw Purcell, he raised his right arm and looked at him with as much pleasure as if he had not seen him for a couple of days. Amoureïa also smiled. Jones was fair with a tinge of red, and she was as dark as it was possible to be. But they both had the same ingenuous expression, the same confiding smile. Purcell stopped and gazed at them. It felt good to look at them.

'Aren't you going to eat?' Jones called out.

'I'm going to Omaata's.'

'She'll strangle you,' Jones said, laughing. 'Listen, I'll give you a tip. When she clasps you in her arms, make the muscles of your back, shoulders and chest rigid, and stay like that while she embraces you. Look, I'll show you.'

He got to his feet, distended his muscles to the utmost limit, held them there and turned scarlet in the face.

'But you're forgetting to breathe,' Purcell said, laughing. 'You'll simply suffocate.'

'Don't you believe it,' Jones said, deflating himself with a noise like a pair of bellows. 'It's a good trick. Try it, and you'll see.'

'I'll try it,' Purcell said.

The first thing Purcell saw when he entered Omaata's hut was his own chair. It was standing in the middle of the room, and Purcell had to make a considerable effort not to be ill-mannered enough to look at it for too long. However, he had not much time to do so. Omaata's arms clasped him and he felt himself engulfed, kneaded and almost swallowed up in her lavish flesh.

'Let me go,' he said as soon as he could breathe.

'My baby,' Omaata cried.

She picked him off the ground like a feather and covered him with a roaring cascade of loving words. But since her breasts were pressed against Purcell's ears, he could hear only the distant thunder of her voice. Clasped to her by her enormous hands, his back and ribs bruised, his head caught between the monstrous globes of her bosom, he was in danger of suffocation.

'You're hurting me,' he cried.

'My baby,' she said tenderly.

But pity merely increased her emotion and she clasped him all the tighter.

'Omaata!'

'My baby,' she cried like a roaring dove.

At last she let him go, but immediately seized him again under the arms and raised him to a level with her face.

'Sit down,' she said, swinging him over the back of the chair and putting him down somewhat roughly on the other side. 'Sit down, Adamo, my baby. I went and fetched your chair so that you'd be comfortable while waiting for Mehani.'

So that was it. What incredible kindness! She had brought the awkward, heavy chair all the way here. But she would forget to return it. It would still be in her hut in a fortnight's time . . . So that he could sit in it for half an hour, she would deprive him of it for a fortnight . . . 'I'm thinking like a *Peritani*,' Purcell thought remorsefully. 'How mean of me! What counts is the warmth, the goodwill . . .'

Omaata sat on the floor beside the chair, one hand behind her on the ground, the other on her knee. She relaxed into that quiet attitude of repose which Purcell so much admired in the Tahitians. How tall she was. Though he was sitting a good foot and a half higher than she was, her huge eyes were on a level with his. Silent and still, she was like a gigantic statue sitting on the steps of a throne.

'The Skeleton came to fetch Jono,' she said, as Purcell glanced round the room. 'Perhaps they've gone hunting. They took their muskets.'

'Do you know what Mehani wants with me?'

'No.'

And she fell silent, happy to say nothing and to watch him. This adoration ended by embarrassing Purcell and he said: 'Haven't you a necklace of pandanus kernels?'

'Yes.'

'But you don't wear it?'

She laughed, and her bright eyes were full of mischief.

'Not today.'

'Why?'

She laughed all the louder, showing her strong cannibal's teeth.

'Adamo is my baby,' she said between two laughs. 'Adamo is not a *tané* I want.'

'Don't be mysterious,' Purcell said.

'There's no mystery. The kernels of the pandanus,' she replied eloquently, 'take on the odour of the skin and emit it with their own scent.'

'Well?'

'It's a very intoxicating mixture. As soon as a man leans forward and breathes it, he wants to play.'

She went on: 'I wore mine on the night of the great rain.'

'Which night?' Purcell said.

Omaata ceased smiling and her face turned melancholy, as if the night she was recollecting was already long ago.

'The night of the *Hoata* on the big canoe. When I danced to have Jono.'

There was a silence.

'Can . . . can a man resist it?'

'There are two things,' Omaata said gravely, 'there's the necklace, and there's the skin.'

Purcell smiled.

'Why are you smiling, Adamo?' Omaata went on seriously. 'The skin must be good too. If it isn't, the mixture isn't good.'

'And if it is good?'

'A Tahitian cannot resist it.'

'And a *Peritani*?'

'Perhaps a *Peritani* like the big chief. Perhaps the Skeleton. But not Jono, Ouili, or the little rat . . .'

She looked at him.

'Nor my pretty little cock with pink cheeks.'

'Me?' Purcell said, raising his eyebrows.

'Don't lie to me with your eyes, my baby,' Omaata said.

She suddenly began roaring with laughter, her body bowed, her huge round shoulders shaking and jerking, and her breast rising with the ample undulations of the Pacific swell.

'I know,' she roared in her cataract-like voice. 'I know about Itia. So does Mehani. So does Ivoa.'

'Ivoa!' Purcell cried, when he could manage to get a word in. 'Who told her?'

'Who, if not Itia?' Omaata said, tears of pleasure pouring from her eyes. 'Oh, my little cock, how odd you look!'

'It's . . . it's indecent!' Purcell said in English.

He went on indignantly in Tahitian: 'But why speak of Itia? I haven't played with her.'

'I know,' Omaata shouted in a voice strangled with laughter, her shoulders shaking as if she had hiccups, and the tears pouring down her huge cheeks. 'O my little *maamaa Peritani,* everyone knows. No one can understand why you're insulting Itia as you are.'

She added: 'However, Itia says you won't resist very long.'

'She said that!' Purcell cried furiously.

'O my little cock with red cheeks,' Omaata cried, her face shining with tears, and unable to stop the convulsions shaking her gigantic body. 'O my little angry cock! I also think you won't resist very long. And Ivoa think so too.'

'Ivoa!' Purcell said.

'Man, what's so extraordinary about that?'

She gradually grew calmer, looked at Purcell with laughing eyes, and extended her large hands towards him, the thumbs spread wide from the fingers and the palms turned to him as if she were bringing him the truth.

'Ivoa,' she said calmly, 'is expecting her baby in two moons.'

There was a silence. The significance of the words gradually dawned on Purcell.

'And yet,' he said after a moment, 'you remember . . . The day we explored the island . . . We were sitting at the foot of the banyan, and Ivoa said to Itia: "Adamo is Ivoa's *tané*" . . . '

'Oh, my stupid little cock!' Omaata said. 'It was only because Itia was paying court to you in public.'

Purcell looked at her in stupefaction. It was not therefore, as he had thought, a jealous reaction but a lesson in manners. 'Do I really understand the Tahitians?' he wondered, suddenly doubtful. 'How many mistakes of this sort I must have made! And what an abyss there is between their ideas and ours! It's clear that the word "adultery" has no meaning for them.'

The doorway suddenly darkened, and Mehani's brown body

appeared, silhouetted against the light, slender, wide of shoulder, his head held high. He stopped on the threshold with a certain majesty. Purcell got to his feet and went to him.

'Adamo, my brother,' Mehani said.

He took him by the shoulders with both hands, leaned forward, and rubbed his cheek against Purcell's. Then, drawing back to the full extent of his arms, he looked at him gravely and tenderly.

'Here I am as you asked,' Purcell said, embarrassed. 'However,' he went on after a silence, 'I don't understand why you didn't come to my hut.'

'We're living through difficult days,' Mehani said with a vague and eloquent wave of his hand.

He let go of Purcell's shoulders and turned to Omaata.

'Undo this earring, Omaata.'

Mehani's single earring was a little shark's tooth attached to the lobe by a liana. Omaata's large fingers took some time to undo the liana's double knot. When she had done so, she pulled on one of the ends she had freed. But nothing happened. The flesh had closed over the liana.

'Take the tooth only,' Mehani said, making a little face, 'and thread another liana through it. Adamo,' he went on, 'you'll have to have your ear pierced.'

'Do you mean to say you're giving it to him?' Omaata cried, as if scandalised.

'Yes,' Mehani said decisively.

His 'yes' prevented further argument. Omaata glanced at him and said tonelessly: 'I'll fetch a liana and a needle.'

She went out of the room and Purcell heard her moving about in the lean-to kitchen.

Since Mehani said nothing and was staring him in the eyes, Purcell said: 'Isn't it the earring your father wore?'

'Yes, that's the one,' Mehani said. 'He gave it to me as a present when I set out with you.'

'And now you're giving it to me!' Purcell said in stupefaction.

Mehani nodded and Purcell looked at him for a moment in silence. He was aware of the importance of the gift, but its true significance escaped him, and he dared not ask. The Tahitian code was very strict. The recipient of a gift asked no questions, showed no pleasure and said no thanks. He remained passive and resigned like a victim.

Omaata came in, holding the shark's tooth on the end of a liana between her teeth. In her right hand she had a sailmaker's needle which Purcell thought needlessly large, in her left a torch which she handed to Mehani. Then, with a slow, solemn gesture, she placed the point of the needle in the flame.

'Turn your head, Adamo,' she said, seizing the lobe of his ear and twisting it away from the neck.

Purcell scarcely felt the prick, but he distinctly heard the slight sizzling of the burning skin. However, when Omaata put the liana in place and tied it, the weight of the tooth pulled at his ear and produced a sharp pain that did not seem to grow less with the passing minutes.

Mehani looked at him with satisfaction. Since he had come into the room, he had not smiled once.

'I haven't eaten yet,' he said.

He turned and went towards the door.

'Mehani.'

He stopped.

'Mehani,' Purcell said, 'the Skeleton came to see me.'

Mehani looked at Omaata and Omaata said: 'I'm going. It's my turn to go to fetch water. I'm going with Ouili and Ropati.'

'And she quickly left the hut.

'He came to see me at Rope Beach,' Purcell said.

'We knew that,' Mehani said.

So they were watching him. Or the Skeleton. In any case, the feeling he had had on coming away from Rope Beach was correct. There were eyes behind every bush now.

'What did he want?' Mehani asked.

Purcell was astonished by the directness of the question. But it was no longer a time for politeness. Mehani's face was grave and tense.

'He wanted to know whether Ouili, Ropati and I were going to join you.'

'And you said "no"?' Mehani said.

'I said, "no",'

'And Ouili?'

'He said "no".'

'And Ropati?'

'He will do as we do.'

There was a silence and Purcell said: 'The Skeleton may forestall your attack.'

Mehani gave him a quick glance, paused as if he were expecting his friend to say more and, since Purcell did not, said: 'That's what we think.'

Then he made a slight inclination of the head and went. Purcell stood there silently for a moment, then he also went out. His ear was hurting him, and he felt the tooth against his cheek whenever he moved his head.

On West Avenue there were pools of sunlight on the black stones of the path and, here and there, striping the ground, the shadows of the palms waving in the wind. How peaceful it all was. The water fatigue had already left. The islanders were either eating or beginning their siesta. Itia must be somewhere in the undergrowth, watching him. Taïata was swearing at Johnson. Mason was walking up and down the 'quarterdeck'. Jono and the Skeleton were hunting. Ivoa was lying on her bed, dreaming about her future child. It was hot. The air smelt of flowers, warm earth, and the nearby sea. Everything was so small, so ordinary, so reassuring. Twenty-seven islanders. It was the smallest village in the Pacific, with its men and women concerned with their plans and their little anxieties: the Skeleton worried about a boil; Vaa concerned with her rank on the island; Ropati with his muscles; Ouili with stones for West Avenue; and he himself, as he had been for the last week, with his sliding door . . .

He remembered Mehani's expression when he had given him the earring; it had been austere, almost fierce. It was no longer the face of a friend, but that of a warrior. He had already seen the same thing in Tahiti. Normally so gentle, these men could turn savage. Their round features and their velvety eyes could show hatred. He remembered Mata, Otou's brother, when he had returned from a fight in the mountain, carrying the head of his enemy by the hair. He had placed it on a pike at the entrance to his hut, and every morning had spat in its face and furiously insulted it. 'Son of a pig,' he had said contemptuously, 'so you wanted to kill me? But you were not the stronger. It is I who killed you. And now there will be no more sun for you. No more fishing. No more dancing. Your head is the calabash from which I drink. Your wife is my slave and I play with her whenever I wish. I do this to her, and this, and again this. And meanwhile you are at my door on a pike!' And yet, Mata was ordinarily the gentlest, politest and most hospitable of men. He had done everything he could to make Adamo happy.

Purcell had not yet reached Jones's hut when he heard someone running behind him. He turned. Still some thirty yards away, Itia was running towards him as fast as she could. Curiously, she was not concealing herself, nor had she emerged from the undergrowth. She was running down the middle of the path in full view of everyone.

'Adamo!' she cried.

At last he was able to make out her face. It was drawn with terror.

'What's the matter?' he cried, taking a few rapid steps towards her.

'The Skeleton!' she shouted, her hand to her breast. She was breathless, her eyes were terrified and her beautiful black face had turned grey.

'Well?'

Purcell set off at a run. In a few seconds he had joined her. He took her by the shoulders and shook her.

'What is it? What is it?' he cried.

'The Skeleton!' she stammered, her bloodless lips quivering. 'The Skeleton and the others... with muskets... at the Tahitians' hut.'

'Good God!' Purcell cried.

He began running like a madman, leaving Itia standing. West Avenue had never seemed so long.

He passed Hunt's hut. At the entrance to Cliff Lane, he saw White's wife, Faïna, standing with her hand against a coconut palm, her face anxious. She looked at him, made a vague gesture as he passed her like a whirlwind, but said nothing.

He was running desperately, his heart beating loudly within his chest, and he was expecting every second to hear the sound of shots.

When he came out into the clearing in front of the Tahitians' hut, he was struck by the silence and stillness that lay over it.

The five *Peritani* of the majority were standing in a line holding the six Tahitians covered with their muskets. Purcell noticed that both MacLeod and White not only had a musket in their hands, but another slung over their shoulders.

The Tahitians had been surprised round a fire in which they were hardening the broad blades of their javelins. They were all carrying these long thin weapons of reddish wood. They looked derisory compared to the muskets of the British. The Tahitians were standing perfectly still and their faces showed no emotion.

'MacLeod!' Purcell cried, breaking into the circle.

'Put your hands up!' MacLeod said, quickly covering him with his musket. 'Put your hands up, Purcell, and go over and stand with the blacks.'

'You're mad!' Purcell said, without moving.

Thin as a reed, bent, panting, his pale face more than ever like a death's head, MacLeod was holding his musket against his right hip. Purcell noticed that his hands were trembling ceaselessly. 'He's going to fire,' he thought suddenly. He slowly raised his hands, and went and stood between Mehani and Teta-hiti. MacLeod sighed and lowered his musket.

'Smudge,' he said in a curiously low, breathless voice, 'keep him covered and, if he moves, give him a ball in the head.'

Smudge put his rat's face against the butt and an eager gleam appeared in the depths of his hard eyes. He was waiting.

'Gently does it, my lad,' MacLeod said without turning his head. 'There must be no killing among whites if it can be avoided. You'd do well to stand still, Purcell,' he went on. 'Smudge would be delighted to marry your widow.'

His hands on a level with his shoulders, Purcell looked Smudge straight in the eye.

'Remember you've only got one ball,' he said coldly.

Just at that moment, there was a sound of breaking branches in the undergrowth behind the *Peritani,* and the grey, terrified faces of some of the women appeared among the trees. Smudge turned pale. He blinked his little eyes, sweat trickled down his nose, and he looked at once malevolent and ill at ease. 'He's frightened,' Purcell thought, 'he doesn't know Omaata's on the water fatigue.'

'Purcell,' MacLeod said hoarsely, 'tell these apes to throw

their weapons on the ground.'

Purcell translated. He saw Tetahiti's glance pass over his head to seek Mehani's. They spoke no word, and yet Purcell felt that they were consulting each other. Then, in the calm, measured tone that was habitual to him, Tetahiti spoke. He was standing almost nonchalantly, one hand flat on his hip, the weight of his body on one leg, his javelin hanging from his hand. He was not looking at MacLeod, and his heavy lids, half veiling his eyes, gave him an absent, thoughtful expression.

'Brothers,' he said, 'it's clear the *Peritani* will fire. But we are six, seven with our brother Adamo. The enemy have only five muskets. Listen carefully. The two men who are not hit must not throw their javelins and begin the battle. They must flee and hide themselves in the bush. And then, one by one, they must kill their enemies. Thus,' he concluded gravely, 'we shall be avenged.'

There was a silence and Purcell said: 'What am I to tell the Skeleton?'

'What you like. That son of a pig does not interest me.'

It was not a pose. It was the literal truth. Tetahiti had accepted his death. Only posthumous vengeance interested him.

Purcell looked at MacLeod.

'They're persuaded you're going to fire,' he said in English. 'And they prefer to die with their arms in their hands.'

'And it took him all that time merely to say that?' MacLeod muttered.

'Yes,' Purcell said, his face firm.

MacLeod felt ill at ease. Confident in his muskets and per-suaded, after the storm on board *The Blossom,* of the blacks' cowardice, he had thought he would reduce them to crying for mercy merely by covering them. Their impassivity astonished him. He had come to make a demonstration, and now found himself engaged in a trial of strength.

'Tell them to throw down their javelins,' he said furiously.

Purcell translated. Tetahiti looked at Mehani and there was a shadow of a smile on his lips.

'Why all this talk?' he said curtly. 'I have already answered.'

'What's he saying?' MacLeod asked impatiently.

'They'll put down their arms, if you promise not to fire.'

I

'I bet he didn't say that,' MacLeod said in a rage.

'If you're displeased with my services,' Purcell said curtly, 'find another interpreter.'

He went on: 'In any case, I advise you to accept. We are seven and, when Baker and Jones arrive, we shall be nine, and you've only got five balls.'

'So you're putting yourself in their camp!' MacLeod cried angrily, his deep-set eyes flashing.

'It's you who put me there,' Purcell said, making a gesture with his hands that were still raised to the level of his shoulders.

MacLeod hesitated. If the blacks put down their javelins without a promise, the concession would be reciprocal and he would not have intimidated them. But if he refused to promise, then he would have to fire. In that case, he could be sure only of Smudge. White had followed him unwillingly. And who could foresee what Hunt and Johnson would do, if he gave the order to fire?

'I promise,' MacLeod said, lowering the barrel of his musket. Purcell translated and, turning to Tetahiti, added pressingly: 'He realises he hasn't frightened you and is looking for some means of departing without losing face. Accept . . .'

'What are you saying to them?' MacLeod asked suspiciously.

'I'm advising them to accept.'

'Adamo is right,' Tetahiti said after a moment. 'We stand to gain nothing by provoking the son of a pig, since he promises.'

He bent down and gently placed his javelin on the grass. The slowness of his gesture was calculated, and one after another the Tahitians followed his example. They were not throwing their arms at the feet of a conqueror, but laying them carefully on the ground, as you put down an object which is precious to you, but for which you have no immediate use.

MacLeod was aware of the veiled insolence of the gesture. His expedition was a failure. He had obtained nothing but a formal concession on the basis of a promise. In a few weeks' time, these same javelins, used just as lovingly, would be menacing him day and night.

He could not make up his mind to go. Waiting for his orders, the *Peritani*, musket in hand, stood where they were, a few yards from the Tahitians and, as the seconds went by, the situation of the British became increasingly difficult. Knowing the women were behind him. MacLeod was afraid of losing face altogether if he retreated backwards. But convinced as he was of the blacks' treachery, he was afraid that, if he turned his back, he would offer a target to their javelins.

As the *Peritani*'s immobility became prolonged, it ceased to be threatening, and became ridiculous. The Tahitians were embarrassed by it as if it were something unseemly. It was another example of the *Peritani* being *maamaa*. There were two alternatives: to fire or go away. But what were they doing standing there like so many posts stuck in the ground?

Suddenly Kori began laughing. Kori was the most spontaneous and impulsive of the Tahitians. It was he who had fired at Mehoro on *The Blossom,* and the moment after thrown himself sobbing into his arms.

'Shut up! ' Tetahiti said in a low voice.

But Kori could not stop. He looked at the yellow man, the Skeleton, the little rat, Jono and the old man lined up in front of him, and the more he looked at them, the more comic they seemed to him. His laugh was a shrill neighing. His hands were on his thighs, his knees bent, his laughing face thrust forward, and his big wide-open mouth revealed his pink tongue and palate.

'Shut up, will you! ' Tetahiti repeated imperiously.

Still laughing Kori turned to Tetahiti and cried as if to justify himself: *'Maamaa! Maamaa!'*

Unfortunately, MacLeod knew the word perfectly well. Horoa said it to him every day. He turned pale, bent down, picked up a little stone at his feet and threw it at Kori's face.

The stone hit Kori in the eye. He uttered a cry of astonishment, bent down with the speed of lightning, seized his javelin and brandished it. At the same moment a shot rang out. Kori dropped his javelin, bent double, took two paces towards MacLeod, and collapsed on the grass, his face to the ground, his arms spread wide. It might have been a signal. All the Tahitians, except Mehoro, began running, and within two seconds had turned the corner of their hut and disappeared from view.

MacLeod threw the musket on the ground, lowered his head, hastily unslung the second and cocked it.

Mehoro, his face grey and his nostrils pinched, was on his knees beside Kori. After a few seconds, he plucked up courage to turn him over. He stayed there a moment looking at him, but without touching him. Then, raising his eyes to Purcell, who was standing pale and petrified two yards from him, he said in a low voice: 'He's dead.' He shook his head and his right hand trailed in the grass beside him. Suddenly he jumped up, javelin in hand. MacLeod fired. The javelin dropped, and Mehoro clutched his stomach with both hands. The blood streamed through his fingers. He watched it flow, his eyes and mouth wide open. Then he turned on his heel, bent double, and began running with slow, short, staggering steps towards the hut. He reached the corner and fell.

'Go and see if he's dead,' MacLeod said, turning to White.

Mehoro had left a trail of red blood shining in the sun on the short grass. After a few paces, White moved away from the trail and made a wide detour across the clearing to reach the body. He stopped a yard from it, crouched down, turned towards MacLeod and nodded. He came slowly back, following the same route, his eyes on the ground.

MacLeod put the butt of his musket on the ground, and leaned on the barrel with both hands. He raised his thin face, which was paler and more hollow than ever. His sides heaved convulsively in his effort to recover his breath, and he could not master the trembling in one of his legs.

Sometimes in Horoa's arms he felt a similar sense of strangeness to that which now troubled his vision. The coconut palms, the grass, the hut, the tree-stumps in the clearing, none of them seemed real to him. His eyes moved over the ground, avoiding Kori's body, and came to rest on the javelins spread out at his feet. By God, he was master of the terrain! He had killed two of the damned apes, and the others had fled like rabbits. But his victory gave him no joy. He felt nothing. Merely a sense of fatigue and emptiness.

Though Smudge had slung his musket, Purcell remained rooted to the spot. He stared at the ground, and his arms hung loose. After a moment, he started and seemed to come to. His eyes met MacLeod's. MacLeod looked vague and besotted as if he had drunk too much.

'So you haven't gone with them?' MacLeod said tonelessly.

Purcell shook his head and MacLeod went on in a low automatic voice: 'I'm sorry about those two. They weren't the worst.'

He seemed dissatisfied with this tone of excuse. He straightened up, pursed his lips, looked round defiantly and went on in a loud, boastful voice that rang false: 'This'll teach the rest to stay quiet. An example had to be made.'

'An example!' Purcell said derisively.

He too, was taking deep breaths and, though he was not particularly hot, sweat was pouring down his cheeks.

'Never fear,' he went on bitterly, 'your "example" will be followed.'

11

Purcell had scarcely finished breakfast when there was a knock at the door. It was White. His yellow face looked wrinkled and hollow as if he had spent a sleepless night.

'There's an assembly in half an hour,' he said rather breathlessly.

Purcell raised his eyebrows.

'I'm no longer a member of the assembly.'

'MacLeod asks you to come all the same. It's serious. The Tahitians have taken to the bush with their women.'

'And he's only just realised it! Where did he think they were going when he fired at them?'

'It was obviously to be expected,' White said, shaking his head sadly.

Purcell looked at him. It was the first time White had emerged from his role of steward and made a comment on events. Since the sharing out of the women he had wholly disapproved of MacLeod's attitude, but had not broken with him.

'White!'

He was already at the door. He turned.

'White, why do you abstain instead of voting against MacLeod?'

White looked at him for a moment as if wondering whether Purcell had any right to ask him such a question. Eventually, he appeared to decide that he had, for he said curtly: 'I don't think MacLeod's behaving properly.'

His voice was low and sing-song, and he spoke more correctly than any other seaman from the ship. His grammar, vocabulary and pronunciation were all correct. The drunken clergyman who had brought him up had taught him those at least.

White went on to make his thought perfectly clear: 'I think he does not behave properly towards the Tahitians.'

He did not say 'the blacks'. Like Purcell, he said 'the Tahitians'. They were the only two British on the island to do so.

'Well,' Purcell said rather impatiently, 'you might have voted against him. You'd have prevented his committing a number of injustices.'

'I didn't want to vote against him.'

'Why?'

White looked at Purcell somewhat doubtfully. He was wondering whether there was not a certain contempt in this persistence, whether Purcell would have asked so many questions of a *true* Briton. However, since Purcell was looking at him calmly and politely awaiting his reply, he felt reassured. He said with a certain solemnity: 'I'm under a great obligation to him.'

'What obligation?' Purcell asked imperturbably.

He was aware of White's hesitation, understood its cause and decided to push his enquiries to the utmost.

'You see,' White said, 'to begin with I was a good deal laughed at on board . . .'

He added quickly: 'Because of my name.'

That was characteristic. He did not say 'because of my yellow complexion and my slit eyes'. He said 'because of my name', as if his name were the only reason.

'Well?'

'MacLeod never laughed at me.'

'He must have thought it dangerous,' Purcell thought. 'And for that, for the abstention, for a good deed that was not one, White is infinitely grateful to him . . .'

'After Russell's death,' Purcell said, looking White in the eye, 'did MacLeod help you?'

Russell was the seaman White had knifed in a fight because he had laughed at him.

'You knew about that?' White said in astonishment.

Purcell nodded and White said, lowering his eyes: 'No, Mac-Leod didn't help me particularly. No more than another.'

He went on: 'You knew and said nothing about it.'

He was silent for a moment, staring at the floor. Then he raised his eyes and said, apparently irrelevantly: 'I didn't like you.'

'Why?' Purcell asked. 'I've never laughed at you.'

'Yes, once,' White said, staring at him intently out of his slit eyes.

He added honestly: 'At least, I thought so.'

'I?' Purcell cried in stupefaction.

'Do you remember when Mr Mason became captain on board *The Blossom,* and I came to tell you the captain was awaiting you for luncheon.'

'Well?'

'You raised your eyebrows mockingly.'

'I did?' Purcell said in surprise.

And suddenly he cried: 'But it wasn't at you I was laughing. It was at Mason, because he was usurping a rank to which he had no right.'

He added: 'And that's what put you in MacLeod's camp?'

White nodded without answering. It was crazy. It was fantastically absurd. The fate of the island had depended on that one facial expression. Without that raising of the eyebrows, White would have voted with him, Jones and Baker: four votes against four. MacLeod could have done nothing at all.

'It's crazy,' Purcell said aloud.

White's face hardened.

'Don't begin all over again,' Purcell cried. 'I didn't say: "You're crazy." I said: "It's crazy." '

'I may be rather sensitive,' White said. He frowned and added: 'People have really laughed at me a lot.'

There was a strange contrast between his mild words and the expression on his face. For this quiet little man to have become a murderer, he must clearly have been tormented in the most appalling way . . . 'And to think,' Purcell thought, 'that merely because MacLeod abstained from tormenting him, White has helped him to bully the Tahitians.' It was disheartening.

'I'm going now,' White said.

Purcell held out his hand. White hesitated, then his jet eyes shone and he smiled. Purcell smiled back and felt a small, crisp, dry hand in his. It replied to his pressure with a certain willingness.

'I'm going,' White repeated, lowering his eyes.

Purcell sat down on the threshold of his hut. He rubbed his neck for some time. He too had slept badly. And he had woken with a headache, a stiff neck, and a bitter taste in his mouth. It was the anxiety . . . Christ, would it never end! The whole thing was spoilt and destroyed. They would have to live with fear. Even at night, behind closed doors . . . And why? Why? He took his head in his hands. It was because MacLeod wanted two acres of land instead of one. He got up and began walking up and down in front of his hut. He kept swallowing and an un-bearable impatience wrenched at his nerves. Two men had already died. How many more would die tomorrow? Ought he not to have allowed Baker to have his way? Buy peace with a single death? 'No, no,' Purcell said almost aloud, 'one cannot reason like that. It opens the door to anything.'

The thought gave him a sense of having recovered himself and he felt more decided. But he was immediately assailed by a new idea which brought him to a halt. He wondered why the principle of respecting all human life seemed to him more im-portant than the number of human lives he might save by renouncing the principle.

But at that point he ceased thinking. He was looking up at the oblique rays of the sun falling through the coconut palms. As long as he was alive, those at least could not be taken from him. It was a splendid scene. The light was tender and curtains of mist were rising successively. The air smelt of damp grass and of the wood fires lit for breakfast. Amid the undergrowth on the further side of West Avenue the flowers were almost aggressively bright, but they did not all yield their scent at the same time. The frangipani opened with the first warmth, and at this hour of the day its rich, sweet scent was dominant.

He returned to sit on the threshold. After a moment, Ivoa appeared. She sat down beside him and leaned her head against his shoulder . . . As she neared her time, she tended to become turned in on herself and less concerned about what was going on in the island . . . A few minutes went by, then Ivoa sighed, spread wide her legs, and leaned her head against the doorpost. Purcell looked at her, leaned towards her, and lightly passed his hands across her stomach which protruded above her bark belt. 'What a world the child's going to be born into!' he thought suddenly. He got to his feet, his nerves quivering, and began walking up and down in front of the hut again. After a while he felt calmer and glanced at Ivoa. Her head was still leaning against the doorpost. There was a fullness and abundance about her, the skin of her face was taut, her complexion glowing with health and her eyes were fixed calmly on the distance. 'What quietude!' he thought enviously. 'What placidity!' Ivoa smiled at him: 'I'm going to lie down,' she said softly. 'I don't feel comfortable anywhere, neither sitting nor standing.' She added with a sigh: 'Not even lying down.' She got heavily to her feet and went indoors.

A few minutes later, Johnson appeared in West Avenue, bald, bent, his musket slung, painfully carrying his thin little stomach before him. When still some distance away, he gave Purcell a little wave of his right hand and came on, dragging his feet on the stones, his neck thrust forward as if to help his progress. His left shoulder sagged under the sling of the musket and, perhaps due to its weight, he was unable to keep to the middle of the path but kept sidling off to the left, so that he advanced in a series of zigzags, like a badly trimmed boat ceaselessly yawing towards one bank of a river.

'I'm a little early to go to MacLeod's,' he said, when he reached Purcell. 'White said in half an hour.'

'A little,' Purcell said. 'Sit down.'

Johnson uttered a series of little sighs, removed the musket from his left shoulder and propped it against the door. When he had done so, he sat down on the threshold.

'Is it loaded?' Purcell asked, sitting down.

Johnson nodded and Purcell went on: 'In that case it'd be

safer to lay it flat on the ground.'

Johnson did so.

'I really don't know what I could do with it,' he said in a hoarse voice without looking at Purcell. 'Suppose a black came out of the undergrowth, I don't even know whether I'd be able to fire. I don't wish anyone any harm,' he went on rubbing his beard with the back of his hand.

Purcell said nothing and Johnson looked at him out of the corner of his eye.

'All I want is a little peace . . . You'll tell me,' he went on, placing his hands on his knees and staring unhappily into the distance, 'that I've not chosen the right woman for it. Christ,' he went on with a feeble access of anger, 'there are times when I feel like taking the musket down and giving her a ball in the face! Good God, why can't she hold her tongue!'

His anger fell away and he looked at Purcell.

'I don't see why I have to carry a musket against the blacks. What have the blacks done to me? Nothing.'

'They can't say as much for you,' Purcell said.

'Me? Me?' Johnson stammered, looking fearfully at him. 'What have I done to them? You're not going to tell me I've done them any harm?'

'You voted for MacLeod.'

'Oh, that,' Johnson said. 'That's nothing . . .'

'Is it nothing to dispossess them of the land?' Purcell said drily. 'Is it nothing to hold them at musket's point as you did yesterday?'

'But it was MacLeod who told me to do it,' Johnson said, his voice quivering. 'O Lord,' he went on, wagging his head anxiously and glancing furtively at Purcell, 'are the blacks angry with me?'

'Probably,' Purcell said.

'Well, I'd never have thought it,' Johnson said, innocently opening his little red-rimmed eyes, and exaggerating his moronic expression. 'Because,' he added, ceasing to rub his beard and waving his forefinger impertinently in front of his face, 'I like the blacks . . .'

Purcell was silent. He was beginning to understand why Johnson had arrived 'a little early'.

'And I want to ask you,' Johnson went on, drawing imperceptibly nearer to Purcell and smiling at him with complicity, 'when you see the blacks – and even if they're in the bush,' he went on, slyly screwing up his eyes, 'it doesn't mean you don't see one or two of them from time to time, since you've remained their friend . . . Well, I'd like you to say to the blacks: "Old Johnson doesn't mean you any harm. And as for firing at you, he'll never do it." You can tell them that, sir. "Old Johnson only carries a musket to obey MacLeod, but as for firing at you – never!" I've never asked you for anything, sir,' he went on proudly, almost meritoriously indeed, as if he had renounced a right by not asking a favour, 'but today it's no longer the same thing. I've got to think of my skin, and that's all I'm asking of you. "Old Johnson," you'll say to them, "means you no harm . . ." It's not that I'm afraid for myself,' he went on, 'old as I am, with pains all over, these spots on my face, and a wife that's much worse even than the first, since she doesn't even allow me to touch her. Well,' he went on with feeble indignation, 'what's the use of a wife, having to put up with her all day, if you can't even make use of her . . .?'

This grievance made him lose the thread of his thought and he was silent for a few seconds, though still waving his forefinger in front of his face.

'What was I saying?' he asked at last, violently rubbing the purple patches in his beard.

'That you're not afraid for yourself,' Purcell said.

'That surprises you, doesn't it? But it's true. I swear it's true, sir. What satisfaction do I get out of life? A stomach that can't digest, soles of my feet that hurt me, pains in my knees, and a wife I can't even make use of . . . No, no, sir, it's not death I fear, it's something else . . .'

He went on hesitantly: 'They tell that when the blacks have killed an enemy, they cut off his head.'

'That's true.'

'Well, I wouldn't like that,' he went on in a low, quavering voice. 'You may well ask what the hell use my head is to me when I'm dead, but all the same . . .'

He shook his head dolefully two or three times.

'Damned savages!' he went on, forgetting the friendship he

had just professed for them. 'They're capable of anything, the bastards! No, no,' he went on, putting his hand to his neck, 'I wouldn't like that. I wouldn't like to be buried with my head, as you might say, in one place and me in another. Suppose,' he concluded despairingly, 'I can't find my head on the day of the Last Judgment, what'd happen then? You'll understand that, sir, since you know all about the Bible and such.'

He stared with frightened eyes into the distance for a few seconds, then leaning towards Purcell he went on in a low confidential voice: ' "Old Johnson," you'll tell them, "doesn't mean you any harm." '

Purcell looked at him.

'Listen, Johnson,' he said severely, 'I'll tell you what you want. You want to make a separate peace with the Tahitians while remaining in MacLeod's camp. Unfortunately, it's not possible. Tahitians don't understand such subtleties.'

'But what can I do?' Johnson cried anxiously.

And since Purcell made no reply, he looked sideways at him and said slyly: 'Must I fire then? Suppose I meet your friend Mehani, must I fire, sir?'

Purcell looked at him in stupefaction. This was blackmail all right. Perhaps old Johnson was not such a good old fellow after all. Because he was unhappy, virtues were attributed to him. Since he lacked character, people shut their eyes to his faults . . . But it did not always pay to find excuses for people. Sooner or later, the effects of cowardice became evident. And they were not pleasant.

Purcell got to his feet. He was disappointed and disgusted.

'You'll do as you please,' he said coldly. 'It's up to you to decide.'

'Well, then, I shan't fire,' Johnson said, looking terrified. 'You can tell the blacks that . . .'

Purcell made no reply. Hunt and Jones had just appeared in West Avenue. He waved to them.

'I'm going,' Johnson said suddenly. 'I don't want to be late.'

He picked up his musket, nodded and left. Purcell did not reply to his nod. He was watching Jones coming along West Avenue. Next to the enormous Hunt, he looked like a little boy trotting along beside his father.

'Did we drive him away?' Jones called, while still some distance off.

He had no weapon, but Hunt, like Johnson, was carrying a musket. White must have transmitted to the majority the order to go armed.

'Did we frighten him?' Jones cried with a laugh.

Purcell watched him approaching. The boy had a wonderful faculty for forgetting! When he had heard of the death of Mehoro and Kori the day before, he had burst into tears. But today he was already on the rebound. For that quick blood, those young muscles, those intact nerves, everything was a pleasure, everything a game.

'Where's Baker?' Purcell asked.

'He went fishing this morning.'

'Alone?'

'He had the hump.'

Hunt was standing beside them, enormous and red, his pale little eyes fixed on them from a great height. He was casually trailing his musket. In his huge fist, it seemed to weigh no more than a conductor's baton.

'Why have I got to carry this about?' he grumbled, suddenly brandishing the musket with a discontented air.

The muzzle was pointing straight at Jones's chest. Jones promptly pushed it down.

'Take care!' he said. 'I don't want to die!'

Purcell looked at Hunt and said carefully: 'It was MacLeod who told you to.'

Hunt turned to him all in one piece as if his neck was screwed to his body.

'And why did MacLeod tell me to?'

'Because the Tahitians must have taken to the bush.'

White must have already told him that the Tahitians had gone, but the news had evidently produced no effect on him. He could not see its connection with the musket he was carrying.

'Today, musket,' he grumbled, staring at the weapon with a querulous, irritated expression. 'Yesterday, musket. Every day, musket. Why?'

Since Purcell said nothing, he went on: 'Yesterday MacLeod said: "Come with loaded muskets." Jono comes,' he went on, tapping the red hair on his chest with his left hand. 'He comes with his musket, but not loaded. Today, too.'

He pointed it at Jones's chest and pressed the trigger. The hammer clicked.

'He frightens me into fits,' Jones said.

'Why should the musket be loaded?' Hunt went on, holding the muzzle in the hollow of Jones's stomach.

'Ask your leader,' Jones said, pushing the weapon away. 'I didn't tell you to carry a musket. He's beginning to bore me,' he went on in a low voice, looking at Purcell. 'Ever since we started out, he's been asking me why. And when I explain, he doesn't listen.'

'I know nothing about anything,' Hunt groaned suddenly, as if replying to Jones's aside. 'And how should I know anything,' he went on, swaying unhappily, 'when nobody ever tells me anything?'

He put his big fist to his mouth and began biting at it, emitting a whole series of plaintive groans. He was like a gigantic bear unable to get rid of a thorn in its paw. And while he went on biting his hand and groaning, his pale little eyes moved constantly from Jones to Purcell as if asking them to explain, once and for all, the hazy, incomprehensible world about him.

'MacLeod will tell you,' Purcell said. 'After all, you don't vote with us, but with him.'

'Vote?' Hunt echoed.

'You raise your hand.'

Hunt docilely raised the hand he was biting.

'Is that voting?'

'That's it.'

He let his hand fall, shrugged his enormous shoulders, and said unhappily: 'I can't know. No one ever tells me anything.'

Then, without waiting for Jones and Purcell, he strode away towards East Avenue. His musket, swinging at the end of his enormous arm, looked like a child's toy.

When Purcell appeared at MacLeod's door, he was surprised by the silence that welcomed him. Owing to the darkness of the room, he could at first see nothing but vague figures carrying muskets. He took a step into the room and stopped in stupefaction. Booted, buttoned, cravatted, and as dignified as if he was lording it in the cabin of *The Blossom,* Mason was sitting in the centre of the room, with MacLeod on his right.

For a second or two, Purcell was speechless. Nor did Mac-Leod say anything. He merely smiled.

'Good morning, Captain Mason,' Purcell said at last.

'Humph!' Mason said, sitting stiffly with his grey-blue eyes fixed disapprovingly on the shark's tooth swinging against Purcell's cheek.

MacLeod smiled, his thin face slit from ear to ear. The muscles of his jaw stood out as clearly and distinctly as in an anatomical exhibit.

'Sit down, Purcell,' he said, his voice vibrating sarcastically. 'Or you'll be taking root.'

Three stools opposite MacLeod had been reserved for the minority. Purcell sat down and, as soon as he had taken his place, he felt strangely naked amid all these armed men. He was making a great effort to conceal his surprise, but his silence and his eyes betrayed him. Mason agreeing to sit with seamen, with the men who had burnt his ship, rejected his authority and nearly hanged him!

'Captain Mason,' MacLeod said, 'Baker is at Rope Beach. He probably won't be back before noon. Since we're all here, except for him, I suggest we begin and that you tell the lads what it's all about.'

So he had taken in sail, too! He was calling Mason 'captain' and giving him precedence!

'My lads,' Mason began at once, 'the past is the past, and I shall not go back over it. There's no point in asking who's been at fault in setting a sail when a squall hits you. With four homicidal blacks in the bush, it's not the moment to quarrel with the quartermaster because he's made a mistake in the course. We're all in a bad way, my lads, the lot of us, and if we hole the hull on a rock we'll all go to the bottom together.'

He paused and looked round at the crew with his grey-blue eyes. He was holding his musket between his legs with his right hand. As he started speaking again, he passed the barrel to his left hand, and placed his right flat on his knee, as if the gesture would lend greater importance to what he was going to say.

'MacLeod,' he went on, 'tells me that you've formed the habit of deciding things by vote and that you wish to continue to do so. Very well. It doesn't seem to me that all this voting has done you much good so far but, as I've said, the past is the past, and I've not come here to criticise, but to decide with you what's to be done.'

'Hear, hear!' MacLeod said politely, as if he were approving a speech in the House of Commons.

'The blacks,' Mason went on in a loud voice, 'can only hope to defeat us by surprise and being two or three against one. It seems to me, therefore, that we should go about armed and as far as possible in groups. Fishing, for example. Suppose that for reasons of security we choose Rope Beach as our fishing place. Three or four men will climb down into the cove, while the others stand guard over the rope. Similarly for the water fatigue. Armed men must be detailed to escort the women. As for the plantations, it's clear they must all be cultivated in common.'

'Temporarily,' MacLeod said.

'Of course. But, for the moment, we need two teams. One team to work; and the other to protect the workers, musket in hand.'

'If I understand you,' Purcell said, 'we're returning to the original system: fishing and cultivation in common.'

'That is correct,' Mason said stiffly.

'In that case, it seems most unfortunate that it should have required a war merely to get back to where we were before. If we'd gone on as we were, there wouldn't have been a war at all.'

'I've already said that the past is the past, Mr Purcell,' Mason said impatiently. 'There's no point in going back over it. I have probably better reason for recrimination than anyone else,' he added, shaking his head, 'but I'm saying nothing about it. I have sufficient strength of will to say nothing. It seems to me that, in our present circumstances, everyone should pocket his grievances.'

'Besides,' MacLeod said, picking up the thread, 'it's understood, is it not, Captain Mason, that when the war's over the land will be divided up again?'

'When the war's over!' Purcell said.

He went on: 'I'd like to know just how you propose to end this "war".'

MacLeod and Mason exchanged a glance which at once put Purcell on his guard. However unlikely it might seem at first, it was clear they had come to an understanding. MacLeod must have gone to see Mason immediately after the murder of the two Tahitians and have persuaded him to come to his help: the sacred alliance, the whites against the blacks, the British against the savages, and so on. Their mutual support was not really so incredible. Mason and MacLeod had nearly killed each other, but they had much in common.

'I'll come to that later, Mr Purcell,' Mason said, 'and you need have no fear that we shall not ask everyone's opinion. We shall even,' he added, addressing the crew on an indefinable note of resignation, regret and contempt, 'vote. We shall vote,' he repeated, slightly raising his hand from his knee, 'since you have made a habit of it.'

Purcell admired MacLeods' ability. He had succeeded in making Mason accept the vote by presenting it, not as a legitimate proceeding, but as a sort of odd custom that had taken root. It was Machiavellian. Mason had no concern for the law, but he was too English not to respect a custom.

'Captain Mason,' MacLeod said courteously, 'you were speaking of the precautions to be taken . . .'

'That's right,' Mason said without looking at Purcell. 'That was what I was speaking about when I was interrupted. I don't much fear attack by day,' he went on with a competent air, 'but it's different by night. The blacks can creep noiselessly up to a hut, set fire to it, and when you come out blinded by the smoke, take you by surprise. I, therefore, propose that all the British withdraw into the Tahitians' hut for the night. It has an open space round it, and it will be easy to clear it still further by cutting down a few trees. Fires can be lit away from the hut to light the approaches, loopholes can be cut in each of the four walls, and sentries posted and relieved every two hours.'

'We'll mount guard!' Jones cried in sudden excitement, and Purcell glanced at him in stupefaction. His eyes were bright and his face pink with excitement. He saw himself at a loophole with a musket . . . He was carried away by the thought of it. 'He too!'

Purcell thought sadly. 'And yesterday he was weeping for Kori and Mehoro . . .'

'But what shall we do with the women?' Jones asked.

'I've thought of that,' Mason said with condescension, as if he were pleased to have been asked the question. 'They'll sleep on the first floor. They'll be safe there and won't interfere with operations. It's lucky the Tahitians' hut has two floors,' he added with an air of satisfaction as if it was in some way a credit to himself.

Purcell looked at Mason and was struck by his expression. At this moment, Mason was wholly happy. His imagination had run away with him. The captain was once more the captain. He was back on his quarterdeck, setting the course. He was at the helm, and taking the crew in hand again, gently and tactfully to begin with. To start with he had even accepted the vote. 'The damned fool!' Purcell thought angrily. 'When MacLeod's made full use of him, a mere vote will send him back to his hut.'

'Captain Mason,' he said aloud, 'I'm not arguing about your proposals. But there's one thing that surprises me: we're in process of going utterly over to war. We're behaving as if we were besieged and making preparations for a siege of indefinite duration. In my opinion, it might be better to seek some means of putting an end to the state of affairs.'

'I see what you mean, Mr Purcell,' Mason said. 'But be assured that we shall not leave the initiative to the blacks. We shall attack.'

He tapped his knee with the flat of his hand and said with decision: 'We shall attack. We shall not be the hunted. We shall be the hunters.'

'Captain Mason,' Purcell said in amazement, 'do you mean to say that you intend to kill the Tahitians?'

Mason looked at him, his grey-blue eyes wide with astonishment.

'Certainly, Mr Purcell, that is precisely what I do mean. It may be regrettable, but there's no other solution. In the circumstances, I consider there'll be no security for the British on the island till we've eliminated the blacks.'

'But that's an appalling suggestion!' Purcell cried, getting suddenly to his feet and staring at Mason, his eyes flashing. 'The

Tahitians have done nothing. Absolutely nothing. They've been bullied and defrauded. Two of their men have been killed. Their only reaction has been to take flight. And now you propose to exterminate them!'

'Sit down, Mr Purcell,' Mason said calmly. 'We're among whites here, and there's no point in getting angry. For my part, I consider that MacLeod has acted in legitimate self-defence and that the blacks . . .'

'He provoked them!'

'Not at all. He was threatened with death, and he took appropriate action. Please sit down, Mr Purcell . . .'

'Everyone knows,' Purcell cried, 'why MacLeod was threatened. He excluded the Tahitians from the sharing out of the land.'

'If you want my opinion, I think he was quite right, the blacks are bad . . .'

'Of course!' Purcell interrupted violently. 'The Tahitians are always wrong. Even when you kill them, it's their fault!'

'Please sit down . . .'

'I demand a vote!' Purcell went on forcibly. 'I don't expect to convince you, nor even to win the vote, but I want everyone here to assume his responsibilities. White! Smudge! Jones! Hunt! Johnson!' he cried in a quivering voice, looking each in turn in the eyes. 'You're going to vote! Captain Mason is of the opinion that the war should be prosecuted until there's not a single black left on the island. I'm against it! It's up to you to choose!'

'Baker's not here,' Jones said.

'I'll grant you his vote, Purcell,' MacLeod said in his drawling voice. 'He's always voted for you and, if he were here, there's no reason to suppose he wouldn't vote for you today. If Captain Mason agrees,' he went on, turning to him, 'I'll put your proposal to the vote. Captain Mason?'

'Go ahead,' Mason said resignedly.

Purcell sat down.

'I put the proposal to the vote,' MacLeod said, laughing silently.

With Mason he could count on six votes, against Purcell's mere three.

'Who's for it?' he said with insulting nonchalance.

'I abstain,' Johnson said at once.

There was a silence and then Smudge shouted furiously: 'What's that you said?'

'I said I abstain,' Johnson replied without looking at him.

He put his musket across his knees, the muzzle pointing at Smudge, and went on: 'I don't advise anyone to touch me.'

The fear of having his head cut off had had an admirable effect! It had even given him courage . . .

MacLeod shrugged. He could afford to lose a vote.

'Who's for it?' he repeated, as if the incident were beneath contempt. 'Will you vote, Captain Mason?'

Mason slowly raised his hand. He seemed to be voting reluctantly, even for his own motion.

'Smudge?' MacLeod said.

Mason let his hand fall and looked up at the ceiling as if the scene held no further interest for him.

'Hunt?'

Hunt raised his hand.

'White?'

White stayed quite still, his eyes on the floor, his yellow, dimpled hands crossed on the barrel of his musket.

'White?' MacLeod repeated.

'I'm against it,' White said in his soft voice.

MacLeod paled and his face tautened. Since White had abstained, he had no longer been sure of him. And now there was an open break. White had gone over to the other camp.

'You've thought it over?' he said reproachfully, with a note of sorrow even in his voice.

He knew White too well to have any hope of intimidating him.

'I've thought it over,' White said without raising his eyes.

'I'm against it!' Jones shouted happily. 'So's Purcell. So's Baker. So's White. Johnson abstained. That makes four votes against four. No majority! Mason's motion rejected!'

He placed his hands on his thighs, turned his elbows out, threw his head back and laughed. There was a long silence.

'Humph!' Mason said suddenly, looking round at them. 'What's going on? . . . What's going on, MacLeod?' he added, turning stiffly towards the Scotsman.

'Your motion has not achieved a majority, Captain Mason.'

'What? What's that?' Mason said with impatience and indignation. 'What does that mean?'

'That it's rejected, Captain Mason.'

'Rejected!' Mason cried, turning scarlet. 'What damned impertinence!'

He seemed on the point of exploding, but controlled himself, and went on fairly calmly: 'Well, what difference does that make? The blacks are still in the bush, and we're still here. I don't see that it makes any difference whether the motion is voted or not.'

'There is one,' Purcell said incisively. 'If you want to go out and hunt them down, you can take with you only MacLeod, Smudge and Hunt. And as far as Hunt's concerned, I can tell you that he has no intention of loading his musket.'

'What's all this?' MacLeod muttered. 'Hunt, isn't your musket loaded?'

'Look,' Hunt said.

He pointed it at MacLeod and pressed the trigger. MacLeod threw himself on the floor.

'Christ!' he said, getting up and rubbing his shoulder. 'Don't play tricks like that, Hunt!'

'It's not very nice,' Jones said sympathetically.

The whole thing was becoming a farce. MacLeod was white with controlled anger. But he dared not ask Hunt any further questions in public. He feared to get a reply that would place Hunt also in the opposite camp. 'I've won all along the line,' Purcell thought bitterly. 'And *it's too late.*'

'Well?' MacLeod said, as if he could read his thoughts. 'What difference does your vote make, Purcell? The blacks are in the bush. They love us about as much as a mongoose does a snake, and it's not your vote that'll throw them into our arms. In my view, the blacks are at this very moment thinking very much as Captain Mason does, that's to say that there won't be any peace on the island so long as our heads aren't decorating the landscape on pikes round their hut.'

'So long as *your* head's not on a pike,' Purcell said coldly. 'After all, who defrauded them over the sharing out of the women? Who excluded them from the division of the land? Who killed Kori and Mehoro?'

'We're not going to quarrel in face of a common enemy,' Mason said gravely, looking reproachfully at Purcell. 'Don't let's forget we're British and must stand together at all costs.'

'Stand together! . . . The common enemy! . . .' He never missed one.

'You'll permit me to reply to MacLeod,' Purcell said, controlling his exasperation. 'He has just suggested that the Tahitians have condemned us all to death. I don't believe it.'

'No one's obliging you to believe me,' MacLeod said in his drawling voice. 'But if you don't believe me, there's a very simple way to find out. Go and ask them.'

Purcell stared at the floor and thought. Did MacLeod's suggestion conceal a trap? Would he be reproached later with having made contact with the 'mutineers'?

'After all,' MacLeod went on, 'you shouldn't have much difficulty in finding them. You know them well, both them . . . and their women.'

Smudge chuckled, and there was a silence. It was evident that Itia's advances were known to the whole island.

Purcell looked up.

'If I try to see the Tahitians,' he said slowly, 'it will not be in my own name, but by virtue of a mandate given me by the assembly.'

'A mandate? What mandate?' Mason said irritably. 'We shall certainly not give you a mandate to go and gossip with the enemy.'

He turned to MacLeod as if seeking his approbation, but MacLeod said nothing. He realised his companions were far from keen for a fight, he feared being abandoned by them, and he counted on Purcell's embassy to persuade them that *all* the Peritani were included in the blacks' resentment.

'If it's merely to go to gossip and rub cheeks with them,' he said sarcastically, 'I agree with Captain Mason that it's perhaps not altogether suitable, either with or without an earring. But if it's to find out about their intentions, then I think it's useful, in time of war, to know what the enemy's intentions are. If Purcell wants to go and risk his precious neck talking to the bastards, I personally think it's an opportunity and, with your permission, Captain Mason,' he added with admirably assumed deference, 'I'm on the whole in favour of it.'

Upon which, he casually raised his right hand, and immediately let it fall again. It was so slight and rapid a gesture that Mason could scarcely regard it as a vote, but as MacLeod let his hand fall he turned to Smudge and winked at him.

'I'm for it,' Smudge said at once.

'So am I,' said White.

Then Hunt raised his hand, followed by Purcell, Johnson and Jones.

'Well, since everyone's agreed,' MacLeod went on at once without asking Mason for his vote or taking note of the result by the usual formula, 'Purcell can go and risk his life in the bush whenever he likes, and with our blessing. And now, if you approve, Captain Mason,' he went on quickly, 'we can turn to something else. There's a water fatigue this afternoon and, in the circumstances, I think we should draw lots for the escort. Smudge, who can write, has put our names on pieces of paper . . . Smudge, pass the hat to Jones.'

'Have you included my name?' Mason asked nobly.

'Captain Mason, I thought . . .'

'Include it,' Mason said.

'That's very decent of you, Captain Mason,' MacLeod said with a devout air.

He got up, went to one of the numerous cupboards behind him, took out the writing-case that had belonged to Lieutenant Simon, and placed it on the table. Smudge drew up his stool, coughed, stuck out his rat's face and, dipping the point of his quill in the ink with the air of a connoisseur, proceeded to trace each letter with painstaking care. The crew watched him in silence, and not without respect.

'There's no reason I should be favoured,' Mason went on, gazing austerely at the ceiling. 'We must all take our share of the common danger . . .'

'Indeed!' Purcell thought irritably. 'I don't remember ever to have seen Mason go aloft in bad weather . . .' He caught MacLeod's eye, and realised that the same idea had also occurred to him. MacLeod was standing behind Mason and the expression on his thin face, far from being one of devout deference, was of such profound contempt that Purcell felt a certain indignation. There was an exasperating side to Mason, but to watch him being relegated to the role of a puppet whose strings were pulled by MacLeod was an odious spectacle.

'How many names am I to draw?' Jones asked, when he had placed Burt's cocked hat on his knees.

MacLeod sat down and turned politely to Mason. He was leaving him the front of the stage and the initiative in minor details.

'Four,' Mason said with his competent air. 'Four will be amply sufficient.'

Jones put his hand into the hat, drew out four papers and put the hat on the table.

'Hunt.'

Hunt groaned.

'You'll go on the water fatigue this afternoon,' MacLeod said.

He was on the point of adding 'with your musket loaded', but kept it for later.

'White,' Jones said.

White nodded.

'Johnson.'

'Me? Me?' Johnson said, looking terrified and putting his hand to his lips.

'You don't think you're exempt, do you?' Smudge said. 'You can shoot as well as the next man.'

'Me? Me?' Johnson repeated feebly, scraping his feet on the floor. He was like a frightened old hen scratching the earth.

'Next,' MacLeod said without looking at him.

'Jones,' Jones said.

And he burst out laughing.

'Hunt, White, Johnson and Jones,' MacLeod said. 'We're all agreed? . . . I think that's all, Captain Mason.'

Mason got up and spread his legs wide as if he feared the ship would roll.

'Men,' he said in a firm voice, 'I'll remind you that we all spend this night in the Tahitians' hut.'

He waved his hand in dismissal. It was over. Purcell went out first with Jones.

'Ropati,' he said, as they walked down East Avenue. 'I'm going to give you a piece of advice. Don't take your musket on the water fatigue.'

'Why?' Jones said, looking disappointed.

It was a game. The most exciting of games. With your musket under your arm, you walked cat-like ahead of the water fatigue, alert, watching for a movement in every bush . . .

'If the Tahitians see you with a musket, they'll put you in MacLeod's camp.'

'Surely not!' Jones said, looking ingenuously at Purcell. 'They like me. I've never had any trouble with them.'

'They won't like you any more if they see you with a musket.'

'Why?' Jones said with a childish smile. 'They'll probably think I'm hunting wild pig.'

'Don't be silly!' Purcell said irritably.

'I'll leave you here,' Jones said, looking put out and squaring his shoulders. 'I'll go by Trade Wind Street. It's shorter.'

'Please,' Purcell said pressingly, 'think it over.'

'I'll think it over,' Jones said over his shoulder.

'I ought not to have said "don't be silly",' Purcell thought. 'He's capable of doing it merely to show he's no longer a child . . .'

'Mr Purcell,' Mason's voice said behind him.

Purcell turned.

'Mr Purcell,' Mason said, 'I've got a couple of words to say to you.'

'I'm at your service, Captain Mason,' Purcell said stiffly.

'Very well then, let's walk. My house is on your way. Mr Purcell,' he added with a suspicion of severity in his voice, 'you're not in step with me.'

Purcell looked at him. It had clearly not occurred to Mason to adjust his to Purcell's.

'Mr Purcell,' Mason went on, 'we have had our little differences. I have not always approved you in the past. I do not approve you any more now. But, owing to the gravity of the situation, I have decided to wipe the slate clean.'

It was typical. Mason was prepared to forgive him for not being always of his opinion.

'Mr Purcell,' Mason went on without even noticing his silence,

'I understand that Mrs Purcell is expecting a baby in June. I congratulate you.'

'Thank you . . .'

'As you know,' Mason interrupted, 'Mrs Mason is in the same case.'

He drew himself up and blushed slightly.

'Mrs Mason,' he added, 'is expecting to be brought to bed in September.'

'Captain Mason,' Purcell said, 'allow me in my turn to . . .'

'I hope,' Mason interrupted again, 'that it will be a boy.'

He stopped and turned to look at Purcell.

'Mr Purcell, it must be a boy,' he went on emphatically, looking Purcell in the eye as if he intended to hold him personally responsible in case of failure. 'As far as I'm concerned,' he went on, 'I have no use for a daughter. I have never made a mystery of the fact that I do not care for the weaker sex. It *is* weaker, and one need say no more. Of course, Mr Purcell, I have nothing against Mrs Mason. As I have already had the honour of informing you, it was a good choice. Mrs Mason is a woman with an inherent sense of dignity. She very much reminds me of my sister. In short, she's a lady. I should not be surprised,' he concluded with a nod, 'to learn that she comes from an excellent Tahitian family.'

He walked on.

'In step, Mr Purcell, if you please.'

Purcell changed step.

'Mr Purcell,' Mason went on, 'I am not a religious man but, since I have learned of Mrs Mason's interesting condition, I have prayed to almighty God twice a day to send me a boy. And I will ask you to add your prayers to mine,' he added in a tone of command.

Purcell screwed up his eyes. To all appearances, Mason thought the prayers of an 'expert' would be more effective than his own.

'I shall do my best, Captain Mason,' he said with perfect gravity. 'But do you not think, since I have no family connection either with you or with Mrs Mason . . .'

'I have thought of that, Mr Purcell. The Lord might indeed conclude that you were interfering in what was no business of yours. But I intend asking you to be the godfather. You will admit that this entirely alters the situation.'

'Evidently,' Purcell said gravely.

'After all,' Mason went on, 'it appears to me that you will make a most suitable godfather. Besides I have no choice. You are the only person on the island, apart from myself, who can be considered a gentleman.'

'Thank you, Captain Mason,' Purcell said without a smile.

'As I have already remarked,' Mason went on, 'this entirely alters the situation. I assume that, as godfather, you are perfectly qualified to ask the Lord to influence the sex of your future godchild. Pray consider that there is already one chance in two that it will be a boy. What I desire is that there should be two chances in two. The demand is not therefore a very exorbitant one,' he went on, as if the Lord could not fail to satisfy so moderate a request.

They had reached his hut. Mason stopped by the gate leading to his 'quarterdeck', and stood face to face with Purcell. He was not going to invite even the godfather of his future son to come in.

His grey-blue eyes turned to the mountain and his face suddenly turned purple.

'Mr Purcell,' he said with sudden emotion, 'I have never forgotten your fine conduct at the time of Jimmy's death.'

It was the second time he had referred to the event since landing on the island.

'Captain Mason . . .'

'It was very courageous of you, Mr Purcell. You were risking your life. That brute would never have forgiven you. He would have let you die in irons.'

His eyes filled with tears, he turned his head away and said in a choking voice, as if suddenly overwhelmed by the tide of his emotion: 'If it's a boy, we shall call him Jimmy.'

Purcell looked down and blushed in his turn. At that moment all was forgotten. He almost felt affection for Mason.

'I would never have dared appear before my sister without Jimmy,' Mason said in a low voice. 'My sister,' he went on, 'has not had a very happy life. As for my life . . . In short, Mr Purcell, Jimmy was . . . our ray of sunshine.'

He uttered the words with some embarrassment as if he considered the metaphor too daring. Then he fell silent, hitched up the sling of his musket, leaned forward to open the gate, and without a word crossed the 'quarterdeck'. Purcell gazed after him.

As he reached the door of his hut, Mason turned. Tears were pouring down his face. He smiled, raised his right hand, and shouted: 'It will be a boy, Mr Purcell.'

'I hope so, Captain Mason,' Purcell cried heartily.

After the midday meal, Purcell looked for his chair and remembered with annoyance that it was at Omaata's. He went out into his garden and crossed the few yards between the hut and the thicket of hibiscus that formed his boundary.

'I'm going to Omaata's!' Ivoa cried, waving to him from the sunny threshold of the sliding doors.

Purcell smiled and waved back. He too was now beginning to talk with his hands. Ivoa moved out of the sun and was immediately swallowed up by the darkness of the hut as if she had disappeared through a trap-door.

Something fell on Purcell's bare foot. He looked down, but could see nothing. He turned towards the thicket of hibiscus and once again something struck him lightly on the leg. It was a little stone. He stood quite still.

He looked round at the giant ferns surrounding his garden.

'Who's there?' he called in a low voice, every nerve tense.

There was no answer, and the silence lasted so long that he almost began to doubt he had served as a target. Just as he was about to start walking again, a third stone hit him on the chest. He suddenly remembered the first day on the island and Mehani lying on the grass in front of the banyan . . .

'Itia?' Purcell said in a low voice.

There was a laugh. Purcell stared at the ferns, but could see nothing. Not a leaf moved. Behind the hibiscus thicket there was a little belt of giant ferns separating it from the trees of the second plateau. It was only some dozen yards wide. But it was so thick that he had never tried to go through it. He went round by Banyan Lane.

'O young woman who throws stones!' Purcell said.

It was what Mehani had said that first day on the island under the banyan. There was a stifled, cooing, excited laugh.

'Come out of that,' Purcell said.

'I can't,' Itia's voice replied. 'I mustn't show myself.'

She went on: 'You come to me.'

He thought it over. Only Itia could lead him to the Tahitians' hideout. MacLeod had been right. Purcell walked slowly round the hibiscus.

'Where are you?' he said, looking at the large leaves of the ferns.

'Here.'

But she still did not show herself. He parted the thick flexible stalks, bent double and entered the thicket. It was dark as night. The air was cool and damp.

'Where are you?' he said impatiently.

The tangled stalks prevented his standing upright. He knelt on one knee. The place was damp, silent and bathed in green obscurity. The ground was covered with moss.

He had no time to see her before she was there, against his chest, all fresh and scented. Her little moist lips moved over his face with the awkward enthusiasm of a puppy. He took her by the arms and held her from him. That was worse. As soon as she was away from him, her scent seemed to strike him in the face. The hibiscus in her hair, the tiarés, the necklace of pandanus kernels . . . Under the big leaves of the ferns, in the damp, confined atmosphere, her scent took on an extraordinary power. 'If the skin is good . . .' Omaata had said. Under Purcell's fingers, Itia's shoulders felt soft and yielding to the touch like those of a child. He could scarcely see her. He felt her and breathed her scent as if she were a fruit.

'I must speak to you, Itia.'

The mere fact of saying it restored his self-control. He reluctantly took his hands from her shoulders.

'Speak!' Itia said.

Purcell's eyes had got used to the dim light and Itia gradually became visible to him. She was kneeling, sitting back on her heels, and in this position her ample, shapely thighs jutted forward, while the white strips of the bark of her skirt fell to the moss on either side. Her round shoulders were leaning forward, bringing her breasts together, and her arms hung down, but her hips

spreading beneath her thin waist forced even her arms into
curves. She was pouting, but her laughing eyes gave the lie to
her lips.

'Speak!' she repeated a little disdainfully, undulating her hips
without moving her narrow waist.

'Itia, listen. We're in a state of war!'

'*Etaoué!*' Itia said, her little round face looking sad. '*Eaoué!*
War is upon us, and many women will become widows . . .'

'Precisely. I want to prevent the war.'

'Prevent the war?' Itia repeated doubtfully.

'Yes, that's what I want. You must take me to Tetahiti.'

'When?'

'Now.'

'Now?' Itia said, looking shocked.

'Why not now?'

'*Maamaa.* It's not the hour to walk in the sun. It's the hour
for a siesta . . . and for play.'

There was a silence, then she undulated her hips again and
went on in a low, soft voice, her brown eyes gleaming in the
shadow: 'Play with me, Adamo.'

He looked at her. What a discovery the word 'play' was! It
summed up a whole people, a whole civilisation! How innocent
it sounded! You played hide-and-seek with Itia under the giant
ferns, and when you had caught her, you 'played'. Adamo and
Itia, naked and childish on the moss like two babies on a carpet
. . . 'Play'! The whole of life was only 'playing'. In the morning,
when it was cool, you 'played' at fishing. In the afternoon,
you 'played' at climbing coconut palms to gather the nuts. In
the evening, when it was cool again, you 'played' at hunting wild
pig. But in the middle of the day, during the belly of the sun,
you sought the shade, and you 'played' . . . The verb had no
need of an object. It was 'play'. It was the pre-eminent 'play'.
The most innocent 'play'.

'No,' Purcell said.

'Why?'

'I've already told you: it's a taboo.'

He said this with a certain embarrassment. That 'play' should
be taboo sounded silly in Tahitian.

Itia laughed.

'Who's taboo?'

'*Eatua's.*'

'Man!' Itia said indignantly. 'You're saying things that are not true! It's the chief or the witch-doctor who makes taboos. It's not *Eatua*. *Eatua* is *Eatua*, and that's all.'

This was heresy! God did not trouble himself with man.

'In the great island of rain,' Purcell said, 'it is *Eatua* who decides taboos.'

And that too, when you came to think of it, was heresy. But how could he make her understand that God was universal?

'Well,' Itia said, 'we're not in the big island here. Your taboo's not valid. Why take the taboo from one island to another?'

But they had already discussed that point. And Purcell had never had the last word in the argument.

'I've said no,' Purcell declared firmly.

Itia sat up straight and her eyes flashed.

'Man,' she said angrily, 'why do you insult me like this? Have I a temper like Horoa? Am I common like Vaa? Am I ugly like Taïata? Look at my breasts!' she said, gently raising them in her little dimpled hands. 'Look at my stomach! Look at my hips!' she went on, undulating them from side to side with her hands raised. 'Look, man! See how big they are!'

And her breasts high, the palms of her hands raised to the level of her shoulders, she watched her hips undulating with a delighted smile as if she were gradually becoming intoxicated with her own beauty.

'Look, man!' she said, her voice low and rather hoarse. 'Look! I've wide hips to receive you and bear you a child!'

'I've given you your answer,' Purcell said. 'And now, please take me to Tetahiti.'

She fell still. Her little round face became stern, and her eyes flashed.

'Man,' she said, her voice shrill with anger, 'if you play with me, I'll take you to my people's hideout. If you won't play, I shall go away.'

Purcell stared at her in astonishment. This was the day for blackmail! After Johnson, Itia!

'I'm very angry, Itia,' Purcell said severely. 'I'm very angry indeed.'

And without thinking that this was hardly the moment to give her pleasure, he repeated in English: 'I'm very angry.'

'Why?' she at once answered in English, shaping her lips with care. She pronounced it 'ouaïé' with no trace of an 'h' and adding an 'é' at the end, but it was so well articulated, and was uttered with such expression, that you could practically see the word issue, rounded and surprised, from her mouth. 'Why?' she went on in Tahitian, with an innocent air, extending her demonstrative hands in front of her. 'If you're kind, I'll be kind. If you're unkind, I'll be unkind.'

She was leaning forward, and with her arms round her knees, her body curved into a ball, she looked like a fruit on a carpet of leaves: round, luscious, scented. 'And I,' Purcell thought, 'I'm the naughty baby, because I won't play.'

'Itia,' he said firmly, 'you'll take me to your people, and that's all there is to it. I won't have conditions.'

'If you're kind, I'll be kind.'

'Good-bye, Itia.'

'If you're kind, I'll be . . .'

'Good-bye, Itia.'

'I shall come back tomorrow,' Itia said calmly, and in her laughing, roguish eyes there shone the absolute certainty that he would end by yielding.

'Good-bye!' Purcell said angrily.

And he left the thicket of ferns with such lack of precaution that he banged his forehead and pinched his right hand between two stems.

As he returned to his hut, he felt the sun beating down on his neck and shoulders. It felt like blows rather than burning. He hastened on, entered the shade of the roof with relief and threw himself on his bed. He remembered that Ivoa had gone to Omaata's. This passion they had for visiting each other! He felt lonely and depressed. In his heart of hearts he was not so sure as he had pretended to MacLeod that the Tahitians did not look upon *all* the *Peritani* as their enemies. He remembered the warrior traditions of Tahiti. When a tribe killed one of your men, it was right, if you could, to massacre it in its entirety. However, the circumstances were different. The *Peritani* were not an enemy tribe with a long past of wars, treacheries and atrocities. Most of them had even been on friendly terms with the Tahitians, and perhaps the latter would admit certain shades of difference into their vengeance. For instance, they might consider that only the *Peritani* who carried muskets were enemies. 'But in that case,' Purcell thought remorsefully, 'I'd have done better to yield to Itia and see them. I could have told them not to go by appearances; that Jones carried a musket merely from childishness; that Hunt did not load his; that Johnson had made up his mind not to fire; and that White had voted against MacLeod . . .'

He saw Jones as he had walked away a few minutes ago down Trade Wind Street, his short nose wrinkled in anger. He would certainly be armed for the water fatigue and, even if nothing happened this time, eyes would be watching him from the bush. Ropati was carrying a musket; Ropati was also against them. 'I ought to go and see him at once,' Purcell thought, 'and suggest taking his place.' But it was hot, and he did not feel like moving. Besides, it was useless. Jones would refuse. He knew what he was doing, he was no longer a child . . . and so on.

The sun and the heat were flooding in through the open sliding doors and, though he was almost naked, Purcell was sweating. He thought of getting up to shut the doors, but he could not be bothered, and merely contented himself with turning his back to the light. He had a strange feeling of certainty that every day that went by brought the islanders nearer to more killings, yet he could not bring himself to believe it. And the others did not believe it either. Baker went off to fish – alone! – and stayed there all day. Mason prayed God twice a day to vouchsafe him a son. Ivoa went to gossip with a neighbour. Itia thought of nothing but 'playing'. And he was taking a siesta, as he did every day. War was upon them, staring them in the face, and no one wanted to recognise the fact.

As each day, at the same hour, he felt sleep coming over him. He closed his eyes and his body settled heavily on the mattress of leaves. He felt torpid, and was sinking little by little into sleep. Suddenly he started up. He felt guilty at going to sleep, as if the lives of the *Peritani* depended on his being awake. 'It's absurd,' he said almost aloud. 'What can I do?' His head felt heavy and his neck hurt. It had been almost too cool under the

K

ferns with Itia, and when he had come out the sun had taken him by surprise.

He closed his eyes again, and slid into sleep. An intolerable uneasiness awakened him. It was the same feeling of having a bad conscience that he had known as a child when he had gone to sleep without having finished his homework. He felt a lump in his throat. There was something he ought to do, but he did not know what. Here he was, lazing in bed, while time was going irremediably by; something, somewhere, had been irrevocably lost; and it was his fault. He did not know whether he was awake or asleep, he had a feeling of nightmare; his thoughts began to go round and round in circles; and a voice was murmuring ceaselessly into his ear: 'Adamo, you ought, you ought, you ought . . .' But what ought he to have done? Of what was he guilty? The voice fell silent, and he sank whirling into the shadows.

If only his thoughts would cease to turn in an oppressive circle, if only he were not so weary . . . If he could go forward and see clearly! There was a green glow in front of him. He was at the foot of the banyan, lost in its verdant maze. He was looking for Mehani. He was going round and round the tree. A shade was fleeing before him, a black athletic back, which bent to pass under a branch. Mehani! He did not even turn round. This had been going on for hours. And suddenly, there he was! There! Above him! His head was suspended in the air all by itself among the leaves, and the face was grey and bloodless, and leaning to one side like Christ's on the cross. He cried: 'Mehani!' The eyes opened with painful slowness, they were already glassy. 'Mehani! Mehani!' Purcell kep crying his name. If he ceased to do so, Mehani would die. Then the thick purple lips opened, and the sad, veiled brown eyes stared at him: 'Adamo,' Mehani said slowly, 'you ought not . . .' 'But what? What?' Purcell cried desperately. 'What ought I not to have done?' . . .

He half woke up. The sweat was pouring from his armpits and down his sides. But his body seemed weighed down by sleep, and he could not move. It suddenly became night. Mehani disappeared, and Purcell saw, quite small, on the edge of the banyan, Jones running, musket in hand. It was not really Jones, but a little boy who looked like Jones and was brandishing a little wooden musket. He turned his head towards Purcell and his freckled face was laughing. 'I shall never catch him,' Purcell thought anxiously. He could not raise his knees to run. He was dragging his heavy and benumbed legs after him. Suddenly, Jones fell. Purcell nearly tripped over his body. He stopped. It was not Jones, but Jimmy, his face smashed by Burt's fist; his nose was crushed and blood was trickling from his mouth. My God, Jimmy! Jimmy! 'I hope, Mr Purcell,' Mason was saying loudly in his ear, 'that it will be a boy.' Mason had taken him by the shoulders. 'Mr Purcell, it *must* be a boy!'

He woke up completely. Large black hands were round his arm and shaking him. The motion made him feel sick. He blinked. The large hands and the dark mass leaning over him were Omaata. He opened his eyes wide and wiped his mouth with his hand. Ivoa was standing beside Omaata. And beside her, Itia.

'What's the matter?' he said, raising himself on an elbow.

The sun was already rather low. He must have slept a long time. He blinked and looked at the women standing motionless at the foot of his bed. Their faces were grey with terror.

'What's the matter?'

'Tell him, Itia,' Omaata said in a whisper.

Itia looked at him, her lips trembling.

'Tell me, Itia,' he said, suddenly afraid.

'Adamo!'

'Speak!'

'They have found the muskets!'

He sat up.

'What are you saying?' he said in stupefaction. 'What muskets?'

'The muskets the chief hid in the cave.'

'What muskets?' he cried, putting his hands to his ears as if to prevent himself hearing. 'What cave?'

And suddenly he cried: 'Mason's muskets? The muskets he hid in the cave? In the mountain?'

'Yes.'

'The madman!' he cried, jumping out of bed and going towards the door.

He stopped and turned pale. Where was he going? What could he do? He looked at Itia.

'They dared go into the cave? What about the *toupapahous*?'

'Mehani went in alone.'

The only Tahitian who did not believe in ghosts! It would be he!

'When?'

'When Avapouhi and I ran away after the sharing out of the *vahinés*. It was Mehani who made us go into the cave. We didn't want to. But it was raining! How it was raining! So we went in.'

He looked at her and said through dry lips: 'How many muskets did Mehani find?'

'Eight.'

'And ammunition?'

'One box.'

That fool Mason! He had carried it all up there with Vaa, so as to 'sell his life dearly', if the frigate returned . . . Purcell was suddenly assailed by an intolerable thought. He cried: 'Omaata! The water fatigue!'

He looked at her. She was trembling in every limb, and her eyes were wild. She was incapable of answering.

'The water fatigue?' he cried, turning to Ivoa.

'It's left.'

'When?'

'A moment ago.'

'What sort of moment?'

'A long moment.'

'How long a moment?' Purcell cried in exasperation.

'The time to go to Blossom Bay and return.'

An hour. They must be almost there. He could never catch up with them. He might shout, but they would never hear.

A mile from the banyan, half way up the slope of the mountain, rocks dammed the stream and formed a little enclosed pool surrounded by bush. It was here the water was drawn. Then, when all the receptacles were full, the party bathed. The clear water running over the black rocks was the recompense for the long march in the sun. Purcell looked at Itia and felt his heart sink.

'They know there's a water fatigue?'

'They know,' Itia said, lowering her eyes.

It was she who must have told them, without thinking any harm! Raha, Faïna and Itia had been wandering about the village since morning, gossiping with the *Peritani*'s women, who knew everything that was going on through their husbands. It was not intentional. It was the custom. Everyone always knew everything in the Tahitian islands! The 'mutineers' were kept informed from hour to hour.

And now they would be waiting for the water fatigue. They would be hidden in the bush on the farther side of the pool, the barrels of their muskets resting on the branches. The *Peritani* would come. They would let the women go down to the pool and would stay on the parapet with their muskets, outlined against the sky. Good God, Purcell thought, the Tahitians would pick them off as if they were targets on a range. 'Jones!' Purcell cried aloud, as if the boy could hear him. A desperate longing to set off running came over him. But to run was crazy! Jones could be no more than some dozen yards from the stream. He would be happy, thinking that when the women had filled their receptacles, he could lay down his cumbrous musket, take off his *pareu*, and be the first to dive into the water, strong, bronzed, happy.

'They'll be approaching the stream,' Purcell said in a low voice.

The three women stared at the mountain. But it was not the mountain they saw. They were seeing the same sight as he was: the four *Peritani* moving slowly across the stones and death lying in wait for them.

'Jono!' Omaata said in a choking voice.

It was true, he had thought of no one but Jones! But Hunt would die too! They would all die, Johnson who had spent his life in terror, White who was so conscientious, Hunt who never understood anything, and Jones! Jones! ...

He looked at Omaata. Her eyes seemed appallingly empty. He went to her and took her by the arm. She was inert and let him have his way. She was shaking her great head, and huge tears were rolling from her staring eyes. Ivoa took her other arm, and Omaata said in a weak voice, like the voice of a very old woman: 'I want to sit down.' And her enormous mass immediately collapsed, as if her legs could no longer support her. Ivoa and Purcell sat down close to her on the floor. After a moment, Itia came and joined them, sitting beside Ivoa, her head leaning against her arm. They were silent, watching the mountain.

The *Peritani* were walking in the sun. From having gone the same way for so long, the water fatigue had made a path through the stones, and they were all in Indian file, silent and barefooted. It was very hot, and they had no desire to talk. Johnson looked fearfully about him. White screwed up his eyes; he seemed calm and melancholy. Hunt was thinking of nothing. Jones was rather frightened. But only a little. The Tahitians liked him. Besides, they had only javelins. And a javelin did not carry far. The sun was biting into his right shoulder. The sweat was running in a continuous stream down his back between his shoulder-blades, and his body was looking forward with delight to the water's caress.

The silence in the room was becoming intolerable. Purcell clasped his hands together. He found it increasingly difficult to breathe.

'Itia,' he whispered.

'Yes?'

'Why didn't you tell me they had found the muskets?'

'When do you mean?'

'Before the siesta.'

'I didn't know it. I only heard of it when I got back to them. I returned at once.'

They made no gestures and spoke in low voices as if they were watching over the dead.

'You must have passed the water fatigue on your way back.'

'I didn't come by the path to the banyan. I went by the bush. It took me a long time.'

There was no use talking. Indeed, everything was useless. But they had to talk and talk. Otherwise they would stifle. Though Purcell closed his eyes, he could see the *Peritani* moving towards the stream, all four of them very much alive. They were thirsty, hot and tired, and they were thinking of little plans for their gardens, for their huts or for fishing. They believed they were alive, but they were already dead. As dead as if they were already stretched out on the stones, a musket-ball in their hearts and their heads cut off.

The sun sank lower, and above the foliage of the banyan, the mountain, lit up on one side only, stood out stark against the sky, and seemed closer and more menacing. Purcell's heart began beating loudly in his chest. He lowered his head, closed his eyes and began to pray. But he gave it up at once. He could not think.

There were two shots in the distance, one immediately after the other, then two more, and that was all.

'Jono,' Omaata said.

Her head held high, her eyes staring at the mountain, she opened her mouth and began to groan.

12

The women returned from the water fatigue at nightfall. They put down their receptacles in the market-place and immediately began the funeral rites. These rites consisted of dances and songs which, far from being sad, were concerned with the single theme of 'play'.

Purcell watched them in stupefaction. There appeared to be no difference in the manner the Tahitians celebrated a birth and mourned a death. In both cases, they exalted what life had to offer them that was most precious. On the few square yards of Blossom Square, lit by dozens of *doédoés* placed here and there on tree-stumps, they danced late into the night to the accompaniment of lascivious songs, and these were the women who had seen their *tanés* die before their eyes only a few hours before. Purcell could not take his eyes off them. What did it all mean? Were they trying to overcome their sorrow at death by making their bodies express the joy of living? Were they making a last homage to their *tanés* of the delights they could no longer enjoy? Or did there lie concealed behind their intoxication a naïve assertion that life was still pleasant for the survivors in spite of everything?

Purcell was sitting on a tree-stump and Ivoa was sitting on the grass between his legs, so that she could lean back. The Tahitians had not allowed the water fatigue to return to remove the bodies, and these were represented by tree-trunks on which the women had thrown sheets made of pounded bark. Amoureïa was not present at the ceremony. Ohou had claimed her as booty after the shooting and, against her will, had kept her with him in the bush. All the women were dancing, except Vaa and Ivoa whose condition forbade it. The singing was becoming more and more frenzied, and Purcell watched the faces of the widows as they passed and repassed before him.

The quarrels between Taïata and Johnson were notorious, but Itihota got on well with White, and Omaata adored her *tané*. And yet, Omaata was dancing as she had danced to seduce Jono on the deck of *The Blossom* at the time of the great rain. Only two hours ago she had been half dead herself, groaning like an animal and her eyes staring. Now she was smiling, her nostrils were quivering and her great eyes were as bright as moons. In the voluptuousness of the dance, Itihota's face wore an identical expression, and even Taïata had lost her severe and sulky air. However different they were in size, proportions and beauty, they all resembled each other in their fixed and ecstatic expressions. They sang in turn, and with a sincerity that banished obscenity, the untranslatable songs in which 'play' was described in all its details. Their voices too were strangely similar, at once shrill and raucous. Once, Purcell's eyes met those of Omaata, and he saw in the impersonal glance she gave him a provocative gleam. It gave him a shock. It was clear that she did not 'recognise' him. At that moment, he was no longer her 'baby' but a *tané* like the other *tanés*. Nor was she Omaata. The vague voluptuousness of her eyes said so; Omaata, Jono and the past were all abolished. She was nothing but a woman dancing because she was alive and because life was nothing but 'play'.

Avapouhi uttered a cry, left the group of dancers and came limping across to Purcell. Her right elbow raised to the level of her shoulder, the forearm horizontal, the wrist supple, she was gracefully shaking her fingers in front of her charming face, as if to give an air of playful exaggeration to the intensity of her pain.

'Aïe! Aïe! Adamo!' she groaned, her mouth half-pouting and half-smiling.

'Show me,' Purcell said.

He got cautiously to his feet so as not to disturb Ivoa, made Avapouhi sit down on the tree-stump and, placing the *vahiné's* right foot against his knee, began massaging her ankle. Ivoa scarcely moved. She placed her head against Avapouhi's thigh and went on singing softly, her eyes fixed on the dancers.

'Where's Ouili?' Purcell asked after a moment.

He had to raise his voice to make himself heard above the singing.

'At home.'

'I'll go and see him.'

'Don't go.'

'Why not?'

Avapouhi slowly lowered her eyes and looked at the ankle. '*Aïe! Aïe!* Adamo!'

'Why not?'

'Not so hard, please.'

'Why shouldn't I go to see him?'

'He won't open the door to you. He's shut himself up.'

'What's he doing?'

'Nothing.'

'How do you mean, nothing?'

'He sits down. He gets up. He sits down again. He takes his head in his hands. When I go to him . . .'

'When you go to him?'

'He shouts: "Go away!" Then he hits the door with his fists. He hits it and hits it! And his eyes are like fire!'

There was a silence. Ivoa stopped singing, ran the tips of her fingers along Avapouhi's thigh, threw her head back to look at her and said: 'You're skin is as soft as silk, Avapouhi. And your smile is gentle too. And so are your eyes.'

Purcell glanced at her. It was difficult to know whether she wanted to change the conversation or whether she had simply not been listening.

'How nice of you to say so,' Avapouhi said slowly.

She put her hand on Ivoa's hair, stroked it and said: 'May *Eatua* bless you with a son. May he give him a loud tongue to call you when you sleep and strong lips to suck your breasts.'

She fell silent. Ivoa encircled her breasts with her arms and closed her eyes, an absent smile on her lips. It was as if the child was already there, naked and lascivious against her, his lips swollen with milk. Avapouhi said nothing. She, too, was seeing Ivoa's little boy, but he was no longer in his mother's arms. He was already walking, belonged to everyone, was passed from hand to hand and was the joy of the island. The child trotted everywhere! He appeared, naked and astonished, at the corner of the path, scarcely taller than the grass. Oh, the child, the child! How soft he was to the touch!

'And now,' Avapouhi said with an expression of extreme happiness, 'I'm going to dance.'

'You won't be able to,' Purcell said.

'I shall,' she said, getting to her feet.

Purcell resumed his place on the tree-stump, his legs each side of Ivoa. Avapouhi took a few steps and uttered a cry. She turned to Adamo and made a face.

'Go to bed.'

'No,' she said with a sudden look of sadness. 'No. I can't.'

She came back to him, sat down by his right foot and leaned against his knee.

A shadow fell between Purcell and the dancers. He raised his eyes. It was Mason, a musket under his arm. He came forward and leaned against the trunk of a coconut palm two yards from Purcell. He did not look at him. And when he spoke, he continued to gaze anxiously round. Standing quite still behind him, scarcely visible in the shadow of another tree, were MacLeod and Smudge. They were also armed. Purcell had not heard them come up.

'Mr Purcell,' Mason said curtly, 'will you make Baker see reason? The fool's shut himself up in his hut and refuses to open to us. After Jones's murder, he ought to realise that his place is with us.'

'He won't open to me either,' Purcell said, shaking his head. 'Give him time to calm down.'

'Time! Time!' Mason muttered. 'We shall be only three muskets against four this night! Because of that fool!'

He went on curtly: 'I do not suppose you will consent to arm yourself?'

'No, Captain Mason.'

'You're deserting us,' Mason said contemptuously. 'If the blacks attack tonight, we shall be only three.'

'Don't worry. They won't attack tonight.'

'How do you know?' Mason asked suspiciously.

'They won't attack on the night the women are mourning their dead.'

'Mourning!' Mason cried indignantly. 'Do you call this mourning? I have never seen anything more disgusting! These savages haven't one single decent feeling. They have nothing *here!*' he went on, tapping his heart. 'Absolutely nothing, and that's the truth! Their songs may be all right. I don't understand them, but I presume they are recommending the deceased to the mercy of the Lord. But their dances! I ask you, Mr Purcell, does one dance when one has lost one's husband?'

'These dances have no doubt a significance that . . .'

'Disgusting!' Mason interrupted, emphasising each syllable. 'They're disgusting, and that's all there is to it. And I'm glad to see that Mrs Mason is taking no part in them. Mrs Mason is a lady. She is contenting herself with singing.'

'I agree that at first sight it is rather surprising, but every people has its own . . .'

'No, Mr Purcell, I have travelled too . . . And never have I seen a woman shake the lower parts of her body to mourn her husband. I am shocked, Mr Purcell,' he went on violently, 'I am inexpressibly shocked!'

He fell silent, drew himself up and assumed a stern and offended expression.

'Are you coming?' he asked stiffly.

Purcell looked at him.

'No, Captain Mason.'

'Do you mean to say you're going to spend the night in your own hut?'

Purcell nodded. Mason glanced sideways at him and said

meaningly: 'You must be very sure the blacks won't do you any harm.'

'I'm not at all sure of it,' Purcell said calmly.

There was a silence and Mason said: 'You could mount guard at one of the loopholes. There are four sides to watch. And there are only three of us. Even without touching a musket you could help us.'

'Certainly not,' Purcell said decisively. 'Count me out. I shall not help you in any way at all.'

'What!' Mason cried furiously. 'Do you intend to remain neutral? Even after these murders!'

Clearly, when the British killed Tahitians, it was an 'example'; but when the Tahitians killed the British, it was murder.

'Even now?' Mason repeated violently.

Purcell looked at him. Pressure, blackmail, appeal to sentiment – it was all there.

'Even now,' Purcell said firmly.

Mason started.

'It's infamous, Mr Purcell!' he thundered.

He cut his protest short, the singing interfered with his indignation.

'We shall speak of this again,' he said, scarcely veiled menace in his voice.

He turned heavily on his heel, and went off down Nor'wester Street with MacLeod and Smudge on either side of him. After a moment, Purcell placed his hands on Ivoa's head.

'I'm going to bed.'

'So am I.'

'I'm not,' Avapouhi said sadly.

When Adamo and Ivoa got to their feet, she took Adamo's place on the tree-stump and watched them go off. How she envied Ivoa! She was expecting a child and her *tané* had the greatest quality in a man: he was kind. Avapouhi sang and watched the dancers, but after a while she felt lonely. She sang louder, clapping to the rhythm. But even so, she still felt lonely. She got up and went to sit beside Vaa. She did not much like Vaa but, to her great surprise, Vaa turned to her and smiled. Perhaps Vaa also felt lonely with her *tané* shut up in the

Tahitians' hut. Vaa was sitting with her back against a coconut-palm. She was humming through her closed lips, and her eyes were sad. Perhaps her *tané* would be killed. Perhaps Avapouhi's. '*Aoué!* We poor women!' Avapouhi slipped her hand under Vaa's arm and, when Vaa did not repulse her, leaned her head against her shoulder.

Purcell and Ivoa had not gone ten yards down Trade Wind Street when Ivoa said in a low voice: 'Let's go through the undergrowth.'

Purcell stopped, listened and whispered: 'Did you hear anything?'

'No.'

She added: 'I'm frightened they'll shoot at you.'

'They won't shoot,' Purcell said.

But he was beginning to be frightened too. He listened again, staring into the shadows in front of him. Nothing moved, except the leaves of the coconut-palms high above his head. The *doédoés* in the market-place shone behind him. He must be offering a sitting target, silhouetted in black against the light. He joined Ivoa in the undergrowth.

'Whom do you mean by "they"?' he asked in a low voice. 'Ours?'

'The others too.'

She pressed his hand to silence him and guided him with certainty through the darkness.

When they were lying on their bed in the hut, the door shut and the sliding-doors fastened as well as they could with ropes, Ivoa said, without moving her head: 'Mehani won't kill you. Tetahiti perhaps not. But Timi and Ohou, yes.'

'Why?'

'It was one of them who shot Ropati. Either Ohou, to have Amoureïa. Or perhaps Timi, so that Ohou should have Amoureïa.'

'But why should they kill me?'

'They know that you loved Ropati and are afraid you will avenge him. But they'll kill Ouili first.'

'Why Ouili?'

'Because they're more afraid of Ouili.'

She fell silent. The night was not as dark as when they had

returned from Blossom Square. A glimmer filtered through the cracks of the sliding-door. Turning his head, Purcell could scarcely see Ivoa's face. All the light seemed to be concentrated on her belly. Smooth, round and large, it emerged like a dome from the shadows.

'I can't bring myself to believe that Ropati is dead,' Purcell whispered.

Ivoa was silent for so long that he thought she had fallen asleep. But then he saw her hand moving lightly over her huge belly.

'Nor can I,' she said, and her hand stopped.

She went on: 'But I don't think of him much.'

'Why?'

'Because I'm thinking of my baby.'

And since Purcell said nothing, she went on: 'Is that wrong?'

'No, it's not wrong.'

After a moment, she said: 'Look! He's kicking me again!'

'I can't see anything,' Purcell said.

'Give me your hand.'

She placed his hand on her belly.

'There! Did you feel it?'

He was astonished at the strength of it.

'Doesn't he hurt you?'

'Yes, a little!' she said, laughing delightedly deep down in her throat.

Then she stopped laughing, silence fell between them, and after a while she said in a different voice: 'Many men will be dead by the time he's born.'

These words froze Purcell like a presage. He said nothing, but his mouth was dry and his heart was beating fast. He was trying to control his fear. A few seconds went by, then he placed his forehead against Ivoa's shoulder and breathed deeply. He was already feeling better. But when he spoke, his voice sounded choked and toneless with anxiety.

'Perhaps I shall be.'

Was it bravado, a challenge to fate? He was at once ashamed at having said it.

'No!' Ivoa said with extraordinary energy, as if his life depended on her. 'No! Not you!'

'Why not me?'

'I shall protect you,' she said with determination.

He laughed but, absurdly, the remark reassured him. And yet, what could Ivoa do?

After that, there was a long silence. Fear had gradually receded like the falling tide, and the thoughts that had pre-occupied him earlier in the evening returned.

'Ivoa,' he asked, 'why those dances?'

'Why all these "whys", O my *tané Peritani*?'

She smiled tenderly in the dark. Oh, Adamo! Adamo! He was never content to live like a Tahitian. He was never at rest. He was always anxious. Always seeking something. Always wanting to know . . .

'Why those dances, Ivoa?'

She shrugged her beautiful shoulders in the darkness.

'What can one do?' she said with a sigh. 'They go. One says good-bye.'

'But why those particular dances?'

He was leaning on his elbow and trying to see her face.

'There are no others,' Ivoa said.

It was disappointing. The explanation explained nothing. He let his head fall back on the bed.

After a moment, he groped down his side to find Ivoa's hand and fell asleep. Ivoa turned towards him and stared into the dark to watch him. Adamo always went to sleep suddenly, like a door shutting.

When his breathing had become slow and regular, Ivoa got noiselessly out of bed, left the hut and went to the lean-to to get the musket Vaa had lent her. It was one of the muskets the chief *Peritani* kept in his hut and Vaa had shown her how to load it. Vaa knew all about the weapon. She even knew how to fire it. The chief had taught her.

Ivoa did not re-enter the hut. Moving some three yards from the lean-to, she slipped into the giant ferns, sat down with her back to a thick stem and, placing the musket across her knees, began her watch. If they came, they would come by the garden. Timi would come with a torch in his hand. He would put it under the kindling in the lean-to. Then he would go into the bushes and wait, his musket aimed at the sliding-doors. And

Ohou would wait in front of the other door. 'No,' she thought hopefully, 'Ohou will not come tonight. Tonight, he has Amoureïa.' If Timi came alone, she was sure she could kill him. She would let him come very close, and before he had time to place the torch she would put the muzzle against his back ...

Her hands flat on the musket across her thighs, her body upright, her head leaning against the fern's stem, she waited. She was not sleepy. Sleep would come towards morning, and then she would have to fight it with all her might. There would be long hours to wait. She would wait. She was not alone. There was the child moving in her belly. And there was Adamo sleeping in the hut. He was sleeping as if there were no war! He had not even a musket! He did not want to kill anyone! She smiled fiercely in the dark. 'Sleep, Adamo!' she thought. 'Sleep, my *tané*! Sleep, my handsome *tané maamaa* ...'

It was scarcely day when Purcell woke up. Ivoa was leaning over him.

'Everything's ready,' she said smiling.

He smiled back at her and was struck by the weariness in her eyes. He became anxious. How drawn she looked! Every day she seemed more wearied by her pregnancy.

'I'm going to wash,' he said.

He washed in the lean-to. He got up, went to the door, opened it, went out and closed the door behind him. At that moment, a shot rang out and a ball whistled past his ears.

It happened so quickly that for a moment he was taken aback. He stared at the undergrowth without realising that it was at him someone had fired. Nor did it even occur to him to go inside.

Then the door opened behind him, Ivoa's hand clutched him, and he found himself inside the hut again with the door shut and his back against the doorpost. He was perfectly calm.

Ivoa looked at him. Her face was grey and her lips were trembling. She suddenly stretched out her hands and staggered. He caught her, took her up in his arms and carried her over to the bed. When he had put her down, he straightened up, relieved and breathless. He looked at her with smiling eyes. They had not exchanged a word.

He went across to the door.

'Don't open it!' Ivoa cried.

He signed to her to have no fear and went to it. The ball had not quite passed through the heavy oak panel and part of it was showing at the height of his chest. Purcell took his knife and began cutting it out. It had all happened in the fraction of the second he had turned to shut the door behind him. His body had been in profile, and the ball had missed him by a few inches. He was surprised, as he cut into the wood, to feel nothing at all. The night before, when Ivoa had said: 'Many men will be dead by the time he's born,' he had had a moment of appalling panic. And now death had brushed past him and he felt nothing.

At that moment a second shot rang out. He took a step backwards.

'Adamo!' Ivoa cried.

But the shot had not been fired at the hut. He ran to the port-hole and risked a glance. Baker was standing in West Avenue, staring into the undergrowth. Smoke was coming from his musket.

A second later there was a knock at the door. Purcell opened it. Baker burst into the room, clutching Amoureïa, who was panting and dishevelled. Ivoa got up, ran to her and took her in her arms.

'I've brought her so that you can translate what she's saying!' Baker said in a rough, imperious voice.

His face was drawn and his eyes haggard. He talked by fits and starts through clenched teeth and with scarcely contained violence.

'I suppose it was at you those bastards fired.'

'I think so,' Purcell said.

He went back to the door and began work again. He had not liked Baker's tone. The 'at you' was disagreeable.

'I was on the path with Amoureïa,' Baker went on feverishly, 'when I heard the shot. I saw something move in the under-growth and I fired.'

He sat down on a stool and reloaded his musket as he talked. Amoureïa and Ivoa were sitting on the bed. They were silent and looked from one man to the other. Purcell was still cutting into the door. The old oak of the panel was as hard as iron. He worked with sureness and precision, striking the handle of the knife with the palm of his hand.

'She escaped from their hideout this morning,' Baker said, indicating Amoureïa with his chin. 'While Ohou was asleep. She came straight to me.'

He added a little more calmly: 'I wish you would translate . . .'

'I've nearly finished,' Purcell said.

He succeeded in getting the point of the little blade into the crack he had made. At the second attempt the ball slid forward but stopped halfway. He gave it more room by cutting round it, and then it fell out of the hole of its own accord and on to the floor. Purcell picked it up, turned it over and over, held it up to his eye and examined it minutely.

'Is there something odd about it?' Baker asked.

'No,' Purcell said, and he put the ball in his pocket.

He brought up a stool and sat down opposite Amoureïa. She at once said in a low, violent voice: 'It's Timi.'

'It was Timi who killed Ropati?'

'Yes.'

'So that Ohou could have you?'

'Yes.'

Purcell glanced at Ivoa. It was a crime of passion committed under cover of war. A little murder in the shadow of a greater. Ivoa had been right.

'Were the others in agreement?'

'Like that.'

'How do you mean "like that"?'

'When Ropati fell, Mehani and Tetahiti were very angry. But Timi said: "Ropati had a musket", and he opened the musket, and inside it was the thing that kills. So Tetahiti said: "That's all right." And he said to the women: "Draw water and go . . ." '

'It's just as well,' Purcell thought, 'that it didn't occur to him to make us go thirsty.'

'And then?'

'Then Ohou said: "I want Amoureïa." I ran away, but Ohou runs very fast. He caught me, threw me to the ground, put his hand on my head and said: "You are my slave!" '

She fell silent and Purcell looked at her encouragingly.

'They cut off their heads.'

It was said without emotion, without a trace of blame. It was the custom. They had respected it.

'And then?'

'They broke the muskets.'

'What!' Purcell said with a start. 'What muskets?'

'The *Peritani*'s muskets.'

'Broke them?' Purcell said excitedly. 'You don't mean "broke", you mean "opened"? They opened the *Peritani*'s muskets.'

'They opened them and emptied them. And then they broke them.'

She mimicked the gesture of brandishing a musket and beating it against a rock. She looked at Purcell in astonishment. It was obvious. You killed an enemy. When the enemy was dead, you cut off his head. Then you broke his weapon.

'And so,' Purcell said in extreme excitement, 'they broke the muskets?'

'Yes, but first they opened them. The yellow man's musket was empty. Then Mehani said: "I regret having killed him." But Tetahiti was angry and he said: "When the Skeleton fired at Kori and Mehoro, the yellow man pointed a musket at us." And the others said: "You speak truth." '

'And they broke the muskets?'

'Yes.'

'The four muskets?'

'Yes.'

Ivoa's eyes never left Adamo's face. She could not understand his astonishment. The Tahitians had eight muskets from the cave. They had quite sufficient.

'Amoureïa,' Purcell went on, 'you're quite sure? All four? They didn't keep one?'

'All four.'

And she went on: 'It was Tetahiti who broke them, one after the other.'

Purcell put his hands in his pockets, got to his feet, walked up and down the room and then went and stared at the undergrowth through the porthole. After a moment, he turned round, glanced at Amoureïa and felt remorseful. Ever since she had come into the hut, she had been nothing to him but a source of information.

'Amoureïa,' he said gently, as he came and sat down opposite her again.

Her hands were resting quietly on her knees, her body was upright, her young face was hard and obstinate, and she looked at Purcell with shining eyes.

'*Tahoo*,' she said without raising her voice.

She repeated *tahoo* several times though Purcell was unsure whether she was demanding that he should avenge her, or whether she intended to do so herself.

'What does *tahoo* mean?' Baker asked.

'Vengeance.'

Purcell scarcely noticed the interruption. He was looking at Amoureïa. How her little face had altered! He remembered her during that first month on the island, when she walked hand in hand with Jones in the wood . . . And suddenly Purcell saw Jones with extraordinary intensity, his short hair, his china-blue eyes, his candid smile. Purcell closed his eyes and leaned forward. It was atrocious. It was as atrocious as an icy blade of sharp steel in his stomach. He bent lower, waiting for the anguish to reach its climax and begin to ebb. It was horrible, it was insufferable to say: 'It's all over.' Over! The word made no sense when it concerned a man! An instant, a day, a task might end, but not a human being! Never again a smile! Never again that tender little light in Ropati's eyes!

'Will you translate?' Baker said impatiently.

Purcell turned to him, looked at him for a moment without seeing him, and then translated. He translated it all, quite automatically and without omitting a detail, not even that of the broken muskets.

'Ask her,' Baker said, 'how long it is since she succeeded in leaving Ohou.'

Purcell translated and Amoureïa looked up.

'The time to go to the banyan and back.'

'Three-quarters of an hour,' Purcell said.

Baker got to his feet and went to Amoureïa, his eyes shining.

'Amoureïa,' he said hoarsely, 'do you want *tahoo*?'

'Yes! ' Amoureïa said.

'*Ouili tahoo!*' Baker went on, hitting himself hard on the chest with the flat of his hand. '*Ouili tahoo Ohou!* And you'll help me! You understand "help"? How does one say "help"?'

'*Taoutourou,*' Purcell said automatically.

'*Taoutourou Ouili tahoo Ohou,*' Baker said loudly, tapping his musket. 'Do you understand?'

'Yes!'

She got to her feet, her eyes full of a savage joy. Baker took her by the hand, threw out his chest, gazed at her wildly, and said: '*Amoureïa taoutourou Ouili tahoo Ohou!*'

'Yes!' Amoureïa cried in a shrill voice.

'Explain to her!' Baker went on feverishly, turning to Purcell. 'She must lead me to the bastards' hideout, and bait the trap for me.'

'You're mad!' Purcell cried, jumping to his feet. 'You can't do that! You'll get yourself killed! And her too!'

'I may get myself killed,' Baker said with a light of triumph in his eyes, 'but I'll get one of them first! I'll get one of them, Purcell! I swear to God I'll get one of them!'

'Baker!' Purcell cried.

'Christ, don't talk to me!' Baker shouted, his face wild with anger. 'It's your fault! All of it! Absolutely all of it! I should never have listened to you! If I'd sent MacLeod to his account the night of the sharing out of the women, there'd have been no war with the blacks, and Ropati would still be alive Christ, it's enough to send one mad! I can't stop thinking of it,' he went on, shaking his head. 'I can't stop thinking that I was all ready to have a go at that bastard of a Scotsman that night and give him his deserts. Christ! If I'd got at him and slit him open, Ropati would still be alive! He'd be in his hut at this moment,' he went on, tears starting from his eyes. 'He'd be sitting by his door having his breakfast, with Amoureïa behind him. And I'd be passing by and say to him: "Are you coming to Rope Beach?" Christ! It's as if I could see him sitting at his table, before the open door, with his gentle smile, and flexing his muscles, the damned little idiot! . . .'

Tears poured down his cheeks and he could no longer speak.

'Baker, listen to me!'

'I won't listen to you!' Baker went on with renewed fury. 'All

I want is for you to translate what I expect her to do. But if you won't, so much the worse, I'll manage somehow! I bet you your watch she'll understand! Amoureïa,' he cried, *'tahoo Ohou!'*

'Yes!' Amoureïa said.

'Tahoo Ohou!' he went on excitedly, his dark eyes flashing. 'We're going to have good fishing this morning, Purcell! There's my bait!' he went on, raising Amoureïa's hand to the level of his shoulder. 'And I swear to God Almighty I'll hook a big one!'

He moved towards the door.

'It's suicide!' Purcell cried, hurrying forward and seizing him by the shoulders. 'I won't let you do it!'

'Let me go!' Baker cried.

They struggled for a moment in silence. Purcell could feel Baker's tense, compact body under his clutching hands. He would not let him go. Baker was holding Amoureïa with his right hand and his musket with the other. He shook his brown head in the effort to escape from Purcell's grasp. His neck was swollen, his jaw jutted and his eyes flashed. He looked like a hound dragging at its leash.

'Let me go!' he shouted. 'You're the cause of it all, you and your damned Bible! Christ, I hate you! And I hate myself for having listened to you! Just look where you've got us with your damned religion! There are already six men dead on the island!'

'Listen to me!' Purcell cried, desperately clinging to his shoulders. 'You'll listen to me whether you like it or not! What you're doing is mad! Nothing else! One against four. They'll kill you for certain!'

'And what the hell do I care!' Baker shouted.

It did not occur to him to let go of Amoureïa to have a free hand, and he was frantically shaking his head and body from side to side to rid himself of Purcell's grasp.

'Let me go!' he cried.

'And what about Amoureïa?' Purcell said. 'You've no right to make use of her! You haven't thought of what they'll do to her, when they've killed you!'

'And why should she go on living?' Baker shouted. 'Ropati is dead!'

'Baker!'

'Christ! Let me go, Purcell! I won't listen to you!' he went on, staring at him with hatred in his eyes. 'It's because I listened to you that the boy's dead!'

'Baker, what you're saying's horrible ...'

'Let me go, I tell you!'

Baker let go of Amoureïa's hand and clenched his fist. Purcell tried to duck, but was too late. He felt a violent blow to his head, staggered backwards, and the wall of the hut seemed to come towards him and hit him in the back of the neck.

He was lying on the floor, his consciousness seemed to be floating in a white mist, he felt no pain, and seemed to be falling backwards like a drowned man. He half opened his eyes. Everything seemed to be merged in puffs of white smoke. He wanted to see! He began blinking, but it required an enormous effort, his eyes insisted on closing for all he could do. Open, shut, open, shut ... No exercise had ever seemed more difficult. He went on blinking, the mist seemed to grow less thick, someone raised his head and his cheek reposed against something soft and warm. The fog began to dissipate, a little light filtered through it, a blurred face appeared. And suddenly his head began to swim, his jaw hurt, and he was unable to think. He gripped Ivoa's shoulders with both hands and managed to sit up. And he remained there, sitting on the floor supported by Ivoa, feeling sick ... A second later, light broke in on his mind with a glacial intensity, everything came back to him.

'Baker!' he cried desperately.

He heard his own voice with astonishment. It was a feeble, falsetto voice, which seemed to him absurd. No one answered. He forced his head round, there was a sharp pain in his jaw, and his eyes moved very slowly round the room. In front of him the hut door stood wide open to the undergrowth.

'Baker,' he said confusedly.

He let his head fall on Ivoa's shoulder, his chest heaved; Ivoa's shoulder was damp under his cheek.

'Adamo,' Ivoa whispered in a tender, singsong voice.

She was clasping her *tané*'s white, fair body in her black arms, and rocking him to and fro. The *Peritani* were *maamaa*. Timi killed Ropati and Ouili struck Adamo! *Aoué*, the war was there like a disease, and all the men were *maamaa*. 'Oh, Adamo,' she thought fervently, 'you alone are good!'

'Help me, Ivoa,' Purcell said.

She helped him to his feet. He felt vague and weak. He staggered and supported himself with his right hand against the wall.

'I'm going to wash,' he said, making an effort to speak naturally.

'Wait a little.'

'No,' he said, staring at the floor. 'I'm going now.'

He left the support of the wall, staggered across the room, went out into the garden by the sliding-door and entered the lean-to.

He had scarcely finished washing when Ivoa appeared.

'*Iore iti** is here,' she said in a low voice, pointing to the hut. 'He wants to see you. He's got a musket.'

Purcell frowned.

'*Iore iti?*'

'Take care. I don't like the look in his eyes.'

Purcell went quietly round the hut and, keeping close to the wall, took a look before entering by the sliding-door. Smudge had his back to him. He was standing facing the entrance door. He had unslung his musket and was carrying it in his hands. Purcell's feet were bare. He went silently up the two wooden steps and entered the hut barely two yards from Smudge.

'Smudge,' he said quietly.

Smudge started violently and turned with fear in his eyes, holding the musket across his chest.

'Well,' Purcell said, his face hard and his eyes watchful, 'what do you want?'

Smudge gradually recovered his breath.

'Mason and MacLeod want you,' he said, showing his teeth.

He stood with his head thrust forward, his eyes shone like little black marbles in their sockets and he talked with a peculiar mixture of arrogance and fear. Though Purcell was unarmed, the way he had come up behind him had frightened him.

'Will you ask Mason and MacLeod to come here?' Purcell said after a moment. 'I was shot at this morning. And I don't

* The little rat.

want to go walking about the island.'

'You don't seem to understand,' Smudge said with an angry sneer. 'I've orders to take you to the Tahitians' hut. You needn't put on airs with me, Purcell. I'm under orders, I tell you.'

'Orders?' Purcell said, raising his eyebrows.

'I've orders to take you there, whether you like it or not.'

Purcell looked at him. Had Smudge really received such orders, or was he inventing them?

'I really don't see how that can be,' Purcell said calmly. 'No one here is in a position to give me orders. Mason and MacLeod can come here if they want to see me. But I shan't leave my hut.'

'They don't want to see you,' Smudge said, drawing himself up with an air of triumph. 'They want to try you. Make no mistake, Purcell, you're no longer a free man. You're my prisoner. If you try to escape, I'll shoot you.'

His hard eyes gleamed with such hatred that Purcell felt a moment's panic. He put his hands behind his back and clasped them. He must be calm and think.

'What am I accused of?' he asked slowly.

'Treachery.'

'Only that?' he said ironically.

But the irony sounded false even to himself. There was a silence and Smudge said: 'Well, are you coming?'

Purcell hesitated, then he looked at Smudge's eyes and the slight quivering of his lips that uncovered his teeth, and he understood. If he went with him, he would not reach the Tahitians' hut alive.

Purcell took two steps backwards, sat down on a stool and, putting his hand behind his back, grasped its edge. The sweat was pouring from the palms of his hands.

'You heard me,' he said. 'I shan't leave my hut. Go and tell Mason and MacLeod to come here.'

There was a second's pause and then Smudge said in a false, shrill voice: 'You'll come with me, Purcell, or I'll shoot you like a dog.'

He put his musket to his shoulder and covered him. Purcell leaned forward, imperceptibly moved his weight from the stool, and grasped it more firmly with the hand behind his back. It was one chance in a hundred. Scarcely one chance in a hundred.

'If you kill me in my own hut,' he said, looking Smudge in the eye, 'I don't see how you'll be able to pretend I was trying to escape.'

'You needn't worry about me,' Smudge said.

His hands were trembling on the musket. He held all the cards and yet something was wrong. He would shoot the bastard, the other two would not make a fuss, and he would have Ivoa. His finger was trembling on the trigger, he longed to press it, but there was something wrong, the bastard was much too calm, something was awry and was not clewing up. His big nose was against the butt of the musket and he scented danger in the air. He stood quite still, ferocious yet prudent, like a rat at the edge of its hole, equally ready to attack or to flee.

'If you're afraid I'll escape,' Purcell said, 'stay here with me and send someone else to fetch MacLeod and Mason.'

'I don't need them to execute a traitor,' Smudge said.

But he still did not fire. Purcell gripped the stool and thought: 'Talk, talk, I must talk, if I don't talk he'll fire.' But the seconds went by, he sought desperately for something to say, but could find nothing.

The silence suddenly became abnormally intense. A shadow appeared on the sunlit floor. It grew and lengthened. Purcell turned his head. Ivoa was standing at the sliding-doors. She was levelling a musket at Smudge.

'Ivoa!' Purcell cried.

Smudge turned his head from his musket and turned pale. He was still pointing it at Purcell, but it was trembling convulsively in his hands, and his little dark eyes, bright as boot-buttons, were staring at Ivoa in terror.

'Ivoa!' Purcell cried.

'Tell her not to fire, sir!' Smudge cried in a choking voice.

Purcell moved quickly across to Smudge, took his musket by the barrel and pointed it upwards. He was now too close for Ivoa to fire.

'Give me the musket,' he said curtly.

Smudge obeyed, turned so that his back was to the door, and uttered a sigh. Purcell was now between him and Ivoa and, though Purcell was armed, he was not frightened of him.

There was a silence. Purcell was surprised to see Smudge so close to him and his chest almost touching the muzzle of the weapon he held in his hand.

'Aren't you afraid I'll shoot you?' he said in a low voice.

All his muscles felt weary and he wanted to sit down.

'No,' Smudge said, his eyes shifty.

'Why?'

'Because it's not the sort of thing you'd do.'

There was a silence and then Purcell said quietly: 'You revolt me.'

But even that was not true. He no longer had the strength for indignation. His legs were shaking under him and all he wanted was to sit down.

'It's my musket,' Smudge said suddenly.

He said it half-plaintively, half-demandingly, like a child whose elder brother has taken his toy away.

Purcell raised the musket, discharged it at the ceiling and gave it back to Smudge without a word. After the shot there was a feverish scurrying among the leaves of the roof. The little lizards were running in all directions. Purcell screwed up his eyes, but could not see them. He felt dull and stupid; there was a heaviness in his stomach.

'Thank you,' Smudge said.

The whole thing was utterly unreal. Smudge had nearly murdered him and now he was saying 'thank you' like a child.

'Iore iti,' Ivoa said.

She was standing two yards away, the musket under her arm, her face like a mask. Smudge winced as if she had slapped him.

'Listen, *Iore iti,*' Ivoa repeated.

She turned her dark eyes on him and said very slowly in English, as if she were repeating a child's lesson: 'You kill Adamo, me kill you.'

Smudge looked at her. He was pale, hypnotised and his lips were dry. Since he said nothing, she said it again without a trace of anger or hatred, as if she were uttering some evident fact she wanted him to grasp: 'You kill Adamo. Me kill you. Understand?'

Smudge licked his lips.

'Understand?' Ivoa repeated.

He nodded.

'You can go,' Purcell said wearily. 'And tell Mason and Mac-Leod I'm expecting them.'

Smudge slung his musket and went off without once looking round. He was small, dejected and contemptible; and he had one shoulder higher than the other. Purcell put out a hand and leaned against the doorpost. He drew a deep breath. He felt sick with disgust.

He turned. Over his shoulder, Ivoa was also watching Smudge going off.

'I didn't dare shoot,' she said regretfully. 'I was afraid of missing him and that he'd kill you.'

The expression in her eyes surprised Purcell. He did not recognise her. She had suddenly become another woman.

'Where did that musket come from, Ivoa?'

'It was lent to me.'

'Who lent it?'

She was silent, stared him straight in the eye, and waited. It was the first time since they had been man and wife that she had refused to answer him.

'Give it to me,' Purcell said.

She shook her head.

'Give it me,' he said, holding out his hand.

She shook her head again and backed away with an agility he had not expected from her in her condition.

'Come on, give it me!' he said insistently, going towards her.

But she quickly avoided him, ran out through the sliding-doors and disappeared into the garden.

'Ivoa!'

He had to make a great effort to run after her for he could scarcely stand on his legs. He turned the corner of the hut and went into the lean-to. She was not there.

'Ivoa!'

He went round the hut and came back to his point of departure. He thought he heard a rustling of leaves in the hibiscus thicket at the bottom of the garden. He ran towards it, his legs trembling. All was still. He went round the hibiscus and entered the giant ferns. He called to Ivoa once again, but his voice seemed to him feeble and smothered. All about him was green, impenetrable shade. He held his breath and listened. Nothing stirred.

Then he fell to his knees, put a hand to the moss and lay down full length on his back. His jaw was hurting and every muscle aching with fatigue. He felt terribly weak and, as soon as he closed his eyes, his head began to swim. He opened them again. Nothing had changed. He rolled carefully on to his side and began taking long, deep, regular breaths. For long minutes he struggled against nausea, but he was unable to control it, and finally it suddenly took him, defeating and overwhelming him. He leaned over, vomited in great bouts, and collapsed. He found himself gasping for air and opened his mouth wide, his sight grew misty and he had the appalling feeling that he was dying.

When he came to, sweat was pouring down his face, his sides, and between his thighs. Then a breath of wind swept over him and he felt a delicious sense of coolness. He was floating on water, passive, at ease, without having to move so much as a hand. He breathed the life-giving air in great gulps, utterly, completely, effortlessly happy . . . Time went by. He was alive, could feel himself living and it was a wonderful sensation. He repeated aloud: 'It's wonderful, wonderful, wonderful . . .' Then his euphoria lapsed. His left leg kicked out suddenly as if he were falling into space, and he thought: 'The others will be coming, the worst is still ahead of me . . .'

Purcell walked round the hibiscus thicket on to the path, and glanced into the interior of the hut. They were there, all three of them, sitting with their muskets between their knees, and with the immobility of actors on a stage at the moment the curtain rises. MacLeod had his back against the entrance door, while Mason and Smudge were each side of the sliding doors. In the middle of the room was an empty stool. 'My place,' Purcell thought. 'The place for the accused . . .'

Purcell walked slowly forward. There was nothing unusual about their appearance. Mason was dressed from head to foot, shod, cravatted, and with his cocked hat at his feet. MacLeod was wearing his white vest; and Smudge was in trousers, naked from the waist up, his right shoulder crooked, the hair on his hollow chest turning grey.

Purcell's bare foot hit a pebble. The three men's eyes turned towards him at the same moment, and Purcell was struck with their lack of expression. Their faces were empty, impersonal, and without a trace of humanity. 'The faces of judges,' Purcell thought, and he felt a cold shiver down his spine.

He quickened his pace, strode up the two steps, and went to the vacant stool. He at once realised why the stool had been placed in the middle of the room. The three men were stationed round the accused to prevent his escaping. 'They're already treating me as an object,' Purcell thought with disgust.

'Sit down, Mr Purcell,' Mason said in a tone of command.

Purcell made as if to sit down but immediately stood upright again. This was his house. No one was going to give him orders in it. He picked up the stool, moved it away from the wall, placed his foot on it, and leaned forward with his right elbow on his knee and his left hand in his pocket.

'Mr Purcell,' Mason said, 'something very serious has happened; your wife aimed a musket at Smudge.'

'So she did,' Purcell said. 'Smudge was aiming at me. Had it not been for Ivoa's intervention, he would have murdered me.'

'It's a lie!' Smudge cried in a shrill voice. 'He was refusing to come, sir! I threatened him, but I had no intention of firing.'

Mason raised his hand.

'Don't interrupt, Smudge. Where does that musket come from, Mr Purcell?'

'I don't know.'

'I'll tell you; it was stolen from me.'

'Stolen!'

'Stolen, Mr Purcell. The addition is simple. There were twenty-one muskets in *The Blossom*; eight French muskets which at this moment are in the hands of the blacks, and thirteen British muskets which were divided as follows on our arrival on the island: Hunt, one; Baker, one; Jones, one; Smudge, one; Johnson, one; White, two; MacLeod, two; and myself, four. You did not have one.'

'That is correct.'

'Due to the four British muskets lost on the water fatigue, the British at this moment have only nine muskets: Baker, one;

MacLeod, two; Smudge, one; and myself four, plus White's second musket, which makes five. In all, I repeat, nine muskets, of which three are here; one in Baker's hands; and five, I repeat five, in reserve in the Tahitians' hut, under the guardianship of Mrs Mason who, I may remark in passing, has behaved most admirably since the beginning of hostilities and in whom I have every confidence.'

He paused.

'Mr Purcell, after Smudge's report, I immediately counted the muskets in Mrs Mason's keeping. I could find no more than four. Mrs Mason was very concerned. She declared that she had neither given nor lent one to anyone. I have complete confidence in her. I conclude, therefore, that, taking advantage of a moment's inattention on the part of Mrs Mason, one musket was stolen from her. Mr Purcell, have you asked your wife where that musket came from?'

'Yes.'

'Well?'

'She refused to answer.'

'And for good reason!' Mason said triumphantly.

And since Purcell said nothing, he went on: 'Have you at least tried to take it from her?'

'Yes. But I've not succeeded. She fled.'

'Fled!' Mason exclaimed. 'Fled, Mr Purcell! And you did not pursue her?'

'Yes, but she escaped me. She has hidden herself in the bush.'

'Mr Purcell!' Mason cried, turning red with anger. 'Do you expect me to believe that a young, active man like yourself can't catch a woman – and a woman who... who... in brief, is expecting a baby...?'

'I'm telling you the truth,' Purcell said dryly. 'I can't oblige you to believe me.'

There was a silence lasting a full second. Mason leaned forward, fixed his grey-blue eyes on those of Purcell and said: 'I do not know whether you are aware of the seriousness of your replies. Avapouhi has just told us through Omaata that Baker has gone into the bush with Amoureïa to set a trap for Ohou. It is madness of course. The result is inevitable. Baker may or may not kill Ohou. But he will certainly be killed himself. The result will be one musket the less for us.'

Purcell's lips formed a thin line and even Mason appeared surprised at the hatefulness of his own words.

'Of course,' he went on, 'I should be distressed if Baker got himself killed. But there are the facts: with him, we lose a musket. This morning we had nine. Nine, less the stolen one: eight. Eight less Baker's musket: seven. Seven muskets, Mr Purcell! Seven against the blacks' thirteen!'

'Thirteen?'

'The eight French muskets, plus the four muskets of the water fatigue, plus Baker's musket.'

'You're wrong,' Purcell said, 'the blacks destroyed the water fatigue's muskets.'

'They destroyed them!' Mason cried, and he looked at Mac-Leod. 'Destroyed them, Mr Purcell! I find it difficult to believe you!'

Purcell straightened up.

'If you find it difficult to believe me every time I open my mouth, I really don't see the usefulness of my answering your questions.'

'Destroyed them!' Mason went on without listening to him. 'But the women of the water fatigue said nothing of the kind.'

'They'd already gone when it happened. It was Amoureïa who told me.'

'It's a pity your only witness should be inaccessible,' Mason said acidly. 'But if it's true . . .'

'It is true!' Purcell said angrily. 'I've sailed with you for eighteen months and I've never given you occasion to doubt my word. Moreover, you're here in my house, and so long as you're in it I'd be obliged to you not to suggest I'm lying.'

He drew breath. He felt much better for having lost his temper with Mason.

There was a silence. Smudge was looking at his feet with an insolent expression. MacLeod, his death's head perfectly still, was staring at the mountain. He was leaning back on his stool, balancing it on two feet, and resting his thin back against the door. Mason had turned scarlet.

'I suggest you calm yourself, Mr Purcell,' he said with an indefinable air of moral superiority. And, as Purcell was about to reply, he turned to MacLeod and went on: 'If what Purcell says is true, I shall be very pleased indeed. It means we shall be fighting the blacks on equal terms with regard to weapons. We have lost our numerical superiority, and it is very important that our fire-power should not be inferior to the enemy's.'

When he had finished, MacLeod nodded his head gravely in assent. Purcell looked from one to the other. He was struck by their air of importance; they looked like two army commanders.

'Let's return to the musket, Mr Purcell,' Mason went on haughtily. 'Do you know how your wife got hold of the weapon?'

'No.'

'Have you any idea what she intends to do with it?'

'Yes.'

'Please tell us.'

'Since I was the only unarmed man on the island, she must have thought it her duty to protect me.'

'Protect you against whom?'

'Against the two rival camps.'

'Is there anyone in the blacks' camp who wishes you harm, then?'

'Yes.'

'Who is it?'

'Timi.'

'Why?'

'He has killed Jones and he's afraid I shall try to avenge him.'

'And in our camp?'

Purcell smiled coldly.

'I'll leave it to you to answer that question yourself.'

'Humph!' Mason said.

He went on: 'Does your wife know how to shoot?'

'No,' Purcell said.

He corrected himself: 'To tell you the truth, I don't know.'

'You said "no" and then corrected yourself,' Mason said suspiciously. 'Why?'

'Ivoa is quite capable of having learnt to shoot without my knowing it. When she covered Smudge, she was holding the musket in the correct way.'

Purcell lowered his eyes. It was just as well that Smudge

L

should not know that Ivoa had been afraid of missing him at three yards.

'Who can have taught her?' Mason asked nervously.

'I've already told you that I don't know.'

There was a silence, and then Mason went on: 'Are you expecting to find your wife?'

'No. I'm not.'

'Why?'

'She knows very well that, if she came back to the house, I'd take her musket away.'

'What do you think she's going to do?'

'Stay in the bush and keep an eye on anyone who comes near me.'

Smudge looked ill at ease and MacLeod looked at Mason.

'It seems to me,' Mason said, 'that if you took a little trouble you could find her.'

'You think so?' Purcell said, pointing towards the bush. 'Look for her yourself, if you think you can succeed in finding her.'

Smudge looked in the direction he was pointing, turned pale and drew his stool back behind the post of the sliding-doors.

'I have some other questions to ask you,' Mason said gravely.

Purcell straightened up.

'I've also got some questions to ask you. Are you in process of trying me?'

'Yes.'

'Of what are you accusing me?'

'Treachery.'

Purcell looked at him and felt a wave of discouragement. That square, stubborn, obstinate face . . . How could one ever make him understand anything?

'So you're my judges,' Purcell said bitterly, looking them up and down. 'All three of you?' he went on, raising his eyebrows.

'Yes.'

'And, at the end of the discussion, I suppose you'll decide whether I'm guilty or not by a vote.'

'Yes.'

'In that case, I challenge one of my judges.'

'Which?'

'Smudge.'

Smudge started and looked at Purcell with a mixture of anger and apprehension.

'Why?' Mason said.

'Because he tried to murder me.'

'Mr Purcell,' Mason said, 'I gave orders to Smudge to bring you to me willy-nilly. If he pointed his musket at you, I consider he was covered by my order.'

'I'm not alluding to that incident,' Purcell said, bending his knee and leaning forward over the stool. 'I was shot at this morning as you know. The ball lodged in my door. I extracted it.'

He removed his foot from the stool, took the ball from his pocket, went across the room and gave it to Mason. They were all staring at him.

'As you can see for yourself,' he said with emphasis, 'it's an English ball . . .'

'I don't understand,' Mason said.

'It's a lie!' Smudge shouted almost at the same instant.

Purcell pointed to Smudge.

'Look at Smudge, Captain Mason! He understood. He understood straight away. The Tahitians have French muskets, Captain Mason! Therefore it was not a Tahitian who fired at me!'

'It's a lie! Smudge shouted, sweat pearling on his forehead.

'Be quiet, Smudge,' Mason said.

He was turning the ball over and over in his hand with a look of perplexity.

'It's certainly an English ball,' he said after a moment. 'But I can't see why Smudge should wish to murder you.'

'Smudge has views about Ivoa.'

'Do you mean to say that Smudge tried to kill you to . . . to marry your wife?'

'Precisely,' Purcell said. 'But he's out in his calculations. If I died, he wouldn't long survive me.'

He glanced at Smudge. He was pale and seemed to be collapsed on his stool. MacLeod was laughing silently.

'I don't understand this affair at all,' Mason said stiffly. 'Why should Smudge covet another man's wife? He's already married.'

Purcell looked at him. In certain matters, the Old Man's ingenuousness was unfathomable. But was it really ingenuousness?

'Why did Timi kill Jones?' Purcell said after a moment.

'That's different,' Mason said haughtily. 'We are British, not savages.'

'Believe me,' Purcell said, 'even in England there are men who kill their neighbour to appropriate his wife.'

Mason blushed, looked away and said with a certain embarrassment and irritation: 'I don't see that there's anything to be gained by considerations of that sort. They seem to me wholly immoral.'

'I'll tell you what I think,' MacLeod said suddenly in his drawling voice, 'the whole thing's pure fiction, and it's based on the story that the blacks destroyed the water fatigue's muskets. And who tells that story? Purcell. Who's he supposed to have got it from? From Amoureïa. And where's Amoureïa? In the bush. In fact, it's only Purcell who says so, and it's not proved. Suppose the blacks didn't destroy anything at all. Timi takes one of the English muskets and comes and takes a pot-shot at Purcell when he opens his door in the morning . . .'

Purcell looked at him angrily. A second before, MacLeod had glanced at Smudge and laughed, now he was flying to his rescue.

'You've forgotten one thing,' he said drily. 'It would be very risky for Timi to shoot at me in daylight from the undergrowth opposite my hut. To get away, he'd have to cross either East Avenue or West Avenue. He'd be quite in the open.'

The tactical argument seemed to have its effect on Mason.

'That's true enough,' he said, his eyes on the ball. 'Nor can one see why Timi should have changed weapons. French muskets are excellent. And less heavy than ours.'

He thought for a few seconds, and then looked up at Purcell.

'Nevertheless, these are merely presumptions and you haven't proved anything against Smudge. In the circumstances, I decide to disallow your objection.'

He spoke firmly enough, but it was clear the incident had shaken him.

Purcell held out his hand and Mason gave him back the ball.

'I shall not ask you,' Purcell said, turning his back on him and going to the table, 'whether Smudge was with you when you heard the shots this morning. I don't wish to embarrass you.'

He took a bunch of bananas from the table, selected one, detached it and began to peel it. Half-sitting on the table, he faced Mason again, perfectly calm and master of himself. His chin hurt a little when he spoke, but all trace of nausea had vanished.

'Smudge was not with us,' Mason said, after a moment's thought.

Purcell bent his head in his direction.

'I'm grateful to you for admitting it,' he said, ceasing to peel his banana. 'And I'm also grateful to you for admitting that there are at least presumptions against Smudge. But that you should still consider that Smudge has the necessary moral authority to be a judge rather surprises me.'

MacLeod was no longer bored. The angel Gabriel had guts! He'd certainly taken the wind out of the old man's sails with his story about the English ball! MacLeod screwed up his eyes and remembered the assembly and the angel Gabriel leading the opposition to him with regret. Christ, there wasn't a dull moment! There was always some manoeuvring to be done against the angel! Always some new attempt to shipwreck him! Those were the days! Those damned blacks had spoilt it all! He clenched his teeth till they hurt. 'Those bastards,' he thought angrily. But they wouldn't get him! No, they wouldn't get this mother's son! Oh no! He'd get away with it! Perhaps he'd be the only one! The only one of all these bastards, black or white, to get away with it! 'The island will be mine!' he thought with a sudden surge of joy. He filled his chest with air, opened his eyes wide and stared at the mountain on the horizon. 'Christ,' he thought, 'the island will be mine!'

The longer the silence lasted the more Mason felt ill at ease. Smudge's absence when the shot was fired had convinced him, but he could not go back on his decision, and he realised how weakened his position was. Meanwhile, he was annoyed beyond words by Purcell's attitude. He had never seen an accused man sit on a table and eat a banana in the presence of his judges. It was positively indecent. Yet, on the other hand, Purcell was in his own house. And it was his table and his banana, after all. He had a perfect right to both of them, and there was nothing to be said about that! For the first time in his life, the respect for forms and the respect for property clashed in Mason, and the resultant shock reduced him to silence.

Purcell began on his second banana. There was no affectation about it. His sickness under the ferns had emptied his stomach, and he was hungry. At the same time, he was aware second by second of what was going on in Mason's mind and, in spite of his danger, he was amused. It was clearly difficult to accuse some-one of high treason when he was sitting on a table eating fruit. So grave an accusation required more ceremony. 'What a comedy of manners!' Purcell thought. 'How men love appear-ances, and everything that gives them power over others! At this moment, Mason would be delighted to have a black cap and a judge's wig on his head to condemn me to death.'

Purcell wiped his fingers on his handkerchief, crossed the room, sat down on the accused's stool, leaned comfortably back against the wall and looked at Mason.

'Mr Purcell,' Mason said at once, 'you have given the im-pression, ever since you've been on the island, of taking sides with the blacks against your fellow-countrymen.'

Purcell shook his head.

'I've defended the Tahitians' interests because they were in-jured, gravely injured; and not only their interests, but their dignity. I would equally have defended the interests and dignity of my fellow-countrymen.'

'Do you therefore consider that the responsibility for this war rests with the British?'

'It rests with MacLeod and with those who voted for him. And it rests with you too, because you became MacLeod's ally after the murder of Kori and Mehoro.'

'Mr Purcell, please abstain from criticising me.'

Purcell raised his eyebrows and said curtly: 'Why?'

Mason sought an answer, failed to find one, and went on peevishly: 'I have myself heard you say that MacLeod did not kill the two blacks in legitimate self-defence. Do you maintain that point of view?'

'I maintain it.'

'From what I have heard, Kori was about to pierce MacLeod

with his javelin when he fired.'

'That's true, but MacLeod had provoked him. He had thrown a stone in his face.'

'Kori had mocked me,' MacLeod said, bringing his stool forward on to its feet and fixing Purcell with his hard eyes.

'I heard Baker mock you in the cruellest way the night of the sharing out of the women, and yet you did nothing.'

'That's different. I'm not going to allow a black to show disrespect.'

'So there are two different standards, are there?'

'Of course!'

'Well, you see to what that system leads: six deaths.'

'These considerations are off the point,' Mason said impatiently. 'From what you've just said, Mr Purcell, I conclude that when the blacks took to the bush, you were in entire sympathy with them.'

'That's not quite true. I don't approve of their having resorted to violence.'

'However, you believe their cause is just?'

'It is just,' Purcell said forcefully.

Mason's grey-blue eyes glittered. He gathered his body together, sank his neck between his shoulders, and leaned his square head forward as if he were about to attack.

'Mr Purcell,' he said emphasising each word, 'I told you last November of my intention to hide arms in a cave. You are the only Briton on the island to whom I confided the plan. The day before yesterday, the blacks took to the bush, and next morning they found my arms. Since you were the only Briton to wish their cause well, I conclude that it was you who told them of the hiding-place.'

Purcell leapt to his feet.

'You're mad, Mason!' he cried violently. 'How dare you bring such an accusation against me? You don't believe in it yourself! I don't want any arms myself, and I most certainly don't want to give them to anyone else!'

'How then do you explain that the blacks found my muskets so quickly?'

'Mehani discovered your cave in November. He used it as a hiding-place for Itia and Avapouhi.'

'Who told you that?'

'Itia.'

'When?'

'Yesterday.'

'At what time?'

'A few minutes before the ambush.'

'Obviously!' Mason said.

Purcell looked at him and his eyes glittered but he said nothing.

Mason went on: 'How do you explain the fact that the blacks knew there was a water fatigue?'

'Their women had been in continual contact with ours.'

'You mean they were spying on us?'

'Not consciously. But Tahitian women are gossips.'

'Mrs Mason is not a gossip,' Mason said stiffly.

Purcell opened his mouth to reply but thought better of it. After all, Mason's admiration for his wife was rather touching. A pity it did not extend either to her sex or her race.

Mason went on disdainfully: 'Has Mrs Purcell been gossiping with Itia?'

Purcell frowned. Of course, Mrs Purcell was a gossip . . .

'I don't know,' he said curtly.

He added: 'The British have nine women. Why do you think it should be mine who told Itia about the water fatigue?'

'Did you tell her about it?'

Purcell sat down.

'Of course not,' he said, shrugging his shoulders. 'Why should I? What would have been the point? You'll soon be accusing me of having organised the ambush.'

'I'm not accusing you of anything of the kind. When the blacks took to the bush, why didn't you tell me?'

'Why should I have told you?'

'So that I could go and take my arms from the cave.'

'So you no longer believe it was I who told the Tahitians of your hiding-place?'

'I don't understand,' Mason said, disconcerted.

'You have just betrayed yourself,' Purcell said, getting up and putting his foot on the stool again. 'You have never believed that I revealed your hiding-place to the Tahitians.'

Mason stared at him, red and blinking.

'Please explain yourself.'

'You can't accuse me both of having revealed your secret and of not having warned you. Either I'm a traitor, or I'm a fool. You must make up your mind.'

'I don't see the contradiction,' Mason said. 'It's precisely because you didn't warn me that I thought you had revealed my secret.'

MacLeod put his head on one side. That was a good piece of helmsmanship! He'd never have thought the old man could surmount that sea so quickly!

'But I didn't even know which cave it was!' Purcell went on angrily. 'I didn't even know you had carried out your plan of transporting arms there. As far as I knew, you had never asked anyone else to give you a hand, and Vaa had refused to help you through fear of the *toupapahous.*'

'Mrs Mason overcame her feelings.'

'How could I guess that?' Purcell said in exasperation. 'I haven't the honour of knowing Mrs Mason as well as you do!'

Mason said curtly: 'We won't talk of Mrs Mason.'

'Really, this is crazy! For the last quarter of an hour you've been accusing me of everything under the sun. By your account, there's nothing I'm not guilty of. Even when I do nothing, I'm guilty! If we're to go into the question of responsibility, don't forget that it was you who taught the Tahitians to shoot, and that it's with your muskets they're shooting now.'

'I repeat, leave me out of this!'

'Leave me out of it! Why should you be privileged in this discussion? And by what right are you my judge except for the weapon in our hands?'

There was a shot in the distance. Purcell became still, silent and pale. In the heat of defending himself, he had forgotten Ouili.

'It sounds as if Baker has sent Ohou to his account,' MacLeod said in his drawling voice.

Mason turned to look at the mountain and said in a low voice: 'Well played.' Smudge also turned his head, but said nothing.

They waited, perfectly still, staring at the mountain. Mason took out his watch, its ticking filled the room. If there was no second shot, it would mean that Baker had succeeded in escaping. Purcell listened in agony. He had never listened for silence with such passion.

There were two more shots, one after the other. Purcell got to his feet and put his hands in his pockets.

'They've got him,' Mason said in a low voice.

'Why do you say that?' Purcell asked violently.

'He hasn't had time to re-load. It was they who fired.'

'They may have missed him.'

'Perhaps.'

'No,' MacLeod said after a moment. 'There were only two shots, and there are three of them. If the first two had missed him, the third would have fired.'

'The third may be busy elsewhere,' Purcell said desperately. 'He may be chasing Amoureïa, for instance.'

'No,' Mason said, 'that's unlikely. They would all three have attacked Baker. They'd deal with Amoureïa afterwards.'

'And don't forget,' MacLeod went on, 'that they've got two muskets each. If they'd missed Baker, we'd have heard more shots.'

'They may not have both their muskets permanently loaded,' Purcell said sharply.

MacLeod shrugged and exchanged a glance with Mason which meant: 'What's the use of arguing? He denies the evidence.' This glance affected Purcell more than all their arguments. He closed his eyes. And he suddenly saw Baker lying livid on the stones, a dark hole in his chest.

Mason was watching Purcell and was struck by his drawn look. He was on the point of saying: 'I am most distressed, Mr Purcell.' But he restrained himself. It seemed to him unsuitable to offer condolences to the accused.

Purcell sat down and placed his hands on his knees. He held his head straight and rigid, the muscles of his neck stood out stiffly, and he stared straight in front of him.

Smudge impatiently pushed his forelock back. Purcell's torpor somewhat restored his courage and he dared at least to move. MacLeod sat with the barrel of his musket leaning against the hollow of his shoulder and he began tapping his knees with his bony fingers. Then he took the fingers of his right hand in his left and began pulling at them, one after the other, only omitting the thumb. When he had finished with one hand, he began on the other. Each time he pulled at a joint, there was a double crack, a slight one and then a louder. Having completed this operation, he looked up and glanced at Smudge. Smudge coughed, stuck out his lower lip, and poked his face contemptuously towards Purcell. After a moment, MacLeod scraped the floor with his feet and looked at Mason again. But Mason avoided his glance. He wanted to go, but reproached himself for it as if it were a sign of cowardice. His duty was to go through with it. He must continue the interrogation, but he could not make up his mind to it. Purcell's stupor reminded him of what he himself had felt at the time of Jimmy's death.

There was a sudden noise by the right-hand corner of the house near the lean-to. Mason seized his musket, turned and fell on one knee. He immediately got to his feet again. It was the women. They came one by one, silent as weasels, and grouped themselves almost elbow to elbow in front of the sliding doors. They did not come into the room. They were all there except Ivoa and Vaa. They formed a black, compact, immobile group, dominated by Omaata's stature. They said nothing. Only their eyes were alive.

Mason frowned, then noted with pride that Vaa had not deserted her post. He gave a slight wave of the hand as if chasing away a swarm of flies and said impatiently: 'Go away! Go away!' None of them moved. 'Omaata,' Mason said with an air of command, 'tell them to go away!' Omaata made no reply. Mason looked at MacLeod as if to ask him to intervene . . . MacLeod shook his head. He had no desire to be subjected to Horoa's eloquence in public.

Mason looked at the women. Their dark, attentive eyes were fixed on him. 'What do you want?' he cried irritably. They made no answer.

Purcell made no move. His attitude was not one of prostration, but of rigidity and contraction, as if he had been struck down with catalepsy. His face was immobile, his wide-open eyes stared unblinkingly, and tears accumulated in them and rolled down his cheeks. The tears were in striking contrast to his impassive, almost petrified face.

Mason looked at Purcell and could not make up his mind to speak. He was haunted by the memory of the ten minutes he had spent in his cabin after Jimmy's murder. He saw himself standing by his table, the open case of pistols, his hands on the lid. He was staring at the porthole in front of him, seeing it without seeing it, unable to think. The lid of the pistol-case slipped from his hands, there was a sharp click, he shuddered, looked down at the pistols, and realised Jimmy was dead . . . Then the world blacked out, he was alone and the dark, cold, icy waters were closing in on him, he was suffocating . . .

Smudge was becoming impatient. He had noticed at once that Ivoa was not among the women. She must be wandering about in the bush round the hut with her musket, making no more noise than a snake, and God only knew if she would shoot him in the back when he went out, for no reason at all, perhaps just to forestall things. He moved on his stool, caught Mac-Leod's eye, and muttered: 'Shall we go?'

MacLeod indicated Mason with his chin and made a face. They would have to wait. The old man was head to the wind with his sails furled. It was clear that he lacked the guts to go on with the case. And the case had been his idea, and what a mess he had made of it! Besides, what the hell had those damned Negresses got into their heads, and what were they doing there, staring at them through their gunports, without uttering a damned word!

'Let's go,' MacLeod said.

He got to his feet so quickly that his stool fell over with a bang. Purcell started, got to his feet, blinked, and with a slow, painful movement, as if his neck was hurting him, turned his head to the right and looked at MacLeod. Then, equally slowly, he turned it to the left, his eyes passed over Smudge, rested a moment longer on the women and finally became fixed on Mason.

'Well,' he said with sudden anger, 'what are you waiting for? Why don't you shoot me?'

MacLeod picked up his stool and sat down. Mason became scarlet in the face.

'We hope, Mr Purcell,' he said fairly calmly, 'that Baker's murder has changed your attitude.'

'What attitude?'

There was a silence.

'I'll be frank with you, Mr Purcell,' Mason went on, lowering his eyes. 'We have only presumptions against you. But,' he added, raising his hand, 'these presumptions are reinforced, and even given the force of proof, by your refusal to join us and fight the common enemy.'

He put his hand on his knee.

'However,' he went on, 'it is clear that, if you decide to change your attitude as a result of Baker's murder, we shall have no further reason to suspect you.'

'In other words,' Purcell cried indignantly, 'either I fight on your side, or you'll declare me guilty! Is that your conception of justice? It's blackmail! Pure and simple blackmail! And I'm beginning to understand why you're bringing this case against me. It's merely to have another musket in your camp . . .'

'Mr Purcell,' Mason said excitedly, 'you have talked of blackmail. If it is blackmail, it's not a form of blackmail that troubles my conscience. I have a proper sense of my responsibilities towards the British here. We are at war, Mr Purcell, and I want to win this war. At this actual moment, it would seem that the blacks number no more than three: Mehani, Tetahiti and Timi. We are four – counting you.'

He paused, picked up his musket with both hands and said forcibly: 'Your presence at our side may be decisive.'

He went on: 'On the other hand, if you refuse us your help, you are deliberately cutting yourself off from our little community . . .'

'And I become guilty!' Purcell cried with biting irony.

'Mr Purcell, your sarcasms don't worry me. I am conscious of doing my duty. The lives of all three of us are at stake. If you refuse to help us, we shall look on you as an enemy and treat you accordingly . . .'

Purcell put his hands in his pockets, walked up and down the room and his indignation fell away. At first sight, it was delirium. Yesterday, Mason had asked him to be godfather to his son. Today, he was prepared to shoot him. But since yesterday, things had changed on the island: the blacks had ceased to be negligible adversaries. They had found the muskets. 'Fear,' Purcell thought. 'It's fear. Even the best become cruel when they're afraid.'

'Even without taking up arms I can be useful to you,' he said, turning and looking at Mason. 'Yesterday, the assembly commissioned me to make contact with the Tahitians. I still intend to do so and to try to restore peace.'

'Peace!' Mason cried. 'Your mind clearly doesn't work like other people's. Do you expect us to live in peace with wretches who have killed five of us?'

'That's just it,' Purcell said bitterly, 'five of us, three of them; perhaps it's time to stop.'

MacLeod shrugged.

'That's just like you, Purcell. Always Bible-thumping, always the little Jesus! No one can be blinder than you! You just put up a little prayer, and the blacks turn white! Another little prayer, they grow wings and there we are! A following wind, ten knots, and a course laid straight for Paradise! Well, I'll tell you what I think, Purcell, I hate those bastards. They're a cowardly, traitorous lot, and there's nothing to be done with them. They're lower than animals, that's my view. Even if those damned blackamoors signed a treaty of peace with their own mothers' blood and in the presence of Jesus Christ himself, I tell you I'd still not trust it. One day or another it'd begin all over again. So, rather than have the jitters all the rest of my life on this island, by Christ it's better to go at it straight away and put an end to it once and for all!'

'All this is leading us away from the point,' Mason said. 'I've asked you a question, Mr Purcell, and I'm awaiting an answer.'

Purcell went to the table, turned on his heel, looked at the women and said in a low rapid voice in Tahitian: 'They want to kill me, because I won't carry a musket.'

'We'll prevent them,' Omaata said.

'Even the one who's on the left of the one who's on your left?'

'Even she,' Toumata said.

Purcell smiled at her. He had not wanted to mention her name in front of Smudge.

'Even the pretty angry mare?'

'Even she,' Horoa said.

'What are you saying to them?' Mason cried angrily.

Purcell looked him up and down and said curtly over his shoulder: 'This is my house.'

He began walking up and down the room again, his eyes on the ground. Pretend to yield? Accept a musket, and take to the bush at the first opportunity? No, he must not come to terms. Not even appear to come to terms. He took a deep breath. His heart was beating fast against his ribs. And there was a cold shiver down his spine.

He went back to his stool and resumed his nonchalant attitude. A foot on the seat, an elbow on one knee, a hand in his pocket. He was aware that the pose, by being prolonged, was becoming affected, but it helped him to keep his courage up.

'Captain Mason,' he said in a low, serious voice, 'you have demanded an answer. Here it is. In the first place, my carrying a musket will do you no good; I don't know how to shoot. In the second, with or without a musket, I refuse to commit the sin of homicide.'

There was no movement in the room. Smudge was sitting in a heap on his stool, his eyes lowered. Mason seemed turned to stone and was staring straight in front of him. Only MacLeod was looking at Purcell. The angel had guts. He had foreseen that the old man would fail.

'If I understand you,' Mason said, 'the answer is "no".'

His voice was passionless and his eyes curiously fixed.

'Yes.'

'In that case,' he went on in a blank voice, 'I know what I have to do.'

And he cocked his musket.

'Take it easy!' MacLeod cried. 'We must vote.'

'Vote?' Mason said in the same blank, automatic voice.

But he lowered his weapon.

'You're not the only one here,' MacLeod said rudely. 'There are three of us.'

Mason looked at him as if he found it difficult to grasp what he was saying. Then he raised his right hand and said absently: 'Guilty.'

'I abstain,' MacLeod said at once.

Smudge had not changed his attitude. His head was hanging, his neck was sunk between his shoulders, and he was silent.

'Smudge?' MacLeod said.

Smudge started, shot a terrified glance at the women and said in a rapid confused voice: 'Not guilty!'

'What!' Mason cried.

'Not guilty,' Smudge said.

Purcell gave a jerky, nervous laugh. It was a farce. An incredible farce. He was saved by his murderer. He sat down, his legs were trembling under him and he could not stop laughing.

Mason was silent, pale and dumbfounded. He looked at Mac-Leod and said blankly: 'What does that mean?'

'That Purcell is acquitted,' MacLeod said.

He had put his thumbs through his trouser-belt; and, tilting his stool back, his head leaning against the door and slightly to one side, he screwed his eyes up and contemplated Mason, his thin lips drawn into a slight smile. The old man had understood nothing. He was a fool of an Englishman. Stupid and stubborn.

The significance of the vote gradually impinged behind Mason's square forehead. His pale face turned scarlet and he started to blink.

'You're betraying me, MacLeod!' he cried.

'I'm not betraying anything,' MacLeod said in his nasal voice. 'We mustn't see traitors everywhere, Captain Mason, or we'll finish up by all going mad on this island. After all, the case was your idea, not mine. All right. Let's admit that had Purcell been afraid of being shot and had agreed to carry a musket, we'd have won. I never believed it, you know, but let's admit it. Another musket was worth the attempt.'

And as Mason opened his mouth, MacLeod raised his right hand and said with dignity: 'One moment, Captain Mason, please. We're all whites here. We can discuss things calmly like gentlemen. As I was saying, if Purcell agreed to carry a musket, we'd have won. Only, there it is; Purcell won't agree, as I foresaw, Captain Mason, and you can't deny it. I know Purcell well. He's got religion. And he believes in it, as hard as the oak of a ship's side.'

'All these considerations . . .'

'Let me speak,' MacLeod said impatiently. 'I've let you have

your say for an hour. It's my turn now. Let's go on. Purcell
refuses. He won't do it. Absolutely not. Homicide, he says? He
has a horror of it. Kill a fellow creature? Never on your life. No
musket for the angel Gabriel! In short, we've failed. And if
we've failed, we've failed, that's what I say, Captain Mason, and
we won't have failed any the less because you shoot Purcell . . .
What do you gain by shooting him? Nothing at all. It won't give
you another musket.'

'There is such a thing as justice,' Mason said.

'Yes,' MacLeod said gradually recovering the sarcastic tone
which was habitual to him, 'yes, Captain Mason, as you say,
there's such a thing as justice, and at the present moment I don't
care a damn for it. Nor do you, with all due respect. And the
proof of it is your telling us that the angel Gabriel gave away
the muskets' hiding-place to the blacks, but permit me – as one
private gentleman speaking to another – to say that I don't know
whether it's justice or truth, sir, but it is difficult to believe, sir.
Let's go on. During the case one says what one says but, after
the case is over, the truth comes out of the well. And there it is,
all wringing wet! Take your feet off it and let it dry! There it is,
I say. If there was any justice left on this island, Smudge would
be swinging at this moment from the highest branch of the
banyan, in the first place (as the angel says) for having tried to
make a target, at an unseasonable time, of one of his fellow citizens, and in the second place for having nearly got himself killed
in the bush by Baker, the bastard (it's Smudge I mean) and
thereby depriving our group of a musket. Let's go on. At this
moment, I simply stow justice away in the locker with the spare
sails. For the moment, I've my own little interests, Captain
Mason. There's my skin, skeleton and organs included. And
from that point of view, I'll say this: I don't see what I've to
gain by putting a ball into the angel Gabriel. But I can well see
what I risk losing . . .'

'Losing?' Mason said.

MacLeod paused. He could afford to. He had so well prepared what he was going to say that no one thought of interrupting him, not even Mason. Purcell watched him, fascinated. What
vitality and truculence! MacLeod was odious, and yet . . . It
was not all avarice, there was something of the gambler in him.

His two long slender thumbs hooked in his trouser-belt, his interminable legs thrown out in front of him, his hollow, expressive face, and the way he looked at this audience with a happy and superior expression . . . The time of his giving precedence to Mason was over. He was taking possession of the stage again. He was playing his part to the utmost. 'Yes,' Purcell thought, 'there's always been something of the gambler about him. But it's with our lives he's been gambling.'

'Of course, I risk losing!' MacLeod went on. 'And not only I. But you and Smudge too. Not guilty, Smudge said. A prudent chap! Seeing as how there's a little lady in the bush with a musket of yours who'd be very angry if anything unfortunate happened to her darling. And perhaps you haven't noticed that there are other little black ladies behind you, Captain Mason, who wouldn't be pleased either, I can promise you. They adore Purcell, it's well known. The angel's their great favourite! They're always cherishing and fawning on him! He's their brother! He's their baby! He's their Jesus! They're mad about him! All of them! Turn round and take a look at them, Captain Mason. They're worth a glance. There's no question now of laughing and singing, or undulating their bottoms to the rhythm! Look at them! Statues. Mouths closed. Teeth clenched. Eyes like razors . . .'

'Are you afraid of the women?' Mason said contemptuously.

'I most certainly am!' MacLeod said emphatically. 'And if you knew them as well as I do, you'd be afraid of them too. They're dangerous, Captain Mason, believe me. I'd rather fight the three bastards over there. And, between ourselves, I've got quite enough on my hands with those three without having the *vahinés* come down on me too. Just suppose I'd said "guilty" of Purcell. Right. I take my musket and I send the angel Gabriel back to his Papa in heaven. What then? What do you think the *vahinés* do? They attack us, you can bet on that, with Omaata in the lead. Or they go and give Vaa a bashing and steal her muskets. And, as a result, there's another armed gang against us in the bush, and one that'll have it properly in for us.'

'All this talk . . .' Mason said, clutching his musket.

He felt a crushing weight on his right shoulder. He looked round. A large black hand was pressing down on him.

'There is no more water,' Omaata said in English.

'Leave go of me,' Mason said furiously and, seizing the giantess's wrist, he tried to make her let go. Omaata did not appear even to notice his efforts. Enormous and maternal, she stood over him from her full height.

'There's no more water,' she repeated, and her voice rumbled like the distant echo of a waterfall.

'What? No more water?' MacLeod cried. 'What about the containers in the Market Place?'

'Upset.'

'Upset?' Mason said. 'Who upset them?'

He ceased struggling. Above him, Omaata's black face shone, immense and lunar, the lips curling, the nostrils wide open, the eyes large and liquid.

'They did,' she said in her deep voice.

'How do you know?' MacLeod cried, getting to his feet.

'Itia said so.'

'When?' Smudge asked, his voice trembling as he, too, got to his feet.

'Just now. They came just now.'

With her free hand she made the gesture of upsetting the containers. Then she went on: 'Itia had this message from them . . .'

'What did she say?' MacLeod cried, his face livid.

'The *vahinés* may come and drink from the stream and the *Peritani* may not. The *Peritani* will drink no more.'

13

Omaata slowly withdrew her hand and Mason was able to move. This new disaster made him feel a need for action. He got to his feet. And as soon as he had done so, he realised there was nothing to be done. The blacks held the only water point on the island. They would wait for the British and shoot them like pigeons.

The four men looked at each other. MacLeod passed his tongue over his lips and the three others at once knew what he was feeling. The thought of lacking water was making him thirsty.

'There's only one solution!' Mason said, his voice quivering. 'It's to go into the bush and attack them!'

MacLeod looked at him, glanced at Smudge and sat down.

'I'm not keen on throwing myself into their arms,' he said in his nasal voice. 'We couldn't take one step in the bush. They'd be warned by the women.'

'Would you rather die of thirst?' Mason asked morosely.

MacLeod shrugged without answering.

'Perhaps we could go to the stream at night,' Smudge said. 'We'd send the women ahead with the containers. And when the blacks showed themselves, we'd shoot them down.'

'Fool,' MacLeod said, 'what have you got on your shoulders? A head or a scuttle? The blacks are no fools. They've proved it. They'd let the women fill the containers without even showing the ends of their filthy snouts. They'd get us on the way back.'

'You talk as if they're bound always to defeat us,' Mason said angrily. 'I don't understand your attitude, MacLeod.'

'I must say, that upsets me considerably,' MacLeod said calmly. 'My attitude's my attitude, Captain Mason, and I can see no reason to change it. We can't defeat the blacks in the bush, that's what I say. We must fight them here.'

Smudge sat down and swallowed.

'And if they don't attack?' he said aggressively. 'What do we do then? Wait for them? Die of thirst?'

MacLeod gave him a bitter, disdainful smile and made no reply. Purcell was silent. He was surprised by the hostile glances the three men were exchanging. MacLeod was crushingly contemptuous, and the odd thing was that Mason and Smudge seemed to be in league against him, as if they held him responsible for the situation.

'Chief of the big canoe!' Omaata said in English.

They turned and looked at her in surprise. In their concern, they had forgotten the presence of the women.

'Listen, O Chief,' Omaata went on, 'we take the containers and we go. Adamo comes. We go to the others,' she went on, modestly lowering her eyes, 'and Adamo says to the others: we give guavas, bananas, mangoes, avocados. You give water.'

There was a profound silence in the room when Omaata had finished speaking.

'Perhaps,' MacLeod said after a moment. 'One wonders what the bastards have had to eat since the day before yesterday. All the fruit and vegetables are on our side, and in open spaces.' He added in a detached voice: 'It might work, I think, if Purcell accepts.'

He did not look at Purcell. He was staring at his feet.

'Why shouldn't he accept?' Smudge said aggressively, and as if Purcell had every reason in the world to risk his life for him.

But he didn't look at Purcell either. MacLeod thrust his legs out in front of him, put his feet together and then parted them at right angles. Then, since the angle was not quite correct, he screwed up his eyes and adjusted it.

'Perhaps Purcell doesn't care for the idea of going off to meet Timi,' he said in a flat voice.

'He's as thirsty as we are,' Smudge said.

Mason was standing and leaning with both hands on his musket. MacLeod brought his feet together and looked up at him. But Mason said nothing. He thought it beneath his dignity to ask a favour of Purcell.

'There's a slight chance it might work,' MacLeod went on indifferently. 'The bastards must be dying of hunger.'

'If they're hungry, they can come and steal fruit from us at night,' Smudge said.

'And we can do what they do at the stream,' MacLeod said, 'wait for them with a musket.'

He went on: 'It may be that's why they're depriving us of water. Perhaps they want an exchange. Give and take. That's my view, my lads.'

He added impartially: 'There's a slight chance it may work, that's what I say.'

This time he looked at Purcell, but he got no response. Purcell was staring into Omaata's eyes. He thought he saw some special meaning in the way she was looking at him, and he was trying to make out what it was.

'Do you advise me to accept?' he said in Tahitian.

'I do,' she said, her face impassive.

He began walking up and down the room. He did not want to

give the impression that his decision depended on the few words he had exchanged with Omaata. He suddenly felt extraordinarily cheerful. All his anxieties disappeared. He felt happy and light-hearted. Even the water no longer presented a problem.

'I'm glad my case has ended so happily,' he said in a clear, cheerful voice. 'Otherwise, I should have been in no position to do you a service.'

He went on with a sudden access of good humour: 'The last time there was a criminal case on the island, Captain Mason was the accused. I'm glad that case also had a happy outcome. Otherwise, we should not have had the pleasure of Captain Mason's company today.'

He smiled at them. MacLeod and Smudge looked at him and Mason blinked and turned scarlet in the face.

'I've already told you,' Mason muttered, 'that I'm not in the least grateful to you for your intervention that day.'

'Of course,' Purcell said amiably.

He felt heedless, happy, amused. 'My God, my God, I've got to put up with these fools.' His thoughts suddenly leapt to Ivoa. He thought of her levelling the musket at Smudge, and felt a peculiar tenderness towards her.

'Have you made up your mind?' Smudge asked, encouraged by Purcell's happy expression.

Purcell looked at him. At that moment, he did not even dislike Smudge. Poor Smudge, poor little rat, how frightened he was of dying of thirst! 'And so am I, so am I! . . . Without a doubt we've got something in common!' Purcell gave a little laugh. He felt ridiculously gay. He was walking up and down the room with a light, rapid step. He felt as if his feet were rebounding from the ground of their own accord. All three of them were expecting him to risk his life. It was a farce. The 'traitor' was to risk his life for the 'community'. 'My God, what fools, what fools!' He stopped and looked at each of them in turn. Smudge was staring at the floor, MacLeod pretending to detachment, Mason gazing at the mountain. In the oppressive silence, MacLeod's stool creaked, Mason passed his tongue over his lips, and Purcell thought: 'They're frightened men. They've got a hollow feeling in the stomach. Their hands are sweating and their throats are dry.'

His exaltation fell away and he said calmly: 'I accept.'

They all turned to look at him. They were relieved, but there was no surprise in their glances. They had expected him to accept. Purcell felt bitter and disgusted. They knew him! They knew exactly what they could expect of him, and they had brought this odious case against him! They had accused him, calumniated him, sullied him!

'I accept,' he went on, 'but on one condition. I refuse to be limited to bargaining over the water. I shall make a bid to restore peace.'

Mason glanced at MacLeod. MacLeod gave a half smile and Mason shrugged.

'Well?' Purcell asked.

'Just as you like,' Mason said.

MacLeod got to his feet, slung his musket, opened the door and, since this made an immediate draught between it and the sliding doors, he held it open to let the other two go out.

There was a moment of embarrassment. Mason did not know how to take his leave.

'Well, that's settled,' he said loudly, looking at no one.

He drew himself up, squared his shoulders, and went to the door followed by Smudge, bent, crooked and looking ridiculously smaller.

As he passed Purcell, he suddenly came to a halt, turned stiffly and said quickly: 'Very decent of you, Mr Purcell.'

Then he went out through the door, Smudge following in his shadow, his eyes on the ground and preceded by his obscene nose.

MacLeod held the door open and looked at Purcell.

'Good-bye,' he said, when the other two had gone out.

But he did not go. He remained standing loosely there, his eyes on Purcell's, his death's head smiling slightly. On the threshold, against the light, one long arm holding the door, the other against the doorpost, his two long legs wide apart, he looked all legs like a spider.

Purcell went across to prevent the door banging, when Mac-Leod should let go of it.

'Good luck,' MacLeod went on, giving him an indecisive half-smile.

He added in Gaelic: 'I hope to see you again.'

It was the first time he had spoken to Purcell in Gaelic. Purcell nodded without answering. He went to the door and took hold of the handle. He had never been so close to MacLeod before, and he was almost frightened by the emaciation of his face. It was the face of a man who for years had not had enough to eat.

MacLeod turned and took a single stride down the two steps.

'Good luck,' he repeated, casting Purcell a last glance over his shoulder.

Then he waved his long skeleton-like hand twice before his face.

'The containers are here,' Omaata said.

Purcell shut the door and turned round.

'And the fruit? The yams?'

'They're here too.'

He looked at her, smiled and felt intrigued. She did not answer his smile. She was maintaining her air of severity and appeared indisposed to talk.

The group went out into East Avenue and turned right into Banyan Lane. Omaata took the lead. Then came Purcell, with Horoa and Avapouhi on each side of him. Taïta, Toumata and Itihota brought up the rear. It was very hot and climbing the hill was hard work.

When they reached the middle of the second plateau, Omaata became rather out of breath. Purcell gained on her and drew level with her. She turned to him and said in a low severe voice: 'Stay behind me.'

As he hesitated, Horoa took him forcibly by the arm and drew him back.

'É Horoa é! ' Purcell said angrily.

She bent towards him and whispered: 'Omaata is afraid the others will fire at you.'

That was why they were surrounding him! The others would be unable to fire without hitting them!

'Omaata! '

'Be quiet! ' she said without turning her head.

She was right. He was the only one of them to show imprudence. They had been walking for half an hour and the 'chatterboxes' escorting him had not said a word. They never so much as moved a stone with their feet. They were controlling even their breathing.

They reached the banyan.

'We'll stop here,' Omaata said in a low voice. 'The others never come here. However, even here we must be careful.'

Since the sharing out of the women, the banyan was thought by the Tahitians to be a place of ill omen, and therefore taboo.

'Taïata,' Omaata said, 'stay at the entrance and keep watch.'

Taïata pouted. Omaata's order would deprive her of the discussion that was about to take place. However, she slipped silently into the grass. Her head reappeared and at once seemed to fade into the outline of a root. It was extraordinary. Even the colour of her face seemed to be the same as that of the wood.

Omaata went in under the banyan. As he followed her into the shade of the leafy rooms, Purcell took out his watch. It was noon. Scarcely four hours had passed since he had escaped Smudge's ball by shutting the door.

It was very dark under the banyan. Omaata went from room to room without stopping, and Purcell had difficulty in following her. Only her bark belt made a light patch in the darkness.

'It's here,' Omaata said.

A shadow detached itself from the wall of foliage and leapt towards Purcell. He took a pace backwards and threw out his hands. But his assailant laughed, ducked under his hands, and took him in her arms. Purcell felt a naked, distended belly against his body.

'Adamo! O Adamo! I thought I'd never see you again!'

She knelt on the moss, took him by the hand and made him sit beside her.

'Ivoa,' Purcell said, taking her face in his hands, 'how do you come to be here? How did you know I was coming?'

She laughed, happy to feel his hands on her face.

'Answer me, Ivoa!'

She laughed all the louder. Always these 'whys'! Always wanting to know! She rested her head in the hollow of Purcell's shoulder.

'When I saw the three *Peritani* with their muskets in the hut, I thought: "*Aoué, aoué,* I can't kill all three of them!"'

There was laughter and Purcell realised that the women were sitting round them in the semi-obscurity. He could scarcely see their outlines.

'Then,' Ivoa said, 'I ran to Omaata's, Itia was with her, and I told them. And Omaata thought and said: "I've got an idea. Go to the banyan with Itia and wait there."'

'And I,' Omaata said, 'assembled the women. I told them my idea, and the women said: "Let it be done as you say."'

She was sitting on Purcell's right. She turned her head towards him, her eyes gleaming in the shadows, and paused dramatically. She was waiting to be questioned.

'And then?' Purcell asked.

'Then I upset the containers.'

'You upset the containers!' Purcell cried in stupefaction.

Omaata threw her head back, the twin globes of her breasts swelled and she laughed like a cataract. However, her eyes remained sad. It was the laughter of pride, not of gaiety. Purcell's eyes had become used to the dark and he could distinctly see the women sitting round him on their heels. He could not hear them, Omaata's laughter dominated everything, but he could see from their lips that they were laughing too. They were proud of having taken part in the trick and that it should have proved so successful.

'You know, Adamo,' Omaata went on, 'that in Tahiti one kills one's enemy. One does not prevent his drinking.'

'But why the trick?' Purcell said.

'To get you out of the hands of the *Peritani* and hide you.'

'Hide me?' Purcell said, raising his eyebrows.

'Till the war is over.'

Purcell looked at the women.

'You were all agreed about this trick?' he said in a different tone.

'All,' Omaata said, 'even the women whose *tanés* are not your friends. However, we didn't say anything about it to Vaa.'

'Vaa is very stupid,' Horoa said, raising her head and shaking her hair. 'She might have betrayed us.'

'Vaa admires the man who wears those things of skin round his feet,' Toumata said. 'She doesn't understand that the chief no longer counts since the big canoe was burnt.'

'The chief himself hasn't understood that,' Itia said.

The women laughed. Itia's wicked tongue!

'However,' Ivoa said, 'Vaa lent me a musket.'

'She lent it to you?' Purcell said.

'Yes, lent.'

Purcell raised his eyebrows, amused. The admirable Mrs Mason had lied to her husband.

'Listen,' Omaata said, 'we're going to hide you in a cave. There are *toupapahous* in the caves. The others are frightened of them.'

'Mehani is not frightened.'

'Mehani is your brother,' Ivoa said.

'Which cave?'

'Mine,' Itia said. 'The one in which I slept with Avapouhi after the sharing out of the women.'

'The cave of the muskets!'

'Do you know it, Adamo?'

'No, I don't.'

'It's a very good cave,' Itia said. 'It has a little spring. With some patience one can fill a calabash.'

There was a silence and Omaata went on: 'You know, the fruit is not for the others. It's for you.'

She added: 'And for Itia.'

'For Itia?' Purcell said.

'Itia will take you to the cave and stay with you there.'

'And Ivoa?'

'Ivoa is carrying a son. She can't climb to the cave. It's a very difficult path.'

'And if I helped her to climb?'

'Ask her.'

Purcell could see nothing of Ivoa but her still profile. Her lips were closed, her expression serious and unforthcoming. She said not a word.

'Suppose I helped you, Ivoa?'

She shook her head and, as Purcell said nothing, added: 'I'm very heavy. I prefer to remain in the village.'

She felt exhausted after her sleepless night. She had but one thought: to go home and sleep for a few hours. Again tonight she would have to watch beside the lean-to with her musket to await Timi. She would know no rest till she had killed Timi.

'Why can't I stay alone in the cave?' Purcell said.

Itia leaned forward and held her hands open in front of her: 'This man is frightened of me,' she said, looking mischievously round at the women.

There were smiles, but they were much more discreet than might have been expected. Ivoa's seriousness and respect for etiquette demanded that they should be.

'Itia will be useful to you,' Omaata said. 'She's cunning. Besides, she'll bring you news.'

'Ivoa can do that.'

'Look at her, man! She can't climb. She can't run. She can scarcely walk.'

'I'll be all right,' Ivoa said.

Purcell lowered his eyes and was silent for so long that the women became alarmed. They made signs to Omaata, and Omaata said in her deep voice: 'Are you angry, O my baby?'

'I'm not angry.'

After that, he was silent, and Omaata went on, her voice hoarse with anxiety: 'Don't you agree to our plan?'

He raised his head and looked at her.

'I agree to your plan, but first I want to see the others.'

'*Maamaa!*' Omaata cried, raising her eyes to heaven. '*Maamaa!*'

And the women echoed it in surprise and consternation. Their *maamaas* rolled out in a long deep crescendo of disappointment and incredulity, accompanied by glances, gestures of the hand and shrugs of the shoulders.

'But you don't need to!' Omaata cried. 'The others aren't preventing the *Peritani* from drinking!'

'I want to make peace.'

The women looked at each other, slapped their thighs with the palms of their hands, and sighed. *Maamaa*. The *Peritani* were either very good or very bad. But they were always *maamaa*. Always.

'Man, it's madness!' Omaata went on. 'Timi will kill you. Or perhaps Tetahiti.'

Tears rolled down Ivoa's cheeks, but she said nothing.

'I've got to try,' Purcell said, taking her hand.

'I've never heard anything so stupid,' Omaata said, raising her voice angrily.

She was leaning against a thick vertical root, and her body was trembling with anger to such an extent that the whole branch was shaking.

'O my stupid little cock!' she grumbled, her voice rolling like thunder. 'O my proud little cock! You want to change the earth and the sky! Those men,' she went on, raising her hands, 'have tasted blood, and now they're going straight ahead killing and killing, and you, you, want to go unarmed and with bare hands to restore peace!'

Purcell waited till the echoes of her voice ceased, and said: 'I shall go, Omaata.'

'Man!' she cried, her eyes flashing with anger.

'Leave it, leave it, Omaata,' Ivoa said, tears pouring down her cheeks. 'I know Adamo. He'll go. He's gentle, but he's not pliant.'

'If you go, I shall go with you, Adamo,' Avapouhi said.

There was a silence. The women avoided looking at Avapouhi. *Aoué,* it was clear she wanted to be certain of Ouili's fate! She was still hoping! Poor, poor Avapouhi! The war was like a disease on the island!

'No,' Omaata said decisively. 'Itia will go to the others and she will say: "Adamo wants to see you." And if the others agree, Itia will go with Adamo. And when the *Manou-faïté* is over, Itia will lead Adamo to the cave. It may be difficult. It may be dangerous. And Itia is very cunning.'

'I will go with Itia and Adamo to the others,' Avapouhi said.

'No,' Omaata said, 'I've got a task for you, Avapouhi.'

The women looked at Omaata and suddenly understood. Omaata was sure that Ouili had been killed and she did not want Avapouhi to see his head on a pike. By *Eatua,* Omaata was wise! She always foresaw things!

'Let it be as Omaata says,' Horoa said, and there was a murmur of assent.

Without a word, Itia immediately got to her feet and left.

'It is the belly of the sun,' Ivoa said. 'Eat, Adamo. You have much fatigue before you.'

While speaking, she peeled a banana and handed it to him.

Purcell had a lump in his throat and the fruit seemed to him mealy and suffocating. After the banana, he ate a mango, then an avocado. The women were talking together in low voices. The continual murmur irritated him and got on his nerves. As the minutes went by, he became increasingly afraid.

He signed that he had enough to eat. He lay down on the moss, put his head on Ivoa's lap and closed his eyes. The women at once fell silent. At first he was relieved. But he could not go to sleep and the silence soon became intolerable. He knew he had a long time to wait before Itia's return, and that his fear would continue to increase. He heard Omaata say in a low voice: 'Horoa, give me your feather necklace.' Then there was the sound of a branch being broken and stripped of its leaves, and that was all. He tried to pray, but after a few seconds his prayer became automatic. He could no longer think, his legs were trembling and his fear increasing. He suddenly felt as if he was stifling under the banyan, panic seized on him and he felt an irresistible desire to get up and flee. He put his hands to his belt, tautened his muscles and felt the sweat run down his body. He suddenly saw himself stretched out, as stiff as a corpse, his eyes shut and his hands crossed on his breast. 'O Lord,' he prayed fervently, 'make it true, make it so that I no longer have to live, and that this nightmare come to an end.' He felt Ivoa raise his head and place it against her breast. He nestled against it like a child, hollowing a place for himself between her warm, soft breasts.

After a moment, the tide of his fear ebbed, his breathing became regular, and he slipped into sleep. When he woke up, Itia was standing before him.

'They agree,' she said, her little round face grave.

Purcell got to his feet. The women did likewise, followed more slowly by Ivoa. Her face was grey and her mouth quivering.

Omaata handed Purcell a stick with a bunch of red feathers tied to the end.

'While you were sleeping, I've made you a *Manou-faïté*,'* she said in rather a hoarse voice. 'Hold it in front of you. Then, Adamo, you will be the bird who flies to ask for peace, and

* The bird which asks for peace.

according to custom the others must not kill you. At least if your embassy succeeds. For if peace is rejected, then you are no longer taboo.'

He took the *Manou-faïté,* and Omaata showed him how to hold it with the feathers pointing backwards, for they represented the bird's tail, and the point of the stick forwards, for it represented the beak. Thus the bird flew while the man walked, and man and bird were one.

Purcell lowered his eyes. He looked at the absurd talisman in his hand. It meant death in case of failure. And how many chances were there of success?

'Do you know the poems in favour of peace?' Omaata went on.

'I know them. Otou taught me them when you were at war. And I was there when the *Manou-faïté* of the Natahiti came.'

'Good,' Omaata said.

She turned to Avapouhi: 'We'll go to the stream to fill the containers. Meanwhile, you'll take the fruit to the cave for Adamo. Then you'll come back here to the banyan and wait for us.'

There was a moment's silence and complete stillness. Purcell clasped Ivoa's shoulder and for an instant placed his cheek against hers. Then he turned to the women and made an inclusive gesture of the hand in farewell.

'I'll come back!' he said loudly and confidently.

There was an affectionate murmur from the women. Adamo! The eloquence of his gesture! How worthy he was of his father-in-law, the great chief Otou!

Purcell blinked in the broad light of day and felt the heat of the sun on his neck. Itia was walking in front of him.

'Did Avapouhi ask you?' he said in a low voice.

'Yes. I told her I didn't know.'

'Killed?'

'Yes.'

'Ohou?'

'Yes.'

'Amoureïa?'

He saw her neck shiver.

'Yes.'

There was a long silence and Itia said: 'You can talk, they're in the camp.'

He took a few paces in silence and then went on: 'Did you see the heads?'

Ever since he had decided to go to see the Tahitians, the idea of this appalling sight had worried him.

'No. They've put them in *poini*.* They'll put them on pikes afterwards.'

'After what?'

'After the war.'

There was another silence, then Itia turned, stopped and said in a different voice: 'But I saw Amoureïa, man! She's hung up by her hands to the branch of an avocado tree. Her legs are tied too. And her stomach has been slit open from here (she pointed to her stomach) to there (her hand went down to between her legs). Man, it was horrible!'

'Who did that?' Purcell said, his throat dry.

'Timi.'

He looked away.

'Let's go on, Itia,' he said in a low voice.

After that, they did not speak for some time. They were about to leave the second plateau for the stony desert of the mountain, when Itia suddenly turned towards a copse of giant ferns. When she reached it, she stood in the shade and seized Adamo's left hand. Her little face was serious and tense.

'Adamo,' she said, her voice trembling, 'after what I saw with the others, I feel ill ... Ill in my mind ... And I have no desire to play. But, if you wish, Adamo, you can ... *Aoué*, it may be the last time you ever play!'

'You're very reassuring!' Adamo said smiling.

He was still capable of smiling! He looked at Itia. He was touched by the naïvety and generosity of her offer. He bent down and touched her lips with his.

'The *Manou-faïté* must fly, Itia,' he said in a friendly way, 'and I cannot stop.'

There was nothing in front of them now but a chaos of black rocks, a burning, interminable desert. Then the bush began. This did not consist of ferns, like that which surrounded the

* Baskets of coconut leaves.

village, but of little palms, six to nine feet high and so close together that Purcell had sometimes to part them with his hands so as to slip between the trunks as he followed Itia. There was not a breath of air, the ceiling of leaves filtered a dim light and the thick swollen trunks were covered with black tufts hanging down like hair. Above his head, Purcell could hear the continuous movement of the palm leaves. It was a hard, metallic scraping sound which was not unpleasant in itself, but became tiresome by its persistence. It lay over you like a threat, filling your ears, echoing within your body. To Purcell it sounded like gigantic insects revelling in the tops of the trees, rubbing their monstrous legs together.

They advanced slowly, yard by yard. Why did the black hairy tufts of the trunks and the noise the big leaves made seem suddenly so important? It was odd. Part of him was afraid. Another part gazed at everything with avidity. The palms gradually grew thinner. Patches of white light appeared in the undergrowth. Suddenly, all became light. The sun seemed nearer, the scraping of the leaves gentler. He felt the sea breeze. In places, the sun's rays even reached the ground, slender as javelins.

'There it is,' Itia said in a low voice. 'Another moment, and we'll be there. Stop a minute. I'm frightened.'

She came to a halt and faced him.

'On the cliff?' Purcell asked.

'No. It's a clearing among the palms.'

She made a circular gesture.

'A big clearing among the palms. There's a rock in the middle.'

A clearing. A cleared space so as not to be surprised. A rock for cover. Mason could have done no better. When it was a question of killing, men were clever.

'It's the camp?'

'No,' Itia said, 'it's not the camp. It's a place in which to receive you.'

They were afraid of a trap. They were suspicious, even of him.

'I'm afraid for you,' Itia said pressing her hands to her cheeks. 'Oh, I'm afraid! I've no water in my mouth.'

'I'm afraid too,' Purcell said.

M

'Oh no! It's not true!' she said looking at him with admiration. 'You're not grey! You're all red!'

He smiled and shrugged his shoulders. He could not tolerate the sun, as she well knew.

'Adamo,' she said, coming close to him, her face grave and tense, and placing a hand on his arm, 'listen! Many *tanés* are dead, others will die, and I want a child! Oh, I want a child! Please, Adamo, if the others don't kill you . . .'

He looked down at her. He was about to say 'no'. He ought to say 'no'. But it suddenly did not seem so important to say 'no' . . . Smudge's ball in his door, Smudge's musket aimed at his heart. Mason cocking his musket. Timi . . . He looked at Itia. He ought to say 'no'. Why? For whom? No! Always no! No to Itia's child! No to Itia's happiness! No to himself! He shrugged impatiently. All these taboos!

'Don't answer,' she said.

Standing quite still with her eyes lowered, she pressed his arm. It no longer occurred to him to be afraid. He was looking at her. The top of her head scarcely reached to his chin. How good she was to look at with her smooth face, full lips, narrow brow and her eyes turned up towards her temples. He threw out his chest, relieved and full of hope. He looked at Itia and was reassured by her beauty. Nothing could happen to him with someone so beautiful beside him. It was absurd, but at that moment there was no doubt in his mind at all. She was beautiful. Therefore he could not die.

'You are beautiful, Itia,' he said in a low voice.

She did not move. All her aggressiveness had fallen away. Eyes closed, arms hanging, she seemed passive, torpid almost. He put a hand on her shoulder, and the other which held the *Manou-faïté* lightly against her back. He clasped her gently to him, his head held high above her, breathing the fresh air from the sea. What a tender light there was in the undergrowth. '*Eatua*,' he said softly, 'thank you for Itia's beauty, thank you for Itia's hair, thank you for Itia's little round breasts against me, thank you for her generosity.'

She threw her head back and looked at him gravely from below, her expression controlled and modest. He smiled at her, then he raised the *Manou-faïté* above her head, the red feathers sweeping Itia's blue-black hair, and said: 'Now we must go.'

When they reached the edge of the bush, a figure emerged in front of them. It was Raha. She turned her back to them and waved her arms above her head. She was facing a long, rounded rock in the middle of the clearing. She smiled at Itia, but she lowered her eyes when Purcell came up to her.

They advanced a few paces in the open, and Itia said in a low voice: 'The muskets!'

They stopped. The three musket-barrels looked brown against the red of the rock. There was nothing else to be seen. Not even the outline of a head. Purcell's heart began to beat wildly.

'Come on,' he said in a low voice.

And, turning to Itia, he added imperiously: 'No, not in front of me. Beside me.'

He went forward, one hand holding the *Manou-faïté* above his head, the other held away from his body, the palm open and turned towards the rock. Itia walked level with him, about a yard away.

There were some fifty yards between them and the muskets. He hurried forward. The clearing was covered with stones which burnt the soles of his feet. The sun weighed on his neck and on his left shoulder; the sweat was running down his forehead into his eyes, blinding him.

When he was five yards from the muskets, Mehani's voice said: 'Go round.'

He obeyed. Beyond the rock was another rock, hidden by the first, then still another, longer and higher. It was at the end of this one that he found the cleft. It was so narrow he had to turn sideways to pass through it.

Mehani was standing in front of him, musket in hand. Timi and Tetahiti had their backs to him, the barrels of their muskets resting on the rock.

'Sit down and wait,' Mehani said impassively. 'You, Itia, go and keep a look out on the south side.'

Purcell felt frozen and abashed by Mehani's coldness and mask-like face. He went forward into the open space. On his left was a corner in the shade under an overhanging rock. He sat down with relief. His feet were burning. He gazed round. The place was about five yards by five, and an almost perfect circle. The rock was breast high almost everywhere, affording excellent firing positions. There was a clear space of sixty yards all round. Itia was playing sentry on the south at the edge of the bush, Raha on the east and Faïna, probably, on the north. On the west, was the cliff. 'They keep better watch than we do,' Purcell thought. 'Our people walk about the village as if in a *pa*,* and it's open on all sides.'

Long minutes went by and Purcell said: 'What's happening?'

'We're waiting,' Mehani said without looking at him.

He sat down opposite him, put his musket on the ground beside him, and crossed his arms. With his eyes lowered and his head on his chest, he looked as if he were sleeping. But Purcell knew better. Mehani's attitude meant that he wished to have no communication with him.

The waiting went on interminably. Timi and Tetahiti stood perfectly still. Purcell could see only their backs.

'What are we waiting for?' Purcell said bluntly.

Mehani opened his eyes and raised his hand for silence. Without turning his head, Tetahiti said, 'Here she is.'

A few seconds later, Faïna appeared at the entrance and came into the enclosure. Timi and Tetahiti turned to her. Mehani got to his feet and went to lean against the rock beside her. Faïna never gave Purcell so much as a glance. She was standing facing the three men, solid and upright. Her breast was heaving with the effort she was making to regain her breath.

'You've been a long time,' Timi said ill-temperedly.

Faïna looked at Tetahiti, but Tetahiti dissociated himself from the reproach.

'They're round the big hut,' she said, addressing him.

'What are they doing?'

'They're constructing a *pa*.'

'How high?'

Faïna raised her arm above her head.

'Have they got far with it?'

Faïna nodded.

'They work fast. Vaa is helping them.'

* A palisade round a camp or house.

And she added: 'They will have finished by tomorrow.'

The three men looked at each other. 'They'll attack tonight,' Purcell thought suddenly, and his heart sank.

'Very well,' Tetahiti said, 'go and keep watch to the north.'

Faïna looked surprised. It made no sense to go and mount guard in the bush since it was clear that the *Peritani* would not leave the village.

'Go,' Tetahiti said impatiently.

She turned and before leaving glanced at Purcell. Now that she had her back turned to the Tahitians she dared look at him.

Tetahiti came and sat down opposite Purcell, his back to the rock, and Timi sat down on his left. Purcell expected Mehani to take his place on Tetahiti's right, but he sat beside Timi, which set the trio a little to Purcell's right. Timi looked displeased and made a gesture of getting to his feet, but Mehani seized him by the arm and silently forced him to sit down again. His heavy eyelids lowered, Tetahiti was staring at the ground. He seemed not to notice the incident.

There was a silence, and Purcell suddenly realised the reason for the long wait. As soon as Itia had told them he wanted to meet them, the Tahitians had sent Faïna to observe the movements of the *Peritani* in the village. Their suspicion irritated Purcell. He had intended to begin his speech calmly, but indignation overcame him and he cried excitedly: 'What does this mean, Tetahiti? Did you think I'd made an arrangement with the *Peritani* to attack you during my embassy?'

Tetahiti opened his mouth, but before he had time to speak, Timi intervened passionately: 'Yes! That's what we thought!' he said sharply. 'And why not? You always betray us.'

'Indeed!' Purcell cried.

'You were in our camp when the Skeleton was covering us, but when he killed Kori and Mehoro, you chose the other camp!'

Purcell looked at Timi. Flanked by Mehani and Tetahiti, dominated by their athletic shoulders, he seemed almost frail, and his round beardless face had something childish about it. But his eyes were hard.

'Timi,' Purcell said, 'I did not choose the other camp. I have not borne arms against you. I tried to dissuade Ouili from going to kill Ohou. And perhaps you know that the *Peritani* are also accusing me of being a traitor.'

'I know,' Tetahiti said. 'Itia told me.'

'If I'm a traitor to them,' Purcell went on making a large figure of eight in the air with the *Manou-faïté,* 'how can I be a traitor to you?'

The argument, and the magnificent gesture that accompanied it, had its effect on the Tahitians.

Tetahiti raised his hand, but allowed a second or two to go by before speaking.

'Adamo,' he said at last, 'when the Skeleton and the others aimed their muskets at us, you were with us, you were our brother. But the Skeleton killed Kori and Mehoro. And our brother Adamo remained with the Skeleton.'

Purcell felt a certain anxiety. Tetahiti seemed to be repeating, though more gently, Timi's grievances. In fact, his complaint was quite different. He was not taxing Purcell with treachery. He was reproaching him with having failed in his duties as a brother. The accusation might seem less offensive. But for a Tahitian it was scarcely less serious.

'Had I come with you,' Purcell said, 'the blood of my brother Ropati would be on my hands.'

'Ropati was carrying a musket against us!' Timi cried, his eyes flashing.

Purcell turned to look at him and stared into his eyes.

'He who killed Ropati did not kill him because he was carrying a musket. *Aoué,* how murder has come from murder! Ohou did not enjoy Amoureïa. He was killed. Ouili did not enjoy his vengeance. He was killed. And now I am told that you are frightened of me and are threatening my life.'

'I am not frightened of you,' Timi said in an insolent voice. 'I am not frightened of a man who resembles those who live in the *farehoua*.'*

'If I am a *houa*,' Purcell said, 'why do you call me a traitor?'

Mehani smiled straight at Purcell in a friendly, mischievous way. The smile faded at once. Clever Adamo. Clever and eloquent Adamo. Purcell looked happily at Mehani's face which

* The house of the 'incapable' (*houa*) in which women, children and old men took refuge in wartime.

had now become impassive again. 'He is therefore still my friend,' he thought, overwhelmed with joy. Everything suddenly seemed easier.

'Tetahiti,' Purcell went on, sure of convincing him, 'listen to me, for I am telling you things that are true. Ropati would not have fired at you. Nor Jono. Nor the old man. Nor the yellow man. Ropati was carrying a musket to play at war. Jono, because he was stupid. The old man, because he was frightened of the Skeleton. As for the yellow man, he had not put the thing that kills into the weapon.'

Tetahiti slowly raised his heavy lids and said disdainfully: 'The *Peritani* have manners we do not understand. They're with a chief and they're not with him. They obey him and they do not obey him. They do something and they do not do it.'

He went on: 'As far as I am concerned, the thing is clear. Those four men were carrying muskets. They were therefore our enemies.'

'I'm not carrying a musket,' Purcell said, 'and yet you look upon me as an enemy.'

'I have not said that you are our enemy,' Tetahiti said, looking him straight in the face.

'A *houa*?'

'You are not a *houa*.'

'A traitor?'

'You are not a traitor.'

'What am I then?'

In Purcell's mind the question was purely rhetorical. It was intended to make his neutrality apparent by a process of elimination. But Tetahiti did not take it thus. He looked at Purcell for a long moment as if he were seeking for the definition of what he was in his face.

'I don't know,' he said at last. 'Perhaps a clever man.'

The reply took Purcell by surprise and struck him like a blow. 'Suppose it's true,' he thought suddenly, 'suppose I'm wrong about myself? Suppose my conduct till now has been nothing but cleverness and opportunism?'

He must speak, answer, not let Tetahiti's phrase go without reply . . . The silence was making him lose face. But he was paralysed by doubt. At that moment, he almost accepted the idea of himself Tetahiti had suggested.

Tetahiti let the silence go on. He saw the disquieting effect his phrase had had on Purcell, but he drew no conclusion from it. Prudent, watchful, he did not like to bind himself too quickly, even in thought. It might one day be necessary to treat Adamo as an enemy. Perhaps. But what was Adamo? It was just like a clever man to stay out of battles. But in that case why risk his life by coming to ask for peace?

Purcell at last remembered the opening phrase he had prepared for the interview. He raised the bird above his head and said: 'I am the *Manou-faïté* and I have flown to you to offer you peace.'

Tetahiti crossed his arms and his strong, lined face assumed an expression of gravity. His attitude clearly denoted that the conversation was over and the ceremony of negotiation beginning

Purcell got to his feet and held the *Manou-faïté* on a level with his shoulder, the tuft of red feathers to the rear, the point of the stick forward.

'I am the *Manou-faïté*,' he began, taking care to give his words a rhythm, 'and I speak in favour of peace. We have had war for three days and eight men have already fallen. *Aoué*, it is too many. Another day, and who can say how many will still be alive on the island? Listen to me, warriors! I am the *Manou-faïté*, and I speak in favour of peace. Why has this war come about? Because there were injustices in the sharing out of the women and the land. But now, *aoué*, there are eleven women for seven men, and quite enough land for all. *Tanés*, do not let us behave like the stupid shark which kills uselessly. Listen to me! I am the *Manou-faïté*, and I speak in favour of peace. A young man brandishes a weapon and feels his strength and his cunning, and he says: "The enemy will be killed, not I!" *Aoué*, war is a hazard. He too will be killed. And then there will be no more fishing for him in the joy of the morning, no more coconut palms waving in the wind, no more siesta in the belly of the sun in which to sleep or play. Warriors, who will remain alive if the war goes on? Who will fecundate the women? Who will people the island when our time is over? Warriors, I speak in favour of peace, and let him who has a tongue make answer!'

He sat down and looked at the three men in front of him. They were holding their muskets on their knees and had naked cutlasses in their *pareu*. They disdained to lean against the rock and sat very straight, showing neither stiffness nor fatigue, and though they were in the full sun not a drop of sweat showed on their foreheads. Their eyes were unfathomable. Though Purcell assured himself that their impassivity was merely ceremonial and prejudged nothing, he felt discouraged.

Tetahiti made a sign and Timi got to his feet. He was to speak first, being the least important of the three. He had been admitted to the council, since he was not noble, only because an exception had been made to the usual custom. To give more force to what he was about to say, he raised his musket above his head in his left hand, and pulled his cutlass from his belt, brandishing it in his right. He stood thus for a full second, on the tips of his toes, like a statue of hatred. He had neither the majesty nor the stature of Mehani and Tetahiti, but he looked as slender and hard as a blade of steel. When he began to speak, he was not content merely to sing the words, he danced them, his feet beating the ground, his eyes flashing, making great thrusts with his cutlass towards Purcell or waving it round his head. There was something adolescent and asexual about his face and figure, which gave the thirst for destruction that emanated from him a peculiarly terrifying quality.

'O warriors!' he cried in a frenzied voice that rose little by little to shrillness. 'I speak in favour of disembowelling the chicken! O warriors, accomplish your mission! Be like the hole in the rock from which the lizards escape! Be like the open channel in which there is an angry shark! Do not spare lives! Let all the *Peritani* perish! Let the tall Skeleton be killed! Let the little rat be killed! Let the chief be killed! Let Adamo be killed! O warriors, I speak in favour of disembowelling the chicken! Burn the huts! Destroy the gardens! Cut down the trees! Reduce the enemy's women to slavery! Trample on them! Let them obey your orders like bitches! Disembowel the women who carry *Peritani* children within them, and let the accursed race be extirpated! O warriors, I have spoken in favour of disembowelling the chicken and let it be done as I have said!'

Timi replaced the cutlass in his belt and sat down. Mehani

immediately leapt to his feet. The son of a pig dared suggest that his sister should be disembowelled! Mehani was grey with anger, and in the effort he made to control himself all the muscles of his magnificent body contracted convulsively. With his head thrown back, his nostrils palpitating, and his eyes furious, he was making such an effort to find his voice that his throat swelled in the most extraordinary way. The dog! The son of a pig! He turned to look at Timi with an expression of such wild anger, that Purcell thought he was going to attack him. But the expression quickly disappeared, he looked straight to his front and with a superlative effort gradually succeeded in relaxing his muscles. It was an extraordinary sight. Throughout his whole body there were waves playing and quivering under his skin, and they grew less with every second that passed as the sea grows calm. Then it was all over, and the dark, bright surface of his skin became as calm as a lake. All his muscles seemed to be sheathed in black, their strength concealed, and his body presented a striking impression of repose and serenity.

'O *Manou-faïté*,' he said in a very slightly hoarse voice, 'who is the fool who talks of cutting down the trees? They are our trees! Who talks of devastating the gardens? They are our gardens! Who talks of reducing the women to slavery? They are our sisters! Who talks of destroying the children they're carrying? O *Manou-faïté*, they are our own nephews! So let no one dare touch the bellies of these women, for fear that warrior attack warrior and kill him!'

Mehani took a deep breath. He felt relieved at having replied to Timi's speech by an unequivocal challenge. He went on: 'O *Manou-faïté*, I speak in favour of peace! I, Mehani, son of a chief, say that only the greedy one be killed, for he is the cause of it all; that only the greedy one be killed, for he alone has killed; that all the rest be spared; that the injustices of the greedy one be repaired; and that the Tahitians live with the foreigners in forgetfulness and concord!'

As soon as Mehani sat down, Tetahiti rose. He stood quite still for several seconds, his heavy lids half lowered, his brows frowning over his imperious nose and the lines each side of his mouth deeper than ever. The *Peritani* guarded themselves so badly that with three against three and equality in arms he was sure of victory. It was from courtesy that he had accepted the *Manou-faïté,* and now he bitterly regretted it. On the eve of the decisive battle, his two companions were throwing challenges at each other. They were threatening to kill each other. Nothing good could come from a *Peritani,* and here was another proof of it. It was Adamo's presence that had provoked the quarrel.

'O *Manou-faïté,*' he said in a grave voice, 'I speak in favour of continuing the war! However, warriors, remember that we are not a tribe against a tribe, but a tribe fighting against itself. And we must take care not to destroy too much . . . O *tanés,* you made me your chief, and I, Tetahiti, chief and son of a chief, say: I shall touch the huts with my head, and the huts will be taboo.* I shall touch the trees with my head, and the trees will be taboo. I shall touch the fences of the gardens with my head, and the gardens will be taboo. I shall touch the bellies of the pregnant women with my head, and their bellies will be taboo.

'O *Manou-faïté,* I speak in favour of continuing the war. It is not for women and land that the warriors are fighting. It is for the offence given and received. It is for the affront suffered. It is because of the superior look of the unjust man! A wound has opened in us, O *Manou-faïté!* If the *Peritani* wish to leave by sea to seek another island, let these unjust men go! But if they remain on this island, let them be wiped out! How can we trust these fickle, incomprehensible men? O *Manou-faïté,* I speak in favour of continuing the war! If the *Peritani* remain on the island, let them perish! Let their death be as a balm to our wound! Let their heads adorn the front of our huts! Let them be cold in the shades while we are warm and living in their women!

'O *Manou-faïté,* I have spoken in favour of continuing the war and let him who has a tongue make answer!'

Tetahiti sat down and Purcell got slowly to his feet. He had hoped that Tetahiti – the most politic and clear-sighted of the three – would propose a compromise solution. But it was now obvious that Tetahiti was sure of winning and therefore did not want peace. His offer to let the *Peritani* depart by sea was almost an insult.

---

* According to the ancient Tahitian belief the head of a chief, being taboo, could communicate taboo to the object it touched.

'Tetahiti,' Purcell said patiently, 'if you were victorious and, when the battle was over, you said: "Adamo, go or die," I would agree to go. Because for me, who has not carried a musket and has not fought, it is not dishonourable to go. But this is not the case with the other *Peritani*. They have arms and would be ashamed of fleeing. You must realise also, Tetahiti, that if the *Peritani* left in the canoes in the cave, they would die. Death by drowning; death by thirst and hunger; or death by hanging, if they met a big canoe from their country.

'Take care, Tetahiti, that after suffering injustice yourself you be not unjust in your turn. Who has offended you among the *Peritani*? One man. Must all the *Peritani* die because of that man?'

Tetahiti listened to this speech with his eyes closed and his face expressionless. When Purcell fell silent, he said courteously, but in a tone that put an end to all discussion: 'Have you finished speaking, O *Manou-faïté*?'

'I have finished.'

Tetahiti turned his head to the left and said: 'Draw the circle in front of me, Timi, the decision must be taken.'

Timi obeyed. In fact, he could not draw it for the ground was stony, and he contented himself with bending down and making a large circular movement in front of his chief with his right hand. This done, he sat down again.

'It is up to you, warriors,' Tetahiti said.

Timi picked up a pebble, threw it into the imaginary circle and said: 'This is the rock for the disembowelling of the chicken!'

Tetahiti frowned. Timi had not been turned from his purpose either by Mehani's challenge or by the taboo he himself had announced. The fool! The insolent fellow! When the war was over, he would have to be punished! Tetahiti veiled his eyes and said calmly: 'Now you, Mehani.'

Mehani threw a stone into the circle and said: 'This is the rock for the restoration of peace.

Tetahiti picked up a stone, put it ceremoniously to his mouth and let a few seconds go by in complete silence. He was marking the fact that his decision was alone sovereign. Indeed the votes were not counted. The chief was the arbiter and his word final.

Tetahiti threw the stone.

'This is the rock for continuing the war.'

Having said this, he raised his heavy lids and looked at Purcell.

'Foreigner,' he said coldly, 'give me the *Manou-faïté*.'

Purcell got to his feet, disconcerted by the order and the tone in which it was given. He hesitated for an instant or two, and then handed the bird to Tetahiti. He had been present at peace negotiations in Tahiti, but the peace had been accepted, and the ambassador had left brandishing the red feathers above his head to the acclamations of the people.

Tetahiti got to his feet, followed by Timi and Mehani. He seized the *Manou-faïté* in both hands, raised it in the air, and bringing it violently down broke it over his knee. Then he threw the two pieces on the ground at his feet and cried in a fierce voice: 'The bird of peace is dead!'

Purcell was suddenly paralysed with fear. The symbolism of the gesture was evident. The destruction of the bird foreshadowed his own.

A second went by. Purcell was incapable of speaking or moving.

Timi changed his musket to his left hand, and drew his cutlass from his belt with his right. Then he pointed to Purcell with the point of the blade, looked at Tetahiti and said: 'O Tetahiti, give me this fish!'*

At that moment, Mehani went close up to Timi and cried in a terrifying voice: 'Taboo!'

The word, as much as the intensity with which it had been uttered, rooted Timi to the spot. Nevertheless, he faced round with courage, looked up into Mehani's threatening face, and said in a shrill voice: 'Why taboo?'

'Look, man!' Mehani cried, shouting each word at the top of his voice. 'Look, man, at the earring Adamo's wearing! It was I who gave it to him! And before me that earring was worn by my father, the great chief Otou!'

Timi looked at the earring in fury. It was true! It was Otou's! He felt he had been outwitted.

'The taboo is not valid!' he cried furiously at last. 'The taboo

* The name given to a man about to be killed.

of a Tahitian chief cannot be communicated to a *Peritani*!'

'And who is this *Peritani*?' Mehani shouted. 'He is the son-in-law of a Tahitian chief! The husband of his daughter! The brother of his son!'

Purcell gaped at them. It seemed that his life depended on this theological quarrel. Could the sacred quality of a taboo be transmitted to a foreigner?

Timi turned to Tetahiti and said curtly, almost arrogantly: 'What does the chief decide?'

Purcell was not looking at Tetahiti. He had recovered his coolness, was balanced imperceptibly on his toes and was watching Timi's slightest movement.

'What does the chief decide?' Timi repeated.

Tetahiti was in a fatal difficulty. He had broken the *Manou-faïté* because tradition demanded it, but without any considered design against Adamo. Nevertheless, the custom authorised the putting to death of the unfortunate ambassador. On that count, he could not but agree with Timi. As for the taboo, he was not at all sure that Timi was wrong. He too had serious doubts on its efficacity since Adamo was not Tahitian. Unfortunately, one thing was clear. By attaching the earring which had touched the head of Otou to Adamo's ear, Mehani had signified that Adamo was his elected brother and that his life was worth more than his own. The sacrifice of Adamo would therefore certainly entail a duel to the death between Mehani and Timi, and in that case the Tahitians would set off to assault the *Peritani* that night with one warrior the less.

'I am the chief,' he said at last, looking Timi in the eye, 'I am not a priest. As to the taboo, I cannot decide who is right and who wrong. Nevertheless, since Adamo is related to Mehani and Mehani considers him taboo, you would be wise to renounce this *fish*.'

A head shorter than the two athletic warriors on either side of him, Timi drew himself up and curved his slender body like a bow. These nobles! These sons of chiefs! They were banding against him! It was clear they wanted to frighten him! But what was their strength worth now that he had a musket?

'My right is my right!' he cried angrily.

A second went by. He seemed to have calmed down and slyly

lowered his eyes. Then, suddenly, with the speed of lightning, he lunged hard at Purcell with the point of his cutlass. Purcell jumped aside, the cutlass struck the rock, and at the same instant Mehani raised his hands high and brought them down on Timi's neck. The blow did not appear to be particularly hard, but Timi was thrown violently forward, his forehead hit the rock and he fell to the ground where he lay motionless, face to the stones.

'Have I killed the son of a pig?' Mehani said.

He looked at Tetahiti. Tetahiti knelt down, turned Timi over and put his head against his chest.

'The fool's fainted,' he said disdainfully.

'Come, Adamo!' Mehani cried, seizing him by the hand.

He was hindered by the passage through the rock which he had to pass sideways. As soon as he had done so, Mehani dragged Adamo after him so quickly that he bruised his chest against the stone. They had not gone ten yards across the clearing when Tetahiti called after them: 'Mehani, don't go farther than the bush!' Mehani ran on, waving his free hand in assent. Purcell turned and saw Itia standing twenty yards away, not daring to join them. 'Itia!' Tetahiti called. 'Bring me some water!' Purcell was bruising his feet on the stones and kept nearly falling. Mehani's pace seemed almost incredible and Purcell felt like a child being dragged along by an adult in some fantastic race.

When he entered the palms, Mehani let him go, but scarcely slowed down, and Purcell was surprised that the trunks did not close in on them as they advanced. No doubt there was a path known only to the Tahitians. Purcell's heart was beating against his ribs, he was afraid of being out-run in the dusk, and he whispered: 'Not so fast, Mehani.'

Mehani slowed his pace.

'Listen to me,' he whispered back. 'I must speak to you. Can you hear me?'

'Yes.'

'Where are you going now?'

'To the banyan.'

'And afterwards?'

'To the cave where the muskets were. It's the women's idea.'

'It's a good idea.'

He went on : 'You're very out of breath. Do you want me to go slower?'

'No.'

'Listen. When we get out of the bush, you must run! Run and not stop till you reach the cave!'

'Yes.'

'You've only got a short start. Timi runs very well. And I can't stop him. I would have to kill him.'

He went on by way of excuse: 'I can't kill him before the fight.'

Purcell ran. He had a stitch in his side and was trying to regulate his breathing.

'After the bush,' Mehani said, 'I'll lay a false trail. It will gain you a little more time.'

The dusk was gradually growing lighter. A few yards farther and the mountain rose before them; at their feet was the stony stretch to the banyan. Mehani turned, raised Purcell in his arms, clasped him to him and pressed his cheek against his.

'Listen,' he said breathlessly. 'Listen. You are going. Listen. Perhaps you'll be killed. Perhaps I shall. Listen, my brother Adamo. I love you. Never forget how much I love you. If I die, I shall think of you, *afterwards*. And you, too, *afterwards*. Promise!'

'I promise!' Purcell said, his voice quivering.

He felt Mehani's rough, rather salty cheek under his lips. He was conscious of a great happiness and also of despair at leaving Mehani.

'I promise!' he repeated.

Mehani released him, then took him by the shoulders and gently and repeatedly banged his forehead against his own. Purcell remembered that he had made this gesture on his arrival in Tahiti when his heart was too full for speech.

'O Adamo!' he said in a low voice. 'O my brother!'

'I promise,' Purcell said, his eyes filling with tears.

Mehani released him and gave him a little tap on the shoulder. His smile was so kind and tender that it almost hurt Purcell.

'Go!' he said. 'Go now! Go, Adamo!'

14

'Here it is,' Avapouhi said, turning round.

Purcell was struggling among the rocks a few yards below her. The path was a sort of gorge, cut straight through the rock, and so steep at the top that you had to use your hands. Purcell was exasperated by the slowness of his progress. He felt he was offering a perfect target to anyone below. He dared not look round. Though he was sweating under the sun, he felt cold shivers running down his spine.

He caught up with Avapouhi, took her hand and pulled her into the cover of a big bush which half concealed the entrance to the cave. He looked down through the branches at the bottom of the gorge. He was standing with his shoulder against Avapouhi's. He was incapable of speech and was astonished by the noise of his own breathing. Apart from a slight shivering of the air above the over-heated rocks, the landscape at his feet was empty and still. He breathed deeply and then turned towards the cave. He was in safety at last.

'Come, Avapouhi.'

'Wait a moment. The basket of fruit!'

She stretched her hand out through the bush, pulled the basket to her, and placed it with a circular gesture against her hip. He looked at her. It was the second time she had climbed from the banyan to the cave in less than an hour, and she was not even out of breath.

'And now?'

'Go straight on, Adamo. I'll tell you.'

The floor of the cave went down for a yard or two, then gradually sloped upwards, amid a tangle of bushes and flowers. The ceiling was pierced with fissures and chimneys which communicated with the air, and here and there there were patches of sunlight on the walls. The tunnel turned to the left, coolness seemed to fall on Purcell's shoulders, the patches of light disappeared gradually giving way to darkness.

'The *toupapahous*,' Avapouhi said, coming to a halt. 'I'm frightened.'

'*Maamaa*,' Purcell said impatiently. 'You spent a fortnight here with Itia! They didn't do anything to you! They're good *toupapahous*! '

After a moment, she said, 'Perhaps they've changed.'

Purcell shrugged.

'You are in no danger with me. I don't believe in them.'

'Is that true?' she said hopefully.

'It is true.'

According to Tahitian belief, the *toupapahous* never perse-cuted people who did not believe in their existence. What was so extraordinary was that in spite of this there were practically no unbelievers in Tahiti.

Purcell walked on and Avapouhi followed him docilely. Not only did Adamo, like Mehani, not believe in *toupapahous,* but she had just thought of a reassuring face: Adamo had hair the colour of honey. The *toupapahous* would never have seen so unusual a human being. Discouraged by his scepticism, discon-certed by his appearance, it was probable that they would re-main quiet, even if their tempers had grown worse since the great rain.

Purcell found himself standing in cold water up to the ankles, and drew back. There was a dark expanse of water as far as he could see. It was gleaming dully in the dark and big round stones emerged from it here and there.

'Itia spoke of a small spring,' he said in surprise.

'There was no water here when we were here,' Avapouhi said, her voice suddenly changing tone. 'It's the malice of the *toupapahous*! '

She was beginning again!

'Listen! ' Purcell said in exasperation.

He took her in his arms; she was stiff and cold.

'Listen! ' he went on solemnly. 'The *toupapahous* don't exist! I, Adamo,' he added in a loud voice, 'declare that the *toupapa-hous* don't exist! '

The speed with which Avapouhi reacted to this declaration surprised Purcell. In an instant, she had melted like butter, her skin had become warm again, her body supple. In the twinkling of an eye she had passed from the extreme paralysis of fear to the most profound calm. She rubbed her cheek gratefully against Adamo's. It was not so much what Adamo had said, but the eloquent tone in which he had said it.

Purcell stepped from stone to stone. When they were too far apart, he let go of Avapouhi's hand and jumped. The roof was not very high and the cave formed a narrow, winding tunnel. A branch of the stream must originally have bored it and then a fall of stone altered its course. And now the water must be filtering through again. When it had widened its bed – after how many years? – it would overflow the slope at the entrance to the cave and rush down in a torrent to the foot of the mountain. This must have been its course in the past. The path by which they had climbed looked like a gorge created by erosion.

'The *toupapahous* are not responsible,' he said, turning round. 'The stream has made a little hole in the rock.'

'The stream's very clever,' Avapouhi said with the tone of respect with which she would have addressed a chief.

He let go of her hand and jumped on to a big flat stone in the middle of the water. The stone tipped forward with a splash, followed by a dull thud. Purcell nearly lost his balance, beat the air with his arms and jumped to another stone. Behind him the two sounds were repeated, the stone splashing against water and then thudding against rock. The stone had returned to its former position.

'Be careful,' he said over his shoulder.

He went on another ten yards. The tunnel turned to the right. On the left-hand wall Purcell saw a round hole in the rock; it was a fairly regular circle and scarcely larger than a porthole. Purcell leaned through it. The opening gave on to another gallery which was less dark than the one in which he was standing and on a higher level. On his side, the lower edge of the porthole was on a level with his hip, but on the other it was at ground level. The second tunnel seemed to run straight and after a fairly well-lit zone disappeared into the darkness. Its floor also consisted of big round or flat stones, but they were perfectly dry. The stream had not regained possession of this particular stretch.

'This is it,' Avapouhi said.

He turned round.

'Here? The other side of the hole?'

'It's quite easy. You'll see.'

She bent down, put her head through the porthole and her hands flat on the ground on the other side. She raised her feet, wriggled her hips and disappeared. It was all done with extraordinary speed. A second later, her head reappeared in the opening.

'I'll help you.'

'No,' Purcell said.

But he managed it much less well than she had. When he got to his feet, he had scratched his stomach.

He found himself in a sort of vaulted chamber, about twelve foot square, after which the tunnel shrank to no more than a narrow passage and was lost in the gloom. The room itself was lit by a fissure which cast a patch of light as large as one's hand on to one of the walls.

'You mustn't go any farther,' Avapouhi said, pointing to the passage. 'There's a pit.'

'Deep?'

She nodded.

'You throw a stone. You wait and wait. And then it goes pouf!'

'Can one go round the pit?'

'We can,' Avapouhi said. 'Not you.'

She spoke without a shadow of contempt. She was stating a fact. Purcell went towards the passage. As soon as he reached the dark zone, he slowed his pace to let his eyes get accustomed to the obscurity. He bent his head, though he realised that the precaution was unnecessary, since the roof was still at least eight inches above it. But when he spread his arms wide he could touch the rock on either side.

'Be careful,' Avapouhi said, putting out a hand. 'It's here.'

'Where?'

'In front of you.'

What eyes she had! He crouched down and saw a dark, almost imperceptible line less than a yard in front of him. He lay flat on his stomach and crawled forward. He groped for the edge of the pit, found it and realised that it spread from wall to wall. There was no way round it. The pit filled the whole tunnel.

He got up. He could not see Avapouhi, but by the scent of the flowers she was wearing in her hair he knew she was on his right.

'Can you really get to the other side?' he asked doubtfully.

'Yes, do you want me to show you?'

'No, no,' he said quickly. 'You've already done it?'

'All three of us.'

'All three?'

'I, Itia and Mehani.'

'When?'

'When the chief came to hide the muskets with Vaa during the great rain. Man! Mehani only had time to throw our bed of leaves into the pit and cross to the other side with us. The chief told Vaa to stay in the chamber and he came on alone into the tunnel. *Aoué!* The *Peritani*'s eyes are not good! We were only a javelin's length the other side of the pit, and the chief didn't see us. Mehani was afraid the chief would fall into the pit and he threw a little stone into it. The stone went pouf! The chief started, then he got down on his stomach like you. He felt with his hands. He grunted' (she gave a striking imitation of Mason's 'humph! ') 'and then he went back.'

'What's on the other side of the pit?'

'You can walk a little way, and then it's finished, the wall's everywhere.'

Purcell turned back. After the total darkness of the tunnel, the chamber seemed almost light.

'Where did the chief hide the muskets?'

'There.'

On the opposite side to the patch of light, a rock jutted out, and between it and the roof, at a height of some nine feet, there was a ledge.

'He can't have found it easy,' Purcell said tonelessly.

He suddenly felt all his fatigue. He only wanted to lie down and stop talking. Above all, to stop talking.

'Why?' Avapouhi asked. 'It's very easy. When the chief left, Mehani climbed up, and brought everything down and unpacked it, the muskets wrapped in oily rags and the things that kill in a box with iron on it. Then Mehani put it all back again, and made us swear not to tell anyone about it, not even Ouili. And he immediately made another bed so that Ouili should notice nothing.'

She fell silent, put one hand to her eyes, dropped to the floor and, the other hand lying open on her knee, began weeping. She wept silently, her shoulders heaving jerkily, and she let the tears roll down her cheeks without wiping them away.

Purcell crouched beside her.

'What's the matter, Avapouhi?'

She took her hand from her eyes.

'You went to see the others. And when you came back you did not tell me about Ouili.'

He turned his head away. He had told her in snatches about the *Manou-faïté* as they ran. But it was true that he had said nothing about Ouili, for indeed what could he have said? And ever since she had met him, she had been waiting for news. She had been waiting for it all through their mad race from the banyan to the cave. And in the cave too, against all hope, she had been waiting for it. And now, hope had suddenly died in her. At last she saw clearly what she had known from the beginning: Ouili was dead.

'Come,' Purcell said, taking her by the shoulders.

He pulled her to her feet, but felt too tired to talk. He led her to the bed of leaves and made her lie down. When she had done so, he lay down beside her. Placing his left arm between her neck and her long hair, he rested his head in the hollow of her shoulder. He wanted to say something to her, but could find no words. He fell asleep.

'Adamo!' a voice said in his ear.

He started, opened his eyes, and was astonished to find Avapouhi in his arms. He noticed the tears on her cheeks. It all came back.

'Have I slept long?'

'No. Scarcely at all. Listen to me, Adamo. I must go. Omaata must be waiting anxiously at the banyan. She doesn't know that Itia has been kept by the others. And Ivoa! Man! Ivoa! She doesn't know you escaped from the others!'

She stood up, her eyes bright. She forgot her own sorrow in her impatience to tell another woman that her *tané* was alive.

'You're quite right,' Purcell said, also getting to his feet.

There was a silence and she said: 'I'll come back. If Omaata permits it, I'll come back.'

He wanted to say 'no', but lacked the courage. He hated the

idea of being alone for long hours in this cold and sinister cave. He took Avapouhi by the shoulders and gave her a little push with the flat of his hand between the shoulder-blades.

She went legs first through the hole, supporting herself on her hands, hollowing her back and twisting her body as she passed through. Purcell leaned down and put his head through the opening. His eyes were not accustomed to the gloom and he followed her with his glance as she jumped from stone to stone. They formed little islands of greyish-white in the black water. Avapouhi's feet made dark patches on them. Above, there was the light patch of her bark skirt and, higher again, nothing but her arms outspread to keep her balance showing black against the paler black of the wall. Purcell could scarcely see her hips move, but he could hear with surprising clarity the rustle of the strips of bark when she jumped. Suddenly a pale light shone on her hair, and the outline of her head appeared surrounded by the faint line of a halo. It was the vision of a second. All the upper part of her body seemed to dissolve, her bark skirt was conjured away, and there was nothing left. The turning had concealed her.

Purcell went back to the bed of leaves, lay down and fell asleep. He woke up again almost at once. He felt very cold and the cave was as silent as a tomb. He closed his eyes again and felt drowsy but could not sleep. Phrases and images kept whirling wildly through his mind. It was intolerable, for he could neither sleep nor remain altogether awake.

After a while he sat up and looked about him. He got to his feet and put his hand to his forehead. In the other tunnel there was a sound like water being slapped with the flat of the hand, followed by a dull thud. The two sounds were so slight that for a quarter of a second Purcell doubted having heard them. Then they were repeated. The splash and the dull thud. He listened, holding his breath. There was complete silence. He suddenly knew what it was. The stone. The tipping stone in the tunnel. It had tipped forward and then returned to its position. Avapouhi had come back. She was the other side of the wall of rock, a few yards from him. 'So quickly,' he thought, surprised. And he bent down to put his head through the hole.

But there was something about the silence that prevented his doing so. Afraid of the *toupapahous,* Avapouhi would have been running. He should have heard her feet skipping from stone to stone and the rustle of the bark strips of her skirt. He went very slowly to the hole and glanced over a ridge of rock with his right eye. Ten yards away, he saw the slender outline of a man standing motionless on a stone with a musket in his hand.

Purcell's mouth went dry and his legs began trembling. He glanced round him. There was nowhere to hide. Nor was there any possibility of flight. In front of him was the pit. Beyond the pit, there was no outlet. If Timi came into the chamber, he would see the bed of leaves and would advance into the tunnel. Purcell saw himself caught in the dead-end like a rat in its hole, and Timi facing him, cutlass in hand. Sweat poured down his sides from his armpits, his hands turned moist and he leaned against the rock wall. He could already feel the cold blade cutting into his stomach.

He made a violent effort to swallow, but his mouth was so dry that his tongue was stuck to his palate. He felt an appalling void in the pit of his stomach, and his body shivered incessantly from his lips to the soles of his feet. The expression 'to tremble like a leaf' flashed curiously through his mind and he understood precisely what it meant. Nothing it seemed could control the trembling of his limbs. Inert, voiceless and paralysed, he felt at once powerless and ashamed in the face of the trembling that shook him. Though he clenched his teeth, his cheeks trembled like a jelly.

Then, from the other side of the hole, he heard the sound of breathing. Timi had managed to reach the hole making no more noise than a cat, but he could not control his breathing. Purcell listened and started with astonishment. Timi was afraid too. He had managed to track him down, but it had required an enormous effort to enter the cave. It was not of Adamo he was frightened, but of the *toupapahous.*

Purcell was huddled against the wall of the chamber, his ear to the rock and his feet a few inches from the hole. He listened to the irregular, whistling breath of his enemy. How badly Timi must want to kill him to have braved the *toupapahous!* Purcell clenched his teeth. There was something repugnant about desiring another's death to that extent. The Tahitian women said that he feared Adamo would avenge the death of his friends. It was not true! Purcell was certain of it. It was hunting down an unarmed man that intoxicated Timi! Vengeance and war were merely pretexts! To torture Amoureïa, disembowel Ivoa and destroy her child, and kill Adamo were intoxicating because they were *easy*! 'The abominable coward!' Purcell thought with sudden fury, and his body ceased trembling. He looked around and felt in his pockets, but he had not even a knife. For the first time in his life, he regretted not being armed.

He saw a largish stone at his feet. He bent down and picked it up with both hands, surprised to find it so heavy. He leaned his right side against the rock and held the stone at arm's length above the hole. He waited.

He waited so long that he almost doubted having seen Timi in the tunnel. But, on the other side of the wall, the breathing was still there, panting and troubled. It was incredible that Timi would come through the hole without at least glancing through it first.

The stone became heavier each second, as he held it tensely at arm's length, and he realised he was bound to drop it. He brought it back against his chest, propped it against the hollow of his stomach and changed his grip, one hand at a time. He had taken his eyes from the hole for the fraction of a second and, when he looked back at it, he saw with stupefaction his enemy's cutlass lying on the stones inside the chamber. Perhaps Timi had put it there so as to have his hands free to come through the hole. Perhaps it was a trap. Purcell's heart beat violently. It was tempting to seize the weapon, but to do so he would have to put the stone down and pass his arm across the opening. It might be that Timi was waiting for him to do just this so as to seize his arm, throw him off balance and bring him down.

Purcell remained still. Timi would come through with his musket, and the musket was long. He would not be able to fire before both he and the musket were completely through the hole. Purcell thought with an access of relief that he would have plenty of time. And he suddenly knew what he must do. Instead of throwing the stone at Timi's head as he had intended, he must use it as a club and not let it out of his hands. He bent his knees and put his right leg back to get nearer the ground, and at the same time rested the stone on his thigh to relieve his arms. He was crouching, gathered behind the stone, ready to hurl himself forward as soon as Timi's head appeared. The stone was wet from the sweat that was pouring from the palms of his hands and he changed his grip once again.

He could still hear Timi's whistling breath and he was surprised at the time he was taking to make up his mind. Perhaps his instinct warned him that danger was near. It was strange that he had not yet put his head through the hole. Purcell raised the stone to a level with his face and flexed his muscles.

It happened so quickly that he had no time to do anything. Timi did not come through the opening by degrees, as Avapouhi had. Instead, he catapulted himself through it with the speed of a tiger jumping through a hoop, his face and chest upwards. He landed on his back, and at the very second he touched the ground, he launched a terrible blow with his musket butt at Purcell's head. The blow was delivered with such extraordinary speed and precision that it was as if Timi had known, before even coming through the hole, that Purcell's face was exactly where it was. But on the instant, there was a clap of thunder in the cave, which rolled and echoed in its tunnels. The chamber was filled with white smoke. Timi gave a violent start, rolled over on to his stomach, clutched the stones with both hands and lay still.

Purcell had scarcely felt the blow from the butt on the stone. He was paralysed with amazement. He stared at Timi lying face downwards on the ground, his fingers clutching, his body slightly twisted to the left. He seemed to be awaiting a blow. Purcell's eyes fell on the cutlass. Its blade gleamed between Timi's legs. Without letting go the stone, or quitting Timi with his eyes, Purcell crept inch by inch towards it. When he was standing above it, he threw the stone hard against the back of Timi's neck, bent down and seized the weapon. He had the hilt in his hand, and his fingers grasped it tightly.

The stone had hit Timi's neck with a dull thud, but not quite accurately. It had rebounded, passed over his head and rolled a yard or two before coming to a stop. Timi lay perfectly still.

Crouching down, his left hand on the ground, his right holding the cutlass, Purcell advanced with infinite slowness, his eyes concentrated on a patch of brown skin above Timi's left shoulder-blade.

He leapt forward with a savage cry. He was lying full length on Timi, both hands pressing the hilt down with extraordinary violence. Then, hoisting his body higher, he leaned his chest on his hands to drive the blade in deeper. Timi lay inert and vanquished beneath him. Purcell pressed down on him with all his weight. He felt a shiver of joy.

Some time passed. Purcell's mind became a blank, and he could hear nothing but the hoarse sound of his own breathing. He thought suddenly: 'That cry was mine.' He got to his feet and his legs felt weak under him. He bent down, pulled the cutlass from the wound and threw it away. He felt an overwhelming desire to see Timi's face. He put his hand on his shoulder, and it felt as slender as a woman's. The skin was soft and yielding under his fingers. He pulled. Timi turned over on his back. There was an enormous hole in the middle of his forehead, and a little trickle of blood was running from it.

Purcell stared at it, gaping for several seconds. Then he understood. The butt had hit the stone he had been holding in front of his face, the shock had set the musket off, and Timi had killed himself with his own weapon.

Purcell staggered over to the bed of leaves and sat down. Beneath the bloody hole shattering his forehead, Timi's eyes seemed alive. The pupils were only half covered by the thick black lashes and they gleamed from the corners of the lids, as if Timi were staring sideways at Purcell. His head and graceful neck were turned slightly away, which gave his glance a sort of sly coquetry. There was no trace of hardness in his face now, and his curved lips were parted in an almost childish smile. Purcell noticed the shape of his eyes for the first time. They were very handsome. They turned up towards the temples like the eyes of a gazelle, but it was the magnificent long black curved lashes which gave his glance so caressing and velvety a quality. It was extraordinary that those eyes should have succeeded in looking so hard. In withdrawing from Timi life had left him only the innate gentleness he had suppressed when alive.

Purcell turned his head away, got to his feet and felt profoundly ashamed. The savagery with which he had hurled himself on the body! The cry he had uttered! And it had been a corpse he had thrust at. It seemed to him incredible that he had not realised sooner that Timi was dead. But he had stiffened his will to such an extent before Timi had come in that he had committed the act blindly, by a sort of inevitable momentum, like a machine. It was horrible and ridiculous, and he felt almost more guilty than if he had really killed him. 'That's what murder is,' he thought with anguish, 'automatism, becoming carried away.' All his life he had been determined to respect life. And yet, when the moment came, he had hurled himself on his enemy howling like a beast! He had thrust in the cutlass with both hands, intoxicated with victory, panting with an overwhelming pleasure!

He felt a damp patch on his chest. He touched it with his hand and his fingers came away dark and viscous. He shuddered with disgust. He went to the hole. Timi's feet were still half in it. He took hold of them, raised them and dragged the body as far as possible from the bed. Timi's head dangled from side to side, bouncing on the stones. When Purcell stopped, it slipped slowly and gently down the left shoulder till the chin came to rest in the hollow of the collarbone. Purcell noticed that the face was turned towards the bed of leaves and that Timi's eyes would follow him when he lay down. He let go of the feet, hesitated a moment, and finally turned on his heel. He did not dare touch Timi's head to turn it away.

Purcell got through the opening with difficulty, jumped on to a stone, lost his balance and fell full length in the water. It was icy cold. He felt as if he were suffocating. He turned over on to his stomach, quickly rubbed his chest and got up. His teeth were chattering.

When he got back into the chamber, he took off his trousers, wrung them out and placed them on a stone. His neck hurt, there was a circle of steel about his chest, and he was trembling from the roots of his hair to his toes. Curiously enough, a cold sweat broke out on his forehead. He tried to jump, but his legs were too stiff to bend. He beat his chest with the flat of his hand, leaned forward and slapped his back and thighs hard. But he could not exorcise the cold from his body. He was numbed to the marrow, and he realised he must take more violent exercise. He lay down on his stomach as far as possible from Timi, and did press-ups. He continued this exercise for two whole minutes, trembling in every limb. Finally he collapsed, breathless. But his teeth were still chattering.

Never before had his whole body felt so frozen. He despaired of getting warm again, and began to feel extremely anxious. He began to do all the exercises he knew or which he had seen Jones do. He did them by numbers, first merely counting aloud, then shouting the figures at the top of his voice. The cold began to yield a little, and it seemed to him that shouting warmed him more than anything else. He started howling. His voice sounded terribly shrill and he did not recognise it as his own. He jumped up and down, bent and straightened up, crouched and thrust his legs out, and above all struggled to get his breath between two howls. Minute by minute he drew nearer to exhaustion, but dared not stop.

In a sudden flash he saw himself as he was: stark naked, beside a corpse in a cave – behaving like a madman and uttering inhuman howls. It was laughable! The trouble to which a man would go to cling to life! He was exhausted and ceased his callisthenics. The roots of his hair froze at once, and the cold seemed to erupt from within his body and flood him from head to foot. He began his exercises again. He was condemned to these ridiculous gymnastics for all eternity! Down! Up! Down! . . . From under his dark brow, Timi's black eyes watched him with a curious light in them, and there was a half smile on his lips, as if he were watching ironically the agitations of the living.

'Adamo,' a voice cried, 'what are you doing?'

He started and turned. Omaata's large black face was staring at him through the hole, which it almost entirely filled. Her lunar eyes were fixed on him in astonishment.

'I'm cold!' Purcell cried shrilly.

'Wait!' she said.

He looked at her incredulously. She got one shoulder into the hole, then the other, forced her huge bust into the chamber, wriggled to get her wide hips through and, stretching and contracting her gigantic body like rubber, succeeded in squirming through the opening. A fragment of rock became detached and rolled on to the ground.

'My baby!' she cried, rushing at him. '*Aoué!* How blue you are!'

For once it was he who nestled against her. He put his arms about her wide waist and had the wonderful feeling of sinking into an eiderdown. It was warm, soft and deep. She began rubbing his back with her great powerful hands, meanwhile pouring out a flood of endearments. She massaged him, slapped him, pinched him and, though it hurt, he voluptuously let her have her way. At each slap, he felt life returning to his skin, his muscles and the mass of frozen organs within him. It was wonderful to feel warm; he had almost forgotten the suppleness, the well-being, the expansion of the pores . . . 'Omaata,' he whispered. 'My baby! . . . My baby! . . .' Purcell listened to her deep voice rolling beneath the roof like a torrent. Even her voice warmed him. She took him by the shoulders, turned him round and rubbed his chest, stomach and thighs. What good hands she had! Big, strong, and yet delicate, they kneaded him like dough, pushing and pulling at his skin, pummelling it, making it roll beneath the fingers. His back sunk in a bath of warm flesh, Purcell felt his chest open and expand like a flower. He could breathe, his heart beat more quietly and he could feel his muscles again.

She turned him round again.

'My baby!' she cooed in her deep voice. 'You're still white! *Aoué!* Where are your red cheeks, my little cock?'

She held him away from her and began giving him little taps. 'You'll kill me!' he cried.

He ducked under her hands and nestled against her. 'My baby,' she said with emotion. Then she suddenly began to laugh.

'You know you frightened me howling like that! Man, I thought it was the *toupapahous*! Luckily, I recognised the *Peritani* words.'

She turned laughing towards the hole and saw Timi's body.

'Man!' she said in stupefaction. 'You've killed him!'

'I didn't kill him,' Purcell said.

She wasn't listening. She went over to the body, seized it disrespectfully by the hair and turned it this way and that.

'I didn't kill him,' Purcell said again. 'It was he . . .'

'What about that?' Omaata said in her powerful voice, pointing theatrically to the hole in the forehead. 'And that?' she went on, pointing to the wound in the back. 'And that?' she continued, pointing to the neck.

She bent down to look more closely at the wound.

'What did you do that with?'

'A stone.'

She let go of Timi's hair, straightened up and gazed at Purcell in admiration.

'Man! You're clever! '

'Listen, it was not I . . .'

'And so,' she went on delightedly, 'you killed the son of a pig! Oh, how strong you are, Adamo! Oh, how brave you are! How cunning you are! And without a weapon! And he with his musket and his cutlass! O my pretty little warrior! O my cock! O Adamo! '

'Listen, Omaata . . .'

'By *Eatua*,' she said, standing over Timi's body, her hands on her vast hips, 'you, Timi, wanted to kill my baby! You wanted to make slaves of the women of your own tribe! You wanted to disembowel Vaa and Ivoa! You rat's spawn! You son of a pig! You cowardly shark! You man without coconuts! You're not even a warrior! You're *houa*! * You're *mahou*! † You're impotent! Well, and where are you now, you excrement? You're cold! You're the fish with dead eyes on the shore of the lagoon! You're the bone gnawed by the tail-less dog! Look at Adamo! Look at that little *Peritani* cock! He's handsome! He's brave! He's cunning! There's not a *vahiné* on the island who does not want to play with him! Look at him! He has hair like honey! He has a pink and white body! He's as appetising as the dough of the breadfruit tree cooked in the oven! He's a great chief! He has many coconut palms in the big island of rain! He has graceful hands like his father-in-law Otou! And you, Timi, what are you now? A lifeless man! A man utterly without importance! A man who's no longer good for anything! A dead fish floating belly upwards! An empty

* Incapable.
† Homosexual.

shell! A dead crab for the sea salters on the beach! ...'

'Omaata!' Purcell cried.

But she was in full swing. She was now bitterly attacking Timi's sexual capacities. She let herself go for two whole minutes with detailed insults about the impotence she attributed to him.

'Omaata!'

'I've finished,' she said simply.

And she came back to him, slow and monumental, her face bright with the sense of a duty performed.

'O Adamo,' she said fervently, as if her admiration for him had increased in proportion to her denigration of the enemy. 'O Adamo! O my baby!'

She began to massage him again. But now that he no longer felt cold, Purcell felt the pain of it.

'I'm warm enough, Omaata.'

'No, you're not, man,' she said, clasping him to her with authority. 'You're warm enough at the moment, but when I've gone, you'll feel cold. You must have great reserves of warmth. Listen,' she went on gravely, 'I'll take that son of a pig on my back and throw him into the sea, and you must never tell anyone you killed him, except Ivoa.'

'But I did not ...'

'No one, you understand. No one!'

'But why is it so important?'

'It is not important if the *Peritani* win. But it's the others who'll win. Turn round.'

'Why do you say that? The others are only two now. And the *Peritani* three.'

'On the sea, the *Peritani* are clever. But not on land.'

'Stop! You're hurting me!'

She laughed.

'*Aoué!* A great warrior like you!'

She went on: 'I shall go and throw away that son of a pig, and send Avapouhi to you.'

'Avapouhi? Why Avapouhi?'

'To spend the night with you.'

'No,' Purcell said stiffly.

'Look at the little cock!' she said, giving him a little tap on the buttocks. 'I don't want you to be alone, man! You'll be eating your heart out with your thoughts, as the *Peritani* do.'

She went on: 'Besides, you'll want to play.'

'No.'

'You'll have a great need to play. When a man has taken life, he has a need to give it.'

'No. I shall want to sleep.'

'Sleep too. Sleep and play.'

'No.'

'That's a *Peritani* no!' she said laughing. 'I shall send you Avapouhi.'

'Send me Ivoa.'

'Man, Ivoa no longer belongs to you! She belongs to her baby.'

There was a silence and Purcell said: 'Well, come yourself.'

The effect of this was extraordinary. Omaata took a pace backwards, drew herself up to her full height, and with quivering nostrils and flashing eyes stared at Purcell.

'Are you angry?' he said in surprise.

'What do you think I am?' she said at last in a voice that was strained with anger.

She was grey with fury, her jaw was trembling and she had difficulty in speaking.

'Omaata . . .'

'I ask you, what am I?' she went on, suddenly finding her voice again. 'I!' she repeated, slapping herself above the left breast.

'The 'I!' and the slap sounded like shots under the roof.

'What am I?' she went on, outraged, looking him up and down. 'An old woman? A cripple? A *mahou*?'

'Omaata . . .'

'And do I smell?'

'Omaata . . .'

'What am I then?' she cried in a paroxysm of rage. 'What am I that a man can sleep all night with me without playing?'

Horribly embarrassed, Purcell stammered: 'But I didn't say . . .'

'You did!' she muttered, giving him an annihilating glance. 'You didn't say it in so many words, but you said it. You said,

N

not Avapouhi. If Avapouhi comes, I'm afraid of playing . . . But you, Omaata, you can come. With you, I'm not afraid. *Aoué! Aoué! Aoué! Aoué!*' she cried suddenly, taking her head in her hands, and her face reflected true suffering. 'That I should hear that! That, I, Omaata, should hear that! Look! Look!' she went on, shaken once again with indignation. 'I'm young!'

It was true, she was young He always forgot it. But how could he tell her that it was her heroic dimensions, her air of authority, the way she had of calling him her 'baby'? . . . And how could he deny it now without his denial appearing to be an invitation?

She turned her back on him and, frowning and contemptuous, seized Timi by the arm and casually pulled his body towards the hole, into which she then began to insert herself.

'Omaata!'

There was no reply. Not even a glance. Omaata disappeared on the other side, and as brutally as if she were avenging herself on him for the outrage she had suffered she pulled Timi through the hole.

Purcell hurried to the opening and put his head through it.

'Omaata!'

She was already moving away, without a word, Timi's body thrown over her shoulder, the dead man's slender legs beating against her back at each huge stride she took from stone to stone.

After a moment, Purcell went and sat down on the bed. He pulled the basket to him and took a mango from it. He had a strange feeling. For the first time in his life he found it difficult to know what he really thought, what he was really worth. Here he was in a cave, sheltered from the fighting, turning his back on both camps . . .

He got to his feet. 'Tetahiti thinks I'm "clever" . . . And suppose it's true! My respect for life, my horror of violence? . . . Who can tell if I've not used these moral reasons to lie to myself? After all, I stabbed Timi. When it was a question of my own skin, I shed blood.'

The patch of light on the rock wall was fading. Outside, the sun must be sinking to the horizon. Purcell felt a damp chill on his shoulders. He walked briskly up and down. He thought of the wonderful warmth of Omaata's big, firm, soft body. And now night was falling and he began to feel cold again.

He tripped over Timi's musket and looked round for the cutlass. He could not see it. Omaata must have taken it. He picked up the musket and remembered the feeling of comfort and security the weapon had given him the day they had seen the frigate. He went prudently into the tunnel as far as the edge of the pit, and hurled the musket into it. The barrel was heavy, and he threw it with such force that he nearly lost his balance.

He felt weary again. He went back to the bed of leaves and lay down, exhausted, his legs trembling. He closed his eyes, but immediately opened them again. However, he must have slept for a while, for his body was shivering with cold. He tottered to his feet and forced himself to walk up and down. It was quite dark, and he counted his paces so as not to walk into the rocky walls of the chamber. Five paces, turn, five paces, turn . . . From time to time, he lost count, and groped for the wall in front of him with outstretched hands, like a blind man. He had a feeling of nausea. He was hungry, but dared not eat any more of the fruit. At times, he felt as if he were sleeping as he walked, and he clenched his teeth to wake himself up. He was afraid of getting off course and falling into the pit.

He suddenly found himself leaning against the wall, his shoulders bowed, his hands on his knees. Sleep must have overtaken him as he was turning round. He blinked, but the inky darkness became no clearer. He no longer knew whereabouts in the chamber he was. He thought of the pit and woke up completely.

It was then that he heard a deep regular sound of breathing. There was someone two or three yards from him. He stood still, terrified. He made so violent an effort to pierce the darkness that his eyes hurt and there was a pain in their sockets. For a few seconds he could hear nothing but the breathing near him and the noise of his own heart against his ribs.

He heard a light rustle of leaves on his left, and at the same moment a frightened voice said: 'Adamo!'

Omaata! It was Omaata! Two yards from him, leaning over the bed of leaves, groping for him and finding nothing. He took a deep breath, but could not manage to speak.

'Adamo!'

He felt a hand touch his chest. There was a stifled cry and the hand was withdrawn.

'It is I,' Purcell said in a strangled voice.

There was a silence and Omaata said quickly, without coming near him: 'Say it in *Peritani*.'

Purcell repeated in English: 'It is I.' And suddenly he understood. The *toupapahous* could not speak English. Omaata was afraid of a trap!

'*Aoué!*' Omaata said. 'You frightened me! You're so cold!'

She went on: 'Man! When I didn't find you on the bed! . . .'

He felt her great hands groping along his arms and across his chest to his shoulders. He uttered a sigh and let himself fall forward, his head against her breast. Omaata was talking, but her voice was no more than a murmur. He fell asleep.

He was woken by a feeling of warmth. He was lying face down on Omaata's firm, elastic body, but his back also felt warm. Something rough, heavy and familiar was covering him . . . A blanket! She had brought him one of *The Blossom*'s blankets. He smelt it. It's folds still smelt of salt, tar and varnished wood.

He was not quite awake. He had the impression of floating in the warm sea of the lagoon at noon, when the sun caressed you gently through the water. His right cheek against Omaata's breast, his hands flat against her ribs, his left knee bent against her belly, he was rising and falling on her gigantic chest to the rhythm of her breathing. Omaata's great hands were reposing lightly on his back and the movement of her breathing was accompanied by an imperceptible pressure upwards as if she were rocking him.

Time went by. He felt as if he were a chick nestling among its mother's downiest feathers, those of the vast warm ruffled stomach, with his head alone appearing in the open air to breathe the freshness of the night. How pleasant the darkness had suddenly become! Here was a cave hollowed out of the mountain, and within the cave a chamber, which lay about him like the shell of an egg, and within the chamber the dark lying

over them like a veil, and in the dark Omaata's big black warm
body. Pushing his head against the giantess's breast, he listened
happily to the powerful beating of her heart, as if its pulsations
were feeding his own sap. Never in his life, anywhere or at any
time, had he had such a sense of well-being. It was so wholly
delightful that he felt like groaning.

'Are you awake, my baby?' Omaata said.

His ear against her chest, he listened to the echo of her voice.
She had scarcely murmured the question, but the murmur went
on resounding like the bass notes of an organ.

'Yes,' he said without moving. 'Have I slept long?'

'Enough.'

With what patience she had borne his weight on her without
moving!

'Are you hungry?'

'Yes,' he said with a sigh. 'Very. Don't make me think of it!'

'I've brought you some food.'

'What?'

'Fish . . . a pancake . . .'

'*Aoué*, woman!'

He woke up completely.

'Where is it?' he said happily, getting up and sitting on the
bed.

'Wait, don't move.'

Her great arm brushed past him and groped in the dark. Then
he became aware that she was putting a *Peritani* plate in his
hand. He put it to his mouth and swallowed its contents with
avidity.

Omaata laughed with satisfaction.

'How hungry you are!'

'Can you see me?'

'No, but I can hear you!'

She had lain down again and he felt that she had bent her
leg so that he could lean his back against it.

She went on: 'Do you want the pancake?'

'Yes.'

He put it to his mouth. That morning he had eaten a similar
pancake, but the memory suddenly seemed to him a very distant
one. He recognised its little sour, rather acid taste with surprise.

'Have you finished?'

'Yes.'

His mind began to work again and he said: 'How did you manage to bring all this up here . . . the plate, the pancake, the blanket . . .'

'I managed,' she said.

He thought he heard a certain curtness in her voice. He turned his head towards her. But it was difficult, when you could not see the face, to judge of an intonation, particularly to judge it afterwards. He said: 'What's the matter with you?'

'Nothing.'

He leaned forward to put the plate on the stones. At the same moment, he felt her put the blanket round his shoulders. He turned his head. From the rustling of leaves behind him he realised she was getting up.

'Where are you going?' he asked anxiously.

'I'm going away.'

He repeated incredulously: 'You're going away?'

She did not reply and he heard the sound of a displaced stone. He was seized with panic, got to his feet and made his way towards the hole.

'Omaata!'

He groped about. She was sitting on the stones, her legs already in the hole.

'No!' he cried, seizing her by the shoulders and making a hopeless effort to hold her back. 'No! No!'

'Why?' she said dully. 'You're no longer cold. You've eaten. You've got a blanket.'

'Stay here!' he cried.

He let go her shoulders and, putting his arm round her neck, he tried with all his might to pull her back into the chamber.

She made no attempt to resist him, but even then he could not move her an inch.

'Stay here! Stay here!' he said beseechingly.

At this moment nothing else mattered, he needed her presence as desperately as if his life depended on it.

'Are you afraid of being cold?' she said at last, and he could not tell whether there was sarcasm in her voice or not.

'No! No!' he said, shaking his head as if she could see it.

And he suddenly said in a choking voice that surprised himself: 'I don't want to be alone.'

There followed a long silence as if she were thinking over her reply. Then she said in a dull, toneless voice: 'Leave go of me. I'll stay.'

When she was standing inside the chamber again, she said nothing, made no movement, did not touch him. After a moment, he took her hand.

'Are you angry?'

'No.'

And that was all. Purcell felt mortally embarrassed. He was sleepy and wanted to get back to the bed of leaves. But he dared not invite Omaata to follow him. A few minutes ago, it had not seemed to him scandalous to be lying on her at full length. But now, even to be standing beside her in the dark and holding her hand had something embarrassing about it.

'We must sleep,' he said hesitantly at last.

And as she still did not move and remained silent, he took a step towards the bed of leaves and pulled her after him by the hand. She stood stock still. He was stopped in his tracks, holding her at arm's length.

The absurdity of the situation suddenly struck him and he wanted to laugh. Here he was, Adam Briton Purcell, third lieutenant of *The Blossom*, thousands of miles from his native Scotland, in a cave, in the dark, naked as the first man and clasping a gigantic brown lady by the hand . . .

'Come, woman!' he said impatiently.

The tone of authority proved effective. It set Omaata in motion and she followed him slowly. When he reached the bed of leaves, he sat on it and pulled her down by the hand. She lay down obediently and made no movement while he drew the blanket over them and put his head on her breast. He waited, his face turned towards her. But she remained silent and inert. The only sign of life she gave was her breathing.

On lying down beside her, he had put his right arm round her waist and, bending his knee, had placed it on her stomach. But as the seconds went by, he became embarrassed by this embrace. It seemed to him no longer innocent as it had been before, nor could he recover the sense of union with Omaata in which he had felt himself fuse with her, as when lying on her body he had had the impression of breathing with her breath. Now they were separate and distinct. Two fragments of the same continent isolated in the ocean. Two islands.

He closed his eyes but could not sleep. His mind was confused and anxious. Timi was floating somewhere under water, borne along by the current, but Purcell saw his eyes fixed on him with a gentle yet sly expression from beneath long lashes. Whether he opened or closed his own, he saw them before him in the dark and felt embarrassed by them, identifying them by some curious quirk of logic with the remorse he felt at having hurt Omaata.

'Are you asleep, Omaata?'

'No,' she said after a silence.

It was a stupid question. She was clearly not asleep. She was there, because he had asked her to stay, lying beside him like a block of stone. She was not even offended any more, merely absent. Perhaps she was thinking of her life on the island now that Jono was dead, of growing old on the island, alone.

'Omaata, why did you say that the others would win?'

There was another silence, as if his words had to travel a long way before reaching her.

'When the others took to the bush,' she said expressionlessly, 'the *Peritani* ought not to have stayed in the village.'

'Why?'

'They didn't know where the others were. And the others knew where they were.'

'What ought they to have done?'

'Taken to the bush.'

'They too?'

'They too.'

'She went on: 'Or built a *pa* at once, and finished it before night.'

'Why before night?'

'If the *pa* is not finished, night falls, and the others attack. When the *pa* is finished and strong, it is almost impossible to attack it.'

'Even with muskets?'

'Man!' she said disdainfully. 'What is a musket? A javelin which fires farther . . .'

Purcell remembered the glance Tetahiti and Mehani had exchanged in the camp.

'Omaata, do you think the others will attack?'

'Not now. It's the night of *Roonoui*. It is very dark. But in the morning. At first light, they'll certainly attack. Before the *pa* is finished.'

'Do the *Peritani* know?'

'I told them.'

Purcell raised his head and leaned over her as if he could see her.

'Why?'

She said without hesitation: 'Jono was a *Peritani*.'

He was not sure he understood the inward meaning of this answer and went on: 'Do you want the *Peritani* to win?'

'No,' she said curtly. 'I want the others to win.'

'Even after the death of Jono?'

There was another silence. Then she said: 'Jono had a musket.'

'You like the others better than the *Peritani*.'

'The others have been gravely injured.'

'And yet you've helped the *Peritani* by warning them of the attack?'

'Yes.'

'Why did you help them?'

'Because of Jono.'

They were back at the same point. He remained unenlightened. Suddenly she said, almost with Ivoa's intonation: '*Peritani*, always why, why!'

And she gave a little laugh which gave Purcell extraordinary pleasure. It was a return to her usual teasing, friendly, almost tender intonation. He gently rubbed his cheek against her breast. She was closer to him again since they had begun talking. Even her body was different; it was softer, more yielding.

He went on: 'Listen. You didn't give me time to tell you. I didn't really kill Timi.'

And he explained what had happened. When he had finished, she thought for a moment and said: 'You killed him.'

'But I've just told you . . .'

'*Aoué,* man, don't be so stubborn. A shark attacks, you hold your knife in front of you, the shark swims on to it. It was you who killed it.'

She added: 'You're a very brave man, Adamo.'

The great deep voice, the warmth, the vivacity – she was herself again.

'I'm a man who has been very frightened,' Purcell said with a note of amusement in his voice. 'From this morning until the death of Timi. And after Timi's death, I was afraid of the cold. And when the cold had passed, I was afraid of being alone. *Aoué,* it has been the day of fear. If fear could kill, I'd be dead.'

She laughed, paused for a moment and then said: 'You're very brave, Adamo.'

She went on: 'I saw you in your hut with the three *Peritani.* And I saw you set out with the *Manou-faïté. Aoué,* I wept when I saw you set out without a weapon with the *Manou-faïté.* So small, so weak, so indomitable! O my little cock! O Adamo! '

After that, he did not know what to say. He pressed his cheek more firmly against her breast and clasped her great waist in his arm. Their voices whispering in the night had re-created a link. It was not the same link as before. That moment would not return. It was something else, a comradeship, an understanding. There was an unexpressed tenderness.

He felt almost too hot and threw the blanket back to his waist. The smell of *The Blossom* at once disappeared and the warm scent of Omaata overwhelmed him. He recognised, one by one, that of the flowers she wore in her hair. There was only one he could not remember, the most penetrating, the most familiar. He ought to have been able to recognise it among a thousand and yet could not name it. It was a subtle, spicy, musk-like, amber-like, ambiguous scent. The scent of a vegetable which had become flesh. At first, you could not tell whether it was agreeable or not. But while you were thinking about it, it insinuated itself like a drug. It was not exuded, but was part of Omaata, of her neck, her shoulder, and the breast against which his cheek was resting. It was an intimate, confined scent. But at the same time, it evoked clear water, great trees with hanging branches, the sand of the lagoon, the belly of the sun. If joy of living had a scent, this was it. But there was a sort of underlying anxiety about its after taste, as if it were suggesting a freshness that was in process of decomposition.

'I'm very comfortable,' he said sleepily.

'You're comfortable, my baby?' she said in a low voice.

It was a murmur like the little surf on a beach in fine weather. She added: 'The leaves are not too hard? Do you want to come on top of me?'

And before he had time to answer, she raised him and placed him on her. The scent at once became stronger, and he lay there motionless, his eyes open. He felt a sense of plenitude and it was delicious. Everything was confused, scent and flesh. His body hollowed out its place and took root. Torpid, but not inert, he felt like a plant swelling with sap.

At the same moment, an odd, irrelevant idea came into his mind and he said: 'Where did the fish come from? The *Peritani* did not fish this morning.'

After a moment, she said: 'Horoa went to fish.'

He followed her in thought from the time she had left the cave. She had thrown Timi's body into the sea, she had returned to her hut, and there she had taken the blanket, the fish, the pancake and . . .

He opened his eyes wide. So that was it! . . . He raised his hand, sliding it gently up to Omaata's neck. He groped. The pandanus kernels were round under his fingers and he felt the liana on which they were strung. Then he hoisted himself up to them, smelt them, raised his head and said: 'You put your necklace on?'

Omaata's breast seemed to contract, there was a tiny little noise and that was all.

'Omaata . . .'

There was no answer. He raised his arm and passed his hand over the huge face above him.

'Omaata . . .'

After a moment, she took his face gently in both hands and placed it against the kernels of the necklace. For a moment he remained there motionless, his hand resting on Omaata's breast. The kernels were sharp against his cheek, he turned on his side and breathed their scent deeply. He felt the scent flow into him, not only by his nostrils, but by all the pores of his skin. After a moment, his head became a void, the walls of the cave disappeared, he was walking on the beach and the nor'wester was whipping his face. He felt he had the power to fly. He stamped imperiously on the sand, spread out his arms, and began to fly through the air, his wings quivering.

15

'Adamo!'

He opened his eyes. Itia was there, standing motionless before him. It was almost light in the cave.

He sat up. He found difficulty in fully opening his eyes. Itia's features seemed blurred. He felt that something abnormal was happening. She said no word. Nor did she throw herself into his arms.

He put out a hand and groped beside him.

'Omaata?'

'In the village,' Itia said in a dejected way.

'What's she doing?'

She shrugged.

'What can she do?'

He looked at the patch of light on the wall. The sun was already high. He had slept a long time. He blinked and his sight grew clearer. He looked at Itia and saw the expression in her eyes.

'Itia!'

'The war's over,' she said dully.

He got to his feet, opened his mouth, but no words came. He knew, he already knew.

'Mehani?'

She looked straight in front of her and said in a low voice: 'All. All. Except Tetahiti.'

She looked away and said resentfully: 'He's not even wounded.'

There was a silence and Purcell repeated with puerile insistence: 'Mehani?'

Itia looked at him. He seemed stupefied, his arms hanging loose and his shoulders drooping. When he spoke, it was in a plaintive, childish voice.

'Mehani?'

She shook her head twice. Purcell felt as if his eyes were starting out of his head, a black veil fell over them, he stretched his hands out in front of him, sank to his knees and then collapsed on his stomach.

'Adamo!'

She ran to him and turned him over. He was pale; his eyes were closed and sunken. She listened to his heart. It was beating irregularly.

'Adamo!'

She began slapping his cheeks. His face quivered and a shade of colour returned. Kneeling with her legs each side of his body, she slapped him harder with both hands.

She stopped, and he parted his lips and said in a strained, pressing voice: 'Slap! Slap!'

She began again, and after a moment he managed to open his eyes. Everything was misty and indistinct. He looked at Itia, and closed his eyes again. The little slaps on his face went on, he whispered: 'Slap, slap.' The taps on his cheeks seemed to set a rhythm for the blood returning to his head. He felt better.

He leaned on his elbow, the nausea was over, but he felt as if he had been knocked out. He said in a low voice in English: 'Mehani is dead.' But it meant nothing. He felt no pain. He could feel nothing. His mind was a complete blank.

Itia lay down beside him and took his hand. She saw him turn his head towards her, his eyes were expressionless.

'How?' he said in a weak voice.

'Yesterday evening. The others surprised the *Peritani* at nightfall. The chief was killed. The little rat and the Skeleton went into the hut. They fired all night. The others were in the trees. They were firing too. At dawn they stopped. The *Peritani* waited a long, long time . . . And when the sun rose, they thought: "Good, they've gone." Then, the little rat and the Skeleton came out of the hut and the others killed them.'

'Mehani?'

'He went up to the little rat too soon. The little rat wasn't dead. Not quite dead. He fired.'

Purcell lowered his head. Killed by Smudge! But no, there was nothing derisive about that. Mehani was dead. That was all.

A few seconds went by. He lay curled up, inert, stupid, thinking of nothing.

Itia said: 'Shall I go on?'

'Yes,' he said feebly, and closed his eyes.

She went on without showing any emotion: 'Tetahiti cut off their heads. Then he sent Raha and Faïna to the camp to get the *poini* which contained the heads. He set up eight javelins round the Tahitians' hut, and on the javelins he placed the trophies. Then the women began shouting and he said: "Why are you shouting? You are not my slaves, but women of my tribe. And these were foreigners who wronged us." But the women went on shouting, and Omaata said: "You are putting the heads of our *tanés* on pikes; you are treating us as slaves." After that, all the *vahinés* talked at once and reproached him. Tetahiti listened patiently to it all, then he said: "These men were foreigners who bore arms against us. They have been killed in war and I have decorated the surround of my house with their heads to do me honour, for I have fought well. With courage and cunning. And I am alive. And they are dead. But you, you are my sisters. I do not look on you as slaves. Whoever wishes to enter my house may do so. I shall treat her with honour." Thereupon, he looked at the women one after the other. It was not a look for play. No, It was something else. He was leaning on his musket, his cutlass in his belt. A great man! an imposing man! The women also looked at him. Then Horoa, who at the time of the Skeleton, and even at the time of Ouili, always played with him a little, said: "Take the head of my *tané* off that pike, and I will enter your house." And Tetahiti said, as if regretfully: "No. It is the custom." There was a silence, and Taïata alone entered his house. And when Horoa saw it, she said derisively (and perhaps also from vexation): "Man, you have made a fine acquisition!" And all the women left him, except Taïata, and of course Raha and Faïna.'

'And you?' Purcell said, raising his head.

'I left too,' she said with a brief flash in her eyes. 'Tetahiti called me back and said: "Itia, my sister, are you going?" I said: "Mehani was my *tané*. Not you. And I do not think you are behaving well." He said sombrely: "I am acting in accordance with my rights. Run after Omaata and bring her back." I brought Omaata back, he looked her in the eye and said: "Where is Timi?" She made no answer. So he said: "Where is Adamo? And why was Ivoa not with the women?" And as she did not reply to that either, he said loudly: "Adamo is my prisoner of war and I shall not kill him. Tell him to come and see me in my house." Omaata said nothing. She went off and, since I did not know where to go, I followed Omaata into her hut. *Aoué*, all the women were there! And when they saw Omaata, they cried: "What shall we do, Omaata?" And some were weeping, though it is not proper to weep. And others were asking: "Where is Timi? Where is Ivoa?" And others again were saying: "What will he do with Adamo?" And Omaata said: "Be quiet! He has said that he will not kill Adamo." '

There was a silence and, since Purcell said nothing, Itia went on: 'Well, what are you going to do?'

Purcell turned to look at her, and she noticed that his features had recovered their firmness.

'Itia,' he said at last, 'tell me the truth. Do you know where Ivoa is?'

'No.'

'Does Omaata know?'

'Perhaps.'

He got to his feet, went and felt his trousers, and was annoyed to find they were still wet. Nevertheless, he put them on.

'Listen,' he said, 'we'll go down. I shall wait at the banyan. You will go and find Omaata.'

He went on: 'But don't tell the other women where I am.'

'And what shall I say to Tetahiti?'

'You'll say nothing. You'll say that Omaata is looking for me. Go ahead, don't wait for me.'

He had almost forgotten how hot the sun was and how bright the light it poured down. He blinked, and clung on with both hands as he went down the steep slope outside the cave. He was alive, and he wanted to think of nothing else.

He could feel the heat of the sun on his head and shoulders, and on his legs through the damp cloth. The whole island was spread out below him like a map in relief, green and multi-coloured in the middle of the dark blue Pacific. He breathed deep into his lungs the air that had passed over the sea, the woodfires of the village and the flowers of the plateau.

He did not go in under the banyan. He took off his trousers, hung them on a vertical root and lay face down on the grass. After a few minutes, he was dripping with sweat, but he lay still for it seemed to him that he would never have enough warmth. There were a few clouds in the sky, and whenever the sun was hidden he felt as sad as if light and warmth had gone for good, leaving the island in the shadows.

Omaata arrived an hour later. She had thought of everything and brought him food. He went a few paces to meet her, looked at her, felt some embarrassment, and took the pancakes from her as if to relieve her of them. Without a word he went back to sit under the banyan, but this time in the shade. He felt his shoulders burning.

'Where's Ivoa?'

'I don't know.'

He looked at her and she added: 'Man, where do you expect her to be?'

'You saw her last night?'

'This morning. When Mehani fell, she rushed to him, fell on her knees, and then got up and went away.'

'Where? In what direction?'

'Towards your hut.'

She had obviously gone to get her musket. Mehani was dead. She would not waste time weeping. She had taken to the bush to protect her *tané* against Tetahiti.

After a moment, he said: 'Does Tetahiti want to kill me?'

Omaata was lying beside him. Leaning on her elbow, she was picking blades of grass and putting them in her mouth one by one.

'He has said that he will not kill you.'

'That's not what I'm asking.'

She gave a little groan. How could she explain to him? Tetahiti did not personally want to kill him. It was more complicated.

Since Omaata remained silent, Purcell went on: 'Do I need to be on my guard?'

'One must always be on one's guard.'

'As much as when Timi was alive?'

'Perhaps not.'

She added: 'Tetahiti has said that he will not kill you.'

He tried to catch her eye in vain.

'Is Tetahiti a man to say one thing and do another?'

She shrugged her vast shoulders: 'Like all chiefs.'

He thought her answer over and said: 'Otou was not like that.'

'In time of peace, no. But in time of war, Otou was very cunning.'

'The war is over.'

'O my baby!' Omaata said, raising her head and turning the light of her large eyes on him.

She took all the blades of grass from her mouth and threw them in front of her.

'The war with the Skeleton is over. But there is another war between Tetahiti and the women. And another war between Tetahiti and Adamo . . .'

'A war with me!' Adamo cried in surprise.

She groaned, lay flat on her stomach and, propping her vast face on her hands, looked tenderly at him out of the corners of her eyes.

'Do you know what Tetahiti is doing at this moment? He's completing the *pa* . . .'

'The *Peritani*'s pa?'

She nodded.

'*Maamaa!*'

'No,' she said gravely. 'No . . . This morning he broke all the muskets, except his own. But there are still two muskets in the island. Ivoa's . . .'

She paused and looked down.

'And Timi's.'

He said at once: 'I threw Timi's into the pit.'

She sighed, but made no comment. He went on: 'Would the women go so far as to kill Tetahiti?'

She groaned. More exactly, she blew angrily through her nose. The *Peritani* always asked these direct questions! Where were Adamo's good manners? Then she looked at him, fair, pink, a large red patch on his shoulders. Poor little cock, he could not take the sun, he understood nothing, he was like a baby among them, and to *whom* could he ask questions? She felt tenderly towards him, put out a large hand and stroked his arm. He turned his head, and she saw his glance. Oh, his transparent eyes, the colour of the sky! Transparent! O my little cock! O Adamo!

'The women are offended,' she said at last. 'I'm very offended myself.'

'But it's the custom.'

'No, no!' she said with passion. 'After a war within a tribe, you do not put the heads on pikes.'

There was a silence and Purcell said: 'Why has he acted thus?'

She shrugged.

'He hates the *Peritani* very much. He's trying to be happy about his victory. For him those eight heads . . .'

She made a gesture and did not complete the sentence. Purcell thrust his chin out and his eyes went cold. Eight heads. Nine, with his. *All* the *Peritani* would be dead. Tetahiti would be really happy . . .

He got to his feet and turned to her.

'Come on,' he said in a determined voice. 'You will go and find Tetahiti. You will say to him: "Adamo says: 'I shall not enter your house, for I do not wish to see the heads of the *Peritani* on pikes.' Adamo says: 'Come to the market place at noon, I shall be there.' " '

She stared at him a moment in silence. *Aoué,* how his eyes could change!

'I shall go back to the village with you,' Purcell went on. 'I shall await his answer in my hut.'

It was only yesterday, almost at the same hour, that he had left East Avenue to turn with the women into Banyan Lane! And now he was back there again, and had already reached the village. On his right was Mason's hut. If, instead of turning left to go home, he went on down East Avenue, he would pass all the huts in the lozenge . . . How well they had chosen the site for the village! The plan had been well drawn; the symmetry lovingly observed; the spaces between the houses properly managed; all the civilised rules had been carefully obeyed . . . How wonderfully successful it had been! The organisation, the effort, the will to create, the ability to foresee, the concern to survive and transmit one's possessions to one's children, all these were admirable. Only a few months ago, there had been nothing here but a virgin wood. And now there were these almost straight 'streets' and 'avenues', each with its signpost and its name, the market-place with its shelter, bell, clock, and the canvas cisterns erected by MacLeod; these solid, if inelegant, huts; these well-fenced, cultivated gardens. Each man with his own separately self-contained home. No one demanding anything of anyone. All the doors of the houses with locks. And farther on, nine parcels of good land on the plateau, belonging to each of the nine British, which should have fed them – and had killed them.

Nine? No, not nine, eight. He could, if he so wished, go and take possession of the parcel MacLeod had allotted him. He lowered his head. There was a dry, bitter taste in his mouth. The only Briton on the island! . . . He felt Omaata's great hand on his shoulder, as he walked beside her, and he slowed his pace as he approached his hut. The deep voice rolled hoarsley in his ear: 'Don't be sad, Adamo.' He shook his head irritably. 'I'm not sad.' He moved away from her side and she withdrew her hand.

They reached his hut.

'I'm going,' Omaata said with dignity.

She left him without a glance, her head held high and her back coldly stiff. He shook his head impatiently. Their susceptibility, their damned etiquette! . . . He opened the door of his hut, and immediately felt remorseful. Solid and monumental, the armchair he had made with his own hands stood in the middle of the room. Before going to the banyan, Omaata had taken the trouble to move it back to his hut, so that it should be waiting for him when he came home and found no Ivoa.

He went out into the garden and walked as far as the hibiscus thicket. He called to Ivoa several times. He was practically sure that she was watching his every move. He knew she would not come out of the bush at his call but he wanted her to know that he was anxious about her.

Still with the feeling that Ivoa's eyes were concealed behind every leaf, he went to the lean-to, washed from head to foot and shaved carefully. He went back into the hut and opened the sliding doors wide. Then, since he felt increasingly nervous, he lay down on the bed facing the light. The sun was high but Omaata did not reappear.

After a while, the women arrived. They spoke not a word and their bare feet made no sound on the stones of the path. However, even before they crossed the threshold, Purcell recognised the characteristic rustle of the bark strips of their skirts. They came in, their eyes grave, bent over him one by one and rubbed their cheeks silently against his. When it was done, they looked at each other. Then there was a sort of rapid, gliding ballet, as if all their movements had been previously arranged in accordance with some definite precedence. Itia, Avapouhi and Itihota sat down on the bed, the first on Purcell's right, the second on his left, the third at his feet. Horoa and Toumata, neglecting the seats or not daring to use them, sat on the floor. As for Vaa, after having embraced Purcell (which she had not done since she had become the *vahiné* of the great chief), she retreated to the door and stood there, like some visitor in a hurry who intends leaving at any moment. These dispositions astonished Purcell. Vaa's distance, the reserve of the two *vahinés* sitting on the floor, and the tranquil air of familiarity of the three women on his bed. That one of these three should be Itihota, White's widow, with whom he had had little contact until then, was still more surprising.

A quarter of an hour went by without a word being spoken. Then Omaata arrived and, not without a certain air of pride and possession, took in the scene with an approving eye. She also came and sat on the bed at Purcell's feet, opposite Itihota.

'Well?' Purcell said, sitting up.

'Tetahiti is waiting for you.'

'Now?'

She nodded.

'Where?'

'In front of the door of the *pa*.'

Purcell looked at her.

'Was it he who said "in front of the door of the *pa*?" '

'It was he. He does not wish to come to the market-place.'

'Why did you take so long?'

She was silent, her expression haughty, her eyes lowered, and her face rigid. 'All right,' Purcell thought, 'my question was out of place. In any case, it was quite useless. It's obvious she took the time to tell Ivoa what was going on.'

He got up and said calmly: 'Come.'

When he reached West Avenue, he took her by the arm and hastened his pace to outstrip the women.

'Listen to me,' he said in a low voice, emphasising his words '*Nothing* must be attempted against Tetahiti. *Nothing.*'

'And if he holds you prisoner?'

'Nothing.'

'And if he kills you?' she said in a hard voice.

He looked up at her. Her face was expressionless. She still bore him a grudge. He rubbed his cheek against her arm.

'Please, don't be angry . . .'

There was a silence, and then she said suddenly in a different tone: 'O my little cock, I'm afraid for you all the time.'

He pressed her arm.

'Remember: nothing must happen to Tetahiti.'

She nodded and said in a low voice: 'I don't want anything to happen to him either . . . But I'm so afraid for you. Sometimes I want to kill him so that my fear should be at an end.'

'No, no,' he said emphatically, 'you mustn't even think of it! '

He added: 'He's frightened too.'

She nodded.

'That's true. He's very brave, but he's frightened. He hasn't laid aside his weapons while working since this morning.'

She went on: 'He's working like a madman with his women. The *pa* may be finished by this evening.'

When they reached the point of the lozenge, Purcell stopped and said without looking at her: 'Rejoin the women.'

He was expecting her to argue, but she obeyed at once. He

went on, the women following twenty yards behind, and turned into Cliff Lane.

The trees became thinner as Purcell approached the Tahitians' hut, the sun was hotter and the sweat trickled down his forehead. He wiped his eyes with the back of his hand, and when he could see clearly again, he saw the *pa*.

It stood on the corner of the path, forty yards in front of him. In fact, it was not more than a rough palisade, some nine feet high and made of long rough posts driven into the ground and bound together at the top. But since the obstacle required the use of both hands and both legs to climb it, the attacker would be exposed and unarmed while doing so. Moreover, though it might be possible to set fire to the *pa*, even though it was constructed entirely of green wood, it was not possible to throw a torch over it to set fire to the hut. The distance was far too great. The *pa* was therefore a very real protection against this form of surprise. And if fires were lit within the enclosure, night attacks could be easily repulsed from the loopholes in the hut.

Purcell was nor more than twenty yards from the *pa*, when he heard Tetahiti's voice.

'Halt!'

Purcell obeyed.

'Tell the women to halt.'

Purcell turned and, raising both hands, palms turned towards the women, shouted Tetahiti's order. There was considerable murmuring among them, but they obeyed.

Purcell turned to face the *pa* again. He could see nothing. Not a face. Not a figure. The gaps between the posts had been filled with branches of thorn.

'Come,' Tetahiti's voice said.

Purcell squared his shoulders and went forward. It was scarcely twenty paces. He held himself very straight and walked stiffly, but he felt soft and weak inside his rigid body. 'Will I even hear the shot?' he wondered anxiously. He was stifling. He realised he had ceased breathing, and he took a deep breath and raised his head. His neck muscles were taut, and he thought derisively: 'The ninth head. I'm bringing him the ninth head . . .'

The *pa* drew near so quickly that he realised he had hastened his pace. He tried to slow down and, from the effort it cost him, became aware of his panic. He was not walking towards the *pa*. He was hurling himself at it.

He stopped two yards from the palisade. As soon as he was still, his legs began trembling. A long time seemed to go by and then suddenly the *pa* moved. More precisely, part of the *pa* moved back and swung open to reveal a gap between two posts. There was something almost threatening about the silence and the suddenness with which the *pa* opened.

'Come in,' Tetahiti's voice said.

'I said I didn't want to see the heads,' Purcell replied.

'You won't see them.'

What did that mean? That he wouldn't have time to see them? There was a silence and then, as if he had understood what Purcell was thinking, Tetahiti went on: 'You can come in. Nothing will happen to you.'

A promise or a trap? Purcell made an effort to control his voice: 'You come out.'

'No.'

'I'm not armed,' Purcell said, putting his hands above his head.

He could see nothing through the posts and the thorn, but he knew Tetahiti was watching his every move.

'No. I don't want to come out.'

It was obvious he was afraid of Ivoa shooting him.

'Behind this door there's another door,' Tetahiti went on. 'You won't see the heads.'

A hall. Or rather a lock-chamber. To isolate visitors or trap assailants. The swinging door was the weak point of the *pa*, and Tetahiti had constructed a second line of defence behind it.

'Let's stay where we are,' Purcell said. 'We can talk here.'

There was a silence. Then the opening between the two posts shut. But this time the door moved noisily. Purcell breathed again. He might be killed. The future would show. But one thing was certain: he would not be a prisoner.

Tetahiti said curtly: 'Where is Ivoa?'

'In the bush.'

'Has she a musket?'

After a while Purcell said : 'Why do you ask me that? You know the answer.'

'What's she doing with a musket in the bush?'

'That you also know.'

Then he thought his answer might sound ambiguous and he added: 'She's afraid you'll kill me.'

He expected a protest, but there was none. He was astonished, almost disconcerted, by the abrupt, very un-Tahitian tone of the questions.

'Where is Timi?' Tetahiti asked in the same curt, imperious tone.

'I don't know.'

It was true too. Literally true. And, improbably, it pleased him to have told only a half-lie.

'Where's his musket?'

Purcell hesitated and was angry with himself for his hesitation. 'I haven't got it.'

It was a stupid answer. It was bound to arouse suspicion.

'Who has it?' Tetahiti asked at once.

Purcell hesitated again and said: 'No one.'

He corrected himself: 'No one, I think.'

That was stupid, too. And the reservation worst of all.

'Has a woman got it?' Tetahiti asked.

Purcell shrugged without answering. The arrogant tone, the brutal, direct questions! It was far from the ceremonial eloquence of the *Manou-faïté*. And suddenly Purcell understood. This was not a conversation between equals. It was the interrogation of a prisoner of war.

Then Tetahiti said: 'You are my prisoner of war and I have the right to kill you. But I shall not kill you. Take one of the three *Peritani* canoes and set off to sea with your wife.'

Purcell did not reply for a moment. He could not find his voice.

'Man, I have spoken,' Tetahiti said.

'Tetahiti,' Purcell said at last, 'I have not borne arms against you. And yet, you now say: "You are my prisoner of war." You also say: "I shall not kill you." And yet you're sending me to drown in the sea with my wife, the daughter of the great chief Otou.'

It was now Tetahiti's turn to be silent. The reasons Purcell had given left him indifferent, but not the allusion to Ivoa's parentage. Otou and his own father had been brothers, Ivoa was his cousin, and Purcell's words placed his cousin's death at his door.

'The *Peritani* are bad,' he said at last with restrained violence. 'You must go! But if my sister Ivoa wants to stay, she may do so.'

The bad faith of this was apparent. Tetahiti could have no doubt whatever as to what Ivoa's decision would be. Purcell felt discouraged. His hatred, his bad faith . . . Understanding seemed impossible.

'Listen,' he said, 'I have not borne arms against you. I came to your camp with the *Manou-faïté*. It is against my will that my wife has taken to the bush. Why do you treat me like this?'

'You're a clever man,' Tetahiti said disdainfully. 'That's why you're still alive. However, you must go. I don't want any *Peritani* on the island.'

There was a silence and Purcell said: 'What will happen if I refuse to go?'

'I shall kill you,' Tetahiti said without a shadow of hesitation.

'Now?'

'Now.'

Purcell looked at the thorns in front of him, but could see neither the glint of an eye, nor the barrel of a musket.

'If you kill me, the women will want to avenge me.'

Tetahiti uttered a little groan which might have been contempt, but he said not a word. He was clearly taking care not to defy the women with words the *Peritani* might repeat. 'He's taking care not to offend them,' Purcell thought. 'If it weren't for that, he would have killed me already.'

Purcell remained silent. He was no longer afraid and his mind was cold and lucid. For some seconds past, he had been very tempted to say: 'The island is as much mine as yours. I am no one's prisoner, and I shall not go.' This attitude had the merit of precision, and yet, at the last moment, he hesitated to adopt it. Face to face with a MacLeod, he would not have hesitated. But MacLeod considered his behaviour from start to finish. You could therefore foresee his actions. Purcell was not sure of Tetahiti's reactions. The Tahitians were capable of calculated behaviour. But they did not always carry out their calculations to the end. On the way, they would suddenly find important reasons for behaving illogically. In the matter of the heads, for instance, Tetahiti, in spite of his reputation, had not behaved prudently. Though he particularly desired not to offend the women, he had turned them against him.

'If I brave him,' Purcell thought suddenly, 'he may very well accept the prospect of an open conflict with the women simply as a point of honour – or for the pleasure of having my head on a pike.'

'Very well,' Purcell said firmly, emphasising his words. 'I will go. But you will have to give me time.'

'Why time?'

'My wife is pregnant. She cannot be brought to bed at sea in a canoe. And before going, I shall have to alter the canoe.'

'What do you want to do to the canoe?'

'Deck it.'

'Why a deck?'

'To protect my wife and child from the weather.'

'How long will that take you?'

'Two moons.'

Tetahiti watched his enemy's face through a crack in a post and did not know what to think. He was relieved that Adamo had agreed to go. Otherwise, he would have been obliged to kill him, and then *Eatua* help him! The women would have fought him like demons! But had anyone ever had the *maamaa* idea of decking a canoe before? It was a trick! A means of gaining time. On the other hand, the women would never let Ivoa go before she had been brought to bed.

'I'll allow you the time you ask,' he said curtly. 'But tell your wife to return to your hut.'

'I shall do so,' Purcell said after a moment.

He waited a few seconds more, but since Tetahiti remained silent, he turned on his heel.

When he rejoined the women, he said in a low rapid voice: 'I'll tell you all about it in my hut.' He walked on, the *vahinés* in his wake. He did not want to have a dramatic scene under the walls of the *pa,* within earshot of Tetahiti.

He walked quickly. He was surprised to feel relieved, almost happy. And yet, to face the sea in a boat with thirty-two inches freeboard! . . . But he would go and take his chance. Since the beginning of the war, he had been hunted like an animal. At sea, he would have to battle alone against the storm, but he would at least be safe from men.

He had a feeling of comfort and security at being back in his hut, sitting with his hands on the arms of his chair and the sliding-doors wide open to the sun. The pathetic scene he had expected did not take place, perhaps because two months seemed so long a time to the Tahitian women that they could not start weeping so far in advance; perhaps also because a certain apathy was becoming evident in their attitude. Their faces showed no sadness, but a sort of rigidity and immobility. They talked little and without animation. Indeed, if they had wept during the morning, their tears were now dried.

The old gaiety scarcely returned when Itia observed seriously that Tetahiti was thirty, therefore old, and might well die before Adamo's departure.

Then another incident relaxed the tension to some extent. The *vahinés* were asking themselves two questions in particular: would Tetahiti have killed Adamo, if Adamo had refused to leave? And had Adamo been right to agree to leave? The discussion was coming to an end when Horoa suddenly began neighing and took Vaa vehemently to task, telling her that having answered 'yes' to the first question, she was stupid to reply 'no' to the second. Indeed, if Adamo was certain that he would be killed if he did not agree to leave, what possible advantage could he derive from saying 'no'? This observation had no effect: Vaa refused to see that the two questions were linked. Horoa indignantly seized her by the shoulders and, eyes flashing, nostrils palpitating, shook her so violently that Omaata cried: '*Aoué!* Vaa is pregnant!' Upon which, Vaa began weeping in self-pity, Horoa said she was sorry, took her in her arms and began to console her.

After that, silence fell on them once more, gloomier and weightier than ever. Omaata got to her feet and said that they must busy themselves with more urgent things, in particular the water fatigue and fishing.

There was a difficult moment when they counted heads for the water fatigue. Eight months before, twenty-seven people had landed from the big canoe. During the last three days fourteen had died violent deaths: eight *Peritani,* five Tahitians and one Tahitian woman. There were now only thirteen people on the island: one *Peritani,* one Tahitian and eleven *vahinés.*

It was decided that Vaa and Ivoa would not be asked to take part in the water fatigue. Tetahiti would not consent to come out of the *pa;* and therefore, by unanimous consent, Adamo would also be excluded, for otherwise it would mean humbling him in relation to Tetahiti. The water fatigue therefore fell to a team of eight women who would have to perform it every other day. Though the prospect was not a pleasant one, it was accepted with equanimity and without complaint.

As for fishing, since Tetahiti would be of no use for that either it was decided, for the same reasons of prestige, not to give this duty to Adamo, but to Horoa, whom MacLeod had taught to fish in the *Peritani* manner, and who would instruct selected companions in this method.

Living arrangements gave rise to further discussion, but it was carried out so discreetly that Purcell had to pay the greatest attention to follow what was going on. Omaata posed the question with precision: were they going to go on living alone, each in her own hut, or were they to live by twos, or even by threes? They all looked at each other, but none of the women seemed prepared to take a stand on the theoretical aspect of the problem. Finally, Itia said that as far as she was concerned she had no house, and that she could either occupy poor Amoureï's hut or, if anyone wished, keep her company. This was said without looking at anyone and with such modesty that it was clear her manners had improved. After that, there was a longish silence during which active consultations were carried out by glances and movements of the head in a code which completely escaped Purcell. Omaata then said that if Itia was not afraid of being crushed when she turned over in bed, she would be happy to share with her. Thereupon, Horoa, still contrite, said that she would like to look after Vaa, either in her own hut or in Vaa's. 'In mine,' Vaa said at once, in a voice that suggested that

Horoa's hut, in spite of its cupboards, was much inferior to her own. There was another short pause, a further exchange of glances and Avapouhi said that, 'naturally', she would be delighted to take Itihota into her hut. This 'naturally' seemed to be understood by everyone, except Purcell. There was then a certain embarrassment, because it was realised that Toumata had not been provided for. There appeared to be reasons, which Purcell could not understand, why neither Omaata nor Ava-pouhi could receive a third person. And it was some time before Horoa, who was busy looking after Vaa, realised that it was up to her to invite Toumata. This she did with a good grace. But everything nearly went wrong when Vaa protested that her hut was too small for three. Horoa was so indignant at this remark that she let go of Vaa's waist, and took her by the shoulders with the evident intention of shaking her again. Omaata intervened. With a couple of words, she installed Toumata in Horoa's hut. Vaa would go to sleep there at night, but remain the rest of the day in her own hut.

It was also decided to return to collective cooking and to re-open the communal oven in the market-place. Purcell wondered whether the women would extend their feeding arrangements to include Tetahiti, but he had no time to work it out. The question was solved at once. Itihota was appointed to take their share to 'those of the *pa*' (this was the tactful way they were designated). Purcell was pleased with this arrangement. It was not only generous. It was intelligent, and was at once a way of making advances and sounding things out.

Purcell did not intervene at all and had the impression that his intervention was not expected. It was clear that a matriarchy was being established on the island and that the women were taking in hand the government of the city without fuss or pre-tension. Everything had been organised rapidly and sensibly, with few words and the minimum of disagreement.

Omaata gave the signal for departure. When all the women had gone out, Purcell stopped her on the threshold. The *vahinés* went on their way without turning round.

'Omaata,' he said quietly, 'I want to see Ivoa.'

She stared at the undergrowth but made no reply.

'Do you hear?' Purcell repeated with a shade of impatience.
'I hear,' she said, glancing at him from her large eyes.

Throughout the meeting her expression had been animated.
But now something in her seemed to have relapsed and her eyes
were sad.

'Well?'

'Man, I know what you want to ask Ivoa. She won't agree.'

'Tell her I want to see her.'

'She won't want to see you.'

'She won't want to see me?' Purcell repeated, half hurt, half
incredulous.

'No,' Omaata said impassively. 'Why should she see you? To
refuse you what you ask of her?'

'What I ask is reasonable.'

'No,' Omaata said, shaking her head, her sad eyes staring
into the distance as if they could pierce the undergrowth and
reach Tetahiti's heart.

She went on: 'No. Not at the moment. Perhaps later.'

'It's for me to judge when it's reasonable,' Purcell said stiffly.

Omaata leaned down towards him and smiled.

'O my little cock, who know the Tahitians better, you or we?'

'I made Tetahiti a promise,' Purcell said after a moment.

'*Aoué*,' Omaata said, shrugging her vast shoulders, 'he'll know
it's Ivoa who has refused to come.'

'How will he know it?'

'I shall say so in front of the women.'

Purcell looked at her in stupefaction.

'Omaata, do you think one of the women . . . But it's impossible! He never comes out of the *pa*.'

Omaata gave a half smile.

'He won't have to come out.'

'Itihota? . . .'

'No, no. Itihota will take him food. That's all. *Aoué*, she's
more silent than a tunny fish! That's why I chose her.'

Purcell said nothing for a moment, and then he thought suddenly: 'The lock-chamber. Not only a defence. An ante-
chamber. The visitor can see Tetahiti without seeing the heads.
Honour will be safe . . .'

He put his hand on Omaata's enormous forearm.

'Is that why you suggested the women should sleep two in a hut?'

'And even three,' Omaata said.

It was clear. She was aiming at the trio in East Avenue: Toumata, Horoa and Vaa. Horoa in particular. Horoa, who 'at the time of the Skeleton, and even at the time of Ouili . . .' One could trust Itia; she knew what went on. He said aloud: 'Horoa?'

'I shall send you Itia, my baby,' Omaata said. 'Itia is to bring you your food today.'

She turned and went off. Purcell was not surprised that she had not answered his last question, but he was surprised that she had said as much as she had. Perhaps she intended to warn him. Perhaps it was her way of telling him that all the women were not to be trusted . . .

After his meal, Purcell made a short siesta. When he woke up, he realised that Itia had gone. He loaded some planks on his shoulder, took his tools and started for Blossom Bay. He had not gone fifteen yards along East Avenue when Omaata, Itihota and Avapouhi joined him. 'They must have been watching for me,' he thought at once. 'My house is well guarded.' The *vahinés* took his planks from him and would even have relieved him of his tools if he had allowed them. Cliff Lane ran parallel to the *pa* for twenty yards and Purcell noticed that the women walked between him and the palisade while they were passing it.

At the foot of the cliff there was a sort of cave, very high and wide, but not very deep. It served as a shelter for *The Blossom*'s three boats. They were protected from the sun and also from the sou'wester, the one violent wind that blew across the island. At this particular point there had been a fall of rock from the cliff. The sand had gradually covered it and now, even at high tide and on rough days, the surf did not reach the cave. Nevertheless, the boats had been prudently moored with a system of ropes and anchors. They had been scraped and repainted in the spring (*The Blossom*, on her long voyage, had carried enough paint to paint her from masthead to keel) and covered with tarpaulins. Six feet above the ground brackets had been set in the rock wall to carry the masts and spars.

Purcell removed the tarpaulins and inspected the boats carefully, testing their hulls here and there with the point of his pocket-knife. There seemed to be no rot. All three boats were sound. Two of them, however, had a few worm-holes. Only one was free of them and, unlike the other two, was clinker built. This was the one Purcell chose.

With Omaata's and Avapouhi's help, he stepped the mast, fitted the boom, and measured the distance between the boom and the floorboards. There were fifty-three inches and he decided to deck the boat at a height of forty-six and a quarter inches, which left a margin of six and three-quarter inches for the boom to swing. As the boat had a freeboard of thirty-three and a half inches at mast-level, it meant raising the deck only fifteen and three-quarter inches, which was modest enough not to imperil stability. Inside the cabin, there would be a height of only some forty-seven and a half inches, which was little but enough to be comfortable when sitting down.

The over-all length was twenty-three feet, and he decided to deck it over for nineteen feet and be content with a cockpit of four feet. In fact, he did not much like the idea of a cockpit, which seemed to him a weak point, since there would be a certain danger of swamping in bad weather. He would have preferred to deck the whole boat from one end to the other, and give access to the cabin by a hatch. But he discarded the idea. In so small a boat with such little freeboard, the helmsman's position would be a very wet and unenviable one.

He at first intended to build the classic form of deck with a gangway each side by which to reach the bows. But, on reflection, he decided to have a flat deck. It would be all of a piece, which would simplify the construction, give greater rigidity, and more room in the cabin below. That point settled, he considered the double curve of the deck: from bow to stern, it must be concave; from port to starboard, convex. At first sight, the longitudinal sheer posed no problems. By prolonging each rib fifteen and three-quarter inches above the side and by joining the ends of the prolongations from bow to cockpit, a satisfactory shape should be obtained. The transversal sheer was more difficult; it was clear that it must be effected by the ribs on which the planks of the deck would be laid, and their curve must be calculated and drawn. Purcell remembered that this curve was called the 'camber', and that he had probably learnt to calculate it, but his memory stopped there. He was suddenly surprised by a regret for MacLeod. He suppressed it, determined to have a look in the ship's library, and postponed the solution till later.

He had brought writing materials with him and began to note measurements so as to be able to draw a plan. When he had finished, he realised there was nothing more for him to do on the beach at the moment, and that it was useless to have brought his tools with him. His first job was to make a plan of the deck, calculate the 'camber' of the ribs, and draw them in chalk on the floor of his hut.

He came out on to the beach and looked for the women. For a moment he could not see them, then Omaata's powerful round shoulders emerged from the great foaming crest of a wave. Two brown heads, looking like children's beside hers, appeared. An arm came out of the water, waved to him and three voices cried in chorus: 'A-da-mo! A-da-mo! A-da-mo! ' The echo sounded from rock to rock all round the bay.

Purcell stood where he was. He was hoping the women would chant his name again. The shadow of the cliff seemed to be extending in front of him as he watched. And he had the impression that he could almost feel the earth turning on itself in space, carrying men and their crimes on its muddy crust. 'A-da-mo! A-da-mo! ' The strange chanting of their voices gave him a shiver down the spine. All his nerves were quivering. The sheer beauty of it hurt. With their long black hair falling over their shoulders, the *vahinés* waved their arms like palms. They were in sunlight, and he was in shade, as if in another hemisphere to theirs, far from them at the other side of the world.

He undressed and ran towards them over the red sand. The slope was steep and he ran down it at a crazy speed. He crossed the line of the cliff's shadow, the beach turned ochre, the sea was azure and diamond, and he scarcely felt a sensation of chill as he dived into it. The breakers bore him up to an incredible height, rolled him in a maelstrom of foam and dark blue water, and with a last great heave returned him to earth.

A little later he was lying alone on the beach. The women were still in the water. Horoa, Vaa and Toumata had joined

o

them. In spite of the lateness of the hour, Purcell could feel the sun on the burns on his shoulders. He turned over on his back, closed his eyes and put his hands to his forehead to shade his eyelids. He pursed his lips. He did not want to think. A moment went by. He could see nothing but the red of his closed eyelids and the circles flowing in them.

He heard the sound of a voice. Purcell started, took his hands from his forehead and opened his eyes. At first, he felt only a vague anguish, a weight on his chest and a lump in his throat. Then the truth suddenly pierced his body like a knife: Mehani was dead. Purcell looked about him. Nothing was changed. The sun was there. The sea. The sand. The voices of the women. The cliff's shadow. And the earth was turning, turning. The earth! What was the use of the earth? He was lying on the sand like a shell. Yes, that was it, like a shell, there was no other word, he was empty, empty . . . He turned over, dug his fingers into the sand, gasping. The sense of absence was appalling, but he could not weep.

After a moment, he got up and went into the sea. Once again, the surf rolled him over, but the blue of the wave seemed to him darker, more frightening. He was relieved when the undertow carrying him out to sea was capped by the incoming wave. As soon as he felt the sand beneath his feet, he began to run to escape the undertow. He stopped, breathless. The women were sitting in a circle on the sand, combing their long wet hair. And, running towards him from the foot of the cliff, he saw Itia, looking tiny on the huge beach, with the great high wall of rock behind her. Just as she reached him, she suddenly changed direction, emerged into the sun, ran a few more yards, and threw herself into Omaata's arms. She stayed there a moment, recovering her breath, then leaned to her and whispered in her ear.

'Adamo,' Omaata said, 'Ivoa won't come.'

The women stopped combing their hair. They all looked at Purcell. He said nothing. He glanced from Itia to Omaata.

'Did you see her?' he said to Itia at last.

Itia nodded.

'I saw her and spoke to her. She won't come. She doesn't want to give up the musket.'

Purcell looked down and made no comment. There was nothing new about this, unless it was that Omaata and Itia had agreed to say in front of the other women that Ivoa would neither come out of the bush nor hand her weapon over to Tetahiti.

'I have more to say,' Itia said, 'but first I'm going to bathe.'

She got up and threw herself into the surf. She disappeared in a huge whirl of foam from which her legs emerged for a brief second, just long enough to show the paler colour of the soles of her feet. The women began combing themselves again with those slow, competent gestures which usually delighted Purcell. He sat down. The black line of the cliff's shadow was gaining ground. It was now no more than a few yards from the *vahinés*, and as the tide was also rising their little group seemed to be cast away on a tiny island of sand that at any moment would be submerged both by sea and shadow. 'I'm obsessed,' Purcell thought, 'I'm frightened of everything.' He looked at the women. They did not lose themselves in vain imaginings. They were so sure of themselves, they knew so well what their role was! He looked at Vaa. To spare her having to raise her arms, Horoa was combing her hair for her, and Vaa was submitting with her head thrown back. She seemed wholly at ease, expansive, blooming, glowing with health and corpulence, reigning among the women as an idol of maternity. That morning, her *tané* had died. Her face still bore the imprint of sorrow, but her heavy, weary features were relaxed. With her lips open in a half smile, and her hands reposing on her enormous belly, she was staring into the distance with an air of happiness.

He turned and saw Itia emerging from the sea, her pretty body dripping water. She came up to the group, looking important, like an actor making his entrance, and when everyone was looking at her, she said, emphasising her words: 'Tetahiti has come out of the *pa*.'

There was no reaction and she went on: 'I saw him! . . . I was going to the beach and the door of the *pa* opened. *Aoué*, I was frightened! I hid behind a bush, and I saw Taïata come out, then Raha, then Faïna, and finally Tetahiti carrying a musket.'

She stopped, looking solemn and as if she was expecting questions, but no one spoke and she went on: 'He shut the door, and he said something to Taïata who remained in front of it. *Aoué*, she was very submissive, I'm sure he's already beaten her! Then Tetahiti went off, following the wall of the *pa* towards the sea, and after a moment he came back on the other side.'

Two or three seconds went by and Omaata said in a low voice: 'So he's finished the *pa*?'

There was an exchange of glances and that was all.

'Had I been in your place,' Horoa said, shaking her mane, 'I should not have hidden myself. I should have shown myself and said: "Once again, man, remove the head of my *tané*!"'

Itia hung her head and put her forearm across her eyes.

'My *tané*'s head is not on a pike,' she said gently.

She was the only woman present who could say as much. She had to say it to do justice to her honour. At the same time, she was very ashamed of seeming to boast.

'It's time to go home,' Purcell said, getting up.

He went over to Itia, put his hand on her shoulder and touched her cheek with his lips.

That evening it was again Itia who brought him his food. By the time he had finished, night had fallen. She lit a *doédoé* in front of the porthole to scare away the *toupapahous,* placed three others on the table so that Adamo could read, and closed the sliding doors.

'Why are you closing them?' Purcell said, turning round. 'It's a warm night, and there's a moon.'

Itia said stiffly: 'Omaata said to do it.'

Purcell looked at her.

'Who gives orders here, Omaata or I?'

But she stood straight and determined in front of him like a little soldier.

'Omaata said: "When you light the lights, you shut the big door."'

'Why?'

'Tetahiti may shoot at you from the garden.'

They thought of everything. And who knew whether the *doédoé* in front of the porthole was not also there to prevent the enemy seeing the inside of the hut? Purcell went on reading. Itia was sitting with her legs crossed on the bed, her hands on her knees, silent and motionless. Purcell could not even hear her breathing. Each time he raised his head from his book, he saw her brown eyes fixed patiently on him. They were sad, but the soft light of the *doédoés* made her little face look smoother and rounder.

'Why don't you go to bed?' he said at last.

He knew how happy it made her to be spoken to in English.

'I go,' she said at once.

And she lay down on the bed. Purcell looked at her.

'I meant at Omaata's.'

'Not tonight,' she said decisively.

She clasped her hands on her breast and lay as motionless as a corpse. Purcell got up and began pacing up and down the hut. This was clearly one of the things that were decided on in the island now without his being consulted. Itia's eyes were fixed on him. He sat down with his back to her and went on reading.

After a moment, he realised he had not turned the page. He got up, shut the book with a bang, walked several times round the room and went and lay down beside Itia. She at once got up, went and blew out the three *doédoés* on the table, leaving the one at the porthole alight, and resumed her place on the bed.

After a moment, he said: 'Itia, are you grieving?'

'Grieving? Why?'

'You know very well why.'

She turned to look at him. By the light of the single *doédoé* he could see no more than the curve of her cheek. Her eyes were in shadow. But from the sound of her voice when she spoke, he realised he had hurt her feelings.

'Why do you ask that? In Tahiti we don't talk of these things.'

She too was like a clam. Impenetrable. 'We don't talk of these things . . .' Jono died. Omaata lamented throughout a whole night. And that was all. She never mentioned his name again. She behaved as if he were forgotten. They all behaved as if they had forgotten their *tanés*. And yet it was not indifference. No, certainly not. Stoicism rather. It seemed strange to apply that austere word to Tahitian women.

In the middle of the night, Purcell was awakened by a slight sound. He opened his eyes and listened. But even when he held his breath, he could not make out where it came from.

Itia made a movement. The sound grew louder. He leaned over towards her. She was weeping.

He remained there a long minute without moving. He was afraid of hurting her feelings again by letting her see that he was aware of her tears. With slow movements, like a man acting in his sleep, he put his arm under Itia's head, and pulled her to him. He could hear nothing now, but he could feel Itia's shoulder shaking under his left hand. A few minutes went by and then she said in a low, quivering voice: 'O Adamo!'

Her shoulder ceased shaking and she lay still. He thought she would fall asleep, but she raised her head, hoisted herself up to his ear and whispered, surprise and despair in her voice: 'O Adamo, everyone's dead! . . . Everyone's dead! . . .'

She sniffed once or twice like a little girl, pressed herself against him and said in a soft, plaintive voice: 'I want to go back to Tahiti . . .'

After a while he felt her grow soft and passive in his arms. He listened to her breathing. It was deep and regular.

After that, he couldn't go to sleep himself. He felt uncomfortable, he was not accustomed to sleeping in a room without air. He got up, went softly to the door and opened it. The moonlight trickled into the hut, and he went out on to the threshold.

He was immediately seized by an enormous arm and hurled into a bush. It was Omaata. He had not hurt himself, for she had thrown herself under him.

'*Maamaa*,' she said scoldingly. 'What are you doing outside?'

'I was taking the air.'

'It's a musket-ball you'll take.'

He felt something hard under his hand. He groped at it. It was a cutlass. She was mounting guard in front of his house, armed and hidden behind a bush! By the slenderness of the hilt, he recognised Timi's cutlass.

'Omaata . . .'

'Talk lower.'

'Do you think he'll attack?'

'Perhaps not. But that makes no difference. You must be guarded.'

'Why?'

'If you were not guarded, he'd know it. He mustn't be tempted.'

There was a silence.

'Omaata . . .'

She looked at him, her huge eyes glowing darkly. Nothing. He had nothing to say. Thanks would have been derisory.

'Go in now,' she said.

She got to her feet and, while he opened and closed the door, she stood on the threshold between him and the undergrowth.

16

Next day, on awakening, Purcell found the calculation which allowed him to determine the camber of the ribs. He opened the sliding doors, pushed his bed and table into a corner of the room, carried his armchair and stools into the garden, and began drawing the plan in chalk on the floor.

The women arrived an hour after sunrise. Purcell asked them not to come in. They went round the hut by the garden and sat down in front of the doors. None of them asked him a question, but from the comments they exchanged in whispers, Purcell understood that there was no doubt in their minds as to what he was drawing. It was clear to them that it was intended to attract the protection of *Eatua* to the canoe.

Itihota appeared towards the end of the morning and told them how Tetahiti had received the dish of fish she had taken him. She was as usual very laconic. He had received it in the lock-chamber, had accepted the dish and been very polite.

The *vahinés* pressed her with questions. Had he his musket? Yes, he had his musket. And his cutlass? He had that too. What was his expression like? Severe. She had said he was 'polite'. Yes, he had been polite, very polite. He had taken her by the shoulders, he had rubbed his cheek against hers, he had not shouted and his gestures had been gracious. And yet she had said 'severe'? . . . Yes, severe: lines each side of his mouth (gesturing with each forefinger to show the lines), wrinkles on his forehead (gestures), frowning (mimicked), his head held high. How severe? Severe like a chief? Severe like an enemy? Itihota hesitated. And since she could not make up her own mind, she got to her feet and mimicked Tetahiti's welcome. Silence. Glances. Had he said nothing? . . . Yes. What? He had spoken! *Aoué!* And she hadn't told them! What a stupid woman! She was a woman out of whom you had to drag information! A woman who was dumber than a tunny! What had he said? He had tasted the fish (the gesture was gracious) and he had said: 'The women of my tribe are clever. They know what they have learnt. And they also know what they have not learnt.' Exclamations. There was no doubt about it: it was a 'caress with words'! He wanted peace! No, he didn't want peace, he was being polite! If he wanted peace, he would remove the heads! The discussion was becoming confused when Itia spoke. It was not a 'caress with words' for all of them. It was a 'caress' for Horoa. What the women had learnt and knew, was fishing. He knew very well that it was Horoa who fished. *Aoué!* The child was right! The child was clever! The child was very cunning! It was a 'caress' for Horoa . . .

Here Horoa stamped her foot, neighed and shook her mane. Perhaps they all wanted peace with Tetahiti. She didn't! She hated him! He was the enemy! He would remain the enemy, even if he removed the heads! If she had been in Itihota's place, *aoué,* she would not have allowed herself to be embraced! Whereupon, Itihota suggested that Horoa should from now on take the fish to those within the *pa,* but Omaata, who had watched Horoa's stampings and pawings with a cold eye, maintained so imposing a silence that no one dared carry the suggestion further.

Throughout the day there was a good deal of coming and going round Purcell's hut, and whether it was by chance or on purpose, Purcell was never left alone, even during the two meals. These were brought to him by Avapouhi. She must have had strict orders for, as soon as night fell and the *doédoés* had been lit, she closed the sliding doors.

On 19th May, Purcell finished the drawings on the floor and began to saw the ribs in accordance with them. In the afternoon, he wanted to check a measurement of which he was uncertain and went down to Blossom Bay, followed by the women. As the day before, Itia appeared on the beach rather late. Her eyes were bright and her round cheeks all swollen with the news she brought: Raha had come out of the *pa*! She had gone to Adamo's hut! She had looked at the things Adamo had written on the floor and at the wood he had cut! . . .

Purcell was bending over the boat and he listened to Itia in silence. From her story it was clear that the intelligence services of both were active. For if Raha had taken advantage of his absence to acquire information about the progress of his labours, it was doubtless not by chance that Itia was always present when the door of the *pa* opened. Purcell wondered whether she carried on her watch twenty-four hours out of the twenty-four, or whether another *vahiné* had been appointed to replace her at night. In any case, it was clear that since the 17th another assembly of the women had taken place without him, and that a number of plans had been made of which he had not been informed.

That day it was Itihota who brought him his midday meal. Purcell was astonished. He had never been on intimate terms with her. Indeed, owing to her taciturnity, it was difficult to have much communication with Itihota. In Tahiti, she had already shown an abnormal propensity for silence, and it had considerably increased through living with White. When Purcell asked her if someone else had replaced her to take their food to 'those in the *pa*', she replied: 'No, it's been done.' She said not another word during the two hours she stayed with him. She came back in the evening, and without a word lit the *doédoés,* closed the sliding doors, sat patiently all the time Purcell was reading, got up when he got up, and lay down when he lay down.

The next morning, immediately after breakfast, Purcell left the house. He had not gone ten yards when Avapouhi and Itia emerged from the undergrowth. Itia cried: 'Where are you going?'

'To Omaata's.'

'I'll go and warn her!'

And she ran off. This haste made Purcell wonder. He hurried on, Avapouhi almost running beside him.

Omaata was sitting on the threshold of her hut, her back

against the door. There was no trace of Itia.

'I want to talk to you. Alone.'

Omaata looked at him. There he stood before her, so small and so resolute. *Aoué,* it was nice when Adamo was angry! She felt a shiver of pleasure which reached down to her belly.

'You're all alone, my baby.'

He turned round. Avapouhi had disappeared.

'In your hut.'

She sighed, got up slowly, opened the door and let him pass in. The room was empty, but the door giving on to the garden was wide open. At the end of the garden the thicket of giant ferns began.

Omaata followed Adamo's glance and smiled tenderly. *Aoué,* he was clever. He had already guessed.

'Omaata,' Purcell said, his eyes fixed on the garden, 'I'm displeased. There are many things the women decide on the island and I'm not consulted.'

Omaata sat down on her bed. She did not want him to feel that he was dominated by her stature during the discussion. When she had made herself comfortable, she looked at him and contented herself with raising her eyebrows questioningly.

'For instance, my house is guarded. I can't take a step anywhere in the island without being accompanied. I'm not saying it's wrong, but who gave the order?'

She made no answer. She contented herself with raising her eyebrows again.

'Itia watches the door of the *pa.* Who decided that?'

She bent her head and, since he was silent, she said: 'Go on, man. Go on. You think a lot with your head. Relieve it.'

He went on: 'The first day, Itia brought me my meals. The day before yesterday, Avapouhi. Yesterday, Itihota . . .'

'Man,' she said gravely, 'they're widows . . .'

'That's not what I mean,' Purcell said looking away and walking impatiently up and down the room. 'What I want to know is who gave the order? Who decides things? Why am I not consulted? Who's going to bring me my meals today, for instance? *Aoué,* I'm certain all the *vahinés* on the island know! Even Tetahiti's *vahinés*! Even Tetahiti! And Adamo does not know!'

'It is I today,' Omaata said.

'You're going to bring my meals?'

He stopped and his anger seemed suddenly to fall away. He turned to her, made a wide gesture with his right hand, and said gravely: 'That it should be you is very agreeable.'

She looked at him approvingly. The gesture, the tone, the gravity. And when he bent his head, the great chief Otou's earring had slid across his cheek. Oh, he was worthy of it! He was worthy of it! She resisted an impulse to get up and clasp him in her arms.

'And tomorrow?' he went on.

'Itia.'

'And the day after tomorrow?'

'Avapouhi. And next, Itihota. And I, after Itihota.'

He was silent for a moment.

'Well,' he went on firmly, 'what I want to know is this: who decided it? Who made the selection?'

He looked Omaata in the eyes and she said reluctantly: 'The three others wanted to as well. But I said no.'

And since Purcell said nothing, she went on: 'Tetahiti would have been humiliated.'

Purcell thought over this answer. The more he thought about it, the more he admired its wisdom.

'But why Itihota?' he said in a low, casual voice. 'I don't know her.'

'She loves you very much.'

He shrugged.

'How do you know? She never opens her mouth.'

'I know it.'

'In fact,' he added after a moment, 'you decide. You alone? You decide everything?'

'No. Sometimes I decide with them all. Sometimes with Ivoa. Sometimes with Itia.'

'With Itia?' he said in surprise.

'Itia is very capable,' Omaata said, nodding her head.

He took a few paces up and down the room, then came back and stood in front of her and said without raising his voice: 'From now on, before you decide anything, I want you to speak to me about it.'

She lowered her eyes and said submissively: 'It will be done as you wish.'

He was surprised by the rapidity of his victory. But was it really a victory? He hesitated a moment, his eyes fixed on Omaata's large face. But no, she had made him a promise, and he must not look as if he were doubting it. He went towards the open garden-door and stood on the threshold, framed in the opening, his eyes fixed on the bush. He was offering a magnificent target to anyone hidden in the ferns, and Omaata said nothing! He shrugged. He had no doubt at all. He came back to Omaata and said stiffly: 'I want to see Ivoa. Do you understand? I want to see her. Tell her so.'

He added more gently: 'Good-bye,' and hurried outside. But if he had hoped to thwart the vigilance of his escort, he was disappointed. It was merely that its composition had changed. Itia had been replaced by Itihota. No doubt Itia had returned to watch the door of the *pa*.

He walked quickly home and immediately set to work again. The cutting of the ribs was a delicate and rather tedious business. It was necessary to go over the same piece several times to achieve the proper curve, and between each cutting to plane the edges flat. To add to the difficulty, the saw, which had been misused by the crew ever since they had arrived on the island, had lost some of its teeth, and from time to time jammed in the wood. After an hour, Purcell remembered that MacLeod had offered to lend him his own tools on Rope Beach, and he decided to go and ask his widow for them.

He left Avapouhi and Itihota at Horoa's garden-gate and went in alone. He noticed, as he crossed the little courtyard in front of the hut, that the portholes were shut. A sound of lively and excited talk came from inside. He went up the two steps and had raised his hand to knock on the door when he heard Vaa's shrill voice saying: 'We must avenge our *tanés*! *Aoué*, it's not difficult to get into the *pa*!' After that there was a silence and Purcell stood there for a moment with his hand raised and his heart beating against his ribs.

His decision was taken, as it were, without his knowing it, for he had the curious impression of learning it as he acted. He knocked on the door, opened it without waiting for a reply and said curtly: 'Vaa, come with me.'

Horoa, Vaa and Toumata were sitting on the floor. They stared at him in surprise. After a moment, Vaa got heavily to her feet and came over to him. Purcell led her into the little garden behind the house.

'Listen,' he said in a low voice, 'I heard what you said. You ought to be ashamed of yourself.'

Vaa's big peasant face was as expressionless as a stone.

'I'm not ashamed,' she said, her little expressionless eyes fixed calmly on Purcell's. 'The chief of the big canoe was a good *tané*. It is my duty to avenge him.'

Purcell looked at her. Her forehead was hard and narrow, her cheeks large and fat, her nose thick and her chin massive. It was discouraging. How could he make a lump of clay see reason?

'It is not for a woman to avenge a warrior,' he said at last.

'Yes it is,' Vaa said shaking her head. 'When there isn't a man.'

He looked her up and down. No, it was not even insolence. She was quite incapable of insolence. Her ideas were arranged in her head like a squirrel's nuts in the hollow of a tree. She brought them out one by one, without reference to anyone.

'Tetahiti has a musket and a cutlass. And what have you got?'

'A cutlass.'

She added: 'I shall kill him in his sleep.'

He shrugged.

'You won't get two yards inside the *pa . . .*'

'I shall kill him,' Vaa said.

'Listen,' he said in exasperation, 'you will do nothing of the kind. I forbid you to do it. And you're going to obey me.'

She looked at him for a full second. The idea that Adamo could give her orders was a new one to her, and she did not know what to do about it. Should she agree or refuse?

A moment went by. She screwed up her eyes. She suddenly looked tired as if from the effort of thinking.

'You're not my *tané*,' she said at last.

'I forbid you to do it all the same,' Purcell said loudly and threateningly.

He had seen the weak point and was throwing all his forces into it.

'You are not my *tané*,' Vaa repeated, as if she were reinforcing her resistance by repetition.

And suddenly she smiled. Her sad, stony face became transfigured. It was a very beautiful smile, bright and warm. It burgeoned wholly unexpectedly on that ungrateful face with its coarse features that did not look as if they had been made for it. But now that it had burgeoned, Vaa was almost beautiful. There was even something agreeable about her stupidity.

'I didn't even always obey my *tané*,' she said, her dazzling smile playing about her lips as she spoke, and then little by little becoming sad.

'What did he say then?' Purcell said in surprise.

She raised her eyes, drew herself up, squared her shoulders, and said in English with the voice and almost the accent of Mason: 'You're a stupid girl, Vaa!'

The mimicry was astonishing. For the space of a second, Mason was present.

'And what did you say?'

'I am! I am!'

Purcell laughed.

'It was what he taught me to reply,' Vaa said simply.

It was astonishing. Who would have thought Mason capable of any form of humour?

'After that,' Purcell said, 'I suppose you obeyed?'

'No.'

'What do you mean, no?'

'No,' Vaa said. 'No, I didn't obey.'

'Why?'

'Because I'm stubborn.'

She clearly accepted no responsibility of her stubbornness. She was stubborn as a stone is round or square. It was her nature. There was no remedy.

'And so you didn't obey?'

'No.'

'And what did the chief do?'

'He smacked my face,' Vaa said.

Purcell raised his eyebrows in amusement. It threw a peculiar light on their relations. The admirable Mrs Mason, of whom her husband was so proud, seemed to be a wholly mythical personage invented for the purposes of prestige. At home, the *lady* was a *stupid girl* whom one smacked to make her see reason.

'And then?'

'Then, I obeyed,' Vaa said, he coarse face lit once again by her ravishing smile.

'Well, you're going to obey me too,' Purcell said firmly.

Vaa's smile disappeared and her face more than ever resembled a fragment of rock detached from the cliff.

'I shall kill Tetahiti,' she said calmly.

'But how?' Purcell said impatiently. 'Can you tell me how? He never comes out of the *pa*.'

'I don't know,' she said. 'I shall go in.'

'But how? Answer me! How will you get in? Over the palisade? *Aoué*, woman, with your belly! '

'No.'

'Perhaps underneath then?'

Irony was lost on Vaa.

'No,' she said seriously.

'Listen to me, at night he lights fires inside the *pa*. He'll see you.'

'I shall kill him.'

'He watches at night, he and his women.'

'I shall kill him.'

It was wearisome. She was incapable of thinking out the means at the same time as the end. She had only one idea at a time and then it was only half an idea.

'Listen, Vaa. He's got a musket. He's a warrior. And you, woman, are expecting a baby. How will you manage?'

'I shall kill him.'

'How?'

'I don't know.'

'How do you mean you "don't know"?'

'I don't know. I shall kill him.'

It was like talking to a wall. Purcell drew himself up, squared his shoulders and said loudly: 'You're a stupid girl, Vaa! '

'I am! I am! ' she replied.

'And now, you'll obey me.'

'No.'

'You'll obey me, Vaa! '

'No.'

He took half a step backwards, judged his distance and slapped her hard in the face.

For a few seconds nothing happened, then Vaa's face softened. The stone little by little became flesh, her eyes lost their flinty immobility, and the delightful smile appeared.

'I will obey you,' she said, her eyes tender.

'Come,' he said, 'you will say in front of Horoa and Toumata that you give up your plan.'

He took her by the arm and led her into the hut.

'Speak, Vaa,' Purcell said.

Horoa and Toumata had got to their feet. They looked from Purcell to Vaa.

'Women,' Vaa said solemnly, 'as concerns him of the *pa,* I shall do nothing.'

She added: 'Adamo does not wish it. I obey Adamo.'

Toumata opened her eyes wide and Horoa forgot to paw the ground.

Vaa looked from one to the other of her companions, put her hand on Purcell's shoulder, leaned her hip against his, and said proudly: 'He beat me.'

MacLeod's box of tools was nearly as long and heavy as a coffin. Horoa insisted on helping Purcell to carry it to his hut; Vaa and Toumata also offered to help; and Avapouhi and Itihota hastened to lend a hand. Purcell returned to his hut with an increased escort and without being allowed to do more than occasionally lay a finger on the lid. The box was placed carefully on the floor. There was, of course, a padlock. Horoa hurried home to find the key, and came running back. Purcell knelt, opened the box and gaped in astonishment. What splendid and wonderful tools! There was not a spot of rust on them, their blades were intact and well sharpened, and the handles were bright and polished . . . The chatter behind him had ceased. He turned round. Ivoa was there. The *vahinés* had disappeared.

Purcell got joyfully to his feet and went to her. But he realised she had come empty-handed. Ivoa had obeyed, but her obedience was also a refusal.

He stopped half way to her, so chagrined and disappointed that he was unable to speak. His eyes went from Ivoa's hands to her eyes. They were the same eyes, and it was the same face, but in the twinkling of an eye they had lost their familiarity.

'Adamo,' Ivoa said gently.

Purcell swallowed. Her features were drawn and hollow, and her belly swollen and shining. She seemed to have difficulty in standing.

'Sit down,' he whispered.

He led her to the armchair and began walking up and down the room. A silence lay between them. She did nothing to break it. He felt sad and powerless. He would have to talk, explain, and convince all over again. What was the use? How many words had he uttered during the eight months on the island to persuade Mason, MacLeod, Baker, the Tahitians? And they had all been useless! He explained and explained . . . It was like banging his head against a wall.

He said sadly and without looking at her: 'You won't give up the musket?'

'No.'

She added: 'It's not the right moment.'

'Why?'

'We think it's not the right moment.'

'Who are "we"?'

'Omaata, Itia, I . . .'

'Why?'

She shrugged, and with her right hand made a gesture of powerlessness. He turned his head away. There were always these mysteries, these ineffable things, these unutterable reasons . . .

'Why?' he repeated irritably. 'The war has been over for four days. And Tetahiti does not come out of the *pa*. Something must be done to restore confidence.'

'Yes,' she said, 'that's true. But not now.'

'Why not now?'

She looked at him. He was staring at her with his beautiful blue *Peritani* eyes. His serious, anxious eyes. She felt overwhelmed with tenderness for him. *Aoué,* poor Adamo, how unhappy he was with that insatiable head of his that was always asking 'why' . . .

'He still wants to kill you,' she said at last.

'How do you know?'

She sighed. There was no end to it. It was always how, why, how . . . Poor Adamo, his head always wanted more . . .

'And do you know when he'll no longer want to kill me?'

She looked at him seriously. No Tahitian ever understood irony.

'No,' she said simply. 'I don't know.'

He paced up and down the room and said without looking at her: 'Well, give the musket to Omaata, and come back here.'

She shook her head.

'In your condition?'

'I'm your wife,' she said proudly. 'It's up to me to guard you.'

He glanced at her and at once looked away again. Ivoa folded her hands in her lap and thought delightedly: 'He loves me! Oh, how he loves me! He wants to take me in his arms, and stroke my belly and the child within. But he's angry,' she thought with amusement. 'He thinks he's angry . . . He's a man and he does not know what he feels.'

'Now, I'm going,' she said, getting heavily to her feet and going towards the door.

She heard him cross the room. He was standing motionless behind her back, and she thought: 'Now, he's going to touch me.' She put her hand slowly on the door-handle, and moved rather father back than was necessary to let the door swing open. But she met nothing but emptiness.

'Adamo,' she said, half turning her head over her shoulder.

He was there at once. She did not turn round. She could feel him behind her with her whole body.

'Put your hand on me,' she whispered.

She leaned backwards, thrusting out her huge, spreading belly. She felt his warm hand moving over the curve of her back, scarcely touching her. O Adamo. O my *tané.*

A few seconds went by, then she said in a choking voice: 'Now, I'm going.'

The door banged and Purcell went on standing there, staring

at the floor. He was alone and had gained nothing.

After a moment, he went back to his planks and started work again. MacLeod's saw was admirable. He worked furiously till evening. Whenever he stopped, he felt a lump in his throat and an overwhelming sadness. The *vahinés* stayed with him all afternoon, but he scarcely spoke to them. At sunset, Omaata brought him his meal. He went to the lean-to and washed. After he had eaten, he felt tired.

He must have gone to sleep over his book, for he found himself on the bed, in Omaata's arms, his head against her breast. The moonlight filtered in through the sliding doors. He closed his eyes again, and felt as if he were sinking backwards into warm, downy shadow.

He stirred and opened his eyes.

'Omaata.'

'My baby.'

'When I came out of the cave . . .'

'Yes,' she said, 'yes . . . your shoulders were all red, my little cock.'

He stammered confusedly: 'You said: "The war is not over . . ." '

He waited. Omaata made no comment, and then something odd happened: Omaata's silence woke him up completely.

He went on: 'Ivoa said: "Tetahiti still wants to kill you." '

She groaned unhappily: 'She said that?'

'Today, when she came to see me.'

Omaata said nothing. He went on: 'Did she say something which is not true?'

'No.'

No denial could have been more laconic.

'You knew it too?'

'Yes.'

'How did you know it?'

'I knew it.'

'How did you know it?' he asked incisively.

Omaata felt a surge of pleasure. Adamo was talking to her severely, like a *tané*. What must his eyes be like!

'He insults the heads,' she said submissively.

'Every day?'

'Yes.'

'All the heads?'

'Yes.'

'Even Jono's?'

'Yes.'

'Even Ropati's?'

'Yes.'

After a moment, she added: 'Tetahiti is not a wicked man.'

It was odd. Why did she say that? What was she trying to make him understand?

He went on: 'Is there a pike waiting for a head between Ouili's and Ropati's?'

'No!' she said with sudden emotion. 'Who told you that? It isn't true! No, no! Tetahiti may have decided to kill you, but he wouldn't do a thing like that! *Aoué!* A pike waiting for a head!'

Her tone made it quite clear that it would have been in the worst of bad taste, a major violation of etiquette, a caddish trick unworthy of a gentleman. Purcell felt a slight twinge of amusement. It pleased him. He took a deep breath and thought: 'I'm not a coward.'

He went on: 'If Tetahiti kills me, what happens?'

There was a long silence, then she said discreetly: 'Very disagreeable things for him.'

Always these silences, these reticences . . .

'What things?' Purcell insisted.

He felt her stiffen in the darkness. This time reserve won. She refused to yield.

'Things,' she said curtly.

Purcell stared as if he could see her.

'Does he know it?'

'Yes.'

'In that case why should he kill me? I'm leaving. There's no point in killing me.'

Omaata gave a little laugh in her throat.

'O my baby, when a man becomes a warrior . . .'

She left the phrase unfinished and went on: 'In Vaa's case, you acted well.'

'You know about it?'

'We all know.'

She added: 'And tomorrow night Tetahiti will know.'

He raised his head again. He was astonished by this information.

'Who'll tell him?'

'You know who'll tell him.'

There was a silence and he said: 'Is she already playing with him?'

'She will play.'

Omaata went on: 'Tomorrow night. Toumata said: "Tomorrow night. Not later." Toumata said: "She won't wait longer. Tomorrow night, she'll go to the *pa*." '

After that, the silence lasted so long he thought she was asleep. But suddenly, he felt her deep chest rise under his head.

'Why are you laughing?'

'*Aïta, aïta*, man . . .'

She went on: 'You'll see tomorrow why I'm laughing.'

She put her large hand on his head and began gently stroking his hair.

In the morning, Purcell finished cutting out the ribs of the deck. A little before noon the women left, and he went and washed in the lean-to while waiting for Itia to bring his meal. He heard the door of the hut open and shut. He dried himself, came out of the lean-to, and put his trousers on in the sun. He stayed there a moment in the warmth. The heat poured into his muscles; he was hungry; and he felt a sense of happiness and well-being. 'Itia!' he called loudly. There was no answer. He went round by the garden; the sliding doors were wide open. With spreading figure and legs apart, Vaa was sitting in his arm-chair. Her belly jutted from the bark strips of her skirt and rested on her thighs. She was contemplating its curve with moist eyes and was kneading her right breast with her left hand.

'Where's Itia?' Purcell asked, frowning.

'I've brought your fish,' Vaa said, pointing to the table.

'Where's Itia?' Purcell repeated, coming into the room. 'Is she angry?'

'No.'

'Why isn't she here?'

'I've brought your . . .'

'I know, I know,' he said curtly, raising his hand to silence her.

He went to the table and smelt the odour of fish and lemon. He was hungry, but could not make up his mind to start eating.

'Listen, Vaa,' he said patiently. 'Yesterday Omaata. Today Itia. Why hasn't Itia come?'

'I've brought your . . .'

He hit the table with the flat of his hand.

'You're a stupid girl, Vaa.'

'I am! I am!'

He sat down, disarmed. He pulled the plate of fish towards him and began to eat.

'Adamo,' Vaa said after a moment.

He looked at her. One large hand was resting on her thigh, and with the other she was rubbing her breast. There was a placid, animal air about her. But there was a certain anxiety in her eyes.

'Adamo, are you angry?'

Her anxiety was something new. Particularly with regard to himself! It was as if Vaa had suddenly forgotten she was the widow of a great chief.

'I'm not angry.'

She thought this over. A few seconds went by, then she said, squaring her shoulders: 'Today, I. Tomorrow, Itia.'

She seemed to be making a desperate effort to explain things.

'Why you today?' Purcell asked.

Vaa's face grew tender, her lips parted, her teeth gleamed, and she seemed almost beautiful.

'You beat me.'

He looked at her, hesitating to understand.

'Well?' he said, raising his eyebrows.

'Yesterday,' she said, her features transfigured by her ravishing smile. 'Yesterday, you beat me.'

He suddenly understood. No doubt this was why Omaata had laughed last night! 'What sacrifices I make for peace!' The thought amused him. He looked kindly at Vaa and immediately the bright flash of her white teeth appeared. She sat delighted in his armchair and smiled calmly and possessively.

'Tetahiti knows,' she said, when he had finished eating.

'He knows?'

'What I wanted to do. Horoa went to him. She told him.'

'Horoa went to him.' There was no trace of blame. It was a fact. An event one stated. As natural as the coming of rain with the sou'wester. As inevitable.

'When?'

'Last night.'

It was astonishing. Not only had Toumata foreseen that Horoa would go, but she had even foreseen the time-limit to her resistance.

'You are my *tané*,' Vaa went on. 'You must defend me.'

Purcell threw her a glance. Perhaps she was not so stupid, after all.

'If Tetahiti wants to kill you,' he said calmly, 'I shall defend you. But if he only wants to beat you . . .'

She put her large hands on her thighs, and gave a little nod of submission. Yes. Blows. Yes. That was just. As far as a beating was concerned, she did not object.

She got up.

'I'm going now.'

He raised his eyebrows.

'You're going?'

'I'm pregnant,' she said with dignity.

'Yes, yes,' he said, blushing and confused. 'Of course! Of course! Off you go!'

'I'm going,' Vaa repeated and, moving towards the door, the bark strips of her skirt swaying about her wide hips, she went majestically out.

Two days went by without any change in the situation. Tetahiti did not come out of the *pa*, Ivoa remained invisible, and the only new event was the use Horoa made of her nights. She made no attempt to hide her comings and goings. Prancing and pawing the ground, she declared that she had not entered the *pa*, only the lock-chamber. As long as Tetahiti had not removed the Skeleton's head from the pike, she still regarded him officially as an enemy. Meanwhile, of course, she played. But she did not enter his hut and she had not chosen him as her *tané*.

On the 22nd, while going down the steep path to Blossom

Bay, Purcell sprained his ankle. He was massaged and bandaged. And it was decided that he should take his midday meal in the cave of boats and not return to his hut till evening. The *vahinés* built him a little hut of branches on the beach in which he could rest during the hot hours of the day.

Taciturn Itihota brought Purcell's first meal to the beach, and would not allow anyone but herself to help him back to the village. Once in his hut, she lit the *doédoés*, put Purcell into his armchair, propped his leg on a stool, and went and fetched him the book he had left on the bed.

Purcell watched her coming and going with pleasure. Itihota was the only one of the Tahitian women who had not long legs, but the shortness of limb, corrected by the extreme slenderness of her waist, gave the lower part of her body something round and compact which, on reflection, seemed agreeable. Her bust was abundant and her head very small, as if the Creator, having devoted so much to her torso, had to economise on materials when moulding her brain. The eyes, in particular, were striking. Instead of being turned up towards the temples like those of the other *vahinés*, they were straight, slightly protruberant, the sockets shallow, the lids rather narrow, and wonderfully alive. From the cheekbones, her face ran down in a narrow triangle to the chin, and in the middle of its delicate contours, the size of the lips, which though lacking in definition were thick and mobile, seemed almost abnormal, particularly since they scarcely ever opened to utter a word. However, they were constantly moving, swelling or pouting and were quite as expressive as her eyes or the bending of her neck.

Purcell could not concentrate on his book. It was Itihota's silence which embarrassed him. She was sitting on the bed, her back against the wooden wall, her hands open on her knees, one leg tucked under her. She had neither moved nor spoken since Purcell began reading. When he raised his head from his book, he did not meet her eyes. And yet, he felt her there. Silent, motionless, her eyes lowered, she had some extraordinary power of making her presence felt.

Purcell shut the book and limped across to sit beside her.

'What are you thinking about?'

She looked at him, bent her neck, and made a little movement with her head: 'Of you, of course. I'm with you. I think of you.'

'What are you thinking?'

She raised her eyebrows, pouted her lips, assumed a serious expression, and made a little gesture of the shoulder that seemed to mean: 'There's a great deal to think about. A great deal.'

'You don't say anything. Why do you never say anything?'

She gave a fleeting smile. But it was only fleeting; her neck was bent, her eyes questioning and her palms lay open. What was the use of speaking? Couldn't they understand each other perfectly well without it? It was astonishing. She did not utter, and yet he understood her. Words lay behind each piece of miming.

'Well,' Purcell said, 'be kind. Say something to me.'

She raised her eyebrows, pouted doubtfully, and looked serious and a little anxious: Say something? What do you want me to say? There's nothing to *say*.'

'Say something to me,' Purcell went on. 'Anything you like. Something for me.'

She seemed to be gathering her strength, then she raised her rather narrow-lidded eyes, and in a low, grave, veiled voice said with emphasis on each word: 'You are good.'

He looked at her. Itihota's silence was effective. As long as it was maintained, it gave her an air of calm and mystery. And as soon as she opened her mouth, what she said gained an added significance. Purcell leaned over and stroked Itihota's cheek with the back of his right hand. He was astonished. How important to him she had suddenly become and with what an economy of means!

There was a violent knock at the door and a voice said: 'It's Horoa.' Purcell froze, the hand with which he had stroked Itihota's cheek still raised to the level of his shoulder. A few seconds went by, then Omaata's deep voice said through the door: 'You can open, Adamo.'

He got to his feet, but Itihota was quicker. Horoa burst into the room as if she had been catapulted into it from outside. With her mane flowing, her chest aggressive and her eyes gleaming, she began pouring out a flood of words, prancing up and down with such impetuosity that everyone moved out of the way to give her room.

'Sit down, Horoa!' Purcell said in a tone of command.

It was exactly as if he had pulled on the reins. She reared and shook her head; her eyes flashed and she began to neigh.

'É Adamo é!'

'Sit down, Horoa!' Purcell repeated. 'Sit down, please. You're giving me a headache.'

'É Adamo é!'

'You're giving poor Adamo a headache,' Omaata said.

'Sit down!' Itihota said.

Horoa was so surprised to hear Itihota speak that she sat down.

'I've seen Tetahiti,' she said at last, her voice almost calm, 'and he said . . .'

She left the sentence in the air.

'What did he say?'

'Listen, man!' she said with renewed impetuosity, and making as if to get to her feet. 'I'll begin at the beginning. The first night, I told Tetahiti about stupid Vaa. He said nothing. The second night, he said nothing . . .'

She shook her shoulders and threw out her chest.

'Then, last night, I got angry . . .'

She made as if to get up, but was not given time to do so. Omaata stretched out her long arm and put her hand on her shoulder.

'And I said: "Adamo is good. Adamo has prevented Vaa from killing you. And you are in your *pa* with your musket and your heads. And you say: 'Adamo must leave or I'll kill him.' You are not a just man . . ." '

She shook her mane and paused.

'Well?' Purcell said impatiently.

'He listened to me looking very severe. *Aoué*, what an imposing air he has! Even I was rather frightened. Then he said: "Adamo is a *Peritani*. He's cunning." '

Purcell looked away. He was disappointed, chagrined. He was a *Peritani*. Therefore everything he did was bad.

'Then,' Horoa went on, 'I completely lost my temper. And I said: "You stubborn man! Adamo is very good! All the women love him!" But he shrugged his shoulders and said: "The *vahinés* keep their brains between their thighs."'

She paused and tapped the floor repeatedly with her right foot.

'"And you, man," I said, "you sit on your brains!" I said it to his face!' she went on getting up so quickly that Omaata had no time to intervene. 'I wasn't frightened,' she continued, pawing the ground, shaking her mane and jerking her hind-quarters from side to side as if she were about to kick.

Then she began her story all over again from the beginning. Purcell put his elbows on his knees and took his head in his hands. He liked Horoa, but at the moment he could not bear her vitality. It depressed him.

'And then?' Omaata said, seizing Horoa with her enormous hand and forcing her to sit down.

'He slapped my face,' Horoa went on more calmly, as if the contact of her backside with the stool had been sufficient to restrain some of her impetuosity. '*Aoué*, what a slap! I fell to the ground. But I gave it him back,' she went on at once, shaking her mane and making as if to get to her feet.

Omaata forced her to remain seated.

'We fought! We fought! And when we had finished fighting,' she said, lowering her voice and closing her eyes with an expression of modesty, 'we played . . .'

'And then?' Purcell asked in exasperation.

'Afterwards, he was in a good humour. *Aoue!* How his eyes gleamed under the moon! And I said to him: "Adamo is *moa*. Adamo has never killed anyone. And he has never carried weapons." Then he frowned and said: "Woman, you're like the drops of water that fall during the rainy season." But he added: "Ivoa has a musket." And I, she cried with renewed impetuosity and almost raising her hind-quarters from the stool, 'I said: "Man! Ivoa is afraid you'll shoot her *tané*." After that he was silent, then he said: "Adamo must leave, but I shall not kill him. You can tell Ivoa so from the nephew of the great chief Otou . . ."'

Purcell quickly raised his head and looked at Omaata. There was a silence. Without doubt, here was a new development. Of course, Tetahiti had already asserted on May 16th that he would not kill Adamo. But never till now had he told someone to tell Ivoa so while emphasising his family links with her. This time, the promise was much less vague. It had been made to an individual and invoked the name of the great chief Otou. Tetahiti continued to demand Adamo's departure, but meanwhile he was making a veiled proposal to Ivoa for a truce.

Next morning, Omaata came to see Purcell with Itia and Ivoa. There was something she wanted to say. Everything was to be decided in the presence of Adamo and with his participation. On the arrival of the three women, the other *vahinés* went off, showing no annoyance at not being invited to take part in the council.

Purcell said he thought Ivoa's musket should be handed over to Tetahiti at once. They listened to him without interruption and, when he had finished, made no objection. He was therefore surprised to discover little by little that the three women were strongly opposed to this plan. It took him some time to understand their point of view. They expressed it more by silences than by words. They agreed that Tetahiti had made overtures. But he would not have made these overtures if Ivoa had not had a musket. The musket was therefore a bargaining point that must be surrendered only with prudence. It was decided that Itia and Omaata should go as ambassadors to the *pa* and find out in the first place whether Horoa had exaggerated Tetahiti's promises. In any case, it would be a good idea to make him repeat them in front of two further witnesses. After that, negotiations could be opened. In any case, there could be no question of handing Ivoa's weapon over to Tetahiti. It would be broken before his eyes. And he must be persuaded to break his in compensation.

Purcell had not thought of bargaining, and he admired the women's audacity as well as their circumspection. Nevertheless, he objected that it was unlikely Tetahiti would consent to destroy his musket. They agreed. But his refusal would enable them, after much discussion, to lay considerable stress on the concession they were making by abandoning their demand. Purcell realised that they thought it important that the discussions should be long and the negotiations arduous. The longer they lasted, the more Tetahiti's promise not to attempt Adamo's life would acquire solemnity, and the more difficult it would be for him to violate it afterwards.

The negotiations lasted from May 24th to June 6th. The first phase was the most critical. Tetahiti, either from principle or cunning, refused to discuss matters with the women. Only with Adamo. But the *vahinés* pointed out that negotiations with Adamo would result in nothing. Of course, Adamo was quite prepared to hand over the musket. He had wanted to do so from the start. (You know how good he is!) But the musket was not in his possession. It was in theirs! It was therefore with them that he must negotiate. A *tané* discussed things with his wife. Why would not Tetahiti discuss things with them? Besides – 'É Tetahiti é!' – what was he doing at that moment?

As Purcell had foreseen, Tetahiti absolutely refused to relinquish his musket. The *vahinés* became indignant, and threatened to break off negotiations. In fact they did break them off, only to renew them. After another week of argument they yielded, giving every appearance of having been defeated and of abandoning the victory to Tetahiti.

Meanwhile, they made an almost theatrical performance of handing over Ivoa's musket. On June 6th they went in procession to the *pa* at noon. Ivoa, Itia and Omaata were in the lead, followed by Horoa, Vaa and Toumata. Purcell walked in the centre between Avapouhi and Itihota. It had rained during the morning, and the 'belly of the sun', falling on the wet undergrowth, made it almost stifling. It was with relief that Purcell emerged into the clearing round the *pa*. Ten yards from the palisade, just where Cliff Lane turned right towards Blossom Bay, was a young banana tree which, though the British had cut it down three weeks before, was already a vigorous shoot three yards high, crowned with a tuft of big leaves. The little group stopped in its shade, and Omaata, carrying Ivoa's musket in the crook of her right arm, called Tetahiti.

Purcell expected him to remain in the lock-chamber where he would be invisible but able to see everything. But he came out into the open before his door with his three women behind him. As a matter of fact, he did not come near them, and carried his musket with the barrel pointed, as if casually, at Omaata's stomach. However, his expression was serene, and when Omaata pointed her musket at the ground, he immediately followed suit.

Omaata made a speech in favour of peace. When she had finished, she broke the musket against a tree and threw the pieces at Tetahiti's feet. Tetahiti signed that he wished to speak and, after a dignified silence, he complimented the women on their wisdom. He congratulated them on showing themselves so capable. He hoped he would never have any but good relations with them. As for Adamo, he was a *Peritani*. Adamo must leave. But he, Tetahiti, a chief, the son of a chief, had made a promise to the daughter of the great chief Otou, and he would keep that promise. If Adamo left on the date he himself had fixed, his life would till then be taboo.

The word had a considerable effect on the *vahinés*. They had not thought that Tetahiti would go so far. But there could be no doubt about it: he had made Adamo taboo, with a definite reference to Otou, whose earring Adamo was wearing at this moment. Adamo was therefore twice taboo: by the earring which had touched the cheek of the great chief Otou, and by the word of Tetahiti, son of a chief and nephew of the great chief Otou . . .

When the emotion had subsided, Tetahiti continued his speech. He had conquered the oppressors, and therefore considered himself chief of the island. As such and in accordance with custom, he gave himself the taboo. Purcell realised that he alone thought there was something slightly ridiculous about this declaration. It was received with grave noddings of the head and a murmur of assent. Then Omaata spoke. She spread herself in polite phrases from which emerged the fact that she assured Tetahiti of her respect and friendship. Then she reminded them, but without dwelling on it, that according to Tahitian custom the taboo was no longer valid if the chief stained his hands with the blood of his family. This allusion was not lost on anyone. Since Ivoa was Tetahiti's cousin, Ivoa's *tané* was a relative of the new chief.

It was doubtful whether this restriction set upon his own taboo pleased Tetahiti. But he gave no sign. Since he had proclaimed himself king of the island, his face seemed even more severe, his features harder and his stature more imposing. When

Omaata had finished speaking, he renewed his compliments, repeating them in various forms, and when everybody was expecting him to take his leave, he paused and suddenly asked the women to leave him alone with Adamo.

There was a ripple of surprise. Tetahiti imperturbably waited a few seconds, then seeing that the *vahinés* made no move, he handed his musket to Raha and his cutlass to Faïna with deliberate gestures. Then, with elegant slowness, he advanced a few paces towards the women and came to a halt, facing them with empty hands.

Purcell felt there was a good deal of play-acting about all this, but all politics, whether good or bad, had a theatrical element about them. And these were good, since they meant negotiations. The women moved away. And Purcell went forward in his turn, with the painful awareness that he was much smaller than the Tahitian and much less graceful in his movements. As he came out of the cool shade of the banana tree he felt all the weight of the sun on his neck.

There was no sign of arrogance or hostility in Tetahiti's expression. Indeed, his severe features expressed nothing. And when he spoke, Purcell noticed that his voice was less harsh than at their last conversation. However, he spoke in short phrases, without bothering about eloquence. He no longer treated Purcell as a prisoner of war. But, on the other hand, he clearly did not consider him an equal.

'When will the canoe be finished?' he asked after a fairly long moment.

'In less than a moon.'

There was a silence. Purcell felt the sun on his neck. There seemed to be a lead band round his head.

'Do you want help?'

'No. Except to launch it.'

There was another silence. Tetahiti shifted his weight from one leg to another, and Purcell thought: 'Now he is going to speak.'

'Where is Timi?'

Purcell blinked. He was very hot. He felt a pulsing at his temples.

'Dead.'

'He was surprised at his answer. Had he decided long ago, without realising it, to reveal everything to Tetahiti, or was it the effect of his physical discomfort?

'Who killed him?'

'No one. He killed himself with his own musket.'

And seeing that Tetahiti was looking at him in silence, he told him of the accident.

'What did you do with his body?'

Purcell made a vague gesture. He didn't want to bring Omaata into this.

'It's in the sea.'

Tetahiti half veiled his eyes with his heavy lids and said flatly: 'What did you do with the musket?'

This was clearly what interested him. This was why he had wished to talk to him. What was the use of breaking Ivoa's weapon if there was another one somewhere in the island?

'There's a pit in the cave. I threw it into it.'

'Which cave?'

'Mehani's.'

'Good,' Tetahiti said.

He turned on his heel. Purcell immediately went back to the banana tree, leaned his head against the young trunk and closed his eyes. He could see only with difficulty and felt as if his head were about to burst.

He felt a fresh breeze against his face. He opened his eyes. Ivoa was fanning him with a leaf. He smiled at her.

'I'm feeling better.'

He heard a friendly murmur round him. *Aoué,* poor Adamo. He couldn't bear the sun, his skin was so tender. He noticed that the women kept their distance, doubtless to give him air.

'Adamo,' Ivoa whispered, 'what did he ask you?'

'He wanted to know where Timi's musket was.'

'Did you tell him?'

'Yes.'

Ivoa shook her head with admiration: 'It was clever to ask you . . .'

Back in his hut, Purcell scarcely ate. He lay down on the bed beside Ivoa, and fell into a feverish sleep. When he woke up at five o'clock with a stiff neck and an aching head, he decided nevertheless to go down to the beach. Ivoa suggested he should go alone. She felt tired, and thought she was near her time. Avapouhi and Itia would stay with her.

Purcell was surprised to have no one but Itihota to accompany him to Blossom Bay. It looked as if the security instructions had been revoked and his escort dissolved. When he appeared limping along the path that zig-zagged down the cliff, leaning on Itihota's arm, the *vahinés* ran to meet him and he noticed Omaata's absence with surprise.

After bathing, he felt fit enough to go to the cave of the boats and begin work. He was alone. Since the sun was beginning to set behind the island, the *vahinés* remained as close to the sea as they could to enjoy its warmth as long as possible.

He had been working for about an hour when Omaata appeared at the entrance to the cave, her monumental black body outlined against the blue of the sky. Purcell looked up and said discontentedly: 'Where were you?'

His scolding tone delighted Omaata. Swaying her vast hips, she entered the cave and came to a halt on Purcell's right, so close to him that she was almost touching him.

'You're comfortable here,' she said. 'You're in the cool.'

Purcell shrugged and pointed upwards with his saw.

'I'm not comfortable at all. There's a draught.'

It was true. There was a large cleft in the roof of the cave which communicated with the air above, and he felt as if he were working in a chimney. Omaata followed his glance.

'If I wasn't afraid he'd kill you,' she said laughing, 'I'd set fire to the boats. They'd burn very well!'

After a moment, she went on teasingly: 'I've been with Tetahiti.'

Purcell gave no sign of having heard her. Since he said nothing and kept his eyes on his work, she added: 'In your cave.'

He carefully drew a line on one of the ribs, stood back and began sawing. She went on: 'With Faïna, Raha and Taïata . . .'

He looked up at her in surprise.

'He went down into the pit?'

'I held the rope. His women helped me.'

He put the saw down.

P

'He found it?'

She nodded. Purcell looked at her a moment in silence.

'He could have left it in the pit. The water would have rusted it.'

She shrugged her vast shoulders. A dark shadow appeared at the entrance to the cave. They both looked round. It was Tetahiti. For the first time since the fighting had ceased he was carrying his musket slung.

'I'm going to swim,' Omaata said.

She went out. Tetahiti stood quite still, staring at the boat. At last he was seeing Adamo's work with his own eyes. Only the framework was there as yet, but it was clear that Adamo was doing as he had said he would. He was decking the canoe.

Tetahiti went to the other side of the boat, put his hands on the gunwale and looked at Purcell.

'You told me the truth about the musket,' he said slowly.

He paused.

'You also told me the truth about Timi.'

Purcell raised his eyebrows inquiringly and Tetahiti added: 'I found the musket-ball in the cave. It was from one of our muskets, not from one of yours.'

After that, the silence lasted so long that Purcell felt embarrassed. There Tetahiti stood with his heavy eyelids half closed, his severe face and his magnificently athletic body. It may have been only the light of the cave, but Purcell thought the lines on his forehead and each side of his mouth had become deeper. What a contrast there was between his wrinkled, bitter face and his body! Every movement Tetahiti made showed off his vigorous physique to advantage, and whenever Purcell raised his eyes to his face he was struck by the contrast of the middle-aged man's head and the young man's torso.

Tetahiti said not a word and with every second that passed Purcell's embarrassment increased. He himself had nothing to say. He dared not set to work again out of politeness. And as he stood there, on the other side of the boat, saw in hand, looking at Tetahiti and waiting for him to speak, he had a vague feeling of being a prisoner before a judge.

His eyes half closed, Tetahiti stared at Purcell without seeing him. His mind seemed far away, preoccupied with sad thoughts, and Purcell suddenly had the despairing feeling that a whole world separated them. The Tahitian seemed so far out of reach! Not even hard or hating, but distant.

Tetahiti tightened his grasp on the gunwale. It was the only sign of emotion he gave. Purcell looked at his expressionless face with anxiety. There were so many injustices, so many misunderstandings, so many dead men between Tetahiti and himself! Purcell's heart sank. At this moment, he hardly cared that he had to leave the island and face the ocean and perhaps death. The real defeat was this wall between them, the Tahitian's conception of what the *Peritani* were like; his contempt and his condemnation.

'It was at that moment,' Tetahiti said, 'that you should have joined us.'

He opened his eyes wide, surprised at having spoken aloud, and Purcell said: 'At what moment?'

'When the Skeleton killed Kori and Mehoro. If you had joined us, Ropati would have done so too; and Ouili; and Jono. Perhaps the yellow man. We would have killed the Skeleton and the little rat. Only them.'

His lids half closed over his eyes again.

'And now,' he said in a hoarse, thick voice, 'there are all those pikes round my house and I'm not happy. I insult them, but except for those of the Skeleton and the little rat, it gives me no pleasure. There have been too many deaths on the island ... Mine and yours ... Because of you.'

'No, not because of me,' Purcell said. 'Because of injustice.'

'Because of you!' Tetahiti repeated emphatically. 'Because of your *moa* ideas!'

'It is not good to shed blood,' Purcell said firmly.

'Man!' Tetahiti cried, shrugging his shoulders with controlled anger. 'I don't like shedding blood either. But it is good to shed the blood of the oppressor. You know the poem. It is a blood you must give your pigs to drink. It is a blood it is delightful to see flow. It is a blood the earth drinks with considerable pleasure. Injustice, O warriors, is a stinking herb. Extirpate it! ...'

Tetahiti stopped as if he had forgotten the rest, and said in a

P*

faltering voice without looking at Purcell: 'If you'd joined us, Mehani would still be alive.'

Purcell's legs were trembling and he clutched at the boat with his left hand. 'Mehani would still be alive!' He remembered Ouili's angry accusation: 'It's because of you Ropati is dead!' Mehani, Ropati . . . How many deaths were being placed at his door! He felt a sudden, appalling fear. Suppose it were true? Suppose Tetahiti were right? Suppos he had been wrong from the beginning? For a few seconds, he felt his mind reel as if the whole basis of his life had been destroyed.

'The day the fighting ended,' Tetahiti said suddenly, looking straight at Purcell, 'I questioned you about Timi, and you said what was not true. And today you have told the truth. Why?'

'That day,' Purcell said, 'I was afraid you would kill me.'

'You were not afraid,' Tetahiti said at once; and he added with an elegant gesture of the hand: 'How could you be afraid, O *Manou-faïté?*'

Purcell bowed his head. It was a generous tribute.

'And today,' Tetahiti went on, leaning forward and looking at Purcell with an indefinable air of accusing him, 'you told me the truth. Twice. About the musket. And about the death of Timi. Why?'

Purcell hesitated a moment before replying. He was looking into himself. It suddenly seemed to him very important to discover his true incentive. And now that he thought about it, the whole thing was obscure. He could find no single incentive, but several, among which he must choose.

'So that you should have confidence in me,' he said at last.

Tetahiti drew himself up, withdrew his hands from the boat, and his bitter, lined face seemed to become even more stony. He turned and looked towards the sea, as if Purcell's presence no longer interested him.

'What difference can it make to you whether I have confidence in you or not,' he said tonelessly, 'since you're leaving?'

17

On June 16th, an auspicious day after the night of the *Tamatea* (the moon lighting the fish at sunset), Ivoa gave birth to a son and called him Ropati.

The *vahinés*, including Tetahiti's wives, seemed to be living permanently in Purcell's garden. They were waiting patiently for the moment when they could hold the first child to be born on the island in their arms for a few minutes. They did not kiss it. In the Tahitian manner, they sniffed the fine little odour of its body. They were never tired of admiring its colour. Its hair and eyes were as dark as a Tahitian's, but its skin, much lighter than Ivoa's, was of so bright a yellow that it looked as if it was made of gold, like that of an idol.

Purcell knew the cult Tahitians devoted to children, but it had never occurred to him that the whole life of the island would be organised round Ropati. This began with Horoa who declared that fishing was not women's business. Why should she go to the rocks and spend several hours a day there, when she could remain in Adamo's garden looking at Ropati and awaiting her turn to sniff him?

For two days there was no fish. Then Tetahiti summoned Omaata. There were only two men on the island, Adamo and himself. Adamo must go on working on his canoe, but he, Tetahiti, the chief of the island, would feed the mother of Ropati. On reflection, Tetahiti must have realised that it would be awkward to carry his musket while fishing, for two days after this decision, he made his peace with the women. He took the *Peritani*'s heads off the pikes, had them placed in *poini*, and sent the *poini* to the widows so that they could be buried with the bodies. After which, he appeared in Ivoa's garden unarmed, asked to see his little cousin, rocked him competently, and when Omaata at last took the child from his arms, he sat down in a dignified way to wait for his turn to come round again.

Now that the whole population of the island was living in Adamo's garden, it seemed simpler to take meals in common again. However, Adamo was always brought his luncheon in the cave of the boats, and Tetahiti took his dinner in the *pa*. Indeed,

Tetahiti left Ivoa's garden every day a little while before Adamo returned from the beach. One of his women must have been on the lookout, for Purcell varied the hour and the path he took in vain. He never succeeded in meeting him.

Once Tetahiti had removed the heads from the pikes, the *vahinés* considered that reparation had been made for the insults they had suffered. However, Horoa and Toumata let a decent interval of several days go by before they went to live in the *pa*. Together with Raha, Faïna and Taïata, they occupied the ground floor of the big Tahitian hut, the first being reserved for Tetahiti. At night he withdrew there, pulled up the ladder, and shut the trap-door. During the day, the ladder was chained up outside the house, and the chain locked with a padlock that had been borrowed from MacLeod. Another padlock shut the trap-door. These precautions, which shocked no one, made the women suppose that Tetahiti concealed his weapons in the room upstairs.

After Ropati's birth, Purcell went later to work and returned earlier. Had he dared, he would have interrupted the work altogether for several days so as to devote himself to his son. But he feared giving Tetahiti the impression that he was trying to delay his departure from the island.

He had reached the last part of his task, and was screwing the planks on to the ribs. Though he intended to make sure that the cabin was watertight by nailing canvas along the top and sides of the deck, and painting it, he did his best to leave as small a gap as possible between the planks so that the damp, as it swelled the wood, might weld them together. But this needed great precision, and it was difficult to effect, since the wood he was using was extremely hard. The good oak of *The Blossom* had hardened with age, and it was not easy to use a gimlet on it. However, in spite of the difficulties of his work and the fact that he was not putting in so many hours, Purcell thought he would finish within a fortnight. His promise to Tetahiti would be kept. He would leave the island on the date he had fixed.

Ropati was scarcely ten days old when he was given his first sea bathe. To the west of Blossom Bay there was a narrow creek, almost closed from the side of the sea. It opened up into a little bay protected from the wind by the overhanging cliff.

The water was always calm and clear, and at high tide the sea reached a little beach of yellow sand, soft to the foot and a delight to the eye. It was there that the *vahinés* went in almost solemn procession, two of them carrying a container of fresh water with which to rinse the baby after his bathe. They entered the sea up to their chests, stood shoulder to shoulder in a circle and joined hands in the centre so as to form a shallow basin in the water. Ivoa slowly lowered Ropati into it. Chubby, fat and sensual, he immediately began to frolic, while the pious murmurs of the women fell on his little golden body like so many caresses. Purcell watched his son over Itia's shoulders. The other *vahinés* – those who had not yet the privilege of touching Ropati – formed a second circle outside the first. His black curly hair was already abundant, his eyes were lively, though half closed because of the sun, and there was a slight smile on his lips. At times Ropati assumed a sort of devout expression which made the women laugh. But it was restrained laughter, as were the exclamations aroused by his slightest movement. Purcell could feel all the emotion concealed behind their restraint. It was as if there was something religious about this first bathe, as if the child, maternity and the joy of living were all being celebrated at once.

A shadow fell between Purcell and the sun. He looked up. It was Tetahiti. Leaning with both hands on Horoa's shoulders, and a head higher than she was, he was looking down at the child. It was the first time for three weeks that Purcell had been in his presence and his heart began to beat. Tetahiti was immediately opposite him. They could have shaken hands by extending their arms above the double circle formed by the *vahinés*. But Tetahiti appeared not to see him. It was only the exaggerated impassivity of his expression that betrayed the fact that he was fully aware Purcell was looking at him. Purcell waited, staring at Ropati every now and then in the hope that Tetahiti would take the opportunity of glancing in his direction. But he was disappointed. Tetahiti did not raise his eyes once.

Purcell turned away, went out of the sea, climbed the rocky side of the inlet and set off for Blossom Bay. He could hear behind him the women's gentle, happy exclamations gradually growing less with distance. He felt excluded from their happiness, excluded from their lives. He went into the cave of the boats and set to work again, a lump in his throat. Tetahiti's whole attitude said as clearly as words that, as far as he was concerned, the *Peritani* was no longer an inhabitant of the island and that he considered him as having already left.

The next day, Itihota appeared in the cave of the boats precisely at noon, bringing Purcell his meal. He was straightening up to smile at her when he saw Vaa behind her, looking shorter and rounder than ever. He was surprised she should have come. She never came down to Blossom Bay now, because in her condition the path was too steep.

Itihota put the dish of fish and fruit on the boat and said: 'I'm going to bathe.'

She went off at once. Purcell looked after her and then turned to Vaa. She was sitting placidly on a pile of planks.

'Well, Vaa?'

'He beat me,' she said after a moment. 'For what you know about.'

'Hard?'

'Very hard. Then he said: "Come into my house. You will be my *vahiné* and the child you're carrying will be mine." Then, I said: "I must speak to Adamo." And he said: "That's true. It is the custom. Go." '

'I don't know this custom,' Purcell said. 'What must I do?'

'If you want to keep me, you go and see Tetahiti and you say: "Vaa is my *vahiné*." If you don't want to keep me, you say: "All right. Go with him." '

'And which do you prefer?' Purcell asked.

Vaa looked down at the ground.

'Which do you prefer?' Purcell repeated.

Silence.

'Well,' he said with a shrug, 'since he wants you, go with him.'

Vaa raised her eyes and her ravishing smile appeared.

'Are you pleased?'

'*Aoué!* I'm pleased!'

She went on: 'He beat me very hard. Not just little slaps like yours. He's a great chief. I shall be the wife of a great chief.'

'When I've gone,' Purcell said, 'all the *vahinés* on the island will be the wives of a great chief.'

'I shall be the wife of a great chief,' Vaa said obstinately.

Purcell smiled.

'You're a stupid girl, Vaa.'

'I am! I am!'

'And you're very lucky. First the wife of the chief of the big canoe. Then the wife of the chief of the island . . .'

'I am a chief's *vahiné*,' Vaa said with dignity.

Purcell smiled. 'Clearly, her marriage with me was a misalliance,' he thought.

'I'm going now,' Vaa said.

And without even a nod, she left the cave. Purcell looked after her. The *vahiné* of a great chief! And only a few weeks ago, she had wanted to murder him.

Purcell spent all day in the cave of the boats with the harsh smell of the sea in his nostrils. The salt and the iodine penetrated everything, and even the freshly sawn wood very quickly lost its pleasant odour. These were his last days on the island. He tried to concentrate on his task and think of what life at sea with Ivoa would be like. But in the evening, when he returned from Blossom Bay and entered the undergrowth, the smell of the earth was there. The tiarés and the hibiscus flowered six months out of the twelve, but June had brought a profusion of flowers whose names he did not know and which at ten yards he could not distinguish from the multi-coloured little birds that fluttered about them. It was an incredible orgy of scents. The stones of the paths were covered with humus and grass sewn with tufts of short-stemmed little yellow flowers. Purcell walked carefully so as not to tread on them. After the hardness of the sand and the rock, the grass was soft and warm under his bare feet.

A little later, lying in the dark beside Ivoa, Purcell listened to Ropati's breathing. Wonderful Tahitian children! Never a cry. Never a tear. Ropati slept naked in his cradle, as silent as a healthy little animal. Since Tetahiti had given him the taboo, Purcell again slept with the sliding doors wide open, and he was waiting with impatience for the moon to emerge from behind a cloud so that he could see Ropati better.

After a moment, he half closed his eyes. Above his head, the lizards which lived among the pandanus leaves of the roof slid from stem to stem with a furtive rustling that sounded just like a puff of wind from the mountain. Purcell tapped lightly on the wooden wall behind his head. The noise ceased at once. He imagined the slender lizards with their long tails hiding between the leaves, their hearts beating with terror under their green skins. Though they had been living with him, concealed and out of reach, for eight months, they were still afraid.

He must have fallen asleep. He opened his eyes again. The moon was shining. He remembered that he wanted to see Ropati and leaned on one elbow. Ivoa stirred in her sleep. She, too, was naked and was lying quite flat, her long hair spread about her head in a black aureole. She was sleeping with one hand holding a breast swollen with milk and the other lying on Ropati's cradle. Purcell stroked her cheek with the back of his hand. For Ivoa there was from now on but one care, one goal, and everything else was secondary. The meaning of her life was established once and for all, without her having to seek it, as he had to, in anguish and confusion.

He leaned over and once again the smallness of the baby surprised him. It would need at least ten years before he filled the solid oak bed he had made for him. Purcell suddenly wanted to laugh. He was really very small. Very small and very fat. And in the moonlight his body had a warm golden-bronze colour that looked almost ancient, as if the twelve days that had elapsed since his birth had sufficed to give it a patina.

'Are you awake, Adamo?'

Ivoa was looking at him.

'Yes.'

'Are you worried?'

'No.'

There was a long silence. He felt he had answered too curtly and went on: 'I was looking at Ropati.'

She turned her head to the left and gazed at the child with slow and scrupulous attention, as if she were seeing him for the first time. Then she said softly and impartially: '*Aoué*, he's beautiful! '

Purcell gave a little laugh, then he drew close to her, put his cheek against hers and they looked at Ropati together.

'He's beautiful,' Ivoa repeated.

After a moment, Purcell let his head fall back on the pillow of leaves. He felt sad and weary. In the silence that followed, the furtive movements among the palm leaves began again.

'What are you thinking about?' Ivoa said.

'The lizards.'

She laughed.

'But it's true!' he said, turning his head quickly towards her.

'What are you thinking about?'

'I like them very much. They've got little legs and they run. They don't crawl. It's disgusting to crawl.'

He went on: 'They're nice. I should have liked to have tamed them.'

'Why?'

'So that they'd no longer be frightened of us.'

He went on: 'I had a plan to tame them. But it's too late now.'

She looked at him in silence, but since she had her back to the moon he could scarcely see her face. A long moment went by. They listened to the lizards.

'It was of the sliding-doors I was most proud,' he said suddenly in a choking voice, as if he were going back to a subject he had already mentioned.

There was another silence, and she said in a low tender voice, slipping her hand into his: 'And the armchair?'

'The armchair was easier. But remember how I worked on the doors.'

'Yes,' she said, 'you worked very hard.'

She fell silent and her breathing altered. Purcell put out his hand and passed it over her face. She was weeping.

He touched her cheek with the tips of his fingers. She at once raised herself on an elbow and waited. It was the rite. He gathered her long spreading hair into a single strand and threw it back on to the pillow, and slipped his arm beneath her neck.

'Are you sad?' he said in a low voice, his face close to hers.

After a moment she replied: 'For Adamo. Not for Ivoa.'

'Why not for Ivoa?'

He went on tonelessly: 'It was a fine hut.'

She put her head in the hollow of his shoulder and said:

'Where Adamo goes, I go. My hut is Adamo.'

'My hut is Adamo!' In what a tone of voice she had said it! A few seconds went by, then he thought: 'Mehani, Ouili, Ropati. Dead. Perhaps after all it's better to leave the island . . .' He shook his head irritably. No, why lie to oneself, he did not really think that, even with all its dead the island was still the island, the only place in the world, the only time in his life in which he had been happy.

He drew back a little to try to make out Ivoa's features.

'Tetahiti said: "When the Skeleton killed Kori and Mehoro, that was when you should have joined us." '

Since she did not answer, he raised her head with his right hand and looked into her eyes. But only the edge of her hair caught the light. He could see nothing but the dark of her irises showing dully against the misty white of her eyes.

'What do you say, Ivoa?'

'All the Tahitians thought that.'

'And what did you think?'

There was no answer.

'What did you think, Ivoa?'

'Adamo is my *tané*.'

She also thought he had been wrong. Once again, he felt alone. Divided from everyone. Blamed by everyone. And struggling with all his might not to feel guilty. He was silent and felt his own silence to be something sad and bitter into which he was sinking.

'Man,' Ivoa said, 'if it were all to do again? . . .'

He was astonished. That Ivoa should ask a question! And what a question! Her reserve, her prudence, her reluctance to discuss important matters, everything he knew of her character contradicted in a few words . . . But perhaps she was merely making an effort to help him?

'I don't know,' he said at last.

He was surprised by his own reply. It was scarcely three weeks since he had again justified his abstention to Tetahiti. But since then doubt must have been burrowing in him like a mole. And there it suddenly and flagrantly was, not as a state of thought you repel, but as an opinion you express.

He disengaged his arm, got up, walked haphazardly about

the room, then went and leaned against the sliding-doors and looked out into the moonlit garden. He had killed Timi, yes, he had killed him, only the intention counted, and since that murder he was no longer clear as to where he stood. From time to time he told himself that the life of a man – whatever his crimes – was sacred. But it was precisely the word 'sacred' which now seemed to lack sense. Why 'sacred'? To permit him to commit further crimes?

This thought affected him profoundly. He went out into the garden and staggered a few steps like a drunken man. The sweat was trickling down his forehead and from his armpits. He had said: 'I shall not kill!' He had thought to choose an exemplary attitude. And it was true, it was exemplary! But the example was useless. No one could afford to follow it. Wherever one was, there was always a criminal to be destroyed: Burt on *The Blossom*, MacLeod on the island . . . and Timi! 'And I killed Timi. No one has been able to follow my "example". Not even myself.'

'Adamo!' Ivoa called.

He returned to the house, staggering as if he had received a shock. He had the same feeling of nausea and bewilderment as on the day Ouili had struck him in the face. He lay down beside Ivoa, and as he was about to slip his arm under her neck, he automatically gathered her hair into a single strand and threw it back on to the pillow.

'Are you not content?' Ivoa said.

In Ivoa's reticent language, 'Are you not content?' meant: 'Are you unhappy?'

Purcell shook his head, and since she continued to look at him, said: 'I'm anxious about Ropati.'

'Why?'

'In the canoe. When we're at sea.'

'I've thought about it,' Ivoa said.

She went on: 'We must give him away.'

He sat up and looked at her in amazement. 'Give him away!'

'Yes,' she said calmly, tears pouring down her cheeks.

'Give Ropati away!' Purcell cried.

'Before we leave.'

There was a striking contrast between her tears and the calm of her voice.

'I've thought about it,' she replied.

'What have you thought?'

'Perhaps in the canoe the wind will fail. And one must eat every day. And one day there's nothing left. And Ivoa has no more milk . . .'

After a moment, he said: 'And who will feed Ropati on the island?'

'Vaa.'

'We're leaving in two weeks' time.'

'No,' Ivoa said. 'Not before Vaa gives birth. I asked Tetahiti.'

He said drily: 'You've arranged everything?'

'Is Adamo angry?' she said, pressing herself against him and raising her head to look into his eyes.

'Yes.'

'Why?'

'You make a decision. And everyone knows about it except me.'

'No one knows,' she said quickly, 'except Tetahiti. And I had to ask Tetahiti before speaking to you. And it is not Ivoa who decides,' she added with a movement of her whole body against his, 'it's her *tané.*'

He realised that his anger was pointless, but he could not master it. He disengaged himself from Ivoa's embrace, got up and paced up and down the room. She was right, she was a thousand times right: a month old baby in a boat! The cold, the weather, hunger . . .

'To whom do you want to give him?' he asked harshly.

'To Omaata.'

There was nothing he could say against that either. His legs felt weak. He sat down on the edge of the sliding doors and leaned his head against the wooden jamb.

'Adamo,' Ivoa's voice said behind him.

He made no reply.

'Adamo!'

He could not answer. She was brave and she was admirable, but at this moment, obscurely and absurdly, he was angry with her. 'As if the whole thing were not my fault!' he thought suddenly in an agonizing flash of remorse and despair. 'The deaths. The departure. They're all my fault.'

He heard her sobbing quietly behind him. He got up and went back to lie down beside her.

As the time for Purcell's departure drew near, a certain discontent became apparent among the *vahinés*, including those who lived in the *pa*. During the long afternoons in Ivoa's garden, tongues wagged even in Tetahiti's presence. No one, of course, dared address him directly, but the complaints were always the same: Adamo and Ivoa were about to leave for Tahiti, and they, poor *vahinés*, would remain behind with only one *tané* among ten of them. *Aoué!* Tahiti! At Tahiti there was a lagoon, and it was never cold as it was here, and the men were kind and never resentful.

This theme was repeated every day in different forms till the moment came when several *vahinés* – among them Horoa – asked Purcell if they might go with him to Tahiti in the second boat. He refused. The second boat was in bad condition. Nor was the third any better. The *vahinés* did not know how to sail a boat. And, in any case, he himself had but a small chance of arriving there.

The dream of seeing Tahiti again was therefore nipped in the bud. Their consternation was so lively that it became a real grievance, and since Adamo – poor Adamo! – could not be blamed, the afternoon conversations took on an added pungency. Another theme appeared: Tetahiti's hypocrisy. The chief dared not kill Adamo, because Adamo had done nothing, but he was sending him to drown at sea with his wife. This view of the facts was developed with such ingenuity and such perfidy that Tetahiti became exasperated, got up without a word, went home and did not reappear in Ivoa's garden next day.

When he returned, he was fawned upon to such an extent he thought his firmness had made the women see reason. But the next day the offensive began all over again. At first it took on a more veiled form: pretty little Ropati, what a charming complexion he had! The Tahitians were too black, the *Peritani* too pale, Ropati was the right colour. *Aoué*, poor *vahinés*, now it was all over: only Ivoa and Vaa would have golden-coloured children!

The next day, Ropati was again praised for the colour of his skin which would henceforth be so rare in the island, but this particular vein had already been over-exploited the day before and was on the point of becoming exhausted, when Itihota emerged from her silence with a new idea. She described Adamo's and Ivoa's life in the canoe and the dangers they would have to run. This theme was elaborated. And though Adamo was at that moment high and dry in the cave at Blossom Bay, and Ivoa in process of feeding Ropati, they were both talked of as already dead. *Aoué!* May *Eatua* protect us! Dead, kind Adamo, who had never done anyone any harm! Dead, gentle Ivoa, daughter of the great chief Otou and niece of Tetahiti's father!

There was much emphasis, of course, on family ties which should have preserved her and her *tané* from this stupid death, and on this basis there was some renewal of the theme of hypocrisy. But Omaata thought it dangerous and cut it short.

The elegy on the deaths of Adamo and Ivoa, which were now considered certain, lasted two afternoons. Then Itia discovered a new subject: Adamo was going to leave. Tetahiti would be the only man on the island and what would happen to the poor *vahinés* if Tetahiti happened to fall ill and die? It at once became clear that disease lay in wait for Tetahiti every moment of his life, and that the ten *vahinés* would very shortly become widows without a single *tané* to feed or protect them. They therefore mourned Tetahiti in his presence. He was even eulogised. And his future widows lamented their fate once he should be dead. This new theme was a peculiarly telling one and it was being exploited to the utmost, when everything was spoilt by Vaa. Pleased with her new *tané* and her position, Vaa had taken no part in her companions' complaints. But the idea that she might become a widow without any hope of marrying again suddenly impinged on her. She was shattered by it. *Aoué,* if Tetahiti died, what would become of Vaa? It was clear that her prospects were being neglected and that she was being wronged. Adamo's departure deprived her of an alternative *tané*. For, after all, a *tané* who was not a great chief was better than no *tané* at all.

Her reaction was immediate. She marched over to Tetahiti,

stood boldly in front of him on her short legs, and supporting her belly with both hands, burst into vehement reproaches.

Tetahiti, who was sitting on the grooves of the sliding-doors, holding Ropati in his arms, did not even raise his eyes. When Vaa had finished, he got up, handed the baby to its mother, slapped Vaa without brutality, turned to the women and spoke with determination. He had made a decision about the *Peritani*, and nothing they could say would make him change his mind. He knew very well that it was easier to make an octopus let go its hold than silence a woman. But if the *vahinés* continued to talk nonsense in his presence, he would go and live alone in the mountain and come back only to make certain that Adamo had left.

This threat silenced them and the silence lasted. But there were still glances, sighs, tears and sad shakings of the head. And, at least when Tetahiti was there, the women used them without restraint.

A week after the incident provoked by Vaa, Purcell saw Tetahiti come into the cave of the boats. He did not greet him, walked quickly round the boat and said without looking at him: 'Is the canoe finished?'

Purcell was irritated by his abruptness. He took a rasp from the tool-box and began to round off the gunwale. After a moment, he saw out of the corner of his eye that Tetahiti was looking at him, and said curtly: 'Nearly.'

'What's lacking?'

'I paint, I put on the canvas, I paint the canvas, and it's finished.'

There was a silence in which nothing could be heard but the little patient noise of the rasp on the wood.

'Why the canvas?'

'To prevent the water coming in.'

Tetahiti passed his hand over the deck.

'But can the canoe sail like this?'

'Yes.'

There was a silence and Tetahiti went on: 'Good. We'll try it out tomorrow.'

'We?' Purcell said, raising his head and staring at him in astonishment.

'You and I,' Tetahiti said impassively.

He turned on his heel, went to the entrance of the cave, said over his shoulder: 'Tomorrow at high tide,' and disappeared.

When he got home that night, Purcell said nothing of this to the *vahinés,* and he guessed from their behaviour that Tetahiti had said nothing either. But when night had fallen and everyone had gone home, he went to Omaata's with Ivoa.

Two *doédoés* – one in front of each open porthole – were burning to keep the *toupapahous* away, but this was mere habit; the moon made everything as bright as day. Omaata was fast asleep with Itia, like a baby, in her arms. Her massive form, crushing the bed beneath her, gave her an appearance of sleeping more deeply than anyone else.

Purcell touched her cheek and she at once opened her eyes. Though they were in proportion to her stature and the size of her face, Purcell was surprised as always by their immensity.

'Adamo,' she said with a smile.

Itia woke up, looking round and slender, stared at them, blinked, and suddenly jumped out of bed and ran to embrace Adamo. She was as happy as a child that Adamo should suddenly have appeared when she was not expecting to see him.

Purcell told them of his interview with Tetahiti.

'Perhaps,' Itia said, her eyes still bright with the pleasure of the unexpected, 'perhaps he's going in the canoe with you to throw you overboard and come back and say: "It was an accident." '

'I'd already thought of that,' Ivoa said.

Omaata raised herself on an elbow, and all her muscles and massive sculptural curves became animated.

'He gave you the taboo.'

'He's cunning,' Ivoa said.

Omaata shook her heavy head.

'He gave the taboo.'

'Perhaps,' Itia said, 'he wants to see if the canoe is a good one. If it is a good one, he'll take it and leave for Tahiti.'

Having said this, she laughed, and her laughter fluttered about the room like a bird. Then she ran to throw herself on Purcell's neck again. But this time she also embraced Ivoa, who heartily returned her caresses, though her face remained grave.

'Tetahiti is not wicked,' Omaata said, staring at Ivoa with her enormous eyes.

'Perhaps he'll kill Adamo,' Ivoa said.

'No,' Itia said, going back to the bed and sitting on Omaata's feet without the latter seeming to be aware of it. 'He's angry, because Itia said: "You're sending Adamo and your cousin Ivoa in the *Peritani* canoe, and they'll be drowned." He wants to see whether the canoe is a good one. He does not want to be ashamed in his heart.'

'The child's right,' Omaata said. 'Tetahiti is very humiliated by the things we've said.'

'Perhaps he's curious,' Purcell said. 'He's never been in a little *Peritani* canoe with a deck.'

'Perhaps he'll kill you,' Ivoa said.

'You're becoming a real *Peritani*,' she said with a smile. 'You worry all the time.'

'They'll be at sea,' Ivoa said. 'The taboo was given on the island.'

Purcell could see from Omaata's expression that the argument carried weight. He suddenly remembered that a taboo lost its force away from the place in which it was given.

'Ask Tetahiti if you can go in the canoe too,' Omaata said after a while.

'I'll ask him,' Ivoa said, and her expression relaxed.

The next morning, as soon as Tetahiti had assembled the *vahinés* on the beach to launch the canoe, she asked him and was met with a curt refusal.

Since Blossom Bay faced north and the wind that morning was south-west, there was no surf and the launching was easy. Purcell handed over the helm to Tetahiti and hoisted the sails, but since the boat was under the lee of the island, they merely shivered. Purcell went aft to the cockpit and put the stern oar in place to haul off Cape Horoa. This was the name they had given to the steep rugged cliff that separated Blossom Bay from Rope Beach on the east. It owed its name to a dangerous fall Horoa had had at the beginning of May when trying to collect terns' eggs.

As soon as they had doubled the point, the sails suddenly filled, the rigging vibrated, and the boat leapt forward. Tetahiti gave Purcell the helm and sat down in front of the cabin with his back turned. The breeze was fresh and the boat heeled considerably. Purcell paid out mainsheet and headed out to sea with the wind astern. The boat steadied and ran before it through the swell.

Looking round, Purcell could see the group of women on the beach of Blossom Bay. It was already so small that he could no longer distinguish their faces nor the tall figure of Omaata. Perhaps they were waving to him, but he could not see it. The island itself was no bigger than an islet crowned with vegetation. 'That's how it will look to me,' Purcell thought, 'when I leave.' The sky had become rather overcast and the sun was hidden. For the first time he felt the spray damp on his naked back. He looked at the wake, pulled out his watch, and glanced at the island again. She was doing seven or eight knots. At this speed, the island would be no more than a black dot on the immensity of the horizon in less than an hour.

While Purcell was looking back at the island, he felt the boat yaw and gave helm to port, then he looked at the bows and corrected to starboard. The wind had freshened, the troughs between the waves were smaller, and the waves themselves higher.

Tetahiti turned. He did not turn altogether, but offered Purcell his profile and the corner of his left eye.

'Ivoa told me you regret it.'

He opened his mouth wide and spoke loud because of the wind, but even then Purcell could scarcely hear him.

'Regret what?'

'Not having joined us.'

He had not said that. Not quite. He had said: 'I don't know.' But essentially it was true. He did regret it. As Tetahiti asked the question, he knew he regretted it.

'Yes,' he said, 'it's true.'

He stood quite still with his hand on the helm and looked at Tetahiti's profile. Ivoa was usually so discreet . . . What was she hoping for? What did it all mean? These questions about the past? The two of them trying out the boat? It was absurd. Since last night everything had been queer and abnormal. It was all happening as if in a dream, inconsequently, disjointedly, incoherently.

A few seconds went by and Tetahiti moved with a deliberate slowness that fascinated Purcell. First he passed his legs over the thwart as if he wanted to face the *Peritani*, and he did face him, but only after a long delay, as if his head were reluctantly following the direction of his body. The spray lashed him, and Tetahiti screwed up his lined and wrinkled face. Between his heavy lids, the dark pupils glowed against the whites of his eyes with embarrassing intensity. He sat there with his austere head resting on his hands and his elbows on his long muscular legs – so smooth and dark that they seemed to be sheathed in black – faced Purcell and gazed into his eyes.

'Adamo,' he said gravely, 'if a big *Peritani* canoe came to the island and did us an injury, what would you do?'

'What sort of injury?' Purcell asked.

'Like the Skeleton,' Tetahiti said in a dull voice.

There was a silence and Purcell said: 'I'd fight them.'

'With arms?'

'Yes,' Purcell said decidedly.

He added: 'But there's only one musket left.'

'There are two muskets,' Tetahiti said.

There was a dark gleam in his eye and he added triumphantly: 'I hid Mehani's.'

He went on in a low, controlled voice, as if he were making a violent effort to dominate his excitement: 'You'd take Mehani's musket?'

'If they did us an injury, yes.'

'You'd fire at them with Mehani's musket?'

'Yes.'

'You, a *Peritani*, would fire on *Peritani*?'

'Yes.'

There was a silence and, since Tetahiti said nothing further, Purcell said: 'Why did you want to come with me in the canoe?'

Tetahiti did not appear shocked by so direct a question. He replied without hesitation: 'To see if it was good.'

'And if it was bad?'

'It's not bad,' Tetahiti said curtly.

Purcell swallowed and tried to catch the Tahitian's eye. But he could not. Tetahiti had lowered his lids as one shuts a door.

After a moment, he passed his legs over the thwart, pivotted on his buttocks, turned his back on Purcell and said over his shoulder: 'There's a lot of water in the canoe.'

Purcell glanced down at the gratings. For some little while the boat had been shipping water. It was not a matter for concern, but they would have to bail.

'Take the helm,' Purcell said.

Tetahiti got to his feet without a word. As he took the helm, he accidentally touched Purcell's hand, but did not look at him.

Purcell unhooked a bailer from under the thwart in the cockpit, lifted up the gratings and started bailing. So as to work the faster he scarcely looked up, but from the whistling of the rigging above him, he judged the wind had freshened again.

He felt Tetahiti touch him on the shoulder. He stood up.

'Look!'

The island was scarcely larger than a rock on the horizon, and behind it, blocking off the whole of the south at sea level, lay a long inky black cloud. Purcell took a look round. The sea was running high and choppy. The waves moving north were now being taken in the flank by others from the south-west and were breaking heavily.

'The sou'wester!' Purcell cried, dropping the bailer.

He realised he had spoken in English. He took the helm from Tetahiti and cried to him through the wind: 'The jib!' Then, as Tetahiti hurried forward, he hauled in the main-sheet and put the helm to port. The boat came up into the wind, and Purcell bore away to diminish the impact of the wind on the sails before edging closer to the wind again.

It was the first time since *The Blossom* had hove in sight of the island that Purcell had seen the terrible sou'wester replace a south-easterly wind without warning. Tetahiti was battling with the jib-sheets. Purcell shouted to him: 'Closer-hauled!' Tetahiti obeyed and, coming aft, replaced the floorboards and the bailer under the thwart.

The boat was set on a good course for the island, but was pitching badly in the chaotic sea and, though carrying very little sail, heeling dizzily. Purcell was sitting on the weather side and Tetahiti came and sat beside him, as if their combined weight could right the boat. The gunwale was completely disappearing under the sea and, leaning backwards, Purcell could see half the hull totally out of the water, while the base of the keel and, at times, the short keel itself appeared through the green transparent sea. Purcell felt as if the boat, as she leaned almost horizontally across the sea, kept her equilibrium only by a miracle and that the least extra push would capsize her into the waves.

He pushed his hand a few degrees to starboard to spill some of the wind out of his sail and handed the helm to Tetahiti, shouting to him through the wind: 'Hold her as she goes!' He plunged down into the cabin and returned with two lines. He tied one round Tetahiti's waist, the other round his own, and made the other ends fast to the stanchion of the thwart.

He took over the helm, brought her up a little, and the boat began to heel again. She rose splendidly to the seas, but shipped great quantities of water. The fore-deck was constantly swept by it, and the foam eddied round the foot of the mast as high as the base of the boom. In spite of the protection of the deck, the water in the cockpit had already reached the bailer.

The sea was becoming continually more confused. It was breaking and foaming in all directions with the feverishness of water boiling in too small a cauldron. But it was fortunately not yet very high, the sky was still clear and, when the boat was balanced for a moment on the crest of a wave, Purcell could see the island. Then she fell into the hollow, and he was blinded by spray as he clutched the helm with his left hand and the gunwale with his right.

Shivering with cold, the water streaming from his naked torso, the wind cutting his face and his hands stiff and blue, Purcell found it a continual effort to regain his breath between two clouds of spray. He had never known so violent a storm on board so small a boat. It was one thing to encounter bad weather from *The Blossom*'s quarterdeck, but quite another to be at sea level and amid the waves, indeed almost as much beneath them as on top of them.

Tetahiti leaned towards him, almost pressed his lips to his ear and shouted, emphasising each word: 'The canoe! . . . Sailing her too hard . . . !'

And he made the gesture of taking in sail. Purcell nodded. It was true. He was driving the boat like a madman. It was crazy to sail in this wind with all his canvas set. But he had no choice.

He shouted back: 'Reach . . . the island . . . before the cloud.'

At the same instant, a great cloud of spray hit him violently in the face, filling his mouth and eyes, and throwing him backwards. He emerged from it, spitting, coughing, half-drowned, his hand clutching the helm, and feeling Tetahiti's shoulder against his own.

He caught sight of the island again. They were tearing through the water, but it had scarcely grown larger since he had gone about. It was hopeless. Drive the boat as he might, it would take him another hour to reach it. And he would not reach it! The sky was already growing dark and the sea turning green. The storm would get there first.

He saw a big wave coming and thought: 'If it doesn't break, I'll see the island.' The bow rose to the wave, the horizon appeared and the black cloud was everywhere. The island had disappeared from view.

'The island!' Purcell shouted, seizing Tetahiti convulsively by the arm.

They had set out without chart, compass or sextant. If they sailed past the island in the dark, they had no means of finding it again. They might wander for days and days in the mist looking for it. Without water, food or clothes! It was the only island within a radius of five hundred sea miles.

'The island!' he shouted again.

Tetahiti stared at him wide-eyed. And for several seconds they gazed stupidly at each other, shoulder to shoulder, their faces nearly touching. There was a strident whistling of wind. Purcell saw the sea to port coming up to meet him. Instinctively, he put the helm over. The mast heeled to within a yard of the water, then slowly came upright. Head to the wind, the sails began flapping violently, and Purcell stared at them, trembling, deprived of thought, unable to move a muscle. It had all happened so quickly. He had only just realised that they had nearly capsized.

'The sails!' Tetahiti shouted in his ear.

And once again he made the gesture of taking in sail. He was right. It was crazy to have waited so long. Purcell handed the helm to Tetahiti, crawled along the deck with the safety-line fast about his waist, and let go the halyards.

He threw out the sea anchor, and spent ten painful minutes in the spray and the pitching, rolling the main-sail round the boom and making it fast. But he was acting and it was all clear; it was almost routine. They were now under bare poles, and the boat was bobbing like a cork to its anchor; they were safe. A great cloud of spray hit him, Purcell hung on tight, sneezed, and thought suddenly: 'Drift!' He could not allow the boat to drift. The sou'wester might last for days. And even if it carried them to the north-east for only a few hours, they would never find the island again. They must keep way on, cost what it might, or at least sufficient to counteract the drift and keep them more or less in the same place.

Purcell crawled back to the cabin, and brought up a small jib. He called Tetahiti. Lashed to the mast, Tetahiti would have to hold him firmly by the safety-line, while he took in the big jib, made the little sail fast to the halyard and bent it to the jib-stay. It was madness to attempt such an operation in the middle of a storm, but Purcell succeeded. When at last he hoisted the sail and returned to the helm, his hands were torn, and he had been so battered by the sea that his head felt empty and bruised.

Bewildered and with the wind whistling in his ears, Purcell stared at the bows without seeing them. The resistance of the helm awakened him. He looked at the little jib. It was strained to bursting point; but it held! It was even making the boat heel. They were making way, gaining on the waves.

He realised he was sitting on the big jib he had just taken in, and it occurred to him to wrap himself in it. He signed to Tetahiti and both of them, fighting the wind that tore it from their hands, succeeded in making a cloak of the sail so that it covered their heads, shoulders and backs. For greater safety, they passed a lashing through the eyelets, pulled it tight and made it fast to the thwart. Purcell had to be able to see to steer, and his eyes and left arm were free of the jib. Tetahiti, on the other hand, disappeared completely within the canvas cage. They were huddled together, like two dogs in a kennel, soaking, shivering with cold.

After a moment, Purcell felt Tetahiti pass his arm behind his neck, place his hand on his left shoulder and his cheek against his.

'Good!' Tetahiti said in his ear.

'What?' Purcell shouted.

Lightning flashed in front of the bows and he closed his eyes. 'The jib! Good!'

Tetahiti must be shouting too, but all he could hear was a thin, distant voice amid the immense cataclysm.

Purcell looked at the jib. It was true, it was 'good'. It had been neither torn nor carried away. Their lives depended on this pocket handkerchief, and it was holding. The boat was sailing into the teeth of the sou'wester. Purcell felt a surge of hope.

'It's holding!' he shouted at the top of his voice, turning to Tetahiti.

Tetahiti then did a surprising thing. He smiled. Purcell saw it distinctly within the shadow of the canvas hood covering his head. 'What a good chap he is!' Purcell thought gratefully. At the same instant, it suddenly became clear to him that sailing as close as possible to the wind was not good enough. It could not be so. They had little sail and little keel. The boat was making way, but crabwise. She was making as much leeway as she was headway. If they continued like this, they ran the risk of passing to the east of the island. Why had he not thought of it earlier? Since he was drifting to the east, he must make up to the west – tack. Short tacks. The shorter they were, the less danger there was of missing the island.

'Tetahiti!' he shouted.

Tetahiti removed his cheek from his and looked at him.

'We must do . . . like this!' Purcell shouted.

And resting his knee against the helm, he freed his left hand and made the gesture of going about. Tetahiti nodded and shouted: 'I'll go!'

As if pleased to have something to do, he immediately slipped out from under the canvas cage, and crawled forward to cast off the jib-sheet. Purcell put the helm over and, to his relief, the boat obeyed and went about. It was splendid! She must be making way, since she had enough to go about.

There was a blinding sheet of lightning and Purcell saw Tetahiti. He was having difficulty in making the jib-sheet fast. Purcell thought anxiously: 'As long as he doesn't haul on it too hard!' He put the helm down to take the wind out of the sail for a second or two to help him.

Tetahiti came back to him, dripping with water, looking spectral in the strange light, the top of his head curiously phosphorescent.

Purcell took out his watch, and waited for another flash to read the dial. Since he could see nothing, the time each tack lasted would have to be fixed arbitrarily. Ten minutes to the west. Six to the east. The tack to the west must be longer, because there was no danger of it taking them farther from the island.

They fell into the routine of tacking; time passed; the storm grew no more violent; they were merely horribly uncomfortable and that was all. The cold, the spray in their faces, the blinding flashes of lightning, the crazy pitching of the hull – there was nothing to be done but wait and suffer. The boat was shipping a lot of water, and Purcell decided to bail. They took it in turns and, after thirty minutes' hard work, succeeded in bringing the water nearly down to the level it had been before the storm. Purcell made fast the bailer and slipped under the canvas beside Tetahiti, who placed his arm round his shoulder and his cheek against his. Purcell took out his watch. It was four hours since they had left the island.

He was abominably cold. His hands were blue, and he could hear Tetahiti's teeth chattering against his cheek.

He turned to him and shouted in his ear: 'Go under the deck!'

Tetahiti shook his head. The lightning ceased and it was an enormous relief not to have to listen to the shattering noise of the thunder. Though the sou'wester continued to whistle and the waves to break, for a minute or two Purcell had an extraordinary feeling of peace and silence. Then it disappeared and he was listening to the wind again.

Tetahiti put his mouth to his ear and cried: 'Anything to eat?'

'No!' Purcell shouted back.

There was a gap in the cloud and the visibility improved,

though it was no more than a cable's length. Purcell tired his eyes trying to see a shape in the mist that might be the island.

He suddenly felt horribly afraid. Suppose they had *already* passed the island? Suppose the island was already behind them? Suppose they were drawing farther away from it with each tack? His heart began beating violently and, though he was numbed with cold, sweat trickled down his forehead.

'Tetahiti!'

A cloud of spray hit him in the face and trickled down inside the canvas. When he could open his eyes again, he saw Tetahiti looking at him. The cold had marked and discoloured his face, but his expression was as firm as ever.

'The island . . . ahead of us?'

'Ahead!' Tetahiti cried without hesitation.

'Why?'

'Ahead . . .'

Tetahiti opened his mouth again, but a violent gust blew his words away and Purcell could only catch scraps of them.

'Much . . . anxiety . . . head . . . alive!'

Purcell looked at the jib again, corrected his course, and stared into the dusk. If only he could see through the mist! There ought to be a special sense to enable one to guess the presence of the places one loved. It was a terrifying thought that they might easily pass within a cable's length of the island and miss it.

He clasped Tetaihti's hand hard. He was right. They were alive. 'It ought to be enough.' The whites were always imagining the future. How much better not to think, to accept the present, and discard one's anxieties!

Everything grew dark. Purcell distinctly saw the black cloud bear down on them. Preceding it, came the rain again, falling in close vertical lines like the lances of an attacking army. The whole sky seemed to open and the rain poured down on the boat with incredible violence, the drops striking their heads like thousands of needles and beating on the deck with a malevolent rattling. For a moment, the pitch-darkness became so sinister and inspissated that the whole world was utterly submerged in it. Then the dark ceiling of cloud grew lighter, the world became grey and woolly, and visibility extended to half a cable's length.

At the same time, a wan cruel light spread over the sea and the green hollows of the waves assumed a repulsive aspect that froze Purcell. Little by little, the ceiling above their heads, which was so low that it seemed to touch the stem when it rose to a wave, split up into clouds of a greenish, poisonous grey. The masthead became phosphorescent, and the centre of the storm burst over them.

The lightning played about them with a rolling and roaring of thunder, casting an intermittent and intolerable white light over the boat, before striking the waves, which assumed green and diabolical shapes against the dark background. The lightning flashes rained down by the hundred in an infinite variety of shapes, broken arrows, zigzags, paraphs, sinuous lines, spiders' webs and huge balls of fire, leaving incandescent tracks on the sea, zones of blood and flame. Purcell was shivering not only with cold but with fear, and he could see a few inches from him – not merely grey, but positively white – the Tahitian's horror-stricken face.

Purcell's face was trickling with water, he felt his features contract, and he began to groan. The appalling cacophony was out of all measure even with what they had had to bear till now. The wind had not freshened, it had even perhaps grown less, as if the rain falling in cataracts had deadened it. But the noise! The noise! It was driving him out of his mind! Lightning flashed on every side at once, as if sky and sea were ablaze, and Purcell had a horribly real and precise impression that the world was coming to an end. The claps of thunder succeeded each other in a terrifying crescendo. They were like mountains collapsing, huge land-slides, a drying up of rivers and yawning fissures cutting towns in half.

Purcell could not longer bear the white, glacial flashing of the lightning. He felt his reason giving way. He put his head under the canvas, and shut his eyes. But strange visions pursued him. He saw the world adrift among the stars and, as it spun, the wild seas submerged the land, whole pieces of continents drifted away, bearing the terrified inhabitants on their thin crusts of mud. The planet was falling apart like a ball of damp sand cracked by the sun. It split into fragments that rained into space, hurling trees, men, and houses pell-mell. Then the stars went out one by one, the sun began to resorb the earth and, reduced to a fiery nucleus, it burst with a gigantic explosion.

Through the canvas, Purcell could feel the rain on his head and he had the ridiculous feeling that his skull was going to break . . . He could not stop seeing the earth cracked, gaping and pulverized . . . He must see nothing, hear nothing and reduce himself to a machine. Screwing up his eyes to protect them against the appalling flashes of lightning, he forced himself to look at the jib. He took out his watch. In a minute, he would to go about. He looked at the dial, then at the jib, then at his watch again . . .

'Tetahiti, the jib!'

There was no reply. Purcell raised the side of the canvas and looked at him. Tetahiti's eyes were closed like a blind man's and his grey face was tortured.

'The jib!' Purcell shouted into his ear.

During a minute, Tetahiti gave no sign, then he emerged from the canvas like an automaton and, stretching his hands out in front of him, groped through the spray to the jib-sheets. He returned, bent double, paddling in the water in the cockpit and his hair crackling with sparks. He sat down again, and started violently at each flash of lightning.

Purcell found it increasingly difficult to breathe. The sky was pouring water down on him by the bucketful; he felt as if he were under a waterfall. There was a lull and Purcell found himself staring at a breaking sea. Its hideous green froze him with terror. He turned his eyes away. A network of lightning flashes struck on his right with a hideous din and he felt such pain in his legs that he thought the lightning had severed them.

Tetahiti began screaming and, for a moment, Purcell thought he had been struck by lightning. His hands clutching the thwart each side of his knees, bent double, his forehead against Purcell's arm, he was literally howling. Purcell could scarcely hear him, but he could feel the breath from his mouth against his biceps. 'He's going mad!' he thought with desperate anxiety; and for a whole minute he fought the desire to scream himself. He put his leg over the helm and, pushing Tetahiti's hands away, began slapping his face. The rain was pouring down on them with such violence that Tetahiti's features seemed vague and deformed. Purcell struck harder. His head still and his eyes closed, Tetahiti let him have his way.

'He had nothing to do,' Purcell thought suddenly. 'His nerves have given way, because he had nothing to do.' He took Tetahiti's head in his hands, put his lips to his ear and shouted: 'Take the helm!'

There was no reply. Not the least sign of life. Tetahiti's face was empty, expressionless. It was finished. The noise had broken his nerve. He was letting himself die.

'Take the helm!' Purcell cried with savage energy.

He was shaking Tetahiti's dangling head between his hands. He besought him. He rubbed his cheek against his. He was almost weeping. In the end, he came out of the canvas, took Tetahiti's hand and placed it on the helm.

He did not see the wave coming. It poured over them and he collapsed in a heap. His head disappeared under water, and he thought: 'I've fallen overboard.' He pulled on the safety-line, his forehead met something hard. He groped at it. It was the cockpit thwart. He got to his knees and tried to get his breath back. A flash of lightning lit up the boat and he stopped in terror. The water had reached almost to the thwart. If the torrential rain continued, the boat would be swamped in less than half an hour. And that would be the end.

He sat down on the other side of the helm. Tetahiti's head emerged from the canvas, his half-closed eyes seemed to be searching for Purcell and he opened his mouth. But this time, he was not screaming. He was talking, shouting words. Purcell could not hear a sound, but from the movement of his lips, he realised Tetahiti was calling him by name. He leaned over and a thin, distant voice said: 'With . . . me.'

'What?' Purcell shouted.

'With . . . me.'

At last he understood. Tetahiti wanted him to get back under the canvas with him.

Purcell put his fingers on the helm beside Tetahiti's and made the gesture of steering. Tetahiti's face seemed to recover some of its firmness. His eyes looked at his own hand, moved to the jib and then returned to Purcell. At that moment, a wave made the boat yaw, and without even looking at the bows Tetahiti corrected it.

Purcell slipped under the canvas. Tetahiti immediately put his arm round his shoulder and his cheek against his.

Sitting as he now was on Tetahiti's right, Purcell realised he had no control over the helm. 'Even if he goes off course!' he thought with a shrug. At each flash of lightning he looked at the level of the water in the cockpit. In ten minutes' time the boat would be no more than a wreck.

A few minutes before, he had been desperately anxious at the thought of missing the island. But with the island lost, the thought of death left him unaffected. He looked at Tetahiti. He was steering perfectly. Perhaps he had been stunned by the lightning? Under the avalanche of the rain his features were calm and concentrated.

Purcell felt weak and apathetic. Two shipped seas shook him one after the other. He clenched his teeth. He must act, act till the end! He took out his watch. Three minutes before going about. He laughed: the last tack! He suddenly ceased to see the dial and there was a sort of blank in his mind. He recognised the cold of the metal against his ear and realised what he was doing. It was childish and crazy. And yet he listened in spite of himself. With a strength and certainty that were extraordinary amid the wildness of the elements, the ticking went indefatigably on, dividing time into precise little slices, as if time belonged to man. Purcell had an extraordinary feeling of security. The little beating sound against his ear was at once ridiculous and wonderful. The life of it! 'I'm going mad,' he thought. But he went on listening, his hand trickling with rain clutching the watch, his head bewildered by the noise and his eyes half-closed.

The rain stopped. Purcell at once slipped out of the canvas and began bailing. He felt no relief or hope. There was something to do. He did it.

Tetahiti relieved him, and for half an hour they bailed in turn. They were too exhausted to talk. For fear of letting the bailer fall overboard, they lashed it to their wrists. From time to time they shipped a sea which made useless five minutes of effort. They paid no attention to it. Little by little they gained on the water.

Visibitlity had improved. They were once again in a zone of white cotton-wool. Purcell felt as if he had already lived through this moment. The memory of his life on the island had faded. He felt as if he had been in the boat for years, famished, shivering with cold, tossed about by the waves.

He was sitting at the helm watching Tetahiti bail. The Tahitian was standing in front of him, his legs spread wide, his calves propped against the thwart, and the safety-line was coiled before him like a snake in the water. His tall body was bent, his long arms were outstretched, and he dipped the bailer into the water in the cockpit and threw the contents to leeward with one circular movement. From time to time he looked up at Purcell as if to assure himself that he was still there.

Tetahiti emptied the bailer to port and stood up. Purcell followed his glance. In the white cloud that covered the sea there was a round patch that seemed whiter and brighter than the rest. It appeared to be slightly above the water line. It was the same effect as the sun trying to pierce a thick fog. But the sun could not be so low on the horizon. It was scarcely past noon.

'A fire! ' Tetahiti shouted.

Purcell stood up, his heart beating and looked incomprehendingly about him.

Tetahiti rushed to him, the bailer attached to his wrist jerking against the sides behind him without his noticing it.

'A fire! '

He took Purcell by the shoulders and shook him. The bailer banged against Purcell's legs and Purcell seized it by the handle. It suddenly seemed very important that the bailer's wild movements should be stopped.

'A fire! ' Tetahiti cried, shaking him violently.

They shipped a sea and it threw them on to the thwart. Purcell got up, coughed and opened his eyes. The bright patch! It was like a veil being torn away. The women had lit a fire on the beach! The island was there!

'Take the helm! ' Purcell cried, making for the deck. He was suddenly brought up short. It was the bailer. He was still holding it and had forgotten that it was attached to Tetahiti's wrist.

He wasted no time undoing the mainsail's gaskets, he cut them. Lying on the canvas the wind was trying to tear from his hands, he succeeded in taking in reefs. He hoisted the sail and made the halyard fast. The boat heeled over. They shipped a great deal of water, but the risk had to be taken. They must drive her to death. If the storm returned, the bright patch to port would be lost in the pitch-darkness.

Purcell took the helm again and was immediately assailed by a terrible doubt. Were they making a mistake? How had the *vahinés* managed to light and maintain a fire in the torrential rain?

'Tetahiti . . .'

Though it was quite useless against the amount of water they were shipping, Tetahiti was bailing. He was bailing with a sort of fury, a stern, determined look on his face.

'Tetahiti . . .'

He raised his head, looked at Purcell and Purcell could see from his expression that he no longer believed in it either. A fire in this deluge! And yet the bright patch was still there, in the same place at water level.

An instant later, Tetahiti was sitting beside him, showing his teeth, his face radiant. He was mad with excitement. 'Adamo,' he shouted, 'the canoes . . . The *Peritani* canoes!' Purcell looked at him and began laughing jerkily, interminably. The cave had served the women for a chimney. They had set fire to the boats.

The mainsail flapped. Purcell saw Tetahiti unlash the stern oar. There was suddenly no more sou'wester. There were no more waves. They were under the lee of the island. Meanwhile, the fog grew thicker. Apart from the bright patch, they could see nothing.

Purcell replaced Tetahiti at the oar and heard him taking in sail behind his back. The pitching and rolling ceased. The boat glided through the water, and its very stability almost made Purcell giddy. He could see nothing, not even the blade of the oar. Everything was white and muffled. He felt as if he were making his way through loose, light, elastic cotton-wool, which joined up again behind him. He was sculling with both hands, looking over his shoulder to guide him to the patch. Tetahiti must be at the bows. He could not see him.

Tetahiti came and took over the oar, and the boat made more

headway. Purcell went to the bows, and with one hand on the jib-stay, the other against the mast, he breathed deeply. His chest heaved convulsively. He could see nothing. Even the water over which they were gliding was invisible. A few minutes went by, then the smell of trees and burning wood reached him. There was a lump in his throat and he felt like weeping.

The keel scraped on the sand, the boat stopped and heeled over to port. He threw out the anchor, jumped into the water and began running up the beach towards the fire. After a few yards, his legs failed him. He fell face downwards on the sand, his arms spread wide, and he pressed his lips to it.

'Adamo!'

It was Tetahiti's voice. It was muffled and anxious. He was looking for him.

'Adamo!'

Perhaps he had not heard the splash when Purcell had jumped into the water as they beached.

'Tetahiti,' Purcell called weakly.

He got up and waited for Tetahiti to answer so that he could walk in the direction of the sound.

'Adamo!'

Purcell began walking, his arms extended in front of him. He could not even see his hands. Everything was white and woolly.

'Adamo!'

He was surprised to hear the voice behind him, but perhaps it was an echo from the cliff. Or perhaps the fog was distorting it.

'Tetahiti!'

Long minutes went by. They could not come together. They must be turning in circles a few yards from each other. There was no point in shouting. The echo falsified their voices. 'Tetahiti,' he said quietly.

And suddenly, quite close to him, so close that it startled him, he heard: 'Don't move any more.'

He turned round. He could see nothing. He stood still and once again Tetahiti's deep, grave voice said: 'Speak . . .'

'Tetahiti . . .'

'Again.'

'Tetahiti . . .'

'Again.'

The voice was to his right, but Purcell resisted a desire to rush in that direction.

'Tetahiti . . .'

He felt a hand on his shoulder. He turned. Tetahiti's tall, athletic figure appeared grey in the mist. Purcell could see the hand on his shoulder fairly clearly, but from the elbow the arm was almost invisible, and the head above it only a dark patch against the white of the mist.

'O Adamo!' Tetahiti said. 'I have found you!'